ACROSS THE STREET

ACROSS THE STREET

A Novel by

Laurie Lisa

ISBN: 979-8-64694-379-9

1

CHAPTER ONE

Alex Carissa and her husband, Jack, had lived in this middle-class Scottsdale neighborhood for almost eighteen years, time enough for the mesquite and imported palm trees to mature and almost provide shade, time enough for the bougainvillea bushes to have grown tall and thick enough to cover the stucco fences that contained each back yard. Most of the back yards had pools (an implied requirement) for Scottsdale, and most of the houses were painted in either a variation of rose or sand. Only a block away from the elementary school, it was an ideal neighborhood to raise kids, and there were many children in this Desert Paradise subdivision. It was the reason why Alex and Jack had decided to settle there when they graduated from the University of Illinois, married, and moved to Arizona—all on the same weekend. They both had teaching jobs, Alex teaching fifth grade at a public school and Jack teaching social studies and coaching girls' soccer at a private school. And with Alex already pregnant with Nick, and Annie following promptly two years later, the choice had been a good one.

They lived in a cul-de-sac, and looking out the window now, Alex could still vividly imagine Nick and his friends gliding by on roller blades, immersed in trying to either score or block the next goal in the nightly field hockey game. She could still see Annie riding by on her pink Barbie Schwinn, plastic handlebar tassels flying as she led a group of girls around the block, to the school and back (as far as she was allowed to go for quite a while). There had been so many themed birthday parties—Ninja Turtles, Superhero (Nick), ubiquitous Barbie, Princess (Annie)—around the pool, and there had been so many Easter egg hunts that started in the house and spilled out into the yard that Alex had assumed they would go on forever. She couldn't remember exactly why or when they had stopped; they just did. It was natural, of course, but she still missed the home-based roles of party planner, tooth fairy, Easter bunny, Santa Claus, nurse, chief counsel, and head honcho. She had been good at them.

She'd only taught for one year; actually, she had only taught from the end of August until February 14, the day of Nick's birth. It seemed fitting that he was born on Valentine's Day because, for her, it was love at first sight. She couldn't bear to leave him with a sitter. (What if he didn't have enough stimulation? What if the babysitter got a telephone call and let him drown in the bathtub?) She couldn't stand the thought of putting him in daycare. (What if he sat in a dirty diaper? What if the other bratty kids took his toys?) So she gladly became a stay-at-home mom. When Annie was born on February 21 two years later, she was the perfect icing on the cake. Alex read to them, played with them, took them on long walks to the park and to the mall, cared for them, and loved them. Later, she was a room mother every year, president of the PTO, presided over homework, cared for them, and loved them. Later still, she was a chauffeur to drum, piano, karate, and dance lessons, to sleepovers and to more trips to the mall. And of course, she cared for them and loved them.

They had been good children—and still were—but lately there had been a subtle shift in the dynamics, as if the very foundation of the home she had so diligently created had started to crack, nothing volcanic, just a tiny filament of a fissure. Alex couldn't quite put her finger on it, but something seemed *off* to her. She was probably being ridiculous, overreacting because she had too much time on her hands. She had gone back to substitute teaching last year, which could take a considerable amount of time off her hands if she was willing to answer a six o'clock phone call and say "yes" to a desperate principal. But it was now June. Jack had gotten his master's degree and moved up to guidance counselor a few years ago and was working through the summer, Nick was working as a bag boy at the local Fry's grocery store, and Annie was babysitting and spending time (too much time?) with her friend. The family dinner had always been an important time of day, but lately even that was up for grabs. Sometimes they showed up, and sometimes they didn't. Alex went to Walmart and bought a crockpot.

She looked at the time on her cell. She would turn forty in thirty-two days, twelve hours, and seven minutes. And so would Sam, in thirty-two days, twelve hours, and five minutes. Where in the hell was she? The moving van, followed by Sam and Chris in their trusty old red Saab should have arrived two hours ago, and Alex had been stationed by her front window for three. Finally, after all these years, she and her identical twin sister were going to be neighbors. They could see each other every day. No more late-night phone calls, each sitting in her separate living room with a glass of wine and a lit cigarette, talking until either Jack on her end or Chris on Sam's end would insist that they hang up and go to bed. No more short visits at Christmas or some other holiday. Sam was going to live right across the street.

It had been Alex's idea for them to buy the house. When Chris had been offered the position of chair of the English Department at Arizona State University and he and Sam were considering the move to Arizona from Champaign, IL, the house had come up for sale. Alex didn't waste any time. The owners hadn't lived in the house very long, which was unusual for this neighborhood, and they seemed surprised when Alex marched across the street with camera in hand, knocked on the door, and asked to take pictures. Because of the awful state of the housing market, the price was lower than everyone expected (which did not bode well for their own house, Jack pointed out) and the deal moved forward quickly.

Surprisingly, Sam had been somewhat reluctant about the move. It wasn't her career that stood in the way. She was a free-lance writer and could work anywhere. Maybe she didn't want to leave Illinois, where she had lived her entire life. They had grown up in a small town in southern Illinois before going to college in Champaign, and there, Sam had fallen in love with one of her college professors. It didn't matter to Sam that Chris was married at the time. She had found her man, and once Sam wanted something, she didn't let anything stand in her way. Alex, when she finally met Chris, had been baffled by the whole thing. He didn't seem like Sam's type: medium height (but slightly stooped), medium build, medium brown hair (now noticeably thinning), and a gentle, scholarly disposition. Frankly, he seemed too nice for Sam. But who was Alex to

judge? Sam and Chris had been married for ten years, so it looked like it
was going to stick.

Alex suspected that the real reason Sam was reluctant to move into this
neighborhood was because of the number of kids. Sam loved kids, and
she adored Nick and Annie, spoiling them every chance she got. It was
the one thing Sam wanted that she couldn't have. Because of her endometriosis, Sam had one miscarriage after another. She finally conceived
in vitro, and the day her daughter Grace was born was the happiest of her
life. It was a difficult C-section, followed by a radical hysterectomy. But
Sam just glowed when they put the baby in her arms. Alex knew. She had
been by Sam's side in the recovery room. Sam had three blissful months,
and then the unthinkable had happened. Chris had finally insisted Sam
see a therapist, but Sam went to two sessions, then quit. That was two
years ago, and Sam still refused to talk about it, not even to Alex, her true
therapist. Alex didn't press her.

"Are you still standing there?" Jack had a turkey sandwich in one
hand and a soccer ball in the other. He had turned forty in March, but he
didn't look it. His dark hair held only a hint of gray, and all those soccer
practices kept him in shape. He ran right beside "his" girls. He was only
five feet nine, but his broad shoulders made him look more substantial.
Her Jack: responsible and dependable, a good guy.

"No, I'm unloading the dishwasher."

"I get it. Ask a stupid question . . ." He grinned, took a bite of his
sandwich, and made a face. "Is this turkey still good?"

Exasperated, she said, "I don't know. Why don't you smell it?"

He did. "I can't tell. Here, you do it." He handed it to her.

"Really, Jack, you're a grown man." She sniffed. "It smells iffy." She
handed it back.

"*Iffy* will have to do. I'm going to be late for practice." He took a huge
bite.

"Aren't you going to stay and say hello to Sam and Chris? They should
be here any minute."

It was his turn to be exasperated. "Look, Alex, I'll greet them when
I get back. They're going to be sticking around for a while." He finished
the sandwich. "You need to calm down."

"I am calm. Excited, but calm." She heard a car and quickly turned
to the window. It wasn't them. It was their neighbor, Amanda Williams,

who parked her brand new Cadillac Escalade and proceeded to unload a mountain of Costco groceries. She must have spent $500, Alex thought with a pang. She and Jack were on a strict budget now that their 401Ks had dwindled to almost nothing, yet the Williams family seemed to be flourishing. But you never knew. This was Scottsdale. Keeping up with the Joneses was an art form.

She probably was being ridiculous as she stood there, doing nothing, when she could be doing something productive—like emptying the dishwasher. And the three cups of coffee she had drunk that morning were paying their toll. "I need to pee."

"Do you want me to stand guard? I can hold down the fort while you answer nature's call."

"Don't make fun of me."

"But it's so easy." Jack flashed his grin again.

She sighed. "I know, I know, but I'm just so excited to be near Sam again."

He gave her a quick hug and a peck on the cheek. "Of course you're excited, and I understand. I've known the two of you for a long time, haven't I? And I love Sam, too, but—"

Alex interrupted. "I don't want a repeat of last night's conversation, O.K.? You better get going."

"O.K.," he agreed. "I'll see you at dinner." He went out the side door to the garage. A moment later, she watched him back down the driveway in their ten-year-old Jeep.

Last night's conversation had almost erupted into a knock-down, drag-out fight, and talking had been the last thing on her mind when she saw Jack taking a shower, stripped down, and joined him. She was lathering his chest, planning on moving down from there when he brought up the subject of Sam.

"Are you planning on spending a lot of time with Sam?" He wasn't really getting with the program. He was still shaving.

"I sure am. It's been eighteen years since I could see her every day."

"Just like the good old college days, huh? The two partying Murphy girls, who could always be counted on to be dancing on the top of the table by the end of the night."

She pressed her body against his and shimmied. "When we party, we party hearty. When we boogie, we boogie-woogie," she sang.

"I remember."

She stopped. This was not going according to plan. "What are you getting at? You can't seriously think we're going to go to bars and dance on tables?"

"I wouldn't put it past Sam."

"Neither would I, but we are soon-to-be forty-year-olds, and I think we've both grown up a little since then."

The lather ran in rivulets down his body. "I'm just worried about her influence over you."

The water was turning chilly. They desperately needed a new water heater but couldn't afford it. "What's that supposed to mean?"

"When you two get together it's like you become a single force, a powerful force."

"We always thought that was a good thing."

"It is, but you can also be a bit exclusive. And bitchy."

"That's it." She opened the shower door, leaving it open so the air-conditioned air would make him cold. She put on her terry cloth robe and began to apply lotion all over her body. She knew what he meant. In the past, she and Sam had been practically inseparable. In the first grade, when their teacher, Miss Anderson, had moved Alex's desk to the opposite side of the room, Alex had cried so loudly that Miss Anderson had finally allowed her to stand by Sam's desk. Sam held up flashcards with one hand and held Alex's hand with the other. And that was a small example. Sam had talked her into doing a lot of things when they were younger. But that was all in the past, and the fact was that now Alex felt a little sorry for Sam, although she would never say that to her face. That would imply that Alex was smug about her own good fortune with her husband and children.

"What happened to all the towels?" Jack stood dripping in the shower.

Damn. Alex had been on her way downstairs to get them out of the dryer when she saw him in the shower. Without saying a word, she went and got them.

"Thanks," he said when she handed him one. "I didn't really want to streak through the house. You never know what teenager will be hanging around."

Alex fully intended to give him the silent treatment the rest of the night.

"Look," Jack said, putting an arm on her shoulder and gently turning her towards him. "I'm sorry. I guess the embarrassing truth is that I feel a little jealous. I know it's ridiculous—and petty—but there it is. Can you continue where you left off before I became a big dick? Pun intended."

Alex, standing by the window, her eyes getting blurry from staring at the empty street for so long, couldn't stand it one second longer. She had to use the bathroom. She ran to the powder room on the first floor. She was washing her hands, idly thinking that she should repaint the walls—they were looking dingy—when she heard the doorbell followed immediately by the opening and closing of the front door.

"Where the hell are you, Alex?" It was Sam.

Alex and Sam sat on Sam's front porch drinking beers and watching the movers unload the van. The two men struggled with an oversized picture of a Hopi woman, her black hair in two coils on either side of her face. The portrait was only one in a series of Southwest artifacts that had been carried into the house: clay pottery, kachinas mounted in glassed cases, and an assortment of woven rugs in bright, geometric patterns.

"Let me get this straight," Alex said. "You bought all this stuff online and *then* moved it out here?"

"Sure did. I looked around my house and decided that all that cherry wood Thomasville crap wouldn't cut it in Arizona, so I had a gigantic yard sale and sold it all dirt cheap."

"That's crazy. It would have made more sense to buy stuff out here. That way, you wouldn't have had to pay more money to drag it halfway across the country."

"I know that, and believe me, Chris sounded like a broken record when he found out what I was doing. But I have my reasons. I wanted to move new things into my new house. You know, a fresh start." She smiled at Alex. "Haven't you missed my day-to-day logic that is, in fact, illogical?"

Alex laughed. "I sure have." They hugged again, which to Alex, had always felt slightly strange. In a way, it was like hugging herself, if that were possible. They were the same height, 5'4", and almost the same weight, with Sam hovering slightly above the 110-pound mark and Alex slightly under. Because they looked so much alike as children, people started to refer to Sam as the "bigger" twin and Alex as the "smaller" twin. Sam retaliated by developing a raging case of anorexia in high school that lasted until sophomore year of college when she started eating more and jogging daily to regain her health. They both still watched what they ate; however, ironically, they both discounted the empty calories in alcohol.

They were relaxed now. They both knew the initial face-to-face meeting involved a thorough inventory of each other's face and body. Alex and Sam couldn't help it. It wasn't like looking in a mirror; instead, it was seeing how the world really saw each woman. The gray and wrinkle tests had been passed. Neither had gray hair because they had both started dying it a few years back. Naturally, they had had dark brown hair with auburn highlights. Now Sam's shoulder-length hair was a deep auburn, and Alex's A-line cut that tapered down to her chin was more a reddish blonde. Granted, each had a few crow's feet faintly etching their blue eyes and maybe the beginning of some fine lines around the mouth, but overall, the inspection had been a success. As Sam had surmised, "Fuck forty. We're still pretty hot."

Chris came out of the house, wiping the sweat from his face with a towel. At fifty-two, he looked better than he had ten years ago. When he got tired of his thinning hair, Sam decided he needed a crew cut. The gray bristles were concealing and flattering. "Sam, do you want to come in here and help me tell the movers where to put everything?"

"Not really."

Chris decided to ignore her. "Is this the normal temperature for June, Alex? What is it? One hundred and five degrees?"

"Something like that, and yes, it's normal, but like they say, it's a *dry* heat."

"Dry, wet, it's frigging hot." Sam took a drink of beer.

"Stop swearing, Sam. It's getting old." Chris did not say this with any conviction.

"*Frigging* is not swearing. *Fucking* is swearing."

"Among other things," Alex said. It was only their second beer, but they both thought it was witty.

"I give up," Chris said, and walked back into the house.

"Is he mad?" Alex asked. "Maybe we should go help."

"He's not mad. He doesn't get mad. Sometimes I think a shouting match is just what we need, but he refuses to raise his voice. Alas, I married a pacifist."

"He's a good guy."

"He is, and you know what? He'd rather direct the movers himself, and except for the kitchen and my clothes, he'll do all the unpacking. He's more particular about that sort of thing than I am." She lit a cigarette. "Where are they? I'm anxious to see my posse."

"They should be here any minute. Nick was supposed to pick up Annie after work."

"I notice you haven't had a cigarette."

Alex raised the sleeve of her t-shirt, revealing a nicotine patch. "Two weeks in. I'm trying to be a good influence on the kids."

Sam laughed. "They're teenagers. They've probably done a lot worse than smoke a cigarette. Did you read that heroin is making a comeback?"

Alex slapped her lightly on the leg. "Very funny. If—" She stopped. What was she going to say? If you were in my position, you wouldn't laugh? Sam would never be in Alex's position.

If she noticed, Sam didn't let on. "Is that them?" She pointed at the white Dodge minivan turning into the cul-de-sac, the old, sometimes dependable, family vehicle. "Is that Annie driving?"

Alex jumped to her feet. "Shit. She is driving. She's had her permit for two days, and she doesn't have a clue. Plus, it's illegal since Nick isn't eighteen."

The van sped down the street, braked too late to make it into the Carissa driveway, backed up with tires squealing, and turned sharply, hitting the pole holding the mailbox at the curb. It toppled to the ground.

"She really is terrible," Sam observed.

Alex ran across the street as Nick and Annie got out of the car, yelling, "Are you all right?" She stopped abruptly, staring as her children got out of the van.

"Uh oh," Annie said. "I think I'm going to need a lot more practice."

Nick bent down to examine the fender. "It's just a little ding, barely noticeable." He straightened up. "Mom, you always said you thought that mailbox looked cheap on that little pole. Now you can get a new one. Problem solved."

Alex was still staring. "Annie, what did you do to your hair?" Annie had left the house that morning with dark brown curly hair that hung to the middle of her back. It was now jet black, perfectly straight, and a fringe of uneven bangs was almost in her eyes. Weakly, she said, "Can you even see?"

"Maybe that's why she hit the mailbox." Sam had also crossed the street. "Come here, you guys, and give your aunt a hug."

Nick and Annie readily obliged. They had always adored Sam, and the feeling was mutual. She spoiled them mercilessly, sending outrageous gifts for their birthdays and Christmas. Last year, she had sent them new cell phones with a two-year prepaid contract, which included the ultimate prize: unlimited texting. Alex thought it was too extravagant, but she didn't say anything. After they had opened the phones, she was pretty sure she would never be able to pry them from their hands. When she had called Sam to suggest that it was too much, she had ended up thanking her. "My pleasure," Sam had said. "You know I'd do anything for those kids." And that had been the end of that.

"You two look great."

"Thanks," Nick said. He looked like his usual self—that is, a typical teenage boy. His jeans were baggy, but not excessively so. His red t-shirt proclaimed, "Nuke the Commies," the result of a recent trend he had acquired of wearing military-inspired slogans. His light brown hair was clean-cut, and thankfully, he didn't have one thing on his body pierced or tattooed. He was a nice, dependable kid.

And so was Annie. Alex now took in what her daughter wore: skin-tight black jeans, a black t-shirt, and black flip-flops. She had even painted her finger and toenails black.

"Thanks," Annie said to Sam and then turned to her mother. "And to answer your question, I dyed it. Carla cut my bangs."

"I don't think Carla should consider a career as a stylist." Nick snickered.

"Shut up, Nick," Annie said. "In the car, you said you liked my new look."

"No, I said, 'Oh wow,' as in 'Oh wow, wait until Mom gets a load of you.'"

"Didn't you think you should ask permission first?" Alex was trying to remain calm. She never raised her voice at her kids, but she was tempted to now.

"It's only hair," Sam said.

"You're not helping, Sam."

Annie seized the opportunity. "Yeah, it's only hair, and it's *my* hair."

"What about those clothes?"

"I borrowed them from Carla. Look, Mom, it's no big deal. We were just experimenting. You know, we'll be sophomores next year, and we want a new look. It's no big deal. Change can be a positive thing."

"She's got a good point," Sam said.

Sam was not helping the situation *at all*. "Go in the house, Annie. We'll talk about this later."

"Give me the keys, Annie. I think your driving lesson is over for the day. I'll park the car in the garage, keep you out of temptation. There's a ton of stuff you could smash into in there." Nick got into the car and opened the garage door. Annie waved at Sam and walked inside.

"I love those kids," Sam sighed.

Alex glared at her. "I didn't appreciate you butting in."

Sam was surprised. "I really didn't see what the big deal was. It is only hair. And I see a lot of kids dressed like that. If I offended you, I'm sorry." She put her arm around Alex's shoulder.

Maybe she was overreacting. "No, it's okay. I guess I was just . . . surprised."

"What you need is a relaxing glass of chardonnay."

"Really, Sam, I need to go inside and start dinner."

"I meant a relaxing glass of chardonnay at your house. I haven't done much unpacking yet, remember? It's hard telling where the wine glasses are buried."

Alex smiled. "That's right. Come on in. We'll drink a toast to being neighbors."

"I'd rather toast being twin sisters."

"I was the one responsible for bringing your parents together," Sam said to Annie and Nick.

It was a week after the move, and they were all gathered around the Carissas' kitchen table, which was cluttered with the remnants of the barbecue Alex had prepared: London Broil, pasta salad, green bean casserole, and grilled vegetable skewers. They had already gone through two bottles of expensive cabernet, compliments of Chris and Sam. Jack and Chris talked at one end of the table, Jack urging Chris to take up golf and Chris urging Jack to retool his investment portfolio. They had never had much in common. Each cared about the other's interests about as much as they both cared about the latest exploits of Britney Spears. Which was not at all. But they were trying.

Alex groaned. "They've heard that story about a hundred times."

"That's okay," said Nick, even though he was watching the time, anxious not to miss *Special Forces: Untold Stories* on The Military Channel. He'd been watching the channel religiously lately, even though he was supposed to be studying for the SAT. He should have taken the test in the spring, but even Jack—his father and guidance counselor—hadn't been able to persuade him to do it.

"Go ahead and tell it, Aunt Sam." Annie, who had announced that she was a vegetarian precisely as Alex placed the beef in the center of the table, had barely touched her food. She'd been sullen all week and was still wearing the black jeans and t-shirt. When Alex refused to wash them, Annie announced that she would take care of it. Her solution? She sprayed them nightly with Febreze.

"I love this story." Sam reached for the bottle of wine and saw that it was empty.

Alex hesitated, but Sam looked at her expectantly. "I'll get another bottle." Alex prided herself on being a good hostess, but she knew the bottles of Vendange on the pantry shelf were going to suffer in comparison to the expensive cabernet. Alex had gotten the Vendange on sale at Fry's for $4.99 a bottle, plus a ten percent discount for buying six. Sam waited while Alex retrieved it and opened it. If she knew how cheap the wine was—and she probably did—she had the grace to not point it out. She poured a glass.

"It was the Saturday of Labor Day weekend at the beginning of our junior year. Alex and I had made the rounds of quite a few parties that night, and for once, Alex wanted to go home when Milton's, our favorite bar, closed at two o'clock. That surprised me because Alex was quite the partier, and at that time, I had a hard time keeping up with her."

"Skip ahead, Sam." Alex had been about to refill her own wine glass but put the bottle down instead.

"Way to go, Mom," Nick said.

"She never tells that part," Annie smirked.

"Anyway," Sam continued, "I had heard about a nineteen-keg after-hours party at Alpha Chi Rho, and I desperately wanted to go because I had a huge crush on the president of the fraternity, Bob Barker." She saw that Annie was going to interrupt. "And no, it was not the Bob Barker on *The Price is Right*. Your mom and I are not that old."

"Yeah, right," Annie said.

"I think Drew Carey is doing a really good job. Have you seen the show since he took over?" Nick asked.

"Stop interrupting, or I will make your lives miserable by dragging out this story and telling every minute detail, including what we had on."

Nick glanced at the clock on the wall. "Our lips are sealed."

"Well, after I convinced your mom that her hair still looked fine—even though someone had spilled beer on it and it was a grossly humid night and it did look kind of soggy—we made it to the fraternity. It was packed. We squeezed ourselves into the room with the keg, but the line was unbelievable. You would think that everyone would have had enough to drink at the bars, but at that time, U of I was ranked the number one college in the country for beer consumption. It was a source of pride on campus."

"Maybe I should apply there," Nick said.

"You lied about my hair?" It was news to Alex.

Sam shot them both a warning look but knew she was losing their interest. "To make a long story short, I saw Bob go by and told your mom I was going after him, big time. She told me she was going home. I begged her to wait and asked her if she was interested in anyone at all there, since she had just broken up with her boyfriend. She pointed at your dad, who walked by carrying a pitcher of beer. He had a mustache and beard and hair down to his shoulders. We couldn't decide whether he looked like Jesus or Charles Manson, and I was so desperate to stay that I was going to overlook the Charles Manson thing, so I went over to him and told him my twin sister thought he was sexy. I pointed out your mom, and he walked over and started talking to her. The rest is history."

"You forgot the part that Dad had a date there, and after talking to Mom, he took the date home and then they went up to his room. Just when he was about to kiss her, she said she thought she heard you calling her, and she left," Annie added.

"And on their first date, Dad picked her up on a motorcycle. They went to a country bar called Stompin' Eddie's, and Mom won a giant turtle raft in a raffle and gave it to him," Nick finished.

"Whatever," Sam said, exasperated. "I like my version better."

Alex laughed. "I told you they'd heard the story a hundred times."

"I'm going to go watch the show now, okay, Mom?" Nick pushed back his chair.

Annie did the same. "I'm expecting an important phone call."

"From whom?" Alex stopped picking up dishes.

"Hold it!" Sam said. "No one's going anywhere yet. I've got some big news."

"She sure does." Chris smiled at her indulgently, as he always did. It was as if he still could not believe that she had consented to marry him.

Alex wondered when Jack had stopped looking at her like that. Two years ago? Ten? She felt a sharp pang of jealousy. She knew Jack loved her and had been faithful to her all these years, just as she had been faithful to him. Perhaps they had become too involved in the kids, work, the house, and all the pressing financial issues that burdened them to make any effort to ignite sparks in the bedroom. They really needed to change that.

"To celebrate Alex's and my big 4-0, we're all going to go on a cruise of the Mexican Riviera!" Sam declared triumphantly.

The Carissa family stared at her. She looked at each of them, her eyes shining.

"Wow," Nick said, breaking the silence.

"I thought cruises were for old people." Annie didn't look thrilled.

"Bullshit." Sam's voice was edging past impatience. "They have tons of things for teenagers to do. There are all kinds of excursions at the various ports, and if you don't want to do that, you can rent jet skis or snorkeling equipment. On the ship, you can eat twenty-four hours a day, go to shows or—her trump card—go to the disco. They're very lax about I.D.s. I checked."

Annie perked up for the first time in days.

"You mean I'd be stuck hanging around with Annie all the time?" Nick asked.

"I'm sure you'll make new friends," Sam snapped.

"We usually go camping for Alex's birthday," Jack said sullenly.

"What a fun time for her." Sam gave Jack a withering glare. She turned to Alex. "What do you think?"

Alex wasn't sure. For the last five years, they had gone camping in the Flagstaff area; it had become a family tradition. Jack, Nick, and Annie loved being outdoors, and they had explored the various canyons in the area. They had more pictures of elk from those trips than of the four of them. For her, it had not been so great, cleaning fish, cooking on an open fire, and sleeping on the hard ground had been a vacation from what, exactly? The idea of escaping on a cruise—no meals to prepare, no laundry or housework—sounded idyllic. The only thing was . . .

"We can't afford it," Jack said. He gave Alex The Look, meaning that the topic was not open to discussion and must be dropped immediately. He was overly sensitive to the fact that Chris made more money than he did.

Alex worried about money, too, but sometimes Jack went too far in equating stupid male pride with financial worth. "It sounds wonderful, Sam, but," she looked at Jack, "we can't afford it."

"That's the best part." Sam clapped her hands, as if she were a little girl standing in front of a present-laden Christmas tree. "It's a gift from Chris and me, isn't it, honey?"

Chris nodded obediently. "She's been talking about this for months."

"Do you see? Everything is taken care of."

"We usually go camping," Jack persisted stubbornly.

"I hate camping," Annie announced.

"Since when?" Jack was incredulous.

"Since last summer when I couldn't get cell phone service in those stupid mountains."

Jack looked like he was going to explode. "You can't get cell service on a damn cruise ship, either."

"They do have internet service," Chris said.

Alex intervened. "It's really a generous and thoughtful gift, Sam, but I think we need a few days to talk about it."

"That would be a problem. I have to pay for the reservations by tomorrow or lose them." Sam looked close to tears.

"Why didn't you mention this sooner?"

"Because it's a surprise. I thought everyone would jump at the chance to go on a cruise. I guess I was wrong."

Alex, Nick, and Annie looked guiltily at each other. Jack remained stone-faced. Finally, Nick said, "Why don't we take a vote?"

"We don't need a vote. It's a wonderful idea, Sam, thank you. I'm sure we'll all have a good time. We were just surprised, that's all." Alex got up and went around the table to hug Sam.

"Are you sure this is what you want, Alex?" Jack's lips drew a straight line, and his left cheek twitched, a sure sign that he was agitated.

Alex looked from him to Nick and Annie, neither of whom seemed too thrilled, either. Then she looked at Sam, whose face was full of hope. "I'm sure."

Nick went into the den and closed the door. He was just in time for his program, which tonight featured an episode about the Green Berets in Vietnam. More than anything, he wanted to join the Marines. You'd think that his parents would have gotten that by now, but as usual, they didn't have a clue, and it had been about a year. The idea started last summer when he had gotten hooked on the series *Generation Kill*, a program about Bravo Company fighting in Iraq. He had recorded all seven episodes and had watched them all at least thirty times. His big fear was that whoever got elected president in November would end the war in Iraq before he had a chance to get there. If that happened, there was still Afghanistan. No one really talked about what was going on there anymore, but it seemed as if it would last at least until he graduated next year. Even Prince Harry had fought there, and the footage of him firing from a helicopter was way cool.

He had no intention of taking the SAT or going to college. So far, he had been able to procrastinate by telling his parents that he wasn't ready for the test and pointing out how competitive admissions to colleges were. As if he really needed to do that. His dad's top priority was to try to get the rich kids at Scottsdale Country Day School into good universities, preferably Ivy League or Stanford. After all, the parents wanted to get the most bang from their buck. The four years of high school at SCDS cost close to $70,000. There were some kids at school on scholarship—smart kids from inner Phoenix—and then there were kids like him and Annie, teachers' kids who got a reduced tuition rate. But mostly, they were rich kids who would go to a good college, maybe work for a while, and then inherit their family's money. Nick couldn't help himself; he was jealous of them. They littered the school parking lot with their Mercedes, Hummers, and BMWs. He drove to school with his dad in their old Jeep.

He texted his best friend Dylan: RU watching?

Dylan immediately texted back: LOL of course dude.

Dylan had been his best friend since first grade, and they had stayed best friends even though Dylan went to Horizon, the public high school in their neighborhood. He lived a few streets over, on Sweetwater, in an aging ranch house that sat on an acre of horse property. It always amazed Nick that there could be horses in the middle of Scottsdale, less than a mile from Paradise Valley Mall, but it was true. Dylan's parents were crazy about horses and boarded other people's horses for a living. They weren't pushing their son to go to college. In fact, Dylan was going to enlist in the Marines with Nick the day after they graduated next spring.

Nick immersed himself in the program. Twenty-two Green Berets along with four hundred Montagnard and South Vietnamese irregulars were trapped in an underground bunker of Lang Vei with 40,000 enemy troops amassed around them. After a massive attack, heroism and perseverance brought out eight American soldiers alive. Satisfied, Nick turned off the TV. That was exactly the kind of thing he wanted to do. It wasn't as if he was bloodthirsty, or anything like that. And it wasn't like he was excessively patriotic, although of course, he loved his country. It was more as if he wanted to be a hero—or at the very least, less ordinary.

It was only a little after ten o'clock, but having nothing better to do, he decided he might as well go upstairs and surf the net for a while. Passing through the kitchen, Nick could see his mom and Aunt Sam sitting on the back patio through the window behind the dinette. They had opened a bottle of champagne and were both smoking cigarettes. That was a shame; his mom had been trying so hard to quit. Oh, well, if it made her happy, it was okay with him. Like the cruise. He was ambivalent about it, but it was her fortieth birthday. The Mexican cruise gave him an idea. He could do some research on Mexican militants and drug cartels.

He went upstairs, and before going into his room, knocked on Annie's door. "Hey, squirt, you want to go out and get some ice cream?" No answer, but he could hear her talking on her phone. He knocked again and heard: "I'll call you back."

Annie opened the door. "Ice cream? That's so nerdy I could puke. It's no wonder you're such a loser."

Nick crossed his arms and leaned against the door jamb. "Hey, I was only trying to be nice. It's not like you can drive yourself. You might forget to stop and plow right into the front window of Baskin Robbins."

"Very funny."

"And speaking of losers, this Morticia get-up might land you on the cover of *Goth* magazine. Wouldn't that be the pinnacle of popularity?"

"Fuck you." She pushed him and slammed the door.

Not wanting her to have the last word, he said, "And you're so articulate, too. You could be the spokesperson for Goths everywhere."

Nick went into his room and slammed the door so hard that the movie posters of *Hamburger Hill*, *Platoon*, and *Apocalypse Now* fluttered against the walls. He didn't know what had gotten into Annie lately. Well, he guessed it had been going on since the beginning of the year when she hooked up with Carla Goldleib, the new girl from Connecticut. According to the grapevine at SCDS (which was extremely short, considering the student population was three hundred), Carla's parents were filthy rich, even by the high SCDS standards of wealth. Since hooking up with Carla, Annie had changed. She and Nick didn't talk much anymore.

The minor confrontation with Annie made Nick restless, and he no longer wanted to sit in front of his computer. He decided to go for a run, get a head start on his cross-country training. This would be his fourth year on the team. At the urging of his dad, who thought sports were almost religious rituals, he had tried basketball, soccer, and lacrosse, but he always ended up sitting on the bench. Then he tried cross-country, and he'd found his match. He loved the solitary nature and rhythm of the sport. It didn't tire him; instead, it made him feel free.

He got the key from the drawer below his computer and unlocked the footlocker he kept in the back of his closet. His well-worn Nike running shoes were on top. Below them, his jersey and shorts from last season. He sat on the closet floor and put on his shoes, and then temptation got the better of him. He lifted the jersey and rifled through his stash: six wallets (with credit cards and cash intact—he'd left behind the drivers' licenses), four watches (one Rolex), and one gold cross necklace. He quickly put the jersey back on top and locked the case. Heart pounding, he stumbled to his bed.

This happened every time. Nick couldn't remember exactly how it had started freshman year. There had been a basketball game going on when he finished his run. No one was in the locker room, and someone had left a wallet in one of the open lockers. The SCDS players didn't ever lock them—everyone was to be trusted. It was like he couldn't help himself. He took the thing, threw on some clothes, and was out of there before anyone saw him. Over the years, people had been accused—usually players from the opposing teams—and one janitor had been fired.

But no one had ever suspected or accused Nick. He was the guidance counselor's son, a quiet, respectful boy who didn't make waves or get in trouble. He was a good kid.

Annie lolled across her bed. She was bored. If it hadn't been for this dinner tonight with her aunt and uncle, she would have spent the night with Carla. If she had her choice, she would live with Carla in her huge house on the west side of Mummy Mountain. Carla was an only child, and her parents traveled a lot—London, Paris, Rome, Stockholm, Hong Kong—so Carla was often left alone with their housekeeper, Rita. Rita didn't speak much English and was addicted to Spanish soap operas. Carla and Annie couldn't figure out if it was only the language barrier or if Rita was also hard of hearing. Whenever they told her they were going someplace, usually the mall, she would smile and nod, then go back to the TV. Once, just for the hell of it, they told her they were going to Cabaret, a strip club on Van Buren Street. Rita smiled and nodded. Language barrier or deafness, either way, it was perfect.

Carla had saved her life. Annie had miserably navigated the first half of freshman year, trying to make friends and joining the debate club. That had been a terrible idea. Speaking before the audience at the first meet, she had developed a stutter, run out of the room, and hid in the bathroom. The experience had not helped her reputation, if you could say that she had a reputation of any kind. At her dad's urging, of course, she had joined the lacrosse team. It was a stupid game, and she had never fully understood the rules. What was "checking," exactly? She had been allowed to quit that after one of her teammates whacked her across the face (on purpose?) during practice and gave her a black eye. Mom had actually been on her side on that one: "What if that girl had knocked out Annie's teeth, Jack? We've spent a fortune on orthodontia!"

So when Carla had arrived at SCDS in January, it had been fate, or karma, or something. They had been standing outside in the parking lot, waiting for rides home. (It was so juvenile to not have a driver's license; it was enforced imprisonment of young adults.) Carla had looked very east coast chic, dressed in Seven jeans and an Armani sweater, her short dark hair in a Posh Spice hairdo. Annie had on Levi's and a sweatshirt.

"I'm dying for a cigarette," Carla said.

Annie wasn't sure she'd been talking to her. "Excuse me?"

"A cigarette. I need a cigarette to relieve the stress of this day." She started to rummage through her oversized Gucci bag.

"You'll get used to it. It's high school, you know. It's really not all that bad."

"Aha!" Carla had found a pack of Capris and a gold lighter in her voluminous purse.

Preston, another freshman, walked by on his way to diving practice. Preston barely cleared five feet, was extremely smart, and if possible, was even nerdier than Annie. "Those things will give you cancer."

Carla feigned surprise. "Really? I tell you, you just can't keep up with modern medical research these days." Preston shrugged and walked on.

"Stupid short shit," Carla said. She turned to Annie. "Do you really like it here?"

"I hate it. Most of these people don't have a clue—and they're boring." Annie's bus pulled up. "Here's my bus. Are you taking this one?" She hoped Carla was. They could sit together and get to know each other.

"I'm waiting for my town car."

"Oh." Annie's heart sank. This girl would probably join the clique of *uber-rich* girls and never give her the time of day again.

"Would you like a ride? We could go back to my place, no one's there, and I'm not in the mood to go home to an empty house." Annie was supposed to go home and babysit for the Williams kids, but she made what her mom would call an irresponsible decision. "I'd love to."

To Annie, it had been a liberating experience. Carla walked her through the rooms of the vast house, pointing out works of art by Picasso, Peter Max, and Renoir, and then suggested they have a drink by the pool, which was located at the front of the house and overlooked the Paradise Valley Country Club, the skyline of Phoenix, and to the south, Camelback Mountain.

Carla rummaged around in the downstairs bar. "What would you like to drink?"

Annie was about to say diet Coke.

"I'm thinking vodka and cranberry would hit the spot. How does that sound to you?"

Annie, who had had one beer in her entire life said, "That sounds perfect."

The girls bonded over vodkas and cranberries (four each), talking about their lives so far, and by the time the town car took Annie home, she felt like they had known each other forever. It was almost like they were soul mates or something, Annie thought drunkenly on the way. No, wait. That sounded like they were *lesbians*, which they most definitely were *not*. Annie had told Carla all about her mad crush on Walter Caldwell a junior.

"Walter?" Carla had laughed. "I don't know if anyone should have sex for the first time with a boy named Walter."

Annie was drunk enough to think this was funny. "Walt. They call him Walt. Anyway, I wasn't thinking about sex with him. I was thinking about a date."

Carla looked at her knowingly. "You are a virgin, aren't you?"

"Yes, and you're not, right?" She already knew the answer.

"No, but it's not like I'm a slut or anything. Only with my boyfriend from back in Connecticut. His name is Drew. He's twenty."

Annie didn't know whether she should be impressed or appalled. "Wow."

When she got home, she got the riot act from her mom, who had to babysit the Williams kids herself. "Where in the world have you been, and why haven't you answered your cell? I'd be absolutely furious with you if I hadn't been so worried."

She had to be careful that she didn't slur. She felt giddy. "Sorry. I forgot. Study group. Battery dead." Head down, she ran up the stairs.

"Come back here, Annie. I'm not done talking to you."

At the top of the stairs, she enunciated, "I have a headache."

The doorbell rang. Thank god it was her mother's turn to host Bunco. She heard the women enter, chatting and laughing, moving into the kitchen and exclaiming over the spread her mother had prepared. Annie was safe this time.

She plopped down on her bed, and even though the room was spinning, she felt happier than she had in a long, long time. The line from that old movie (*Casablanca? Planet of the Apes?*) popped into her head: This is the beginning of a beautiful friendship.

He shouldn't be doing this. He knew that. But he was so damn frustrated with Sam waltzing in here and taking over, announcing that they were all going on a Mexican cruise. Jack's relationship with Sam had been a complicated one from the very beginning, and he thought it was in both of their best interests to avoid each other. It had been easy enough when she lived hundreds of miles away, but now she was across the street, practically in his family's lap. He knew that having Sam close made Alex happy, and he was glad for that. He also knew that he should have come up with a better idea than camping for Alex's fortieth birthday. He would have loved to whisk her away for a romantic weekend—maybe San Diego—but money was tight, which was another reason he should not be installing PokerStars on his computer right now.

He got up from his seat at the dining room table and peeked around the hall into the kitchen. Through the window, he could see Alex and Sam on the back patio, drinking and smoking. They'd be at it for hours, maybe until dawn. It had happened before. On one holiday visit years ago, he had gone to bed while the girls were drinking champagne, and when he awoke at six o'clock the next morning, the girls sat in the same place at the kitchen table. The only difference was that they had switched to Bloody Marys. He made himself a deal. He wouldn't say a word to Alex about her smoking, and in exchange, he could play five hands of poker online.

He sat back down at his computer. The program wanted his username and password. He typed in what he always used: Matilda (after the dog he had as a child) and 050290 (his wedding date). When the program asked for his credit card number, he hesitated. What were the chances of identity theft? Surely, these kinds of programs were regulated. He knew that Mac, the junior class history teacher, played all the time, and he had mentioned that Chris Moneymaker, the 2003 World Poker champion, had started out on PokerStars. Jack fished his wallet out of his back jeans pocket and pulled out the MasterCard with the least amount of credit remaining: $200. He had no intention of spending that much. He would limit himself to $20.

"I'm going for a run, Dad," Nick said from the doorway, jogging in place.

Jack eased down the computer screen, not wanting his son to see what he was doing. "Isn't it a little late?"

"I feel the need for speed. Thought I'd get a jump up on training."

Jack smiled. He loved that Nick was so into running. Being in a sport was good training for life. "All right, then. Be sure to grab a reflective jersey from the garage."

"Will do." And he left.

He was a good kid, Jack thought, although he had been lacking in the motivation department this last spring. He should have taken the SAT. It was strange. He could corral all the other juniors into getting into the college spirit, but not his own son. Jack wasn't one to push his children— he left that up to Alex—but unknown to Nick, Jack had signed him up to take the test at the end of July. They had to get the ball rolling if there was any chance of Nick getting a scholarship, and getting a scholarship was a necessity.

It was a good thing that Alex left the financial matters of the household to him. She would be terrified if she knew how much their 401K had dwindled over the last year. She did know, of course, about the second mortgage he had taken out on the house because, as co-owner, she had to sign the papers, too. With interest rates so low, a lot of their neighbors had done the same thing. And apparently, it was a hot topic of conversation on the local Bunco circuit, so she was easily persuaded to take the equity out of the house. They had put the money in the bank, unlike many of the neighbors who had purchased new cars, renovated their homes, or gone on fancy vacations. They were saving for a "rainy day," Jack had told her. He hadn't told her he was afraid that, very soon, it was going to pour. This recession was a real bitch to the middle class.

He won his first two poker hands. He was playing with three men and one woman, and none of them seemed to know what they were doing. This was like taking candy from a baby, and maybe he would actually win a little cash. They really needed a new hot water heater. Then he lost the next three hands. So much for him becoming a professional poker player and making millions of dollars. He heard a loud thumping coming from upstairs.

Annie. She was probably listening to the new local band she had just discovered called Vistilance. Not wanting to get up and go upstairs and lose his momentum in the game, he texted her to turn it down. Surprisingly, she did so. She was certainly going into teen terrorism with a vengeance these days. Being around teenagers for a living, he knew it wasn't uncommon, and he had reassured Alex that this phase would pass. He wished that being a teenager wasn't so hard on his daughter, that she was more like the wholesome, athletic girls on his soccer team, but it wasn't turning out that way. He had seen how she had struggled to fit in during her first semester, and how she had become more outgoing when Carla Goldleib started at SCDS. He secretly watched his kids at school. He knew what was going on.

An hour later, he shut down his computer when he heard Alex come into the kitchen. He went in to say goodnight and found her rummaging in the refrigerator. "What are you looking for?" he asked.

"I thought we had another bottle of champagne." She turned to face him, eyes bright, face flushed, obviously tipsy.

"Don't you think you've had enough?" he asked mildly.

"We're just going to have one more glass. We're having such a good time." She came over and hugged him. "I feel so happy."

Jack kissed the top of her head. He loved his wife more than anything, and he was glad to see her happy. She had been feeling down the last few months. She said she wasn't depressed; she couldn't explain it; perhaps it was turning forty. "I think there's another bottle in the refrigerator in the garage. I'll go get it for you."

"Oh, thank you, Jack, you are a wonderful husband." She gave him a smoke-tinged kiss on the lips. "I promise you we won't make a habit of this." She stared at him with drunken earnest. "Are you sure you're all right with the cruise? Honestly, we don't have to go if you don't want to. I'd be okay with that."

How could he disappoint her? He could swallow his pride for a week to make her happy. "No, I think we should sail the high seas and celebrate your birthday in style. Ahoy, matey!"

"I love you, Jack," she said.

"The feeling's mutual. I'll get the champagne." It was the least he could do, considering he had just lost $200 they couldn't afford to lose. He would pardon himself this one time, but he was never, ever going to gamble again.

Across the street, Chris roamed through the downstairs of his new house with a box in his hands. The box contained various mementos he had collected over the years—a paper fan from Hong Kong, a silver-plated Statue of Liberty from New York, a small carved totem pole from Alaska, and assorted other knickknacks he had accumulated over a lifetime. (Chris didn't like to throw anything away.) He was trying to decide where to discreetly place each item, to put his stamp on this new house that Sam had bombarded with southwestern furniture and artifacts. It probably wouldn't do any good. Sam thought his collection was a "bunch of junk," and she would probably throw everything back into the box and hide it in the garage in the morning.

The only room in the house that was familiar to Chris was his office, which held his scarred oak desk, lumpy leather chair, and floor to ceiling bookshelves filled with books. After being a professor of American literature for twenty-five years, he had amassed an impressive collection. It had taken him two full days to restore these books to their proper, alphabetical (by author) order. If Sam had even suggested that he not move his office intact, he would have stood his ground. It was the one argument she could not win.

He indulged Sam. She laughingly joked that she was his "trophy wife," even though he was only twelve years older than her; however, that was how he thought of her. He first met her when she was a senior and enrolled in his Women in Literature class. She was beautiful, intelligent, and full of life, but of course, nothing could happen between them because she was his student. And he was newly married to Rita. That had been a mistake. He and Rita had both wanted to get married, had felt that it was the proper stage in life to do so, but the marriage was basically over on their honeymoon to Spain when they realized they had nothing in common, and furthermore, didn't really like each other. They divorced amicably a year later, and he was free to pursue Sam, who was then in graduate school and no longer his student.

They had lived together for six years and been married for ten. When Sam was about to turn thirty and decided that her biological clock was not only ticking but moving forward at warp speed, he had wanted to marry her but was not so sure about the baby. At forty-two, he was pretty much set in his ways. But as usual, Sam was persistent, and Chris obliged. He had plenty of time to get used to the idea—eight years. At first, when Sam couldn't get pregnant, they hadn't been concerned. Then another year passed, then another. They were both tested. His sperm count was on the low side, and Sam had endometriosis. He suggested adoption, but Sam was determined to have her own biological child.

They went to three fertility experts in Chicago, then to one in New York followed by one in L.A. During that period, Sam had four miscarriages.

It was a terrible time. With each pregnancy, Sam's hope had skyrocketed, only to be unbearably crushed when the blood started to flow. Her grief was all-consuming. She wouldn't get out of bed for days, and even the doctor-prescribed antidepressants didn't help. Finally, they turned to in vitro fertilization. The first two attempts failed. They had just enough money for a third and final try, although Chris didn't tell Sam that. Luckily, he didn't have to. Sam got pregnant, and when she made it through the first trimester, they were cautiously optimistic. After the second trimester, they could finally breathe normally, and with each passing week, their excitement mounted. And when Sam went into labor only two weeks early, they could believe. And then they had Grace.

Grace was a beautiful baby—a dark-haired, perfectly formed joy. He fell in love at first sight, and the force of that love surprised him. However, he suspected that his feelings for Grace were surpassed by Sam's. Literally, it was almost impossible to pry Grace from Sam's arms. If it had been even remotely physically possible, Sam would have become a marsupial, grown a pouch, and carried that baby everywhere. It took Chris a month to convince Sam that it was not healthy or safe for the baby to sleep between them in bed, then another month before Sam could be persuaded to not sleep on a chair in the baby's room. Chris put six baby monitors in Grace's nursery and one in every room in the house, and only then would Sam consent to let the baby sleep unattended, although she still got up often in the middle of the night to make sure the baby was breathing. Really, Chris thought it was something of a miracle that Sam didn't crawl into the crib and sleep with the baby.

On a Saturday night a month later, they had a party. It was supposed to be a quiet affair, a few colleagues and their wives and a group of ten graduate students from his seminar on Native American literature. But it was the end of the semester, a warm spring night, and everyone seemed giddy with excitement. The graduate students drank a lot, as they always did when offered free booze, and Chris, too, was in the mood to celebrate. He had just had a book proposal approved by Garland Press. Even Sam, after parading Grace around before putting her down at 11:00, had finally started to relax. She was drinking Benedictine and brandy, her first since the baby was born, and she wasn't carrying the baby monitor around. This, too, was a first. Finally, Chris thought, things were becoming normal.

More people showed up. Evidently, the graduate students had invited some of their colleagues, who likewise were lured by free drinks, and the party grew louder. Chris didn't mind. He was flying high. It had been a successful semester, he and Sam had a beautiful baby girl, and Sam was finally happy.

Sam came up just then. "This was a wonderful idea, Chris. I'm having a great time." She had another full snifter of B&B in her hand. "I haven't felt this happy, or tipsy, in a long time." She smiled beatifically and kissed his cheek. "I'm going to sneak upstairs and check on Grace. I'll be back in a sec."

Tess, one of his graduate students, stood nearby. "Can I go with you, Mrs. Connor? I know I've already seen Grace, but she's such a pretty little girl."

"You don't need to suck up now, Tess. The semester's over," Sam said.

"Oh, I," Tess stuttered.

Sam laughed. "I'm just kidding. Of course you can see my little angel." She took hold of Tess's arm.

Chris watched her thread through the crowd, weaving slightly, holding her glass carefully (but still sloshing). She went up the stairs, holding onto Tess's arm for support. He checked his watch. It was after two o'clock, yet no one seemed willing to leave, to let the night go. That was always the sign of a good party.

And then he heard Sam's piercing, agonized scream. All sound in the room stopped. For Chris, it felt as though his heart stopped beating, as if time itself froze.

Then Tess stumbled down the stairs, her face drained of color. "The baby. Grace," she said.

Chris dropped his glass and ran toward the stairs—still feeling like he was moving in a slow-motion dream—as the primal scream went on and on and on.

The mister system had started to drip into puddles at the edge of the patio, yet Sam and Alex barely noticed. They were cool, slightly damp, and Alex had just opened another bottle of champagne. Sam looked at her cell phone. It was not quite midnight. "What were we talking about before you went in?" she asked.

"I don't remember. We've talked about everything so far: junior high, high school, college, and all the boys we dated or wanted to date. You'd think we get sick of talking about our past, wouldn't you?"

"You'd think so, but I don't."

"Me neither."

"We are continually revising our shared history. It gets better that way." Sam shook a cigarette out of the second pack of Virginia Slims Superslim Menthols on the table. She wanted to talk to Alex about what was really on her mind, but the time wasn't right yet. Would it ever be the right time? She handed the pack to Alex. "Want one more?"

Alex took one. "You are such a bad influence on me." She lit the cigarette and inhaled deeply. "But it feels so good. I can't believe you actually live across the street."

Sam couldn't believe it either. It had been more of a non-decision than a decision. After sleepwalking through the past two years, fueled by Xanax, Prozac, and valium, she had walked by the baby's room one dreary March afternoon, and for the first time since that terrible night, stepped in. The pink, blue, and yellow Care Bears were still stenciled on the walls, along with the cherub wallpaper that fringed the top of those four walls. The crib was made up with the fluffy pink checked comforter, and the carousel mobile hung above it. Sam peered into the crib. The baby wasn't there. Grace wasn't there.

Sam dropped to her knees. She had thought she was out of tears, but she was wrong. She cried and cried. Later, after the sun had gone down and Sam lay in utter darkness, Chris found her. He gently pulled her up and took her downstairs and tucked her in on the living room couch. He went to the kitchen and made her a cup of ginseng tea. It seemed to take a long time before the kettle boiled. It usually irritated her that he made tea the old-fashioned way instead of using the microwave as she did. Now, she was too tired and numb to care. She didn't feel anything.

Chris brought her the tea and sat down on the coffee table in front of her. "We can't go on like this," he said.

"I know." She took a sip of tea. It was too hot. She handed it back to him. "I'd rather have a brandy."

He went to the well-stocked bar in the corner of the room and poured a snifter full of E&J. Handing this to her, he said, "I think we should move.

I've been offered a position as head of the English Department at Arizona State University. Just think, Sam, you'd be close to Alex and her family."

She wanted to be close to Alex and her family. She had thought about it many times, but could she handle it? She loved Nick and Annie dearly, and that was the problem. Each time she had seen them since . . . the accident . . . it only made her own loss that much greater. It was a terrible thing, she knew, to be so insanely jealous of her own sister.

"Life is so unfair," she said. The day before, lying in bed and flipping listlessly through the TV channels, she had landed on *Maury*. As it so often was, the tabloid talk show's topic was paternity. Tearful and/or angry young women were there to determine the fathers of their babies. Those cocky young men could go around impregnating girls as easily as if they were dropping seeds into richly fertilized soil. One in particular, the "baby daddy of Champaign" (right here, in her own town!), had fathered eight children and didn't seem to want any of them. Briefly, excitedly, she wondered where he lived. Perhaps he had magic semen, super-duper sperm, that could make anyone pregnant. Her heart pounded furiously. She could call the show and find out his last name. Maybe he was in the phone book? Maybe she could Google him? She reached for her phone, then stopped, scared.

That was when she knew she was going crazy. She had crossed the line.

Chris had been talking for some time, carefully articulating his argument for the move to Arizona. "I really think it's a good idea, Sam. It could be a fresh start, and maybe, just maybe, Alex can give you something that I can't."

"Like a baby?" she asked. She finished the last of the brandy.

"Sam," Chris said gently, "you really need to move on."

The idea began. She and Alex, being identical twins, had the same DNA. Why hadn't she thought of this before?

"I can't bear to see you this way any longer. You know I'd do anything I could to make you happy." Chris took her hand and kissed it.

She left it there, caressing his lips with her fingertips. "What the hell, let's do it."

"I just don't know what's going on with Annie," Alex said. "Instead of her usual As and Bs, she got Cs and Ds. Jack didn't even want to ground her, saying that a lot of freshmen get off to a rocky start. As usual, he left it up to me to be the bad guy." She looked at Sam, who wore a glazed expression. "Sam, are you listening?

Sam started. "Of course I'm listening. It's only hair." She'd really been gone there for a moment or two. Thank God Alex was here to pull her back into the present. She had been living in the past for too long. She must make a new start.

"You were not. I was talking about Annie's miserable grades," Alex accused. She poured more champagne into their glasses. "Maybe it's time to go to bed."

"I don't want to go to bed. I've spent enough time there lately, thank you very much."

"I'm sorry." Alex looked at her with sympathy.

It enraged Sam. "I don't need your sympathy, Alex." She reached for a cigarette and knocked over her champagne glass. It fell to the concrete patio floor and shattered. She started to cry. "It's all my fault," she choked.

Alex bent down to pick up the pieces. "Don't worry, honey, it was a cheap glass I bought from Walmart. I might have even bought it at the Dollar Store. A dollar, that's all it cost."

Despite the tears running down her face, Sam started to laugh. "I wasn't referring to the glass, you dummy. I thought twins were supposed to read each other's minds. Boy, did you veer down the wrong path."

Alex straightened up. "I know what you meant. You meant Grace, and it wasn't your fault, Sam. Sudden Infant Death Syndrome is no one's fault. You didn't do anything wrong."

"I was drunk. What kind of mother would do that when she has a three-month-old baby upstairs?" The tears started again. Would they ever stop?

Alex leaned over and hugged her. "You were a good mother, Sam," she said softly. "Unfortunately, accidents happen."

"But why? I put her to bed on her back, so how did she end up suffocating in the mattress?"

"I don't know how these things happen, but I do know that it's not your fault."

Sam let Alex comfort her in their rocking hug. It had been a long time since they held each other like that, too long. When they finally let go of each other, Sam said, "I'm glad I finally told you. I felt too guilty and embarrassed to tell you before."

"I'm glad, too, Sam, but you know I would never judge you."

"I know. Let's not talk about this anymore. As Chris so often points out, I need to move on, make a fresh start."

"That's a good idea. I could use a fresh start myself."

Sam reached for the champagne and drank out of the bottle. "Why?"

"Do you want me to get you another cheap Dollar Store glass?"

"No, since I'm not standing in an alley with a paper bag around this bottle, I think it'll do."

Alex laughed. "Yeah, you know I don't care if you're a wino."

"Back to you. Why do you think you need a fresh start?"

"It's hard to explain, but things around here have been different lately. On the surface, everything seems the same, but underneath, it feels like some force is gaining momentum." She shook her head. "I'm probably just being paranoid."

"Nick and Annie are growing up—"

"And they don't need me anymore," Alex finished.

"Sure they do. They just need you in a different way." Sam took another swig from the bottle. Growing up: Grace never had the chance. There would never be birthday parties, holidays, sleepovers, schools, puberty, or graduations. All that had been over before it began.

"Maybe the cruise will make us all feel closer again," Alex said hopefully.

"It will, and it's going to be great."

"Thanks again, Sam, but I do feel bad that you're paying for everything. We could pay you back in installments or something."

"The layaway cruise plan? Not an option. It's my gift to both of us."

"Guess what? From me, you're getting the boxed DVD gift set of all the *I Love Lucy* episodes. Would you consider that a fair gift exchange?"

"I certainly would. I've always wanted the complete *I Love Lucy* collection." They both laughed, and she reached across the table and squeezed Alex's delicate hand, identical to her own.

"I love you, Sam. You know I'd do anything for you."

Sam's hope surged. "I love you, too, my darling sister." She raised the champagne bottle. Alex raised her glass. "This is a toast: Fuck you, forty." They clinked, bottle to glass.

2

CHAPTER TWO

It was the first full day at sea on the Royal Caribbean Voyager, and the six of them met at the buffet breakfast at 9:00 a.m., as they had agreed to do at dinner the previous night. It promised to be a sunny, windy day at sea, unlike the day before, when they had boarded the boat under dark clouds and drizzling skies. Sam felt personally responsible for the weather because this had been her idea, after all. Instead of lounging by the pool, they had toured the boat *en masse*, walking through the shops on the promenade deck, the nightclub, the sports facilities, the various bars, the gym, and the ice rink. They had all had dinner together, as they would every night at their assigned table, and had then gone to the wine bar and listened to Vicente, a very drunk piano player. By the end of the evening, Sam had felt exhausted, as if she had led a group of grade school children on a very long and rather boring field trip.

"I have an idea," Sam said as the waiter set down their drinks. She pulled the day's itinerary from her purse, and she could swear she heard Jack groan. She looked pointedly at him. "I think we should all do our own thing today. There's entertainment by the pool, rock climbing, an art auction, the casino is open, and a lot of other activities. Basically, there's something for everyone."

"Now, that's what I call a good idea," Jack said.

"Fine by me," Nick said.

"I think I'll go to the art auction and drink the free champagne." Chris did air quotes around the word "free."

"I'm thinking about the pool," Alex said.

"Me, too," Sam said. "What about you, Annie?"

"I haven't decided yet." She looked pale, and her dyed black hair hung limply around her face, begging to be washed.

"A suntan would kind of ruin the ghostly Goth effect, wouldn't it?" Nick asked.

"Shut up, Nick!"

"Stop it, both of you." Alex rummaged in her purse. "Are you feeling all right, Annie? You look a little under the weather. It might be seasickness. I brought some Dramamine. This boat was really rocking last night. Did anyone else feel it?"

"I'm fine, Mom," Annie said with exaggerated patience.

"Let's get something to eat." Jack rose from the table and headed toward the buffet station. Chris and Nick followed.

Alex pushed the bottle of Dramamine across the table. "Keep it just in case, honey. I think I'll get something to eat, too." She went in the direction of the others.

Sam studied Annie. She knew a hangover when she saw one. "Late night?"

"Yeah. I couldn't sleep, so I decided to walk around. I met some kids on the Lido deck, and they bought me a few beers. I didn't even need the fake I.D. my friend Carla got for me. You were right, Aunt Sam, they're really lax about underage drinking on the high seas." She took a tentative sip of orange juice and shuddered. "You won't tell Mom, will you?"

Should she? Sam wasn't sure about the proper protocol in a case like this, but Annie's eyes were pleading, she wanted Annie to trust her, and this was a vacation. "I won't tell."

"Thanks." Annie hugged her. "You are such a great aunt."

Sam held the hug for as long as she could. Annie was at such a vulnerable age, and something was clearly bothering her. Perhaps she could get Annie to confide in her. Maybe she could help, but would that be a betrayal of Alex? She wasn't sure.

"I'm going to go puke." Annie abruptly left the table.

The others came back to the table, their plates heaped with scrambled eggs, bacon, sausage, and waffles. Except for Alex. She had a small muffin and some fruit. It was the same thing Sam had planned to eat. They were both careful about their weight, and now that they were turning forty, it was probably a good thing. Even during her pregnancies, Alex had not gained a lot of weight and had quickly lost it. It would be a plus for Sam's plan.

"Where's the Bride of Frankenstein?" Nick asked as he shoveled scrambled eggs.

"Nick," Alex began.

"Your mom's right, Nick. You've got to stop picking on your sister. She's just going through a phase, and as a family, we have to support her," Jack said.

"She went to lie down." Sam motioned to the waiter for more coffee.

"It figures. When you come in—"

"How do you like your rooms? The junior suites have a lot more room than you think," Sam interrupted.

"And a balcony. They're absolutely great." Alex turned to Nick. "What were you going to say?"

"Nothing," he mumbled through his food.

Chris pushed his chair away from the table. "I'm heading over to the internet station to check my emails since the boss," he nodded and smiled at Sam, "wouldn't let me bring my computer. Anyone want to come with me? Nick?"

"That'd be great."

"I'm off to the rock gym. I've got to work off some of this breakfast." Jack leaned over and kissed Alex on the cheek. "Have fun."

"Why is everyone in such a hurry? I haven't even eaten yet." They were supposed to relax and spend quality time together on this vacation, and Sam knew it had been her idea to let everyone go separate ways today, but still, what amount of time had passed since that suggestion? Fifteen minutes.

"Don't sweat the small stuff, sis." Jack playfully punched Sam's arm as he walked by.

"You're lucky she didn't punch you back," Chris said, joining Jack.

"Don't I know it." They laughed.

"I would not have punched you," Sam called after them, although she had at one time thought that Jack needed a swift kick in the balls. But that had been a long time ago.

"I'll stay with you, Sam. I've barely started to eat," Alex said.

"Assholes." Sam looked at her sister. "No teenaged boys included in that group."

"No offense taken."

Sam had naturally assumed that Alex would stay with her, just as she always had. "Thanks, honey. We need a rum drink, preferably one with a ridiculous paper umbrella. Let's get this party started."

After Nick checked his emails (one from Dylan, but he hadn't been expecting any others), he put on his running clothes and tried to jog around the outdoor track that circled the top deck of the ship. Apparently, a lot of people had the same idea. He tried to dart around the mothers pushing baby carriages, the old ladies in sun hats and Rocket Dogs strolling around the path, and the other mismatched cruisers in varying stages of walking/jogging, but he couldn't get his heart rate up to a satisfactory level, so he gave up and went to the gym. It, too, was crowded, and as he patiently waited for a treadmill to free up, he couldn't help thinking that the crowd of exercisers—many overweight—probably never exercised at home. Starting a workout routine on vacation was definitely doomed to failure.

He ran his ten miles and returned to the stateroom to shower. Annie lay motionless on the bed. He threw a dirty sock at her, but she didn't move. Concerned, Nick went over to check on her, bending down to her mouth, which was slightly parted. He could feel her breath on his cheek. He could also smell its sour mix of beer and vomit. He should probably ease her onto her side to make sure she didn't drown in her own puke, but he didn't want to wake her. Despite looking rather green—he could start calling her Herman Munster—she seemed peaceful, and for once, she wasn't yapping off about something or calling him a loser. He loved her, of course, but he liked her much better passed out.

They had bickered constantly since getting on the boat. No surprise there, but they were in such close quarters that his escape routes were limited to the small closet or the bathroom. Unlike his parents and aunt and uncle across the hall, they were in an interior room without a balcony, which was a good thing. Annie was a slob, and her unpacking consisted of placing her large suitcase on a precious piece of floor, opening it, and digging through it like a puppy, throwing clothing everywhere looking for something to wear to dinner. When she went out the night before, he could have taken all her stuff and tossed it over the imaginary balcony, letting the dolphins play with her hot pink Victoria's Secret bras and thongs. Instead, he folded everything up and put it in the closet.

He decided to check out the pool, first stopping at the buffet for a hamburger and a hot dog, thinking that he might as well get his money's worth. The pool was crowded; a half-naked body sprawled over every deck chair—old, young, fat, and thin, all glistening with sweat and suntan oil. The sight of all that exposed flesh embarrassed him, and he was about to go back inside when he heard his mother call "Nick!" He would swear that she had some kind of maternal radar. How in the world could she pick him out of that mass of humanity? Reluctantly, he searched the crowd, spotted her and Aunt Sam, and made his way over to them.

They had prime seats, right in front of the makeshift stage. They both wore bikinis—weren't they too old?—and Nick averted his eyes from their bodies and concentrated on their faces. Mom patted the edge of her lounge chair. "Why don't you have a seat? They're about to start the men's Best Legs contest."

He sat down gingerly. "Nice seats."

"We had to fight and claw for them," Aunt Sam said.

"No, we didn't," Mom said.

"Well, I did give that obnoxious woman a little push when she said we didn't get here first, and I told her that you can't put a towel on a chair, say you are *saving* it, go eat lunch, and then expect the chair to still be yours." She was drinking a pink drink, and so was his mother.

Aunt Sam held hers up. "Bahama Mama, the drink special of the day. Do you want one?"

"No, thanks." It was Nick's opinion that everyone in his family drank too much. He didn't particularly like the taste of alcohol, even though he had only had a few sips, and he hated how stupid it made everyone. More importantly, he disliked that alcohol made people lose their self-control. His eyes wandered over to a group of four girls about his age frolicking in the pool. Their swimming suits didn't leave much to the imagination, and he quickly looked away.

"Checking out those girls over there, are you, Nick?" Apparently, Aunt Sam wasn't drunk yet. "That little blonde is really cute."

"I wasn't checking them out."

"Leave him alone, Sam. You're embarrassing him." Mom rubbed his arm. "He's still a little shy around girls. It's perfectly natural."

He felt his face turning red, and her touching him in public made it even worse. She had said on many occasions before that he was a *late bloomer*, as if that accounted for the fact that he had never had a date. He knew it was more than that. He could look at a cute girl and not feel anything at all, and that couldn't be natural, could it? But he was certainly not attracted to boys either. Tentatively, he had discussed this with Dylan, who also had never had a date, and they had done some research on it and come up with the possibility that they might be asexual, not attracted to either sex. They had pondered this, not too worried, figuring that it would save them a lot of time, drama, and money in the long run.

Luckily, he didn't have to say anything else because the Best Legs contest started. Three paunchy, middle-aged men, a fraternity type who acted like he thought he was Adonis, and a ten-year-old boy paraded around the stage, flexing and bowing. The women in the crowd yelled and cheered like the specimens before them were male strippers. To the side, a young man in his early twenties slipped off his jeans and bounded onto the stage. The crowd went wild. He was good-looking in a wholesome, all-American way. And he had a prosthetic leg, metal, with a springy looking rudder at the end.

"Would you look at that?" Mom clapped furiously.

"You've got to love a guy with a sense of humor," Aunt Sam said.

Nick sat riveted. The metal leg gleamed in the sunlight as the guy pranced around the stage with the others. Given his crew cut, Nick would bet his life savings ($600, not counting the stolen stash) that the guy was military. Each contestant gave a short speech, and Nick was right. He was a Marine and an Iraq veteran. Adonis, naturally, was an Alpha Tau Omega.

The winner was determined by applause. The three middle-aged men got decent applause—mostly from their wives—the ten-year-old got a larger outpouring, followed by Adonis. When the emcee held his hand over the Marine, the crowd went wild, stamping their feet and clapping.

"Go bionic man!" Aunt Sam yelled, and the crowd took up the cheer.

Nick, too, was on his feet, clapping and yelling. This guy was a hero, and everyone here recognized that. This was what he wanted. He would prefer not to get his leg shot off in the line of duty, but he would have no control over that. Perhaps he could find this guy later and talk to him about Iraq. Maybe he could ask for an autograph, or would that be too lame?

"That was great," Mom said after the hero was declared the winner and everyone sat down again. "I'm so glad bionic man won."

"Are we having fun yet?" Aunt Sam picked up her drink.

Nick had had enough of the sun and of them. He stood up and said, "He is not a bionic man. He is a United States Marine." He left before they could say another word.

Nick had hoped the Marine would get a trophy for winning, but all the guy got was a lousy drink coupon.

Chris sipped champagne at the art auction held in a small auditorium. He sat alone at a small red-clothed table at the side. He had previewed all the art, looking for something to put in his office, still the only room Sam hadn't touched with her Southwest decorating spree. The Picasso limited edition prints and the Peter Max mixed media works interested him the most, but they were way out of his price range, and he wasn't interested at all in the sports or Disney cartoon prints that they were currently auctioning. Too bad that he didn't have his computer to check out the prices of some of the smaller Peter Nixon or Kandinsky prints that were coming up for sale. He had no way of knowing whether he would get a good deal.

This cruise was not his idea. He had given into Sam, as he always did, but she didn't seem to realize how much it was going to cost. In their marriage, it was his responsibility to worry about money, not hers. After all the fertility experts and IVF treatments, their savings account had been nearly depleted. He had started to build it up again, then he had to deal with the cost of the move, the recession had taken its toll, and now this. But he was willing to soldier on, to bear the expense just to make her happy, and when things finally settled into a routine again, he could once again start to save money for their retirement.

But now Sam had another idea. Last night, after an interminable dinner with the Carissa family (he had absolutely nothing in common with Jack the jock), they had been sitting on their balcony, sipping wine. It was windy, but the sea was relatively calm, and the stars shone vividly in the black skies. He felt contented and relaxed, and therefore, Sam caught him completely off guard.

"I'm going to ask Alex to be a surrogate for me."

He hoped he hadn't heard her correctly, that the wind had distorted her words. "What did you say?"

She repeated, "I'm going to ask Alex to be a surrogate for me. I mean, for us."

Was she drunk? Had she taken a valium? He thought they had put this all to rest two years ago. "You're joking, right?"

"No, I've never been more serious. I don't know why I didn't think of this before. We're identical twins with the same DNA. Her eggs are the same as mine—if I still had any. So, with your sperm and Alex's egg, we could have another baby that would be genetically the same as if it were really you and me. Don't you see?"

Oh, God, he should have forced her to stay in therapy. "I don't see that at all, Sam. This is not a good idea. In fact, it's a ridiculous idea."

"It's not ridiculous. It's brilliant. Oh, I almost forgot. I bought you some cigars today." She went into the room and came back with an expensive Cuban Cohiba and handed it to him. "I know you like a good cigar."

Did she think this was a done deal, that she could start handing out cigars like a new proud parent? "I don't want a cigar, Sam, and I want you to listen to me."

"Very well. I'll smoke it myself." She lit the cigar.

"What in the world would make you think that I would agree to this? Or Alex? Or Jack? Or Nick and Annie? This would be a huge imposition on everyone, especially Alex."

"I know Alex will do it for me."

"You don't know any such thing."

"Yes, I do. I know her as well as I know myself. She would. Especially if we paid her."

"What?"

"I think she would carry our baby out of love anyway, but I know she and Jack are having some financial issues, and the money could be the icing on the cake. I've thought it all out."

He didn't know what to do with her, probably never had. She was used to getting her own way, but this was an exception, a very big exception. "This is not going to work, Sam. I love you very, very much, but this is out of the question."

She put the cigar down and knelt before him. She reached for his hands and looked directly into his eyes. "I know you think I'm crazy, but I've never been more sane. I've given this a lot of thought, and I know how many risks are involved, but I want this more than anything in the world. This is our very last chance for a baby, our very last hope. All I'm asking for you to do right now, Chris, is think about it. That's all, just *think* about it. Would you do that for me?"

He suddenly felt exhausted. The pleading in her eyes drained the energy from him. "I'll think about it, but—"

She threw her arms around his waist and buried her head in his lap. "Oh, thank you, Chris, thank you!"

She had thanked him in bed, and it had been such a long time since they had made love that he was surprised and gratified by the intensity of it.

"More champagne, sir?" The waitress startled him.

"Oh, no thank you. I think I'll be going." He got up and passed by the Peter Nixon prints on his way out. The beautiful women dressed in flowing gowns of red and gold looked like they were dancing. Sadly, he was never going to be able to afford them.

Jack walked through the casino. He had no intention of playing, had purposely not brought any money with him. He watched the blackjack players for a while. The table seemed to be hot; everyone had a stack of chips in front of him. His heart started to beat faster. He really wanted to play. He and Alex had brought three hundred dollars spending money for the trip. It wasn't much, just enough to get a few souvenirs at each port. It was in the safe in their room, and perhaps he could borrow from it and pay back the money when he won. But what if he lost? What would he tell Alex? No, it was better to find something else to do. He reluctantly walked away, through the smoke-filled air and past the rows of clanging slot machines. And then, almost hidden in a corner, he saw the ATM machine.

When he got back to the table, there was a new dealer, an attractive brunette with a British accent. "Good luck, sir," she said as she changed the hundred into chips.

She didn't bring him luck. Twenty minutes later, he went back to the ATM. He won the next seven hands. He had made his money back, and he knew he should leave, but Jack had a gut feeling that he was on a winning streak. He started to relax, began to order Bacardi and diet cokes and chatted with the other players. The table grew more boisterous. They were all on vacation, after all, and everyone wanted to have a good time. He barely noticed his dwindling pile of chips.

"Where have you been?" Alex said when he returned to the room at 7:30.

"Walking around." It wasn't exactly a lie. After the cash machine rudely flashed the message that he had exceeded his daily limit on withdrawals, he had taken a walk around the ship, feeling flushed, slightly nauseous, and ashamed. What had he done? He should tell her now, before it was too late. She'd be angry, but she'd get over it when he told her that he would never be so reckless again.

"We need to hurry. Even though our dinner seating isn't until 8:30, it's formal night, and we've all agreed to meet downstairs at 8:00 for a family picture." She went into the closet and came out with a plastic garment bag. "I rented a tux for you. Sam said that Chris was wearing one, and I thought it would be nice if you had one, too. You haven't worn one in years, and you always did look so nice in a tuxedo."

He finally noticed what she had on: a strapless, floor-length, navy blue sequined dress. "Where'd you get that dress?" He wanted to say: How much did it cost?

"T.J. Maxx. I thought I told you about it. Do I look bad in it? Maybe it is a little too tight."

"No, you look beautiful." She did.

"Thank you. Now go prettify yourself." She pushed the garment bag into his arms.

He did start to feel better when they all met downstairs at the photographer's station, dressed to the nines. Even Annie had put on a nice sundress and piled her black hair on top of her head.

"You look much better," Alex said to her.

"The Dramamine did the trick."

"I thought it would." Alex turned to Nick, dressed in a black suit and a red tie. "You look great."

Jack felt a lump in his throat. His children looked so grown up.

"It's our turn," Sam said, looking stunning in a gold dress. "Let's position ourselves on the stairway."

"Wait a minute," Jack said. "I thought this was supposed to be a family picture."

"It is a family picture," she said. "Aren't we all in the same family?"

Jesus, she was pushy. "I want a picture of the four of us." He motioned to Alex, Nick, and Annie.

Sam looked hurt. "Well, of course, you can do that. I just wanted a picture of all of us together."

"Fine," he said. "Then we'll have a picture taken of the Carissa family." He would stand firm on this point. He had four people in his beautiful family, and for one time on the trip, he wasn't going to let Sam fucking interfere.

Alex, sitting on the stage with Jack next to her, was acutely embarrassed. She didn't know how she had gotten roped into this ridiculous situation. It had started at dinner when they were discussing the evening's entertainment. Sam mentioned that the Marriage Game sounded like fun.

"It's a game show with three couples, the newlyweds, the oldyweds, and the goldyweds," she read from the ship's itinerary. "It's like the *Newlywed Game*. Remember that show with Bob Eubanks? It was a scream."

"They have a new version on GSN hosted by Carnie Wilson," Annie said. "It's not as funny as the old one. She doesn't joke around as much as the other guy." She picked at her filet.

"Aren't you supposed to be a vegetarian?" Nick had finished his dinner and was eyeing her mostly untouched meat.

"I quit doing that. I forgot one day and had Taco Bell for lunch. It is very hard to maintain a healthy lifestyle in this culture. I mean, there's a fast food place on almost every corner. It's like they're tempting you on purpose."

"Oh, brother," said Nick.

The waiter came to the table. "Is everything satisfactory here?"

"Is it possible to get seconds?" Nick asked.

"You can order as much as you want."

"Great. I'll take another steak, please."

"Oink, oink," Annie snorted.

"Wouldn't it be more like moo, moo?" Nick said.

"Let's get back to this game show thing. Who wants to go?" Sam looked around the table. Everyone gave a varying degree of assent: okay, yeah, sure, sounds like fun, why not?

They were some of the first to arrive, and Sam marched them down to the first row of the auditorium. Immediately, a young blonde man with a Hollywood smile came over to them. "Hi, I'm Allen, the emcee. I'm looking for contestants for the show. Who's a married couple here?"

"Not interested," Jack said.

He hadn't said much at dinner, and Alex was getting irritated at him. "Not interested in being on the show, or not interested in marriage?" she asked.

Allen laughed. "You two must be married. I think you'd be perfect for the game."

"We're really not interested," Alex said as politely as she could. She wished that Allen, with his toilet-bowl-white, capped teeth, would quit hovering. The other people filing into the auditorium were staring.

"Why not?" Sam said. "Be adventurous, take a risk, it's a once-in-a-lifetime experience."

"Then you do it," Alex snapped.

"But Allen doesn't want Chris and me," she smiled sweetly at Allen. "He wants you. Isn't that right, Allen?"

"That's right."

"Oh, for Christ's sake," Jack muttered.

"Don't push, Sam," Chris said.

"I think you should do it," Nick said, grinning. "It's not very often you're allowed to laugh at your parents."

"For once, I agree with Nick," Annie said. "Just don't say anything really embarrassing, like anything to do with sex. That would be too gross for words."

"What do you say?" Allen asked.

Alex and Jack looked at each other, and defeated, they rose and followed Allen backstage.

So now they were the oldyweds, sitting in the middle of the stage with the giggling honeymooners on their right and a couple celebrating their fiftieth wedding anniversary on their left. Backstage, they had been separated and asked questions and were now trying to match each other's responses. They were terrible. They hadn't matched each other once, much to the delight of the audience. At least Jack had gotten into the spirit of the whole thing, remarking at one point: "I really don't know this woman at all. I just picked her up at the piano bar an hour ago." The audience cheered. Alex was mortified.

"And now for the twenty-five-point bonus question," Allen said. "We'll start with the couple with the least amount of points—in this case, a big fat zero—the oldyweds, Jack and Alex. Let's see if they can get one question right. What do you say, audience?"

"You can do it. You can do it," they chanted. Alex looked at Nick, Annie, Sam, and Chris, who were chanting along with the rest of the crowd. They were all traitors, she thought, but she mustered a smile. She didn't want them to think she was a bad sport.

"Jack, in what direction does the living room in your house or apartment face?"

Jack grinned. "Well, Allen, you think this would be an easy question, don't you? But let me tell you a story so you can see what I'm up against here."

"Don't you dare tell that story, Jack." She really was terrible with directions, but did the whole world have to know about it? Apparently, they did. Jack started the story of the family vacation to Seattle.

"I won't say that Alex is lousy with directions. That would be too mean." He patted her knee. "I'll just say she is *directionally challenged*." The crowd snickered. "So, I hadn't let her drive the whole trip. But on the way home, driving from Seattle to Portland, I got sleepy and decided to let her drive. It was easy enough. All she had to do was follow the route south. I fell asleep, and when I woke up, we were crossing the Canadian border."

Nick stood up and made a megaphone with his hands around his mouth. "Welcome to Canada! It's a true story!" The audience cheered.

"To answer your question, Allen, the direction our living room faces is east." Jack turned to Alex. "What did you say, honey?"

She clutched the card on her lap. "I'm not turning this over."

"You can do it. You can do it," the relentless audience chanted. Alex could hear Sam screaming above all the others. "You can do it! You can do it!"

"Come on, sweetheart, you might as well get it over with."

She glared at Jack, then defiantly stood up and waved the card for all to see: WEST.

The crowd went wild. Alex had never before made a spectacle of herself in public and realized it wasn't so bad after all. In fact, it was exhilarating, her own fifteen minutes of fame.

Annie waited for Adam on the Lido deck, leaning against the ship's railing, pretending to look at the stars. He was one of the boys she had met the night before, and from what she could remember, they had really hit it off. She vaguely remembered making out with him, but after four beers, three shots of tequila and part of a joint, she couldn't be one hundred percent sure. She might have dreamed the kissing part. And she wasn't quite sure if he had actually asked her to meet him tonight at midnight either, but just in case, she had left on her nice dress from dinner. It would be her first date, if he did, in fact, show up.

Out of habit, she reached into her purse for her cell phone to check the time. Damn. It wasn't there. Duh. She had left it in the room because they didn't have any cell phone service on the ship. She was a master at texting. Sometimes she and Carla texted each other forty times a day. Not having that valuable means of communicating was painful, like losing a limb or something. Well, maybe that was a dramatic way to put it, but she did know this: Her hands felt very, very empty. She had even reverted to biting her nails today, just to give her hands something to do.

He was late. She was sure of that because she had forced herself to wait until five after twelve before she came on deck. If he didn't show up, it would probably be just as well. It would solve her quandary about whether meeting Adam would be unfaithful to Walter. Walter, the golden-haired captain of the lacrosse team, the love of her life, who had almost smiled at her on the last day of school, giving her hope and her life new meaning. Carla told her that pining for a boy for an entire year, without receiving one iota of attention from said boy, was enough. She told Annie she needed to move on, but Annie was having a hard time doing that.

However, if Adam didn't show up, she was really going to be pissed. Being stood up on a first date went on the "You're a Loser Because . . ." list. Embarrassingly, it would be her new number one. And now she would have to spend the rest of the vacation avoiding him, which would be a problem since she didn't remember exactly what he looked like.

"Hey, there." Someone tapped her shoulder. "Sorry I'm late. I had to do the family thing. Grandparents' sixtieth anniversary and all that."

She turned. Adam didn't look anything like the picture of him she had in her head. He was tall, probably over six feet, really skinny, and had a mild case of acne. He was no Walter. "I was about to leave," she said, thinking that she should. He had been so much better looking in her imagination.

"Please don't. I've looked forward to seeing you all day." He smiled, showing perfect teeth, and the smile lit up his dark brown eyes. "You look very pretty."

He looked much better. All she had to do was keep him smiling. It was kind of too bad that she didn't have that stupid joke book Nick used to have as a kid. Wait a minute. Did he just say she was pretty? "All right. I'll stay."

"Good. We should get this party started." He pulled a joint from his pocket and lit it with a Bic lighter. He inhaled and handed it to her.

Because she had been allowed to have a glass of red wine at dinner after her mom had grudgingly said "yes" at Aunt Sam's insistence, the pot immediately made Annie feel light-headed. However, it also made her feel relaxed. Her nervousness eased away. "So, where are you from?"

"Yeah, I suppose we should get all that crap over with. I'll give you the Cliff Notes version. I'm from Newport Beach. I feel like I'm an only child, but I'm not. I have a brother who's way older than me. I was my parents' midlife mistake baby. I just finished my sophomore year at Santa Barbara. What about you?"

She did a quick calculation. Adam would be twenty. Wow, he was the same age as Drew, Carla's boyfriend. Maybe this was some kind of sign. But what was she going to tell him, that she was a sophomore in high school? She stalled for time. "What's your major?"

He took another hit and laughed. "I haven't declared yet. It's a great source of consternation to the parents. You know how that goes."

"Oh, sure," she said. "And then you never major in what they want you to, so what does it matter?"

"That is so true. I knew last night that I liked you, uh—"

"Annie," she supplied.

"Annie," he said. "Sorry about that. I was pretty wasted last night."

"Me, too. I haven't been that wasted since the last party I was at. You know, you come home from school, and you have to deal with the parental issue." Technically, she hadn't even told one lie yet. She could get away with this through simple *omission*.

"Exactly!" He handed her the last of the joint. "It's so nice to find someone you can talk to, Annie. You're really special."

She was glad it was dark because she was sure she flushed pink with pleasure. He had said she was pretty *and* special.

Two boys—or were they men?—clomped noisily across the deck. "Hey, Scumbag, do you want to go to the disco with us?" the taller one asked. He eyed Annie. "You're the girl from last night."

"I am." Like with Adam, she didn't recognize them, but she knew that they, too, were not high school boys.

"My cousins," Adam said by way of introduction. "No, we're going to hang out together tonight."

"Got you." The shorter one winked. "Good luck." They walked away, and as they reached the end of the deck, Annie heard them burst into laughter.

"Ignore them. They're already drunk. And of course, they're jealous."

"Why would they be jealous?"

Adam put his arm around her and started to steer her away from the railing. "Because you're so adorable."

Another compliment. This was really turning into her night. "Where are we going?"

"I thought we'd hang out in my room for a while. I've got some tequila."

"Okay," she said. It wasn't like he could take her any place she couldn't escape from. This was a boat, after all, not someplace in the desert, and she liked him. She really wanted to make out with him. And try to re-member it this time.

As they walked down one flight of carpeted steps to his stateroom, she had this thought. Adam was the first man; Adam was her first boy.

"It's our birthday eve," Sam shouted over the whipping wind. A big chunk of hair blew into her mouth. She removed it and glanced over at Alex, who looked as if she was holding onto the edge of the truck for dear life. She shouted again, "Today is our birthday eve!"

"Only if we live until tomorrow," Alex shouted back. "I can't believe I let you talk me into this."

Alex needed to learn how to go with the flow more. When the man had offered to take them on a quick one-hour tour of Mazatlán for twenty dollars, Sam had been eager to go, but not Alex.

"Do you think it's legal?" Alex had whispered to Sam.

"He says he's originally from Texas," she had whispered back.

"What does that have to do with anything? It's a rickety truck with makeshift benches around the side."

"I don't think that most vehicles in Mexico have roll cages." She smiled warmly at the driver. "Just give me a minute here, please." She took hold of Alex's arm. "We're holding up the tour."

Alex didn't budge. "What if he's a human trafficker?"

"You watch too many Lifetime movies. Where's your sense of adventure?"

"I don't have any."

"You used to."

"You're making me mad," Alex warned.

"Fine. Go watch the others snorkel. Go sit on the sidelines. I should buy you some knitting needles and a shawl."

"Fuck you, Sam." And Alex got into the truck.

It had been a whirlwind ride. They had seen the highlights of Mazatlan, but the driver hadn't even stopped long enough for Sam to take pictures. Still, it was something exciting to do, unlike Cabo where they had spent the day lying on the beach. However, she could tell by Alex's face that she was still mad. She needed to make amends. Sam scooted closer to her on the seat. "Honey, you don't need to hold on so tightly. Take my hand. I'll make sure you don't fall out of the truck."

Reluctantly, Alex gave Sam her hand. "You and your crazy ideas. I probably should have gone snorkeling."

"But the tour is almost over, and you did it."

The truck screeched to a stop, narrowly missing a motor scooter that looked as if it was transporting an entire family. Sam and Alex—the only ones not holding onto the side of the truck—landed on their behinds on the truck's bed. They looked at each other and started to laugh.

"I think we're done here," Alex said.

"You are so right." Sam pulled her to her feet. "And look," she said, pointing at the corner restaurant, "we're right in front of Senor Frog's. I think it's time for a margarita."

"It's happy hour somewhere," Alex said.

They hobbled down from the truck, crossed the street, and went inside. The bar was dark and cool and crowded with tourists. Wearing sombreros, about twenty of them had formed a conga line that snaked through the tables.

"Apparently, some people started happy hour as soon as they got off the boat this morning," Sam said as they settled onto two empty bar stools. "Two stiff margaritas and two shots of tequila," she told the bartender.

"We need to catch up," Alex added.

Sam rummaged in her purse and found her cigarettes. She handed one to Alex and lit up. "Right now, I'm loving Mexico. You can smoke anywhere. Remember the good old days when you could sit in a bar with a drink in one hand and a cig in the other? God, I miss those days."

"We're getting old."

"Stop it. We are not. We are in the prime of our lives."

"Face facts, Sam. We are officially middle-aged. Look at that girl over there." She pointed to a voluptuous young blonde wearing cowboy boots and a holster. She went from table to table selling tequila shots. "I will never be that girl."

"So, the truth finally comes out. Your true ambition in life was to be a shot girl in a chain restaurant in Mexico. What a heartbreaking missed opportunity."

"Knock it off, Sam. You know what I mean. It's like doors closing. Suddenly, you realize that many things in life are no longer an option. You go along, living your life day after day, and—Bam! You wake up and realize your life is half over, and you have no idea how it happened."

Sam did know what she meant, but at this stage in her life, she chose to be positive. The world was still full of promise, and perhaps, if she played her cards right, she could have another baby. She had been waiting for the perfect moment to broach the subject with Alex, but this obviously wasn't it. "I refuse to participate in your pity party. We need more margaritas."

"You're right. I'm being selfish, wallowing, and whining." Alex picked up the fresh margarita and took a long drink. "My liver is going to be the size of a watermelon by the end of this trip."

"You're exaggerating. Maybe a small cantaloupe, though?"

"That's a much better analogy," Alex said, brightening.

The conga line—which had doubled in size—danced by them. "Why don't you two pretty ladies join us?" A balding, perspiring man shouted. He was at least sixty.

Sam and Alex looked at each other. "Will you let me borrow your sombrero?" Alex shouted.

"Sure!"

They jumped off the bar stools and joined the line. They danced through the bar three times, shouting *ole! ole! ole!*, and when they returned to their stools, they were both sweating. However, Sam noted, Alex was smiling broadly.

"I think we should move to Mexico," Alex said. "I could do this every day. Why worry about your kids and your mortgage when you could live in Mexico and drink tequila and dance?"

"I'll come with you. We could make money teaching English."

"Too boring. We should learn to make silver jewelry and sell it on the beach."

The blonde selling shots approached. "Would you two care to buy a shot? They're a buck apiece."

"How old are you?" Alex asked. Up close, the girl looked no more than eighteen.

"Excuse me?" she said.

"Never mind." Sam reached into her purse for a ten-dollar bill. "She's just jealous because you have her dream job."

"Excuse me?" she said again.

"Ten shots," Sam said, handing her the bill. The girl moved onto the people motioning for her at the other end of the bar.

"Not very bright, is she?" Alex poured salt between her thumb and forefinger, licked it, took the shot, and then bit into a lime.

"You don't have to be bright when you have boobs that big." Sam took her shot.

"Do you know what a lot of the girls at SCDS are getting for their sixteenth birthdays? A boob job."

"That's disgusting."

"I know, but it's practically becoming an epidemic among these little rich girls. Have you ever seen that reality show called *My Super Sweet Sixteen*? Those little princesses want so many things."

"Not only do they want them, they think they deserve them. I wrote an article on the Entitlement Generation a few months ago. These kids have no sense of reality, and they don't have the patience to climb up through the ranks."

Alex drank another shot. "It's appalling."

"I know."

"But yet, I feel sorry for them. In this terrible recession, how are they ever going to know how to cope?"

Before Sam could answer, the mariachi band approached them and asked if they wanted a song. "La Vida Loca," Sam said.

After the song and a couple more shots, it was all a blur to Sam. She wasn't quite sure how she and Alex ended up dancing on a table, but it felt like old times: free, uninhibited, and happy.

Jack and Chris didn't share their enthusiasm when they burst into the bar and spotted them. "What in the hell are you doing?" Jack demanded.

"When we boogie, we boogie woogie," Alex slurred.

"The boat leaves in ten minutes," Chris said as he pulled Sam down from the table. "Have you not noticed that the bar is practically empty?"

When Sam looked around the bar, she was surprised. All the other tourists were gone. "We lost track of time."

"We have to hurry," Jack said, steering Alex toward the door.

"I think a taxi would be a good idea." Alex leaned heavily against his shoulder.

"There are no taxis. We're going to run."

"I don't think that's a good idea," Sam said. She could now feel the tequila sloshing around her stomach. When was the last time she had eaten?

"It's the only way," Chris said. "We don't want to get left behind."

Making an awkward line by putting their arms around each other's shoulders—Sam, Chris, Alex, and Jack—they stumbled/ran toward the boat. The boat was in sight when they heard the blast of the horn, the signal of the impending departure.

"Shit!" Jack said. "I'm going to run ahead and tell them to wait. You three keep moving!" He ran towards the boat.

"Bossy, isn't he?" Sam tripped over a rock.

Chris caught her. "This is serious, girls. We don't want to have to catch a plane to meet the boat in Puerto Vallarta." He took hold of both of their arms and propelled them forward.

"We must run like the wind. We must run like Jack. Isn't Jack beautiful when he runs, Sam?" Alex hiccupped.

"God help us," Chris said, but somehow, he managed to get them to the ship.

Jack stood at the top of the walkway, motioning to them. "Come on, come on. They held the boat for us."

"That was lovely of them," Sam said as they stumbled up the walkway.

"This is like walking the plank," Alex said.

"It is! It's like we're pirates or something." Sam linked her arm through Alex's.

Chris, right behind them, still pushing them forward, said, "You walk the plank off the ship, not onto the ship."

"What, honey?" Sam said.

"Never mind."

They made it through security, apologizing to the people there. "We just lost track of time," Sam explained.

They got into the elevator. Chris pushed the button for their floor and took a handkerchief from his back pocket to wipe his brow. "You two are dangerous when you get together."

"Out of control," Jack agreed.

Sam and Alex looked at each other. "I think I need a nap," they said simultaneously.

Neither Mom nor Aunt Sam made it to dinner. No surprise there. Nick overheard his dad and Uncle Chris talking, and it sounded like they had been pretty wasted. Really, they seemed to be getting a little too old for that kind of thing, but he suspected that turning forty made women out and out crazy. But he had missed them at dinner. Dad and Uncle Chris didn't talk much, and he couldn't rib Annie, who seemed preoccupied. He couldn't even make a snide comment about her clothes, since she had on another nice sundress. Something was up with her, and he planned on finding out what it was. To amuse himself at dinner, he had ordered two appetizers, two entrees, and two desserts. No one seemed to notice.

Outside the dining room, Chris said, "I think I'll call it an early night and go check on Sam. Good night, everyone." He walked away.

"Are you going to check on Mom?" Nick asked his dad.

Jack was staring toward the casino. "Yeah, sure. In a minute. I need to walk off some of this dinner first."

"I really think someone should see if she's all right," Nick persisted.

"Really, son, she's fine. She was snoring like a truck driver when I left for dinner."

"But—"

"Look, Nick, if you're so concerned, you can go and see for yourself." He reached into his back pocket. "Here's the room key. I'm going for a walk." He started off, then turned back. "I want you both in your room by twelve. No exceptions."

Nick and Annie stared after him. "What's with him?" Annie asked.

"I have no idea." Their father was usually so easy going, but come to think of it, he had been tense the last couple of days.

"Well, I'm off," Annie said.

"Where are you going?"

"That, my dear brother, is none of your business."

He planned to make it his business. He had seen the crowd Annie had been hanging out with, and they were too old for her. Neither of his parents had been paying much attention to what he and Annie did in the evenings, which was highly unusual, especially for his mom, who practically kept a log book of where they went, who they went with, and when they got home. Nick decided it had to do with the ship. It was like they were in an entirely different world with an entirely new set of rules. So, if his parents weren't going to take the time to check up on Annie, he would take on the job himself.

"You might want to rethink your plan on covering up that hickey. The makeup doesn't quite do it. What about a scarf?"

"Oh," Annie's hand flew to her neck, and she blushed.

"I know it's a little warm, but you might consider a turtleneck. It's a big sucker."

Annie gave him the finger and stalked off, still holding her neck.

That exchange gave him some satisfaction, a modicum of control. His original plan for this reconnaissance mission had been to trail her—at a discreet distance, of course. And to always be prepared, as he had learned in his years of being a boy scout. But now he would have to develop an alternative plan because he had to check on his mom. And he should probably check on his dad, too. This was good training for the military. Maybe he would end up in Intelligence after his combat duty? It was something to think about.

He quietly let himself into his parents' room and tiptoed to the bed where his mom was indeed loudly snoring. He stared at her. Mascara had smeared below her eyes, giving her a raccoon-like appearance, but she still looked pretty. When he had been in grade school, he had always felt proud when his mother showed up at school for a PTO bake sale or a conference with his teacher. He always thought she was the prettiest mom in his class. He had continued to think that until last year when she went to one of his cross-country meets. He was at the starting line when he overheard one of the senior boys call her a MILF. He had pondered what that meant during his race, and it hindered his performance; he finished seventh. He called Dylan as soon as he finished. Dylan, equally uninformed, asked his older brother and came up with the definition: Mother I'd Like to Fuck. Nick was appalled. That kind of attitude broke all the laws of social decency. Since then, his mom's appearance at school functions made him extremely uncomfortable. He felt bad about it, but he couldn't help it.

He grabbed one of his dad's baseball caps and left the room, deciding that the first objective of the evening should be to see what his dad was up to. He already had a hunch. Every time they walked by the casino, Dad looked like he was itching to go inside. Even Mom had commented on his behavior, saying that he looked like he was trying to fight a magnetic pull when he walked by. Dad had laughed, saying that he did enjoy watching people waste their money. Mom said that better be it because they certainly didn't have money to throw away and that she would rather flush money down a toilet than step a foot inside a casino. Dad had laughed again, but it sounded kind of nervous.

Nick knew he was too young to enter the casino, but no one was standing guard. He pulled the baseball cap low over his eyes and slunk in, keeping to the machines on the back wall where few people were playing. His dad wasn't there. He breathed a sigh of relief, and then he heard a cheer, and within the various voices, he heard his dad. He sidled up to the middle row of slot machines and peeked around the corner. His dad was sitting at the blackjack table, a pile of chips in front of him.

The guy next to him slapped him on the back. "Good timing. You bet a hundred and hit a blackjack."

"I know. I was feeling lucky." Jack took a sip of his drink.

"You're on a streak."

"Yeah, if I was smart, I'd take the money and leave now."

"You ain't that smart. None of us are," the guy said. The people at the table laughed as the dealer began a new game.

Nick hurried out of the casino, his mind reeling. Mom would be furious if she knew that Dad was gambling. On the other hand, would she be happy if she knew he was winning? Maybe he was trying to make money to buy her a fancy birthday present, or maybe he was going to use the money for a down payment on a new car. They certainly needed one. Gambling didn't seem like such a bad thing when you won, but what if you lost all your money? The one thing he hadn't considered about his mission—and Nick could see now that it was the most important—was what he was going to do with the information he gathered. It was a moral dilemma.

He needed to find Annie. Maybe she would know what to do about Dad, although he highly doubted it. She would probably think it was no big deal, and maybe, it wasn't. Still, he felt a growing sense of urgency to find her and make sure she was all right. Since he hadn't been able to trail her, he had to try to think like her. Where would she go? It was a no-brainer. She would head for the party scene. She had proudly shown Nick her fake driver's license that Carla had gotten for her, not caring when he pointed out that she didn't look anything like the girl in the photo. Nick headed for the nightclub.

Again, no one was standing at the entrance checking I.D.s, and Nick slipped easily inside, threading his way through the packed room. The bass on the disco music was so loud that it felt like the room was vibrating, and to Nick, it smelled like sweat and desperation. How could anyone in his right mind think this was fun? Nick slowly circled the room, being constantly jostled and blocked. He checked out the dance floor. No Annie. The pounding music was starting to give him a splitting headache. He would check out the bar, then he was out of there.

Annie wasn't at the bar, but the one-legged Marine who had won the Best Legs contest was sitting on a bar stool drinking a beer. People surrounded him, yet he seemed strangely alone. Nick had been looking for him for the past couple of days, and now, in the last place Nick would expect to find him, there he was. Nick was slightly disappointed that a United States Marine would be in such a sleazy place, but he would let it go. Finding Annie would have to wait. He really wanted to talk to this guy.

Nick tapped him on the shoulder. "I think you're a hero." Thankfully, there was a lull in the music, so he didn't have to shout.

The Marine looked up from his beer and stared at Nick with bloodshot eyes. Up close, he looked older than Nick had originally thought. "There ain't no heroes, kid." He had a twangy southern accent.

"Sure there are," Nick persisted. "All our military personnel in Iraq and Afghanistan are heroes. They're fighting for our freedom. They're fighting against global terrorism."

"What planet are you from, kid?"

This was not going at all as Nick had imagined it. "Well, obviously, I'm from the planet earth." It was such a lame thing to say.

But the guy laughed. "Yeah, I guess you would be." He lifted his empty beer bottle toward the bartender. "I'll take another."

The bartender shook his head. "I think you've had enough, sir."

"I have so fucking not had enough. What kind of a shit hole place is this? I'm on vacation, man. I'm on my freaking, fucking honeymoon. And I need another drink." He pounded on the bar, then lunged toward the bartender.

He missed, and Nick realized that he was quite drunk. Nick caught him before he hit the floor. "Hey," Nick said as he helped him to his feet. "I'll be glad to help you to your room." The deafening, throbbing music started again, so the Marine just nodded.

Nick had the Marine's arm slung over his shoulder as he half carried/ half dragged the guy towards the elevator. "I'm Nick," he said when he had the guy propped up against the wall of the elevator. "Where to?"

"Dwayne. Press two. I'm in the bowels of the ship."

There were so many questions Nick wanted to ask Dwayne. Where had he served in Iraq? How many missions had he been on? What was his job as a soldier? How did he lose his leg? But looking at Dwayne's flushed and sweating face, he knew better than to start on that track. He thought it would be more sensible to try to become his friend. Then maybe they could have a real conversation tomorrow.

"So, you're on your honeymoon," Nick finally said as the doors to the elevator opened.

Dwayne snorted. "The fucking bitch." He allowed his arm to be swung over Nick's shoulder again as they made their way down the galley hallway.

The poor wife was definitely not going to have a good time with her new husband tonight. According to Nick's rules, a man should not get drunk on his honeymoon. To break the awkward silence, Nick asked: "How did you two meet?"

"On the internet. The fucking bitch."

"I really don't think you should be calling your new wife that."

"Oh, yeah?" He stopped walking and turned to face Nick. At this low level, the boat was really rocking, and Dwayne swayed back and forth. It seemed as if Nick's comment had opened the floodgates. "We've only known each other for two months, but she seemed like the perfect match for me. She said she didn't care if I only had one leg; she loved me for myself. She said we'd be together forever. What a crock of shit. You want to know how long *forever* lasted?"

Nick didn't really want to know how long *forever* lasted. And it did feel like they were in the bowels of the ship. It was claustrophobic, and the rocking boat was not being kind to the double dinner he had eaten. He needed to get Dwayne moving. "How long?"

"Forever lasted five days, twelve hours, and thirty-two minutes." Anger propelled Dwayne down the narrow corridor. Nick followed.

Dwayne's room was at the very front of the ship. He fumbled with the key. "So, I get back from snorkeling today—she didn't want to go—and she's gone." He finally got the door opened and swung it open. "Vanished. All her stuff is gone."

Nick peered into the tiny room. He had a fleeting thought: Maybe she had upgraded to a better room? This one was awful, probably the cheapest one on the boat.

"I know what you're thinking," Dwayne said.

Nick fervently hoped that he didn't.

"But she wasn't abducted or left at port," Dwayne continued. "She never swiped her Sea Pass card, so she has to still be on the boat. I know she met another guy and shacked up with him. I just know it."

The seas were getting rougher, and Nick needed to end this conversation and get out of there. "I'm sure you'll find her."

"Oh, I'll find her all right, and when I do, I'll kill her."

"I've got to go. This boat is rocking hard." Nick turned and ran.

"It's probably the bitch fucking the shit out of someone with two legs!" Dwayne screamed after him.

Nick found the stairs and ran up the six flights of stairs to his room. He opened the door and went immediately to the bathroom and found the Dramamine Mom had given to Annie. Annie. He had forgotten all about the reconnaissance mission to trail her, but she was already in bed. Wow. She'd actually listened to Dad and came home on time. It was just as well. What if he had found out that she was doing drugs or something like that? Would he tell Mom and Dad? And what about Dad gambling? And what if a dead woman was discovered on the boat? Would he go to the authorities and tell them what Dwayne had said?

Sometimes a person could have too much information. It created a moral dilemma.

She knew she had told them "no gifts" for her birthday. She had told them that being all together on a glorious cruise vacation would be more than enough to celebrate her fortieth birthday. At the time, she had probably meant it. At the time, she thought they wouldn't listen to her. But they had, and now, for some stupid reason, she felt slighted. Didn't she always make a big deal out of their birthdays, buying gifts, baking elaborate cakes, throwing parties? Didn't she always have a celebratory birthday breakfast (blueberry pancakes, waffles, Spanish omelets) waiting for them when they awoke? Alex, standing in front of the bathroom mirror, shook her head. She was going to have to let go of these negative thoughts. Being hungover didn't help, and neither did her image in the mirror. She would swear she had a couple more wrinkles around her eyes and mouth.

At least she could commiserate with Sam at breakfast. They were all going to the El Eden jungle outside of Puerto Vallarta today, and the others had already left to pack swimsuits, towels, and sunscreen. "I feel like I was expecting a parade, and the organizers decided to take the marching bands and floats to another county fair," Sam said as she nibbled on a piece of toast. She, too, was hungover.

"Majorettes. Don't forget the majorettes." Alex sipped strong black coffee.

"Dear God, no. Never forget the majorettes. Do you remember?"

"How could I forget one of the most humiliating experiences of my life?"

They had both been majorettes for one year in their small-town high school marching band. The mothers of the majorettes had sewn the gold and blue strappy outfits. Their mother was many things, but a seamstress was not one of them. She had merely tacked down the tiny shoulder straps. By the end of the first block, Sam and Alex were holding up the short dresses with both hands, batons swinging in the crooks of their elbows. They heard snickers from the crowd along the parade route, but it didn't occur to either of them to drop out. Their boyfriends of the moment thought it was hilarious—and probably a little enticing, too, that hint of seeing a bra. They, at fifteen, thought it was mortifying, but now it was just one more funny shared memory.

"I think you can dread an event so much that when it actually arrives, you're disappointed that it isn't worse." Sam found a Tylenol in her bag and handed one to Alex.

"It's the same thing when you anticipate an event so much that when it arrives, you're disappointed that it isn't better." Alex took her pill with coffee. "We are getting philosophical in our old age."

"If you say we're old one more time, I'm going to have to slap you. I've never done it before, but there is a first time for everything." A woman passed pushing a stroller, and Sam looked longingly at the baby nestled inside. "A lot of forty-year-old women are having babies."

"I know. I used to think it would be awful to have children almost grown and then start all over again with the bottles, the diapers, the ear infections."

"Do you still think that?" Sam asked tentatively.

"I don't know. A friend of mine, Sadie—she's forty-three—just had a baby. She had two older children, but tragically, her sixteen-year-old son died in a car accident two years ago. He was hit by a drunk driver. She was a wreck, as any mother would be. Her grief was terrible to witness, and I'm ashamed to say that a lot of her old friends quit coming around, including me. You know how it is. You—" Alex stopped herself, appalled. How could she be telling this story to Sam? Sam had lived through this heart-wrenching situation. She didn't dare look at Sam. "You can slap me now."

Instead, Sam took Alex's hand. "It's okay. Really, Alex. Did people think the baby was a kind of 'substitute' child, a replacement for the one she'd lost?"

Alex looked up, relieved that she hadn't either insulted or hurt Sam. "That's exactly what a lot of people thought, but it didn't turn out that way at all. I think that baby girl saved Sadie's life. She's beautiful, and in no way a substitute for the son Sadie lost. And frankly, it wasn't anyone's business but Sadie's family."

Sam's face glowed. "That's a wonderful story. It's like I've been telling you. There's always hope."

"Of course there's always hope. When did I say there wasn't?"

"Let's not bicker. There's something I've been meaning to talk with you about. Something important."

Sam's urgency alarmed Alex. "Is something wrong? Are you and Chris all right? Is something wrong with your health?"

Sam laughed. "No, it's more like a brilliant plan I want to share with you."

The Carissa family noisily entered the dining room, followed by Chris, his pale, thin legs exposed below Bermuda shorts. Alex wondered how he could have stayed so white after all the outdoor activities—50 SPF sunblock? For the thousandth time, she wondered what had attracted her twin sister to Chris. It was not stunningly handsome looks. It had to be his inherent kindness. He was certainly that.

"Time to go, birthday girls," Jack said. "The zip lines are hanging in wait." He carried a large duffel bag.

"Mr. Gung Ho is ready to fly," Chris said dryly. "I packed your things for you, honey," he said to Sam. He kissed her on the forehead.

Jack didn't offer a kiss to Alex, which made her feel slighted all over again. "I'm having second thoughts." Not only was she bad with directions, but she was beginning to be afraid of heights. Hanging onto a bar and zipping above the tree line on a thin wire cable was not her thing.

"Come on, Mom. It'll be great. It's where they filmed the movie *Predator*. It's like a historic site." Nick was bouncing on his heels, anxious to leave.

"The filming location of an Arnold Schwarzenegger action movie is not a historic site, doofus." Annie punched him lightly on the arm. She was in a very good mood today. "But please, Mom, you have to come. This is one of the highlights of the trip. That's what the brochure says anyway."

"I'm not so sure about this either. Maybe Alex and I should hang out by the pool. We were in the middle of a conversation." Sam had been looking forward to the adventure, but she had been so close to asking Alex to do the most important thing in her life.

"You're always talking," Nick said.

"All the time," Annie added.

"Please, Alex." Jack dropped the duffel bag and got down on one knee in front of her and took her hand.

"What are you doing?" Alex asked. People were staring. "It's a little late to be doing a formal proposal." His actual proposal twenty years earlier had taken place in the emergency room at McKinley Health Center at Illinois. He had twisted his knee during an intramural soccer game and was being fitted for crutches while she waited beside him. When the nurse left the room, he turned to her and said they made a pretty good team. He then asked her if she wanted to try out for the all-star team. She said sure, why not? He had to explain later that he had asked her to marry him. She said she'd known that, although she hadn't.

"We are proposing," he nodded toward Nick and Annie, "to make this the best birthday you have ever had. We wanted to surprise you and Sam, but I think it might influence your decision if you knew that the kids and I arranged for a cake and champagne to be waiting. So, will you please come?"

Alex was both touched and relieved. How had she ever doubted them? "My answer to your proposal is *yes*."

"All right!" Nick yelled.

"You're coming, too, aren't you?" Alex asked Sam.

"The cake is for both of you," Annie said. She gave Sam a hug. "This is a family celebration."

"I wanted to go all along." Sam got up.

They left the dining room in a noisy group, but Alex managed to whisper to Sam. "What did you want to talk to me about?"

"Later. We'll talk later."

Alex then forgot all about it. Sam tended to be overly dramatic, so it was probably not even particularly important in the scheme of things.

El Eden jungle was everything the brochure promised it would be, lush and densely green with foliage. The others had been content with one zip line ride across the canopy of trees and were now swimming at the base of a glorious waterfall, but Jack and Nick were going for another ride. Jack was proud that at least Nick seemed to have inherited his sense of adventure. They waited patiently in line to get strapped in.

"This is quite an adventure, isn't it, son?" Jack said.

"It sure is. I wonder if it's the same sensation you get when you jump out of an airplane?"

"I don't know. We'll have to try it sometime. There's a skydiving place west of town. I'll look into it when we get back."

"That would be great. I think it would be good training for me." Nick moved to the front of the line, and a man began to put on his harness.

"What do you mean by 'good training'? Are you planning on becoming a professional skydiver? I don't think there are a lot of employment opportunities for that particular profession." Jack laughed. You could never tell what teenagers would come up with. In some ways, they were wise beyond their years, but in other ways, they were totally clueless.

Nick kept his eyes on the man's hands as he buckled the straps of the harness. "No, I'm planning on joining the Marines."

Jack felt like he had been punched in the gut. He knew that Nick had been interested in all things military for the last year or so, but he had assumed it was just a phase. After all, who couldn't be affected by the wars in Iraq and Afghanistan? They had been huge political and ethical issues for some years now. No, Nick must be joking. He knew how much his parents wanted him to have a college education. He knew that they expected him to go to college. "You're taking the SAT next week. I signed you up."

Nick was poised on the edge of the platform, ready to take off. "No, I'm not."

"Joining the Marines is not an option. You're taking the test."

"I hope you can get a refund," Nick said.

And then he was gone, flying down the cable, growing smaller and smaller as Jack watched him go.

Dinner had been terrible. The tension was so thick you could cut it with a knife. Annie now knew what that expression meant, and it was all her fucked-up brother's fault. His sense of timing had been perfect. Perfectly awful. Why did he have to pick today to drop the bombshell that he didn't want to go to college? And then why did Dad have to blab to Mom on this of all days? She had cried through most of the dinner, and by association, Aunt Sam looked on the verge of tears, too. When Uncle Chris, the only one at the table who was calm, said that in today's economy joining the military might not be such a bad idea, she thought her dad was going to punch him out.

"You're only seventeen, Nick. I don't think you've given enough thought to all the implications of such a decision," Mom had sniffled.

"We'll work through all of this when we get home." It was taking Dad a great deal of effort to remain calm.

"Will you promise me that, Nick? Please?" Mom had asked.

Nick sat resolutely, arms crossed, but he threw Mom a birthday bone. "Sure."

It was obvious to Annie that he was lying, but at least they finished the dinner with an uneasy truce. It was a good thing there was only one more day at sea before they reached port in L.A. Things were getting weirder and weirder. It seemed to her as if everyone's personality had changed in the last week. Dad was not the easygoing man he usually was, Mom was not constantly checking up on her kids, Nick was causing waves, and she was actually being nicer. She wondered if when they reached land, everyone would instantly revert to normal.

She knew she was ready to get off the boat. Things with Adam were getting complicated. She had enjoyed their first two dates, the partying and the make-out sessions, but then he started to get more demanding. She had thought she would have sex with him. It would be better to do it with someone who didn't go to school with her or who didn't live in her town. That way, if she didn't do it right, no one would be the wiser. And it would certainly be something to tell Carla about when she got home. However, she surprised herself. When things got hot and heavy last night and they were both in their underwear on his bed, she changed her mind. With a great effort, she pushed him off her. He'd gotten angry, storming around the room in his Hanes jockey shorts, and called her a *cock tease*. She was frightened, but oddly, the sight of his skinny white legs gave her an almost irrepressible urge to laugh. She gathered her clothes and went into the bathroom to dress, and when she came out, he was all apology and sweetness. He'd been like that the whole trip, nice one minute and snidely mean the next. He had a Jekyll/Hyde personality.

And he was too old for her. She didn't get many references that he and his creepy cousins made to music, or to science fiction movies, or to sports teams, or to their stupid prep school. They were in college, right? Shouldn't they be more grown up than that? She didn't want to be one of those girls—and she knew many—who were so desperate to have a boyfriend that they would date anyone, regardless of his appearance, personality, or in one case, his hygiene. One of the most popular girls at SCDS was dating a greasy-haired boy from a public high school who smelled really bad. Everyone else held their noses when he was around, but she didn't seem to notice.

Yes, there were many reasons to break up with Adam, and she was going to do it tonight. *Breaking up* might be an extreme expression in this case. It might be more appropriate to say that she was going to quit *hanging out* with him during the last two nights of the cruise. It was her first romantic fling, and she thought it had been worth it, despite his schizophrenic personality, his age, and the fact that he made her feel uneasy. She chalked it up to her lack of experience—*zero*, in fact—guessing that most people felt uncomfortable at the beginning of a relationship.

Once again, she was waiting for him on the Lido deck, and once again, he was late, and once again, she was going to continue to wait for him. She felt she had to make some kind of closing remarks, kind of like she used to do during her short stint on the debate team. She could say something like: "I had a lovely time with you on this cruise. I wish you all the best in your future endeavors." No, that would sound like she was some debutante from Georgia. She'd probably say something like, "I had a great time getting to know you on this trip, but I should spend the rest of the cruise with my family." That was bad, too. Maybe she'd have one drink with him, so she could relax and say what was really on her mind: "You're a pompous ass. I find you a little frightening. And by the way, I'm only fifteen."

"Hey, doll," Adam said as he came up behind her. He put his hands on her shoulders, turned her around, and gave her a proprietary kiss on the lips.

"You're late," she said.

"Honey," he said. "I'm never late for the party. That's because I *am* the party."

Of course, he had his goon cousins with him. Annie still didn't know their names, but they had been with her and Adam most of the time during the last week, and of course, they laughed at Adam's stupid jokes. She figured they were such loyal subjects because Adam was the one who always supplied the booze and drugs. She should have known that they would be with him during the first part of the evening, before she and Adam went down to his room. She didn't want to embarrass him in front of his cousins by telling him to *shove off.* After all, he had supplied her with a lot of booze and drugs, too. She'd have one drink with them and then she'd leave.

"I've got a special treat for you tonight," Adam said, waving a large water bottle in front of her.

The goon twins did their creepy laugh, and Annie wondered if she was missing some phallic reference or something. "A water bottle? Gee thanks. It's what I've always wanted."

"No, silly girl. It's very expensive rum. The water bottle is how I sneaked it onto the ship. It's not easy to do, you know." He had obviously been taste-testing the rum already.

"Forget declaring a major. Your true vocation is to become a smuggler."

"Ha, ha. I'll tell that one to my probation officer."

The goon twins thought this was beyond hysterical, and again, Annie felt like she was left out of the loop. Maybe he really did have a probation officer? They didn't know each other well at all, now that she thought of it. This was so definitely going to be the last time she saw the three of them.

"Let's go to that cabana area by the workout room. You know, where all the fat old farts lounge around in the hot tub. It's quiet there." Adam led the way.

Annie followed, relieved that he didn't suggest going to his room. It would be easy to have just one drink and then beg off with a headache, or better yet, cramps. That would do it.

The area was more enclosed than the deck and not nearly as windy. They settled on some chaise lounges in the far corner. "Did you bring the stuff?" Adam asked.

"I've got it taken care of," one of the goon cousins said.

"What stuff?" Annie asked. She was not going to smoke any pot tonight, and she didn't want to be tempted.

"The glasses and the diet coke," the other goon said.

This was odd. They usually just passed around the bottle. "So, we're going to have cocktails like proper adults tonight, are we?" Annie sat at the edge of the lounge chair. She didn't want to get too comfortable.

"Nothing's too good for my girl," Adam said. His back was to her as he mixed the drinks on the small table. "You moron. You forgot the ice."

"We've got the important stuff," goon one protested. Adam looked over his shoulder and glared. "You know, the booze." he finished.

Adam passed out the glasses. "Cheers." He raised his glass.

The others did the same. "Cheers," they said.

They talked idly. Adam told a story about a guy in his fraternity who got drunk at a party and held his girlfriend out the window by her ankles. Big mistake. The girl had at one time been the national junior black belt champion. When he finally hauled her up, she cornered him and began delivering kicks and punches that missed his head and all his vital organs by millimeters. Then she gave a kick that landed on the most vital organs of all: his balls. They began another equally stupid fraternity story about more people that Annie didn't know and couldn't care less about.

Annie sipped her drink. She was barely halfway done with the drink, but she was already feeling quite drunk. Adam must have made them super strong. She needed to slow down. She reached toward the table to put down her drink, and it felt as if she were moving in slow motion. She almost missed the table, but Adam caught the drink.

"Whoa, baby. You must have had some wine at dinner before this."

She shook her head. "I didn't have anything to drink at dinner," she thought she said, but they were looking at her strangely. Maybe she hadn't said the words at all. She was having trouble moving her tongue and mouth.

"Why don't you just sit back and relax? Enjoy the evening, honey." Adam situated her on the chaise and handed her back the drink. "There's plenty more where this came from." The goons laughed.

Annie nodded. She needed to get out of here, but she felt so drunk and disoriented. She looked around the cabana area, which was becoming blurry. She could signal for someone to help her, but it looked like all the people had floated away. She tried to focus her eyes on Adam. She would ask him to take her to her room, but she had difficulty discerning Adam from the other two. They were growing smaller, and her head was growing heavier. She heard a glass hit the floor.

It was the last thing she remembered before she passed out.

Chris, Jack, Sam, and Alex sat at a small table for four in the crowded ka-raoke room. If the surroundings were supposed to be plush, with the red velvet chairs and heavy brocade drapes, they had missed the mark, Chris thought. The place looked tacky, or maybe he just thought that because he was in a rare bad mood. Before this cruise, he had had no idea that seven days could be so long. He missed his computer, he missed his office, and he missed his book-lined shelves. The only bright spot right now was that it was intermission, and the horrible renditions—three of them—of "I Will Survive" had ceased.

"I think we should do a group song," Sam said. She was animated, trying too hard to have a good time and to make sure everyone else had one, too. "Maybe something by the Mamas and the Papas?"

Chris suspected she had gone back to the room after dinner and taken a valium. He'd have to count the remaining pills when he got back. It was how he kept her in check. On occasion, he had flushed a few down the toilet. "I think we've had enough excitement for one night." He knew where she was headed with the Mamas and Papas suggestion. It was prob-ably a segue into her proposing her grand plan of surrogacy, and he had asked—no, begged—her not to bring up the subject tonight. Things were tense enough already.

"It's only midnight," Sam protested.

"Most people would think that was a late hour," he said. He looked at Alex and Jack sitting stonily silent. He knew that Nick's ill-timed an-nouncement had sent a shock wave through all that they had counted on for their son. However, the boy was young and would probably change his mind by next week.

"You'll sing with me, won't you, Alex?" Sam asked. "We need to lighten up the mood around here."

Alex looked at her with red-rimmed eyes. "You exhaust me, Sam. I want nothing more than for this awful evening to be over." She started to rise.

Sam put her hand on Alex's arm. "I'll come with you. We'll take a bathroom break, refresh ourselves. I bet I can talk you into it."

"I bet you can't. Even if I could carry a tune, and neither one of us can, I wouldn't get up on that stage."

"I'll come with you," Sam said again, and followed Alex out the door.

"I got a nasty little sunburn today," Chris said, trying to break the ice. He almost wished that the awful caterwauling would start again. He wouldn't have to feel the responsibility of making conversation with Jack.

"I think Alex brought some aloe lotion," Jack said stiffly. He drummed his fingers on the table and finished yet another drink, then he turned to look directly at Chris for the first time since dinner. "Can I ask you a favor?"

"Sure."

"I need to borrow a couple hundred dollars."

"Wow." It was probably the last thing he expected Jack to ask. As full as he was of macho pride, it was a small miracle that he agreed to come on the trip at all because Chris was paying.

"I can probably pay you back tomorrow."

"I'm not worried about you paying me back. I mean, if it's some emergency." In all the years he had known Jack, it was the first time he had seen Jack blush.

"I think it's an emergency." He gulped from the fresh drink the waitress had sat down. "Well, actually, it's not. I've been foolish. I've lost some money in the casino and want to win it back. I know I can. It's only a matter of time." He saw the skeptical look on Chris's face. "It's okay. Forget it. I shouldn't have asked."

Chris reached into his back pocket and pulled out his wallet. He carefully counted out ten twenty-dollar bills and pushed them toward Jack. "It would probably be a good idea to keep this between the two of us."

Jack stared at the money as if he were afraid to touch it. "I really should not have asked you."

"I can keep a secret."

Jack tentatively fingered the money. "This trip is making me crazy. I'm definitely more of a land person. I need to get back on a soccer field."

"I'm sorry you're not having a good time," Chris said dryly.

Jack looked up. "Oh, no, I'm having a good time. It was very generous of you to invite my family, and I see how happy it's made Alex. Until today, that is."

Thankfully, the horrible karaoke started again, and it was difficult to communicate over the noise. This time, it was two young and very drunk women trying to sing "Mockingbird." Jack fidgeted in his chair. It looked as if it was taking all his willpower not to run to the casino and blow more money. As soon as the song ended, he scooped up the money, said "thanks, buddy," and left.

Chris sat alone at the table, his migraine throbbing in time to the music. Sam and Alex still hadn't returned from the restroom, and it was now 12:15. What would he tell them when they asked where Jack had gone? He wasn't going to tell them the truth. Like he had told Jack, he could keep a secret. He didn't think it was a good idea for Jack to be gambling, but who was he to judge? Like everyone else, he had secrets of his own. He pushed his chair away from the table and stood up. Avoidance was the best course of action in this situation. He wouldn't have to tell the girls anything if he wasn't here. He was going to bed.

"These damn pantyhose," Sam said when she snagged them on her wedding ring as she was pulling them down to use the toilet. Two women were chatting loudly at the sink.

"What did you say?" Alex asked from the adjoining stall.

"Nothing. I'm just complaining about pantyhose." Sam took off her shoes and peeled the hose the rest of the way off. The two women left and the restroom was suddenly, eerily quiet.

"What a day," Alex said. "What do you think Jack and I did wrong? Did we push Nick too much academically?"

In Sam's opinion, both Alex and Jack were overreacting. Nick couldn't join the Marines for months and would probably change his mind before then. Since she wasn't face-to-face with Alex, she felt freer to say what she really thought. "It's not the end of the world, Alex. In fact, it's quite a noble thing to want to defend your country."

"That's easy for you to say. It's not your child who wants to be in the range of bullets and bombs," Alex snapped.

Nick wasn't her child, and on this night of her fortieth birthday, Sam would give anything in the world to change places with Alex. Even going through anguish was better than not feeling anything at all. "Would you be a surrogate for me?" The words just popped out. After all the weeks of waiting for the perfect moment to ask Alex, after all the imagined perfect scenarios of time and place, the secret, harbored words escaped from her lips in a bathroom stall precisely when Alex flushed the toilet.

Sam flushed the toilet in her stall. She was holding her breath. Had Alex heard her? But when she opened the stall door and stood face-to-face with Alex, Sam knew that she had.

"What did you say?" Alex asked.

There was no backing down now, and Sam felt tears come to her eyes. "I'm asking you to be a surrogate mother for me."

Alex's expression was dazed. She turned and washed her hands at the sink. Sam followed. They stared at each other in the mirror, their eyes riveted on each other's faces.

For forty years, Sam had known every thought, wish, and dream her sister had, but this time, she didn't have a clue what Alex was thinking. Alex was still washing her hands, squirting soap from the dispenser for the third time. Sam walked to the paper towel dispenser and got them each rough cardboard-shaded squares. She handed one to Alex, and for once, she waited patiently, wondering if Alex could hear the thumping of her heart.

"How long have you been waiting to ask me this?" Alex finally said.

"A long time. Weeks. Months. I'm not sure. I was waiting for the perfect time."

"And you think this is it?"

"No, of course not. It's like the words themselves decided there is no perfect time and decided to come blurting out all on their own. I know that this is a huge favor to ask of you." *Please, God*, she silently prayed, *let her hear me out*.

"Asking me to be a surrogate for you is more than a favor. A favor is lending someone a punch bowl or picking up your neighbor's kids from school or agreeing to substitute for someone who can't make it to a Bunco game. This is a little bit different than that. I'd say it's more in the realm of a life-altering experience."

Sam nodded. The tears were coming dangerously close to falling. "Yes, I know."

An older lady tried to push open the bathroom door with her walker.

"Let me help you with that." Alex held open the door as the woman inched into the room.

"Thank you, dear," the blue-haired woman said.

"My pleasure." And Alex walked out.

Again, Sam followed as Alex walked up one deck to the Whiskey Saloon and went directly to the bar. Sam hung back, not knowing what to do. What if Alex never wanted to see or speak to her again? In all her imaginings, she had never considered that possibility. Not having Alex in her life would, quite literally, break her heart.

The bartender set down a champagne glass in front of Alex and one in front of the empty stool next to her. "I know you're there, Sam," Alex said, not turning around.

Sam took the empty seat. "Are you mad at me?"

"I'm feeling a lot of things right now, but I don't think anger is one of them. *Confused* might be the operative word here." She clinked her glass against Sam's. "To fucking forty. Notice the absence of *fabulous*."

"Duly noted."

"So, I'm guessing this terrific family cruise could be considered a generous bribe."

Sam decided that, at this point, honesty was going to have to be the best policy. "You could look at it that way. I wish you wouldn't, but you could."

"I don't know if I could handle being pregnant again. I wasn't one of those glowing, radiant moms-to-be. I was more of the grouchy, heartburn-stoked with swollen ankles variety."

Sam felt a surge of hope. Alex was thinking about it. "Just remember that Johnson's baby lotion smell of a newborn."

"Or the stench of a guacamole diaper."

"Rocking a baby in your arms.

"Trying to soothe a screaming, colicky baby at two in the morning."

"Looking at a peacefully sleeping baby in his crib."

"Trying to get the baby to sleep."

"I'm only asking you to think about it, Alex. That's all. Would you do that for me?"

Alex finally turned to look at her. "I always thought I would do anything for you, but I never counted on this."

Sam took her hand. "Just think about it, okay?"

"I'll think about it, but that's the extent of my promise at this point."

"That's good enough."

After a few more glasses of champagne, and after Sam had persuaded Alex to go back to the karaoke parlor and sing a duet of "I've Got You, Babe," where Sam was Sonny and Alex was Cher and they were laughably awful.

And after they hugged goodnight before going into their staterooms, Sam felt better than she had in a very long time. Perhaps there was a chance for true happiness after all.

Someone was tugging on her arm, trying to pull her up to consciousness, but Annie was having trouble cooperating. She felt as if she were swimming in the murky depths of the ocean, and the tentacles of seaweed kept entangling her limbs. She wasn't frightened; she was just so very tired. She didn't have the energy to break free and rise to the surface and the light.

"Annie, wake up. It's really late, and I need to get you back to the room," the male voice said.

Annie felt arms around her, and with their embrace came a jolt of panic. She opened her eyes and looked at Nick's concerned face. "What are you doing here?" she said slowly, her tongue thick.

"What am I doing here? What are *you* doing here? It's two o'clock in the morning, and I've been looking all over for you. I passed through this room three times before I spotted you passed out here in the corner," he said with disgust. "I was sound asleep an hour ago when Dad came to check on us. I lied and said you were in the bathroom. So, get up. I've got to get you home."

Annie tried to follow what he was saying, but he was talking so fast that his words seemed to evaporate before she could comprehend them. Her mind was fuzzy, but she had heard the last part. "Yes, I want to go home." She wanted her own bed.

"Well, then, get up!"

She tried to raise her head from the chaise, but everything started to spin. "I don't think I can."

"I can't believe you." Nick was getting angry. "What all did you drink, smoke, swallow, or snort to put you in such a wasted state? You make me sick. I should leave you here. It would serve you right."

"Please, Nick." She tried to reach her hand out to him, but it fell weakly. "I need your help." What had she taken to make her feel this way? She knew what a hangover felt like, but this was far worse. Now that she was awake, she felt as if she had been clubbed over the head.

"You're pathetic, you know that? And you look like a slut lying out here. I'm out of here." But he didn't move.

Oh, God. A slut. That rang a bell. Did she have an argument with Adam, and did he call her that? She couldn't remember what had occurred the night before, but she knew that something had. Everything felt all wrong. "I think something terrible has happened." She started to cry.

"What do you mean?" He was instantly beside her on the chaise, trying to console her, but her tears only increased. "Is it that guy you've been hanging around with? Did he do something to you? If he did, I'm going to kick his ass."

"No," she managed to say, even as her suspicions grew. She couldn't have Nick involved in any of this, and she couldn't let anyone know. "Could you go get me a glass of water, Nick? I think it would make me feel better." She needed time to think.

"I'll be right back," he said.

Parts of the evening were starting to come back. She was pretty sure she only drank one drink. She had planned on breaking up with Adam. The goons had been there. She gingerly sat up. She didn't feel sore, and she couldn't see any bruises, although it was too dark to be certain. By the time Nick came back with the water, she had made up her mind.

"I mean it, Annie. If that skinny, pimply creep did anything to you, I'm going to inflict some serious damage." Nick, too, had made up his mind.

"No, no, it wasn't anything like that at all. You were right. I got drunk and made a fool out of myself. I just said something terrible happened because I was so embarrassed." Her trembling hand could not get the water glass to her lips.

"I don't believe you."

"Really, Nick, I've behaved like an idiot. Let's forget the whole thing."

"You always behave like an idiot." He helped her to her feet.

"That's me. The village idiot."

"Don't forget your purse." Nick picked up her black tasseled evening bag from the floor by the chaise.

Leaning on Nick, she slowly made her way across the deck. "Do you promise you won't tell anyone?"

"My lips are sealed on one condition. You won't do this again."

"It's a deal."

Back in their room, Nick used the bathroom first and got into bed. Annie stood under the lights for a long time, looking at her smeared make-up and her bloodshot eyes. She didn't look any different, but her face wasn't the true test. She reached under her sundress and pulled down her panties, not looking at them until they slithered to the floor, and there was the undeniable proof: the bloodstain.

Adam, her very first boyfriend, had drugged her and raped her in front of his cousins. Had that been his plan all along? Did he pick her out because she looked like an easy target? How could she have been so stupid that she didn't notice what a horrible person he was? The futile tears began again, and she wanted to throw something. She grabbed her purse and started to beat it against the sink. The tiny silver clasp sprang open, and the three Polaroids fell out.

The three of them. Annie wished she were still unconscious, swimming in the murky, seaweed depths of the ocean. She wished she never had to wake up because there was no going back now. She could never go back.

At fifteen, she had already been stamped on the forehead with raging red ink: DAMAGED GOODS.

3

CHAPTER THREE

Alex needed to escape the laundry. Since returning from the cruise three days before, the members of her family had slowly unpacked, resulting in a steady mound of dirty clothes on the laundry room floor that never seemed to diminish in size. It was getting on her nerves. She should have told them that if every dirty, smelly article of clothing was not in the laundry room the day after the cruise, she was not going to wash, dry, and iron it. She should have told them that she was not the slave labor of this household. But she hadn't, and really, if she thought about it, she *was* the slave labor of this household. Since everyone else had a job this summer—Jack coaching, Nick bagging groceries, and Annie babysitting—she was the laundress. And the cook. And the maid.

Of course she had always done the menial household chores and had even enjoyed them at one time. So why did she have this sudden resentment? It all boiled down to Sam, who had blown into town, swept them all off on a cruise (which was, in fact, bribery), and totally disrupted the balance of her family. Alex knew she wasn't being fair, or completely honest either. Nick and Annie had been acting like typical teenagers before Sam moved across the street, distancing themselves from her in their perfectly normal progression toward adulthood. It was her problem, this inability to let go, and she was going to have to get over it.

She had been thinking in this vein all morning, which might or might not explain why she was now in front of her computer on the Cherished

Surrogacy website. Since Sam's *request* on their last night on the boat, Alex had been avoiding her. Alex had tried to convince herself that Sam hadn't been serious, but she knew better than that. The obvious answer would be to tell Sam that it was a ridiculous idea because of a variety of reasons: Alex was too old, she had already raised her family, and Jack would never in a million years go for the idea. Still, the naked pleading/hope in Sam's voice, eyes, and face haunted her. She knew how much pain Sam had gone through—and she wanted Sam to be happy—but was it her responsibility?

The site predictably had pictures of pregnant women and babies, many of them twins. Her eyes were drawn to the center of the page with the capitalized heading: AT CHERISHED SURROGACY WE MAKE SURE SURROGATE MOTHERS HAVE A POSITIVE EXPERIENCE, AND THAT THEY ARE RECOGNIZED AND RESPECTED FOR THEIR ROLE. "How very warm and fuzzy," Alex said aloud. Then she started to read the individual stories of the three Surrogates featured in the center of the page. There was Gina—standing in profile in a white shirt, her belly bulging— featured in a 2006 *Washington Post* article, who gave birth to twins. There was Tammy (another bulging belly profile in a pink shirt), who was helping an older couple become parents after years of disappointment.

But the Surrogate who most caught Alex's attention was Gloria, who was pictured in a bathtub, surrounded by bubbles, her pregnant stomach protruding like the rump of a baby whale. The caption read: Wisconsin Surrogate defies convention and happily carries twins for gay dads returning from Afghanistan. Alex's heart lurched with the triggers: "twins," "Afghanistan." Just as she had been avoiding Sam since the cruise, Nick had been avoiding her, and they had not yet had the family discussion about, as Jack termed it, Nick's "misguided career aspirations." She clicked on Gloria's name to read her story in greater detail.

"I thought I'd come over for a cup of coffee," Sam said from the doorway of the den.

Alex started. She felt guilty, as if she had been caught in some unsavory act. "I didn't hear you knock."

"That's because I didn't knock. You should lock your front door, Alex. You never know when a weirdo will show up in this picturesque, suburban neighborhood."

"That's pretty brazen of you. What if Jack and I had been having sex on the kitchen table?"

"Number one, I would assume that you would lock the front door if that were the case. Number two, I know he isn't here because I've been looking out my front window and know he left an hour ago. And number three, I'm being a coward. I was afraid if I knocked and you came to the door and saw me, you'd slam the door in my face." Her voice wavered.

"I would never do that."

"May I come in?"

"You might as well. In a way, your timing is perfect."

"What do you mean?" Sam walked to the computer and saw the screen. "Oh," she said softly.

"Pull up a chair, and I don't want you to say one damn thing until we're done reading Gloria's story."

According to Gloria, she had always wanted to be a surrogate. After having four children of her own, she knew first-hand the joys of parenting, and so, she wanted to "give back." Her husband was totally supportive, as were her children (ages 15, 13, 7, and 4), but her father took some convincing. Eventually, he came around, and Gloria began the process: the application, the physical examination, and the psychological evaluation. She was accepted into the program and then got to choose her parent. Edward and Nathan, gay soldiers returning from Afghanistan, piqued her interest. They talked on the phone, met in person, and "really felt a connection." She began the hormone injections, had the procedure, and got pregnant on the first try. Abracadabra! She gave birth to twins Gordon and Gideon thirty-two weeks later. The twins were early but strong and healthy. For Gloria, it had been a totally rewarding experience.

"Do you think this is for real?" Alex asked. "It sounds just a tad too smug for my taste."

"I think Edward and Nathan are the lucky ones. It was a perfect match. I mean, they only implanted two embryos because they didn't want to have a whole litter of babies. And yet, both embryos developed. Amazing." Sam stared at the picture of the twins on the screen.

"I find it highly doubtful that Gloria's four-year-old would be *totally supportive* of the whole thing. A child that young wouldn't have any idea what was going on," Alex said drily. "Let's go get the coffee now."

Sam followed her into the kitchen and perched on the bar stool at the center island. "Why were you looking at the Cherished Surrogacy web site, Alex?"

"Curiosity. That's all. Don't get your hopes up, Sam. I still find the whole idea of surrogacy to be—"

"Distasteful? Unnatural?" Sam interrupted as she stirred vanilla flavored creamer into her coffee.

"No. More like gross." Alex sat down on the stool next to Sam. "Gloria harbored and nurtured a stranger's sperm in her body. What if Edward or Nathan was actually a perverted psychopath?"

"Don't be ridiculous, Alex. They screen the prospective parents, too, and it seems to me that Gloria did a generous and unselfish thing by having children for those two men."

"Look, Sam, this whole concept of surrogacy is virgin territory for me. Do you mind if I play the devil's advocate a little while longer?" Alex got up and paced nervously around the kitchen, picking up stray cups and plates and loading them into the dishwasher.

"Be my guest." Sam's eyes followed Alex's every move.

"And once a woman has her family, I don't understand how she would willingly want to be pregnant again. I was not *in bloom* or *glowing* when I was pregnant. I had swollen ankles, heartburn, hemorrhoids, and splotchy skin. And during the last two months, I was a raging bitch. Don't you remember?"

"No. I remember you being happy and excited."

Alex continued as if she hadn't heard Sam. "I have a smiley face scar on my lower belly and a tuft of skin that hangs over it that no number of sit-ups in the world will ever tone up. I'd get liposuction if I could afford it." She rummaged in the cabinet below the sink for dishwashing detergent.

"You'll never get lipo. You're afraid of hospitals." Sam sat rigidly on the stool, not moving.

"Right. That's another thing. I'm deathly afraid of hospitals. My blood pressure surges just walking into one. Damn. I'm out of Cascade. I'll have to use regular dish soap." She filled the soap container, slammed the door shut, and turned it on.

"Alex," Sam said tentatively. "You only need a drop or two of regular soap or else—"

"*I'm not done yet!* And what about Mother and Dad? Did you think of them when you dreamed up this scheme? You know how small-town they are. They'd be all worried about what everyone in the church would think." She finally sat down.

"They're hardly ever home anymore."

Since their father had retired from his position as a grade school principal two years earlier, he and their mother had purchased an R.V. and begun traveling the country with no planned itinerary. If they liked a place, they stayed awhile. It had surprised Alex and Sam at first, since their parents were conservative Christian people who never missed church on Sundays. But their parents warmed to the idea of traveling, then embraced it wholeheartedly. The only problem was that many of the campgrounds Paul and Emily stayed at had lousy cell phone service, so their parents were difficult to contact. This had irked Alex and Sam in more than one conversation. Their parents—once so loving and attentive—now seemed to not give a damn. Sam put it this way: "It's like they're the children now. They're out playing and refuse to come in when they're called to dinner."

"That's beside the point. I'm sure they'll have some opinion on me carrying your baby. Did you think of that?"

"I need a cigarette."

"I knew it! All you've thought about so far is how happy a baby would make *you*. You haven't considered how this baby would affect everyone else in our family."

Sam got up and went out the back door to the patio. Alex saw her light a cigarette through the window, and even from her vantage point, she could see how Sam's hands shook. She followed her out and helped herself to the pack on the table. Her program for quitting had fallen by the wayside since Sam's arrival.

"And that's another thing. If I got pregnant, I'd have to quit drinking and smoking." She inhaled deeply. "Neither of which is a bad thing, but again, I'd be the one making all the sacrifices."

"That's enough, Alex," Sam said quietly. "You've made your opinion abundantly clear. No, I didn't think about how many people would be affected if you carried my baby. I was thinking along the lines of you and me being in this grand plan together, with the result being a beautiful baby. I wasn't even really thinking about the fact that Chris, of course, would have to be a major contributor. Isn't that odd? I was so caught up in my selfish dream that I couldn't see clearly. I'm sorry." She stubbed out her cigarette. "I should be going. I've got a deadline to meet by Friday. Thanks for the coffee."

"Wait a minute." The words were out of Alex's mouth before she could stop them. She didn't know what she would say next. She only knew she couldn't let Sam leave just yet, not like this. It felt like something was breaking apart here, disintegrating before her.

"Really, I have to go. I've wasted too much of your morning already." She opened the patio door and stepped inside.

"Wasted my time? You haven't wasted my time! I was playing the devil's advocate! You know how I can get on a subject and rant and rave." She was almost pleading, but for what? For Sam to stay? For a chance to start over?

Sam called from the kitchen. "I hope your devilish little hands don't mind getting wet. Your dishwasher is overflowing."

Alex bounded into the kitchen. "Oh, great. This is just perfect." Sudsy water gurgled out of the top, sides, and bottom of the dishwasher. The entire kitchen floor was already underwater, and the foaming bubbles were inching rapidly toward the living room. Alex sloshed to the appliance and turned it off.

"I tried to warn you about the dish soap," Sam reminded.

"I know. I was preoccupied."

"Where do you keep your mop?"

"Mop? I need a Wet Vac or some other industrial appliance. It's going to take the rest of the morning to clean up this mess."

"It won't take that long. I'll help."

"I thought you had a deadline?" Alex took off her flip-flops, waded to the utility closet, and got the mop and a bucket.

"It can wait. Some things are more important than work." She squeezed Alex's arm. "Look at the bright side. You'll have a clean kitchen floor when we're through."

They began to clean, talking amiably about inconsequential subjects— who they were rooting for on *Survivor*, the pre-fall sale at Macy's, where Sam should buy her patio furniture—and once or twice, Alex imagined she saw the tight rounded belly of Gloria peeking up through the bubbles on her kitchen floor.

People were so inconsiderate. If anyone had bothered to ask Nick what he had learned this summer working at Fry's, it was that fact. He was rounding up discarded carts in the parking lot in 110-degree heat, but given the black tar, it was probably closer to 120. The grocery store had cart deposits, but many people were too lazy to walk the few measly steps and place their carts between the rails. So, Nick spent countless hours each day rounding up the stray carts and banding them together like a long snake to take back to the front of the store. That was one pet peeve. The other was discarded food. People would decide they didn't want the Ruffle potato chips they had impulsively snatched from the snack aisle by the time they reached the dog food and would leave the chips wedged between the Purina and Pedigree bags. It was a fact. People were so inconsiderate.

"You're going to break my eggs," the old woman said when Nick gently placed the egg carton on top of her meager bagged groceries. She had bought tins of cat food, a quart of milk, a box of generic high-fiber cereal, and two potatoes. She had on a pilled black sweater despite the oppressive heat.

"No, ma'am, I've carefully placed them on top. They should be fine." Nick thought she must be close to one hundred, and she had a single gray hair growing out of a mole on her chin.

"If I have one cracked egg, I am going to hold you personally responsible, young man. I'll come back and complain."

"Yes, ma'am. Have a nice day." She slowly wheeled the cart away. He hoped she hadn't driven to the store herself. She was so hunched over that there was no way she could see over the steering wheel unless she had a booster seat. He would have felt sorrier for her if it hadn't been such a long day.

"It's five o'clock, Nick. You get out of here now, and don't have too much fun tonight, okay?" Loretta smiled at him as she started checking out the next customer in line.

Loretta was his favorite cashier. She had died blonde hair—it must be, the roots were black—and long fingernails which didn't get in her way at all. She had been nice to Nick from the very beginning and even sat with him in the breakroom if they were there at the same time. She smiled constantly, and Nick didn't know how she did it. Her husband was in jail for something to do with methamphetamine, and her seventeen-year-old daughter had just made her a grandmother. When Nick had tentatively asked Loretta if she thought seventeen (his age!) was a little on the young side to become a parent, Loretta had looked at him blankly and said: "What do you mean? I was sixteen when I had my first."

He didn't know why he had told the white lie. When Loretta had in-nocently asked what his "red hot" plans were for tonight, a Friday, he had blurted out that he had a date. Naturally, Loretta assumed he meant a girl. Who wouldn't? But he was going to hang out with Dylan, and they'd probably watch the Military Channel on TV. It's what they usually did on a Friday night. He said goodbye to Loretta and walked quickly out of the store, untying his apron as he went.

He planned on driving straight to Dylan's house. In the week since the cruise, he had spent most of his time there. Dylan's parents didn't seem to mind at all. Unlike his parents, Mr. and Mrs. Taylor were totally laid back, and their house was proof. Mrs. Taylor didn't believe in housekeeping. Clothes were strewn over the living room couch and chairs, and the kitchen had empty cereal and cracker boxes and dirty dishes crammed on every surface. Opening the refrigerator was risky business. Sometimes you'd be blasted with the smell of sour milk, or if you were brave enough to open one of the mystery aluminum foil packets, you might find a reasonably new leftover or a stuffed green pepper so decomposed that it resembled a furry dead rodent. Still, Nick felt at home at the Taylors', and being there was much preferable than being at home where the looming *discussion* of Nick's plans hung over the place like a thundercloud.

He was almost to Dylan's when he remembered that Mom said she needed the car tonight. She was going to give Annie a driving lesson, of all things. Good luck with that. Annie had not improved her driving skills one bit since her run-in with the mailbox. Mom was either incredibly brave or incredibly stupid. Given it was his mom, he'd go with naively brave. You'd have to really love Annie to get in the same car when she was behind the wheel. In her hands, the automobile was truly a lethal weapon on wheels.

He pulled into the garage. He was just going to run in and drop the keys on the counter then leave quickly. Dad was clearly not at home—his Jeep wasn't here—and he didn't feel like talking to Mom. Since his an-nouncement on the cruise, she had been almost too nice to him. It was like she thought that if she made things nice at home (cleaned his room, fixed his favorite lasagna dinner), he would change his mind about joining the Marines. It made no sense, but that's the way it was. It made him feel terrible because it made him want to avoid her, so it was a relief to find that she wasn't home either. The house was quiet. He put the keys on the counter; then he had a great idea. He'd put helmets on the front seat of the car. He had a couple of old bike helmets up in his room. It would be a great joke, and as a bonus, it would make Annie livid.

He bounded up the stairs and ran smack into her, knocking her down. "You idiot!" She screamed.

"Sorry," he said, extending a hand to help her up.

Annie slapped it away. "You could kill someone when you charge up the stairs like that. You need to have more respect for other people's personal space."

"Hey, at least you're talking to me. Calling me an idiot is your first utterance since the cruise." When he thought about it, Annie hadn't been talking much to anyone in the family. When she wasn't babysitting, she was holed up at Carla's, much like he had been at Dylan's.

"I've been busy." She got up slowly, as if everything on her body ached.

"Yeah? Doing what?"

"None of your business." She edged past him toward the stairs.

"You haven't passed out on any more chaise lounges lately, have you?" He meant it as a joke and was going to laugh. Then he saw her face. Her eyes widened, a flitting look of fear, and then her whole face went blank. It was as if someone had given her an electric shock. "Annie, are you all right? I was only joking. I swear I haven't told Mom and Dad about that night, and I never will."

Annie gained some composure, but her face was still deadly white. "What night? I don't know what you're talking about."

"The night . . ." and then he got what she meant. They were supposed to act like it never happened. He hadn't realized she'd been that embarrassed. "I'm an idiot."

"At least we agree on something." She turned and went down the stairs.

"Hey, try to remember which pedal's the brake and which one is the gas. And please, dear sister, try not to kill our mother when you get behind the wheel of that car," he called to her descending back. Without turning around, she flipped him the finger, which relieved Nick. She was acting normal.

After that, he decided that the helmets on the front seat weren't such a great idea. He grabbed a couple of DVDs from his room and jogged over to Dylan's. "Hey, buddy," he yelled as he let himself in the front door.

"Hi, Nick," Mrs. Taylor said from somewhere in the house. He found her at the cluttered dining room table looking at a horse magazine. Her long gray hair was in a ponytail, and her face, weathered from the sun, made her eyes appear even bluer.

"Hello, Mrs. Taylor. Where's Dylan?"

"He's in the barn, honey. I finally got that boy to do some work. He's feeding the horses. You can go on out and help him." She lifted her coffee cup. "You want to get me a refill on your way out?"

"I hate these damn horses," Dylan said when Nick found him in the barn. He had his mother's blue eyes, and like her, his long brown hair was in a ponytail. He was slight, and his small, sinewy biceps bulged as he forked hay into a stall.

"I'm supposed to help you," Nick said. He didn't care for horses either, and he was pretty sure he wouldn't last long breathing in the odor of musty hay, rotting wood, and horse crap.

"Perfect timing, dude. I'm done." Dylan grinned.

"What are you so happy about? Feeding the horses usually makes you cranky."

Dylan continued to grin.

"Stop it, Dylan, you're weirding me out."

"Come on, I'll show you." Dylan went to the back of the barn. A row of shelves held assorted bridles, horseshoes, and just plain junk. "I was pissed off about having to be out here, so I came back here to punch the wall."

"That was stupid."

"You think so?" He removed two wooden slats. "Look in here."

Nick stepped closer and peered in. "Guns," he said.

"Two rifles, dude. Colt Accurized Flat Tops."

"Who do you think they belong to?" With all his fascination for things military, Nick had never actually shot a gun. Hell, he hadn't even held a real one because Paintball guns didn't count. The presence of the guns was both thrilling and frightening.

"I don't know. Probably my dad, although he's never mentioned them."

"Wow," Nick said.

"I know," Dylan agreed as he carefully replaced the boards. "Now the question is: What are we going to do with them?"

Jack should have showered, and he should not have scheduled this appointment for eleven o'clock when soccer practice ended at ten thirty. He had slapped on some deodorant in the car on the way to the bank, but he still felt pungent. The loan officer sitting across from him, dressed in a nice black suit, crisp white shirt, and red striped tie, was surely not impressed with a guy with disheveled hair and sweats asking for a personal loan. What had he been thinking when he made the appointment for this time of morning?

"I'm afraid that we're not going to be able to accommodate you." The loan officer looked like a teenager playing dress-up to Jack, yet he held Jack's application and the promise of much-needed money in his hands.

"Is there anything I need to do differently? Maybe I can fill out another form?" Jack tried to keep the desperation out of his voice. His gambling on the cruise had certainly dipped into their savings, which was not much to begin with. His Jeep and the aging van needed some work done, not to mention the decrepit water heater, which had taught each member of the Carisa family to shower in two minutes. All the added expenses were going to deplete what little they had left after his 401K plummeted with the ongoing recession. They would literally be living paycheck to paycheck.

"I'm sorry, Mr. Carissa, but the bank isn't giving out personal loans at this time. It has nothing to do with your application. It's the economy. After the government bailout, we're all trying to get back on track. Is there anything else I can help you with?"

"No, no, thanks for your time." Jack shook his hand, and now he didn't care that he hadn't showered. It hadn't made any difference at all. Banks were not giving out money. Period. What was he going to do?

He called Alex on his way to the car, asking her if she wanted to meet him at My Big Fat Greek Restaurant for lunch. She didn't know anything about Jack applying for a loan, and he didn't plan on telling her. He knew that eating out was an expense he should avoid, but at this point, another twenty-five dollars down the drain was irrelevant.

He was sitting on the front patio under the misters when he saw her walking across the parking lot. Even after all these years, just the sight of her made his heart beat faster. She had on a short denim skirt and a white tank that showed off her tan. She had on black Old Navy flip-flops, and Jack thought she looked beautiful. She didn't look forty, that was for sure.

She waved when she saw him and walked quickly to the table. She bent down and kissed him on the cheek before sitting down next to him.

"What a nice surprise. The two of us haven't gone out for lunch in a long time. I was just about to fix us some bologna sandwiches when you called."

"Sorry about the sweats. As soon as practice was over, I had the idea to ask my beautiful wife out to lunch."

"You must have had a long practice. I hope you didn't work those poor girls too hard."

"Oh, no, I had some paperwork to attend to." It wasn't exactly a lie, but he still squirmed uncomfortably in his chair.

The waitress came to the table, handed them their menus, and asked for their drink orders. "I'll have a red wine sangria," Alex said. "It feels like a special occasion," she said to Jack.

"Water for me," he said.

"Oh, if you're not going to drink, then I'll—"

"No, that's okay. I'll have the sangria, too." He mentally added twelve dollars to the bill, but what did it matter? Alex looked so happy, and they might as well drink to the damn recession. After the waitress brought their drinks, they ordered: a gyro salad for Alex, a turkey club for him.

Jack looked out over the parking lot, which was an advertisement for wealth with its assorted collection of BMWs, Mercedes, Lexuses, Cadillacs, and Audis. And the crème de la crème was the Bentley parked across from the jewelry store two stores down in the strip mall. Where did these people get their money? He supposed that some of it was inherited, some self-made, and some of it a good show. He knew for a fact that a lot of North Scottsdale people leased their cars, and he also knew that a lot of them were being repossessed. He had also read about a lot of McMansions being foreclosed upon in this wealthy area. It was the same old story. People spent more money than they had, and now, after years of a booming economy, people were forced to pay the piper. However, you wouldn't know it from looking at this parking lot.

"Is something the matter?" Alex asked.

"I've been thinking," he said, reaching for his sangria and finding that it was empty. Alex poured some of hers into his glass. "With Nick graduating next June—"

Alex's face fell. "We're not going to talk about Nick now, are we? I thought we were going to enjoy our time together. We so rarely have a date night anymore. I miss them."

When the kids were little, they had made it a point to have a date night every other Saturday, hiring a babysitter and going out to a nice dinner or a movie. It had been a very, very long time. He felt a pang of guilt. Why had they stopped?

"Besides," Alex continued. "I think Nick will change his mind once the school year starts and the kids in his class start getting their acceptance letters from colleges across the country. It's always an exciting time for the seniors. He'll see. We just have to wait. And that's all I'm going to say on the subject. Let's enjoy our lunch."

The waitress set down their food, and they each ordered another drink. There went another twelve bucks, he thought. He sighed and picked up his sandwich. "I wasn't going to say anything about Nick's misguided career aspirations." Alex started to interrupt, but he held up his hand. "I was going to say that you'll have even more time on your hands this fall. You might want to think about getting a full-time job."

Alex's mouth was full of salad as she stared at him, slowly chewed, and swallowed audibly. "What do you mean by 'even more time' on my hands?"

Had he actually said that? He had meant to say, "some time on your hands." "Don't get defensive on me. I only meant that now that the kids are older, you have more time to do other things." The color was rising in her cheeks, and her eyes flashed as he scrambled to placate her. "I know how hard you work, with the cooking, cleaning, shopping, laundry, and all the other things you do—which are many, I know—but just think about it," he finished lamely.

Trying unsuccessfully to control her wavering voice, Alex said, "You know I substitute every time that damn phone rings at six a.m., and you also know that no school district is hiring right now because of all the budget cuts and state and federal funding going down the toilet."

"Of course, I know all that." It was his turn to flush. He was choking on the big fat foot he'd stuck in his mouth. He thought he could just throw out the idea of her contributing a little more monthly income to the household, but he was going about this in the wrong way.

"What do you propose I do? Flip burgers at McDonald's?"

"Alex."

"Fry ground beef at Taco Bell? Waitress or tend bar, although I understand those jobs are hard to come by, too? Maybe I could get a job in the housewares department at Macy's? Eventually, I might work my way up to floor manager. I'm very good at taking directions, you know."

"You are blowing this all out of proportion. I thought maybe you'd like the idea of getting out of the house more. I didn't mean to offend you. I only made a casual observation." He was going to be in the dog-house now, but he knew he deserved it. He reached for her hand, but she snatched it away.

"Thank you for a lovely lunch, Jack." She pushed her half-eaten salad to the center of the table. "Are you going to pick up the check, or should I contribute my share?" She reached for her purse, then stopped. She looked at him, all trace of anger gone. "This is about money, isn't it?"

"No." He blushed as she continued to stare. She knew him too well. "Yes," he said.

"Are we broke? Be honest with me, Jack. Are we?"

"No, not yet."

"What about our savings?"

"We've been slowly eating away at our savings for some time now; you know that. Every time we have an unforeseen expense, more is gone." He would never, ever tell her about the hundreds he had lost gambling lately. He was too ashamed, and he was sure she would never understand. Why should she? He didn't understand it himself. "I'm concerned that we don't have a large enough emergency fund. That's all."

She reached for his hand and stroked his palm. "A lot of people are in this position, honey. It's just the way things are right now, but we'll do what we always do. We'll work it out together. You'll see. Everything will be fine. A few years from now, we'll look back at this stage in our lives and be grateful for all that we do have."

God, he loved her so much. He'd told her more than he had planned, but of course, he hadn't told her everything. It was his responsibility to make things better, and he would. "I want to get you home right now." He signaled to the waitress.

"Really?" She said coyly. "I have some time on my hands."

"There's no reason to be so sullen," her mom said.

Annie was pressed against the passenger seat door, as far away from Mom as she could get. It was humiliating to have her mom drive her to

Carla's house. She had a permit; she should be driving. She was never going to get better if she didn't practice, but after her last lesson, Mom refused to let her drive on busy Tatum Boulevard. "An unmitigated disaster," Mom had told Dad after the lesson. Nick, of course, was snickering as he inhaled cereal at the kitchen table. So what if she had gone off the road a couple of times (eleven, actually)? So what if she hadn't seen that kid on the bicycle when she was trying to make a right turn? He came out of nowhere, and if Mom hadn't grabbed the steering wheel, she *might* have hit him. Anyway, after that she was shaking so badly that Mom had driven home. She hadn't let Annie behind the wheel since, which was why Annie was so furious with her. Bad things sometimes happened, but you had to get on with it. It was her new motto: *Get on with it.*

It wasn't easy. It wasn't easy at all. Annie was having nightmares about a night she couldn't remember, a night she refused to acknowledge. As soon as she was back in the land of the technically civilized, she had tried to find Adam on Facebook. She wanted to see if he had posted any pictures on his site, which would have made him the worst human on the planet. It was impossible, of course, since she didn't know his last name, but it was some comfort that he didn't know hers either. They hadn't even exchanged phone numbers. At times, it was almost possible to believe that the boy had never existed. At times, it was almost possible to believe that the night had never happened. So, when she would wake up in the middle of the night sweating and shaking and crying uncontrollably, she would bury her face in the pillow until she calmed herself. Then she would take a valium that she had stolen from Aunt Sam's medicine cabinet. (She'd never miss them; she practically had a pharmacy.) *Get on with it.*

They were at the top of the hill at Carla's front door. She reached for the duffel bag in the back seat and got out, slamming the door to make her point.

Mom rolled down the window. "I love you, too, sweetie."

Annie didn't look back as she walked to the front door and rang the bell. Rita let her in and in her broken English directed her to Carla's room. Carla was sprawled on her king-sized bed reading a stack of fashion magazines, but she jumped up squealing when she saw Annie. The girls hadn't seen each other since the end of June when Carla's parents had whisked her off for a vacation on St. Martin. She had just returned late the night before. The girls hugged fiercely.

They excitedly jabbered the preliminaries: "God, I've missed you." "You look so tan." "Did you have fun?"

"I was so bored," Carla said. "The cell service sucked, and the freaking villa didn't have wireless. How was your cruise? Did you meet someone?"

Annie blushed. She had spent a considerable amount of time trying to decide what to tell Carla. Her best friend knew everything about her, but Annie couldn't bring herself to tell the story of Adam out loud. If she did, it might really be true.

"You did! I can tell by your face. Tell me everything, and I mean it. I want details." She pulled Annie down on the bed.

So, Annie told her about Adam, the high school junior from the Netherlands. His English wasn't the best, but somehow, they understood each other perfectly. He was tall and blond with cobalt blue eyes and a smile to die for. They had jet skied on a shore excursion and taken moon-lit walks on the Lido deck. Their time together had been romantic and beautiful, but sadly, they both knew it couldn't last. The distance between them was too great; they were continents apart. They parted tearfully on the last night of the cruise, and the next morning as she left her cabin, she found a single red rose by her door.

"Did you do it?" Carla asked.

"What?" Annie had been so caught up in her story she had forgotten Carla was even there.

"Sex," Carla said impatiently. "Did you do it? Remember, we decided it should be the goal of your trip to lose your virginity."

Annie hesitated, unsure how this story should end. Would sex make it better or worse? Wouldn't Adam from the Netherlands be a perfect gentleman and respect her for herself, or would their passion be so over-whelming that making love was a natural conclusion?

"You did it!" Carla decided for her. "Don't hold out on me." She reached into her nightstand and got out a joint. She lit it, took a deep drag, and handed it to Annie.

All Annie's resolve to never drink or do drugs again immediately flew out the window as she took the joint. She didn't have even the slightest hesitation. She inhaled and immediately felt better. "It was magical," she said. A few more hits and she was really going to believe this story.

"Your first time?" Carla was skeptical. "It usually hurts."

"No," Annie insisted. "It was perfect."

"Well, he must have had a pencil dick or something because the first time usually hurts." She was as insistent as Annie.

"Now you're being gross. Adam was . . . a normal size." She wasn't sure what a normal size was, and she was starting to feel uncomfortable with the whole subject. "Let's talk about you now. How's Drew?"

"Oh, that reminds me." She reached for her phone and sent a text. "I've been texting him every ten minutes. I don't know why he isn't answering. He should be orgasmic with joy that I'm back in the good old USA. That brings me to another question. Did you have an orgasm?"

Shit, why wouldn't she let up? The pot was making her sleepy. "I don't know."

"If you don't know, then you didn't have one," Carla said with authority. She patted Annie's arm. "Women rarely do their first time. That will come later."

"I'm hungry," Annie said.

She and Carla went downstairs to the large, well-stocked, walk-in pantry. Annie always wondered why the Goldleibs kept so much food on hand when they were constantly traveling. And Carla certainly didn't eat much, although she was trying to get over her seventh-grade anorexia and had gained enough weight to reach a hundred pounds. But considering she was five feet five, she was still very skinny. As they gathered Cool Ranch Doritos, Double Stuffed Oreos, a box of Cookie Crisp cereal, and diet cokes, Carla chattered nonstop. She acted high, much higher than one half of a joint should have made her. She might not be taking her meds, Annie thought. Carla had been diagnosed as being bipolar, but she disagreed. "Have you ever seen me depressed?" She had asked Annie. Annie had not.

They dumped the food in the middle of the bed and sat cross-legged as they tore into the food. Annie took a huge handful of chips. She was famished, despite having a huge bowl of leftover spaghetti and meatballs for lunch. She wasn't at all happy with her body (breasts too small, ass too big), but she didn't really worry about weight at five feet four and one hundred and twenty pounds. Carla took an Oreo, licked out the creamy center, and threw the chocolate cookies toward the wastebasket. She missed, and Annie knew she wasn't going to get up and properly place them in the trash. Carla knew Rita would do it.

Carla's phone vibrated. "Drew, of course! It's about time!" She checked the message.

Annie continued to eat, waiting for Carla to tell her the message from Drew, probably some sappy "I luv luv luv u," or some slightly dirty sexual reference. However, Carla just sat, staring at the phone. "Is something wrong?" Annie finally asked.

Carla looked up, her eyes glassy. "I can't believe it. Drew just dumped me. How could he do that to me? He was supposed to fly out next week, and I thought he was going to give me a promise ring. What the fuck is this?"

"Maybe he's just playing a joke? A really, really bad joke." Annie didn't like the look on Carla's face.

"He says he's given it a lot of thought and that I'm too young for him. How can that be? I wasn't too young for him when we started dating, and we're the same age difference now. It doesn't make sense." Even though her lips moved, she looked like she was in a trance.

Annie didn't know what to say. Carla had known Drew her whole life. Their parents were the best of friends and often traveled together, and apparently, no one thought the difference between Carla's and Drew's ages had been a big deal. In a creepy way, it was kind of like an arranged marriage. In an even creepier way, it was like they were sister and brother. "He'll probably come to his senses," Annie said, unconvinced.

"No, he won't!" Carla screamed. She threw her phone against the far wall. It hit with a crack that sounded like a gunshot. "That prick! He text-dumped me! That is the lowest of the low!" The trance was gone. Carla was out of bed, running around the room, knocking the collection of ceramic dolls off her dresser, pulling pictures of ballerinas off the wall. She ran crazily around the room, holding a fistful of hair in each hand as if she wanted to pull off her scalp. And all the while, she screamed.

Annie tried to intercept her once, but Carla just knocked her to the floor. So she waited, and when Carla finally collapsed into Annie's lap, exhausted and moaning, she held her. Annie didn't talk. She didn't quote her new motto—*get on with it*—because it was too premature for the newly fragile Carla. And she didn't tell her that everything would be all right.

She no longer had faith in that meaningless, catch-all consolation.

Chris sighed as he got off the phone with his mother, eighty-five-year-old Louise. He had dutifully made his biweekly phone call, and predictably, Louise had regaled him with a litany of complaints. Her arthritis was acting up, her joints ached, she was sure she had a near stroke the previous night, and she was convinced that her neighbor was stealing her morning paper. This was nothing new. Louise had been complaining nonstop since he moved her into the assisted living facility in a western suburb of Chicago two years before. She had refused to live with him and Sam, much to their relief, so Chris, being an only child, did the best that he could. Golden Manor came highly recommended, but Chris suspected that no facility would make Louise happy. The truth of the matter was that she was angry at being old.

Still, Chris felt guilty. He had also called with a half-formed plan to delicately steer the conversation to money. He knew exactly how much Louise was worth since he took care of her finances. Plus, she had received $250,000 from the life insurance company when his father died years before. He had never asked her for money before, but if Sam went ahead with her surrogacy plan, he was going to need more than he had saved. But after Louise had gotten around to complaining about the food—not fit for a pig to eat—he knew he couldn't do it, not yet. Chris sighed again. Sometimes the women in his life were just too much.

Sam wasn't home, and since he was feeling guilty anyway, he went to his computer and logged on to a porn site. It had started as a lark. He was a normal man, after all, and who didn't occasionally check out the Porn Stars website? But as the weeks turned into months during Sam's mourning period, he found himself spending more and more time watching pictures of naked women and subscribing to various sites. He started checking into chat rooms, using an alias, of course. It was harmless entertainment. He wasn't actually going to meet any of the women he chatted with, so it wasn't like he was committing adultery.

And then Sam found out. It was right before they moved to Arizona. He hadn't heard her come into the house, nor did he hear her enter the office. He didn't know she was in the room, or how long she had been standing behind him when she yelled, "What in the hell are you doing?"

He put his hands on the screen, trying to cover the particularly graphic scene of two women having sex. "I didn't hear you come in," he stammered.

"Obviously." She had her hands on her hips, feet apart, a stance he recognized as a warning to a knock-down, drag-out fight.

"I was just looking."

"And why do you need to do that? It's so perverted, Chris."

She went on and on. It was disgusting behavior. It devalued women. It devalued her. It made her feel dirty, and it made her feel like he didn't think she was enough for him. She continued to rant after he turned off the computer and went to the bar to pour a stiff scotch. She finally wound down after he poured her a drink and led her to the couch. In the end, he apologized and promised to end the "porno trash," as Sam termed it. In a conciliatory gesture, she promised to quit smoking.

Neither one kept the promise.

This time, he heard the door slam and Sam's loud clamoring in the kitchen. "Chris, honey? Where are you?"

He exited the site and met her at the door to the office. She dangled the car keys in front of him, back and forth in front of his eyes. "What are you doing?" he asked.

"I'm hypnotizing you."

"What have you done that you need to hypnotize me?" She probably made some outrageous purchase or dinged the car in the mall parking lot.

"I volunteered your services."

"Oh, great. What committee am I going to be on now?"

"Nothing like that. I volunteered you to give Annie a driving lesson."

"No," he groaned. "I'd rather be on the Scottsdale Beautification Committee with a bunch of cackling women who have nothing better to do than argue about petunias."

"Now, now, no need to get nasty. Alex and I decided that you're the logical choice. You're the most patient of all of us." She tossed him the keys. "Besides, you're the only one left. Giving sweet little Annie a driving lesson has terrorized the rest of us. It's your turn."

"You don't value my life very highly, do you?" Of course he would do it. Sam insisted, so he would do it. That was the structure of their relationship, and it was fine with him.

"Yes, I do, sweetie. You're the love of my life." She kissed him quickly on the lips and gave him a tiny push. "Annie's waiting for you in the car."

Sam had tried on twenty pairs of shoes before deciding on gold high-heeled Nine West sandals. Alex dutifully tried on a few pairs, but she didn't buy anything. She had been quiet since her spat with Annie a few minutes before. The purpose of this trip to the mall was to buy school clothes for

Annie, but Annie wasn't having any of it, saying the clothes at Dillard's were too "old lady like," even though Sam thought the clothing in the junior department was quite stylish. Alex had finally given in, sending Annie out into the mall to Charlotte Russe and Forever 21 with her credit card and the promise that Annie would not spend more than $200. They would meet up at Z'Tejas in an hour for a late lunch.

"Your sole is not really into this, is it? And I hope you got my witty joke. I meant s-o-l-e," Sam spelled.

Alex slumped back against the chair. "I don't know why every discussion with Annie has to turn into a confrontation. I'm worn out."

"It started in the car on the way here when you wouldn't let her drive—again. She's never going to get better if you don't let her practice."

"I know, but she's just so awful."

"She sucks," Sam agreed.

"She's driving impaired."

"She's a menace to society," Sam added.

Alex laughed. "Well, now that we have that out of the way, I feel better."

"Let's go directly to lunch and have a glass of wine." Sam paid for her shoes.

"I need five minutes. I have to get a birthday gift for Sadie's little girl. She's turning two." She started toward the escalator and the children's department on the second floor. "I'll meet you at the restaurant."

"No, I'll go with you." Sam knew that Alex wasn't sure how she would react to all the baby clothes, the fluffy pink dresses and little blue corduroys, but she could handle it now. She knew she could. However, when they reached the department filled with racks of tiny clothes, her heart started to beat faster, a premonition of a panic attack.

"Are you all right?" Alex gave her a worried look. "I'll be quick. I've already decided to get her a little bikini and a sun hat." She walked quickly to the carousal of swimwear and raked through the merchandise.

Sam couldn't help it. She was drawn to the little girls' section, the toddler size two. She imagined that would be Grace's size now, wouldn't it? She had been a petite baby, but maybe she would have blossomed into one of those plump little toddlers, with chubby cheeks and a waddling walk. Sam would never know. All those years had been snatched away from her. That familiar black hole of despair began to bloom in the pit of her stomach.

A hand clasped her elbow. Alex. "We have wine to drink." She firmly guided Sam out of the department, out of the store, and into the restaurant. They were seated at a table in a dark corner, and Alex ordered two St. Michelle chardonnays. They didn't speak until the wine arrived.

Sam took a drink and felt like she could breathe again. Had she been holding her breath that whole time? It didn't seem possible, but now she was taking gulping breaths into her empty lungs. "Thanks for rescuing me. That was a close call."

"That's what I'm here for."

"Thank God."

"Excuse me! Excuse me!" A woman trilled gaily. She was trying to maneuver a large, expensive-looking double stroller through the tables. The woman was what Alex and Sam had come to call the Scottsdale Barbie doll: tall, slim, dyed blonde hair, and fake boobs impossibly large for her slender frame. She also had on the requisite cleavage-showing top and tight Capri pants. "My fault! My fault!" She called as she continued to bump into tables and chairs.

"Talk about terrible drivers," Alex said. "She's making a spectacle of herself."

"Those poor babies are probably shell-shocked." Sam had plenty of time to peek into the stroller as the woman tried to maneuver by their table and ran over Sam's foot. The two children were probably two and one, dressed in blue and pink. They were of Asian ethnicity; their dark brown eyes were open wide, yet calm. "They're adopted," she said when they had finally passed.

"I guess the twenty-something trophy wife didn't want to ruin her figure." Alex studied the menu, her newly acquired reading glasses perched on the end of her nose.

"That's a really bitchy thing to say," Sam said, reaching for the cornbread the waiter sat down and ordering two more glasses of wine.

"Do you think we could have one conversation that doesn't end up being about babies?"

Sam felt as if the breath had been knocked out of her again. Couldn't Alex sense that she was still in a fragile state? "I was only making a simple observation."

"You could still adopt, you know." Alex went back to studying the menu.

Sam felt like ripping the menu out of her hands. "You know I want my own biological child. You can so blithely suggest adoption because you have *two* biological children. Plus, you know that Chris and I have looked into it. The process is complicated, time-consuming, expensive, and a lot of times, disappointing. Plus, I think Chris might change his mind altogether if we waited that long. I know I only have a certain amount of time before my nagging expires." Alex continued to study the menu. "Damn it, Alex! Don't you know what you want? We've been here enough times before! Order the fucking Santa Fe chicken enchiladas like you always do!"

"I didn't know that nagging had an expiration date. I've learned something new here today." Alex looked like she was trying to keep a straight face.

"Are you trying to goad me, or are you just being nasty?"

"Neither. It just seems to me that if my twin sister asks me to carry her baby, I have a right to make suggestions or offer opinions occasionally. Doesn't that seem reasonable to you?"

"I need a cigarette." She got up. Alex remained seated. "Aren't you coming?"

"No." She lifted the sleeve of her shirt, revealing a nicotine patch.

"Oh." Sam pondered the significance of the patch when she was outside smoking furiously, standing the requisite distance from the doorway. Did it mean that Alex was seriously considering the idea of carrying a baby? Was that why she was trying to quit smoking—again? Sam was exhausted from thinking about all of it. It had seemed like such a simple plan in the beginning.

When she got back to the table, Alex was putting her phone back into her purse, and she had ordered more wine. "Annie's late, and she's not answering her phone."

"She probably just got caught up in shopping or hooked up with some friends. You've got the car keys anyway."

"Right." Alex took a big drink of wine. "I'm going to say one more thing about the baby idea, and then we're done for a while, okay?" Sam nodded. "Are we absolutely positive that we're identical and that we share the same DNA?"

"I always assumed so, but it's not like we're mirror images of each other." This thought had never occurred to Sam. For some reason, she thought of the Olson twins, those adorable little girls on *Full House* who grew a conglomerate worth billions and seemed to have become dissatisfied adults. They had looked alike—and still did—but it turned out that they were fraternal twins.

Sam reached for her purse. "There's only one way to find out. We need to go to the source." She dialed.

"Good luck getting hold of the footloose folks."

The phone rang and rang. Since their mother wasn't savvy enough to set up voicemail, the ringing could go on for some time. Finally, she answered. "Hello, Mother?" Sam said. The connection was bad, static crackling. "I'm sitting here with Alex, and we have a question: Are we really identical twins?"

"I can't hear you," Emily's voice cackled. It was so loud that Alex had no problem hearing her.

"Jesus," Sam muttered.

"Are you taking the Lord's name in vain, Samantha?"

Sam mouthed to Alex: How in the world did she hear *that*? "Do you know for a fact that Alex and I are identical?"

"Well, the nurse told me you were. I was there, of course, but in those days, they used general anesthesia. If you're asking me if I saw the actual amniotic sac, the answer is *no*."

"Thanks, Mother, that's all we needed to know."

"What's this all about? Talk fast because we're crossing over—" The line went dead.

"Saved by the bell," said Sam, hanging up the phone. "That's good enough for me. What about you?"

"I don't want to take a DNA test. I know in my heart that we're identical, so that's good enough for me." She reached for Sam's hand.

"You guys are in public," Annie said. She was laden with shopping bags.

"You're late," Alex said, letting go of Sam.

"You're drunk," Annie countered.

"We are not. We're tipsy." For the first time, Sam noticed that their waiter had not been attentive about removing empty wine glasses.

"You two have way too much fun together."

"Sit down." Sam pulled out a chair. "We'll finally order some lunch."

"I think we better get going. A monsoon is rolling in. The sky is practically black, and the wind is already blowing like crazy."

Sam and Alex insisted on finishing their last glass of wine before they followed Annie to the parking lot. It was going to be a powerful monsoon, one with whipping rain and gusts of wind powerful enough to knock out power lines and uproot trees. The rain would start any minute.

"Give me the keys, Mom."

Alex looked at Sam, and Sam nodded. Neither one of them was in any shape to drive. They got in the car, Alex in the front passenger seat and Sam in the back. Sam made sure her seat belt was secure. Annie did okay in the parking lot, but when the rain started in earnest, she kept running off the road, correcting jerkily when she returned to the pavement. She drove slowly, and the normally ten-minute drive took twenty, but they made it home. When Annie parked crookedly in the driveway, all three breathed a sigh of relief.

"You see, Mom? I'm perfectly capable of driving a car, even in torrential weather." Annie couldn't keep the pride out of her voice.

"Good job, honey," Alex said.

"Excellent, kiddo," Sam said. "I'll see you guys later." She opened the door and made a dash for her house across the street. Even that short distance left her drenched, but she didn't care. It had been a promising afternoon.

Nick and Dylan had used stealth and guile to complete this mission, even though they didn't need to. They had secreted the guns out of the barn in an old duffel bag with Nick standing guard at the entrance. They had pilfered aluminum Coke cans and Miller Lite beer bottles out of the recyclable bin by the back door, constantly looking over their shoulders, moving quickly and quietly. They breathed a sigh of relief when they were safely in Dylan's battered Toyota truck, heading for the desert outside of Cave Creek. It had been a successful mission so far, they agreed, and it didn't matter that no one had been home at Dylan's—or was expected home for another couple of hours. They had used stealth and guile.

Nick had researched how to unlock the safety clip and load a Colt Accurized Flat Top. Even though he had spent hours looking at pictures of guns on the internet and watching war movies, holding a real weapon in his hands was an entirely new experience. He was glad Dylan's back was turned as he set out bottles and cans on the makeshift rock table they had constructed. Nick's hands were shaking, and he was sweating. It was a little after seven o'clock in the evening, but the desert was still hot, dry, dusty, desolate. They had driven pretty far out to ensure that they wouldn't run into anybody off-roading or riding dirt bikes. Since they didn't have permits for the guns, what they were doing was probably illegal. Neither he nor Dylan had mentioned this fact.

"I think we're ready for target practice, dude," Dylan said, walking over to Nick. "Do you think we're the right distance from the targets?"

Nick estimated that they were about twenty feet away. Would a glass bottle shatter and spew shards their way? He should have researched that. "I think we should move a little farther back." They walked a few feet backward.

"This is great," Dylan said. "We're finally going to see what we're made of. We'll see if we have the makings of great soldiers."

"Yeah," Nick said with unconvincing enthusiasm. What if he was terrible? What if he had no natural talent for gunmanship? It seemed to him that it was an essential part of being a soldier. "You shoot first," he said to Dylan.

"No, you go first."

"You should have the honor. They're your guns." They both stood, holding the rifles slightly down and away from their bodies at an awkward angle.

"Technically, they're not my guns. They're my dad's. I think."

Obviously, Dylan was just as nervous as he was, but Nick wouldn't call him on it. Best buddies didn't do that. "Why don't we shoot at the same time?"

"That sounds good. You aim at the far left target, and I'll aim at the far right. Ready?"

Nick lifted the gun to his shoulder and centered the beer bottle in his sights. He closed his eyes and squeezed the trigger. The shotgun blasts thundered in the desert, amplified by the dry air. The kickback of the blast pushed the butt of the rifle painfully into his shoulder. He opened his eyes and choked on the dust. Dylan was doing the same. When the dust settled, they looked toward the targets. Both were still standing.

"We must have hit the ground," Dylan said. His eyes were still watering.

"It was only our first try. We just need to practice."

"Dude, I think we're going to need a lot of practice," Dylan said, raising his gun.

They fired three more rounds before Nick hit the beer bottle. It exploded with a satisfying sound of ruptured glass. Adrenaline pumped through his veins. What an excellent feeling, a fusion of power and control! He could do this all day and never get tired of it. It must prove that he was destined for the Marines.

"Nice shot," Dylan said glumly.

"It's your turn. You can do it, Dylan," Nick said, although he was both thrilled and relieved that he had struck first.

Eventually, Dylan hit a few bottles, and Nick hit more and more. When he hit five in a row, they decided to call it quits for the evening. It was dark by then, and they had been shooting by the light from the Toyota's headlights. Dylan was worried that they were running the battery down and would have to call someone to come and get them. They'd be in big trouble then.

Nick reluctantly agreed. He felt like he was just getting warmed up. "This was a blast. If we lived in the Old West, we would have been gunmen like Billy the Kid."

"He was on the wrong side of the law, dude. We would have been like the Earp brothers."

"You're right. We would have been the good guys." Nick was swinging his rifle back and forth like he had been handling it all his life.

"Hurry up, Nick." Dylan climbed into the truck. "Is your safety on?"

It wasn't. Nick had been too exultant to think about it. He pointed the gun toward the ground to be safe, and he meant to click it on, but it was dark, he really wasn't familiar with guns, and he inadvertently squeezed the trigger. He heard the blast and felt the pain at the same time. "I'm shot!" he screamed.

Dylan ran over. "Shit, shit, shit," he said. "Are you hit?"

"My foot. I shot my foot!'

He felt the seeping blood and the searing pain as Dylan helped him to the truck. He didn't know that pain could feel like this. Up until now, the most pain he'd experienced had been a badly sprained ankle. This was like a red hole sucking him down, down, down. But he couldn't pass out. He couldn't do that to Dylan. He gritted his teeth as Dylan managed to get off his bloody Nike and wipe at his foot with some rags he found in the back of the truck.

"Good news, dude. You have all your toes," Dylan said as he examined the foot, "and there's no bullet. You shot off a little chunk of your heel."

Nick forced himself to look. The bleeding had subsided to a trickle, and he had indeed shot off a small part of his right heel. All that pain for that tiny piece of insignificant flesh? His babyish reaction would be embarrassing if it still didn't throb so darn much. He had not done a good job of being brave under fire, if this stupid mistake even counted as that. What decent soldier shot his own stupid, stupid foot?

"I'm taking you to the emergency room." Dylan started the truck. "You'll need an antibiotic."

"No, you can't do that. Don't emergency rooms have to report gunshot wounds? We don't have permits. We'll be in deep shit."

"I have to do something. This is all my fault. I'm the one who found the guns, and I'm the one who suggested we go shooting in the desert." Dylan sounded like he might cry.

"This is so not your fault. I was careless." He lightly punched Dylan on the arm. "What you can do is let me spend the night at your house." He wasn't about to take the chance that his parents would be home watching a movie or something in the family room. They would call him in and ask about his night, where he'd been, who'd he been with, and if he'd had a good time. He couldn't be nonchalant about it with only one shoe and a bloody rag tied around the other foot.

"I don't know," Dylan said doubtfully. They had finally reached the highway.

"Look, it really doesn't hurt anymore," (which was a lie), "and I just remembered that we have almost a whole bottle of amoxicillin in the medicine cabinet from Annie's last ear infection," (which was true).

"Well, all right," Dylan reluctantly agreed. "I'll take you to my house, but it's against my better judgment, dude. I'm only doing this because you're my best friend, and I don't want you to get in trouble."

"Thanks, Dylan. You know you're my best friend, too." He breathed a sigh of relief. He had an entire night to figure out what to do about his foot and his parents. "Let's drive through Taco Bell on the way home. My treat." He was suddenly ravenous, which must surely prove that he wasn't in that bad of shape. Right?

How could the kid think he wouldn't find out? For crying out loud, he was a guidance counselor. He could smell a cover-up a mile away. When Nick had come home limping from Dylan's, he had explained it away as a sprained ankle. Jack had been on his computer typing out various plays for his soccer girls, and frankly, he was preoccupied. He had barely glanced up from his keyboard. "Go put some ice on it. You know that."

"Sure thing, Dad."

However, Nick was still limping a couple of days later, and it didn't look like a sprained ankle to Jack. The kid was practically walking on tiptoe, and that was not an ankle injury. The four of them had been having dinner at the kitchen table, which was a rarity these days. Jack had grilled some hamburgers, and Alex had made potato salad. It felt like old times, and everyone had been in a good mood. "Let me look at that ankle, Nick. It should be getting better, but I notice you're still limping."

"It's fine. I should be able to go for a run tomorrow." Nick chewed furiously on his second burger.

"Please don't make him take off his shoe at the dinner table. That would be so gross. I'm eating." Annie picked at her small helping of potato salad.

"I agree with Annie," Alex said. "Can't it wait until after dinner?"

Jack was growing certain that something fishy was going on. Nick had always come to him with his various minor injuries before. "I think I should take a look at that ankle," he insisted.

"Really, it's nothing." Nick's face had gone white.

"Come with me to the den," he said, rising from the table.

It had been a shock when he peeled off Nick's sock and band-aid. The wound was scabbed, and it looked like a small triangle of Nick's heel had been sliced open. It didn't take much coaxing to get Nick to tell him the whole story. He confessed like a convicted felon, the words spilling out of him: the guns, the desert, the shooting practice. Jack grounded him for two weeks, and then he drove him to the emergency room.

The truth of the matter was this: He had a conflicted attitude about the whole episode. On one hand, he was angry at Nick for his reckless and potentially dangerous actions and even more upset about how secretive his once open and trusting son was becoming. On the other hand, he understood. He had grown up on a farm in central Illinois, and he and his buddies often went target shooting in the empty pastures. However, they had gone with their fathers' approval. Most of the time.

Alex's attitude toward the event was clear-cut. She was extremely upset. When they got home from the emergency room, with Nick on crutches and a filled prescription for a strong antibiotic, she screamed at him for doing something so dangerous. Then, predictably, she cried and hugged him. Nick stoically withstood her tirade and did not resist her desperate hugs. He looked exhausted and finally excused himself, hobbling up the stairs with surprising agility.

Alex went to the phone. "I'm going to call Dylan's parents. How could they leave guns laying around?"

"I don't think that's a good idea."

"How can you remain so calm? Our son could have killed himself." She started to dial.

He took the phone from her hands. He had to practically wrench it from her hands. "Nick is embarrassed enough as it is, and it's not going to do any good to get Dylan in trouble."

"I don't care if Dylan is grounded for life. Something needs to be done." She glared at him.

"Something has been done. Nick is going to be fine. Thankfully, he missed his Achilles tendon, so he won't need surgery. He's learned his lesson. I guarantee it."

"You can't guarantee anything."

That was true, but he was ninety-nine percent sure that Nick wasn't going to go shooting again. He also hoped—but didn't dare bring up the subject—that Nick was now cured of the idea of joining the Marines. This whole incident very possibly could have a positive side. "I'm going to pour you a glass of wine and a scotch for me. I think we deserve it after this evening." One glass of wine wasn't enough. Alex polished off an entire bottle before she accepted a drunken serenity.

And now they were in phase two of Nick's "punishment." Jack was driving Nick to Saguaro High School to take the SAT. They made this agreement while they were waiting in the emergency room. Nick, realizing he had no bargaining position at that point, had reluctantly said he'd take the test. He hadn't said a word on the entire drive.

"Are you nervous?" Jack said as they pulled into the parking lot of the school.

"What's there to be nervous about? It's just a stupid test."

"It's a very important test. Your score will help determine what university you'll go to and whether you get a scholarship. I think U of A would be a good choice for you. They have an outstanding cross-country team, too."

"Spoken like a true guidance counselor."

"What's that supposed to mean?" Jack turned off the engine.

"Nothing." Nick opened the door. He got out and hopped on his left foot to the back seat, opened the door, and got out his crutches.

Jack got out of the car. "I really want to know what you meant by that remark."

Nick didn't turn around, but Jack heard him distinctly. "I meant that sometimes it's more important to act like my *father*."

Jack wanted to call after him that of course he was his father. But he didn't. He was stopped by the determination of his son's strides as he quickly approached the building. He wanted to believe that his son would appreciate the fact that his father had insisted he take this test, an important preliminary step towards his future. He wanted to believe that one day in the future Nick would thank him. Maybe he wanted to believe these things too much. As far as he knew, Nick hadn't even brought a pencil.

It had been a disastrous double date so far, and of course, it had been Carla's idea. After two days, Carla announced that her *grieving process* for Drew was over. She maniacally went about finding them dates, making lists of various eligible boys from St. Andrews Catholic Prep School and making phone calls. Carla thought they should start off with the Catholic boys because they were probably nicer, and therefore, would be a good launching pad for future public school boys. So far, there hadn't been any niceness at all. Carla's date, Mike, and Annie's date, Cameron, had barely spoken. Rather, they acted like they had been forced against their will to participate in this exchange. Carla overcompensated by chattering endlessly, and Annie felt the beginning of a headache behind her right eye.

They had gone to the Phoenix Zoo. Again, Carla's idea. Annie had loved the zoo as a child, but she hadn't been there since a sixth-grade field trip. She decided she hadn't missed much. The zoo was crowded and hot on a late Saturday afternoon. The boys insisted on walking fast, ahead of them, and the girls' carefully applied makeup melted under the sizzling hot sun. Still, they tried to keep up with the boys as they whizzed by the giraffes, elephants, tigers, and through the blessedly cool indoor snake exhibit. The only thing that seemed to interest the boys was the orangutan cage, which inspired their first unsolicited comments: "Holy shit! Look at their shiny red asses." (Mike) "They must be butt fucking each other 24-7." (Cameron)

"*They* must be butt fucking each other 24-7," Carla had whispered to Annie. "We are way too attractive to be ignored like this."

"This is not going well," she hissed.

"We have to try harder," Carla said.

So, Annie now sat in a booth at Denny's with a smile plastered on her sunburned face. She smiled as the boys squirted water at each other through their straws. She smiled when the harried middle-aged woman set a plate of greasy onion rings in front of her, and she smiled when Cameron, in his exuberance to beat Mike to the ketchup bottle, accidentally elbowed her painfully in the breast.

She kept smiling when Cameron announced that he had to take a piss and Mike said he'd go with him. They shoved each other on the way to the bathroom. Mike's final shove knocked Cameron into their poor waitress, who dropped a tray of drinks. They both thought this was hilarious.

Then she stopped smiling. "If you weren't my very best friend in the whole world, I'd be so pissed at you right now," she said.

Carla, too, had stopped smiling. She slumped against the back of the booth. "You have every right to be mad. They're jerks."

"Let's get out of here. I'll call Nick to come and get us." Annie reached for her phone.

"No!" The color rose in Carla's cheeks. "I don't care how bad this is. I'm not sitting at home alone on a Saturday night. I'd bet anything that Drew's out with some new slut, and I refuse to be the dumped girlfriend wallowing in heartbreak." Her voice rose higher. "I refuse!"

In Annie's opinion, Carla had nowhere near completed her *grieving process*, but she didn't want to make her feel worse. "All right, Carla, we'll play this out to the bitter end. And I'm emphasizing *bitter*."

The boys returned. "Hey, we just found out about a party," Cameron said, looking happy for the first time. He was almost cute when his brown eyes lit up.

"Do you want to go?" Mike asked.

"I'm definitely up for a party." Carla stood up.

"I'm always up for a party," Annie said, noticing that Cameron finally looked interested in her.

A few drinks later, Cameron was definitely interested in her. The party had started hours earlier as a pool party, and of course, the parents of the household were out of town and their son, a St. Andrews senior, seemed to have invited everyone he had ever met. "We need to catch up," Cameron said as he surveyed the drunken teenagers in the pool, scattered around the backyard, and gathered around the kegs.

Annie hadn't had any alcohol since the cruise, but she didn't want to think about that now, and the only way to do that was to drink—and drink fast. As long as she mixed her own drinks, and as long as she kept her drink in her hand at all times (not setting it down, not letting it out of her sight), she would be safe. It was amazing, really, what alcohol could do. The boys who had been so aloof before were now hanging all over Carla and her. Cameron was acting like her boyfriend, his arm slung around her shoulder, his beer casually sloshing on her flip-flops as he gestured with the punch line of a series of funny, dirty jokes. When Annie announced that she had to go to the bathroom, Cameron gave her a sloppy, beer-soaked kiss on the mouth. She shuddered involuntarily, but he didn't seem to notice.

On the way back from the bathroom, she stopped at the outside bar to refill her vodka tonic. There were bottles and bottles of booze, but she couldn't find any tonic. She filled the cup to the brim with vodka. She would sip it the rest of the night. It would be her last drink. She would not let herself get drunk and lose control. She could handle her alcohol.

"What took you so long?" Cameron asked when she finally found him.

She had been wandering around for some time, getting more and more disoriented. "Where's Carla?" she asked.

"She and Mike went to find a bedroom," he smirked. "I think we should do the same."

"Why?"

"Oh, come on. You've been coming on to me all night. You know you want it."

Annie thought it had been the other way around. Wasn't he the one who had been hanging all over her? Did he think she wanted to have sex? Did he love her? The questions made popping sounds in her brain, which caused a wave of nausea. "I think I should find Carla. We should go home."

"Don't be a bitch," Cameron said, but he followed her inside.

Annie started knocking on doors. There were so many of them in this large, large house. "Carla!" she called, again and again.

She reached the end of the hallway and turned, running into Cameron. He pushed her against the wall roughly, smashing his body against hers. "Don't!" She thought she had screamed, but it came out as a whisper. He roughly pulled down her shorts and jammed a finger up her vagina.

"You know you want this," he said.

Why did they all think that?

What was wrong with her?

She vomited right into Cameron's face.

Her dear niece showed up on her doorstep looking like a cross between a bedraggled orphan and a punk rocker. Her newly chopped black hair stuck up in uneven spikes, and some of those spikes had been dyed pink. Her clothes had gotten baggier, and she wore a dark hoodie, even though it was sweltering. She looked both terrified and defiant.

"You've got to help me, Aunt Sam." Annie's pleading blue eyes were rimmed in black eyeliner. Beneath the smudged eyeliner were dark circles.

Sam stifled the urge to say that she looked like a train wreck. Instead, she calmly said, "I see you've been experimenting with your hair again."

"Carla thought I could use a new look, but she didn't really know what she was doing." Annie didn't tell Aunt Sam that Carla had been drinking straight vodka and passed out before she finished.

"Obviously." Annie's hair stuck out in uneven spikes, and she looked close to tears. Sam opened the door wider. "Of course I'll help you. Come on in."

She put down newspapers on the kitchen floor, settled Annie on a chair, and wrapped a towel around her shoulders. "Your mom and I used to cut each other's hair all the time in high school. Has she ever told you that?"

"Mom," Annie groaned. "She's going to kill me."

"She's not going to kill you." Sam snipped the roughly cut spikes, trying to even them out. What had the girls used, a knife?

"Right. She'll just ground me for life."

Sam smiled. Teenagers were so dramatic. Every little incident was high drama. It was too bad that they couldn't appreciate the youth, the freedom, the endless possibilities ahead of them. She and Alex had had a blast in their small southern Illinois high school. They had been major-ettes, cheerleaders, class officers and straight-A students. They thought they had been invincible as they headed off to college, with plans to con-quer the world, to become rich and famous. What had happened? Life, that's what. Marriage, mortgages, bills, and children . . .

"Is my hair looking any better?"

Annie's question startled Sam out of her reverie, which was about to take a dangerous turn. "Sorry, honey, I was thinking about how much fun high school is."

"You're not serious, are you? High school *sucks*."

"Oh, honey, don't say that. Freshman year is tough, but it gets better, especially after you start to drive."

"We both know how that's going," Annie said glumly.

"You're getting better."

"Yeah, I've gotten good enough to be bad."

Sam laughed. Annie didn't join in. "Give it time."

"I don't have time."

Sam stopped cutting. What in the world did Annie mean by that? She had been blathering on about the glory days of high school, offering empty platitudes, when she knew that kids these days faced all sorts of pressure, the pressure to get into the right college, the pressure to belong to the right group. She knew that the suicide rate among teenagers had skyrocketed in the last few years. Suddenly, she felt afraid for Annie.

"What do you mean about not having time?" She asked carefully, hand-ing Annie a mirror.

"School starts next week, and Dad won't let me drive to school until I can parallel park. That is so *not* going to happen." She looked in the mirror. "Hey, it looks pretty good."

Sam was relieved at this simple explanation, but still, looking down at Annie's mirrored reflection, she could see that Annie's black-lined blue eyes did not look the same as they had at the beginning of the summer. They looked, somehow . . . haunted? Sam was probably reading too much into this. Maybe the child had had a bad night's sleep. It wasn't like she had any personal experience in raising a teenager. Then she got it. Another new look, another new haircut. This had to be about a boy. Hadn't Alex said that Annie was going on a date?

She took the towel from Annie's shoulders and folded it. "We're all done here. You look gorgeous."

"Thanks, Aunt Sam, you're a lifesaver." Annie hugged her.

"Hey, Annie, your mom said you were going on a date last Saturday. Did you have a good time?"

Annie pulled back sharply, and her mood—which had been almost happy—abruptly changed. "It was fine."

"I didn't mean to pry." But apparently, she had. It was like a light switch had gone off behind Annie's eyes.

"It was a double date with Carla. We went to the zoo. It was boring." Annie said in a rehearsed voice.

"Well, good."

"Do you mind if I use your bathroom, Aunt Sam? I think I just got my period."

"You know you don't have to ask." Annie started toward the powder room off the kitchen. "You'll have to use the bathroom upstairs. That one's broken. I expect the plumber any minute."

"Great."

Sam took the towel outside and shook out the hair. Then she called the plumber and asked why in the hell he was two hours late and got the usual response that he was delayed by the job before hers. She emptied the dishwasher. Still no Annie. Maybe she was feeling ill? She called up the stairs.

Annie came down immediately. "I was looking at the pictures on your nightstand," she said. "Where was the one of you and Uncle Chris on the beach taken?"

"South Beach. That was on our honeymoon. Uncle Chris had a lot more hair then, didn't he?"

Annie smiled wanly. "I guess. Well, I've got to go. Thanks for the haircut."

She was out the door before Sam could finish calling out, "Good luck."

Sam went into her office. She needed to finish the article on the new members of the city council for *Scottsdale* magazine. She sat down and stared at her computer, but she didn't write. She was thinking of Annie. She had only been here for around a half hour, but Sam felt exhausted. The girl could run hot and cold within the span of a minute. Sam was convinced that something was bothering her, but then again, she had thought the same thing on the cruise, and Annie had seemed happy enough then.

And why had Annie spent such a long time upstairs? She had seen those pictures before. Something didn't add up. "Oh, God," she said.

She ran upstairs to the bathroom and opened the medicine cabinet. She moved the ibuprofen, band-aids, and assorted cold medicines and face cleansers. The three musketeers, as she called them, were still there: Valium, Prozac, Xanax. She opened each bottle. They looked as if they contained the same level of pills, but she couldn't be sure. She hadn't taken the Prozac in a while, and when was the last time she had a Valium? She thought it was Tuesday. The only person who would know if any pills were missing would be Chris. She knew that he counted the pills on a regular basis and that he sometimes flushed some down the toilet. What he didn't know was how many prescriptions she had for each.

Should she ask Chris for the pill count? And if she did find out that some pills were missing, what should she do?

The doorbell rang. The plumber had finally arrived.

Alex didn't give Annie the reaction she probably expected when she walked into the kitchen. "I see you cut your hair again," she said as she molded the ground beef into a loaf. "Would you set the table?"

"Sure," Annie said uncertainly, "but I'm not going to be here. I'm babysitting the Williams kids tonight, remember?"

"Oh, that's right." Alex hadn't remembered. "Set it for three then."

Nick hobbled in on his crutches. "Nice hair," he said to Annie.

"Buzz off," she said.

"Grow up," he said. A car honked outside. "That's Andy. I'm off, Mom."

And Alex hadn't remembered that Nick had a pre-season cross-country meeting at Pizza Hut. It was questionable whether he would be healed enough for the season, but Nick insisted that he had to go. Who was she to argue? It didn't do any good, and it was becoming increasingly clear that her opinion wasn't much valued around here anymore. She was tired of feeling tense all the time, like she was walking on eggshells around her children. She needed a hobby, or a project, or something to keep her occupied. Maybe she should start training for the P.F. Chang Rock and Roll Marathon? Maybe she should have a garage sale?

"It's fine, honey," she said to Jack when he called a few minutes later saying that he had run into Bob Cotsall at the school and wanted to know if she minded if he went out with him for a beer and some wings. She took the partially cooked meatloaf out of the oven, covered it in foil, and stuck it in the refrigerator, pulling out a half-opened bottle of wine at the same time. She rummaged through the junk drawer to find the hidden pack of cigarettes before she went out to the patio.

She could call Sam, but she wasn't going to. She needed time alone to think. Of course, it seemed as if she had plenty of time alone these days, but she always tried to be busy: folding laundry, pulling weeds from the flower beds by the front door, making phone calls for the PTO, grocery shopping—sometimes it felt as if she had spent half of her adult life in the aisles of a grocery store searching for the cheapest brand—cooking, and cleaning. For the longest time, she thought she had been happy, but now it was starting to look like a rather paltry, pathetic existence. Her family meant everything to her, but it was time to face the truth: They no longer needed her like they used to. A corner had been turned; a new phase needed to take flight.

And then came Sam, proposing this outlandish idea that Alex should carry her baby. Was it fate, God's will, karma, or stupidity? Alex didn't know. The best way to characterize her feelings at this time could be embodied in one word: *confusion.* Alex poured a second glass of wine, ripped off the nicotine patch, and lit a cigarette. She inhaled deeply, and the poisonous gas felt wonderful in her lungs. She needed to quit once and for all. Maybe smoking was just one more sign of her inherent weakness? Whatever. She continued to puff on the cigarette.

One thing she was certain of was her love for Sam. It was amazing that, during the course of her cajoling and subtle pleading, Sam hadn't brought up Alex's secret, her biggest regret. Sam had helped Alex through the ordeal, and then they had vowed never to bring up the subject again. Sam had been true to her word. She might have used the incident to make Alex feel guilty, to tip the scales in her favor, but she hadn't.

Sam had been true to her word.

It was her first and last one-night stand, and it had been completely out of character for Alex, something she had never, ever considered doing. But then, the entire Saturday night on that April day at the end of sophomore year had been out of character for her and Sam. It was the first warm day of spring, and the entire campus seemed as if it was in an ebullient mood. People were out in force, playing Frisbee on the quad, walking around in shorts, baring their white legs to the sun for the first time that season, and sitting jacketless on sagging front porches drinking beer. She and Sam had been invited to one of those parties—by a friend of a friend—and had spent a good part of the afternoon drinking beer in their shorts and halter tops and flirting with the boys. It had been a heady experience for them, since most of the boys were seniors and seemed so much more mature than the freshman and sophomores they had dated that year. When someone suggested that they meet later that evening at the Illini Tavern, she and Alex accepted without hesitation.

They had never been to that bar before. Instead, if they didn't have dates, they tended to gravitate to the Greek bars, especially Milton's, where the clientele favored the late eighties, preppy look. The Illini Tavern, on the other hand, was a small, dark, narrow bar favored by upperclassmen and quite a few local middle-aged men who seemed to have permanently staked out claims on specific bar stools. Freddy Fender's "Wasted Days and Wasted Nights" poured from the jukebox, and the air was heavy with smoke.

"How could we not have known that this place existed?" Sam said over the din when they walked in the door. No one carded them as they entered, which was a good sign, although many bars on campus looked the other way when nineteen-year-olds drank.

"I don't know. It's a great place," Alex said. The floor, sticky with spilled beer, caused her to step out of one of her sandals, but that only added further charm to her impression of the Illini Tavern.

They saw the group they had partied with earlier in the day by the bar. Neither she nor Sam could remember who was who, and as they put on their makeup before coming to the bar, they had dubbed them the "B" boys because all their names started with the letter B: Brad, Brent, Brandon, Barry. The boys poured Sam and Alex beers from one of the pitchers lining the bar. It was all very convivial, very friendly. And then he walked in.

"It's about time you got here, bro," one of the B boys said. He gave him a brotherly hug. "This is my brother, Dave, up from the farm in Assumption," he said to the girls.

"I'm surprised your name isn't Buford or Buck or Biff," Sam said.

"What?" Dave said.

"I'm just kidding." Sam was grinning happily, drunkenly. "We've been joking about all the names here that begin with B."

Alex barely felt the not-so-subtle elbow jab that Sam landed in her ribs. She realized she had been staring, probably with an open mouth, at this stunningly handsome man. He was tall, slightly over six feet, with sapphire blue eyes and ebony hair that curled slightly over his ears. His smile, with perfect teeth, lit up his face. She had never seen such a good-looking person. "I'm Alex," she stammered.

"Hey, Alex," he said with a sexy drawl as his eyes passed over her body. Apparently, he liked what he saw. He got a beer and led her to a table in the corner.

The rest of the night passed all too quickly as she and Dave talked and talked. He was twenty-four and had graduated from U of I two years earlier. He ran his father's farm and led the local 4-H group. Alex barely heard his words as she stared at his beautiful face. When he finally took her hand, it felt like a current of electricity passed through her entire body. She knew she was going to sleep with him. She wanted to sleep with him.

"Are you sure?" Sam whispered to her right before she followed Dave out of the bar.

"I'm positive."

Sam didn't look convinced. Neither of them was a virgin, but each of them had only slept with one boy: her high school boyfriend. "I'll come over to the house with you."

"That would be incredibly embarrassing. It would look like you're my watchdog or something."

"Well, aren't I?"

"Not tonight."

"You don't even know him," Sam persisted.

"Aren't you always telling me that I need to be more adventurous?"

"Yes, but—"

"I'll see you in the morning, Sam."

Alex knew it was a mistake as soon as they got back to the boys' house. She was the only girl, and she uncomfortably joined them in a couple shots of tequila. Dave took a large swig from the bottle before he led her to a messy bedroom with an unmade bed and a sour smell. She heard a burst of laughter from the other room when Dave shut the door, and she knew they were laughing at her. She wracked her brain to see if she could think of any way to get out of this. But then he kissed her, and everything seemed all right. She had never been kissed like that before. Thankfully, he didn't turn on the lights, and they undressed quickly and slipped beneath the rumpled sheets. They didn't speak, it was over quickly, and just as quickly, the person she had just had sex with, the person she didn't really know, fell into a drunken, snoring sleep. Alex lay in bed next to him, not touching him, until the noise from the other room finally ceased. She hurriedly dressed, slipped out the front door, and ran to the dorm room.

It was 5:00 a.m. when she got there, and Sam was immediately awake when the door closed. "Thank God. You're alive."

"Of course I'm alive." Alex was close to spilling the tears she had held back for the last three hours.

Sam turned on the light and saw Alex's face. She immediately got out of bed and came to her. "What's wrong? He didn't hurt you, did he? If he did, I'm going to personally go over there and beat the shit out of him. I don't care how big he is."

"No, no, nothing like that. I just feel so . . . cheap."

"Isn't that part of the definition of *one-night stand*?" As Alex's face crumpled, Sam took her in her arms. "I don't know why I said that. I would never think you were cheap."

"What a stupid thing to do. He wasn't even very good, as far as I could tell. I will be humiliated if I ever run into him again."

"That's not likely. He doesn't live here, his brother—one of the B boys—will be graduating next month, and we won't go near the Illini Tavern. We'll pretend like the night never happened." She patted Alex's head.

Alex left the embrace and started to undress. She was going to take a long, hot shower. "Thanks, Sam, we'll pretend like it never happened."

"Like *what* never happened? I have no idea what you're talking about."

Alex turned at the door, basket of toiletries in hand, and smiled at her. "I'm already starting to feel better." She opened the door.

"He did use a condom, right?" Sam called from the bed.

How could she have been so stupid? She had so desperately wanted the whole thing to be over, had been so concerned about the boys in the other room that she hadn't even thought about it. "Maybe he put one on when I wasn't looking?" she said to Sam.

"Did you go to the bathroom or something?"

"No."

"Then I think you'd know." When Alex buried herself under the covers, Sam said, "There's nothing to be upset about. Chances are good that you're not."

They left it at that. But for Alex, the next two weeks were the longest in her life. She went to class, studied, worked her assigned hours in the dorm's cafeteria, and laughed with her friends, but always, there was a cloud of dread hanging over her. She had been in the exact middle of her cycle and could very well have been ovulating. She had trouble sleeping, and when she did fall asleep, her dreams were an uncoordinated mismatch of body parts: baby heads, torsos, arms, legs, and hands, floating around a large mouth with rows and rows of shark-like teeth.

When her period was five days late, she and Sam stood outside the Walgreens on Green Street. "I can't do this," Alex said.

"It'll be a piece of cake." Sam led her inside. They went to the pharmacist counter in the back and asked, mumbling, for a pregnancy test. "It's for a friend," Sam said to the white-clad, middle-aged woman.

"Uh huh," she said as she rang up the purchase.

"What a bitch," Sam said when they were outside. "It's 1988, for shit's sake. A lot of unmarried women have babies."

"Why don't you just shut up?" Alex said.

Sam ignored her. At the corner, as they were waiting for the light to change, she reached into the sack and pulled out the box. "It says here that you're supposed to take the test the first thing in the morning."

"Put that back!" Alex looked around to see if anyone was watching. There was only one couple nearby, and they seemed to be totally engrossed in each other.

"Sorry. I can understand why you're tense. Do you want to go to a bar? It is time for Friday happy hour." It was an event they never missed.

"No, I'm going to take the damn test now."

The community bathroom was deserted when Alex locked herself in the stall. Sam stood outside and read the instructions. Alex was supposed to pee into a miniature test tube, which wasn't easy. Then, furtively, they took the test tube to their room and propped it up in a tray that came with the kit. Sam set her alarm. They waited for the required fifteen minutes in a silence that was finally broken when the alarm buzzed.

"I can't look," Alex said.

Sam got up and lifted the tube, peering at the bottom. She compared it to the illustration on the box. She stared at it for a long time.

"Well?" Alex finally asked when she couldn't stand it any longer.

"There's a donut shape on the bottom."

Alex hadn't read the instructions. "What does that mean?"

"It means that you and I are going to be parents."

"Oh, God, no!" Alex ran to the bathroom and vomited.

It took some time before Sam could coax her out of the stall and back to the room. She had been crying so hard that she was now hiccupping uncontrollably. Sam propped her up on the bed and brought her a glass of water. When she could speak, she said to Sam: "I can't believe this is happening. I remember feeling sorry for all the girls who got pregnant in high school. I thought their lives were over. Now I'm in the same situation."

"Not really. Most of those girls got married."

"It's certainly not an option here. I don't even know the guy's last name."

"We could go back to the house and ask the B boys. We could rent a car and drive to Assumption and tell the jerk that he's going to be a father." Sam paced the room. "He has a right to know, doesn't he?"

Alex felt like she was in a bad dream. She desperately wished that she could close her eyes, open them, and this whole thing would go away. She looked down at her flat stomach. It just couldn't be true. She knew that someday she would have children, she wanted children, but it absolutely could not start like this. "I'm not telling Dave."

"Okay, we'll scratch that idea." Sam continued to pace, thinking aloud. "Maybe we should call Mother and Dad? They'd throw a fit, of course, but then they'd realize they were going to be grandparents and forgive you. They'd probably make some biblical allusion to the Virgin Mary, and then they would move you back home and watch their wayward daughter like a hawk."

Alex started to cry again. "I don't want to leave school."

At this point, Sam started to cry, too. She went to the bed and stretched out next to Alex. "I don't like that idea either. If you quit school and moved back home, I'd go with you. I don't want to be here without you, and I vehemently don't want to go back home."

"I've made a mess of things," Alex sniffled.

"A perfect solution would be this: They would let you stay in school, you would conveniently have the baby over next winter break, and they would keep it and raise it as their own."

"Fat chance," Alex said.

"I know. I'm grasping at straws here."

They lay silently, holding hands until Alex spoke next. "You haven't mentioned an abortion."

"We don't believe in abortion," Sam said. "I can't stand to think of it. You know how I love babies."

"I can't stand to think of it either, but I don't see any other choice." Her heart felt like it was going to break. A couple of years ago, they had shown a film on abortion at their Methodist church back home. The graphic images of aborted fetuses still haunted her.

"I know we're too old to *run away*, but maybe we could disappear for a while, go to Florida or something. We could get jobs, you could have the baby, and then we would finish school and—"

"Raise the baby together? What would we do for money? Who would stay with the baby while we were in school?"

"I know the idea has a few flaws."

"I'm going to have to get an abortion, Sam. We both know that." They started to cry again.

"I know."

Sam went with Alex to the Planned Parenthood facility in Champaign two weeks later. After it was over, when Sam joined Alex in the recovery room, they vowed never to cry or talk about it again. They shook hands, hugged each other, and kissed each other on the lips.

And Sam had been true to her word.

Since that day in May 1988, Alex had not allowed herself to think about the abortion. And she had never told Jack, who she met in the fall of that same year. But now, with the advent of Sam's proposal, her general sense of an unfilled dissatisfaction, and wine-fueled reverie—she had opened another bottle of wine sometime while revisiting the memory—she did think about it. For some reason, she imagined the baby as a boy. He would have been born in the early part of January. If he had arrived early, he could have been a New Year's Day baby.

Oh, my God, she thought with a start. He would have turned nineteen this year, a young man. Maybe he would be in college studying pre-law, or maybe, somewhere along the way, he would have been acquainted with his biological father and be farming the family farm in Assumption, Illinois. He could even be married and have a child of his own. There were so many options for this son who had never been given the chance to live.

Tears streamed down Alex's face, and wave after wave of guilt washed over her. She had done a terrible thing; she had taken the life of her own child. But she had been so young. It had been the right thing to do, hadn't it? If she had had that baby, she would not have married Jack and not have given birth to Nick and Annie, and it was this family that was her true destiny. That's what she had always believed, but had she only deluded herself? By burying the abortion so deeply in past memory to avoid feeling the shame and guilt, had she completely missed the *point*?

It was time to make amends for that lost baby. And for Grace, as well.

She was a little unsteady on her feet as she went through the house to the front door. The doorbell rang just as she opened it.

Jack stood there. "Sorry, honey, I forgot the garage door opener, and I didn't have a key. Hey," he said, looking at her, "have you been crying?"

"Never mind," she said, brushing past him.

"Are you mad because I went to Hooter's with Bob?"

"No."

"Where are you going?"

"To Sam's."

"I'll wait up for you."

"Don't bother."

Another monsoon was on its way. The wind was lashing at the trees, and she felt an occasional fat drop of rain as she crossed the street and knocked on Sam's door.

Chris opened the door, and it seemed as if he were more intuitive than her own husband. "She's on the back patio."

Sam's patio was a replica of her own with its almost-empty bottle of wine and heaping ashtray. Sam was staring at the lit pool. She, too, had a tear-streaked face. "Alex," she said.

"I'm going to do it. I'm going to carry your baby. You deserve it, and I deserve it." She took hold of Sam's hands and pulled her to a standing position.

"Are you sure?"

"I'm absolutely positive."

"Oh, Alex, I love you so much."

"I love you too, Sam."

Like that long-ago pact, they hugged and kissed each other on the lips.

"You'll see," Sam whispered between sobs. "Everything is going to be perfect."

4

CHAPTER FOUR

"This school sucks," Carla said. She picked at the lunch Rita had packed her: a chicken and bacon wrap with ranch dressing, a small bag of Baked Lays, a banana. "This week has been *excruciating*. I don't know how I'm going to make it through this whole year."

It was Friday of the first week of school, and Annie and Carla were sitting on one of the picnic tables in the center common area of SCDS. It was way too hot to be sitting outside, but they had decided they couldn't face all the "morons" and "stupid people" who had elected to eat in the comfortably air-conditioned cafeteria. Annie, out of necessity, had to take off her black hoodie, which she almost never did in public these days. She looked down at her own lunch—a hastily prepared peanut butter and jelly sandwich on two crusts of plain white bread—and sighed. "Are you going to eat the other half of that wrap?" she asked.

"Hell, no," Carla said, handing it over. "Rita's trying to fatten me up again. I keep telling her to stop it, but she refuses to listen to me."

"Maybe you could gain a pound or two?" Annie said hesitantly. Since her breakup with Drew, Carla was eating even less than usual.

"Whose side are you on?" Carla snapped.

"Yours, of course. I'm always on your side." Not only was Carla dwindling away, but she was also very bitchy these days. Drew had moved quickly on, as shown on his Facebook page. He had plastered pictures of himself with a new, strikingly pretty brunette at some fraternity party. As Carla pointed out, he hadn't even had the decency to block Carla from his page. According to her, he had wanted to rub her face in the fact that he had a new slut for a girlfriend. It had been the last straw for Carla. She had thrown a major fit that night. At one point, Annie had considered calling 911 because Carla was close to convulsing.

"I just had a feeling I'd be bored to tears today." Carla reached into her backpack and pulled out a water bottle. She took a sip and handed it to Annie.

Annie's water bottle was empty, so she took a big gulp. "Oh, my god, Carla!" she choked. "You brought vodka to school?"

"Actually, it's gin. I'm getting rather bored with vodka, along with everything else."

"Do you know how much trouble we could get into?" They would definitely be suspended if they got caught. "You should pour it out. Now."

"Really, Annie, you sometimes disappoint me with your lack of enthusiasm for my bright ideas." Carla took another sip.

"Carla, my father is the guidance counselor here. Do you know how disappointed he would be?" She looked nervously over her shoulder, and as if on cue, Dad came out of his office and headed toward them. "Put it away now!"

For once, Carla did as she was told.

"Hey, girls, what are you doing out here? It's still a little hot for a picnic." He stood at their table smiling warmly, his hands in his pockets.

Annie loved him; she really did. He had always been a great dad. However, after the last episode with Cameron, she found that she was leery of all males, which unfortunately, included him. After she vomited all over Cameron at that horrible party, as he stood dripping and swearing in front of her, Carla had magically appeared, called Cameron a *filthy pig*, and then led Annie outside where she called Rita to come and get them. Carla didn't ask Annie any questions, only held her as she cried most of the ride home. She had been a wonderful friend. Later that night, as they lay in Carla's bed watching a movie, they had come to the consensus that *all* boys were filthy pigs.

"Hi, Dad." Annie didn't look at him as she started gathering the remnants of her lunch and stuffing them in the crumpled paper sack.

"Hello, Mr. Carissa," Carla said politely.

"How is the first week of classes going, girls?" Dad looked like he was waiting for an invitation to sit down and join them, but there was no way Annie was going to ask him. It would be humiliating if he did that and some of the kids walked by and saw him sitting with them.

"Splendidly, Mr. Carissa!" Carla said with exaggerated enthusiasm. "It's all such interesting . . . stuff."

Annie hunkered down on the bench. What was Carla doing?

"Is that so, Carla, even physics?" Dad said with a laugh.

"Well, maybe not so much *that* class."

Annie knew that Carla had planned on skipping *that* class after lunch. She threw her lunch sack at the nearby garbage can and missed. She almost mumbled *shit* but stopped herself in time.

"I'll get that for you, honey." Dad walked over to the sack, picked it up, and dropped it in the can.

"Thanks," she mumbled. She stood up. "Are you ready, Carla?"

"Sure." She stood up, too. "Nice talking to you, Mr. Carissa."

"We have some studying to do," Annie said. It was a total lie.

"Is that so?" He didn't sound convinced. "Well, I certainly wouldn't want to stand in the way of that." He turned to go, then came back. "Annie, I thought on the way home we could stop and rent a couple of movies for tonight. We haven't had a family movie night in a long time."

She wanted to *die*. She didn't even want her best friend to hear her dad say lame shit like that. A family movie night? Did he still think she was in third grade? Why not shout out to the entire world that she didn't have a date, didn't have anything better to do on a Friday night than hang out with her parents and brother? "Maybe," she said.

She and Carla walked quickly away and ducked into the nearest restroom. For some reason, she was having a hard time breathing.

"Is he for real?" Carla got out the bottle of gin and took a sip.

"If there was any justice in this world, I would be adopted." She wanted to splash cold water on her face, but it would smear her black eyeliner. She reached out her hand for the bottle.

"You know that I'm adopted, right? Or did I fail to mention it during the last year?" Carla took a long swig from the bottle.

"Oh, God, Carla, I'm so sorry. I didn't mean anything by that remark." She had really stuck her foot in it this time, but she'd had no idea. "I hope I didn't offend you."

"No offense taken. I probably didn't tell you because I don't think it's that big of a deal. It's the classic story. My parents were getting old, early forties, and couldn't have kids, so they adopted me, the unwanted product of a poor unwed mother."

Annie swallowed hard. Carla was getting that crazy glazed look in her eyes again.

"And of course, the moral of the story is: I was wanted. I was cherished. I was one of the lucky ones, don't you see?" Carla went to the door, looked out, and seeing no one, lit a cigarette.

Annie's unease grew. They could get in a shit load of trouble if anyone walked in on them.

"At least that's the ideal scenario," Carla continued. "I don't think Ron and Marge, the parental unit, had a clue what they were getting into. They would have been better off adopting a dog with a lifespan of twelve years or so. They didn't know it at the time, but that was about the length of their attention span."

The bell rang, and Annie was relieved. "We'll talk more about this later tonight, okay, Carla?"

"No, we're done talking about this—forever."

"Whatever you want." Annie found a couple pieces of gum in the outside pocket of her backpack and gave one to Carla. "We need to get to class." She took Carla's elbow and steered her toward her classroom.

"Because of your dad, I have to go to that fucking physics class. You know he'll check."

"I know."

If they walked unsteadily across the campus, no one said anything, and no one stared, but then again, most of the students ignored them most of the time. She and Carla preferred it that way. The little bit of gin she had drunk made her feel stronger than normal. It was like she and Carla had an invisible force field around them as they threaded their way to class. They passed Walter, the former love of her life, and he actually smiled at her. Normally, she would have been beside herself with happiness (that made smile number two!), but now she smiled back knowingly and walked past with head held high (she hoped!).

It was too bad that Walter was, in all probability, a filthy pig.

Sam had been floating on air for two days now. To say that she was simply happy would have been the understatement of the decade. She knew that she was talking—and thinking—in hyperbole, but she couldn't help herself. Alex had agreed to her plan, and everything was going to be perfect. She knew she was getting on Chris's nerves, but frankly, he was starting to annoy the hell out of her. He was not jumping on the bandwagon of her enthusiasm and had instead chosen to be his usual frustrating, rational self. The voice of reason.

"Alex is going to do it!" Sam had burst into the living room the minute Alex left the other night, unable to contain her joy.

He looked up from reading his book. "Do what?"

"She's going to have our baby, you idiot. What else would I be talking about?" She was out of breath. She had thought he would be jumping up and down with her. What was wrong with him?

"Sam," he said as he put down his book on the coffee table. He patted the couch. "Come here and sit down."

Reluctantly, she did so. She knew she wouldn't like what he had to say, and a sudden fear gripped her. What if he had changed his mind?

"First of all, I am not an idiot."

"I didn't mean that. I'm sorry. It just slipped out of my mouth."

"Sometimes, Sam, 'you need to pause a moment before sharing thoughts.'"

She said the statement in unison with him. It had been the comment on her report card from her second-grade teacher, and she had laughingly told him about it years ago. Unfortunately, it had come back to haunt her. He used it on her when she was being particularly obnoxious, treating her like the child she was probably behaving like. It was maddening. "Alex has agreed to be a surrogate for us," she said calmly, stubbornly. "I thought you would be excited."

"Getting Alex to agree is only the first step."

"I thought you would be excited," she repeated. She took a deep breath. "You haven't changed your mind, have you?"

"No, sweetheart, I haven't." He took off his glasses and rubbed the bridge of his nose. "We need to discuss all the elements involved in this."

"Oh, that," she said, relieved, "we've been through this before."

"Yes, we have, but I think we need to lay all the cards on the table one more time."

"All right," she sighed. She needed to at least hear him out one more time if it would make him happy. Let's face it: She needed his sperm. She walked to the bar and poured them each a snifter of brandy.

"Jack not only needs to agree with this, but he also has to be totally on board. Nick and Annie need to agree. At their age, it could be quite embarrassing to have your middle-aged mother walking around pregnant."

"I resent being called middle-aged."

"Shut up, honey." He took a sip of brandy. "Your parents should be told."

"They should be thrilled to have another grandchild."

"And last, but certainly not least, is the question of money. You know how expensive the procedure is and—"

She couldn't help herself. She interrupted again. "I don't care if it takes every last cent we have, Chris. I'll try to get more writing assignments. We can borrow against the house. We could ask your mother, although we both know what a tightwad she is. Hell, Chris, I'll sell a kidney!" She couldn't sit still. She was off the couch, a bundle of excited energy.

"Look, sweetheart, we need to talk about every single detail. We should probably have a contract drawn up."

"We don't need a contract. Alex promised me, and we never break our promises to each other. We're family. We're sisters. We're twins."

"There's no talking to you tonight, is there?"

"No, let's go to bed to celebrate."

And they had, and she had been floating on air for two days, which is why she had so readily agreed to help Alex with this sweltering, disgusting, endless yard sale. Who in their right mind would come out in this heat to look at another person's junk? She just didn't get it. She also didn't get how Alex could have saved so much useless crap in the years they had been in the house. She would swear that Alex had worn in college a few of the blouses hanging on the makeshift clothesline strung between the front porch columns.

It was ten o'clock in the morning, and they had been at this since seven, when they started dragging out the stuff from the garage where Alex had carefully marked prices on pieces of masking tape. Annie was manning the cash register/cigar box and looked as bored as Sam felt. Jack had left about an hour ago for some meeting at school, and Nick helped people take the bigger items (a scuffed bookcase, a sagging chair, a couple of broken floor lamps) to their cars. Her job was to police the front yard to make sure that no one stole anything, which to Sam, seemed like an utterly pointless endeavor. They should be giving this crap away.

"Do you have microwave?" a tiny Hispanic woman asked Sam in broken English.

This was the eleventh microwave request of the morning. It must be the hot item at yard sales, and she wanted to shout at the top of her lungs: No, we don't have any damn microwaves! We didn't have microwaves to begin with, and we will never, ever have any microwaves to sell! Instead, she said as sweetly as she could muster, "No, ma'am, sorry."

"Hey, Sam, could you help me bring this out? I forgot to put it out earlier," Alex yelled from the garage.

Sam went into the garage, glad for the chance to get out of the scorching sun. "What have you got?"

Alex was trying to pry something out of the back corner. "The kids' old crib. I can't believe I've kept it this long."

Sam felt a moment of panic. Maybe Alex had changed her mind. "Don't you think we'll be needing that soon?"

"This old thing? A couple of slats are broken, and it's so rickety I don't know if it would be safe for another baby. I'll sell it for five bucks."

Sam helped her drag the crib to the yard. Immediately, a very pregnant woman who had been milling around walked over. "How much for the crib?"

"Five dollars, but I have to warn you that I'm concerned about the safety. A couple of slats are broken," Alex said.

"My husband can fix anything," the young woman answered.

Sam had another one of those moments when she didn't *pause a moment before sharing thoughts.* "I'll pay ten."

"Eleven," the young woman said.

"Fifteen," Sam countered. Suddenly, she felt that she had to have that crib.

"Twelve," the young woman said dubiously.

"Twenty," Sam said, her voice rising.

"Sam." Alex's voice was stern. "What are you doing?"

"I need that crib."

"No, you don't." Alex turned to the woman. "You can have the crib for free. Nick, would you help this lady carry it to her car?" She then dragged Sam back to the garage. "What in the hell were you doing out there?"

"I don't know what got into me. I might be going crazy."

"You've always been crazy."

"I'm becoming a nervous wreck. I really want to get this process started, but of course, it's up to you, whenever you're ready."

"Now that I've made up my mind, I really want to get going on this, too. I just can't decide how to tell Jack and the kids. It's all I've been thinking about."

Sam put her arm around Alex's shoulder. "I think Chris and I should be with you when you tell Jack. We can tell the kids after that."

"I could use the moral support."

"I was thinking more along the lines of it being three against one. Why don't you come to dinner on Monday night?"

Alex nodded, and Sam hugged her tightly. Finally, Sam thought, they were on their way.

Nick hated not being able to run. Even though he was no longer on crutches, the so-called experts—i.e., his mom, his dad, and his coach—thought it was in his best interest if he didn't compete. It was making him stir-crazy. Coach Everett thought he was doing Nick a huge favor by letting him be the cross-country team manager, but really, it only made things worse. His big task was to stand at the finish line and record the individual times, times Nick knew he could beat if someone would let him run. Sure, they'd give him a lousy letter at the awards banquet at the end of the season, but it wasn't the same. It was the only sport he was good at, and he was missing his entire senior year.

The one bright spot in the whole wretched scenario was that no one knew what had really happened to his foot. They all just assumed it was a sports injury, and he wasn't about to dispel that notion. If his teammates found out that he'd shot himself in the heel, they'd never let him live it down. He still couldn't believe it either. How stupid could you be to do something like that? Dylan, being the good buddy that he was, hadn't said anything along the lines of: "You're a real asshole," or worse yet, "You'll never be a good soldier." No, not Dylan. Instead, he had quietly put the guns back and suggested that the next time they went target shooting, they might want to consider going to an actual shooting range.

Nick was the only one in the locker room fully clothed and not sweating. The other twelve guys on the team were showering, flicking each other with towels, and just generally horsing around. Nick had turned in the times to Coach Everett in his office and was now picking up towels, another one of his stupid jobs. The other guys didn't exactly exclude him. "Missed looking for your back out there, Carissa," Andy had said, which was nice, considering that Andy usually beat him. "Missed kicking up dust in your face," Corey said, which was an asshole thing to say, considering that he was the worst runner on the team.

Still, Nick felt oddly left out, made worse by the fact that he was now a kind of locker room maid. The guys thought nothing of tossing their towels everywhere: on the floor, on top of lockers, even leaving them wet and soggy under the shower heads. He sighed. He didn't want to be here all night, waiting until everyone was gone before he retrieved those wretched towels. He didn't care if he got wet. He stepped into the shower room.

"You fucking moron! What are you doing?" It was Corey, standing naked under a stream of water.

"I'm getting the stupid towels," Nick said.

"In your shoes?"

Nick looked down. He hadn't thought about taking them off. In fact, he didn't want to take them off, revealing his bandaged heel. These runners would know that it wasn't any type of sprain.

"You're making a giant mud puddle in here. It's fucking unsanitary. Get the hell out!" The others in the shower echoed Corey's sentiment.

"Fine," Nick said. "You can pick up your own stupid towels."

He had had enough. It was rare that he was in such a bad mood, and he knew it was because he couldn't run. He dumped the towels he carried into the dirty laundry hamper, told Coach Everett he had to leave because he had an appointment (not quite a lie—he and Dylan were going to the movies), and went to his locker to get his backpack. He passed jerk Corey's locker on the way to his. Glinting enticingly from its perch on top of Corey's clothing was his class ring. Without really thinking about it, with only a cursory glance over both shoulders to see if anyone was looking, Nick grabbed the ring, jammed it into his pocket, snagged his backpack, and was out the locker room door in a kind of hobbled jog.

His heart pounded as it always did when he had taken something that was not his, that was not supposed to be his, but this time he felt something he hadn't felt before—shame. He had thought he was through taking things, and one night a few weeks back, he had even entertained a half-baked notion to somehow give all the things he had stolen back. There, he had finally admitted it to himself. *Stolen.* He stole things. He was a thief.

Head whirring with all these shameful thoughts, Nick barreled around a corner of the building and ran directly into a small compact body barreling around the corner in the opposite direction. The impact knocked them both flat.

"I'm sorry," Nick said when he could get his breath back.

"Ouch," Jennifer Sang said when she was able to speak.

"Are you hurt?" Nick looked at her tiny frame for evidence of damage. She was barely five feet tall and probably weighed all of ninety pounds. "I don't see any blood."

"I think I have internal damage. I'm pretty sure my kidneys are bruised."

Alarmed, Nick said, "I'll take you to the emergency room. I'll carry you to my car."

Jennifer laughed, a pleasant, soft tinkling. "I'm kidding you, Nick. I just got the wind knocked out of me. I'm fine."

She looked fine, with her waist-length, straight black hair trailing along the ground and a smile that lit up her dark brown eyes. "Let me help you up." Nick extended his hand and brought her to her feet. He had been right. She seemed to weigh almost nothing.

"Thanks. And by the way, I'm sorry, too. I should have been watching where I was going."

"Wow. Apology accepted. When I knock my sister down, she calls me an idiot."

"Is this a habit of yours? Knocking people down?"

"I hear it's as tough to kick as smoking," he said, hoping he didn't sound too lame. But Jennifer laughed again. It made Nick's heart feel light, her laughter. What was not light, however, was her backpack. He discovered this as he bent down to get it for her. "I think your backpack weighs more than you do."

"I know. It's all the Advanced Placement courses I'm taking. I'm studying like crazy and basically bring my entire locker home every night."

"You could develop some serious back problems." He regretted saying that as soon as it was out of his mouth. Was he her chiropractor or something?

Jennifer didn't seem to mind. "You know, I've thought about that, too."

They started to walk toward the parking lot. Nick was scouring his mind for all he knew about Jennifer Sang. He knew she was smart, her dad was some kind of surgeon, and she was on student council, he thought, but maybe she was a class officer. They were starting their fourth year in this small high school, and he barely knew her. Of course, he didn't really know any of the girls in school, and for the first time, he wondered if he had been missing out on something. Jennifer certainly seemed nice enough.

"This is my car." She stopped at a sporty Lexus.

It figured, Nick thought. She was probably one of those stuck up girls who only pretended to be nice.

As if she could read his mind, Jennifer said, "Actually, it's my mom's. Mine's in the shop again. It's an old VW bug, but I think it's so much better than this pretentious thing."

"That's mine over there." Nick pointed toward the Jeep. "Actually, it's my dad's."

"Do you ever go off-roading in it?" she asked as she opened the car door.

"No. Do you go off-roading?" Nick wondered if she would need a booster seat to see over the steering wheel.

"No, I've never been." She blushed. "I was just trying to make conversation. I haven't had much practice. I mean, I haven't had much practice with a boy. With conversation." She blushed an even deeper shade of pink.

"Me neither. With a girl. With conversation." Evidently, the blushing thing was contagious. Nick ducked his head.

"Well, I'm off to study now," Jennifer said reluctantly. She got in, closed the door, and started the ignition.

Nick just stood there, rooted to the spot. She looked so tiny in the car, and it did look like she was sitting on a cushion or something. It felt like something was incomplete in this situation, but he had no idea what was lacking. He raised his hand to wave.

She started to back out, stopped, and rolled down her window halfway. Only the top half of her face was visible. "Would you like to go to a movie sometime?" The words rushed out.

Nick nodded.

"Good." She rolled up the window and sped out of the parking lot.

It was a few minutes before Nick willed himself to walk toward the Jeep. What had just happened here? Would going to a movie with Jennifer be considered a date? Maybe she meant that a whole group of people would go. He should probably ask his mom about all this, but for some reason, he wanted to keep it private until he could sort things out in his head.

He searched in his pants pocket for his keys and felt the lump of Corey's class ring. Shame rushed in to crowd out all the other confusing thoughts. He was never going to do that again. He was never going to steal. He needed to get rid of this ring. A row of bushes lined the parking lot, and he threw the ring into the nearest one, but on the way home, it didn't seem like the best idea. The *best* thing to do to absolve his guilt would be to put the ring back in Corey's locker. He was going to do it. It would be the start of his atonement. He turned the Jeep around.

It took Nick almost an hour to find the ring, but he refused to give up. His jeans were covered in dirt, and his hands were scratched from crawling through the bushes, but he finally found it, the gold glittering and waiting in the beam of the flashlight.

"Yes, Mother," Chris said yet again. He had probably repeated this phrase twenty times during their five-minute conversation. It was the same every phone call, and he hadn't expected it to be any different today. He listened absently to her stream of complaints and grudges, staring out his office window at the students snaking their way through the campus three stories below. He had decided to call from his office because he didn't want to take any chance that Sam might overhear this conversation. He didn't like to keep things from her, but this was too important.

"And when that old goat Mr. Peterson took out his dentures for the third time at lunch, I'd had enough," Louise continued. "I marched over to the lunchtime supervisor—who is totally worthless—and asked her, 'Are you running an insane asylum here?' And do you know what she said?"

"Mother," Chris finally interrupted, "I actually called for a specific reason." He might as well stop her now. She could go on in this vein for hours.

"Christopher, I am not finished yet," Louise said indignantly.

"Fine," Chris sighed. "What did she say?"

"What did who say?"

"The lunchtime supervisor."

"Oh, never mind. I've lost my train of thought."

Chris seized his opportunity. "Mother, I'm calling to ask you for a favor." He might as well be direct. Louise had never been a generous person, not even to her only son, and this wasn't going to be easy.

"What kind of favor?" Her voice was clouded with suspicion.

"I'd like to borrow some money." There, he'd said it. The line was silent as long seconds ticked by. "Mother, are you still there?"

"I'm still here," she snapped. "You make a good living, so what would you *like* to borrow the money for?"

Chris paced his office, clutching his cell phone so hard that his fingers were going numb. "Let me rephrase the request. I *need* to borrow some money."

"Are you going through some kind of mid-life crisis and decided that your life isn't worth living unless you buy an exotic sports car, or even more ludicrous, run away to some tropical island and retire in luxury?"

"Of course not." The humiliation of this conversation was making him feel ill.

"Unless you need the money for bail—say, for example, you got caught smuggling heroin into the country, which I highly doubt—I can't think of one earthly reason why I should lend you money."

It wasn't surprising. At eighty-five, she could still dish out the sarcasm like a pro. "Please give me a chance to explain."

He heard a sharp intake of breath. "Is this a health issue? Are you ill, Christopher?"

So, the old girl did have a tiny glimmer of compassion. Maybe they could get somewhere now. "No, I'm fine. It's Sam—"

"Is she ill?" she interrupted.

Chris considered his approach. It was a fine line. While Sam was not physically ill, it could be argued that this last chance to have a baby was crucial to her mental health. But would his mother, a no-nonsense, frugal woman with unflappable, inherent, Puritanical values, even consider this as a viable option? Plus, he had to add in the fact that Sam and his mother had never been close, and on a few occasions, had been downright antagonistic. He took a deep breath. He really had no choice but to tell her the truth—or at least part of it. "Sam wants to try for a baby again."

"Oh, that," Louise said tiredly. "Why doesn't she just let it go? That woman has been a broken record for years on the baby subject. I told her in no uncertain terms ages ago that I had no interest in being a grandmother, a granny, a nana, or whatever else those women choose to call themselves. Frankly, most children are just a nuisance."

"We wouldn't count on you to babysit and bake cookies," Chris said dryly. It wasn't helping his cause, but he couldn't help himself.

"Wait a minute. If memory serves me—and frankly, it hasn't been all that sharp recently, I'm sure I'm getting Alzheimer's—Sam doesn't have a uterus. So what in the world are you talking about?"

"We want to hire a surrogate."

"That's ridiculous," Louise sputtered. "I'd be rolling on the floor with laughter if the whole idea were not so distasteful, or if my arthritis wasn't acting up so much. Did I already tell you about that?"

Chris had not expected her to be turning cartwheels with delight after hearing about their plan (if her arthritis wasn't acting up so much, that is, he thought snidely), but he was reaching his limit with her. He had always tried to be a dutiful son, but the truth of the matter was that she had been and still was a mean-spirited woman. This conversation needed to end. "Will you loan us the money or not, Mother?" Louise was chuckling and mumbling *surrogate* on the other end of the line. "Yes or no?"

"Well, in all probability, I would have said *no*, but after last week, the reality of the situation is that I now can't."

A red flag went up for Chris. What did she mean that she *now can't*? Chris knew that she had enough in her retirement account to live at the outrageously expensive Golden Manor for another three or four years, but what he thought she could spare was a part of the $250,000 life insurance policy she received after his father died. He paid her monthly bills and received her bank statement in the mail every month. With a sinking feeling, he realized he should have insisted that she open an online account so he could have greater access. She'd said there was no need, and he'd thought she wouldn't do anything foolish.

"What did you do, Mother?" His voice wavered; he feared the worst.

"You remember Dorothy, don't you?"

"Yes." Dorothy had been Louise's faithful housekeeper for years, a tall, thin, black woman with an equally surly personality. Chris thought that's what had kept them together for so many years, their matching disdain.

"She came to visit me a couple of weeks ago, and we were talking about old times and such, and then she just broke down. In the thirty-five years that woman worked for me, I never saw her cry, so I knew it was something serious." Louise paused.

"Can we please get through this story?" Chris spoke to his mother with more impatience than he had ever shown towards her.

"It was her grandson. It seems that he has been accused of shooting a rival gang member on the south side of Chicago, and she needed some money for bail and an attorney. Dorothy said he was innocent, and I believed her. That woman never lied to me, as far as I know, although that particular grandson seemed to be something of a derelict from the time he was a little boy."

Dear God, he thought. "How much did you give her and when?"

"Last week. All of it." Her tone was almost defiant.

"All $250,000?" His throat closed up, and he couldn't speak for a moment. He had never consciously thought of that money as his inheritance, but it must have been in the back of his mind because he now felt shockingly betrayed. "What day? I still might be able to stop payment on the check."

"Oh, I don't think so."

His mother was maddening. "And why would that be?"

"Dorothy drove me to the bank, and I took out the money in the form of a cashier's check, so I'm quite sure the transaction is complete. Then she took me to lunch, her treat."

"Mother," he squeezed out of his clenched throat. "Didn't you think about me at all?"

"Well, Christopher, you have a very good job, and I've always taught you to be self-reliant, haven't I? I wouldn't have been a very good mother if I hadn't taught you to depend upon yourself. That's why I probably would have never lent you money in the first place. You'll thank me for that one of these days."

"Goodbye, Mother." He might never speak to her again.

"It was a delicious lunch. Dorothy took me to IHOP," Louise said as Chris clicked off his phone.

Jack was on his back on the concrete of his driveway under the dilapidated Honda Civic owned by his colleague Bob. The idea had occurred to Jack on the night they went to Hooters for wings and beer. Bob had been complaining about the estimated cost of fixing the suspension on his decade-old car, and Jack had mildly offered that he knew a thing or two about fixing cars because he had interned at a mechanic's shop during one college summer. They had had a few beers by that point, and Jack had gone on to say that he always fixed his own cars. (No mechanic with an inflated price was going to get his hands on an automobile owned by Jack Carissa—no way, man!) Bob had said, then why don't you take a look at mine? He said he'd pay a reasonable rate. And right there and then was the birth of this idea. Jack could pick up some extra cash by working on cars during the evenings and on weekends when he wasn't coaching.

Jack wasn't sure it was such a good idea now. The car was a disaster, and at the repair price that he and Bob had agreed upon, he estimated that the man-hours it would take to get the job done would put his wages in the neighborhood of five bucks an hour. Yet he couldn't go back on his word. Bob was a friend. And he couldn't not finish the job, no matter how long it took. He had his pride, after all. He said he would fix the car, and he would. A drop of oil plopped onto his face from the leaking engine, and Jack wriggled out from under the car, cursing. Among other things, he would need to borrow a dolly from someone.

The front yard was strewn with tools, and as soon as Bob had dropped it off, Jack started to get dirty looks from the passing neighbors. It seemed as if they thought this dilapidated car in his driveway was going to immediately make the value of their homes plummet. He knew this wasn't the type of Scottsdale neighborhood that had car parts sitting in front yards. No, it was the kind of neighborhood that prided itself on well-kept lawns and trimmed hedges, a neighborhood where the pristine outer façade of a house could mask any number of messy dysfunctions going on behind closed doors. Still, it was only a car that would temporarily be in his driveway. The hope of making a business out of this was fading fast. He would need to rent shop space, and he couldn't afford it.

Amanda Williams pulled up in her gleaming white Cadillac Escalade. She rolled down her window. "What are you doing, Jack?"

Here we go, Jack thought. Remain calm. "I'm working on a buddy's car."

"How long do you think that *thing* will be here?"

"I'm not sure." Jack couldn't tell if her lips were pouting or injected with an obscene amount of collagen.

"This is why we need an HOA." Even though it was growing dark, her perfectly streaked blonde hair threw off golden highlights.

"Why don't you work on that, Amanda?"

"You can be sure that I'm going to ask the other neighbors what they think about this."

"Be my guest," Jack said, "but could you do me a favor?"

She looked dubious. "What kind of favor?"

"Just wait to ask the neighbors until after I put my old brown suede sofa on the front porch, okay?"

He didn't think it was possible, but those lips grew even more fish-like as she drove away. Jack had to give Annie a lot of credit for putting up with this prissy woman as an employer all summer long, and he hoped the kids took more after the Williams dad, a guy who spent most of his time on the golf course.

Before Jack could even get back to work, their old van came around the corner. Shit, what time was it? He had planned on cleaning up the yard before Alex and the kids came home from an unusual joint expedition to the mall. Alex needed to get an anniversary present for her parents, Nick needed a new pair of jeans, and Annie wanted to get a second piercing in each ear. This, of course, had prompted a discussion the night before. Alex didn't think it was necessary, and Jack had pointed out that two piercings in each lobe were better than one on the nose or eyelid. However, Jack had "neglected" to tell Alex about his new business venture, harboring the secret hope that she would be happy about it. Now, he was about to find out.

Alex parked in the street because there was no way she could get into the garage. "What are you doing?" she asked as she got out of the van.

"I'm working on Bob's car." How many times was he going to have to state the obvious?

"What a mess," she said as she surveyed the yard. "Couldn't you have done this at his house?"

She had a point there, one he hadn't considered. "I kind of had the idea that I'd start a mechanic business." She looked more than skeptical. "A lot of people work out of garages," he defended himself.

"Cool," said Nick. "Can I help you? I've always wanted to learn more about cars."

"You're not working out of the garage, Dad, you're in the driveway," Annie unhelpfully pointed out.

"I know that, Annie," he said with exaggerated patience. "I'm in the process of getting . . . organized."

"You can't do this here," Alex said. "What will the neighbors think?"

"I already know what the neighbors think," he snapped. "I had a few words with Amanda Williams."

"Oh, great." Alex looked toward the lit windows of the Williams house. "Let's go inside. I don't want them to see us arguing."

"We're not arguing. Yet." All he wanted to do was pick up some extra money for his family, and it was turning into an overblown affair about something that people did all the time: take care of their automobiles.

"I'll pick up the tools, Dad," Nick offered.

"Thanks, son." Jack was truly touched. They hadn't talked much since Nick took the SAT. The scores should be coming any day now, and then it would be time to talk about applying to U of A.

"I have homework to do," Annie said as soon as they were inside. She headed for the stairs, texting as she walked.

Jack and Alex were alone in the kitchen. "What's really going on, Jack?" she asked.

"I just thought I could make a little extra money, that's all."

"What are you not telling me? We're making the same amount of money we always have. I know the recession has hit everyone hard, but we're managing, aren't we?" She looked him directly in the eyes.

"Of course we're managing." Jack had to avert his gaze. He opened the refrigerator door and pulled out sandwich makings: bologna, cheese, mustard. She trusted him, and he couldn't let that trust waver. He had to take care of his family.

"I'll stop going to my hairstylist. Briana has become too expensive. I don't mind going to Great Clips, and I can color my own hair—unless you prefer grey streaks." She laughed.

He tried to laugh with her; the trying hurt. "No, honey, there's no need to do that."

"I've thought of something I might like to do. I'm going to look into selling Avon. Don't try to dissuade me. I do think I need to contribute more to this family financially."

"I'm not going to try to dissuade you." He had made two sandwiches, and there was no way he was going to even take a bite of one. It wouldn't have gotten past the lump in his throat.

"Good, it's settled." She kissed him on the cheek. "I'm going to start researching it right now." She turned at the doorway. "I'm sorry about the mechanic business, but I really don't think it would work out. We don't have the space."

"I know."

What had he been thinking? Something along the lines of, *desperate times call for desperate measures?* He wrapped the uneaten sandwiches in foil and put them in the refrigerator, tomorrow's lunch. He thought he might go into the den and read a bit, transport himself somewhere else for a while. He glanced at the day's mail, which he hadn't gotten to yet. The MasterCard bill was on top. It was the bill he had been dreading the most. He took a deep breath, willing himself to get it over with, then tore it open. He stared at the amount due with numb shock. The cash withdrawals from the casino seemed to go on for a long time, taunting him. He had to stop gambling. He would stop.

But how was he going to make back the money he had already thrown away?

So far, the dinner on her back patio had been pleasant enough, considering how wound up she was. Her hands were shaking so much that Sam was surprised she hadn't knocked over her wineglass by now. Alex wasn't in any better shape, Sam noticed. Her hand had wobbled with each forkful of salmon that went into her mouth. Chris had been reserved and polite, his usual demeanor, during the idle dinner chitchat. Only Jack seemed relaxed and like he was having a good time. She had fixed him four scotch and waters, plying him with drinks, thinking that it would make it easier on him when she dropped the bombshell. Tonight was going to be the night she laid all her cards on the table, and as she saw it, Jack was the only obstacle in her way.

The sun had just gone down, and she nodded at Chris, who got up to turn on the pool light and the Jacuzzi, which bubbled to life. "It's finally a cool enough night to get in the Jacuzzi. Don't you all agree?"

"I certainly do," Chris said in a wooden voice. He would have made a terrible actor.

"Sounds like a good idea to me." Alex, too, could have used some acting lessons.

Jack yawned and looked at his watch. "It's getting late. We should probably be going."

"Late? It's only eight o'clock," Sam said, alarmed. She had this evening perfectly planned, and the plan was to get Jack totally relaxed—drunk, actually.

"It's a Monday night, and I have some conferences scheduled before school tomorrow."

"But we all already have our swimming suits on." Sam shot a pleading look at Alex.

"Come on, honey. You've been tense lately, and a relaxing soak in the hot tub would do you good." Alex massaged his shoulder.

"Well, maybe we could stay for a few minutes."

"Great!" Sam said with too much enthusiasm. "You two get in, and I'll go get a bottle of champagne. Alex, can you help me carry the plates into the kitchen?"

Under the glare of the kitchen light, Alex was pale. "I don't think I can go through with this, Sam. I feel like I'm involved in a plot to ambush my own husband. I think I should tell him alone." She put the dirty plates in the sink.

"You might back down if you told him alone."

"I might," Alex admitted.

"The idea just takes some getting used to."

"He's not going to agree to this."

"We'll see." Sam popped the cork and poured out four glasses of champagne.

They joined the men in the hot tub, sinking down into the warmth of the frothy bubbles. Even Sam felt some tension instantly slip away. She had meant to put on some soothing music but had forgotten. Looking over at Jack, who looked like he was almost asleep, she decided to skip it altogether. She didn't have much time until he was totally catatonic. "Are you awake, Jack?"

"Mm," he mumbled.

"We have something important to discuss with you." Sam had thought about starting the conversation with general talk about IVF, how all the movie stars were doing it, how even gay men were hiring surrogates to have their babies. But that seemed corny and shallow now, sitting in this hot tub, on this night, with her very future at stake. She'd get right to the point. "Jack, are you awake?" He didn't even mumble a reply this time. His chin dipped below the swirling water.

"Wake up, honey." Alex shook Jack's arm.

"Sorry. I must have dozed off. I could get used to this. It's better than a massage." He straightened up. "How much did this thing set you back, Chris?"

"I don't know how much they cost. It was here when we bought the house," Chris said, calmly sipping his champagne.

"I should start using the whirlpool in the boys' locker room after school. I wonder why I never thought about it before."

"You can come over and use this one any time you want," Sam said impatiently.

"That's generous of you, Sam. How much does your pool guy charge to maintain it?" he asked Chris.

"Shit," Sam said.

"I'm going to be a surrogate for Chris and Sam's baby," Alex said. There was only the sound of the swirling water.

"Come again?" Jack sat up.

"I'm going to carry Sam's baby." Alex didn't look at Jack. She stared straight at Sam.

"You can't be serious. You're all playing some kind of practical joke on me, just because I fell asleep, right?"

"I had the same reaction when Sam first came up with this idea," Chris said. "But they're deadly serious."

Now Jack looked directly at Sam. "And when, exactly, did you come up with this idea?"

"A few months ago, but Alex only agreed a week ago, so it's not like she was really keeping anything from you."

"Yes, Sam," he said icily, "that's exactly what it's like." He turned to Alex. "Why didn't you tell me?"

Sam was surprised. It wasn't the reaction she thought would come from Jack. He seemed more hurt than angry. "I told her to wait until we could all tell you together. It was my idea. The whole thing is my idea. You see, Jack, since Alex and I are identical twins, we carry the same DNA. So, if Chris's sperm fertilized Alex's egg, we would end up with the same biological baby as Chris and me."

"Of course the whole thing was your idea. It always is." He stood up. "And in case your scheming little brain is wondering, the answer is *no.*"

"Sit back down, Jack." Alex tugged at his hand.

He stood there uncertainly. The jets went off, and the night went quiet. Chris reached over to press the start button, and the water came writhing back to life. Jack sat back down abruptly. "I don't get it," he said.

Alex moved over and then onto his lap, straddling him, looking as if they were getting ready to make love in the midst of all the turbulence. "This is something I really want to do. I want to do it for Sam and Chris, and I want to do it for myself. For quite a while now, I've felt like something is lacking in my life." Jack started to protest. "Oh, it's definitely not you or the kids. There's something inside of me that needs more. I can't explain it any better than that, but can you try to understand?" She kissed him.

"I can't wrap my mind around this. This is too much." He put his arms around her.

"I know." Alex kissed him again.

Seeing her opportunity, Sam interjected, "This is the greatest gift she could ever give to Chris and me, to all of us. There would be another member of the family to love and be loved by, a new life. A new sacred life on this earth," she finished, her voice inflamed with passion.

"Tone it down, sweetheart," Chris said to her.

"And we'll pay you!" It was Sam's trump card, even though Chris had specifically asked her not to mention money—or any form of payment—tonight.

"Sam," Chris's voice held a warning.

"What?" Alex disengaged herself from Jack but remained close to his side.

"Of course we'd pay you. All surrogates get paid, plus their medical bills."

"Sam," Chris said again.

"You never mentioned money to me before, and frankly, it's insulting. It's like you would be paying me for services rendered. I wouldn't want to take your money." Alex was trying to keep her composure.

"But don't you see, Alex? It's the only thing I can give back to you, and it's such a minuscule thing compared to what you would be doing for me," Sam pled.

"I'd have to think about it," Alex said.

"Please." If she hadn't been in the hot tub, Sam would have fallen to her knees.

"How much are we talking about?" Jack asked

"Jack!" Alex said, appalled.

"I'm the one being bulldozed tonight, so I think I have the right to hear the entire proposition."

"I think everyone here needs to hear the entire proposition." For Chris, it was a forceful tone.

"What are you talking about?" Sam didn't want him to impede the progress that she hoped she had made so far.

"There isn't a lot of money to work with here. I've been trying to tell you this for the last few weeks, Sam, but you refused to listen."

"But—"

"Don't interrupt me again, Sam," he said sharply. "The move was expensive, the cruise was expensive, and the recession has dwindled our 401(k) dramatically. We can't take out a second mortgage because, obviously, we don't have any equity in a house we've lived in for a couple of months." He paused to take a gulp of champagne.

"And you can't take out a personal loan these days," Jack said. Alex looked at him questioningly. "Later," he answered.

"Furthermore, we don't qualify for a loan for the IVF or IUI at Alternate Fertility Care of Arizona—ironically, we make too much money—and the interest rates on their financial payment plan options are exorbitant, increasing the cost of a 3-cycle procedure from around $23,750 to much higher." Chris drained the rest of his champagne. "So you see, if we pay Alex and Jack, which I would absolutely insist on doing, pay the IVF cost and the medical bills . . . Well, there isn't enough money."

Sam was stunned, even though she could recall a number of times when Chris had tried to talk to her about money, and she had refused to listen to him. And now she refused to give up. She would not release this last chance to have a biological baby. She could not go on if this last hope died. "What about your mother? Louise has money. We can ask her."

"I already did," Chris said softly, knowing that everything he had just revealed was breaking her heart once again. "Apparently, she gave away my father's life insurance money to a former housekeeper's murderous grandson."

"Oh, my god!" Sam buried her face in her hands and wept. "It can't be over," she sobbed. "It just can't be!" This could not be happening; there had to be a way. Alex was by her side, rubbing her head, her back. There must be something she hadn't thought about, something that could give her this baby she so desperately wanted. And then it came to her.

"Alex and Chris can sleep together."

After the collective gasp in the Jacuzzi, Jack was the first to find his voice: "Over my dead body."

"We're only talking about the mechanical act of intercourse, not romantic sex or anything like that. It would be an animalistic act."

"I see, Sam," Jack's sarcasm was thick, "it would be more like a 'wham, bam, thank you, ma'am.'"

"In a sense, yes, but the good thing about it would be that there has never been, nor will there ever be, any romantic feelings between Chris and Alex. It would be purely clinical."

"I think this heat and the champagne are going to your head. Let's get out now." Chris tried to pull Sam up by her arm.

She slapped his hand away. "We're not done here yet. Alex, what do you think?"

Alex finally let out her breath. It seemed as if the conversation was floating through the steam around her and not connecting to any reality that she could grasp. Sam, in her desperation/hysteria/possible insanity, had just proposed that Alex sleep with her twin sister's husband. In truth, she hadn't been looking forward to the hormone regimen and the actual IVF procedure, but this was impossible, wasn't it? For some reason, the vision of Chris's skinny legs on the cruise came to mind, and of all the thoughts churning in her mind, the one she blurted out was this: "I'm not physically attracted to Chris."

"Perfect. Well, I guess I might be a little insulted under normal circumstances, but in this instance, it's just *perfect*." Sam's speech was rapid, pleading. "What do you think, Chris, honey?"

"I think you need to take a Valium, or a Prozac, or *something*."

"I think, Sam, that you need to be *committed*." Jack got out of the hot tub.

"Where are you going?" Sam asked.

"I'm going to get the bottle of scotch."

"Good idea. Bring another bottle of champagne, too."

They were silent, watching Jack walk into the house. They didn't speak until he came back carrying the bottles and slipped into the hot tub. He filled Alex's glass and passed the bottle to Sam. He took a gulp from the scotch and passed it to Chris, who also took a long drink.

Finally, Alex turned to Sam. "You surprise me every time. Each time, I think you can't get closer to the edge, and yet you take the final step and fall into the ravine below. What are you thinking?"

"This is my last chance."

"I know that. And I really wanted to be a surrogate for you. I had pledged myself to the idea, and strangely enough, when Chris was talking about the money—or rather, the lack of it—I felt oddly disappointed. I felt that something was being taken away from me, too. I wanted to be pregnant with your baby."

"Really, Alex?"

"Really. From the bottom of my heart."

Sam moved over next to Alex. "I love you so much."

"I love you, too."

"This is all very touching." Jack slurred slightly. "I get the twin shit, the sisterhood, the DNA and biology, but what Sam's proposing is the prostitution of my wife. Chris, I know we don't often see eye to eye on things, but you have to agree with me on this—although I sure as hell didn't hear you say anything about finding my wife unattractive."

Chris needed to choose his words carefully. "I'm as blindsided by this as you are, Jack, and you have every right to be upset."

"Damn right I do."

"I would do anything for Sam, but I know this is asking for a lot."

"The understatement of the year, Dr. Connor."

"If we did do this, we would be paying for the surrogacy services."

"That's my point. Prostitution." Jack took the bottle of scotch back from Chris and downed a quarter of the bottle.

"No, we would be paying for the *surrogacy* services," and delicately, he added, "I know that money is a little tight for you right now."

Jack's mind flashed back to the cruise and the loan. He had forgotten all about paying it back, and Chris hadn't said a word. Not about the repayment, and not about his gambling. "I'm a guidance counselor at a private school. Money's always tight."

Alex's mind was still whirring. They could use the money. They desperately needed a new water heater, and the tires on her car were bald. Still, she would feel bad taking the money. This was something she wanted to share, to give, but she really didn't know if she could sleep with Chris. Maybe he could put on a Jack mask? She almost giggled, and knew she was getting a little loopy from the champagne. "What if it didn't take the first time?"

"Then that would be it."

"Couldn't we make it twice?" Sam bargained.

"No, one try. Then it's over, Sam," Chris said firmly. "We would have tried everything in our power, and then it would be over."

"I still say *no*." Jack got out of the hot tub. "It's time to go home now, Alex. This has been a hell of a night."

"What do you say, Alex?" Sam asked tentatively.

Alex climbed out of the tub. Her body looked like a wrinkled prune, and her insides still churned like the water in the hot tub. "I honestly don't know, Sam. I can't think right now, and I really need to have a long talk with my husband, alone."

Jack took her arm and escorted her across the street and up the stairs to their bedroom, only pausing to say goodnight to their children. They silently stripped off their cover-ups and wet suits and climbed into bed. They lay apart until Jack reached over and put his hand on Alex's hip, a familiar and comforting gesture.

"I can't stand the idea," he said in the darkness.

"For me, it's about not being able to wrap my mind around it, like you said earlier."

"Oh, I can imagine it vividly. That's the problem."

"It wouldn't be like that. It wouldn't be like the way you and I make love."

"Are you saying you're going to do it?"

"I don't know what I'm going to do. But I certainly don't want to do it over your *dead body*." Her very feeble attempt at humor fell flat. "We could use the money."

"Yeah, we could use the money, but the important things in life don't have to be about the damn money."

"No," she agreed in the darkness. "It seems to me that the important things in life should be about love."

"Is something wrong, Mom?" Annie had walked into the living room when she got home from school to find her mother sitting on a chair, the plantation shutters closed and the room darkened, staring vacantly into space. This was highly unusual; her mom was always busy doing something.

Startled out of her reverie, Alex got quickly to her feet. "Oh, no, honey. I'm just tired. I didn't sleep very well last night. How was school?"

"It is what it is." Annie went into the kitchen to get a snack. Her mother followed.

"I feel like we haven't had a good mother/daughter talk in a while. Do you have a few minutes?"

Oh, great, Annie thought. She was having the crappiest year ever, and now Mom wanted to talk. What did she want to know? Was it really worth her while to know that Annie had just flunked a geography test? Or would she like to know that she had been pilfering Valium from Aunt Sam to help her get through the day? Aunt Sam might have caught on. When Annie went over there yesterday, the bottles had been moved, but also, if Aunt Sam knew about it, she hadn't told Mom. And on top of everything else, maybe her mom would like to know that Carla was getting crazier every day?

"I don't really have time right now, Mom." The disappointment in her mom's face made her feel a flash of shame. Annie probably did need to talk to her, but she also knew how shocked and disappointed her mom would be if she knew some of the things Annie had been up to.

"Oh, that's right. The first dance of the school year is tonight. That's always a big event of the fall semester."

"Hm." How could she possibly think that? The gym was decorated with stupid blue and gold crepe paper streamers and balloons. It looked like a second-grader's birthday party. She wouldn't be going at all if her father hadn't volunteered her and Carla to be on the refreshment committee. It was so lame. It was so *humiliating*. They were supposed to make sure the refreshment table didn't run out of cookies and soda and whatever other crap they were going to have. The whole thing made it even more obvious that she and Carla didn't have dates.

"What are you going to wear? That was always one of the high points for me, picking out what I was going to wear before a big dance."

Sometimes she would swear that her mother went to high school in the 1950s instead of the 1980s. "I'm going to borrow something from Carla."

"Oh." Again, the disappointed voice. "Do you need a ride over there?"

"No, Carla's birthday was two days ago. She's got her driver's license now." This, probably more than anything else, had contributed to her wretched day. As ashamed as she was about it, the fact was that she was insanely jealous of her best (really, only) friend. "She should be picking me up any minute."

"Is she a safe driver?"

"She's better than me, but then I suppose everyone is."

Mom ignored the obvious. "I still haven't met her parents yet."

Annie had only met them once in the nine months she had known Carla, but she didn't want her mom to know how little supervision Carla had. "I'm sure the Goldleibs would like to meet you, too." Annie was pretty sure this wasn't even remotely true.

Thankfully, a car honked. "That must be Carla. Gotta go."

She rushed out the front door, then stood stock still on the porch. Carla was seated in a baby blue BMW convertible, a jaunty beret on her head. It just figured that her parents would get her a new car for her sixteenth birthday, but Carla hadn't said a word about it.

"What do you think?" Carla beamed. It was the happiest she had looked since her breakup with Drew.

"Wow." Annie opened the car and got in, inhaling the wonderful new car smell of leather and polish. "Why didn't you tell me you were getting a car?"

"I didn't know. The parental unit is in Bangladesh, I think, and I got the diamond earrings on my birthday, so I thought that was that. Then this was sitting in the driveway when I got home from school. Sometimes they actually surprise me in a good way."

"Wow." It was all Annie could manage. The hideous jealousy was rearing its ugly head.

"Just think of all the freedom we have now. We don't have to rely on stupid Rita or stupid what's his name, my driver."

"Tom," Annie supplied. Really, Carla should know the name of her driver by now. It was a matter of simple courtesy. She looked at the house in time to see her mother backing away from the front window. "I think my mom's watching you. Sorry."

"I see her, but don't worry. I'm pretty good at this." Carla backed cautiously down the driveway.

And surprisingly, Carla was a good driver. She drove within the speed limit and used her blinkers for lane changes. Annie was impressed and told her so. Carla shrugged it off, saying that she had had a lot of practice in St. Marten over the summer. Her good mood was contagious, and Annie started to think about the fact that they really would have a lot of freedom now. It was something about the wind in her hair and the looks they got from other people on the road. Whatever the reason, she suddenly felt more grown up. No matter that it wasn't her car or that she wasn't the driver. She *felt* more adult, if only by association with Carla.

But walking into the gym automatically erased that newfound sense of maturity. They were put immediately to work by a bossy senior named Marianne, who had obviously crowned herself the Queen of Refreshments. After giving them a dubious glance, she sent them over to the cafeteria to haul trays of cookies back to the gym in a kid's wagon.

"This is bullshit." Carla teetered on her high heels and flung the pink boa back over her shoulder. "It's bad enough that we're at the refreshment table, but this means of transport is just adding insult to injury."

Annie also struggled up the hill, the wagon in tow, in her impossibly high black stilettos. At Carla's house, after they shared a joint, it had seemed like a hilarious idea to dress outrageously, in short, tight miniskirts, high heels, and feather boas. Annie's boa was fluorescent green, and now as the dope was wearing off, Annie was sure that it looked like a freakish alien had vomited around her neck. "Let's just make it through this stupid night."

"I think we should spike the Kool-Aid punch."

"I don't want to get into trouble."

"I don't want to get into trouble," Carla mimicked in a high, whiney, childish voice.

"Well, I don't." Annie could feel her neck sweating underneath the boa. She hoped the green dye didn't come off on her skin. "My dad is the—"

"I know, I know. Jesus, Annie, you don't have to remind me of that all the time." She stumbled. "Shit."

"Besides, you drive now, and you don't want to drink and drive."

"We should be poster women for not drinking and driving."

She stopped, and Annie stopped, and they looked at each other, Carla in her red leather mini and Annie in a black one. They started to laugh—it seemed hysterical, for some odd reason—and Annie wondered if the dope hadn't completely worn off.

When Carla could finally catch her breath, she said, "You don't have to worry about me getting into an accident. I will die of *boredom* before this sorry excuse for a dance is over."

Inside the gym, it was crowded and hot. People were gyrating to the D.J.'s selection of music, which certainly leaned more towards the Jonas Brothers than Social Distortion, which was one of Annie's favorite bands. They arranged the food on the table as Marianne instructed them to do, then stood there uncertainly. Annie was sorry to see the task end. This was the part of a dance she hated most, the waiting. You were supposed to look like you didn't have a care in the world, like you didn't care if someone asked you to dance or not, like it didn't matter. But it did matter to Annie, and if Carla would admit it, she cared, too. The apprehension gathered into a tight knot in Annie's stomach.

Preston, the snide asshole who hadn't grown even an inch over the summer, came over to the table. He looked them over as he took a chocolate chip cookie. "This isn't supposed to be a costume party."

"Go away, you little twerp." Carla flung her boa so that it tickled him in the face.

"You look like prostitutes."

"No self-respecting prostitute would let you get your scrawny little dick within ten feet of her—"

"How's it going, girls, Preston?" Dad's timing, once again, was impeccable. Annie had to give him that. She elbowed Carla in case she hadn't seen him yet.

"Hi, Dad." Annie wished he would go away.

"Hi, Mr. Carissa," Carla and Preston said. Preston walked away after he greedily grabbed four more cookies.

"You girls are looking very . . . dramatic tonight. Very nice. Are you having fun yet?"

He looked so earnest, her dad, dressed in a black polo shirt and khaki pants. He didn't look as ancient as other men his age. In fact, in the darkened gym he looked pretty young because she couldn't make out the faint crinkles around his eyes. If she told him the truth, that this dance was just another notch on the totem pole of her *humiliation* at this school, she knew his face would crumple.

"Yes, sir," Carla supplied.

God bless her, Annie thought. Carla could come across in a crunch. She really was a good friend.

"Jack." It was Mr. Raymond, the boys' P.E. teacher. He whispered something into her dad's ear.

"Have a good time, girls. I've got to go. Duty calls." He winked and walked away.

"I wonder what that was all about?" Annie helped herself to a cookie.

"I could make out part of it. It sounded like someone—I couldn't quite catch the name—brought in some alcohol."

"You could make that out?"

"My hearing is very astute, especially when it comes to booze of any kind. We should find out who it is and go have some fun with that guy."

"We're running low on cookies, you two." Marianne stood in front of them, arms crossed.

"Sorry, your majesty, but these two maids are off duty. Come on, Annie, let's dance." Carla dragged her to the dance floor in the center of the gym.

"With each other?" But if Carla heard her, she didn't let on.

They threaded through the crowd to the middle of the gyrating bodies. It was a Flogging Molly song with a good beat, and Carla began to dance with exuberance. Well, Annie was not sure if she would call it dancing. It was more like Carla was *flailing*, arms waving, legs kicking out from her body as far as her tight little skirt would allow. Normally, Annie would be acutely embarrassed, but she now understood Carla's goal for the evening. With the choice of attire and the wild dancing, she was determined to make a spectacle of herself. It didn't really take any thought at all. Annie started imitating her movements with equal exuberance. Carla expected it, and she should. They were a team.

They danced the next four songs, through stares, and possibly, some laughter. (But who could tell for sure? It was quite loud.) As the fifth song, a slow one, came on, Carla linked her arm through Annie's, and they bowed. "The show's over," Carla said. A few couples around them actually applauded.

"That was great!" Annie's face felt flushed, and her heart was still pounding. She had probably, in some people's view, made a fool out of herself, yet she felt oddly liberated. In the scope of things, did it really matter what other people thought of them? She should try not to care so much, but it was hard for her.

"On that note, I think we should go." Carla mopped her forehead with the pink boa.

"I think that we should dance some more. That was super fun."

"No, it's time to go," Carla said with finality. As was happening so often lately, Carla's mood had changed abruptly.

Annie knew it was useless to try to argue with her, not that she ever did. "Okay, okay, I just need to grab a book out of my locker. I'll meet you at the car."

The lockers at SCDS were outside, and Annie's was across the courtyard from the gym. There wasn't as much lighting as she would have liked, and she tried to talk herself out of any anxiety by reminding herself that the school had a security guard. Still, she jumped when she felt the tap on her shoulder. The heavy science book was in her hands, and as she spun around, she had the fleeting thought that she could use it as a weapon.

"Sorry, I didn't mean to scare you."

It was Walter, her Walter. She had noticed him at the dance, of course. She always noticed him. Her mouth went dry. He was standing about a foot away from her, and even though it was pretty dark, she knew exactly what the honey blonde hair and blue eyes looked like. "Oh, yeah," she croaked brilliantly.

"I didn't mean to scare you. I was just grabbing something out of my locker, too—it's over there—and I saw you standing here."

She didn't have to follow his pointing hand with her eyes. She knew where his locker was. Of course she knew where it was. "Oh, yeah." Her lack of conversational sparkle or wit was *humiliating*.

"I just wanted to tell you that I liked your outfit."

Which reminded her of the stilettos. She wobbled a little. "Thanks." Maybe this was some kind of a joke? Maybe his friends were hiding in the bushes and would suddenly jump out and say, "We dared him to talk to loser Annie Carissa! Here's your five bucks, man!"

"I was thinking you should have worn the pink feather thing. It would have matched your hair." He pointed at a pink-tinged spike of her short hair.

"I never thought of that. I keep forgetting about my hair, and then I'll look in a mirror, and I'm, like, whoa, I have pink hair." It still astounded her. She tried to wear it brazenly, confidently, but the truth was that it still shocked her when she least expected it.

"It's nice." He smiled.

It was her third smile from Walter, and this time, she smiled back. "Thanks."

"I'll see you around."

"Sure." She watched him walk off, still not completely believing that this exchange had occurred. Could it be that he was a nice guy and not a filthy pig? Would he ever talk to her again? As she walked slowly toward the car, the only thing that she was totally sure of was that this brief, baby conversation with that boy had only whetted her appetite. She wanted more.

She couldn't wait to tell Carla, but when she got in the convertible, she changed her mind. Carla had been crying, and now she was trying to smoke her skinny Capri menthol cigarette. She hiccupped smoke.

"Let's get to your house," Annie said.

Carla only nodded, and they drove home in silence. Annie felt like she was bursting with something close to happiness, but she also felt guilty that Carla was so low. She certainly didn't mention that the wind in her hair (that Walter liked!) felt especially good in the hot, dry night.

Alex couldn't make herself go into the low ranch-style building. She had driven by it many times when she took the back way to Costco. It was located on a tiny side street and looked identical to its neighbors in its dilapidated, nondescript condition, except for the neon sign in the front window, which read: PALM READER. She had always thought it was rather amusing and wondered what kind of people went to a palm reader. In her imagination, she saw an older, heavyset, turbaned woman—Madame Florencia, perhaps—sitting at a round table, a crystal ball nearby. Madame Florencia was probably a school cafeteria worker or a greeter at Walmart who dabbled in psychic melodrama on the side. It had always made Alex smile.

Until today. She didn't think it was funny today. The green neon light was on, and Madame Florencia must be inside, waiting to read the palm of someone like Alex, who was so confused that she didn't know which way to turn. Would Madame Florencia truly be sympathetic to Alex's insomniac, heart-wrenching indecision, or would she say something conciliatory and pat, just biding time until she held out her liver-spotted hand for the crumpled twenty-dollar bill that Alex would thrust upon her? Or worse yet, would she say something horrible was going to happen to Nick, or Annie, or Jack, or Sam that would drop the bottom out of Alex's world, leaving her in a dreadful state of anxiety for the rest of her life, just waiting for the inevitable shoe to drop? Alex backed out of the narrow driveway and went on to Costco.

Alex wished she had better dreams. Unlike Jack, who dreamed in vivid colors, she had fragmented, black and white dreams that never seemed to relate to anything in her life, at least not that she could determine. Perhaps a dream analyst could make some sense out of the jigsaw pieces that floated around in her subconscious, but she certainly wasn't going to go looking for one. She checked her horoscope in the newspaper each morning, but it was always so vague that she promptly forgot if she was supposed to have a two-star or four-star day. She had once, long ago, been at a party that had a Tarot Card reader (an ordinary woman without a turban), and because everyone else was doing it, she had sat down at the table, a cocktail in hand, and watched the woman lay out the cards. When she saw the card that looked like a skeleton, she had gotten up, saying, as if it were a joke, "I don't want to know how my life will turn out. I'll let God surprise me."

She shouldn't have stopped going to church. Maybe it all boiled down to that. Jack had not been brought up in any particular religion, and she was raised as a Methodist. Yet once the children were born, she insisted that they go to church every Sunday. She had Nick and Annie baptized in the Methodist church. She had faithfully driven them to their religious classes when they were young, and both were confirmed in the church. When the kids reached middle school, she had told Jack that the ball was in his court, that it was time for him to take some responsibility for their children's religious upbringing. Jack, who had stopped going to church ages ago, naturally did nothing. Now, since they were nothing more than Easter and Christmas congregants, she would feel ashamed to ask a pastor, a reverend, or even a priest for any kind of spiritual guidance.

When she got home, she put away the Costco groceries, the case of diet Coke, family pack of pork loin chops, bulk toilet paper and paper towels, three-pack of Ragu pasta sauce, and other mega food portions. She had to quit going to that store; she couldn't get out of there without spending at least a hundred dollars. Jack had tried many times to convince her that she didn't save money buying in bulk. Instead, they just used things faster, or ended up with a gallon jar of olives or salad oil slowly rotting on their shelves. But she loved going to the warehouse-style store, and it usually made her feel better. But not today.

Today, she was looking for an answer. Time was running out. She would be ovulating in another week, and this would be it for her. She might get up her nerve to sleep with Chris once, but that was it. *Might* was the operative word. Right now, she couldn't even fathom it. She tried to focus on the possible end results, the baby, Sam's happiness, the fact that she had done something noble, good, and kind. Then the image of Chris's skinny white legs would pop into her mind, emblematic of the fact that she would, in fact, be committing adultery. Not prostitution. *Adultery.*

She had stopped at Starbucks on her way home from Costco and ordered a venti Kenyon coffee and gulped it down. It wasn't a good idea. She had caffeine jitters on top of her anxious agitation. Her hands were trembling, and her heart pumped furiously as she paced through her house. She needed to sit down and try to relax. She sat in front of her computer, and it seemed as if she had no control over her shaking hands. On their own accord, they did a Google search on "palm reader" and ended up at a web page for Read My Palm Online. At this point, Alex thought, why not?

The site had an animated woman whose cleavage was trying to burst out of a long red dress. Alex had no idea what that had to do with palm reading, but she clicked on the continue button. She held up her left hand—it was difficult to keep it still—and tried to click on the correct responses to the shape of her heart line, her life line, and her head line. The lines on her palm were so faint that she had no idea if she was describing them accurately. When she got to the next section, the destiny line, she was alarmed by the asterisked notation that said not everyone had a destiny line. Shouldn't everyone have a destiny line? It was alarming to think that someone wouldn't, but when she looked at her hand, she couldn't really see one. Panicked, she pulled out a magnifying glass from her desk drawer. Yes, there it was! She had a faint line leading straight up her palm to her middle finger. She continued to the end of the program, and of course, the website wanted her credit card number so it could email her the results of her success age, the evaluation of her future, her financial turnaround dates, her love life turnaround dates, the most important ages of her life, and her lucky numbers.

Jack found her face-down on the computer, sobbing. "What's wrong, honey?" He pulled up a chair next to her. "Besides the obvious," he added. He gently lifted her head and put it on his shoulder.

She held out her hand. "Look at my hand, Jack. There's something wrong with it."

He looked closely. "Did you hurt yourself? I don't see anything. Maybe it's a paper cut? Those can hurt like hell."

"No, Jack! I don't think I have a *destiny line*. I tried to find one with a magnifying glass, but I think I just made it up. It would be terrible not to have a destiny line." She wiped her eyes with the back of her other hand, which didn't seem to have a destiny line either. They were both traitors.

Instead of asking what the hell she was talking about, Jack looked at the computer screen and saw the site. "What does it mean if you don't have a destiny line?" he asked calmly.

"It sounds like you're just this doormat of a person, a person doomed to a life so ordinary that you don't even rank a lousy *destiny line* on the palm of your hand." His presence was starting to calm her.

He saw that she hadn't filled in her credit card information. "But you don't know for sure, do you?"

"No," she admitted.

"Look, honey, some people might believe in this type of spiritual stuff, but frankly, I think it's a bunch of bologna. And I can tell you from first-hand experience that you are light years away from being ordinary."

"Really?" It was amazing that he could love her with snot running from her nose and her crazy rant about the mythical destiny line. She was already acting like a pregnant woman whose hormones were out of whack.

"Absolutely." He kissed her temple.

"I've been trying to find the answer."

"Me, too," he said simply.

"What are we going to do?"

"I think we should talk to the kids, see what they think about the whole idea. Well, not the whole idea. I think we should omit the part that Uncle Chris himself might be the means of *in vitro*." He shuddered involuntarily.

Of course. They should talk to Nick and Annie. They were the source. They could help find the answer.

"Dinner," Jack called up the stairs.

Alex had ordered pepperoni pizza from Domino's. She opened the two boxes and placed it in the middle of the kitchen table and got out paper plates and napkins from the pantry. That was going to be the extent of her dinner preparations for the evening. Exhausted, she slumped into a chair.

Nick and Annie trooped down the stairs, bickering as usual.

"Quiet down," Jack said.

"He started it," Annie said.

"Why don't you grow up?" Nick said.

"Can I take the pizza up to my room? I have homework to finish." Annie plopped a slice on the thin paper plate.

"Yeah, right. She's probably on Facebook." Nick helped himself to four pieces.

"No," Jack said. "We're having a family meeting."

Both kids startled, the pizza suspended halfway to their mouths. They glanced warily at each other, then at their parents. Annie spoke first. "Who's in trouble?"

"No one's in trouble," Alex said. She gratefully took the glass of wine that Jack handed to her. "We have something very important to discuss with you."

"This sounds ominous." Nick resumed eating.

"Not at all." Alex handed a napkin to Nick. "It's actually very . . . exciting."

"We're getting a new car," Annie guessed.

"Probably not," Nick ventured. "We're probably supposed to be overjoyed about a new water heater. Am I right?"

"You're not only not in the game, Nick. You're not even in the right ballpark." Jack sipped at his scotch and looked at Alex. He nodded.

She took a deep breath. "I'm thinking of being a surrogate mother for Uncle Chris and Aunt Sam's baby." There, the words were out, and Alex could feel the weight of them as if they were encapsulated in a cartoon bubble over her head. The kids stared at her. She could see Nick's half-chewed pizza in his open mouth.

"You're talking about in vitro fertilization? Why?" he finally said.

"This is the last chance Aunt Sam has for a biological baby of her own. You know how sad she's been since she lost Grace, and since we're identical twins, we have the same DNA. So, in a sense, my eggs and Uncle Chris's sperm will create the same baby she could have had herself. Biologically speaking."

Silence. Then Annie said, "Aren't you too old to have a baby?"

"I'm not ancient," Alex said, although she wasn't really offended. It was, after all, a valid question.

"You're not ancient, Mom, but you are *forty*."

"Your mother is aware of how old she is, Annie." Jack sat with his arms folded across his chest.

Alex wished that he would help her out here, but she also knew that this was her gig, her responsibility, her decision. "Like I said before, this is Aunt Sam's last chance to have a baby."

"Why doesn't she just adopt one?" Annie asked. "There are all those extra babies in places like China and Russia."

"*Extra* babies?" Nick's voice was heavy with sarcasm.

"You know what I mean," Annie snapped. "Unwanted babies. Babies who need a good home."

"That's the first thing I suggested to Aunt Sam, too, but she has her heart set on a biological baby, and that points to me." Alex glanced at Jack. Neither his position nor his expression had changed.

"But you'll be walking around *pregnant*." Annie shuddered.

"That's the idea." Alex got up to pour another glass of wine. She knew what direction Annie's train of thought was taking her. If her mother was pregnant, it would seem to be obvious to everyone that her mother—God forbid!—had had sex. To a young teenager, that was mortifying.

Annie's next question was predictable. "What would I tell everyone?"

"The truth. Surrogacy is not that uncommon these days." Alex sat back down at the kitchen table. "You know how devastated Aunt Sam was when she lost Grace. No mother should have to go through something like that. I would like to try and make her happy again, but there's no guarantee that this will work. The IVF procedures don't always work, and we're only going to try it one time." When she again glanced at Jack, his expression had finally changed. He looked as if he might explode, yet he kept his mouth clamped tightly shut.

"I love Aunt Sam a lot, but I still think the whole thing is kind of gross. You have this baby—and from everything I've seen on TV and the movies, it is not a fun experience—and then you hand it to her and say, 'here's your present.' So basically, you do all the work, and Aunt Sam gets the easy part."

Alex couldn't help it. She laughed. "Trust me, Annie, pregnancy and birth are the easiest parts of motherhood."

Nick finished his fourth piece of pizza. "I think it's cool, Mom, that you would want to do that for Aunt Sam and Uncle Chris."

Alex smiled at him gratefully. "Do you really?"

"Yeah, it might be fun to have a little kid around. You know, they get so excited about Santa Claus and the Easter bunny and stuff like that."

The holidays when Nick and Annie were children were some of Alex's fondest memories. "Little kids get excited about almost everything."

Annie elbowed Nick. "Spoken like someone who's never babysat. Try it, and then tell me how much you like little kids."

"You have no maternal instincts." Nick elbowed her back.

"I'm fifteen. I think Mom and Dad would be a little concerned if I had maternal instincts right now."

Jack finally opened his mouth. "Damn right we would."

Alex felt the beginning nudges of a headache. "Can we get back on track? This is a serious subject, and I need to know what everyone thinks."

"I have one more question," Annie said, "and it's probably going to sound dumb, but—"

"I'll bet a hundred dollars it's going to sound dumb," Nick interrupted.

Annie, for once, ignored him. "Will it be like you and Aunt Sam share the baby? I mean, will you have the baby for a week, and then Aunt Sam has it for a week?"

"I win," Nick said. "That is definitely a dumb question."

"She can ask all the questions she wants," Alex said to him. Then, to Annie, "No, honey, the baby would be Aunt Sam's and Uncle Chris's. I'll be the aunt, Dad will be the uncle, and you and Nick will be the cousins. Any more questions?"

"Just one. What do you think, Dad?"

They all turned to stare at Jack. He remained silent for a long minute. Then, looking directly at Alex, he said, "I'm leaving this decision up to your mother."

Now the three of them stared at her. Alex swallowed hard. Of course there couldn't be guarantees on something of this magnitude; it couldn't be black or white, yet she wanted some answer that felt solidly right. She didn't want to sleep with Chris—the thought made her feel nauseated, in fact—but she was afraid that Sam would lose it if she backed out now. She didn't want to hurt Jack or damage their marriage in the process either, and she wanted her children to be happy about and comfortable with her decision. What she wanted, and probably wouldn't get, was everyone's total approval and support.

"Well?" Jack prompted.

"Maybe we could take a vote," she said weakly.

"Maybe we should flip a coin?" Jack sounded facetious, but Alex knew there was an underlying fury.

"I'm okay with it," Nick said.

"I'm sure I'll get used to the idea," Annie said.

Alex rubbed her forehead. The headache was full-blown now. The kids' lukewarm response was disappointing but not surprising. She needed to face this fact: It was her body, and ultimately, her decision. "I'm going to think about it some more. I'll let everyone know tomorrow." She would be ovulating in five days. Time was running out.

Everyone left the table, and Alex cleared the paper plates and pizza carton. When she was sure they were all at their various evening tasks, she sheepishly rummaged in her oversized Target hobo purse for a quarter. She found a sticky, lint-coated one at the bottom. Silently, she called "heads." And flipped the coin.

"You've barely spoken to me in the past twenty-four hours." Sam sat across from Chris in a back booth at Cochran's, their neighborhood bar and grill. She had suggested that they go out for dinner, and when he seemed reluctant, she had insisted. She couldn't stand to be in that house for a long evening of tension-filled silence.

"What do you want me to say?" Chris studied the menu.

"Anything. Something."

"I think I'll order the black and bleu burger." He closed the menu.

"Are you making a joke?" Chris's sense of humor, which rarely surfaced, tended to be of the subtle, sarcastic variety. Was he suggesting that her idea of him sleeping with Alex was making him "black and blue"—i.e., somehow emotionally bruising him? She didn't blame him if that was the case. She had really asked him to go out on a limb this time.

"No." He just calmly sat there, hands folded on the menu.

It was maddening. "I wish you would yell at me or something. Go ahead. I can take it."

"I am not going to yell at you."

"Why in the hell not? I deserve it. I am an atrocious wife, an awful sister. I want my husband to impregnate my twin sister so that I can have a baby. Maybe Jack is right. Maybe I should be committed."

Sam was interrupted by the waitress bringing their beers and taking their orders. The bar was noisy and hot. Sam felt perspiration dripping down her sides, probably staining the black t-shirt she was wearing. This place was very hot. The whole damn state of Arizona was disgustingly hot. It was the beginning of September, but there was no sign of any relief from the relentless heat.

She flagged down their waitress. "Is the air conditioning in here broken?"

"No, ma'am."

"Do you think you could turn it up?"

"I'll ask the manager," the waitress said.

"She'll ask the manager," she repeated to Chris, as if he hadn't heard, as if he wasn't sitting right there, across from her, drumming his fingers on the plastic tabletop. "Why won't you talk to me?"

"What do you want me to say?" Chris said again.

She wanted to reach across the table and shake him, shake words out of his mouth that would let her know what he was thinking, what he was feeling. "Let's not go through that verbal banter again, okay? I want to know how angry you are at me."

"On a scale of one to ten, I'd rate it a five."

A five. She could work with that. He wasn't level ten furious, although a five rating was high for her mild-mannered husband. "Good."

Again, the waitress. Her sense of timing was atrocious. She sat Sam's taco salad in front of her and asked if she could bring them anything else.

Sam stared at the big glob of sour cream adorning the top of her salad like a fattening beret. She was not going to be able to eat it. She told the waitress no, she couldn't bring them anything else at the moment.

Chris seemed to have no problem eating. He doused his fries with ketchup, carefully piled the garnish on top of the burger, then neatly cut it in half. He was a neat and precise diner, her husband. Actually, he was neat and precise about everything he did, even making love. Her heart quickened. That was it. He had to have been insulted that she could so blithely offer his sexual services without showing any trace of possessiveness or jealousy. In the hot tub, without any forethought, she had basically said to everyone present, "Here's my husband's penis, Alex, please use it wisely."

"You're not eating," Chris observed.

"I will be jealous," she said.

"What?" Chris pointed to his black and bleu burger. "If you're jealous of this sandwich, you can have the other half."

"No, I mean I will be jealous when—if—you sleep with Alex to create our baby."

"I knew what you meant, Sam, and the fact is that you will not be jealous in the least. You want a baby so badly that you will not let anything, and I do mean *anything*, stand in the way."

Chris delivered the remark matter-of-factly, mildly, but it was meant to sting. It didn't. Because it was true. "I wish I wasn't like this."

"It's too late for that now. Since we lost Grace—"

"Please don't talk about her." Sam felt that all too familiar wave of sorrow wash over her. Would it never cease?

"Since we lost Grace," Chris persisted, "you have grown more and more determined to replace her."

"I'm not trying to replace her!" She wasn't. She could never replace that precious little girl. How could he think that?

"And now you have the ball rolling, and it's too late to go back now. Too many people are involved, and the stakes are too high."

The guilt should have punched her squarely in the stomach, but it didn't. She was too far gone, and she knew it. She could not let go of this obsession; she just couldn't. It was deeply ingrained in her psyche, it was a train out of control, and it had become her life's goal. "What do you want me to do?"

"Nothing. I know you can't do anything about it now."

She had wanted him to talk to her, begged him to tell her how he felt, but of course, she had secretly harbored the hope that he was totally supportive of the idea and fully on her side. Obviously, that wasn't the case, but as he said, it was too late to go back now.

Chris's eyes softened. "Did I hurt your feelings, honey?"

He was still her mild-mannered husband. "No." She had to just come out with it. "Are you going to have sex with Alex or not?"

"You only have one script in your head." He handed a credit card to the waitress before she set down the bill, not giving her time to speak.

"Yes or no?"

"It's a catch 22, isn't it? Damned if I do and damned if I don't."

"No, it's not like that. Please don't put it like that." She was not a particularly religious person, but his interpretation had an ominous note of judgment that she didn't want to acknowledge.

"Sam, be realistic for once. The odds of Alex getting pregnant are not great. She's forty, and I'm fifty-two, but to force you to let go of this unhealthy, all-consuming obsession, I will have sex with Alex. I will have cold, mechanical procreation as you prescribe. But only once. And then it will be over. We will never try for another child. The process will be complete, and we will never, ever talk about it again. Do you understand?

"Yes," Sam said, "I understand."

Chris was going to do it.

It was a coincidence, or a sign, or just plain bad luck. Unable to sleep, worried that his tossing and turning would awaken Alex, who had finally fallen into a fitful rest, Jack had wandered down into the den and armed himself with the TV remote and a tumbler of cheap scotch in the recliner. Flipping through the channels, he landed on *The Big Chill*. He should have changed it right then to one of the numerous episodes of *Law and Order* that seemed to be on every other channel. But he didn't. He was drawn unwillingly into the story of the college roommates who reunite for a classmate's funeral, who end up having a good time despite the sordid circumstances, and then inevitably, the end when Glenn Close's character asks her husband to sleep with her best friend. The best friend desperately wants a baby, and Glenn Close is atoning for her affair with the guy who committed suicide.

Atonement. While her husband is upstairs having sex with the Mary Kay Place character, Glenn Close is wrapped in a blanket on a chair on the porch, a sly half-smile playing around the corners of her lips. What was she thinking? That everything was even-Steven now, that her past mistake was now erased from the slate because she allowed her husband to sleep with someone else? What would she say to her husband the next evening in the intimate privacy of their bedroom, something along the lines of, "Whew, I'm glad that's over with—now we can get on with the rest of our lives?" Could it be that simple?

Of course not. It was a movie, not real life. Jack got up to pour himself some more scotch, knowing that he shouldn't. He was drinking too much these days. It was the pressure. The pressure was really getting to him. At work, he was meeting with all the seniors, helping them make lists, narrowing down the colleges and universities they would soon apply to. Each student would come into his office clutching a list of possible schools, and after he reviewed their SAT scores and GPAs and extracurricular activities, he would evaluate which schools were a "stretch," "realistic," or "stretch/ realistic," and offer his own recommendations. Every senior had signed up for an appointment, eager for his help. Except his own son.

Nick's SAT scores had come in the mail today. Not wanting to interfere with Nick's privacy, Jack had placed the envelope on Nick's desk upstairs. Nick hadn't said a word about it, but Jack supposed that their dinner conversation had something to do with that. He would give him until tomorrow evening to say something before he took matters into his own hands and demanded to know how Nick had scored. Nick's future was at stake here, and damn it, he was going to make sure that Nick made the right decision. He was not going to join the Marines. He was going to college. Period.

And then there was Annie. Both her geometry and science teachers had dropped by his office to casually mention—as a professional courtesy, really, since it was early in the semester—that Annie was not doing well in their courses, that she seemed preoccupied and unfocused. When he had her alone in the car coming home from school yesterday, he had broached the subject, asked her if there was anything she needed to talk about or if anything was wrong. She stared straight ahead, pink-tinged hair standing up in spikes, saying "No, Daddy, I'm just off to a rocky start." Then, when he casually mentioned, almost as an afterthought, that perhaps she should broaden her circle of friends and not hang out exclusively with Carla, she tuned out and shut down. She didn't say another word and turned up the radio.

He knew the teenaged years were difficult, a roller coaster ride of hormones, self-esteem issues, and social maneuverings. He had seen it all before, and he wasn't overly concerned about his children right now, but he knew one thing for certain. He was going to keep his eyes wide open. He hadn't mentioned any of this to Alex yet. She didn't have as much experience around teenagers as he did, and it would only cause her more distress.

As would their financial situation. Coming to this point in his thought process, Jack's stomach began to churn violently, and he choked on a slug of scotch. They were mired in debt, and it was all his fault. *His fault.* If he hadn't started to gamble, they could have financially hung on with their fingernails. But a quick stop at the Talking Stick Indian Casino after a board meeting, or a golf game, or a soccer match, or a trip to Home Depot—the list went on and on—had racked up the credit card debt. He couldn't believe how much money he had lost since June, and still he couldn't shake off that terrible need to play one more hand of blackjack or put another twenty in a slot machine, always hoping against hope that he would win, he would make the money back, and it would all be over. It never was. He was locked in a vicious cycle.

Jack dropped his head into his hands, glad he was alone so that no one could witness this, his despair, the culmination being that his wife was probably going to sleep with another man in a feeble attempt to have a baby for her twin sister. And he was going to let her do it.

He was going to let her do it. He could not think of another way out of this terrible situation that he had gotten his family into. Oh, he had tried. He had lain awake night after night, trying to come up with some solution, some plan to come up with more money, but he had come up empty-handed. He was on the verge of failing them all. He was a terrible husband, terrible father, terrible man.

He was crying now, not a masculine, controlled seepage of tears, but a full-blown, narcotized spillage. Maybe everything would have been all right if Sam hadn't moved across the street. He would have liked to place the blame squarely on her shoulders, but it wasn't fair, and it wasn't right. He and she had always had a prickly relationship, starting at the beginning

when he first began dating Alex. There was a mutual attraction that neither wanted to acknowledge. It was perfectly normal, right? That whole
guy with twins fantasy. He'd heard plenty of guy/twin/sex jokes from his
Alpha Chi Rho fraternity brothers, way too many jokes. He tried to laugh
them off, but secretly, he was pleased. Dating a twin seemed to give him
an elevated status among his brothers, and he liked it.

Of course nothing happened. Not then. God help him. The alcohol was rushing through his brain, unearthing something that he had
refused to acknowledge for years, something that should not have happened, something that he had talked out of memory. Another drunken
night. A mistake.

God help him. *Atonement.*

5

CHAPTER FIVE

They arrived in separate cars, Alex and Jack in the Jeep and Sam and Chris in their Saab. That way, the couples wouldn't have to talk to each other on the way up through those stark towns that dotted the desert with names like Nothing, Arizona, through Wickenburg, Kingman, and Laughlin, through desert and mountains, across the Colorado River, and then another sixty miles before reaching their destination. The couples had barely spoken to each other during the last twenty-four hours when decisions had been made and preparations completed. Tensions ran high, but it was an easy agreement to drive separately and plan on arriving at around 7:00 p.m. And so they had. Alex and Jack pulled up in front of the Bellagio within ten minutes of Chris and Sam.

Las Vegas. It had been her idea, of course, but her inane joke about "what happens in Vegas stays in Vegas" fell on deaf ears. Even though this whole thing about to transpire had been her grand plan, her need, Sam was as nervous as everyone else. It was better to be on neutral ground, a Switzerland of emotion, she thought. Vegas, with its neon and largesse, was more surreal than neutral, but it would have to do. Ironically, Louise—the stingy bitch—loved to gamble and flew to Vegas once a month or so. Sam had badgered Chris to call Louise (very much against his will) to ask if they could use points on her Player's Reward Card to get their rooms comped for a "mini-vacation." Surprisingly—maybe because she had given away her son's inheritance?—she agreed.

They checked in, and because each had only brought a small bag for their short, two-night stay, there was no need for a bell cap. They walked in silence through the massive lobby and clanging casino to the elevator. It was a stroke of luck that they were on separate floors. Being on the same floor would have been too close, too conspicuous, too uncomfortable.

As the elevator doors opened to let out Alex and Jack on the twentieth floor, Sam tapped Alex's arm. "Meet me in the Fontana Bar?" she asked, timid.

Alex stared straight ahead. "I might as well," she said. "I plan on getting very, very drunk tonight."

"Aren't we all?" Jack took Alex's hand possessively as he led her out the elevator's open doors.

Sam was in her room for less than five minutes, five long minutes, as she watched her husband meticulously unpack his toiletries, hang up two shirts and a pair of jeans, place his underwear and socks in a drawer, and discreetly put the copies of *Playboy, Penthouse,* and *Hustler* in the bathroom. The magazines had been her suggestion. She wanted her husband to have sex with Alex—she fervently did—but she also hoped that he would need some extra enticement, that his reluctance would need additional stroking, so to speak. His job was simply one of procreation, a continuation of the species, her species. She kissed him quickly on the cheek and left him without saying anything. What more was there to say at this point—don't think about what you're doing, get it over with quickly, good luck? She, too, desperately needed a drink.

The Fontana Bar overlooked the hotel's dancing waters on its eight-acre man-made lake. Every so often, large fountains would spurt upwards, reminding Sam, at this point in time, of giant semen ejaculations. She needed to get her mind off the upcoming event. It was going to be impossible, but she would try. She fished her vial of Valium out of her purse, shook out two tablets, and washed them down with the pink Cosmopolitan that the excruciatingly handsome waiter placed in front of her. (He looked like a younger version of Brad Pitt with George Clooney's coloring. Could there be a better combination for the male species?) She spotted an ashtray and remembered gratefully that she could smoke in this bar. In Vegas, you could smoke practically everywhere. It was a comforting thought. She lit a Virginia Slim Superslim Menthol and greedily inhaled the slender feminine-looking cigarette.

A burst of high-pitched female laughter came from the corner. It was unmistakably a bachelorette party. The bride-to-be wore a short white veil and held up a red, filmy, transparent Frederic of Hollywood negligee, the source of the laughter. She was young, probably early twenties, flushed with excitement and alcohol. "I could never wear something like this!" she said.

"Sure you could, Angel," one of her friends said. "You have the body for it!"

No, she didn't, Sam thought. She looked to be thirty pounds over-weight, and Sam couldn't imagine how she could squeeze her thigh into the fragile little garment. But that didn't matter. They were all so young. Their illusions had not yet begun to erode.

"No, I mean, Billy won't let me wear it. He says he wants me to be totally naked all the time. He wants me to clean the house in the nude!"

This brought more peals of laughter and another disturbing image to Sam's mind. She truly hoped that the girl would be happy with Billy, but really, they only had a fifty-fifty chance like everyone else, didn't they? And if she walked around naked all the time, wouldn't that take away any last vestige of mystery or romance in Billy's eyes? The thought of chubby Angel on all fours, scrubbing the kitchen floor, her pendulous breasts almost touching the floor . . .

"I hope they comp the minibar." Alex plopped on the high bar seat next to Sam and swiveled it towards her. Her eyes were bright. She reached for one of Sam's cigarettes.

"I don't know if the hotel takes care of that or not. The items are outrageously expensive. How much did you drink?" It was ridiculous to feel this niggling of irritation at her sister right now. Why did she raid the stupid minibar when she could go downstairs and drink for free if she put a couple nickels into a slot machine?

"I can tell you what's left." She motioned toward the bartender. "Everything that is not alcoholic is left. Jack drank most of it, but I did have a couple, three of those adorable little bottles." The bartender came over. "I want one of those." She pointed to Sam's fresh Cosmo. When he left, she said, "My god, did you ever see anything so beautiful?"

"You're pretty drunk."

"Uh huh." Alex nodded emphatically and lit another cigarette. Her first was still smoldering in the ashtray.

"Maybe you should slow down a little?" Sam suggested cautiously.

"No, my dear twin sister," she patted Sam's hand, "I do not think I will do that." She gulped at the Cosmo as if she were parched. She hiccupped. "Here's a thought. Why don't I take that gorgeous bartender boy upstairs? Think what a beautiful baby we could make."

"You really are drunk."

"I wish you would stop stating what is glaringly apparent. But let's get back to the topic at hand. I mean no offense to Chris or his genes or his DNA or anything like that, but just think about it, Sam, if you only have one shot at it, wouldn't you rather have a baby who looks more like a movie star than a stodgy professor?"

The sweetness of the Cosmo coating her tongue tasted like dread. "Are you backing out on me, Alex?"

"Hell no, Sam! I'm only trying to give this little egg its best option." She finished her drink. "Well, I'm off." She squirmed her way off the high stool and smoothed her dress.

She couldn't let her go like this. It wasn't right. It was awful. What had she done to her sister? "Let me walk you upstairs."

Alex cocked her head, squinted her eyes at Sam. "To which room?"

Sam hesitated a fraction of a second too long.

"That's what I thought." She turned, caught her heel on the carpet, and reached for the bar to steady herself.

"I'm going with you. You need help walking."

"You are not going with me. This is my show now." She took off her shoes. "I should have never worn these high heels. Don't know what I was thinking." She stuffed the shoes in her oversized purse. "No good in looking like a tramp, is there?"

Sam watched her walk out of the bar, head high, only wobbling slightly now that the shoes were off. Her heart thumped loudly in her chest; fear and longing kept equal pace. The time to call after her was now, the time to stop everything was this moment, but she didn't act.

Sam watched Alex go.

Alex couldn't find the elevators. She wandered through the maze of the casino, down one row of slot machines to the next. It was endless. She kept searching for the corners of the casino, reasoning that the hotel personnel would put them there, forcing you to enter the casino, tempting you to plop a coin in one of their hideous, hungry machines. She marveled at the number of senior citizens who were dutifully glued to their machines, robotically pressing the "spin button" over and over again, methodically losing their retirement funds, pensions, and social security checks. But who knew? Maybe these graying citizens had horrible children who mistreated them, or worse yet, ignored them. Possibly, they had worked hard all their lives, only to see their accounts and home values plummet in the last couple of years, and in their own quiet, stubborn way were saying, "Fuck you, Mr. President, you can take care of us in our tarnished golden years. The United States government owes us that."

She tripped over an old woman's oxygen tank, stubbing her toe. "Shit! Sorry."

The old woman was not a grandmotherly type. She snarled at Alex, a cigarette dangling from the corner of her mouth, her face crisscrossed with wrinkles. "Watch where you're going, you drunkard."

"You'd be drunk, too, if you were heading upstairs to try and have your sister's baby."

The woman shrugged and turned back to her screen with its brightly lit images of red, white, and blue 7s. "Get away from my machine, or I'll call security."

"I wouldn't dream of touching your filthy machine," Alex said, offended, yet she hurried off. The intensity of the old woman's stare at the twirling sevens was somehow frightening, or perhaps, she was just frightened in general. Totally frightened. Scared shitless.

She rummaged in her bag for a tissue to wipe her sweating forehead. Instead of a tissue, she discovered that she had lost a shoe along the way. She only had one shoe in her purse. She had no idea how that had happened. She hadn't stopped or put it down that she could recall, but then again, her brain was not really functioning right now. She couldn't let it function, couldn't even contemplate what she was about to do. She felt absurdly nostalgic about the shoe. She had bought the black pumps at TJ Maxx to wear to Nick's eighth-grade graduation. She had loved these shoes. She had worn them to all the important events of her life in the last three years: her anniversary dinners with Jack (the one time of year they really splurged on an expensive dinner), a friend's wedding, the annual Christmas parties they attended. And then she remembered. She had also worn them to Grace's funeral.

She slumped down onto the nearest empty stool in front of a slot machine, holding the remaining shoe in her hand. It conjured up that dark May afternoon immediately. It was painful to think of it even now, even though over two years had passed. The white baby-sized casket surrounded by dozens of colorful spring flowers that seemed obscene in their opulence. The dark thunder clouds splitting open over the cemetery, pelting the ground, splattering mud over the tiny box before they could reach the burial tent. Sam falling on her knees, frantically swiping at the splatters with the hem of her mourning skirt. Afterwards, the reception at Sam's house where even the food tasted like loss. No one knew what to say. No one knew what to do.

"Can I get you a drink?" The cocktail waitress' silicone breasts were barely corralled by her halter top.

"By all means. I'll take a . . . Wild Turkey." It somehow seemed appropriate. "Make it a double."

"You are playing, aren't you?"

Alex knew she had to play to get the "free" drink. She rummaged in her purse once again. "I just got here." She found a crumpled five-dollar bill and held it up. "See? I'm playing."

The cocktail waitress walked away. Alex inserted the bill into the money slot. The machine spit it out. She tried again. The machine spit it out. "This is ridiculous," she said to the machine, yet she and the machine repeated the strange battle of wills until the cocktail waitress reappeared and handed Alex her whiskey. She took a long drink and tried to push the money into the slot once again. It rejected the bill. It rejected her. And the whiskey was a very bad idea. Bile rose into her throat, and she really needed a bathroom, immediately.

She asked directions from a kindly looking white-haired lady who ended up leading Alex to the restroom (only a few feet away, a stroke of luck). She was the nicest woman ever, Alex thought, and she told her so. She told her she was a Good Samaritan and gave her a kiss on her powdered cheek before she rushed into the nearest pink-tiled stall and vomited. She knelt in front of the toilet bowl for what seemed like a long time before she had the strength to stand up and drag herself to the sink to splash cold water on her face. Neither the vomiting nor the cold water helped her feel more sober. She was still hopelessly drunk.

She stared at herself in the mirror. "You are a mess," she said. It was certainly true: stringy, sweaty hair, flushed cheeks, crazed eyes. "How can I go through with this now?"

"Is this your shoe?" The young blonde had just emerged from the stall Alex had been in. She glanced down at Alex's bare feet and extended the black pump.

"Yes, thanks." She fled the bathroom, shoe in hand. Maybe this was the sign she had been looking for all along? The black shoe with its eerie power to bring up the thought of Grace's funeral, of the precious baby girl herself. She would do this not only for Sam, but also, in memory of Grace.

She walked with purpose—weaving some, but with purpose—towards where she thought the front desk was. And it was actually there! She asked for the Connor's room number, which she no longer remembered, and they gave her directions to the elevator.

She now stood in front of room 2303. She took deep breaths. *You can do this, you can do this, you can do this*, she chanted. *This is for Grace, this is for Grace, this is for Grace.*

She knocked on the door.

They said they were going to a fertility clinic in Las Vegas. It was all so bizarre and frantic as they rushed around getting ready to leave. Annie asked her mom why they had to leave so suddenly, and her mom gave her a vague answer about this specialist who had an unexpected cancellation. He wouldn't have another opening in months, and they needed to take advantage of the situation immediately. Her mother gave this explanation as she tossed clothes into a duffel bag. It sounded suspicious to Annie, and it looked suspicious, too. Mom was usually a very meticulous packer.

"You know what this means, don't you?" Carla sprawled on the family room couch, her feet propped up on the coffee table next to the bottle of rum she had brought over.

It was strange to see Carla in her home, comfortable and drinking. They almost always hung out at Carla's house where there was no supervision. (Rita didn't count at all.) More than once, Annie had snuck a furtive glance over her shoulder, as if she expected her mom and dad to come in the door any second. She knew that Nick was working and wouldn't be home until after ten o'clock, but still, she felt uneasy. She took a sip of her rum and coke.

"Hey, earth to Annie. I said, you know what this *means*, don't you?" Carla leaned forward to slosh more rum into her glass.

Annie resisted the impulse to go and get a paper towel to wipe up the stray drops. "What are you talking about?"

"It's every teenager's dream. Parents out of town, empty house. It's so obvious."

Annie knew what Carla was getting at, but she decided to play dumb. "I don't get it."

"Yes, you do, Annie Carissa. It's party time!"

"I can't do that. My parents would *kill* me if they found out." They wouldn't kill her, of course, but they would ground her until she was thirty.

"They won't find out," Carla said with confidence.

"How can you be so sure? What if people trash the place like they did at that awful party we went to a few weeks ago?" Annie shuddered at the memory. "By the end of the night, there was puke everywhere. Including my own. I can't take that risk."

"That party just got out of control. We could only invite a few people. We could have a nice, civilized party—with a lot of alcohol."

"The alcohol is the problem." Trouble seemed to follow drunk teenagers. It was a known fact.

Carla misunderstood. "We don't have to buy it. My parents have enough booze to inebriate the entire country of Yemen, wherever that is."

"Wouldn't they notice the missing bottles?"

"No. Rita always replenishes the liquor cabinet before they get home from their latest trip, and she won't tell. She takes bottles, too." Carla was leaning toward her now, getting excited at the prospect.

"Then why don't you have the party?" To Annie, this was the obvious thing. Carla's parents were always out of town. Her house was always empty, but out of sympathy, she didn't point this out. Carla was lonely in that house; she had told Annie that often enough.

"My parents have all that expensive artwork and furniture and stuff."

"Are you saying my parents' stuff is a bunch of crap?" Annie looked around. The couch did look kind of shabby, and there weren't any expensive works of art. Her mother hung family pictures on the wall. It was very *middle-class*, if you asked Annie.

"No, no, that's not what I meant at all. My parents would know if there was one pinprick of a spot on their Persian rugs or one picture a millimeter ajar. I love your house. It feels lived in."

Annie reached over and picked at a loose thread on the arm of the couch. "It looks lived in, too. If we're going to have a party, and I am very much against the idea, it should be at your house. If we have a nice, civilized party, then nothing would get messed up, right?"

"We can't have a party at my parents' house," Carla said, her voice flat. "Why not?"

"I don't want to tell you. It's too *hideous*."

"Oh, come on, Carla, it can't be that bad." Carla tended to exaggerate everything, and Annie was used to calming her down. "And you know you're going to tell me sooner or later. We tell each other everything." Well, we tell each other *almost* everything Annie thought. There were some things that would never be voiced into recognition. She got up and started to pace, trying to keep a step ahead of the memory of that boy on the cruise.

"My parents—I mean Ron and Marge—hate me."

"No, they don't." Carla's parents might be a little neglectful, but Annie doubted that they hated their only child. A parent wouldn't give a BMW to a child they despised.

"You don't know what it's like, Annie. When they're gone, I really want them to come home, and when they do, it's terrible. Everything I do is wrong, and then all I want is for them to leave again. They come home, we fight, they leave, they send me presents, they come home, we fight, they leave. It's a vicious cycle."

Annie was startled to see that Carla was crying. Carla hardly ever cried. She rushed to the downstairs bathroom and came back with a wad of toilet paper. "Sorry, no tissues." Annie had noticed that her mother had stopped buying little things like that around the house: tissues, hot dog buns, Herbal Essence shampoo, and Doritos. They now used toilet paper to wipe their noses, bread for their hot dogs, Suave on their hair, and ate generic chips.

"Marge—and who would have seen this one coming?—went snooping in my room. And guess what she found?"

"Uh oh." Annie imagined the drawer with the pot and pills.

"Bingo. She found my stash." Carla's tears stopped abruptly. She was angry.

"So, are you grounded?" It was Annie's parents' favorite form of punishment.

"Duh, Annie, I'm here."

"Oh, right." She hated when she said stupid things in front of Carla, but she seemed to do it all the time.

"No, my parents wouldn't do something as mundane as grounding me. No, not Ron and Marge Goldleib. To teach their adopted daughter a lesson, they had something much better up their sleeve. They installed surveillance cameras."

"Surveillance cameras! Are you kidding me?" That must have cost the Goldleibs a small fortune, although there was no question in Annie's mind that they could afford it.

"I shit you not. Surveillance cameras inside and outside the house. Talk about trust issues. Obviously, I do dabble in drink and drugs, but they don't need to know everything I do, do they? They're only my parents."

"So they can see everything you do?" It would be *terrible* having her parents know her every move. It would seem like she was in prison.

"Not quite. I threw quite the temper tantrum when they wanted to install one in my bathroom. Can you imagine taking a shower with a camera watching you?"

Annie couldn't. The thought of a camera seeing her naked body made her blush.

Carla refilled her glass. "Once I pointed out the lewdness of such a thing, they backed down. Really, it's a form of *child porn*, I said to them. The guy checking the tapes would see their sixteen-year-old daughter in all her natural glory. What if he published them on the internet, and I became a freak show like Paris Hilton or Pamela Anderson? It would disgrace the Goldleib name, and it would be *all their fault*." She fished a pack of cigarettes out of her purse. "Can I smoke in here?"

"On the patio." Annie followed her out the back door.

Carla lit her Capri. "Anyway, that was the best part of the whole conversation, the porn part. I'd never seen Ron look so terrified. His face went bright red, and I thought he would have a heart attack. It was great."

"So what are you going to do now?" Annie thought of the many hours they had partied in Carla's room. She was going to miss it, too, lounging around in that pretty room that looked as if it had been decorated for an eight-year-old princess, with its ceramic ballerina dolls and pink eyelet comforter. It had always struck her as odd how child-like the room was. Carla had lived in the room for less than a year, but it looked as if it had been transplanted from a past era of Carla's life, one in which she didn't grow up, always remaining the Goldleibs' little girl. If it struck Carla as unusual, she didn't mention it.

"Duh, once again, Annie. I'm going to do everything I've been doing before, but now it's going to be done in the bathroom. And in my car. And other places outside of the house. When you think of it, they've really put me at a *higher risk* for accidents by installing the fucking cameras."

"You do have a really large bathroom," Annie said.

"Exactly. I'll show them."

"Wait a minute. If we do have a party, how are we going to get the alcohol if there are security cameras everywhere?"

Carla gave her a wicked smile. "This is when it comes in handy to have bigoted, idiotic, alcoholic parental units. Marge only found pot and pills in my room—which is highly unusual but also lucky—so it didn't seem to occur to them that I also might be drinking. Given their nightly habit to imbibe a few, they weren't too keen on the idea of being seen on tape celebrating their nightly happy hours, and I do mean *hours*. That tape, too, might get in the wrong hands. So, they decided that they would just keep the liquor cabinet locked at all times. Problem solved. Case closed. *Voila!*"

"Okay, so the liquor cabinet is under lock and key. I'll repeat my question: How are we going to get the booze?"

"Oh, ye of little faith. I have a key, of course. I had it made right after we moved in when it was just laying around on top of the bar. It didn't even cross their minds that I might have a key, the idiots. All I have to do is put a few bottles in my backpack and walk right past the next camera. Rita will probably hide her bottles in a basket of laundry or something, and she'll keep replacing the bottles every time Ron and Marge come home."

Carla stubbed out her cigarette. "Let's go inside and get the SCDS directory. Almost everyone puts their cell numbers in it. We can start texting invitations for tomorrow night."

"I still don't know about this." Annie felt uneasy. So many things could go wrong, especially the one she feared most. "What if no one shows up?"

Carla paused, her hand on the doorknob. "I suppose that's a possibility. You and I don't have a chance in hell of winning any popularity contest at SCDS. However, if I know human nature, and by that I mean the nature of your average teenager on the lookout for free booze, they will come. Remember the movie *Field of Dreams* when Kevin Costner hears that voice saying, 'Build it and they will come'? I say, 'Provide alcohol, and they will come!'"

"We'll only invite four or five people, right?"

"Ten, max. And listen, Annie, we can invite Walter, your prince charming. I hear he likes to party, and his best friend, Jacob, is hot. We can invite them."

As she followed Carla into the house to rummage for the directory, she knew she had given in. Once Carla got an idea into her head, it was like trying to stop a runaway train. And for the first time, the idea of a party gave her a little thrill of excitement. Maybe Walter would come to her party, and they could talk, and he could see that she was an interesting person, if she didn't say anything stupid, and he would ask her out. Yes, maybe a party was what she and Walter had needed all along.

"That girl over there has her eye on you, sugar," Loretta said as she drummed her long ceramic nails on the cash register. Tonight, they were decorated with black skulls and crossbones. "She's looked at every magazine on the rack, and I highly doubt that little thing has an interest in *Motorsports Magazine*.

It was an unusually slow night at Fry's, and Nick hated when it was slow. The minutes dragged by. He much preferred to have a steady stream of customers to keep him busy bagging groceries. He had thought about asking if he could leave early. With his parents out of town and Carla at their house, anything could happen. Mom had specifically told him he was in charge, so the blame for anything stupid happening would fall squarely on his shoulders. And when his sister and her best friend got together, *stupid* was their middle name.

"Yeah, right," he said, distracted. The odds of a girl looking at him were something like a billion to one, and probably, it was a girl who was waiting around for a chance to shoplift something meaningless from the store, like a tube of lipstick or a pack of gum. It happened all the time.

And he had other things on his mind. He had finally opened his SAT scores and was totally surprised. They were pretty good, 1620, and he hadn't even tried. He hadn't even taken a pencil into the test and had had to borrow one from a girl who was so nervous she threw up in the middle of the exam. Yet Mom and Dad would think they had died and gone to heaven when they found out his score. But that was the strange thing. They hadn't asked. Instead, there was a last-minute decision to go to Las Vegas to see some special fertility doctor, hurried packing, and a quick departure. After all the nagging he had endured during the last few months, after he had taken the stupid test, and after the results came, his parents hadn't asked how he had scored. It was weird, vaguely unsettling, and he had to admit, a little disappointing.

"I know a crush when I see one," Loretta said. "She's cute, babycakes. Some kind of Oriental, I think—Asian, or Chinese, or Japanese. Those people all look alike to me. I know that's a bad thing to say, but I'm just a hick who's never been out of Arizona, so that's my excuse. I'm—what do you call it? *Politically incorrect.* That's the term. Politically incorrect. Boy, that came out of nowhere. Sometimes I surprise myself."

During Loretta's rambling, Nick looked toward the magazine stand. It was Jennifer. Their eyes met briefly before she glanced back down at the magazine in her hands. It was now *Men's Bodybuilding*, and it was upside down.

"Do you know her?" Loretta asked.

"A little. She goes to my school."

"Why don't you go on over there and talk to her? We're so slow tonight that I could take care of everything with one hand tied behind my back."

"No, that's okay. It's my job to stay here. I'll just . . . stay here." He knew how weak the excuse sounded as he felt his face go hot.

"Oh, go on, Nicky doll. The poor thing has been standing there for thirty minutes."

"I said I'll stay here."

Loretta sighed dramatically. "Ah, young love," she said. "It's totally wasted on teenagers. If I had a young man looking at me like the way she's looking at you, I'd be all over him in about five seconds."

"We're not in love." Nick tried to look busy by straightening the paper bags that were already perfectly stacked.

"And you never will be if you don't go over and start a conversation with that little girl. Get your pretty boy bootie over there *now*."

Nick knew he didn't have a choice. Loretta would not let this drop. "I'll be right back."

"You'd better not be, pretty boy," Loretta said.

Nick could feel her eyes boring into his back as he made his way to the magazine stand. He was so inexperienced at this that the last thing he needed was an audience to witness his awkwardness. No, the last thing he needed was *Loretta* as his audience. He would have to make this quick, although the mere twenty feet to Jennifer seemed like a vast distance.

"Hi, Jennifer. Nice to see you when you're not flat on your back." If it were possible to catch those words in his bare hands, he would have strangled them.

"What?" Jennifer's blush matched his own.

"I meant," he cleared his throat, "that it's nice to run into you without running you *over*." He glanced over his shoulder and saw Loretta watching them. She smiled and nodded encouragingly.

"I didn't know you worked here." Jennifer put the *Men's Bodybuilding* magazine back on the rack with the cover face down. It didn't help much. The back cover featured a Viagra ad.

"Yeah, I've worked here for over a year. It doesn't pay a whole lot—"

"I did know you worked here," Jennifer interrupted. "I asked around."

What was he supposed to say to that? The ball was in his court. Think, he told himself. Think of something to say. "Oh."

Jennifer seemed equally at a loss for words. She stared at her feet, her toenails painted a muted pink.

"Do you need help finding something?" At the very least, he reasoned, he could be helpful in this, their second awkward encounter. "I know where almost everything is in this store. Sometimes, when we're not busy at the registers, I help stock the shelves."

"No, that's okay. I've already done my shopping." She held out her hand. A mangled Snickers bar looked as if she had been holding onto it for dear life.

The candy bar got to him. She was as nervous as he was, this cute girl who had, it seemed, come to the store to see him. Why would she do that? He had caught a glimpse of her from time to time at school during the last week. Always, it seemed that she had been looking at him, but when he caught her eye, she smiled nervously and looked away. He cleared his throat again; it sounded a little like he was strangling. "That one looks damaged. I can get you another one."

"No, I'll pay for this one. I'm pretty sure I'm the one who damaged it."

"That Snickers looks like it was run over by a car. Let me get you another one. They're right inside the check-out aisles."

"No, I'll pay for this one." Jennifer finally looked him in the eye. "It's the honest thing to do. I was so nervous to talk to you that I didn't realize I was squeezing it so hard."

Her glossy black hair hung in a sheet down her back to her waist, and she had the whitest teeth he had ever seen. But the best thing to Nick was that she had just said she was *honest*. He didn't know a lot about girls, obviously, but the guys talking in the locker room made it sound like most girls were lying and deceitful. And that was some of the nicest things they said. But then again, a lot of the guys were gigantic jerks.

"If you want to pay for that one, I'll buy you another one. I insist." He needed to stop talking about the stupid candy bar, but he couldn't help himself.

Jennifer helped him. "I don't care anything about this candy bar. In fact, I don't even like chocolate. I've been wandering around this store for more than an hour—so I, too, pretty much know where everything is—but I was trying to get up the courage to ask you."

She put a hand on his arm (not the one with the candy bar), and he felt a low-grade heat make itself up his forearm. "Ask me what?" He managed to squeeze out the three little words around his thick tongue.

"About a movie. We talked about going to a movie, and I wondered if you would want to go tomorrow night?" Her words rushed out, and her face was three times as pink as her toenails, but she held her head high, her jaw at a determined angle.

"Of course he wants to go, honey. Some fellows are a little slow on the uptake, like our boy Nicky here, but they may very well be the ones worth waiting for," Loretta called from the cash register. "Trust me. I am a *professional* when it comes to men. Granted, a lot of my men have been scumbags, but I still consider myself highly trained in that particular area."

Startled, Nick turned to look at her standing there with her arms crossed over her ample chest. The woman must have astounding hearing. But he wasn't mad at her. In fact, he was somewhat grateful. She was still smiling encouragingly. He turned back to Jennifer. "I would like to go to a movie."

"With you, add *with you*," Loretta contributed. "I'll say it once again: Youth is wasted on teenagers."

"With you," he added.

Jennifer's smile lit up her small oval face. "Well, that's great."

Nick lowered his voice so that x-ray hearing Loretta couldn't snoop. "I've never been on a date before, so how do we do this? Do I pick you up, or do we meet there, or what?"

"This is my first date, too," Jennifer whispered, "and I already thought about that. Why don't we meet at the theater, and since it'll be rather awkward for both of us, why don't we each bring a friend? How does that sound to you?"

"It sounds great," he whispered back. He could invite Dylan and get his take on this whole thing. He needed another perspective, and he couldn't talk to his mom and dad about it, not yet. They'd be full of questions, and he didn't have any answers right now. Not a one.

When he opened the door, she fell into his arms, sobbing hysterically. He picked her up and laid her gently on the bed, then went into the bathroom and brought back a damp, cool washcloth and put it on her forehead. It was going to take her a while before she could speak, and he didn't have anything to say either. After polishing off the mini bar, he had walked the gaudy Vegas strip, trying not to think about anything, trying not to picture what his wife was doing at that very moment. After that, he had come back to the room and sat in the darkness, crying. He was ashamed of himself, for crying, for every mistake he had made in the last few months, for his lack of courage to tell the truth.

Now, Jack simply stared at his beautiful wreck of a wife. Her face was red and puffy, and gray mascara rivulets stained her cheeks. She exhaled sour breath with every sob. Her red dress ("If I'm going to be a whore, I might well dress like one," she had said on her way out the door, already disturbingly drunk) had stains trickling down the front. Her right knee stuck out from a gaping hole in her pantyhose, and she was wearing only one shoe. This mess of a wife would seem alarming to most men, Jack knew, but not to him. He was relieved. He knew that she hadn't slept with Chris, and instead, had probably wandered around the casino—she wouldn't have left the casino, not with her terrible sense of direction and fear of getting lost—trying to drink herself into conviction. But it hadn't worked.

He got another damp, cool cloth from the bathroom and replaced the first. Her breathing was starting to return to normal. He sat on the side of the king-sized bed where she looked so tiny, dwarfed by the expanse of plush white comforter. He took her hand, kissed the palm. "You need to get some rest," he said.

"I didn't go through with it," she said. She clung to his hand.

"I know."

"I lost my good black shoe. Could someone explain how that can happen? One minute, it's in my purse, the next minute, it's gone, vanished into thin air. It was Grace's shoe. I tried to find it, but I couldn't. No, that's not right. I think I went into the bathroom and threw up instead. Oh, God, what a failure I am."

"You're not a failure." She was either still drunk or emotionally overwrought. Probably both, and either way, she was wasted.

"Sam is going to be furious with me." More tears, but these were silent tears of exhaustion.

"Forget Sam." If he wasn't so tired himself, he would have felt anger at the mention of Sam's name. She was the one responsible for the state his wife was in, lying emotionally drained on this ridiculously enormous bed. "It didn't work. We'll pack up and go home in the morning and put this all behind us."

"But I promised Sam that I would try to have her baby."

"That was before you knew they didn't have enough money for the IVF procedure. I'd say that put a noticeable kink in the plan."

"I told her I would do it."

"You tried, and that's enough."

"No, I didn't try. Getting drunk and wandering around a casino and crying over a lost black shoe is not trying."

"Let's call it a night, okay? I think we've had enough of this day." Jack took off his shirt and pants, planning on getting into bed and holding Alex in his arms all night.

"And what about the money?"

"I'll come up with something." As usual, the mention of money made that sickening ball of guilt in his stomach flare up. He had already started to count on the money. He didn't want to, but he had.

"I know we need the money, Jack. Not only do we have to think of our monthly bills, but we've got a child going to college next year."

If only it were that simple, he thought. "I'll come up with something," he said again. What he could possibly come up with was anyone's guess.

"When did life get so complicated?"

"When your twin sister moved across the street."

"That's not funny." Her voice was hard.

"I'm not trying to be funny. I'm serious." And it was so obviously true to him. In the few months that Sam had lived across the street, their lives had become so much more chaotic, unpredictable, *messy*. But Alex didn't see Sam that way, and he knew she never would. He had accepted the truth years ago: When it came to Sam, Alex was blinded by love.

"I reek," Alex said, sitting up.

"You smell fine to me," Jack said. It wasn't true, but he just wanted to hold her, fall sleep, and wake up to a new day. This one had certainly kicked everyone in the butt.

"I reek of failure. I'm going to take a bubble bath." Alex stripped as she made her way to the Vegas-sized Jacuzzi tub in the bathroom. She stopped, turned, and gave him a smile. Granted, it was small, almost imperceptible, but it was her first smile of the day. "You can join me if you want."

He didn't need a second invitation.

For all her careful planning, Sam had forgotten to come up with a sign, the message signaling that the coast was clear. She should have told Chris to call or text, but knowing Chris—who for all his brilliance in academia was a complete moron when it came to cell phones—the phone was probably nestled in the bottom of his briefcase, uncharged. She had spent the last two hours in front of a nickel poker machine, trying to make her mind completely blank as she played one nickel at a time, trying not to think about what was going on upstairs in room 2303, hoping that *the act* had all been over in five minutes. She could call the room from the phone in the lobby, but that seemed wrong somehow, like an invasion of privacy. But whose privacy? The thought made her shudder.

Since there was obviously no protocol or etiquette in a situation like this, she decided to go up to the room. She was tired, and for no reason that she could think of, she felt absurdly close to tears. She stood outside the door, hand fisting to knock, but that also seemed like an inappropriate thing to do. She pressed her ear against the door, but it was eerily quiet. Oh, God, what if they had fallen asleep? Alex had been quite drunk, and she was sure Chris would have taken something to calm his nerves, a Valium, or maybe a brandy. What if she walked in and they were still in bed, entwined in each other's arms, looking like lovers? What if the mechanical intercourse had turned into something more? The Cosmos she had had earlier churned painfully on her empty stomach.

She had to know. Quickly, before she could change her mind, she dug the room key out of her purse and inserted it into the lock, once, twice, three times before the blinking light turned from red to green and let her push open the door. She took a deep breath and prepared herself for the worst. What if they had betrayed her? What if the whole thing was a disaster, and it was all her fault? She walked in, letting the door bang heavily behind her.

The room was totally dark, no lights, the curtains tightly drawn. She fumbled her hand along the wall, looking for a light switch, ready to illuminate whatever had happened in this room during the last two hours. She could hear Chris's gentle snoring and the hum of the mini bar, but that was it. Her fingers found the light switch.

Chris lay on top of the made bed on the side he always slept on at home. He was on his back, hands clasped on his stomach, fully clothed in his jeans and button-down white shirt. He still had his brown loafers on but had carefully put a towel under them so as not to dirty the comforter. Except for the fact of his snoring, he looked peacefully—terrifyingly—dead.

"What?" He stirred, blinking against the light.

"Oh, Chris," she said, moving towards the bed. "You have no idea what terrible things were going through my head before I opened the door."

He sat up and reached for the bottle of water on the nightstand, took a sip, and cleared his throat. "Oh, I think I have a pretty good idea. I know first-hand how your vivid—or maybe I should say *colorful*—imagination works."

She realized how thoughtful it was of Chris to remake the bed and put his clothes back on. It was just like him to think of things like that.

It would have been very uncomfortable to come in and see him asleep in bed in his pajamas, something that hadn't occurred to her before now. "Thank you for making the bed."

"I didn't." He took another sip of water.

"Then, Alex—"

"No."

"You called maid service."

"Guess again."

"I don't understand," she said, although she was beginning to.

"Alex didn't show up, Sam."

Just ten minutes ago, she would have felt a complete and utter rage towards Alex that would have fueled her disappointment, but now, the disappointment was tinged with relief. She had not spent enough time on the details of the plan. The trip to Vegas had been sudden, and her usual attention to detail had flown out the window somewhere around Nothing, Arizona.

"You didn't try to call her?"

"Why would I do that?"

"To see where she was."

"This is her decision, Sam, not mine and certainly not yours."

"I'm going to call her." She fished in her purse for her phone.

Chris took it out of her hands. "No, you are not."

"Oh, Chris," she wailed as the tears finally came.

He pulled her slowly down to the bed and put his arms around her. "They say everything happens for a reason. Maybe we can believe it just for tonight."

"I used to believe that. Alex and I said that to each other all the time when we were growing up." Her tears were dampening his white shirt, and she could feel the heat of his skin under her wet cheek. "And then your baby dies, and you don't know how there could possibly be one single reason for that happening. There is absolutely nothing good; in fact, it is fucking *atrocious*. Then you start to question the possibility of hope and happiness because you can't see out of the black hole of despair."

"I know," Chris patted her back, "but let's believe it for tonight."

Sam felt sleep dragging her down. "Maybe it's karma. The karma wasn't right tonight."

"You could have a point there," Chris said.

Chris must have been drifting off, too, or else he would never have attributed anything to karma. He was too practical. "You know what?" Chris mumbled.

"Tomorrow is another day. Name that famous quote, Mr. Professor." No reply.

"Scarlett O'Hara. Everyone knows it's from *Gone with the Wind*." During the summer between seventh and eighth grade, she and Alex had fallen in love with the novel, reading it, discussing it, and acting out key scenes. Alex always played Scarlett, and Sam played Rhett, mostly because she liked to say, in a fake-deep voice, "Frankly, my dear, I don't give a damn." It had been one of the best summers of their young lives.

Sam's last hazy, half-formed thought before she fell asleep was this: Scarlet O'Hara wasn't the nicest person, but she usually got her way.

Chris debated whether to tell Sam that he saw Alex and Jack on the other side of the restaurant's outside patio, by the pool. Jack had obviously been swimming. He had on the hotel's white terrycloth robe, and his wet hair was slicked back from his face. Alex had a cover-up on over her swimming suit and oversized black sunglasses perched on her delicate face. They were a handsome couple, and no one looking at them would suspect that anything was amiss on this sunny Saturday morning in glittering Las Vegas.

Jack flashed a charming smile at the waitress as she placed two Bloody Marys on the table, and Chris felt a pang. It was no wonder that Alex found it so repulsive to sleep with him. With a handsome and athletic husband like Jack, she probably viewed her sister's husband as some aging, myopic, sedentary specimen of mankind. It was not that Chris was jealous of Jack's charm—not at all. In fact, he thought Jack was a little on the shallow side, too liberal in his politics, uninformed in financial matters, and frankly, not all that bright. And it was not as if he wanted Alex to be attracted to him, her sister's husband. It was perhaps the only thing that Sam had been right about so far. Physical attraction would only complicate an already convoluted situation. Still, he would be negligent if he didn't acknowledge that Alex had hurt his feelings last night when she didn't show up. He understood her reasons—they were obviously valid—and he didn't want to feel this way, but unfortunately, he did.

"What are you staring at, Chris?" Sam had on dark sunglasses, too, trying to conceal her bloodshot and puffy eyes.

"Nothing." He picked up his menu. He was starving. It was ten o'clock, and it had been an exhausting morning. When Sam had awakened at seven, she had immediately started in on how she needed to talk to Alex and ask her what was going on, ask her if she was still going to try to do the surrogacy. One step ahead of her, he had hidden her cell phone, which infuriated her. She had torn apart the room before she found it taped to the bottom of the desk drawer.

"Aha," she said, manic. "You think you're so smart?" And then she saw that it was dead. "Damn it, Chris." She stalked to the room phone and was equally frustrated when the front desk said that the Carissa room had requested that no calls be put through.

"Leave them alone," Chris said in a soothing voice. "Give them some privacy." Sam was just going to make things worse.

"I have to talk to Alex." She had thrown on a sundress and run a brush through her hair. "Tomorrow is not another day. Tomorrow is today. Today is THE day."

Chris didn't usually recommend it, but he said, "Why don't you take a Valium."

"I don't need a Valium. I need Alex."

He followed her to Alex's room, and despite the Do Not Disturb sign, she pounded frantically on the door until he made her stop. Then he followed her to the front desk where she asked if the Carissas had checked out ("No, they haven't") and followed her through the casino as she kept muttering, "They have to be here somewhere." Then he followed her to their room and watched helplessly as she cried as if her heart had been broken. He had not seen her cry like that since Grace was taken from them.

And now they were ordering breakfast—an omelet for him, fruit and toast for her.

The waitress brought more coffee, and Sam lit a cigarette with trembling hands. He wished she would quit, but it was another argument he had lost to her a long time ago. She had quit when she was pregnant with Grace and didn't touch a cigarette until . . . *after*. Everything had gone to hell *after*, and he didn't blame her. In fact, he had come close to smoking a cigarette a few times, too, and he had suffered bouts of asthma as a child.

A woman laughed, and Sam straightened in her chair, her twin radar notified. "That's Alex. She's here." She craned her neck, looking left and right.

"Don't turn around," he said.

So, of course, Sam turned around. "There they are! I'm so relieved. I'm going to go over and talk to Alex." She turned back around, stubbed out the cigarette, and grabbed her purse.

Their food arrived. "No, you're not going over there. You're going to sit here and eat your breakfast, and you're going to let them eat theirs in peace."

"Stop treating me like a child."

"Stop acting like one." He said it calmly, but it stopped her in her tracks.

She hung her purse on the back of her chair. "I've become a raving lunatic, haven't I?"

Chris took a bite of his Denver omelet and then buttered a piece of toast.

"You could disagree with me." She stabbed a piece of cantaloupe with her fork.

"I could."

She sighed. "I don't know why you put up with me."

"Because I love you."

"You are a very patient man."

He was a patient man. He supposed growing up with a mother like Louise, who was moody, irrational, sometimes even cruel, had contributed to this. If you looked at it in that light, he could almost credit her for doing something right in the childrearing department.

"What are we going to do?"

He was a patient man, a patient man with a plan. "You're going to the spa. I've booked you a massage for two o'clock."

She put down her rye toast without taking a bite. "I'd love a massage, Chris, but I don't know if it's such a good idea."

"Did you plan on spending the day following Alex around, just like I followed you this morning?"

Her face said that she had.

"Not an option, Sam. You're going to get a massage, and you're going to relax."

"But—"

"We're going to give fate a fighting chance today and see how things unfold."

"I don't like this idea."

"That's too bad." He had decided early that morning that they were going about this conception thing in entirely the wrong way. Emotions were controlling everyone when what they needed was detachment—along with some secrecy. He had left a note for Alex at the front desk, asking her to meet him at a motel just off the strip at three o'clock. He had also instructed the front desk to send up a "complimentary" golf pass to Jack's room. With both Sam and Jack occupied, he could meet with Alex on more neutral ground. It was the only way he could see this thing even having a chance, and even now, that slim chance would depend on: 1) Jack believing that the golf pass was complimentary (and Chris knew that Jack always kept his golf clubs in the back of his Jeep, and 2) Alex not saying anything to Jack and then actually showing up at the hotel. Arranging everything had cost him more money than he would have liked, but he was doing it for Sam. It had always been clear to everyone that he would do anything for Sam.

"I suppose I could use a massage," Sam said as she rubbed the back of her neck. "The muscles in my shoulders are as hard as rocks."

"Good," he said as they stood to leave. "Maybe we should throw in a facial, too."

"Oh, Chris," Sam said as she took his arm. "You really are too good to me."

"Relax. People will come," Carla said. "What high school kid doesn't love a party when the parents are out of town?"

Annie watched as Carla arranged their assortment of booze on the kitchen island. She had managed to smuggle an impressive variety of vodka, gin, tequila, scotch, and other alcohol that Annie had never heard of. Carla didn't volunteer the information on how she had smuggled out the bottles under the watchful eye of the surveillance camera, and Annie hadn't asked. She didn't really want to know.

Annie was nervous, as Carla could see, and she had a hard time trying not to fidget. She was afraid of two things: that people wouldn't show and that too many people would. No, make that three things. She was also afraid that people—i.e., boys (if they showed!) would trash her house. She hadn't told Nick about the party, and she hoped he would spend the night at Dylan's as he usually did. What would he do if he found out? Would he tell Mom and Dad? They would go ballistic if they knew she had hosted a party with *alcohol*. Annie supposed she was actually nervous/scared about a million things. This was probably not a good idea. Once again, she had let Carla talk her into something she didn't particularly want to do. But then again, Carla's adventures usually worked out okay, didn't they?

"Here, try this." Carla handed her a red paper cup filled with ice and an amber-colored liquid.

"What is it?" The drink smelled sweet.

"Amaretto. You're going to love it."

Annie took a sip. It tasted a little like syrup. "It's delicious." Like magic, the drink soothed her nerves as it made its way down her throat. She took another, larger sip. The power of alcohol. *Amazing.* She flipped the blonde ponytail over her shoulder; the wig was starting to feel slightly less uncomfortable.

"You really do look like Madonna," Carla said, "except I don't think she would wear cutoffs and a tank top. I brought you another corset like the one I have on." Carla wore an identical blonde wig and had attired herself in an outfit like Madonna wore on the Blonde Ambition tour. The black, tight corset had pointed breasts, which only accentuated Carla's flat chest.

She should have said an emphatic *no* to the whole Madonna theme when Carla had shown up with the costumes and CDs, but as usual, mousy Annie had gone along with Carla's game plan. It was growing worrisome to Annie, this increasing need Carla had to dress up in some outlandish costume. On Friday, she had gone to school dressed as Princess Diana, complete with a blue satin gown and a tiara. People had laughed at her, of course, but Annie stood loyally by her side, uncertain whether Carla was trying to get attention or the opposite: trying to make her own self disappear. Either way, the whole situation was confusing to Annie. And it was freaky, too. Princess Di was *dead*.

"In the name of Madonna, this wig is as far as I'm willing to go," Annie said. She poured herself another amaretto. "Plus, I don't think she dresses like that anymore. She's got kids."

"Yeah, she's ancient now, but I'm dressed as the younger version of Madonna, the slutty one." She adjusted the pointy bra. "Besides, this outfit makes my boobs look bigger."

No, it didn't, Annie thought. The pointy cups stuck out like empty ice cream cones on Carla's bony chest. They heard a car pull into the driveway.

"Showtime! Put on the tunes, Annie. I'll get the door."

They had invited ten people, six boys and four girls. At first, they weren't going to invite any girls. In their opinion, most of the girls in their grade were first-class bitches, but Carla had pointed out that it would look odd if they were the only girls. "We don't want it to look like we're setting ourselves up for a gang bang," she had said.

Annie had turned abruptly away, not wanting Carla to see the expression on her face, which was a combination of fear, revulsion, and shame. "No, we don't want it to look like that," she had said. "We just want a nice, quiet party."

"We'll see," Carla had answered.

Carla had been right about one thing, though. Everyone they invited came, even Walter. Drinks were poured, the music was playing, people were laughing and joking around, and it was . . . *awkward*. It soon became clear to Annie and Carla that their party was only the preliminary party of the night for their more popular guests when Jacob loudly announced that the late-night party at Cole Watson's house was going to be awesome. Annie and Carla glanced at each other. Carla's eyes blazed with fury. Even though it was their party, they were still, once again, excluded. They stood together at the kitchen island and drank.

Nina Romano walked over to refill her cup. With her long black hair and brown eyes, she was one of the prettiest, and most popular, girls in school. They had invited her because she had always been kind of nice to them. Well, maybe *nice* wasn't the proper word, Annie thought. She had never been overtly mean, and as far as they knew, she had never talked about them—at least not in their hearing.

"Are you guys supposed to be twins or something?" Nina sloshed vodka into her cup, and Annie realized she was already drunk. Maybe their party was only one in a *succession* of parties these people were going to tonight.

"We're dressed like Madonna," Carla snapped. "That should be obvious."

Nina looked Carla over. "Oh, right." She wobbled slightly on her wedged sandals. "I didn't get the text that this was supposed to be a costume party." She looked at the others sitting in the family room. "I guess they didn't either."

"It isn't a costume party." Carla, uncharacteristically, blushed.

"Then why are you dressed up? I don't get it."

"We're dressed up because we wanted to be . . . *festive*."

"Festive? Is that a word?" Nina blinked.

"Explain it to her, Annie." Carla poured a hefty dose of rum into her glass.

Annie didn't know why they were trying to look like Madonna, but she had to remain loyal to Carla, as always. "Because we wanted to express our creativity?" she ventured.

"Exactly! Annie and I are very creative people."

Nina laughed.

"It's not funny!" Carla slammed her drink down on the counter.

"Well, it is a little funny. They're supposed to be Madonna," Nina called over her shoulder to the others.

"I thought they were supposed to be Vegas drag queens," Jacob said to the group.

His voice wasn't loud, but Annie and Carla heard. They looked at each other. So, they had been talked about at their own party. Annie felt the shame like a fiery ball in her stomach. They did look ridiculous, and she wished she could disappear, just vanish from the spot in a puff of smoke. She reached up to take off the wig.

"Leave it on," Carla hissed into her ear. "We are not going to let them win."

Win what? Annie wanted to ask, but she left the wig on.

"You look good as a blonde, Annie," Nina slurred. "Maybe you should try that color the next time you dye your hair."

"Um, thanks," Annie said. Maybe Nina was going to be nice after all, and maybe the party could still be salvaged. Carla glared at her, and Annie knew that she shouldn't have acknowledged the semi-compliment.

Walter walked up. "Hey, Annie, do you guys have anything to eat?"

She finally had Walter come to her house, only to find out that she was a terrible hostess. She had zero experience being a hostess, it was true, but her mom had always said that if you were going to serve people alcohol, you should also give them something to eat. In her anxiety about the party, she had forgotten this one basic rule. "I could make some popcorn," she said.

"We don't have any popcorn," Carla said.

"I think we do."

"No, we don't," Carla warned.

"Well, do you or don't you?" Walter smiled at Annie.

Annie looked at Walter's smile, the smile she longed for, and then at Carla's fierce scowl. The decision was not easy. She shrugged. "I guess we don't have any."

"No big deal."

Nina flung her arms around Walter's neck. "Kiss me, Waltie. You are so cute!"

"You're drunk, Nina," Walter said as he tried to remove her arms.

"That's never stopped you before." She puckered her lips.

"Cut it out, Nina." He loosened her stranglehold, but then had to catch her before she hit the ground.

"I think we should be heading out," Jacob said, coming into the kitchen, the others close behind.

"Yes, why don't you all go to your next precious party." Carla marched to the front door and opened it.

The group put down their cups and shuffled toward the door with mumbled, indistinguishable goodbyes. Two of the girls were holding Nina up. Carla scowled at each one as they left.

Only Walter was left. "Thanks for the party, Annie."

"Sure," she said. Now that she had him alone, she needed to say something important, something that would make him stay and talk, something that would make him choose her over his shitty friends.

"Come on, Walt," Jacob called. "We're running late."

"Sorry," Walter said, but then he turned and joined his friends, leaving Annie standing there with her last lingering hope for the evening evaporating.

Carla slammed the door. "They are all pieces of shit!" she shrieked.

Annie recognized the dark mood coming on. They were becoming more frequent. "It's not the end of the world, Carla. Let's go outside and smoke a cigarette."

"It was a fucking *disaster.*" Carla poured a glass full of whiskey and gulped it down. She was breathing heavily. "Why do I set myself up for their shit? They are revolting human beings."

"Just calm down, Carla. They are revolting, and we shouldn't waste any more time even thinking about them." She should try to get Carla into bed before she drank more. She wanted to go to bed herself and mull over the events of the evening. Walter had said *sorry* to her. At least he had some manners.

"I hate them all." And then Carla picked up the first bottle and shattered it on the floor.

"What do you think?" Nick asked Dylan. They had escaped to the movie theater's bathroom to confer. So far, so good, Nick thought. Everyone had bought his or her own ticket, and now the two girls were standing in line to get popcorn.

"I think she's fat." Dylan thrust his hands in the pockets of his baggy jeans and rocked back and forth on the balls of his feet.

Nick had hoped that Dylan wouldn't have noticed, which was ridiculous. Melissa, the girl Jennifer had brought along (her best friend since preschool, she explained) was quite . . . hefty. "She's a little on the plump side, but she seems very nice."

"A little on the plump side? Do you need glasses, dude? The girl is *enormous.*"

"Come on, Dylan, she's not that bad."

"Is that so?" Dylan cocked his head. "If you think that she's 'not that bad,' then you can take her, and I'll take the tiny Asian girl."

"Her name is Jennifer."

"Whatever, dude. I'm not going back out there."

Nick felt a wave of panic. "But what would I tell them?"

"Tell them I'm sick. Tell them my house caught on fire. Tell them I'm a psycho. I don't care."

This was so unlike Dylan, who was usually easy going about everything, but Nick had to concede that he had a point. Dylan was super skinny, and Melissa was rather hefty, and together, they would make an odd couple. He tried another approach. "It's not like Melissa is your date."

"Then what would you call it?"

"It's a group thing. We're just four people seeing a movie."

"Yeah, right," Dylan said, unconvinced.

"I'd do it for you," Nick said, and he meant it.

Dylan sighed. "I know you would, dude. I guess I'm being unreasonable, but she is SO FAT."

"The theater will be dark."

Dylan sighed again.

"I'll give you my new *Marines in Training* DVD." It had taken him a month to find it on Amazon, but if it would get Dylan to stay, he'd give it to him. He didn't want Dylan's walking out to make a bad impression on Jennifer, and more than that, he didn't want to be stuck talking to two girls all night by himself. He didn't think he could handle that yet.

"Aw, dude, you don't have to do that," Dylan said, softening.

"Yes, I do."

Dylan sighed one more time. "What are friends for? *Semper fi, amigo.*"

They walked out, joined the girls, and made their way into the theater. Dylan lagged behind, but at least he was still there. To Nick's relief, the screen darkened immediately, so there was no need to make conversation. Jennifer sat quietly beside him, daintily chewing her popcorn. She offered him some, but he declined, afraid that he would chomp too loudly. This was a new experience, sitting beside a girl in a darkened theater, and he didn't want to make any mistakes. Although, as it turned out, he had already made a mistake. It was some awful chick flick/romantic comedy, and it was totally predictable. Nick was pretty sure he heard Dylan groan a couple of times. Lesson learned: Never let a girl choose the movie on the first date.

After the movie, the four of them stood awkwardly in front of the theater in the warm evening. Dylan yawned noisily. "I'm beat."

"But it's still early," Jennifer said.

Nick checked his phone. It was only nine o'clock, and he didn't want to go home yet. He hadn't had a chance to try to talk to Jennifer, and he knew he wasn't going to get any better at it if he didn't practice. "We could go get something to eat," he suggested, and was glad he did when Jennifer gave him one of her smiles. She had super white teeth, and he liked that. (If he ever had a "type" of a girl, it would have to be one with great teeth.)

"I have to be up really early in the morning," Dylan said.

Nick shot him a look. "We're only talking about a few minutes."

Dylan must have really wanted the *Marines in Training*. "Well, okay."

"There's a McDonald's a couple of miles from here. They're fast," Jennifer said.

"I'm on a diet," Melissa said.

Nick glanced at Dylan, willing him not to say something like: A diet, dude? What's up with the milk duds you had to go get halfway through the movie?

But he didn't. Instead, he said to her, "They have healthy stuff like salads."

"I know that, but if you're going to go to McDonald's, what's the point of eating something healthy?"

"I hear you. If you're not going to go for the large fries and Big Mac, there is no point." Dylan actually smiled at her.

She smiled back, and she had great teeth, too. "I'll have to use my will-power," Melissa said. "But I have to tell you that I'm not all that good at it."

She wasn't good at it at all. She ordered after Dylan and duplicated his large fries and Big Mac. It was Nick's turn. He turned to Jennifer. "I'll buy." It seemed like the least he could do. After all, she had bought her own movie ticket and popcorn.

"You don't have to do that," she said.

"I'd like to."

"It's not necessary."

"We've had this conversation before," he said. She looked confused. "The Snickers bar."

"Oh, right. We hardly know each other, and we're already in a conversational rut." She looked up at him, smiling shyly.

"How do you suppose we get out of this conversational rut?"

She cocked her head, looking thoughtful. "I think we need to practice."

"That's exactly what I was thinking."

He started to like her more when she ordered a cheeseburger and diet coke off the dollar value menu. He'd thought he had another twenty in his wallet, but it turned out to be a ten, so her kind frugality saved him a whole lot of embarrassment. They joined Dylan and Melissa at a table where they were deep in conversation. Once Dylan had discovered that Melissa's father was a retired brigadier general and that she had visited most Marine bases in the country and around the world, he was a goner.

He couldn't stop asking her questions, and Melissa was nice enough to answer them all.

And so it finally happened. He and Jennifer had a real conversation that wasn't tinged with a stuttering awkwardness. He learned that she was an only child, that both her parents were one hundred percent Korean (but not "traditional"), and that her father was a cardiologist and her mother was a dermatologist. She had traveled to Korea, Vietnam, Thailand, China, and Japan, where her father often lectured at universities. They made a trip to New York twice a year so her mother could shop, but she hated to shop. She was interested in Greenpeace and environmental issues and said she was a Democrat just to aggravate her Republican parents. Her parents wanted her to major in pre-med and go to Stanford, but she wasn't sure she wanted to do that. She didn't know anything about sports.

When he told her about himself, he couldn't help thinking that his life seemed rather paltry compared to hers, but she listened avidly. He told her about running cross-country, his family, and his interest in all things military. (He didn't tell her about the stealing, the gun accident, or not wanting to go to college. Later, he would ponder whether what he left out was more important than what he told her.)

They stayed at McDonald's for close to three hours when Melissa, with embarrassment, said she still had a 12:00 a.m. curfew and needed to get home. Nick would have liked to maybe give Jennifer a kiss on the cheek or a quick hug, but he didn't do that because the other two were there. Perhaps, next time, he and Jennifer could go to the movies alone.

"That wasn't so bad," Dylan said when they were in the van. "Melissa actually knew a lot about the Marines."

"Thanks for sticking it out, buddy. You're a good friend." Nick was feeling an emotional high from the evening. It had really gone well with Jennifer.

"No problem."

They were almost to Dylan's house when he remembered. "I need to swing by the house and get some cash. I didn't bring as much with me tonight as I thought I did, and if we go to the shooting range tomorrow, I'm going to need it."

As if he didn't hear him, Dylan said, "She was so nice that I could almost forget she was fat."

Chris opened the door, and there stood Alex. She was wearing a blue sundress and a look that came close to being defiant. She walked into the small room, which was slightly on the seedy side. He had booked this room in a small motel just off the strip because it was cheap. And it looked it. But really, what did it matter at this point? They just had to go through the motions and get this over with. He remembered when he and Sam had tried so hard to have a baby, when making love became mechanical and a means to an end. In a very strange way, this was the same thing.

"I'm here," Alex said, throwing her big purse on the nearest chair.

"I can see that."

"What do we do first?"

"I'll have to check the instruction manual," he said testily. This wasn't his fault, and she knew it.

"Sorry. I'm tense and nervous, and I know you don't want to be here any more than I do."

No, he didn't, but he at least had the courtesy not to point that out. "We're both here because we love Sam."

"Yes, we love Sam." She sat primly on the bed.

The silence stretched between them. "Should I put on some music?" He had thought about bringing a bottle of wine, but that seemed somehow too intimate, inappropriate, and it would necessitate conversation, wouldn't it? However, right now, he wouldn't mind downing a glass as fast as a fraternity boy on spring break downed a beer.

"I guess music would be okay."

Chris fiddled with the radio on the nightstand, but all he could find was a country music station laced with static. "This is the best I can do."

"It's fine. It's noise." Alex got up and rummaged in her purse. She produced two minibar bottles of Jack Daniels. She handed one to him.

"Thanks." He took it gratefully. They each upended their bottles: one long, neat shot.

Alex walked over and closed the curtains completely. Not a scrap of sunshine permeated the murky room. "Okay," she said. "I'm ready."

He wasn't. The seedy room, the scratchy sound of the radio, the shot of Jack Daniels, the circumstances. This tableau was quickly becoming an achingly bad country and western song. It was a good thing he had brought the magazines with him. Otherwise, there wouldn't be a chance of anything happening down south, and of course, there couldn't be any

help from Alex in that department. It would be just one more thing joining the inappropriate list.

"If you'll excuse me," he said, walking to the bathroom. Once inside,
he locked it, which seemed rather childish. What was Alex going to do,
barge in on him? He was behaving like a teenage boy who was afraid his
mother would find him beating off in the bathroom. He was fifty-two
years old, yet at this moment, he felt as if he were fifteen.

He opened the *Playboy* to the centerfold. Of course, she was young,
blonde, and had large silicone breasts, the stereotypical idea of every man's
fantasy. But not his. He flipped through the magazine until he found a
brunette, but she reminded him of a student he had taught last semester,
so she wasn't going to work at all. He tried *Penthouse*, but it was more of the
same. All the impossibly young women stared at him with sultry, vacant
eyes, already assuming what a man would do when he saw their ripeness.
He felt ashamed for both them and him.

Time was passing, and he was getting nowhere. He closed the magazine and pulled out a picture from the small duffel bag he had brought.
It was a picture of Sam and him on their honeymoon in South Beach. She
looked so young and beautiful in her yellow bikini, her skin tan and her
expression full of hope. He looked pale and slightly paunchy standing
next to her, and once again marveled at the fact that Sam had chosen him.
Of all the men she could have married, she had chosen him.

He stared at her face and remembered the wonderful week that they
had spent in Miami, the long walks on the beach, the romantic dinners,
making love all night. They had been so happy then, before all the problems trying to conceive, before the endless treatments and testing, before
they lost Grace. He concentrated on the idyllic time they had BEFORE.
He stroked himself until he was close to climaxing, then zipped up his
pants, and opened the bathroom door.

Alex was asleep on the bed. Just perfect. He didn't want to clamor on
top of her like some Neanderthal, but time was of the essence here. "Alex,
please wake up." He shook her shoulder.

"Oh, sorry." She was groggy, but when she saw his face, she seemed to
realize where she was. "I took a sleeping pill last night, and I guess it still—"

"We need to do this now."

"I understand." She shimmied out of her underpants but left her dress
on. She averted her face.

He didn't look at her as he climbed on top, lifted her dress the minimum amount necessary, and unzipped his pants. He closed his eyes.

It was over in less than a minute.

He zipped up his pants and got quickly out of bed, still not looking at her. "You can use the bathroom first."

She grabbed her panties and went into the bathroom. He went to the curtains and opened them completely, letting the sunshine in. Even though it had just happened, and he was practically still in the moment, it was already starting to feel like a dream. They had specifically followed Sam's plan, and it was now over. Of course he knew that the chances of Alex getting pregnant were slim to none, and he had certainly told Sam that enough times, but as usual, she didn't want to listen. He would cross that bridge when they came to it, and then, maybe, Sam would realize that they weren't meant to have another baby. Maybe Sam could finally find some peace of mind about the loss of Grace.

Alex came out of the bathroom. She picked up her purse and stood uncertainly by the door. "I guess I better get going."

"Yes, I'm going to check out of here immediately."

She looked around the room, really noticing her surroundings for the first time. "This place is really a dump, yet somehow, it was entirely . . . appropriate."

"Appropriate, yes." He smiled at her for the first time.

She smiled back. "I don't know about you, but I feel relieved."

He did feel relieved, a tremendous amount of relief that it was over. "We played our parts," he said.

"Our parts," she echoed, nodding. "Yes, we did." She gave him a small wave as she went out the door.

Sam didn't feel relaxed after her massage. She felt rejuvenated, energized, and hopeful. As the masseuse pummeled the tight muscles in her neck, Sam concluded that everything was going to be all right. She only needed to talk to Alex, to reassure her that she was doing the right thing. She had no doubts about Chris, none at all, but Alex had been resisting her. She could understand the resistance; of course she could. She knew, if she fully admitted it to herself, that she would feel the same—doubtful, apprehensive, worried—if she were in Alex's position. However, Alex had promised her, and when she and Alex made a promise to each other, they kept it. Always.

Sam's phone was fully charged now, and she had tried to call Alex twice and texted her three times. Alex hadn't responded, and Sam certainly didn't want to annoy her any more than she had already. She had already pushed her sister to the edge. She knew that, too, but she couldn't help herself. She so desperately wanted this baby. This baby would make her world whole again. This baby would keep her from going crazy. This baby would make her happy.

She was out of cigarettes. She had been smoking way too much, but didn't everyone smoke too much, drink too much, and just in general *excess* in Vegas? She went into the gift shop to buy a pack. As she was paying, she heard the unmistakable sound of her sister's voice. She would know it anywhere. It came from the back of the store, so that's where she went.

"Love you, too," Alex said as she ended the call, "but you still have a curfew, even if I'm not there, Annie." She put the phone back into her purse and saw Sam. "That daughter of mine is going to turn my hair snow white before the end of the year."

Sam gave an inward sigh of relief. So, Alex was speaking to her. Everything was going to be all right. "Teenage girls keep Clairol in business."

"I suppose so." Alex sorted through the souvenir t-shirts.

Sam decided to get right to the point, but her voice was tentative. "Do you want to talk about last night?"

"Nope." She held up a t-shirt. "Do you think this is tacky?"

"That's horrible. Only a gaudy old woman would wear that one."

Unfortunately, a grey-haired woman down the aisle from them was wearing an identical flamingo patterned t-shirt. She glared at Sam.

"I'm sorry. I didn't mean you," Sam said to her.

Alex tried to stifle her laughter. "You have a big mouth, sister."

"Don't I know it." Alex held up another t-shirt, and Sam shook her head. Alex seemed more relaxed than she had been lately. She was even smiling. "So, what did you do today?" she asked conversationally.

"I had sex with your husband," she said.

Sam felt as if she'd been slapped. Alex was nonchalant, dismissive. "Excuse me?"

"I said, I had sex with your husband."

"But you were supposed to do it tonight." Sam was trying to grasp the situation. She should be ecstatic, swinging from the rafters with happiness, but she wasn't.

"I know, but that obviously wasn't working. Chris thought it would be better if we met at a different place, a kind of neutral territory."

"So you got a motel room?" That made it so much worse. If they had sex in her room, and she knew what was going on, that was one thing. But sneaking off to a different motel made the whole thing so tawdry, like it was an actual affair.

"That's right. The deed is done."

Again, Alex's tone was so dismissive, and Sam, who knew her so well, couldn't tell what was going on here. Maybe Alex was thoroughly angry with her. She asked, "Are you mad at me?"

"Not anymore. I feel like a huge weight has been lifted from my shoulders. Maybe I'm just shell-shocked after the emotional roller coaster we've been on the last couple of months. Who knows?"

"I don't know what to say." It was probably the only time in her life she had been rendered speechless.

"I thought you'd be thrilled," Alex said. She picked up the two t-shirts she had selected.

"I am. I am. I'm just a little taken aback."

"Not everything can be in your control, Sam." Alex started towards the register.

Sam followed. "I know that."

"No, you don't, but you need to learn it."

"So, you really did it?" It was starting to sink in. All the months of longing were over. She didn't like it at all that they had changed the venue on her, but she refused to let herself dwell on that aspect. There might be, at this very second, a baby on the way.

"Mission accomplished." Alex paid for the t-shirts. "Let's go get a drink."

Jack sat in the bar, still in his sweaty golf clothes. He was on his second Bud Light but was thinking of switching to scotch the next time he ordered. And he would order another. And he would get drunk the second night in a row. He hated this place, and he hated the reason why they were here.

He had been proud of himself for not once going to the tables or a slot machine, despite the mounting panic he was feeling. Maybe, he thought, he didn't have a gambling problem. He was in Las Vegas, the gambling capital of the world, and he hadn't bet a dime.

When the complimentary golf pass arrived, he knew it was just what he needed: fresh air and physical activity. Granted, it was odd that he, a nobody, would get a free pass to a prestigious golf course, but he didn't care to question it. He got teamed up with three other guys about his age, and after the first two holes, he knew he was a better player than all of them. When one of them, Frank, suggested a "friendly wager," Jack had been all in. Surprise, surprise. All three of them turned out to be 8 handicappers, and he got his ass whipped. It was such a transparent set-up that he should have seen it coming. It was such a well-known scam that it had become a stereotype. The stereotypical scam had duped him out of five hundred dollars.

Jack raked his fingers through his hair. He had dug his family into a deep financial hole. They were upside down in their house, their savings were on the verge of depletion, he couldn't get a personal loan, and the thought of declaring bankruptcy was unthinkable. They would lose their house, and Alex and the kids would be mortified. He wouldn't be surprised, too, if declaring bankruptcy would cost him his job. The rarefied world of SCDS would not condone a faculty member with such a publicly messy financial record.

And so he had let his wife prostitute herself to make money. He was the only one of the four who thought of the whole business as *prostitution*. Alex thought of it as *adultery*, but it was adultery aimed toward a greater good—a bundle of joy for her twin sister. Hell, in his opinion, Sam, and especially Chris, were too old to start a family. He knew it was a common occurrence these days. Many of his kids at SCDS had older parents, but the fact was that Chris would be around seventy before this hypothetical kid graduated from high school. That was too damn old.

He hoped Alex wouldn't get pregnant, and chances were good that she wouldn't, but then again, who knew how fertile she was? He had had a vasectomy years before, after Annie was born and they both decided that their family was perfect with two children, a boy and a girl. He wouldn't, couldn't think of Alex being pregnant, blowing up in front of his eyes, carrying another man's child. Hadn't anyone else thought through the details of this detestable plan? Conversely, though, if Alex didn't get pregnant, they wouldn't get the money. It was a lose/lose situation for him.

"I'll take a scotch," he said to the bartender. He helped himself to the trail mix on the small saucer on the bar. He had difficulty swallowing the dry mixture. He hadn't had anything to eat since breakfast, but he wasn't hungry.

He shouldn't be spending money, drinking at this bar, but at this point, did it really matter? He couldn't face the possibility of going up to his room and watching Alex get dressed. It had almost killed him last night, and truly, his heart had hammered so hard that he thought he might be having a heart attack. He was going to take this night one drink at a time.

"I thought I might find you here." Sam slid onto the stool beside him.

God help him. She was the last person he wanted to see tonight. He stared into the mirror behind the bar at the woman who looked so much like his own wife, but who was so much less kind, less thoughtful, *less nice.*

"Buy me a drink?" she asked.

"No, I can barely afford my own."

"Okay, then, I'll buy you a drink."

That would solve the problem of how he could afford to get drunk tonight. "I'll take you up on that." He downed his first scotch and ordered another.

Sam ordered a glass of white wine and lit a cigarette. "How're you holding up?"

He felt the flush of anger rising up his neck. "How the hell do you think I'm holding up? My wife is getting ready to fuck your husband—all because of you—and I'm drinking myself into oblivion. What does that tell you?"

"You're angry."

"And you're a genius." He fervently wished she would go away before he said or did anything that he would regret, before he called her a raging bitch or punched her in the face. The violence she could inspire in him right now was frightening, and it was a fury directed towards both her and him. Why had he even thought this plan was feasible? Why was he going to allow his wife to sleep with another man? Oh yeah. The fucking money.

Sam didn't say anything.

"And would you move that fucking ashtray to your other side? The smoke is blowing right in my face."

Sam moved the ashtray. "Do you want me to apologize? I've been doing a lot of that lately."

"Don't do me any favors." He finished his drink and ordered another. "This is still on your tab."

"It seems like the least I can do."

She wasn't behaving normally. Even Jack, in his agitated state, could see that. "Are you having second thoughts as you sit here commiserating with the other spouse who isn't getting ready to procreate?" He said it meanly, wanting to hurt her.

She flinched. "No, I'm not having second thoughts. It's too late for that."

Suddenly, Jack knew what he was going to do. "You know what? I don't think it's too late. I should never have let this go so far. It's *insane*. I'm going upstairs right now to get my wife and take her home." He stood up, and his head spun. He had had a lot to drink in a very short period of time.

"Sit back down, Jack." Sam gently tugged on his arm.

He did, but only because he needed to gather his wits about him before he marched upstairs and took Alex home where she belonged, with him.

"It *is* too late, Jack. Alex and Chris did it this afternoon while you were golfing and I was getting a massage. It's done."

"It's done," he repeated. He felt like someone had kicked a soccer ball hard into his chest. He was having trouble breathing. While he had been on the golf course, his wife had been with Chris. All along, he realized, he had secretly thought that Alex wouldn't go through with this, that she would see that it was an idiotic plan concocted by her crazy twin sister. He knew she loved Sam deeply, but he had truly thought that she loved him more. He had been wrong.

"If it makes you feel any better, I'm not feeling all that great right now either. They actually rented a motel—"

"Will you shut up!" he yelled. The people at the bar stopped talking and stared.

"Don't make a scene," she said.

He forced himself to lower his voice. "I'll make a huge fucking scene if you don't get out of here right now. I mean it, Sam. I've had enough. I don't want to talk to you, listen to you, or even see you. Get out."

Without a word, she pulled out two twenties from her billfold and left them on the table. She might have whispered *sorry* on the way out, but knowing Sam, probably not.

Jack waited a few minutes, ensuring that Sam didn't come back. She had left enough money for him to afford another drink. He ordered it, but even that was not enough to keep him from drowning in the waves of fury, shame, and sadness that washed over him. When Alex found him, he had his elbows propped up on the bar, his face in his hands. He was mourning for everything he had lost.

Annie was on her knees, trying to get the bloodstains out of the carpet with a wet rag and a can of Spot Shot when Nick and Dylan walked in the front door.

"Whoa, dude!" Dylan said.

"What happened here?" Nick said, then with a rising panic he called, "Annie, are you all right?"

"Do you think we should call the cops?" Dylan crunched on a shard of glass with his boot.

"Don't call the cops," Annie said, getting to her feet. "I'm in the family room."

Nick and Dylan walked in and surveyed the broken glass strewn throughout the room, the overturned furniture, the blood, and Annie with her tear-stained face and the Madonna wig askew on her head.

"Annie, are you okay?" Nick asked again. "Do I need to call an ambulance? Did someone break in here?"

"Is he still here?" Dylan asked, excited. "I wish I had a gun, but I bet Nick and I could take him with a couple of kitchen knives."

"No one broke in here." Annie fought back tears. Despite herself, she was touched that Nick showed so much concern for her. After the events of this awful night, someone was being nice to her. But it didn't last long. Nick, the Boy Scout, suddenly realized what must have happened.

"You had a party," he said, all sympathy gone. "What an idiotic thing to do. Those stupid rich kids don't have a clue how much it costs to clean up the houses they trash. Haven't you heard those stories, Annie? All the guys brag about what they've done on the weekends on Monday morning, and next Monday, they're going to be bragging about trashing *our* house. You know Dad will hear about this."

Annie had thought about that but then dismissed the idea. No one was going to be bragging about coming to her and Carla's loser party. All the snobs were probably too embarrassed to mention that they had briefly stopped by the Carissa house. It had been boring, and she and Carla, in their matching wigs, were only an oddball footnote in their Saturday night. "No one's going to be talking about this," she said.

"Of course they will. I'm surprised Amanda Williams didn't call the cops. It must have been pretty loud. You are such an idiot."

The tears came then. "It wasn't like that."

"Lay off her, dude," Dylan said. "She's crying."

"We only invited ten people, and they only stayed an hour." She couldn't bring herself to tell Nick that they thought her party was a joke. As she was cleaning the bloodstains, trying to get them out before they set, she had been mulling over what Carla had said before she went ballistic. Why did the two of them keep setting themselves up for this shit? They were *never* going to fit in. And Annie didn't want to try anymore.

Nick picked up a piece of broken bottle. "I don't get it. It looks like a tornado went through here."

"It was Carla." Annie had seen a few of Carla's tantrums before, but she hadn't ever seen one like tonight: Carla breaking every bottle, splattering the walls with sticky booze, Carla overturning furniture and pulling at her hair in anger and frustration, Carla picking up a shard of glass and running it over her wrist. It had taken all the strength Annie had to calm her down, find her meds in her purse, and practically carry her up to bed. She had been passed out for a couple of hours now.

"Carla did all this? I knew she was a little nuts, but this looks like major crazy."

"Don't try to set me up with her next, dude. I'd rather have a fat one than a crazy one." Dylan gave a low whistle as he surveyed the mess.

"She's not crazy." Annie would always defend Carla, but it was getting harder. "She just had a bad night."

"That's the understatement of the year."

"And what does Dylan mean by—"

"Nothing," Nick said quickly.

Her brother was up to something, and normally, she would try to pry the information out of him. But not tonight. She had a long night of cleaning ahead of her, and she was already exhausted. The only thing keeping her going was to focus on her anger. Carla had been right about that, too. The kids at SCDS were *revolting* human beings.

Nick went to the hall closet and got a broom and a dustpan.

"Where's your vacuum?" Dylan asked.

"You guys are actually going to help me?" She'd be grateful to them forever if they helped. Well, she would probably be grateful until the next time they insisted on watching the stupid military channel when she wanted to watch *The Bachelor.*

"Yeah, we'll help," Nick said, starting to sweep.

Annie wondered if there was a trick involved. "So, are you going to help me and then tell Mom and Dad?" At this point, with her frayed emotions, she didn't care so much.

"I should tell them. You're only fifteen, and you had a drinking party. There are so many things that could go wrong in that scenario."

"I know." But the last thing she had expected was Carla to cause a problem. She understood where Carla was coming from, of course, but still. It was her house Carla had trashed. She knew Carla would apologize profusely in the morning and then try to give her money. She would refuse, Carla would insist, and then she would take it and everything would be squared up in Carla's mind. Annie had gotten used to this arrangement.

"But I'm not going to tell them. This one was mostly Carla's fault."

"Do you promise?"

"I'm pretty good at keeping your secrets." Nick looked up from the section of tile he was sweeping.

It was true. He hadn't said another word about the state he found her in on the cruise, nor had he questioned how she got there. She was trying her best to forget the little she remembered about that night, but every so often, a flicker of a memory—a comment made by Adam, or a grey-tinged image of one of the other two—might appear. It would have been so much worse if her brother hadn't found her. And once again, he was helping her out, cleaning up after another mess.

It was another disaster diverted, wasn't it?

She felt a little choked up, so she just nodded at him.

Nick went back to work with the broom. "You need to get to work on those stains, Annie."

6

CHAPTER SIX

Alex already knew. She had known when she woke up that morning, and it wasn't because her period was two days late. That had happened many times before. No, it was a feeling in her gut, a deep-seated knowledge within herself that she remembered from her pregnancies with Nick and Annie. So really, peeing on the EPT stick was just a formality.

"What's taking you so long?" Sam called from the other side of the bathroom door. She had come over with the test as soon as Alex telephoned her.

"I didn't know you were going to come running over here armed with a pregnancy test when I called. I had just gone to the bathroom."

"Turn on the faucet. The sound of running water always made you pee when you were a kid. Remember that trip to Niagara Falls? You peed your pants." Sam was talking fast. She was excited.

"I was eight," Alex said, but she got up from the toilet and turned on the water. The old trick still worked. She trickled on the stick. She hurriedly washed her hands and opened the door.

"Are you?" Sam asked.

"You read the directions with me, Sam. With this digital one, we wait three minutes before it says "pregnant" or "not pregnant.""

"Three minutes!" Sam made it sound like a lifetime.

"They've come a long way with these tests since the last time I took one." Or since the first time she took one, back in college. She and Sam had had to wait for fifteen minutes, or was it twenty? It was the only other time Sam had been present when Alex was waiting to see whether she was pregnant, which was probably why this scenario had a sense of *déjà vu* about it. But this time, the important difference was that Alex fervently wanted a positive reading. As they had all agreed, this was the only chance they were going to take, the *one shot*, as Jack had grudgingly, angrily said on the way home from Vegas. He hadn't talked about it since.

Alex sat down on the edge of the bed, the stick in her hand. Sam sat close beside her, their legs touching. They stared intently at the stick.

"This is a fucking long three minutes," Sam said.

And then it appeared clearly: *pregnant*.

"You're not going to be allowed to swear around the baby." Alex stared at the stick until tears clouded her vision. She had known she was pregnant, but she still couldn't believe it.

"Thank you, God!" And then Sam jumped off the bed, laughing and crying at the same time. "You are my hero, Alex, my wonderful sister." She pulled Alex from the bed, and they jumped up and down like they did when they were small and excited by the prospect of birthday or Christmas presents.

When they finally calmed down a little, they made their way down to the kitchen, and Alex poured them each a cup of coffee. Sam stared at it dubiously. "It's decaf," Alex said. "I had a feeling."

"Once again, I'm going to tell you how wonderful I think you are. Thank you for putting up with me these last months. I know I've been awful. Even Chris, who professes his undying admiration for me, was pushed to the edge."

"You've been something of a bitch." Alex smiled at her over the rim of her coffee cup.

"Language." Sam smiled a huge smile. All trace of the tenseness that had surrounded her had disappeared. "You'll be around the baby a lot, too, you know."

Alex didn't want to spoil the euphoric mood, but she felt that she had to bring it up. "This is marvelous, sweetheart, but you know that we're not in the clear until the three-month mark."

"Believe me, I know that."

Alex felt a stab. She had been thoughtless to say that after all of Sam's miscarriages, but still, they needed to face reality. She was a forty-year-old woman, after all.

"And we have to get through the amniocentesis, too, but I have such a good feeling about this. I really do. Everything is going to be perfect. I just know it." Sam's face was bright with conviction.

Alex chose to believe her. She was healthy, and she didn't have a history of miscarriages. In fact, she rarely caught colds. "To the baby." They clinked cups.

"I'm going to be with you every step of the way for the next nine months."

"I'm pregnant, Sam. I'm not in some kind of rehabilitation program." Alex laughed.

"We should start an exercise program."

"We both hate to exercise."

"I know, but we could start walking through the neighborhood in the mornings like a lot of the women in this neighborhood do."

"You make fun of those women with their spandex shorts and tiny dumbbells. What do you call them—the fickle, fricking brigade? You've said you've wanted to mow them down with your car."

"I know, but I'm changing my ways. I'm going to stop smoking, stop drinking, eat only healthy, non-processed foods, and exercise. In short, I'm going to be pregnant with you."

"Except for the fact that you won't gain weight, get stretch marks, or have heartburn."

"If I could, we wouldn't be in this situation."

Once again, Alex felt as if she had put her foot in her mouth. During the time Sam had been going through her fertility problems, Nick and Annie had been small, and they hadn't been able to see each other as much as they liked. Alex still felt guilty about the flights she hadn't taken (and couldn't afford), the trips to the emergency room that she hadn't gone to, her sister's hand that she hadn't held when she was going through all that pain. It was a big part of the reason that she, as Jack put it, let Sam "run all over her." She didn't see it that way. To her, she was now making up for all the times she had been absent in Sam's life when Sam needed her most.

The huge smile had returned to Sam's face. "This is a miracle, Alex. It really is."

"I know." Against daunting odds, they had become pregnant.

Sam's eyes gleamed. "Do you think it's too early to start thinking about names?"

Alex laughed. "Since we've only known we were pregnant for ten minutes, that might be jumping the gun a bit."

"We're pregnant," Sam said with wonder.

"We're pregnant." Alex nodded her head. She wasn't going to point out once more that there were still a lot of risks involved. She would let Sam relish this moment. She put her hand on her flat stomach. She would do everything in her power to nurture this miracle.

Jack stared across the desk at his son. His easygoing Nick sat with his arms crossed and his jaw clenched. "Excuse me?"

"It's not like this is headline news, Dad. I told you on the cruise that I don't want to go to college. I want to join the Marines."

"And I believe I told you that joining the Marines is not an option." Nick was the only senior who had not signed up for a single counseling session. This morning at breakfast Jack had told him to be in his office at ten o'clock. Period. He had thought this whole fantasy Marine phase would be over with by now. The school year was only one month old, but college choices and applications were the main topics among seniors in this school. At SCDS, everyone—one hundred percent—went to college. It was a college prep school, for god's sake.

"I don't understand why it's not an option," Nick said stubbornly.

Jack took a deep breath, trying to calm himself. "I'll tell you why. To get ahead in this country, and especially in this economy, you need a college degree. Look," he pointed at the open folder in front of him, "your grades are decent, and you scored well on the SAT. You could get into a number of good schools."

"I know you want me to go to U of A, and I know you want me to get a track scholarship, but I'm telling you, I don't want to do it." Nick started to gather his backpack.

That was exactly what Jack wanted. "Sit back down."

Nick slumped back into the chair.

"Your foot is healed now, and even though you're missing this season, you could start training again. I'll run with you. I know it's been hard on you not being a part of the team."

"Running cross-country has nothing to do with this." Nick's ears were growing red.

"Then forget about the scholarship. Your mom and I will be able to swing the tuition." Jack didn't know how, but they would thrash out that problem when they came to it.

"You're not listening to me."

"I am listening. I just disagree with you." It was his job to get these kids into colleges, and he'd be damned if his son was the one student in the history of SCDS that didn't go.

"I know what I want." The flush was spreading down Nick's neck and across his cheekbones.

He looked so young to Jack. "You're only seventeen, Nick," he said as gently as he could.

Nick tried to keep his gaze steady, but he was blinking rapidly. "I'll be eighteen when I graduate."

As if his own father didn't know that? These kids, so technologically savvy, were still awfully naïve. "There's a war on, Nick. Your mom and I don't want you over in Iraq or Afghanistan. We love you very much, and we can't stand the thought of you putting yourself in harm's way." Jack refused to allow himself to envision Nick in a combat zone or driving a Hummer over a land mine. He refused.

"I want to fight for my country, Dad. Most people think that's noble. It's not like when you were growing up, and everyone was against the Vietnam War."

Despite himself, Jack almost smiled. "I was five when the war ended, son. It's not like I was out protesting."

"Whatever. You get my point."

"Actually, I don't. I think that's the topic of this conversation."

Nick finally broke the gaze and looked out the window, his arms still folded, still defensive.

Jack tried another approach. "You could go into the military after college. Then you could go in as an officer instead of a private." In four years, Jack was certain, this fantasy would be over.

Nick turned back from the window. Earnestly, he said, "But the war might be over by then. One of the guys running for president is already talking about withdrawing the troops from Iraq."

"And you don't think that's a good thing?"

"It's a good thing if we're . . . winning," Nick faltered.

"You don't have any idea what war is like, Nick."

"Yes, I do. Dylan and I watch the military channel all the time."

"I didn't serve in the military, Nick, but I know this: War is not glamorous, and it's not a game. And unlike the programs you see on TV, it's not edited for content."

"I've got to go now," Nick said as he stood.

"We're not done here."

"I've got a history test next period. Do you want me to miss it?"

Jack looked at his watch. The next class would be starting in five minutes. "No, go ahead."

Nick walked quickly to the door. All traces of his limp had vanished, Jack was glad to notice.

"I'll tell you what. We'll get on the computer tonight and look at the campus, okay?" U of A had a beautiful campus, and after showing Nick that, he could segue into the application process.

"I've got to work tonight."

"Tomorrow, then," he said, but Nick was already out the door.

Jack was still thinking about the conversation when his phone rang. He had to dig under the sheets of Nick's transcript and SAT scores to find it. "Hello?"

"We're pregnant," Alex shouted.

For a brief, blessed second, he had no idea what she was talking about. They were going to have a baby? That brief, blessed second didn't last long enough.

"Sam is over the moon, as you can imagine." Alex, too, was obviously excited.

"Sam belongs on the moon," he said. His heart felt like a rock. In the last couple of weeks, he had convinced himself that Alex would not be pregnant and that everyone would forget about Vegas. That had been his fantasy.

"Stop it," Alex giggled. "What time are you going to be home tonight? We can celebrate with a glass of milk."

"I'll be late. I'm going to the board meeting," Jack lied.

"I'll wait up."

"Don't bother, honey. I've got to go now." He hung up. There wasn't a board meeting, but he was going to avoid going home for as long as possible. He did not want to celebrate this pregnancy with a glass of milk.

No, he'd stop at Cochran's pub, where he ran a tab, and celebrate the end of his fantasy with a few scotches.

"So your mom's knocked up, huh?" Carla languished against the pink leather headboard of her Princess bed, a bottle of vodka in one hand, a cigarette in the other.

"So she says." Annie took a sip of her own drink. It was three o'clock in the afternoon on a Saturday, and they were both already well on their way to getting smashed. They had tried sitting out by the pool, but even though it was the beginning of October, it was still well over a hundred degrees, so they had decided to skip the tanning and get drunk. Well, to be more accurate, Carla had made this their afternoon goal, and Annie had agreed. Carla had been drinking even more heavily since their disastrous party. They both had.

Annie was on the floor, leaning against the side of the bed. She took another drink. "It's creepy, isn't it? I'm almost sixteen, and I'm going to have to watch my mother blow up like a beach ball. It seems unnatural somehow." What she really thought was that it was gross. She knew her mother had done IVF—not technically sex—but it was still *gross.*

"I don't know." Carla flicked her cigarette in the general vicinity of the ashtray on her nightstand, not noticing, or not caring, that she missed it entirely. "I actually like kids, believe it or not. I always wanted to have a brother or a sister, but Ron and Marge only wanted to adopt one: ME. Lucky, wasn't I?"

"This kid will be my niece or nephew, not my brother or sister—at least I think that's right." The whole identical twin DNA thing made it a cloudy issue to Annie.

"Ron and Marge wouldn't even let me get a puppy," Carla went on as if she hadn't heard Annie. "They let me have a goldfish, which is not exactly a child's idea of a warm and fuzzy pet. The damn thing was so tedious; it just swam around and around this tiny plastic palm tree that I planted in some rocks at the bottom of the bowl. I was bored in twenty minutes, but it took him two days to *die* of boredom."

Annie thought it was a good idea to change the subject. She didn't want to contribute her hamster story into this conversation. She had really loved Speedy, even though the wood shavings at the bottom of the animal's cage had given her a fungal infection under her right thumbnail, which eventually fell off. And she didn't want to tell Carla about the nice funeral service her mother had planned for the hapless hamster, complete with a lovely eulogy that had made them all cry. And she wouldn't tell Carla that they had then all gone to Peter Piper Pizza, her favorite place, and had pepperoni pizza and played arcade games. That kind of story made Carla sad, angry, or both, which was the worst.

She got up off the floor and settled in next to Carla. "What happened with the surveillance cameras? You were going to tell me yesterday, but then you forgot."

"I didn't forget. It's a tedious story."

This was obviously Carla's word of the day: *tedious.* "Tell me anyway."

Carla sighed dramatically as she lit a fresh cigarette off the smoldering butt of the first. "It's not even really a story. I threw a fit, saying the parental unit didn't trust me, that they must not love me if they were going to have professionals spy on me, yada yada yada." She snapped her fingers. "So they took the cameras down, just like that. No arguments, no fuss, no nothing."

"Well, that's a good thing, isn't it?"

"They were in a hurry. They had to catch a plane to Thailand, or Taiwan, or something."

"So you won, right?" It looked to Annie like Carla's eyes were starting to fill.

"I guess so, but here's the weird thing. I was kind of disappointed that they gave into me so easily. I didn't want the fucking cameras around, but then again, it seems that if they really cared about me, they would have kept them up—saved me from myself, you know what I mean?"

"Sure," Annie said uncertainly. Even when the cameras had been up, Carla had done the same things she always did, drinking, smoking, dabbling in drugs. She had even told Annie that it had been more exciting because it forced her to be more creative.

Carla gave her a hard look. "You don't have a fucking clue what I'm talking about."

"Yes, I do."

"No, you really don't. You have this *Pollyanna life* with the perfect nuclear family, so you don't know what I'm talking about." Carla's voice was growing louder.

Annie felt her face grow hot. Why was Carla getting angry at her? What had she done? "You know I don't have a perfect life. My parents are clueless, and my brother is a fucking nerd." She felt a pang as she said this. Carla was forcing her to denigrate her family in her own defense. She sometimes felt that about her family, but not all the time.

"Oh, grow up, Annie. You can be so simple at times."

Annie got off the bed. This was their first fight, and she didn't know if she was more mad or more hurt. "I don't deserve this, Carla Goldleib, and I don't know why you're attacking me. Who do you think you are that you can treat me, your best friend, like this?"

Surprisingly, Carla backed off. "I'm a nobody, and you're not only my best friend, but you're also my *only* friend."

"You shouldn't talk to me like that."

"I know. It's the vodka talking. I really should go back to gin." She smiled wanly. "I truly am sorry."

It was becoming a daily occurrence, Carla's frightening mood swings. Still, Annie loved her like a sister and couldn't stay mad at her. Like Carla had said, they were best friends and the *only* friends each other had. "It's okay."

"No, I was a bitch. Let's have another drink, but I'm switching to gin. Let's go down to the well-stocked bar, the only thing in this house that my parents know how to nurture."

Annie followed her downstairs to the granite bar in the family room. "It looks like a liquor store in here," she said as she gazed at the rows of bottles standing behind the glass-fronted cabinets. "Isn't there more alcohol here than there used to be?"

"Yeah, my parents just had a giant party a couple of weeks ago. Didn't I tell you about it? They had all sorts of bigwigs here. Visiting dignitaries and that sort of crowd. I could have sworn I told you about it."

"No, you didn't." It seemed odd that Carla would forget to mention something like a party.

"Yeah, the parental unit paraded me out for about an hour and told me I could have a glass of champagne. Little did they know what I had already consumed upstairs."

She giggled as she poured them hefty glasses of gin and tonic.

Annie looked around the opulent room, once again struck by the artwork and the ornate furniture. "What, exactly, does your dad do for a living?"

"I'm not sure. I think it has something to do with the import/export business. He's never really told me, and I've never asked."

Annie thought it was strange that Carla didn't know what her own father did, and she told her this.

"Why? What does it matter? He obviously makes a ton of money, and he's not in jail, so I'm assuming it's legal. Now, Marge, she's another story. I know what she does. She's a Stepford wife, following Ron wherever he goes, and of course, her number one job requirement is that she always looks perfect. The woman has had so much plastic surgery that she can barely stretch her face into a smile. You've met them, haven't you?"

Annie nodded. "Once, briefly, in passing. They were on their way somewhere." She remembered a tall, striking couple. Mr. Goldleib had handed Carla a credit card and an envelope full of money "for emergencies." She and Carla had gone to the mall as soon as the Goldleibs' car turned out of the driveway.

"Then you know all there is to know about them. They're always *in passing.*" Carla flopped down on the overstuffed couch. "This is so *tedious.* Even drinking is getting tedious."

Annie's stomach rumbled. It was getting close to four, and they hadn't eaten lunch yet. "Aren't you getting hungry, Carla?"

"No. I'm not eating."

Annie wasn't going to point out yet again that Carla was alarmingly thin. She knew it wouldn't do any good. "Do you mind if I go upstairs and get something to eat?"

"Suit yourself."

Annie went upstairs and into the pantry. As usual, it was loaded with food. She grabbed a bag of Doritos (the authentic chips, not the generic, tasteless chip her mother bought) and a box of granola bars and took them downstairs. Maybe she could entice Carla to eat something.

"We need to find something exciting to do," Carla said. She hadn't moved from the couch.

"We could watch a movie." Annie tore open the chips. She offered the bag to Carla, but she shook her head.

"That's not very exciting. I bet the popular kids don't sit around watching movies on a Saturday evening."

"Some of them might."

Carla frowned at her over her glass as she finished her gin and tonic. "I guess we're not authorities on what popular kids do."

She was right. They didn't know.

"I have an idea." Carla sat up. "Sometimes, when I'm bored, I go into Marge's closet and try on her clothes and shoes. She's got everything in there—Chanel suits, Jimmy Choo shoes, the works."

"I don't want to do that."

"Why not?"

If Annie remembered correctly, Mrs. Goldleib was also incredibly thin. Although Annie was, as her mother told her, *a normal size*, she didn't want to risk the humiliation of not fitting into a Chanel suit, even though she had no idea what that was. "I don't think her clothes would fit me."

Carla looked her over. "You might be right, but that's not the point. I always manage to *accidentally* tear off a button or put a small stain on the hem of a skirt. Marge can never figure out what happened. That's the fun part."

Carla walked to the bar and poured herself another drink. Suddenly, she was animated. "I have an idea. We could take a road trip!"

"Now?" Carla was in no condition to drive, even if she thought she could.

"Why not? We could go to San Diego, sit on the beach, try to hook up with some surfer guys." Carla paced excitedly.

Annie stated what should have been as clear as glass to Carla. "We've been drinking."

Carla went on, caught up in her own idea. "I have a credit card. We could get a nice hotel on the beach. Hell, if we really like it there, we don't need to come back!"

Annie choked on a chip. "Are you talking about *running away*?" This was outlandish, even for Carla.

"I hadn't thought about it in those terms, but yes, I guess that's what it is. We could run away!" She spoke rapidly, and her pacing became more frantic.

"I have to babysit tomorrow afternoon." It was such a loser thing to say, but she couldn't think of anything else.

"So what? Running away means relinquishing your responsibilities, doesn't it?"

"I suppose so." As usual, Carla was moving way too fast for her. In all the times she had been unhappy at home or at school, and there were *many*, Annie had never even considered running away. She had always thought of it as a rather cowardly thing to do, but Carla would probably see it as Annie's lack of vision.

"Really, Annie, what do we have here? We hate school, our parents are ineffectual, we don't have any friends—except for each other—and we don't have boyfriends." Carla's voice rose to a crescendo. *"We don't have boyfriends!"*

Carla triumphantly stating that glaring fact didn't make it any easier to bear. "But Walter—"

"Walter isn't your boyfriend," Carla interrupted. "He barely acknowledges your existence." She saw the stricken look on Annie's face. "Sorry, honey, but it's true."

Hurt, Annie said, with as much disdain as she could muster, "You can't be serious."

"Oh, but I am." Carla started to twirl, sloshing her drink all over the tiled floor. "We have nothing to stay here for, nothing to come back to. We should run away. I'm dead serious."

She was trying so hard not to annoy Alex, but she hadn't done a very good job in the two weeks since they discovered they were pregnant. She had bought her a cookbook, *Healthy Recipes for the Mom to Be*, which Alex had placed on her counter without even looking through it. "I know what I'm supposed to be eating, Sam," she said. "I don't think things have changed that much since the last time I was pregnant." She had knocked on Alex's door early one morning, ready for a brisk walk around the neighborhood. When she had finally persuaded Alex to join her, they made it one block before Alex vomited on the sidewalk. Sam took her home, put her to bed, and offered her saltines and ginger ale, but even that seemed to annoy Alex. "Just go home, Sam. I'll feel more sociable when I get past this morning sickness."

Obviously, it was her fault that Alex felt sick as a dog, and obviously, she could understand why Alex didn't want to be around her right now. What wasn't obvious to Alex was how fervently Sam wished she were in her place right now, nausea and all, which is why she was overcompensating, which is why she had become such an annoyance. When she tried to explain all this to Chris, his uncharacteristic answer was: "You're really not being any more annoying than usual."

Her first instinct was to run across the street and tell Alex what Chris had said, hoping it would make her laugh. But she couldn't do that. She was going to be strong for Alex any way that Alex wanted, and right now, Alex wanted her privacy. Sam looked at the clock on the wall of her office. It was Monday morning, and it had been twenty-three hours since she had seen her sister. She missed her.

Yesterday morning, restless, she had gone for a drive. Aimlessly, she ended up on Lincoln Avenue and passed by a row of churches: Methodist, Unitarian, Presbyterian, Valley Christian. On a whim, she braked and turned into the parking lot of Valley Christian, even though the last time she had been in a church was for Grace's funeral, or so she was told. She didn't remember it at all. In fact, during that time entire months were blocked out; she had no memory of going through day after day. She sat in her car and watched the families go in, all casually dressed, many with bibles in their hands. She wanted to go in and be a part of that congregation, but she had a deep-seated feeling that she wasn't *worthy*. Who was she to pretend to be a devout Christian among these people? Instead, she bowed her head, said her thanks to God as best she could, and drove away.

Instead of working on the article for *Arizona Magazine,* she got up and went to the window and looked across the street at Alex's house. The house was quiet. Jack and the kids had left for school about an hour ago. Sam wondered what Alex was doing. Was she still in bed? Did she feel better? She wanted to go over there so much that it was a physical ache in the center of her chest. But she wouldn't allow herself to go, not yet.

Sam went back to her computer, but she was still not able to concentrate. She read the news, went to a couple of celebrity gossip sites (Brad and Angelina had how many children now?), and ended up on Overstock. com. The site had an amazing array of baby products, so many new ones since she had last shopped for a baby. Before the morning was out, she had purchased many items. Some of them had especially lovely names: Cherry Elite Oval Bassinet with White Eyelet Bedding ($132.99), Fisher-Price Zen Collection Cradle Swing ($140.59), Eddie Bauer Complete Care

Play Yard in Michelle ($129.99), and Disney Music and Lights Walker in Happily Ever After ($47.03). Sam especially liked the name of the walker for its promise of *happily ever after.*

Sam microwaved a Lean Cuisine for lunch, and after she ate it, out of habit, she walked out onto the back patio for a cigarette. The pack wasn't there, and the frustration she felt made her either want to cry or pick up a lawn chair and throw it into the pool. She really needed a cigarette. She had been so good for the last couple of weeks, trying to keep her promise to Alex that she wouldn't drink or smoke for the duration of the pregnancy. However, just to be on the safe side for a moment like this, she had kept a pack with two lone cigarettes buried in the bottom of her purse. She really needed a cigarette. She could go get one and just smoke half. No one would ever know. She went inside and picked up her purse.

She couldn't do it. It would be a betrayal of Alex, and she would not let herself do that to one of the most important people in her life. She threw the purse against the wall and heated up another Lean Cuisine. She should make herself gain weight with Alex, out of a sense of duty and for emotional support.

It had been a long day. It was 12:30. Sam went back into her office and picked up her phone. Usually, she would have talked to Alex and/or been over at her house three or four times already. She had never really noticed how much time she spent with her sister since she moved across the street. Alex was a huge part of her everyday life now, a routine that had seemed so natural and right after all the years they had lived apart. This time, they had only been apart for twenty-seven hours. She missed her sister.

Since the day was going nowhere, Sam decided to call her mother. She hadn't spoken to her in over a month, and when they did talk, it was never about anything substantial. Even though Alex wanted to wait three or four months to tell their parents about the baby, Sam could at least drop a couple of hints.

"Hello?" her mother finally answered, her voice accompanied by the perpetual static of her ancient cell phone.

"Hi, Mom, it's me, Sam."

"Just a minute, dear." In the background, Sam heard her mother say to her father, "Paul, you need to pull over *now.*"

"Is something the matter, Mom?"

"We're just having a little glitch. The policeman following us with his lights on wants us to pull over, but your father doesn't think he was speeding." In the background, again, "Paul, you need to pull over *now*."

"Don't you think he should pull over, Sam? A policeman does not turn on his lights for just any little old reason, right?"

"Right. He should pull off to the side of the road."

"You tell him that, dear."

She must have handed Paul the phone. "I was not speeding," he said gruffly. "I have the wheels calibrated and the odometer in tip-top shape, and I am not exceeding the speed limit."

"Please pull over, Dad."

"Oh, all right, but it goes against my principles." He handed the phone back to his wife.

"I should probably go now, dear, but one more thing. We're coming out for a visit!"

So, she and Alex would be giving them the news in person, and without a drink to fortify themselves before the big announcement. The thought made Sam nervous. Emily and Paul were old-fashioned, straightforward people. "When?"

"Soon. Bye now. Give my love to everyone." She hung up.

Sam needed to talk to Alex about the visit. They needed to come up with a strategy. She went to the window again, wondering if she could *will* her twin sister over.

Maybe she could. Alex was crossing the street, and Sam, relieved and grateful, hurried to open the door for her.

Chris knew he shouldn't have answered the phone. It had been a grueling day so far. First, he had had to confront Sam about all the packages from Overstock.com. They arrived that morning, and they littered the living room.

"What did you buy?" he asked Sam just as she was getting ready to open the first box.

"A little of this, a little of that," she said vaguely.

"'A little of this, a little of that,' has to be shipped back."

"But why? Our baby is going to need all this lovely furniture." She stood with her hands on her hips, ready for battle.

"The baby," he said, looking at the box nearest to him, "does not need a Zen Collection Cradle Swing. What in the world is a Zen Collection Cradle Swing?" It sounded unnecessary and ridiculous to him.

"I'm not quite sure," she admitted. "But it sounds like it would be very soothing to a baby."

He walked over to another box. "And a Cherry Elite Oval Bassinet? A baby is in a bassinet for what length of time? Two or three months?"

"What do you suggest we do? Put the baby in a dresser drawer like our great-grandparents did out on the lonesome Prairie?" Her blue eyes flashed.

She could not have her way on this one. "How much did all of this cost?"

"I don't know," she said stubbornly.

"Yes, you do."

"Okay, I do, but I'm not telling you."

"We are on a budget now, Sam. You know that." When he gave Jack the first check tonight, it would be only the first slice taken out of their nest egg. He was dreading that encounter thoroughly, and it was why he had awakened in such a foul mood.

"But the baby is going to need at least some of these things." She looked longingly at all the boxes.

"Renee Rosewall in my department had a baby a few months ago. She's always talking about all the stuff she has in her garage. I thought we could ask her to borrow some things. Later, when the time is more appropriate."

"You want our baby to have a borrowed crib and layette?" Sam put her hand over her heart dramatically.

"This is what you wanted, Sam, and now you're going to have to play by the rules."

She took a deep breath. Truthfully, she had tried to be more compromising in the last few weeks. "You're right. I'll send everything back today. We'll worry about what we need later."

Perhaps he had won this small battle with Sam, but he was never going to win the war with her. He knew it, and he didn't mind, but in the financial matters of this arrangement, she was going to have to abide by what he said. He refused to go into any more debt over this, not in this deplorable economy.

Then, after teaching his two classes, he had had a long line of students waiting outside his door during office hours, all with the same question:

What was going to be on the midterm exam? It was still a couple of weeks away, and he had promised them a study guide, but still, they came in fear. It was natural, he supposed. Since it was his first semester at ASU, they couldn't rely on former students to tell them how difficult his tests were, or if he was a strict grader. And certainly, no former tests of his lurked in the filing cabinets of fraternities, ready for a fresh batch of freshmen to peruse. He had tried to be patient with all of them, even though it seemed the students acted younger and more insecure every year. Had technology taken away their self-confidence, along with their social skills?

The last student left, and then his phone rang. He didn't want to answer it; he recognized the number of the Golden Manor. But what if it was an emergency? What if one of Louise's imaginary illnesses had become a reality?

"Hello, Mother."

"You didn't call me last Sunday night," she said accusingly. "What's wrong?"

"Nothing is wrong, Mother. I've just been very busy."

"Huh!" she said.

"Why aren't you calling from your cell phone, the one Sam and I gave you for Christmas?" He wouldn't have answered if it had been that number that popped up on his screen.

"That stupid waste of money? It doesn't even work. I think it needs a new battery or something. Just a minute." She said in the background, "I said to wait your turn. I'm busy here." She returned to Chris. "It's that annoying Mr. Peterson again, the man who likes to take out his teeth. He's been following me around like a mangy hound dog."

"Maybe he likes you," Chris said, thinking that if that were the case, the poor old man must be a glutton for punishment.

"This phone station they have here smells like urine. I'll have to have a talk with the janitor. He seems to be the lazy sort."

"Is there anything particular on your mind?" he asked, hoping she would avoid the subject of her health (not likely) or zero in on the purpose of her call (not likely either).

"Yes, I do have a purpose, Christopher. I always have a purpose. I'm calling to find out when I can expect my thank you note for getting you those rooms at the Bellagio. Did it get lost in the mail?" she asked tartly.

Chris groaned inwardly. He was a fifty-two-year-old man, yet as Louise's son, he should have instinctively known that she would demand a proper, formal thank you note. "It's on the kitchen counter," he lied. "I'll mail it tomorrow."

"A prompt thank you note is always proper etiquette."

"Yes, Mother."

"Get away, you old coot!" she shouted, not bothering to turn her head away from the phone.

"Anything else, Mother?" He yearned for this call to end.

"Did you have any luck?" she asked.

Well, how should he answer that one? "We had some luck," he mumbled.

"Christopher," she said, echoes of a stern teacher in her voice, "what is really going on?"

"What do you mean?" He felt like a trapped kid caught in a lie.

"I know you don't like Vegas, I know you don't like to gamble, and I believe we had a ridiculous conversation not so very long ago about you wanting to borrow money so that your wacky wife, at the age of forty, could have a baby via a surrogate. I might be in the early throes of Alzheimer's, but my memory is excellent."

"Sam is not wacky," he stalled.

"Christopher," she said.

What the hell? Why not tell her? She had never approved of anything he had ever done. "We are having a baby via a surrogate. Alex volunteered. She's pregnant. We're hoping that everything goes well."

"What in the world are you thinking? I thought you would give up on that preposterous idea when I wouldn't lend you the money. You two are too old to have a baby. It is very selfish of you."

"It turns out we didn't need your money, and it's what we want." He could hear her heavy breathing on the other end of the line. He had actually gotten to the old woman, so he thought he'd take it a little farther. "Whatever happened to Dorothy's grandson, the one you so selflessly donated to the cause of proving his innocence?"

"Oh, that." Louise paused. "He confessed everything. Guilty as sin." She paused again. "But that is not the issue here, Christopher. We are talking about you and Sam, a surrogate, and a baby . . ." By the time she had finished with her rant, she had worked herself up to her normal, righteous anger. "What do you have to say for yourself, Christopher?"

"Congratulations, Granny," and he hung up the phone, smiling.

Nick emptied the dishwasher and then went upstairs and knocked on his mom's bedroom door. "Is there anything else I can do for you, Mom?"

"Come in, honey," she said.

He opened the door and walked in. She was sitting up in bed, reading a book. "How are you feeling?"

"Much better now, sweetheart. In fact, I feel kind of guilty sitting here and reading in the middle of the day. I don't remember the last time I did this. I should probably get up and make myself useful." Even though she was still pale, her smile was bright.

"There's really nothing to do, Mom. I cleaned up the kitchen and put in a load of laundry. Didn't the doctor say you should get plenty of rest?"

"Yes, he did. I'll use that as my excuse for being lazy." She reached out and took his hand. "I don't know what I'd do without you, Nick. You really are a special son."

"I don't know about that," he said, embarrassed.

"You really are," she said firmly. Then, "Do you happen to know where Annie is? She's not answering her phone."

"She's probably at Carla's."

"Probably." His mom looked thoughtful. "She does spend a lot of time there, but I'm glad that Carla is such a good friend to her."

"Uh huh," Nick muttered, but he wasn't at all sure about that. It seemed to him that Carla was a bad influence on Annie, but every time Carla made an appearance in this house, she pretended to be all sweet and innocent. She could be the next Meryl Streep; she was that good an actress. And a diva. She was a good diva. She had never even bothered to thank Dylan and him for cleaning up her mess after the party. And surprisingly, Annie had been right about something. He didn't hear anyone at school mention the party the next Monday morning.

"Have you and Dad—"

"I've got to go to the meet, and I'm staying at Dylan's tonight," he interrupted. "In fact, I'm late now. Gotta run." And he was out the door before she could say another word about the U of A application and the rapidly approaching deadline. He knew that he couldn't keep bolting every time one of his parents mentioned college, but he had no intention of filling out the application. It was totally frustrating that Mom and Dad were not respecting his wishes. In a few months, he'd be eighteen and a grownup. Didn't they understand that?

He was going to the school, but he wasn't going to the cross-country meet. To the disappointment of Coach Everett, he had quit the job as manager/maid/ass-wipe. No, the reason for today's trip to the school was because Nick had decided that it was finally time for an important mission. He was going to put Corey's ring back in his locker under a pile of dirty jock straps, or in a running shoe, or ideally, in a crack in the dinged metal. Corey's outburst when he discovered that his ring was missing had died down quite a while ago, and of course, his wealthy parents had bought him a new, better one, but that was not the point. It was too late to give the other things back to their rightful owners because they had all since graduated, but this was one thing he could do to make amends for being a . . . *thief.*

And it was all because of Jennifer. Certainly, he hadn't told her about this sporadic bad habit of his, this desire that came out of nowhere to take things that didn't belong to him. It baffled him. He wasn't that kind of person. He didn't want to be that kind of person. What would Jennifer think of him if she ever found out? She would be disappointed, of course, and probably even repulsed. He couldn't take that chance.

It wasn't like they were a couple or anything like that, not exactly. They had been to the movies a couple more times, but Dylan and Melissa were always along. Surprisingly, their relationship was moving along at a much faster pace than his relationship with Jennifer. Not only did Dylan not make any more references to Melissa's weight, but he also told Nick that he had kissed Melissa in the dark theater when Nick and Jennifer had gone out to the lobby to get a refill on their popcorn. Nick had felt a pang at this discovery, a pang that he only later realized was jealousy. He didn't want to be jealous of his best friend, so he brushed off the feeling by telling himself that he and Jennifer were just taking things slowly, that they were taking the time to really get to know each other before getting to anything drastic like *kissing.* Their first kiss would be special because the time would be right.

When Nick got to the school, the parking lot was nearly deserted, just as he had hoped. The meet had ended a couple of hours earlier, and it was a Saturday, so he was counting on the locker room being empty. He fingered the ring in his jeans pocket and took a deep breath. He was nervous—no doubt about it—but he was finally going to do the right thing. He approached the locker room, trying to act nonchalant.

He passed the janitor coming out of a classroom. He tried to force his voice to be calm, but it squeaked adolescently when he said, "Forgot a book, Al. Big calculus test on Monday. I really need that book."

As if Al cared. He nodded and said in his thick Spanish accent, "Big test."

Al went into the next classroom, but just to be on the safe side since he had been seen, Nick went to his locker and took out the heavy book. No one else seemed to be around, so he hurried to the locker room. He really wanted to get this over with.

He stopped just inside the door. He could see that Coach Everett's office was dark, and he let the familiar smells of sweaty dampness wash over him. Until now, he hadn't realized how much he missed that smell. Al had obviously not gotten to this room yet, and the air also held a faintly sweet, musky odor, which must have been left by the assortment of cologne the guys put on after their showers.

Quickly, cautiously, he went to Corey's locker. He quietly lifted the handle of the unlocked door. And a riot of dirty clothes, running shoes, and jock straps fell to the floor. In a panic, he scooped up the jumble and tried to stuff it back into the locker. As soon as he could get an arm's worth in, some stray sock or shirt would jump back out. After what seemed like minutes to him (but was probably only thirty seconds or so), he had the stuff precariously stacked. He reached into his pocket and pulled out the ring. He would bury it in the middle of all Corey's crap, and he would think it had been there all along.

"What are you doing? I always thought you were a pervert, and guess what? I was right." It was Corey, coming toward him, his right fist tightly clamped.

Trapped, Nick said the first thing that came to his mind. "All your stuff fell out of your locker, and I was just putting it back."

"Yeah, sure. My jockstrap managed to open the locker all by itself? It's a pretty talented garment, but I don't think it—" He was right next to Nick and saw the ring in his hand. "You fucker! You're the one who stole my ring!"

"No, it wasn't me. It was right here with all your stuff." Nick was sweating profusely. "You must have misplaced it."

"I know damn well I didn't *misplace* the ring. You took it, Carissa, and you're going to pay."

"No," Nick said again. "No, no, no." What would happen to him? Would he be expelled? It was a fleeting thought, unbidden: He definitely wouldn't have to go to college then.

Corey wrenched the ring from Nick's hand, but unfortunately for Corey, it was the hand that held his joint. So that was the smell. It hadn't been cologne after all. Smoking pot on school grounds was also punished with expulsion.

"You've been smoking pot," Nick accused in an attempt to divert the attention away from himself.

"So what? You stole my ring."

"I'm putting your ring back," Nick said.

"Your ass is mine, Carissa. Wait until everyone in the school knows what you're really like."

"You're high," Nick said. "Wait until everyone in school knows about that." Corey's eyes were glazed, and he didn't look Nick directly in the face.

"No one gives a shit. But you, you're a thief. I bet you stole all that other stuff, too."

The fear that shot through Nick was sharp. He didn't say anything. Instead, he put the ring on top of the jumble and forced the door closed. He turned back to Corey just in time to see the fist coming straight toward him.

Having never been in a fight before, he was shocked at how much his face hurt as he fell backward to the floor. Corey, being stoned, had lost his balance with the swing and had also fallen to the ground. It was pure instinct—no thought or feeling involved at all—that caused Nick to reach for the heavy calculus book he had put on the bench in front of the locker and hit Corey in the face.

"That's enough." Coach Everett's voice said from somewhere behind Nick.

And that was the end of the fight.

Jack was bent under the hood of the old van, trying to change the battery, and he didn't see Chris as he crossed the street. He was grease-stained and unprepared. So far, he had been able to avoid seeing both Sam and Chris since the *incident* in Las Vegas. So far, since Alex wasn't showing, he could almost pretend that nothing had happened. So far, he hadn't been forced to look Chris in the eye since he had fucked his wife. In the past few weeks, he had become a master at avoiding his own feelings.

And then Chris said, "Hi, Jack."

Jack bumped his head on the raised hood of the van. "Damn it!"

"Sorry. I didn't mean to surprise you," Chris said.

Without quite looking at the man that he wanted to punch in the nose—and he could so easily beat him up without breaking a sweat—Jack busied himself wiping his hands on a shop rag. "What do you want?"

"I wanted to give this to you personally."

Since Jack was not looking directly at him, he didn't know what Chris held in his hand. "Give me what?" As far as Jack was concerned, Sam and her husband could never repay him.

"The check, Jack, the first installment. It's what we agreed on."

"Oh, right, the recompense, the compensation for my wife's services," Jack said sarcastically. He threw down the shop rag. "I don't want it."

"Come on, Jack, we have a verbal agreement: after the conception, three months, six months, and the birth. I don't blame you for being angry—I really don't—but we all agreed, and now the pregnancy is a fact. Take the check, Jack."

Jack finally looked at the check in Chris's proffered hand. He wanted to make a statement by grabbing the check, ripping it into tiny graffiti pieces, and throwing them in Chris's face.

"Please, Jack, just take it. This is what we agreed on."

The damn agreement. But it seemed so long ago, back in another time when Jack wasn't angry, or hurt. He took the fucking check and stuffed it in his pocket.

Chris stood around awkwardly, obviously wanting to leave but then seeming to think he shouldn't rush off after his deed had been completed. "What are you doing?" he finally asked.

"I'm changing the battery." Jack picked up the shop rag from the floor and again wiped his greasy hands on it. Why didn't the guy just go?

"I don't know how to change a battery," Chris said, taking a step closer to the car, pretending to be interested.

"You didn't grow up on a farm."

"No, I'm a suburban boy through and through. I never took any auto repair courses in high school. Or shop."

As if that wasn't obvious enough just by looking at him, Jack thought. "Yes, well, I should probably get back to work." Jack willed him to leave.

"How's the soccer team doing?"

"Pretty well." So far, it had been a mediocre season, but Jack wasn't going to tell him that.

"I wouldn't mind coming to a game sometime. When are they?"

This was getting painful. "It varies."

"Maybe you could let me know—"

"Will do," Jack said quickly. Why in the hell didn't the guy just leave?

Chris tried another subject. "Did you know that the girls' parents are coming out soon? As usual, they didn't specify a time."

Jack hadn't known that, but then again, he hadn't had many conversations with his wife lately. *His choice.* Still, Chris didn't need to know that either. "Uh huh."

"I don't know where they'll want to park their RV—"

Jack interrupted; he couldn't stand one more second of this intolerable non-conversation. "You know what? I think we're done here. I need to get back to work."

Chris looked relieved. "Oh, sure. Right. I'll be going then. Use the money wisely." He turned abruptly and walked quickly out of the garage and across the street.

Jack had never seen the man move so quickly before. Chris had practically galloped across the street, an almost impressive gait for such an unathletic man. Jack didn't have time to spit out the words: What in the hell do you mean by *use the money wisely*? Who was he to say how Jack was supposed to use this cursed blood money that his wife had risked so much for? He took out the check from his pocket and looked at it. It was the amount they had agreed upon those long weeks before. And then he remembered. He had borrowed that two hundred dollars from Chris on the ship. And he had never paid him back. It had been completely erased from his mind until just this second. He hadn't thought about the loan once since they left that awful cruise. Well, one thing was clear now. The first thing he was going to do with the money was pay Chris back. He was not going to be indebted to Chris and to Sam. It was the other way around. They were indebted to *him*.

He went back to work, but his mind was not on the project at hand. It was filled with too many other anger-fueled thoughts. He wished he had someone to talk to about everything that was going on. Before, he had always had Alex, but that was out of the question now. He had acquaintances, quite a lot of them, but they were more of the beer-drinking, "let's go catch a game at the bar" type of guys. Rarely, if ever, did they speak to each other about personal problems or trouble at home—unless it was obvious, like Bob's divorce. And even then, they had all agreed that Bob's wife was a bitch for cheating on him, and he was better off without her. Not once did they ask Bob how he was feeling or if he needed to talk about it. They should have, Jack thought now.

He wished he could call his parents, but they had been dead for almost five years now, killed by a drunk driver on a two-lane back country highway on the way home from their first vacation in twenty years. They had gone for a worry-free weekend to a gospel concert in Paducah, Kentucky, forty-eight hours of freedom from the farm that they were about to lose, that they had been about to lose for as long as Jack could remember. God knows that not one of their sons would ever help them out, but surprisingly, they had never seemed bitter about that.

Lucas and John, Jack's older brothers, had been born wild. They were nine and eight years older than Jack, and by the time he was born, they had formed an unbreakable bond that he could never penetrate and never really wanted to. They were always getting into trouble at school for fighting or doing something stupid like sneaking a pig into someone's locker, or getting caught at beer parties at Boss's Lake, an old strip mine pit. He had never been close to them, and except for a random Christmas card, he never heard from them (and he was sure neither had computers, let alone a Facebook page). They were still living wandering lives. He thought Lucas was in Oregon lumberjacking and John was on some ranch in west Texas. Both were divorced. Lucas had a daughter and John had two sons, but he couldn't be sure of any of that after so many years. It was a damn shame that he had lost touch with his family, an unforgivable shame.

If his mother had still been alive, maybe things would be different. She had certainly loved Jack, and it wasn't any great secret in the family that he was the favorite. His older brothers didn't care—really, he was almost invisible to them, an annoying, pesky, little brother—nor did they acknowledge that he excelled at sports and got decent grades. It was his mother, and to a lesser degree, his father, who doted on him and praised him and was ecstatic when he got a scholarship to U of I. He was the first one in his family to go to college, and his mother must have bragged to everyone in the town, including the preacher, the postmaster, the butcher, and her quilting circle. It had been the greatest achievement in his life— until he met and married Alex. Small wonder that he wanted the same for his kids, now that he thought about it.

His phone rang. He was really starting to hate the damn thing, and it seemed that lately, it only provided unwelcome news. No one really needed to know where he was 24/7, but when you had teenagers, you always, always answered your damn phone. "Carissa," he barked.

"Everett," the coach barked back, but then again, his voice was always a bark. "I thought I'd call and give you a heads up, one coach to another."

"Sure," Jack said cautiously. Coach Everett was another one of his acquaintances, but they usually only talked about Nick.

"There was a minor scuffle here. Your boy and Grosman got into it a little, but it's all taken care of now. Frankly, they could each stand a lesson on how to throw a punch. Know what I mean?" He chuckled.

"Nick got into a fight?" Nick had never been in a fight before. He hadn't even been close. And what had he been thinking? Fighting on school property could lead to suspension, and depending on the cause, even expulsion. Nick's college career could have been gone in a second, a one-two punch.

"No harm done, Carissa. It's a done deed."

"But what were they fighting about?" Jack just could not fathom why Nick would fight. Did it have to do with all his military crap?

"What do all boys fight about? Absolutely nothing." Coach Everett chuckled again. "Anyway, it's all taken care of. No big deal. It didn't happen. We have to take care of our players, don't we?"

"Of course."

"Good. I'll see you on Monday." He hung up.

Jack stared at the dead phone. What in the world was going on with his son?

Her son had a swollen black eye.

Her husband had an angry red face.

Her daughter had a frightening pink Mohawk.

Alex hadn't been under the weather for very long with morning sickness, only four weeks, give or take a day or two. Yet look what things had come to in her nominal absence: a black eye, a red face, a pink Mohawk. She was feeling better now, stronger every day, and she would take control of the situation. They were all living in the same house, but they were not communicating. That was the problem in a nutshell. They needed to communicate with each other, and it was going to start today.

The first order of business was to get to the bottom of Nick's face. She, like Jack, was bewildered by the whole thing. She couldn't remember a time when her son spoke an unkind word to anyone, let alone threw and received punches. He and Annie sometimes bickered, but that was normal between siblings. Now he sat on a stool at the kitchen counter holding a bag of frozen peas over his left eye. The peas would have to do. They didn't have any steak in the freezer to thaw out and put over his eyes like they did in the old black and white movies that she loved to watch on TCM.

Jack was pacing, his face red with anger. "What were you thinking? You know better than to fight, let alone on school property. You could have been suspended, or worse."

"It all happened so fast. I was putting Corey's clothes back in his locker—they had fallen out, I don't know how—and he accused me of stealing. I think he thought I stole his class ring or something." Nick banged the bag on the counter to loosen the frozen peas and placed it back over his eye.

"That's ridiculous," Alex said, feeling a bit heated herself, not at Nick but at this Corey kid who could accuse her son of such a preposterous thing.

"He's an asshole, that Grosman kid. He's got a sense of entitlement you wouldn't believe, but that's not the point, Nick. You need to think about the consequences of your actions. You could have sabotaged your future." Jack got a beer out of the refrigerator.

"It all happened so fast," Nick said again.

Alex wished she could have a beer herself, but of course, she would not. She hated to admit it, but it bothered her that something about Nick's story didn't quite ring true. He was obviously not a thief. "So, in a sense, Corey provoked you without a reason?" She knew there was a lot of bullying going on in public schools these days, but it didn't happen much in the private schools. At least this is what she had always believed, that it didn't happen at SCDS.

"Maybe I should call his parents—" Alex began.

"No," they said in unison.

"You can't still think that's a solution to a problem, not when Nick is seventeen. I'll call them both into my office on Monday morning," Jack said. "It can be handled in a professional setting."

"No!" Nick said too quickly, too loudly. "I mean, thanks for the offer, Dad, but Coach Everett took care of it. He made us apologize and everything. I just want to forget about the whole thing."

Jack's dismissal of her hurt, but she would deal with that later. What the two needed, Alex thought as she looked at them, was some time together. They hadn't even gone running together since Nick's accident, something they used to love to do. They hadn't gone fishing or golfing either. They needed time alone, and they needed to communicate, not simply glare (Jack) or avoid eye contact (Nick). She told them that.

Neither one answered. She should be getting used to it by now with Jack, but she wasn't. She had expected that, after Las Vegas, he wouldn't want to touch her for a while. And of course, he hadn't. But she had thought that by now he would be willing to be in her presence, willing to talk to her like they used to, talk about everything that happened in their days, talk about anything they found interesting. But he hadn't. She missed him. She missed him very much.

"What's happened has happened," she said. "Nick's eye will heal, and really, nothing serious happened. I'll say it again: You two need to spend some more time together. Why don't you go look at the U of A website? You've been meaning to do that for a while now."

Jack perked up instantly. "I think that's a great idea. What do you think, Nick?"

Nick looked as if he'd been trapped. "I guess so."

Jack didn't—or refused—to see Nick's reluctance. "I'll show you the campus, and then we can move onto the application. It'll be great."

And then Annie walked in.

The three of them gaped as she walked nonchalantly to the refrigerator and took out a gallon of milk, then opened the cabinet to get a glass. Her hand trembled slightly as she poured. "What?" she said.

"Jesus," Jack said as he slammed his empty beer bottle on the table. "What the hell?"

"What have you done?" Alex could have cried at the sight of her. Her beautiful daughter with a shocking pink Mohawk. The bare skin on each side of the strip of hair glistened pink from the recent razor, looking like the bald head of a baby who was wearing some kind of funny hat. Her ears, perfectly normal-sized ears, now looked disproportionately large on her head. Her downcast eyes, Alex knew, were rimmed with a thick coat of eyeliner. The hand holding the glass sported chipped black nails.

"Hello, Baldy," Nick said, trying, not successfully, to suppress a grin.

"Jesus," Jack said. His inflamed face had drained of color.

"It's only—"

"Don't even think of saying it," Alex warned. "I might have conceded to Aunt Sam on that point once, but not this time."

Nick had removed the bag of peas from his eye. "I know I've said it before, but you need a friend who has more talent as a hairstylist."

"For your information—not that it's any of your business, jerk—Carla and I went to a barber."

"Jesus." Jack seemed incapable of muttering anything else.

"What in the world possessed you to do this?" First, her son gets into a fight, and then her daughter waltzes in looking like this. Was everyone going crazy?

"We have our reasons," Annie said. She drained the milk and poured more to keep from meeting any of them eye to eye.

"You and Carla could start a rock band," Nick offered. "Last I remember, you could play a mean kazoo in the fourth-grade talent show. And I use the word *talent* loosely."

"Oh, shut up!" Annie exploded. "You wouldn't know what was cool if it punched you in the face." She finally looked at him. "Oh, I see it already did."

Jack had finally found his voice, and the too-bright color had returned to his face. "No daughter of mine is going out in public looking like that! What will people think?"

"I don't care what people think."

"You'll scare little children," Nick said.

"That's enough, Nick," Jack said. He took a deep breath, trying to compose himself. "Of course you care what other people think about you.

Everyone does. You have to interact with other people in this world, and unfortunately, your appearance makes the first impression. What impression do you think you'll make when you look like *that*."

Annie gave a long, maddening shrug.

"You talk to her, Alex." Jack practically growled.

Alex hated the Mohawk as much as Jack, but they weren't getting anywhere like this. Communication was the key, but right now, it seemed as if they needed practical solutions. "This isn't the end of the world, you guys. It's far from an ideal situation, but I repeat: It's not the end of the world. Annie can wear a wig until her hair grows back."

"I'm not wearing a wig." Annie braced herself against the counter, perhaps preparing herself for a fight.

There wasn't going to be any fighting or any more yelling. "Fine. A hat."

"She could wear a mask," Nick piped up. "Better yet, a paper bag with hole cutouts for eyes. Forget the mouth."

"You're not helping, Nick," Alex said as calmly as she could.

"Would you make him shut up!" Annie cried.

"Why don't you go up to your room?" Jack said.

"Sure thing." Nick made a quick escape up the stairs, off the hook again from starting the college application.

"You're grounded," Jack said to Annie. "Indefinitely."

In a falsetto, babyish voice, Annie said, "Since you don't want a daughter of yours going out in public looking like this, I guess I can't go to school. Right, Dad?"

"That's it." Jack slammed his fist on the counter, making Alex and Annie jump.

Again, trying to diffuse the situation, as always, the mediator, Alex said, "Why don't you go get some air, Jack? I'll talk to Annie."

He looked suddenly lost, uncertain, a slowly deflating balloon.

"Look," she went to her desk and rummaged through the drawer. "I cut out a coupon for the driving range. Go." She gave him a little shove. He might have been too angry to argue, or perhaps, he was too spent. But he went.

"How long do you think I'll be grounded for?" Annie said.

"I don't know."

"Dad can be so unfair! It's only *hair*." She looked as petulant as a two-year-old about ready to stamp her foot.

"It's not only Dad, Annie. I'm upset with you, too."

And then the child won out; all the bravado was gone. She collapsed into Alex's arm like a limp doll—make that a troll doll, Alex thought as she looked down on the Mohawk. Alex knew she should be stronger, hold her ground, but Annie felt good in her arms. When was the last time they had hugged? It had been too long. She let her cry it out, stroking her shoulders, her face, anything but her head.

After a while, Alex said, "I think I need to get out of the house, too, get some air. Let's go somewhere." She did feel like the house was suddenly closing in on her. She and Annie needed to get out, find some impartial territory somewhere together.

"But I'm grounded," Annie sniffled. Her eyeliner was a mess.

"I'll make an exception. Go wash your face."

Annie complied in record time, although she had hurriedly, sloppily reapplied her eyeliner, and she was driving the van slowly, very slowly (literally, pedestrians were passing them) through the parking lot of the strip mall. Alex remembered seeing a new gelato place in this mall recently and suddenly had an acute craving for a raspberry gelato. She directed her to the far end of the lot where there were three empty spaces in a row, a good—but not one hundred percent—guarantee that Annie wouldn't sideswipe another car.

Alex hadn't expected the reaction to Annie's Mohawk. How could she? She had barely had time to process the startling look her daughter sported. They were in the heart of Scottsdale, a bastion of both fashion and conservatism, and of course, her daughter drew stares, whispers, mutters, and the occasional outright guffaw. Annie held her head up high and stared straight ahead. Alex wished she had had the foresight to bring a hat, not that Annie would wear it, but it would make Alex feel as if her daughter had some sort of protection against the rude stares.

They settled themselves outside, away from the crowded shop but not far enough away from a table of boys in their Boy Scout uniforms. One started the cowboy western version of the Indian war cry, patting his mouth with his fingers, and of course, the rest of the table took it up.

After the longest thirty seconds that Alex could remember, Annie turned around and gave them the finger.

"Annie, don't do that."

"It made them stop, didn't it?" She took a bite of her lemon gelato.

Actually, it didn't. Alex could see over Annie's shoulder that it was the arrival of their troop leader to collect them that had made them stop.

Alex let her raspberry gelato melt. She no longer had an appetite for it. Across the parking lot, she could see a bar that she and Jack used to frequent years ago when the kids were little and they would splurge and get a babysitter for a night. She missed being with Jack.

She really wanted a glass of wine.

Annie didn't seem inclined to start a conversation, so Alex thought she would begin one with something innocuous. "How's sophomore year so far?"

"I hate it! Carla and I both hate it."

Alex was surprised by her vehemence. "But why?"

"Because Carla and I are freaks."

"You are *not* a freak, Annie." But this was Alex's unasked question: If she thought she was a freak, why did she do that to her hair?

"Whatever. You don't know what it's like these days."

True, she hadn't gone to school with all the technology the kids had these days, but teenagers were teenagers, people were people. "Then tell me what it's like."

"It's *complicated*." Annie looked up from her devoured gelato. Her eyes were glassy.

Probably from all those tears, Alex thought. "Would you like to change schools?" Alex didn't want her to leave the school with its stellar academics, but certainly, she and Jack had talked about it before. Even though they got a discounted tuition, they really had to struggle to make the payments.

"Carla's parents won't let her transfer out of SCDS."

"So? I know that Carla is your best friend, but you don't have to do everything that Carla does. Dad and I just want you to be happy."

Annie widened her glassy eyes. "Are you going to eat that?" She pointed at the melting ice cream with her tiny plastic spoon.

Alex pushed it to her side of the table. It was too bad for Annie that she wanted to change the subject. Alex persisted: "Did Carla talk you into the Mohawk?"

She shook her spiky head. "No, it was a mutual decision."

"Why?" It was the pivotal question.

"We wanted to make a statement."

"What kind of statement?"

"You know, that we're way cool, that we're *individuals*."

Alex needed some serious help understanding this logic. "So, first you tell me that you think you are a freak, and then you go get a Mohawk that will draw attention to you, probably negative attention?"

"You just don't get it, do you?"

"No, I don't. Enlighten me."

Annie sighed like a martyr. "It's *complicated*."

It was a good thing the table separated them because she couldn't reach Annie's shoulders to give them a good shake, to make her tell Alex what was wrong, to make her listen to reason. Alex probably wouldn't have done that even if she could reach. She needed to be supportive of her daughter in this difficult time. She grabbed both of Annie's hands. "I only want you to be happy, Annie. We've always been close, and you know you can talk to me about anything, right? Anything at all."

"Sure, Mom." She was looking at Alex but didn't seem to see her.

"We can work together to make things right, to make you happy."

Annie swallowed a laugh. It came out as a snide little snort.

"There's nothing funny about this, Annie."

"Oh, Mom, you're such a *Pollyanna*!"

Alex withdrew her hands. "Is that so?"

Annie dug into her jeans pocket for her cell and checked the time. "Do you know what that means?"

"I know what that means," she said more sharply than she intended.

Annie lowered, softened her voice. "Oh, no offense, Mom."

"None taken. Shall we go?"

When they got back to the car, Alex held out her hand. "I'll drive."

Annie didn't object, perhaps sensing, perhaps not, that she had gone too far and hurt her mother's feelings. Annie had been going through a rough phase for a while now, but it was as if the pink Mohawk had erased any vestiges of the sweet young woman she really was. Alex refused to believe that the sullen, pink-haired girl sitting in the car beside her was an obnoxious alter ego of her daughter; it just couldn't be. This outlandish persona was an ugly, temporary facade.

They had forgotten to put up the reflecting dashboard covers, and the car was unbearably hot. It was difficult to breathe.

"It's like a furnace in here," Alex said, rolling down the windows and cranking the air conditioning up as high as it would go in the old van.

"Or like hell."

They were almost home when Alex said: "I don't think you should see Carla anymore."

Sam was looking out her front window at her sister's house, again. It seemed as if she was doing a lot of that lately. It wasn't that she was jealous of her sister, not at all. It was just so much more interesting over there, with the comings and goings of Alex, Jack, and the kids. There wasn't much going on over here, and she was beginning to think that this house was too big for just Chris and her. She couldn't wait for the baby to come and fill up all the empty spaces in this house—and in her life.

But today, she had a valid reason, a mission for being nosy. Earlier, Alex had come to her front door, looking tired and drawn. "Jack and I have made a last-minute decision to go camping up in Oak Creek Canyon. We need an overnight getaway."

"Good for you." Alex had intimated that she and Jack weren't getting along very well. She probably hadn't meant to make Sam feel guilty, but Sam knew it was her fault anyway.

"Nick is going to be over at Dylan's for the night, so will you keep an eye on Annie?"

"You know I'd love to." Maybe she could take Annie to the movies or shopping.

"She's not going anywhere. She's grounded, under *house arrest* as she calls it."

"What for?"

"Have you seen her Mohawk?"

"No," Sam lied. She had seen it, of course, through the window.

"And don't you say, *it's only hair.* I'm sick to death of that phrase. Besides, it's not really about her hair. It's about her attitude, which stinks, and learning that her actions have consequences. That's Jack's new mantra to the kids: Every action has consequences."

"I'll keep an eye on her. Actually, I'd love to go over and spend some time with her." She'd bought a couple of new DVDs at Target that she hadn't watched yet.

"No. She's supposed to be alone. She's not supposed to be having a good time with her aunt Sam."

Sam raised her right hand. "I promise to keep an eye on the prisoner and not go over there. Tell me, is she wearing an ankle bracelet to monitor her every move?"

"Very funny." Alex turned to go and muttered just loud enough for Sam to hear, "I wish."

Sam had watched Alex and Jack leave, and Dylan picked up Nick a little after ten o'clock. It was now nearing noon, and there was no sign of life over at the Carissa house. She had promised not to go over, and had meant every word at the time, but now she was feeling sorry for the girl. It seemed rather harsh to keep her penned in like that. Annie was a sweet girl, and really, Alex sometimes overreacted when it came to her children. It *was* just hair, after all. Who would even give a damn in another month or so?

She let the curtain fall. She was getting hungry, and she bet that Annie was, too. She hadn't promised not to bring her food. Surely, it wouldn't be against Alex's law to run to Taco Bell and pick up some of Annie's favorite food, nachos and a chicken quesadilla. She would just ring the bell and hand the sack to Annie, see for her own eyes that everything was okay. Alex couldn't get mad at her for that.

Ten minutes later, she was ringing Alex's doorbell, which seemed strange. She almost always walked right in. The smell of fake cheese wafted up from the bag, making her mouth water and her stomach feel queasy. "Annie," she called. No answer. She had a strange feeling that the house was empty, which was ridiculous. Annie was in there.

"Annie," she called again. This time she rang the bell and pounded on the door. "I know you're under house arrest, so I brought you lunch." No answer. Maybe the girl was pouting up in her room, or more likely, she was plugged into her iPod, listening to the loud alternative rock music that she favored. If that was the case, she couldn't hear a thing.

She tried one more time. "Annie, open the damn door!" No answer. Well, the girl could be obstinate, there was no doubt about that, but Sam still felt a rising anger. She was trying to be a good aunt, and her niece was ignoring her.

And then she had another thought. What if something was wrong? What if a stranger had broken into the house and abducted Annie, or worse? What if she was lying beaten and broken and bleeding on her bedroom floor? And then the most terrifying thought of all: What if

Annie had done something to herself? With quaking hands, Sam found the door key on her ring of keys and let herself in.

"Annie," she called as she walked through the eerily quiet house and into the kitchen. The kitchen, too, seemed unnatural. It was too clean. No crumbs dotted the counter in front of the toaster, and there wasn't a single dirty plate, cup, or spoon in the sink. It wasn't that Alex was a bad housekeeper, but she certainly wasn't anal about it. Maybe this was part of Annie's punishment?

The quiet was unnerving her. Not even a television murmured in the background, and Sam was feeling a rising panic. The girl must be in her room. She called her name again as she bounded up the steps to Annie's bedroom door. Not even bothering to knock, and expecting the door to be locked, she grabbed the doorknob with both hands and gave a push. The door was not locked, and the force of her push flung it against the wall with a shuddering bang. But Annie wasn't there. Her bed was neatly made, and the usual piles of discarded clothes and books had been put away. The sight of this pristine teenaged girl's room terrified her even more.

Sam made a quick but thorough search of the rest of the house, looking under beds, into closets, and behind shower curtains. It was a frantic game of hide and seek, but she, the seeker, didn't even know if someone was hiding. She went outside and walked the perimeter of the property, finally daring to approach the pool. At first sight, the deflated blue raft hovering near the drain at the bottom of the pool looked like a dead body. She would swear that her heart stopped for a moment.

Her panic fully stoked and her mind racing, Sam went back into the house. Where could Annie be? I was only gone for ten lousy minutes, Sam thought to herself, how could she have just disappeared? She was a terrible aunt if she couldn't do this one thing right. Alex had trusted her, and she had let her down. She was supposed to be Annie's guardian, her watch person, and she had *lost* her.

There was only one place left to check. She went to the garage and opened the door. Like the rest of the house, it seemed eerily empty, but it only took her a split second to realize why. Both cars were gone. Alex and Jack had taken the Jeep, and Nick had been picked up by Dylan. That meant only one thing. Annie had taken the van.

How could she have done such an irresponsible and dangerous thing? She didn't even have her driver's license yet, and on the road, she was a menace to herself and to others. Sam's fear was now tinged with rage. She went back to the kitchen, got her phone out of her purse and started dialing, once, twice, three, four times. It went to voicemail each time. Of course the little shit wouldn't pick up. Mommy and Daddy were out of town, and the Mohawked teenager was out for a joy ride.

But what if she got into an accident? Again, an image of a bloodied Annie came to mind. Sam sank into the chair at Alex's desk and put her head in her hands. Think, she told herself. Be calm. You are the adult in this situation. She could get in her car and go looking for the girl, but it seemed futile if she didn't have a clue where Annie would go. Then she had an idea. Annie's best friend. Alex had been worrying lately about how much time Annie spent over there. What was her name—Cindy, Marla, Carla? That was it. Annie's friend was Carla. Sam opened the desk drawer and found what she was looking for, the school directory. Unfortunately, the directory alphabetized the entire student population from K to 12, not according to class, and Sam didn't have a clue about Carla's last name.

She was about to give in and call Chris, who would probably tell her to calm down and wait, when her phone rang. "Hello?" she said frantically.

"Aunt Sam? It's me." Annie's voice was hesitant.

"Where in the hell are you?" Sam's heart lurched. Annie was alive.

"I'm in a little bit of trouble." Her voice was barely audible over what sounded like traffic in the background.

"Are you all right?" Sam said, realizing that was the question she should have asked first.

"I'm okay. It's the stupid van. It won't start."

"Where are you?"

Annie told her she was at the Shell station at Scottsdale and Thunderbird Roads. She hadn't made it very far. The gas station was only four blocks away.

"I'll be right there." Sam grabbed her purse and ran to her car. She pulled into the gas station four minutes later.

Annie was leaning against the hood of the car, her arms folded and her face sullen. She had on short shorts and a tight T-shirt, which was the opposite of her usual baggy jeans and hoodie. Frankly, she looked a little slutty, a little scared, and a little scary.

Sam parked behind her and walked over. "What are you doing here, Annie?"

"I was getting gas."

Sam glanced at the pump. Annie had put $1.00 of gas in the van. "That's not what I mean, and you know it. What are you doing driving the van?"

"I'm not driving the stupid, fucking van. It won't start." She said it loud enough that the young man lounging against the gas station doorway could hear. He had a scorpion tattoo on his forearm.

Fine, if she wanted to play it that way. They would get to the bottom of this when they got home. She took a deep breath. Be calm, she told herself. You are the adult here. "What's wrong with it?"

"That guy over there," she pointed toward the scorpion tattoo, "said I needed a new battery after he tried to start it with those cable things. But I told him my dad put in a new one the other day. So he doesn't know what the hell is wrong with it. He told me to call AAA, but I don't think we have that. Hell, I don't even know what it is."

"I have my card here. I'll call them, and we can have it towed to Scottsdale Auto Repair." She found the card in her wallet and made the call. They waited until the car was towed away, and then Sam drove them home.

"Can I come into your house?" Annie asked when they pulled into the driveway.

"You're under house arrest, remember?"

"Come on, Aunt Sam," Annie cajoled. "Just for a minute."

It came to Sam then what she was after. "They're not there anymore."

It was as if a mask came down on Annie's face. "I don't know what you're talking about."

"The pills. I moved the pills."

"What pills?" Annie got out of the car and slammed the door, hard. She slung her large canvas bag across her shoulder and stalked across the street.

The ungrateful little *bitch*, Sam thought. She hadn't even bothered to thank her for getting the van towed. She deliberated about a second before she followed her across the street.

Annie was already digging into the soggy nachos and congealed cheese, eating sloppily, as if she was starving. "What are you doing here? I'm grounded, remember?"

Sam got right to the point. "Where were you going, and why? It's illegal for you to be driving, and you could have hurt yourself or someone else."

Annie shrugged.

Sam took her by the shoulders and turned her so that they were facing. She wasn't going to coddle her like she suspected that Alex always, eventually did. "Answer me, Annie."

"It's really none of your business."

She wanted to strangle her. No wonder Alex was beside herself these days when it came to Annie, who could turn from sweet, to surly, to downright hateful in the blink of an eye. It was beyond maddening. "Oh, I beg to differ. I'm the one who just rescued your skinny little ass."

"It doesn't really matter now, does it? I'm home, safe and sound."

Sam gave her a little shake, not nearly as hard as she would have liked. "Tell me." Up this close, right in Annie's face, she could see how dilated her pupils were. "Have you been drinking?"

"Have you?"

She really did want to wring her neck. And she did remember that she had poured a little—not even a shot, probably—of amaretto in her coffee a few hours before. "Where were you going?"

Annie wrenched her shoulders out of Sam's grasp and turned again toward her food. "To Carla's house."

"Why?" Annie was taking some kind of drug. Sam would bet on it. Why hadn't Alex noticed?

"She was having a bad day."

"She was having a bad day, so you decided to illegally drive a car to her house?"

Now Annie stared at her in disbelief. "Wouldn't you? Oh, never mind. I already know the answer to that one. You'd do anything for my mom, right, anything at all?"

Well, of course she would, but that was completely different.

"Oh, wait a minute. I think I've got it turned around. I think it's my mom who would do anything for *you*. Isn't that the correct version? I mean, she is going to have your baby, and I'd say that was pretty *generous*. You're really lucky she loves you so much. There's probably not much chance that she'll decide to keep the baby when you inevitably fuck things up."

The slap hung in the air. Afterward, Sam couldn't remember if she had actually hit the little bitch or just wanted to so badly that she felt it viscerally. She loved her niece, she did, but the girl was like a ticking time bomb. And she was acting like a *bitch*.

"I'm not going to take you to get the van in the morning, and I'm not going to pay for it." She remembered Jack's mantra. "You're going to have to learn to deal with the consequences of your actions."

Or maybe not. The next day, as Sam was looking out her window—she really was going to stop looking out the damn window so much—the van arrived followed by a black town car. A girl with a Mohawk—it must be the infamous Carla—got out and went into the house. She was inside the length of time it took the driver to smoke a cigarette, and then she climbed into the town car and drove away. There was no sign of Annie.

"It needs to be romantic, honey," Loretta said as they sat in the break room at Fry's. "That first kiss needs to be romantic."

"Okay," Nick said doubtfully. He was fascinated by Loretta's crimson nails tapping on the Formica tabletop. Each nail had a sparkling little jewel in the center. They looked like diamonds, but Nick knew they couldn't be. You didn't make enough money at Fry's to afford real diamonds on your fingernails.

"Look at me, sugar. I'm trying to help you out here. Old Loretta has been around the block way more times than once or twice, honey, and I know what I'm talking about. God, I wish we could still smoke in here. Those were the days when I really looked forward to my breaks. Me and my Camels."

Who was losing focus now? He had tentatively asked Loretta what she thought he should do about his first *alone* date with Jennifer, skirting the issue of the kiss. But Loretta had instinctively known what he was talking about. He hadn't gone to his mom or dad for advice, not yet. There was too much tension in the house right now, and he wanted to keep this thing with Jennifer to himself for a while longer. "What do you mean by *romantic*?" he asked Loretta to get her back on track.

"You know, someplace special to you. Where do you like to go?"

He tried to think. In the movies, couples always went to expensive restaurants with tuxedoed waiters and white tablecloths, but he thought a couple of teenagers would look stupid doing that, ordering Cokes and trying to order off a menu they didn't understand. Well, Jennifer probably *would* understand it. But where did he really like to go? "Dylan and I like to go to the shooting range," he finally said.

"No, sugar boy, that's way off track. Headphones and paper people targets with holes in their guts? I don't think so." Loretta ran her crimson nails through her overly bleached blonde hair. "Someplace else."

Nick was drawing a blank. They had been to the movies a number of times now, and nothing had happened, even though they had been in the dark, close enough for their shoulders to touch. He refused to take her to the mall. He hated the mall, and besides, he didn't think there was anything romantic about that. He supposed he could ask Jennifer where she would like to go, but he didn't want to do that either. He wanted the setting for this date to be his idea.

Loretta saw the confused look on his face and reached over to pat his hand. "Maybe I can help you out here, sweetheart. What about a picnic? On my first date with my husband, and I'm talking about my first husband, not the asshole who is currently incarcerated—and my second lousy husband, boy, I am not *ever* going to go there with you—we went to a park and had a picnic. It was a nice night, and we had stopped at the 7 Eleven for some good things to eat: salami, pork rinds because they were his favorite, and some dessert . . ." She paused, then snapped her fingers. "Hostess cupcakes, that's what they were. We spread out a blanket by this little pond and ate our supper under the stars."

Nick wasn't going to comment on the lack of nutrition in this remembered picnic. He liked Loretta too much to chastise her on her choice of junk food. "Then what did you do?"

Loretta paused for a second. "We took a walk. Yes, we took a walk through some trees that circled the pond."

"And then you kissed?"

"Of course we kissed. That's what comes natural, honey." She patted his hand again.

"And then what did you do?" Nick wanted to know this part most of all. Would there be an awkward silence afterward? Would they be embarrassed? What if they had clicked teeth or something, and Jennifer's mouth was bleeding?

"Oh, well, you know." Loretta waved her hand in the air and shrugged. "The usual."

"I really want to know," Nick persisted.

"Well, we had a flask. Did I mention that? One thing led to another and suffice it to say—is *suffice* a word? I've been trying to improve my vocabulary—nine months later Molly was born."

"Oh," Nick said, alarmed. He hadn't expected that ending.

"Now, now, honey. I gave you more information than you needed, didn't I? Me and my big mouth. You're a good boy, and you're not going to end up like old Loretta here. And let me tell you a secret. She wants to kiss *you* as much as you want to kiss *her*."

"Really?" That put a whole new spin on things. He felt the pressure in his chest give a little. Could it really be true?

Loretta nodded. "I guarantee it, sugar boy." Loretta looked at the clock on the wall above the vending machine and started to gather her lunch things. "Just do what comes natural." She stood up. "And don't slobber."

So Nick had followed Loretta's advice and was now sitting in Tempe's Town Lake Park. He and Dylan had researched all the parks in the area and decided that this was the best one. And it had a lake, just like in Loretta's story. They were sitting at a wooden picnic table by the lake, since he had forgotten all about a blanket. But Jennifer said she didn't mind, that she would *go with the flow*. He liked that about her. He had remembered to bring Subway sandwiches, offering Jennifer a choice between the turkey and the cold cut combo. She said she liked both, so they split them. He liked that about her, too.

They were talking about general stuff, and things were going great when Jennifer said, "Someone told me that awful rumor about you and Corey getting into a fight."

"Really?" Nick feigned nonchalance, but he could feel his ears growing pink. He knew that there would be rumors—it was such a small school—but he and Corey certainly weren't commenting. Since The Episode, as he called it, he and Corey had formed an uneasy, silent truce. When they passed each other on the way to class, they exchanged a slight nod and quickly averted their eyes.

"It's terrible how gossipy SCDS is. People make up such crazy things that couldn't possibly be true. I told the person who told me—and I'm not naming names and starting gossip myself—that it was not true."

A rowboat went by just then, Nick's lifeline. "Would you like to go rowing?"

"Sure. I've never been in a rowboat, but I'll go with the flow. Literally." Jennifer laughed.

So, they had been outfitted with orange life jackets (Jennifer was in a child's size, the only one that fit her) and were gliding across the smooth lake. Nick was trying to maintain a smooth manly stroke, but he had to admit that his arms were starting to ache. Before, when he had been in a rowboat on camping trips with his family, most often with his dad, they had taken turns rowing. Even his mom, on the rare occasions she could be talked into getting on a boat, took her turn with the oars. Even Annie rowed one time, but she didn't really count as a girl. However, he was not going to let Jennifer row; he would be the man here.

"This is so romantic," Jennifer said. She looked cute, even in a life jacket, and she smiled sweetly at him with her white, white teeth.

Bingo! Nick rowed with renewed strength. She had said the perfect thing. "It is nice, isn't it?"

"Oh, look at those swans over there." She pointed toward a group circling a little bit away. "They're beautiful. They look like a picture."

"They sure do," Nick said, willing his underarms not to perspire. He didn't particularly like swans. Like geese, they could be mean and try to snap at you.

"Do you think we could paddle closer?" Jennifer asked.

"I guess so." There wouldn't be any harm in getting closer, but not too close. He rowed nearer.

"They really are beautiful. I've never been this close to a swan before." She extended her arm toward the nearest one.

"Be careful, Jennifer, they can be mean."

"Don't be silly. Look at how graceful they are."

And before he could stop her, before he grasped the situation, Jennifer was leaning over the side of the boat in a half crouch, stretching toward the swan.

Of course the boat capsized. He was underwater, swallowing the fishy-smelling pond before he bobbed to the surface, sputtering. Where was Jennifer? He instinctively panicked, but she was right in front of him, having bobbed to the surface at the same time he did.

He reached her in two strokes. "Are you all right?"

"I'm perfect."

And then he kissed her. It was as simple and natural as that. (Loretta had been right again!) There was no awkwardness when the kiss ended. They smiled and giggled. Maybe they giggled with relief, or maybe it was with happiness. Nick didn't know, and right now, he didn't care. He didn't think he had slobbered, but it was hard to tell because they were so wet.

It took some effort to get the boat righted and hoist Jennifer over the side—even little girls weighed a ton when they were sopping wet—before climbing in himself. He rowed back to the rental shop, and as they talked about what had just happened, about how they had capsized the rowboat, they started to laugh. They were cracking up, practically rolling on the ground with laughter when the guy behind the counter gave them some towels. He thought it was pretty funny, too. "I guess you christened the lake," he said.

Between fits of giggles, they chanted this all the way home from their excellent adventure: "We christened the lake! We christened the lake!" Someone overhearing them might have thought that they had had a flask along, just like Loretta. But it wasn't so. They were high on something else entirely.

He walked her to her door. "I had a wonderful time," Jennifer said. She hadn't even bothered to run a comb through her wet hair, yet she was still beautiful.

"Me, too." Nick kissed her again, like it was the most natural thing in the world.

Chris was going from room to room, watering his plants, with Sam in close pursuit. He resented this. It was his "alone time," time to think about his job, money, Sam, sometimes (rarely) his mother, and recently, he almost dared to think about the coming baby. So, Sam following him was not a good thing. But he didn't tell her this. He didn't want to hurt her feelings, which seemed especially fragile now that Alex was pregnant. He didn't think that Sam had really prepared herself for the fact that she would not be carrying the baby. In theory, she might have accepted that fact. In practice, she had not.

"So, should I tell Alex about Annie?" Sam asked for what seemed like the hundredth time. She had been asking for three days now.

"Of course you should. Annie acted irresponsibly and put herself and others in a dangerous position." His flowing ivy plant was looking a little peaked. He needed to buy more plant food.

"But nothing really happened. She got home safely, and somehow, had the van taken care of."

"If you were her mother, wouldn't you want to know?" He walked toward the office.

"Oh, I don't know, Chris," Sam said with exasperation. "I don't think it would have done my mother any good to know about the beer party Alex and I went to senior year in high school. You know how anti-drinking my mother is, so what would have been the point to tell her we got a little tipsy? She thought we were coming down with the flu the morning after, and we didn't correct her. No harm done."

Chris was tired of this conversation. Annie had always seemed like a sweet kid to him, and he knew he would rather not have known about her latest escapade. "Then don't tell her."

"But I have to think about what's in Annie's best interests. If she's heading down the wrong path—and every indication says she is—wouldn't it be better to stop her now?"

"Then tell her mother." He walked into the family room, Sam on his heels.

"Annie would never forgive me. She's already furious with me, and I don't know why. All I did was try to help her, and she turned on me. I didn't handle it well, not at all." She walked over to the bar. "I need a drink."

"Then have one." He was barely listening to her now.

"I can't have a drink because Alex can't drink."

"Then don't have one." Who did she think she was kidding? He knew she had been sneaking amaretto into her coffee, among other things. She was drinking a lot of coffee these days.

"I can't." She followed him into the kitchen. "You have too many damn plants."

"I like my plants. You've known that for years." He finished watering the herbs (basil, parsley, oregano) that he had planted in ceramic pots on the windowsill and then emptied the remaining water into the sink.

"I love you, but it's not a very manly hobby." She stood in front of the refrigerator, debating on whether to open it, perhaps willing it to open by itself and pour her a glass of wine.

"Should I be more like Jack and work on cars?"

"God, no." She gave into temptation and got out the wine.

She was probably thinking the same thing he was. Jack had come home yesterday, triumphantly driving a Lexus. A Lexus. Jack had used the first installment to buy something completely unnecessary. Granted, they needed a new vehicle, but it was unfathomable to Chris that Jack would buy a luxury car when a used Toyota Camry would have been more appropriate.

Alex had called Sam and him over to admire the car, and Chris had feigned excitement along with the rest of them. Jack, defensively, privately pulled Chris aside to tell him it was a 2006 model just off lease, the interest rate was rock bottom, it would hold its value better than most cars, etc., etc. Chris just nodded and left as soon as it was appropriate. The only good thing about it was that Jack had not blown all the money gambling. He didn't know with absolute certainty that Jack still gambled, but he had a strong suspicion that he secretly did. Jack still owed him two hundred dollars from the Mexican cruise.

Sam took a big gulp of wine and popped a piece of Nicorette gum into her mouth. She made a face. "Ugh," she said, "these taste terrible together."

"But it's better than you smoking."

"I know, I know. I'll get used to it."

Chris also knew that she had been sneaking cigarettes in the backyard by the side of the house. The mints she chewed on couldn't disguise the smell emanating from her hair. It was the dance they played. She tried to hide things from him; he always found out. He pretended not to know; she pretended that he didn't know. It had been going on for years, and it suited them. It was basically harmless.

But this business with Annie was not harmless. Probably, it was a secret that should not be kept. However, he understood Sam's indecision. She wanted to enlighten Alex, but she didn't want to betray Annie. She wanted to help, but she didn't want to overstep her bounds.

"Maybe I could take Annie shopping, you know, get on her good side. Maybe she would open up to me?"

"Good idea. Reward her bad behavior." Chris really wanted to get into his office and get online. How many more days was he going to have to patiently listen to her waffling?

"You're right. That would be inappropriate. I'm such a failure as an aunt." She popped in another Nicorette and chewed furiously.

There was a new site Chris wanted to check out. He had gone for almost a week without looking at any porn, and he was going to reward himself. Five minutes. That's all the time he would take.

"You're supposed to say: You're not a failure as an aunt."

"You're not a failure as an aunt." Chris poured himself a glass of wine and topped off Sam's glass. "I have some work I need to catch up on."

"But I haven't decided what to do!" Sam practically wailed.

"Just make a decision. Be done with it. This is consuming too much of your—and my—time." He had been patient long enough.

"You're right." Sam squeezed his hand. "I've been bothering you long enough. I'm sorry. I can be such a mess sometimes." She leaned into him, nestled her head against his shoulder.

This was another integral part of their dance. In the space of a breath, Sam could become so sweet and loving, the person she truly was deep inside, and he would melt. "I love you." He stroked her auburn hair.

She sighed. "I love you, too." She stepped back and looked into his eyes. "I've made my decision. I'm going to keep it to myself for a few days, see what happens. There's no need to jump in with both feet until I know more." She gave his chest a playful push. "Go on and do your work now, honey. I've kept you from it long enough. I know you love what you do, but you work too hard sometimes."

"Okay," he said, leaving the kitchen quickly before she could see any trace of guilt in his eyes. He really didn't have any work to do at all. It was yet another secret. He hurried to his office, closed and locked the door.

The secrets were accumulating.

7

CHAPTER SEVEN

Christmas had always been Alex's favorite time of year. Granted, it had taken her a few years to get used to Christmas in Arizona. With temperatures sometimes hovering in the mid-70s, Saguaro cacti strung with twinkling lights, and fat inflatable Santas sitting in yards of sand, the images weren't even close to her remembered Christmases in the Midwest. But she had adapted and now even embraced the season in this warm climate. Jack had hung the icicle lights above the front porch, and the Christmas tree—fake, she had conceded on that point—in the living room was decorated with heirloom ornaments, as well as ones her children had made in grade school: snowmen made of cotton balls, popsicle crosses covered in yarn. To her, these child-made, bedraggled ornaments made the tree perfect.

She was a little over three months pregnant. She had made it safely past the first danger point and felt incredibly healthy—and almost perfectly content. The busyness of the season had kept her occupied and feeling useful, and it had also taken away from the time she fretted about her family. She had baked dozens of cookies and distributed them to the neighbors and the Christmas bake sale at school. On three different days, she had helped one of the homeless shelters in the area distribute boxes of food to needy families. She had gone to the women's shelter and wrapped gifts for the children. She had even volunteered at the Salvation Army to be a street corner Santa, but that had been awful. Standing in front of Walmart, wearing a red felt Santa hat and ringing the little bell to try to entice (or guilt) people to drop their spare change into the tin bucket had depressed her. In this economy, people couldn't really afford to be as generous as they would like to be, and it showed in their drawn faces as they hurried by her, most of them not even glancing her way.

In the spirit of the season—actually, in a desperate attempt to draw her family closer—she had announced at dinner one night that they would have an old-fashioned Christmas. They would ignore the commercialism of the season and buy inexpensive presents no more than fifteen dollars, or better yet, homemade gifts for each other. Everyone should spend an hour a week helping people less fortunate than their family. The announcement had not been unanimously accepted. In fact, the announcement hadn't gone over well at all.

"That sucks," Annie said. "My computer is on its last legs, and I was going to ask for a new one." Since her hair had started to grow out, she had taken to wearing a purple scarf tied tightly around her head. Alex thought, but didn't say, that she looked like a cancer victim.

"But I already bought a present for you and Dad, and it cost way more than that," Nick protested.

"You can take it back," Alex said, but she was touched by his thoughtfulness.

"No, I can't. It's a gift card."

"Wow," Annie said, "you really put a lot of thought into that one, didn't you?"

"Shut up," he said. "Fat lot of good it does to do things ahead of time."

"It's a nice idea, Alex, but I can't afford an hour a week to feed the homeless, or whatever." Jack swirled the scotch in his glass.

"Why not?" she asked. Jack wasn't home much these days, blaming work and coaching, but she knew the real reason was that he wanted to stay away from her.

"I just can't. End of discussion."

"If Dad's not going to do it, then neither am I," Annie said.

"I'll try, but—"

"Fine. Scrap the whole idea," Alex said, interrupting Nick.

Maybe it was naïve of her to think that an old-fashioned Christmas was still possible in this day and age. Alex had just watched *Christmas Vacation* with the Chevy Chase character insisting on an old-fashioned Christmas, with hilariously disastrous results, but she refused to heed the warning. She was still going to do it, if only to prove that it was possible.

She had learned that it was possible, although it took a hell of a lot of work. Originally, her idea was to knit a sweater for each of them, but it had been years since she last knitted and yarn, along with everything else, had gotten so damn expensive that she would have been way over her self-imposed fifteen-dollar limit. Each member of her family was getting a wool scarf and hat made by her own hands. Which they would never wear. Which made the project utterly useless.

Still, she was keeping her spirits up. "Everything is going to be fine. We're going to have a wonderful Christmas," she said to the baby as she patted her slightly rounded abdomen. Lately, she had begun talking to the baby when no one was around. "Mommy's going to take care of everything," she would say. It helped her to feel more connected to the child—she was starting to imagine a girl—who was growing daily inside her. And she needed this connection, this reminder that it was real, since everyone else in her family was blatantly ignoring the fact of this baby. Occasionally, one of them would glance at her stomach, then quickly away.

Except for Sam, of course, who wouldn't shut up about the baby, Sam, who had recently, irritatingly, started to call her Baby Mama. They had been going through Alex's old maternity clothes they found in a box in the back of her closet. They were sadly outdated and probably hadn't been very attractive the first and second times around: shirts with bows and Peter Pan collars, a white t-shirt with a black arrow pointing down at the mound with "BABY" in block letters, cotton pants with stretched-out panels, a single plaid dress that looked like a giant blanket.

"My Baby Mama is not going to be seen out in public wearing this crap." Sam threw the dress onto the pile of discards, which was the entire contents of the box.

"Why are you calling me that?"

"I don't know. I guess I've been watching too much *Maury*. He's always having these shows where young girls are trying to find out the paternity of their babies, i.e., the Baby Daddy. You're my Baby Mama."

"It's not exactly the same thing."

"Of course not. But I like the sound of it, don't you?"

"Not really."

"Oh, lighten up, Alex. It's a term of endearment." She stood up. "We need to get you some decent maternity clothes."

"I'm not going to need them for a while." She had, though, taken a stroll through Target's maternity section. Even there, the clothes were expensive, especially considering the short time she would be wearing them.

"How much weight have you gained so far?" Sam, unlike her family, stared intently at her belly. If she could get a hold of X-ray glasses, she would undoubtedly wear them.

"Four pounds." She was right on track with the weight gain chart in her old copy of *Expectant Mothers*.

"That doesn't sound like very much. When I was pregnant with Grace, I had already gained ten pounds. Are you eating enough?"

"Yes, I'm eating enough." They had had this conversation before. Her sister was replaying the same soundtrack again and again.

"I gained forty pounds with Grace." Sam was staring out the window. "I didn't worry about it at all. Me, who was a pioneer for anorexia nervosa. Do you remember, Alex?"

"How could I not?" Sam had gotten down to eighty-eight pounds her junior year of high school. She had become the "smaller" twin, which had been her goal. It had taken her years to come to terms with the disease. But Alex doubted that a person ever truly *got over* anorexia.

"I would have gladly gained forty more pounds for Grace. It was such a privilege to be pregnant with her." Her shoulders shook.

Alex went to her and turned her gently around. Sam's eyes glistened with tears. "Are you all right?"

Sam nodded. "I'm good." She leaned her head on Alex's shoulder. "I just talked about Grace without falling apart, without sobbing, without wanting to scream. I think that's a first."

Alex stroked her hair. "That's really something." Maybe, at last, Sam would start to heal.

"And it's all because of you, Alex." She lifted her head. A smile played at the corners of her mouth. "You're my Baby Mama."

Sam had the Christmas carols blasting as she wrapped the final present and put it under the tree. Alex had warned her not to buy too much, that they were cutting down this year, but Sam couldn't help herself. Nick and

Annie knew that they could count on their aunt Sam for good presents. She had bought them a PlayStation and a couple of video games. Alex couldn't get mad at her on Christmas, a *holy* day. Knowing Alex, she would wait until later to let Sam have it, but by then, it would be too late.

Besides, she needed, somehow, to get back in Annie's good graces. Annie had managed to avoid her for almost two months now, and Sam still couldn't understand why Annie was so angry with her. She hadn't told Alex about Annie taking the van, or about the pills. No, she had bided her time, waiting to see if anything else was up with Annie, but the girl seemed to be keeping a low profile, flying under the radar. Which didn't mean that she wasn't up to something. It just meant that she hadn't been caught. Yet.

It was December 23rd, and it was time. Sam went to the closet and got out the stocking she had been hiding and hung it on the mantel. It was for the Baby, and she had stuffed it with a baby brush, rattles, two small stuffed animals, bibs, and some teething rings. The baby brush was blue because she had begun to get the feeling that Baby Mama was carrying a boy. She didn't particularly care what the sex of her child was, but the premonition was growing daily. He was a boy.

This was going to be the best Christmas she and Chris had had in a long time. They were going to be with family. Past Christmases with Louise didn't count. She was such a bitchy old lady who would offer to take them out to a nice restaurant in the city if they would drive up to get her. Then, they would sit awkwardly around a table, listening to hypochondriac Louise talk about her various ailments and spout forth venom about everyone else on the planet. The check would arrive, and Louise would excuse herself to go the restroom, where she would hide for at least thirty minutes, ensuring that Chris paid the bill. That way, the stingy old lady wouldn't have to open her padlocked pocketbook.

Sam was even going to cook Christmas dinner, her first. She didn't cook much past the basic baking of chicken, a box of Rice-a-Roni, and premade salad in a bag, but that didn't mean that she couldn't. Hell, if you could read a recipe, you could cook, right? She was a little worried about the twenty-three-pound turkey, but she had gotten instructions from the internet. Thinking about the turkey made her realize that she hadn't put it out to thaw. She hoisted the heavy bird out of the freezer and lugged it to the counter. She consulted her instructions. Shit. The bird was supposed to have started thawing four days ago. She ran cold water into the sink and plopped in the bird, hoping it would hurry the process and she wouldn't have to go out and buy a gigantic microwave to defrost it. Did they make microwaves that big?

The reason she didn't hear them was Johnny Cash's version of "The Little Drummer Boy." She turned from the sink, and there they were: her parents, Emily and Paul Murphy, the early retirees who traveled all over the United States in their Intruder RV. They hadn't bothered to tell her they were coming for the holiday. The last time she talked to them, her mother had vaguely said they would be coming "soon."

"You can hear that music from the street," Emily shouted. She looked good at 64, with her gray hair styled in a short bob—she had her hair done at the local Beauty College in whatever town they stopped in—and a sweatshirt with an embroidered face of Jesus. She seemed a little shorter and a little rounder since Sam had last seen her.

"The door was unlocked, Samantha. You live in a big city now, and you should keep your door locked at all times. I don't want to be lying awake at night thinking of your unlocked door." Paul, at 65, had lost most of his hair, and he wore a hearing aid, but his blue eyes still twinkled behind his glasses.

"What a surprise," Sam said. She should have said it was a nice surprise, but her mind was reeling. In three months, she and Alex had still not planned what they would say to their parents about the baby. They were staunch Midwestern Methodists, so their opinion on surrogacy could go either way. Sam loved her parents, she really did, but they also made her uneasy. Around them, she felt like a perpetual teenager. She turned off the music and went to hug them.

"Why didn't you call? I could have had the guest room all made up."

"Oh, that," Emily said, waving her hand. "We're free spirits now, your dad and me. We just let that rolling camper take us wherever she wants to go. Besides, we can sleep in her." She looked around the room, taking in every detail, probably noticing every crumb or stray glass.

"She's like a horse, that RV," George nodded.

So their traveling home now had a gender. "Does she have a name?" Sam was joking.

"Ginger," they said in unison.

"We were over in Bakersfield, and on a whim, we decided to come over to good old AZ and surprise our girls. We know how you like surprises, Samantha," Emily said.

Sam *hated* surprises. Did they no longer know her at all? It was like that stupid vehicle had changed their personalities. They had been strict parents, not that she or Alex had ever given them anything to worry about. They had been good students, popular and respectful, but by the time they got their driver's licenses, they were rarely home. And then they went off to college and never looked back.

"I'd like a tour of your house, Samantha. It looks," she spied a Kachina doll in a case, "Southwestern."

This might have been a little dig. Her mother's house was all chintz fabric and Precious Moments figurines. She remembered the stocking. Her mother's eagle eye would spy it, and she'd start asking questions. "Why don't you show me Ginger first?" She gave them a little nudge towards the door. "I'll be right out."

It didn't take long to tour the RV, but her parents pointed out every knob, strip of "real" wood, and appliance as if they were marvels of science. ("Look at this shower head," her mother said, "it's hand-held.") Her dad was especially proud of the satellite dish that he could extend with a crank. She supposed that they should be proud. They had taken early retirement—her dad had been a grade school principal, and her mother had been the school secretary—and sunk their life savings into her. Ginger.

Then, it was a tour of her house with her parents shuffling behind her as she walked briskly through the rooms. She only stopped when her mother would ask her how much something cost, replying: "I don't remember." She longed to get away to call Alex, to warn her, but she knew that Alex and her family, at Alex's insistence, had gone to see the student production of *A Christmas Carol* at SCDS.

Now they were sitting at her kitchen table drinking coffee, even though it was 5:00 and should have been happy hour, in Sam's opinion, and eating the box of holiday cookies that Sam had bought at Fry's. Her mother arched her eyebrows when she saw the box because, of course, Sam had not baked this year (or any year). The time was crawling by, and she wondered where Chris was. He had probably pulled into the cul-de-sac, spied Ginger, and turned around. She didn't blame him. He got along fine with her parents, but they still held it against him that he had been married before.

Emily took a tiny, precise bite of her cookie—she was still the slowest eater Sam had ever seen—before she started another story: "Do you remember that girl in your class in high school, Candace Marshall?

Sam stirred her coffee, nodded. She vaguely remembered a girl with thick glasses and mousy hair, but she had never had any classes with her and would never recognize her now.

"Well, she married the cousin of that Gluck boy from church. You have to remember him. He was in your confirmation class."

Sam nodded. She was confirmed in fourth grade and had no idea who that Gluck boy was, let alone his cousin.

"Well, she had a daughter, Lucy, who was in my vacation Bible school class for a couple of years. A sweet, sweet girl, but she was mildly retarded—"

"Mentally challenged." Dad put in his two cents.

Sam saw him reach up and turn down his hearing aid after his contribution to the story. Lucky guy.

"Mildly retarded. Well, she turned sixteen a couple of years ago and dropped out of school. She started to work at the truck stop out on I-57 outside of Bensonville, and then guess what happened?"

"I have no idea." Sam knew that her mother kept up with the local gossip back home from the women in her Red Hatters group. With *them*, she would communicate.

Her mother had reached the climactic point of the story. "She got arrested. Guess what for!"

"I have no idea." Couldn't her mother intuit that she didn't care, that she was dying of boredom here? She had a raging headache now.

"Okay, spoil-sport, I'll tell you. For prostitution! She was servicing (this in air quotes) *all* the truckers. You know how the truckers park in lines? She was going down the line and servicing (air quotes) *all* of them."

With her mother looking at her expectantly—expecting what, Sam didn't know—she could think of absolutely no response. And then, bless her heart, Alex and her family walked in.

"Look who's here," Emily cried. She nudged her husband. "Paul, it's the grandkids!"

Her mother, who could talk for hours about gossip that meant absolutely nothing to Sam, had not once mentioned her other grandchild, her lost one, nor had she asked Sam how she was feeling. To her, time healed all wounds, life went on, Jesus saved.

"Sorry," Alex mouthed, meaning she was sorry for not being there for the initial parental onslaught.

Sam gave her shoulders a slight shrug, meaning she knew it wasn't Alex's fault She hadn't known they were coming either.

Alex winked, meaning they were in this together now.

Jack had always liked his in-laws. He and Paul, especially, had always had a lot in common, talking about the state of education in the country (dismal, they thought, but there were so many things that could be done, if only there was more money), or about cars (they both liked to "tinker" around with their own automobiles). Emily, he knew, could be a little overbearing at times, a little too zealous in her religious beliefs, but she had a good heart. Since his own parents had passed, Paul and Emily were the closest thing he had to parents.

But this visit was not going especially well. Paul and Emily's unexpected appearance was adding more tension to an already tense situation. At least it was a tense situation for him and had been ever since Sam moved across the street and decided to run the show. He could feel the stress in the knotted muscles of his neck and back. He longed to ask Alex to give him a back massage like she used to do, but he wouldn't, not yet. It would be too intimate, too much like it used to be. It would make him want her again, and he had sworn to himself that he was not going to make love to his wife while she was carrying another man's baby.

Would most men have left at this point, bailed out? Was he too weak to do that, or was he too responsible? He preferred to think that he was too responsible. He had a family to take care of, a family that he loved, and he was not one to quit when the going got rough. And the going had gotten very rough indeed. And of course, he couldn't ignore or forget his responsibility in this deformed scenario.

When Alex had asked Nick, Annie, and him to do volunteer work this holiday season, he had said that he didn't have time. He had set the stage for the others to back out of doing something good, something noble, this Christmas, and he had felt like shit when he saw the hurt in Alex's eyes. However, he had been telling the truth. He hadn't told anyone that he had taken a night job at the temporary Christmas tree stand on the corner of Indian Bend and Pima. He spent his evenings hauling trees to cars and then tying them to the top, always looking over his shoulder for fear that someone he knew might see him. He was an educated man, yet he was working for minimum wage and the rare tip to supplement his income.

He had only gone to the casino a couple of times in the last two months, always losing, always regretting it as he walked out the door with empty pockets and a maxed-out credit card. Stupidly, he always started with such high hopes. He didn't understand it, not at all. He had always been frugal with money, so what in the hell was wrong with him? He knew he wasn't an addict. It wasn't that. It was the fact that in the darkened, smoky casino, he could lose himself, forget about his problems for a while, and focus all his energy on the cards in his hand. He had started to play poker with the "big boys," the men who made their living playing cards, which meant that he didn't have a chance in hell of winning. Yet he still wanted to play.

A few of the regulars were women, and one, Cookie, had made a habit of sitting next to him whenever he showed up. She had bleached blonde hair, a little dry looking, but she was attractive in a *used* kind of way. While other players silently stared at their cards, raised or folded, she whispered comments about them to him, snide comments that he found amusing. At first, he thought she was trying to help him out, but then it dawned on him that Cookie was flirting with him. *Before*, he would have politely told the woman that he was married and moved to another table. Now, he flirted back and had bought her a couple of drinks when they took a break. He was flattered. He needed to be flattered right now, and nothing more would come of it. He was sure.

Alex nudged Jack with her elbow. White candles were being passed down the pew. In his reverie, he had completely forgotten he was in church. At the insistence of Emily, they were all in church, and glancing to his left and right, they all looked decidedly uncomfortable. It was sad but true; they hadn't been to church in years. Sunday mornings, to him, meant golf.

So, at breakfast that morning (the eight of them together, again at Emily's insistence), when Emily asked, "What time is church?" They all stared at her blankly.

"We are all going to church," Emily said. "We are celebrating the day our Lord and Savior was born. It is our duty to go. No, it is our *joy* to go."

Her words hung in the air until Nick piped up. "I'm taking a Bible as Literature course, and Dr. Mitchell said that Jesus wasn't actually born on this day. The Hebrew calendar is different from ours and—"

"The Bible as Literature? What nonsense. The Bible is the *Bible*, and that's that. It is the Word. If the Bible says that Jesus was born on this day, then He was." She primly folded her paper towel and placed it by her plate. Since Alex hadn't known that her mother would arrive, she hadn't bought napkins. Hence, they were using paper towels.

Right then, Nick was the only one with any guts in the family. "Actually, the Bible doesn't say that Jesus was born on December 25th."

"Oh, hush. Of course it does. We're going to church."

Emily, the law, the Word, had spoken, and they were all here, lined up like ducks in the wooden pew: Emily, Paul, Annie, him, Alex, Nick, Sam, and Chris. Annie, her head swaddled in the purple turban, was sulking because Nana had taken her cell phone away at the beginning of the service when she caught her texting. Nick was actually reading the Bible, probably looking for any mention of Jesus's birthdate, and the rest of the adults, except for Emily, were staring at the pastor with glazed eyes, thinking other thoughts.

Jack bowed his head, as if in prayer, but he was fiddling with the paper on the candle. It was there to catch the dripping wax, but it looked like a little skirt. He knew many churches held a candlelight ceremony on Christmas Eve, but it had always seemed dangerous to him. How easy it would be to drop the candle or hold it too close to a hymnal and have the whole church go up in flames. All semblance of holy serenity would be gone when people knocked over each other as they stampeded to the exit like frightened cattle.

Nick closed the Bible. Too loud, he whispered, "I was right. It does *not* say when Jesus was actually born."

Luckily, Emily, like her husband, was starting to lose her hearing. Her head was slightly raised. It appeared that she was looking at the crucifix, bobbing above a sea of poinsettias, at the front of the church. She probably was.

Alex patted Nick's hand and gently whispered, "Let it go, son."

His son. Jack loved him so much, and he was such a good, decent kid. A good, decent kid who was misguided about his future. Nick had been quite adept at avoiding the entire college application process with hollow excuse after hollow excuse. Finally, without Nick's knowledge or consent, Jack had filled out the U of A application himself and mailed it in. He had called a friend of his in the Admissions Department, and it was almost a certainty that Nick would get in. They should hear any day, and then together (although Jack had already started), they could begin to work on scholarship applications. Nick would be angry at first, but Jack knew that he would get over it, and by the time next fall rolled around, Nick would be excited to go to Tucson.

Alex's gentle nudge came again. It was time to rise with the rest of the congregation for the final song. They sang "Silent Night, Holy Night" as the flame was passed person to person, lighting candle after candle. Annie's went out when she turned to light his. "Damn," she said. She turned to her right and lit it again with Paul's, then succeeded in lighting Jack's.

He turned to Alex. Her eyes were wet with tears. "This is lovely," she said. "We should go to church more often."

He lit her candle. He should have said something meaningful then, or something comforting. But he didn't. "They don't do this every Sunday," he said.

Her tattoo itched. Was that normal? Annie sat in the rubble of wrapping paper in Aunt Sam's living room and tried not to scratch it. "Thanks for the gifts, everybody. I love everything." She did love the PlayStation. She and Nick had been careful not to let their true glee show and acted like they didn't see Mom's pursed lips and the shake of her head she pointed at Aunt Sam. If Aunt Sam was trying to get back in Annie's good graces after she had nosed into her business, she had a good start going with this gift, even though Annie couldn't remember exactly what had happened that Saturday because Carla had given her an Ecstasy tablet to make it through the long weekend of her house arrest. Nana and Poppy's Christmas gift was a seventy-five-dollar gift card to J.C. Penney's. Annie wouldn't be caught dead wearing anything from that store, but she figured she could buy some stuff—maybe sheets and towels—return them for cash, then go to Old Navy.

Christmas at home this morning had been pretty lame. Since they were only doing cheap gifts this year, there was no need to get up early like she used to do when she was a little kid. She'd wake up at 5:00—that is, if she'd gone to sleep at all—and then be forced to wait two agonizing hours. (The Rule: No Getting Up Before 7:00 a.m. Mom thought it would make Christmas last longer if they didn't start at the *crack of dawn*.) It was ten o'clock when she meandered down the stairs this morning, enticed by the smell of the cinnamon rolls that Mom baked every Christmas. She got a scarf and hat from Mom, two CDs from Dad (Social Distortion—she couldn't believe he knew that), and a curling iron from Nick.

"Very funny," she said to him.

"I thought so," he said.

"Christmas," Mom reminded.

Annie couldn't stand it any longer. She excused herself to go to the bathroom. She locked the door and carefully lifted the bandage from her left hip. The black jagged half heart with BFF inside looked a little pink and swollen, but the tattoo guy said that was normal. She and Carla had debated about where to get the tattoos. Originally, they had considered putting them on their sides, but as Carla pointed out, that would outlaw any possibility of wearing a two-piece bathing suit in the near future. It was imperative that the tattoos not be seen by their parents, so that left boobs, butts, and hips. Hips it was.

The research they had done said that the hip was one of the most sensitive areas to tattoo. No shit, Sherlock. She thought she was going to pass out at one point, but Carla held her hand the whole time, as she had done for Carla, who had gone first, naturally, and had gotten her half-jagged heart on her right hip. Carla, with bravado, had said it didn't hurt, but Annie knew how hard she had gripped her hand. Afterward, they were giddy with excitement.

"I can't believe we did that!" Annie said, relieved and exuberant at the same time. She would always remember that she got her first tattoo with Carla on Christmas Eve.

Carla's headscarf was aquamarine, and it looked like her outfit's goal for the day was to channel Paris Hilton with a pink t-shirt that said *that's hot*. "We are amazing!" She pawed in her oversize bag until she found a cigarette.

"And we are brave!"

"Well, those three shots of tequila from my trusty flask probably helped with that." They got into Carla's BMW. "Are you sure you can't come to my house for a little while?" Carla asked for the hundredth time. Her exuberance was beginning to fade.

"I can't. I've got to do the church thing with the grandparents, and there's no way I can get out of it." She had already explained this to Carla, but Annie knew she was disappointed just the same. Since Carla's family was Jewish, they had already celebrated Hanukah and had no plans for tonight. In fact, her parents were leaving for Dubai at five o'clock, and Carla would be alone.

"You could come to church with us." Annie didn't know why she hadn't thought of this before. It was so obvious.

"It's okay. I don't want to butt in on your family." Carla started the car.

"Everyone would *love* to have you join us." Annie wasn't entirely sure about this. Her mom could get all weird about the *family* thing, but surely the spirit of the holidays would prevail, wouldn't it?

"A Jew girl does not need to be sitting in a Christian church on Christmas Eve. It's probably against my religion or something. I should have paid more attention during my bat mitzvah and learned something. I had the best party, though. All the other kids said so."

In the bathroom, thinking about Carla being alone on Christmas, Annie felt a wave of sadness for her best friend. Annie had always thought Carla had it made with parents who traveled all the time and left her pretty much on her own. But it did seem callous for them to leave their daughter alone during the holidays.

"They don't see me," Carla had said on more than one occasion.

"Sure they do," Annie said. Carla was always hard on the parental unit.

"I could shave my head, and they wouldn't notice." And she had a point. Her parents did not say one word about Carla's Mohawk as they rushed away to another destination. Not one word.

Annie decided to call her instead of texting. She could sing a silly Christmas song, like "Rudolph, the Red-Nosed Reindeer" in a squeaky voice like the Chipmunks. Maybe it would cheer up Carla and make her laugh. But the phone rang hollowly, and Carla didn't answer. Annie decided she would try again later, but now she needed to get back to her family. She had been in the bathroom long enough. She flushed the stool and went out.

To wait, and wait, and wait. Aunt Sam's dinner was supposed to be at 2:00, but when she had put the turkey in, it was still partly frozen. The Costco appetizers, mini quiches, buffalo wings, and vegetable tray, were long gone, the empty plate practically licked clean. The men—well, they were all men except for dorky Nick—were in the den watching football, Dad and Uncle Chris pounding down the scotch. Obviously, no one was going to offer her an alcoholic drink, so Annie found a box of Ritz crackers in the pantry and settled herself on a kitchen chair to watch the women. Really, it was like watching a soap opera.

Aunt Sam opened the oven door to stick in a meat thermometer. "Not even close," she said, slamming the door shut.

"You should have put out that bird to thaw sooner," Nana said.

"I know that now, Mother. It's the first time I've cooked a turkey." She opened the oven door again.

"It's never going to get done if you keep opening that door," Nana said.

It was comical. All three women were hovering around the stove like it was some huge deal. It was like a Greek tragedy or something. Who knew? Maybe they thought they could put a band-aid on the turkey and make it *well*. Annie giggled. She was enjoying herself.

"It doesn't matter what time we eat," Mom said. The voice of reason, her mom.

"But everything else is getting cold," Aunt Sam argued. She poured a glass of champagne from the open bottle on the counter.

"How many glasses of champagne have you had, Samantha?" Nana sounded suspicious.

"I'm not counting, Mother. It's Christmas." She snapped out *Christmas* like it was a swear word.

"Look at your sister. She's not drinking. She's finally realized that alcohol doesn't do a person any good. I'm proud of you, Alexandra." Nana patted Mom's shoulder affectionately. "It's about time."

"Well, there is a reason that I'm not—"

Aunt Sam stepped in front of her. "Why don't you make yourself useful, Mother, and go fill the water glasses?"

"You know I want to be useful, but it's too early to fill the water glasses. All the ice will melt, and I like ice in my water." Today, Nana's sweatshirt had a glittering nativity scene across her ample chest. (Why didn't I inherit those? Annie wondered.)

"Fine. You can refill your glass again right before dinner. How's that?"

"I'll leave my glass empty for the time being," Nana grumbled. "No use wasting water. You girls live in a desert now, and you should know how important it is to conserve water." She filled a plastic pitcher with ice from the dispenser and water from the sink.

"Use the filtered water, Mother, that lever on the left. I showed that to you yesterday." Aunt Sam's face was red, and Annie didn't know if it was caused by heat from the stove or Nana.

"Too late now." Nana carried the pitcher into the dining room.

"She's driving me crazy!" Aunt Sam hissed.

"Why did you cut me off?" Mom hissed back. "Let's get this over with."

"I want to wait until everyone is sitting at the Christmas dinner table. I want the announcement to be special."

"So, you want to wait until next week?"

"*Et tu, Brute?*"

Annie stopped munching on the crackers and sat up straighter. Nana and Poppy didn't know about the baby? That would certainly explain why they hadn't said anything about it before. Since they never talked about the baby in her family, it hadn't seemed all that strange. Now it did. But why hadn't Mom and Aunt Sam told Nana and Poppy? They were ultra-religious, that was for sure, but it seemed to Annie that they would love to have another grandchild. Maybe Methodists were against surrogacy? She would have to look this up, and if she had gotten a new laptop for Christmas, she could have done it right then. But maybe her mom and Aunt Sam were afraid of Nana? Annie liked this idea. It made the whole mother/daughter playing field much more even. Or maybe something else was going on? She wouldn't doubt it. Everyone had been acting funny since that trip to Vegas. *Sin City.* She couldn't wait until she was old enough to go.

Nana came back into the kitchen and sat down in the chair next to Annie's. "Since we have a lot of time here, Annie," she looked at Aunt Sam, who promptly filled her champagne glass, "let's talk."

Uh-oh. Nana's full one-on-one attention made her nervous. She could kind of see why Mom and Aunt Sam would be a little afraid of her.

"How's school?"

"Fine."

"Do you have a boyfriend?"

Annie blushed. "No."

"When I was your age, I had quite a few admirers. Poppy was the only one who got lucky."

What did that mean? He got to marry her, or they had . . . sex? She wasn't going to ask. She reached in the box for another handful of crackers.

"Don't spoil your dinner, Annie. It will be ready eventually."

At that, Aunt Sam yanked open the oven door, jabbed the turkey with the oversized thermometer, then slammed the door shut again.

"That's a pretty scarf," Nana said, fingering the silk. "Is that the new style? Poppy and I watched that MTV channel the other night—it was the only channel we could get in the RV park—and I think one of those unladylike girls had one on. Is it the new style?"

"I don't know. I just like to wear it." In agreement for once, no one in her family thought that Nana needed to know about her hair.

"It's looking a little soiled. Why don't you take it off? I can hand wash it." She looked at Aunt Sam. "We have time."

"I hate all turkeys," Aunt Sam said, slugging down her champagne.

"That's okay." Annie tried to gently tug the silk from Nana's fingers. "It's Christmas."

"I need something to do," Nana said with more force. "Give me the scarf, Annie."

Panicked, she looked at Mom. "There's absolutely no reason to do that now, Mother. Like Annie said, it's Christmas." Mom started toward the table.

"I insist."

Annie stood up. She needed a way out of this situation. "Mom's pregnant with Aunt Sam's baby!"

Mom stopped dead in her tracks, and Aunt Sam knocked over her champagne glass.

"Jesus Christ," Nana said.

They forgot all about the turkey in the commotion that followed. Chris, Jack, Paul, and Nick raced to the kitchen when they heard the shattering of glass and the shriek that followed. Chris imagined the worst. In Sam's growing frustration with her mother, she had snapped and hit Emily over the head with a champagne bottle. Sam had tried so hard to make this Christmas perfect, despite Chris's quiet insistence that there was no such thing as a perfect Christmas, and then her parents arrived and derailed her. As everyone knew, Sam didn't like to be derailed.

However, when he got to the kitchen, the broken glass was a shattered Waterford goblet on the floor, and there was no blood streaming down Emily's face. Emily had her hand over her heart and was muttering, "WWJD. WWJD. WWJD."

Chris looked to Paul. "What is she saying?"

"What Would Jesus Do."

"What's going on here?" Jack asked.

"Is Nana having a heart attack?" Nick had his ever-present cell phone in his hand. "Should I call 911?"

"Nana is not having a heart attack," Alex said. "She just found out about the baby."

"Is Annie pregnant?" Paul asked, glancing at her with sorrow in his eyes.

"No, Poppy! Mom's pregnant with Aunt Sam's baby." Annie looked shaken.

Sam looked mad, and Chris suspected that she had not been the one to spill the beans. She had planned to make the grand announcement during dinner. "Annie told Nana," she said, trying to keep her voice under control.

"I need a glass of water," Emily said dramatically as she sat down.

Sam reached into the cupboard for a glass.

"My glass is the empty one on the table," Emily said, fanning herself with her hand.

Sighing, Sam went and retrieved the glass and filled it. "Aren't you happy that you'll be having another grandchild, Mother?" she asked.

"I don't understand what's going on here," Emily said.

"Alex is the surrogate for Chris's and my baby," Sam said. She kept clenching and unclenching her hands, which meant she *really* wanted a cigarette.

"Let me explain," Alex said.

She patiently told the agreed-upon version of the story, about the identical DNA, the decision to go to Vegas to a fertility clinic, and the miracle of her getting pregnant the first and only time. Of course, Alex didn't tell her parents what had really happened in Vegas, and of course, she didn't tell them that she was being paid for her services by Chris. So the story seemed skewed to Chris. Alex came across as noble, while Sam was the selfish one who wanted another baby.

"You can think of it as a kind of Immaculate Conception," Sam said hopefully.

"Don't blaspheme, Samantha Marie Murphy. Jesus was not conceived in a test tube," Emily said sharply.

Chris saw that he wasn't the only one who was trying to hide a smile at the image that statement brought to mind.

"We will be blessed with another grandchild, Emily." Paul stood behind her and patted her shoulder.

"I am happy about that. Another grandchild will indeed be a blessing, but our girls are forty—no spring chickens."

"Many women are having babies in their forties, and even their fifties," Alex said. "And the doctor says that I'm the picture of health."

"Yes, all those movie stars who have money to burn and think it's the thing to do, to accessorize with a baby." Emily shuddered. "I don't buy those trashy magazines, but sometimes the line at the supermarket is long, and I might glance in their direction."

"This is good news." Paul kissed Alex and then Sam on the cheek.

"Aren't you happy, Mother?" A tiny note of pleading crept into Sam's voice.

"Are you sure you're strong enough to do this, Samantha? When our little angel passed, your father and I feared for—"

"Grace." Sam interrupted. "My daughter's name was Grace."

Tears came to Emily's eyes. "I know that, dear. I know that."

"And this baby is not a replacement for Grace."

"Not at all," Alex added.

Uncharacteristically, Emily remained silent.

"If you're thinking along the lines of: If Jesus wanted me to have a baby, I would have been able to have another one . . . just stop it. I think God wanted this baby on earth, and that's why he made Alex and me identical twins."

Emily remained silent.

"What's the matter, Mother?" Alex asked.

"I'm hurt," Emily said. Her voice was childish, petulant.

"Why?" Sam was trying hard not to explode.

"You should have told me sooner. I'm the grandmother of this baby, and you shouldn't have let three months go by without telling me."

"We never know where you are," Alex said.

"That doesn't matter, Alexandra. You could have found a way to let me know." She crossed her arms over the nativity scene on her ample chest.

It took another two hours for Sam and Alex to cajole their mother out of her hurt mood, and Chris couldn't tell if it was real, imagined, or manufactured. Emily did like to be the center of attention, but he had had enough. He wandered back to the den with the rest of the men where he pretended to be interested in the Cardinals versus the Steelers. Another scotch, and he couldn't keep his eyes opened. To Chris, sleep was preferable to football any day of the week.

It was after five o'clock when Sam awakened him. "Time to eat," she slurred. "That damn turkey is finally ready."

"Sorry I didn't help," Chris said. At the very least, he should have mashed the potatoes.

"That's okay, honey. You're on clean-up duty."

Alex couldn't rouse Jack from the chair. Chris looked at the Glenlivet bottle. It had been full that morning; now it was almost empty. Jack was really drinking too much these days, and Alex was pretending not to notice. "I'll make him a plate," Alex said. "He can eat later."

They quickly ate the Christmas dinner that Sam had prepared, and frankly, it was terrible. The turkey—stubborn and then forgotten—had overcooked to the consistency of beef jerky, the potatoes were lumpy, and even the rolls were burnt. Emily and Paul had decided, with just a look between them, that they would leave that night.

"Your father and I have decided that we need to visit the Grand Canyon again. If we leave soon, before dark, we should be able to make it to Flagstaff," Emily said.

No one protested. No one said, "But you can't leave on Christmas," or "You just got here." Chris couldn't tell whether Emily was hurt by their ambivalent response or not. She didn't make her feelings known. She wolfed down her food., which was something of a small miracle because she was normally a painfully slow eater. Then, in a flurry of goodbyes, she corraled Paul out to the RV.

And they were gone.

"Merry Christmas," Sam said as they all watched the retreating RV. Everyone, that is, except for Jack, who was still passed out in the chair.

"I'll help clean up." It was clear that Alex was exhausted.

"No, that's all right," Chris said. "You go on home." He would clear the table, load the dishwasher, and scrub the pans. He alone would clean up the mess.

Nick knew what it was, but he couldn't believe it. He had planned on rushing upstairs to change clothes before he met Jennifer at Starbucks, but he had made a quick detour through the kitchen to grab a snack. The waiting white 8" by 11" envelope with the U of A logo in the corner might as well have been a stop sign. He knew enough from listening to the other seniors talk that a letter-sized envelope from a college meant that you were rejected or wait-listed. A large envelope like this one meant that you had been accepted. He had been accepted by U of A, and he hadn't even applied.

His father had. He had gone behind Nick's back, even though Nick had repeatedly told him that he wanted to join the Marines after graduation. Nick felt a surge of helpless rage. He couldn't ever remember being mad at his dad before, but he was mad now. Blood-boiling mad. He was going to be eighteen in a few weeks, a grown-up, yet his parents were still treating him like a child. He grabbed the offensive envelope and took it to his room where he stuffed it in the back of his closet. He knew it wouldn't do any good to put it there, that his parents had undoubtedly already seen it, but it still made him feel better to treat the envelope like trash, like it meant nothing at all.

He had to jog to Starbucks. Of course, there was no car available, which further fueled his helpless rage. He had already had to walk home from Fry's, since his mom had the Lexus and had gone to the after-Christmas sale at Target to stock up on Christmas decorations for next year, and his dad had taken the Jeep to who knows where. The van, which was supposed to be "his" vehicle, was in the shop yet again. His parents had given him a broken-down heap that only ran half the time. Thanks a lot, Dad and Mom.

He counted on Jennifer to get him out of his foul mood. She could always cheer him up, even though he disliked their new habit of meeting at this coffee shop. He thought it was a waste of money to spend close to five bucks on a cup of coffee, especially since he didn't really like the taste. But Jennifer was hooked on her venti mocha lattes, so Starbucks it was. This was their third meeting here this Christmas vacation, the only times they had seen each other. Jennifer had relatives from Korea in town, and her parents insisted that she stay close to home.

She was sitting at a table by the window, the absurdly large cup of coffee in front of her, and she smiled when she saw him. His spirits lifted.

"I have some exciting news," she said.

"What's that?" He slid into the chair across from her.

"I got into Stanford!" Her face was flushed.

"Oh." They had mostly avoided talking about college plans. Well, he had avoided talking about it, changing the subject every time she brought it up. He had known that her parents desperately hoped that she would get into Stanford, her father's alma mater. But Jennifer had acted ambivalent about the whole thing—until now.

"You don't sound very joyous for me," she said, almost pouting.

He was supposed to be *joyous* for her? That was a stupid word to use in this situation. Another first for the day: At this moment, he thought Jennifer could be childish. He had recognized this before, of course, but had thought it was endearing. Not today. "Congratulations," he mumbled.

"I thought you'd be happy for me." Now, she was pouting.

"I'm *overflowing* with *joyousness*. Can't you tell?" His voice didn't sound at all like his normal voice. It was angry, surly.

"What's the matter with you? Did something happen at work?"

"No." Work had been busy, which was good. It made the time go by faster. (Nick suspected that a lot of the shoppers were trying to escape relative-crammed homes.)

"Then what is it?"

"Nothing. Can we change the subject?"

"Oh," she said knowingly. "Don't worry, Nick. You'll be hearing from colleges soon. I know you'll get into a good school." She totally misunderstood the situation.

"I don't want to go to college," he said, finally admitting the truth to her.

"What?" She was incredulous. "Everyone at SCDS goes to college. After all, it is a college-prep school."

Sarcastically, he said, "Then I will be *notorious* in SCDS history. I will be the first student *ever* who did not go to college."

"But what would you do?"

She had no imagination. "I want to join the military. Specifically, the Marines."

"But you could get killed!"

"I could get killed by a car crossing the street. I could get struck by lightning. I could get pulverized by perverts. What's your point?" He thought he loved her, but he was being intentionally mean to her. He didn't care.

"I don't want you to get hurt," she said quietly.

"I could get murdered by a home invader. I could fall down a well. I could have a brain aneurysm," he went on.

"Nick—"

"I could get croaked by a foul ball. I could have a heart attack. I could get trapped in a burning house." He didn't seem to be able to stop himself.

"That's enough," she said, her voice barely audible.

He had hurt her feelings and should apologize. It was the right thing to do. He got up and got a paper cup of water from the glass jug on the counter. Lemons floated on the top. He drained the cup and poured another. He took his time, thinking what he should say to her. They had just had their first fight, and it was all his fault. When he turned back toward the table, Jennifer was gone.

He ran outside. She was probably in her car, waiting for him to say he was sorry. But that, too, had vanished. He reached into his pocket for his phone. He held it in his hand and stared at it, then put it back. He would text her later.

He went to Dylan's; he needed to talk to his best friend. He found Dylan in his back yard—supposedly, according to Mrs. Taylor—cleaning their murky green pool. Instead, he was sprawled on a tattered blue chaise, arms folded behind his head, the bud of his iPod plugged into his ear. Nick nudged him awake and immediately began spilling his story of his dad's betrayal and his first fight with Jennifer.

Dylan, always a good and faithful listener, nodded sympathetically. "Rough day, dude."

"What do you think I should do about U of A?" Nick worriedly broke a twig into tiny pieces and threw them into the pool. It was so dirty that a few more pieces of debris wouldn't even be noticed.

"Don't sweat it. You're not going to go. You're going to join the Marines with me. That's always been the plan."

That was easy for Dylan to say. His parents were supportive of him joining the military. He would be following in his dad's artillery footsteps. "But what about my dad?" Nick asked.

"Look, dude, when you're eighteen, you can quit school and just go. You don't need his permission to sign up." Dylan pushed his old sweater up his skinny arms.

"And not finish high school?" Nick had never, ever considered that.

"We could get our GEDs instead. I feel like this next semester of senior year is a big waste of time anyway. I'm only waiting for you." Dylan had turned eighteen two weeks before, and he was a mediocre student at best.

"I can't do that. It would just kill my parents."

Dylan shrugged. "Fine, dude, we'll finish high school, and the day after we graduate, we enlist. We'll just go to the recruiting office, sign up, and that will be that. No one can stop us then."

Nick thought that Dylan had a good point. "You're right. I can just play along, act like I'm going to do what they want me to do, then enlist."

"Vanish," Dylan said. "*Vamoose.*"

Okay then, their Marine plan could probably work after all. All he had to do—and really, it was a little bit daunting—was act for the next five and a half months. He half-heartedly wished Carla gave acting lessons. He could use her help in that department. "What do you think I should do about Jennifer?"

"You're going to have to apologize, man. Chicks get off on that kind of thing," Dylan said knowingly.

When did Dylan become an expert on *chicks*? "Yeah, I'm going to text her later tonight, as soon as I think of what to say."

"Nah, dude, you have to show up at her door. Maybe bring her a present or something." Dylan took the rubber band from his scraggly ponytail and flicked it at a dead gecko lizard floating on the pool's surface. "Bingo," he said.

"Flowers?" He had never gotten Jennifer a present before. What if she had expected something for Christmas, and he had just blown her off? Annie was right. Sometimes, he could be the world's biggest dork.

"That would be perfect, man. Chicks dig flowers."

The question begged to be asked. "How come you're such an expert on *chicks* all of a sudden? The last I knew, you were as knowledgeable as me. Which is to say that we don't know squat."

Dylan grinned. "I've been initiated, Nick old chum."

"Wait—"

"Did the deed." Dylan nodded.

Nick digested this information. Dylan and Melissa had had *sex.* "When?"

"Last night. Melissa said it was her Christmas present to me, and I shit you not, man, you could have knocked me over with a feather. I didn't see it coming, but of course, I didn't say no." Dylan couldn't stop grinning.

"Where?"

"In her bedroom. Her parents were at a party."

"Wow."

"I know."

Nick hadn't even gotten to the point of imagining sex with Jennifer in his daydreams yet. Once again, Dylan had jumped ahead—way ahead!—of him on the relationship ladder. Nick was somewhat appalled, somewhat titillated, somewhat jealous. He knew he shouldn't ask, but: "How . . . was it?"

"I'm going to be a gentleman about this. I'm not going to kiss and tell. Or you know what and tell."

Nick nodded. He would expect nothing less of Dylan. "Right."

"But it's a lot messier than they let on in the movies."

Nick had one more question. "Are you in love with her?"

Dylan looked thoughtful, then shrugged. "I don't know about that, dude, but I think it's fair to say that I'm *in like* with her."

Nick nodded once again, trying to absorb all this new information. A few short months ago, he and Dylan had not been interested in girls at all. "Nick's just a late bloomer," his mother had said to Aunt Sam. Maybe it was time to tell his mother about Jennifer, ask her for advice as well as Loretta. One thing he knew for certain was that he needed all the help he could get.

Oh, he knew one more thing for certain. He had to apologize to Jennifer and hope she would accept—if she was still *in like* with him.

Alex didn't know why she had agreed to come to this neighborhood holiday party thrown by Amanda Williams. She didn't even like the woman, who was pretentious to a fault. She was always talking about how much money her husband, Curtis, made; yet it was a secret as to what Curtis actually did for a living. With her bleached blonde hair down to her butt (probably an implant) and her breasts the size of cantaloupes (definitely implants), she was a walking stereotype of the Scottsdale woman that she and Sam called Barbies. But the thing that irritated Alex most was that silly Amanda didn't even know that she was a stereotype. No, Amanda thought she was stylish and beautiful.

"I'm not going," she had said to Jack only an hour before. She had been feeling odd all day—not ill, certainly, just off, *funky*.

"We should go," Jack said. "All the neighbors will be there, and we've been neglecting our friends since Sam moved across the street."

That was true. Sam hadn't really expressed an interest in socializing with the other couples in the neighborhood. Alex had invited some of her friends over for coffee shortly after Sam moved to Arizona to introduce her. Sam had put on a good face, but after the women left, she told Alex that she had suffered through it and found their housewife talk to be utterly boring.

"Besides, you know how they love to show off. The booze will be expensive stuff," Jack said.

The last thing Jack needed was more booze, but as was her modus operandi these days, she would hold her tongue and get through this holiday season without making waves. "The alcohol does not give *me* a reason to go." Was he going to persist in ignoring this pregnancy until the end?

"They employ our daughter, and it's almost impossible for a teenager to get a job these days."

This was true, too, and the reason she finally agreed to come. Jack was also right that most of the neighbors were there: the Millers, the Udalls, the Shapiros, the Westmores, the Carters, the Walkers. She had made the rounds and joined in the usual chitchat about their middle-class lives: How was your holiday? How're the kids? How's the golf game? How's the job? What's your mortgage rate now that you've refinanced? What do you think about a Black president? (Oh, sorry, let's leave politics out of a holiday party!) Do you think this fucking economy will ever improve?

Alex stifled a yawn as she walked around with a glass of sparkling cider. She felt dowdy and underdressed compared to the other women in their sequin dresses and high heels. She was at the point in her pregnancy that everything was getting tight. She hadn't been able to button her good black wool slacks and had ended up wearing an old elastic-waist skirt that would have been more appropriate to go bowling in, but at least it concealed her burgeoning belly. No one knew she was pregnant yet, and she wanted to keep it that way for as long as possible. These people, her dearest friends, were a nosy and gossipy bunch, and she dreaded their prying questions.

Alex was about ready to call it quits when Sam arrived at 8:00. The party had started at six, and it wasn't the type of party that you were supposed to be fashionably late for. "Where've you been?" she asked Sam.

Sam had spotted her immediately and made a beeline for her corner with Chris in tow. "I thought I'd wait until this group had knocked back a few. Maybe they'll be more interesting."

Sam looked stunning in a sleeveless red sweater dress that she had ordered from Victoria's Secret, and Alex felt even worse about her appearance. "I'm barely," Alex looked around and whispered, "pregnant, but I already feel like a frump."

"You look fine." Sam had noticed her skirt and couldn't help herself from biting her lip. "We need to do the big M shopping."

"You better not have planned a grand announcement, Sam. I mean it."

"No way. Tell these snippy bitches? I don't give a flying fuck—oh, hi, Amanda. Lovely party."

Amanda had come up just then with a tray of champagne. "I can't find my serving girl anywhere," she pouted, and with her lips newly collagenous, she looked like a well-dressed fish. "It's so hard to find decent help these days."

"What movie is that line from?" Sam asked with feigned politeness. "I know I've heard it somewhere before." She took a glass of champagne from the tray.

"Excuse me?" Amanda arched her perfectly plucked brows.

"I'm going to get a bite to eat," Chris said, probably not wanting to be around just in case any kind of catfight ensued.

"This is a really nice party," Alex interjected. "Did you repaint your living room?" If there was one sure way to divert Amanda, it was to get her talking about how much money she had recently spent.

"Why, yes, I did," Amanda said, pleased. "It cost an arm and a leg, but Curtis got such a large bonus this year that I thought: What the heck? I owe it to my family to create a lovely and serene environment. Mint green is such a soothing color, don't you think?"

"Yes," Alex said while Sam choked on her champagne.

Curtis called to his wife to join a group of his golf buddies, and she sashayed over to him, hips swiveling in her tight dress.

"What planet is that Stepford Wife from?" Sam looked at the walls. "Mint green, my ass. It looks like there's moss growing on her walls."

The color was indeed terrible, but Alex didn't want to egg on Sam. "You need to play nice, Sam. These people are our neighbors."

"I know, but really! Parties like this one make me ashamed to be part of the Keeping-up-with-the-Joneses middle class. They're so predictable."

"The parties or the middle class?"

"Both. People will drink too much. Men will flirt with other men's wives, and the wives will flirt with their best friends' husbands. Secrets will be told in confidence, but they'll be all over the neighborhood by tomorrow. Approximately half of the couples here will be fighting by the time they get home."

"Then why don't you go home?" Alex was slightly offended. She had always liked being part of the middle class and being a part of this neighborhood. She genuinely liked these people, excluding Amanda, of course.

"Because *you're* here, Alex." Sam snagged another champagne glass from a passing tray. (It seemed that the missing service girl had reappeared.) "I'm going to go back on the wagon after the holidays. I promise."

"I really don't care, Sam." In fact, alcohol sounded repulsive to her these days, but she didn't think it had anything to do with her pregnancy. No, it was watching her husband drinking to excess on the few nights he was home. It was as if he wanted to forget her, or maybe even obliterate her from his consciousness. She looked over at him standing by the makeshift bar in the corner of the living room, scotch in hand, talking and laughing (flirting?) with Greta Udall. It was painfully true; he was Sam's stereotype.

Alex felt slightly queasy. She reached out for Sam's arm.

"Are you all right?" Sam asked with concern.

"I don't think the shrimp dip agreed with me." The queasiness was starting to feel more like actual pain.

"I'll take you home."

"I think I should use the bathroom first." It took sheer will for her not to clutch her stomach. "Will you help me to the bathroom?"

Sam led her to the powder room on the first floor where there was a line of four women. "Do you mind if Alex cuts ahead?" she asked. "She isn't feeling well."

Normally, Sam's pushiness would have embarrassed Alex, but tonight she was grateful as the women let her go to the front of the line. When the door opened, she pushed through. Sam followed.

"Sam, I don't need you in here with me. Are we sorority girls who have to follow each other into the bathroom to moan and complain about the bitch who is trying to steal their boyfriends?"

"I'm helping you," Sam said. "Don't try to stop me."

Sam turned her back, and Alex pulled down her underwear and sat on the toilet. The pain was lessening somewhat, but she had broken out in a sweat. And then she saw the streak of blood in her panties. "Oh, my god," she said.

"What?" Sam asked, not turning around.

"Don't panic," Alex said, although panic had already taken control of her heart, making it beat rapidly. "I'm bleeding—just a little, not a lot." Alex knew that some women spotted during their pregnancies, but it had never happened to her before. And was this pain—cramping, she realized—normal? Something told her it couldn't be.

Sam, of course, didn't listen to her. "No!" she screamed. "This cannot be happening, not again!" She wrenched open the door and shouted at the top of her lungs. "Someone call an ambulance! *Now!*"

Alex could hear the women outside the door murmuring: What is it? Did she fall? Is she drunk? Is she ill?

"Someone call a fucking ambulance!" Sam was now hysterical. "Alex is having a miscarriage!"

It was the first time Jennifer had been to his house. For some strange reason, it seemed to Nick like a big step in their relationship. There was something really personal about letting someone see where you lived, where you ate your meals, where you slept, and God forbid, where you went to the bathroom. But Jennifer had asked, and he was so relieved she wasn't mad at him—"not at all!" she had said—that he agreed to bring her here. Plus, he knew that his parents were at the Williams' holiday party, so there wasn't the added pressure of having to introduce Jennifer to them as his girlfriend. His dad would wonder why he hadn't seen them together at school (because they made it a point *not* to be seen), and his mom would fall all over her, asking questions, questions, questions. It was better this way.

It was a new experience to see things through Jennifer's eyes. The comfortable plaid family room couch that he had always loved to sprawl over when he watched TV now looked a little shabby to him. So did the furniture in the den, the curtains in the kitchen, and the towels in the powder room. His mom hadn't bought anything new for the house for quite a while now. How had he not noticed this before? Jennifer lived in a new house in a new subdivision, and since both her parents worked, they had it professionally decorated. It was so obvious that his family had not. Nick tried to shake this thought out of his mind. He loved his house. It was . . . homey.

"This is very nice," Jennifer said, taking in every detail. She walked over to the collage of pictures on the family room wall. "You were such a cute little boy! How old were you in this one?"

She was looking at him sitting on Santa's knee wearing tiny cowboy boots and a miniature Stetson. For the first time, it seemed to him like a weird thing to dress your kid in when he was going to see Santa Claus. Shouldn't he have had on a Christmas sweater or something? "Two, almost three," he said, walking over to her.

"You look like such a happy family," she said wistfully.

She was studying the large picture in the center, the family picture where they all sprawled on a white furry rug dressed in matching denim shirts. He had been eight in the picture, and he still remembered the plush softness of that rug and how they had all giggled uncontrollably when the photographer suggested that pose, which seemed like an outlandish idea. Yet it had turned out to be the best picture of them and the one his mom bought. His mom still stared at that picture a lot. He had seen her do it many times when she thought no one was around. And like Jennifer, Mom, too, would have a wistful expression on her face.

"Where's your bedroom?" Jennifer asked suddenly.

Nick felt the all too familiar stupid blush rising into his cheeks. "Upstairs."

"Do you mind showing it to me?" She saw the redness on his cheeks. "I mean, if you don't want to, that's okay, too."

"No, no, of course I don't mind." Had he left dirty underwear on the floor? If he had, he would have to kick it under the bed before she noticed it, like they did in the movies. He highly doubted this, however. He was usually neat, or if you listened to Annie, he was *anal*.

When they reached the top of the stairs, he pointed at Annie's closed door. "This is my sister's room. I'm not going to show you that. It's probably radioactive."

Jennifer giggled.

He loved to make her laugh. "Seriously, she could raise pigs in there, and it would be a step up on the cleanliness ladder."

Jennifer giggled again.

He was on a roll now. "Seriously, the smell would improve if she—"

"I can hear you." Annie's voice came from behind the closed door. "You and Dylan get away from my fucking door. And Dylan, you giggle like a girl."

"In here." Nick practically pushed Jennifer through the door of his room. That was a close call. He had thought that Annie was gone, and there was no way he wanted her to know about Jennifer. He would never hear the end of it, and she, being Annie, could spoil everything. He quickly closed and locked the door behind them. "Don't pay any attention to her," he said to Jennifer.

And then Annie was pounding on his door. "Hey, bro, can you lend me ten bucks? Carla will be here any minute, and I'm flat broke—unless you want to count that lame J.C. Penney's gift card. Ha!"

He had to get rid of her, fast. He fumbled for his wallet and took out a twenty, all he had. He unlocked the door and opened it a crack, blocking the view into his room with his body. "Here." He shoved the bill through the crack. "It's all I have, so don't ask for any more."

"Wow, thanks," said Annie. "But I only asked for ten, so I only owe you ten." A car horn honked. "Gotta go." Annie bounded down the stairs and slammed the door on her way out.

"That was nice of you." Jennifer sat on the bed. "I think you're a very good brother to her."

"Well," Nick said, feeling guilty. He hadn't been nice. He had only wanted to get rid of his sister.

"I like your room." Jennifer surveyed the movie and military posters on the wall, the war books on his desk. "It makes me understand you better, and I think that's essential, don't you?" Her dark eyes were serious.

Nick nodded. Essential to what? He didn't really understand what she was getting at. "I sure do. It's essential."

Jennifer smiled, seeming to sense Nick's confusion. "I think it's essential to our relationship that we know everything about each other. Before, when you said you wanted to join the military, I didn't understand, but now I think I do. It's part of who you are, Nick, a good and noble person who wants to do the right thing. You want to stop terrorism and defend your country. What could be nobler than that?"

Nick felt a rush of emotion that he had never felt before: gratitude, happiness, excitement, tenderness. He looked at this lovely, earnest girl, and he felt all of this rolled into one. "I love you," he said.

Jennifer's eyes welled with tears.

Nick rushed to the bed and sat down beside her. "Should I not have said that?"

She shook her head. "No, it's not that. It's that I love you, too. I have since the first time I saw you, I guess. But I really knew when you ran into me and knocked me down, strange as that sounds."

It didn't sound strange to Nick at all. In fact, it made perfect sense. He kissed her, and they continued to kiss as if they couldn't get enough. Somehow then, they were lying down, and he was touching her small breasts, her soft skin. Nick didn't stop to think. His body knew what Loretta meant when she said to do what came naturally.

"I want to make love," Jennifer said when they finally stopped for air.

Nick also wanted to make love. Desperately. Unlike Dylan, he knew that he loved this girl, and that it would be something beautiful. "Are you sure?"

"Very." She ran her hands down his naked back.

"But I don't have," he didn't want to say *rubber*, "protection."

"It will be okay, just this one time. We'll have to trust each other."

"I trust you," Nick said.

"I love you," Jennifer said.

The Goldleibs sure knew how to throw a party. Annie had never seen anything like it: the caterers in their white starched shirts and black pants, the pounds of shrimp and lobster tails, the ice sculpture of an angel in the middle of the laden dining room table. "This is amazing," she said to Carla, "but why didn't you tell me it was black tie? I am definitely underdressed." Not only was she wearing jeans, but she also couldn't remember the last time she had put them in the laundry.

"It doesn't matter. We're not going to stay long. Marge and Ron demanded that I make an appearance at this stupid party, and that's all they're getting out of me." Carla, too, had on jeans, and a red and white Santa hat covered her stubbly head. She grabbed two glasses of champagne from a passing server and handed one to Annie. "Drink fast. Moms and Pops should be making their dramatic entrance at any moment."

Annie did as she was told, and it was a good thing. In less than a minute, Mr. and Mrs. Goldleib were descending the curving staircase, arm in arm. They could have been in a fashion spread for *Vogue* magazine, he in a tux and she in a flowing, strapless white gown. They were both incredibly tanned with hair that looked as if it had just been professionally styled (and probably had been).

"The Armani twins," Carla said. "They make me want to puke."

"Wow," Annie said. She couldn't even begin to imagine her parents dressed that glamorously. Even if they had money, Annie highly doubted that they could pull off such a grand entrance. It just wasn't Mom and Dad's style.

Carla snatched two more glasses from yet another passing tray. "Seriously, you need to chug before Margezilla makes her way over here. It ain't gonna be pretty."

Annie really, really wished that Carla had told her how formal this party was. If Mrs. Goldleib got mad at them for looking like slobs, Annie couldn't blame her. She and Carla didn't look like they were from the wrong side of the track. Oh, no. It was much worse than that. They looked like they could be from *underneath* the track. She quickly sniffed her underarm. Not good. "Why don't we go upstairs and put something else on?"

"No. I'm doing the command performance my way."

Carla could be so stubborn. Annie sighed. She'd support Carla, of course she would, but she might as well make the best of the situation. "Let's raid the buffet. I'm going to get some shrimp and go stand in a corner. Come with me, Carla." She already felt a little light-headed from gulping the champagne, and food would be a good thing right now.

Besides, she was starving; she was *famished*. She had decided to go on a hunger strike that very morning when her mom got on her case for not emptying the dishwasher, of all stupid things. Her mom's hormones were all out of whack, and in the long run, in the *grand scheme* of things, who would ultimately care if she emptied the dishwasher this minute or in the next hour? "You're still walking a thin line," Mom had said to her. Yeah, right. She would show her. She didn't come downstairs for lunch—leftover turkey sandwiches, which she loved—and she didn't nibble at the Christmas cookies or the fudge or the fruitcake, which she didn't particularly like but would pick out the berries soaked in rum. No one had seemed to notice. What was the *point* of a hunger strike if no one noticed?

Mrs. Goldleib spotted them eventually. She walked crisply over to them, her high heels tapping on the marble floor. Her face was a mask, but her blue eyes burned with fury. "Why didn't you dress for the party, Carla?"

"We didn't discuss dress code." Carla hadn't touched her shrimp, but she had grabbed two more glasses of champagne.

"Our annual holiday party is always black tie. You know that." Mrs. Goldleib looked as if she wanted to reach out and slap Carla's cheek.

"I'm not planning on staying long," Carla said.

"I want you and your friend to march upstairs and put on an appropriate dress. Now." Mrs. Goldleib was trying hard to maintain control, but her voice shook.

"Her name is Annie."

Annie thought that it might be a good idea to reintroduce herself. "I'm Annie Carissa, Mrs. Goldleib. We met once before."

Carla's mother didn't even glance in her direction. "You are not asked to do many things around here, Carla, but I insist on this point. You will go up and put on something appropriate. All of our friends and business associates are here, and you must make a good impression."

Carla stood rooted to the spot, and she and her mother glared at each other. "I don't give a *flying fuck* about impressing your friends and business associates."

Marge Goldleib flinched at her daughter's language, but her voice grew even colder. "The Republican senator is here, the Secretary of State is here, and we expect the Governor to make an appearance before the evening is done. You *will* go up and change clothes now, young lady."

Annie had to stop herself from opening her mouth and uttering another lame *wow*. If that many important people were here, she certainly didn't want to look like a slob. "Come on, Carla, let's go up. Your mom does have a point." She took Carla's arm, and surprisingly, Carla allowed herself to be led upstairs.

She exploded when they were safely in her bedroom. "Whose side are you on, Annie? 'Your mom does have a point,'" she mimicked in a high squeaky voice. "Really, Annie, you could have been more supportive of me." She flopped down on the bed, reached into her nightstand, and pulled out a joint.

Why did Carla always have to question her loyalty? Hurt, she said, "You know I'm always on your side. How many times do I have to tell you that?"

Carla sighed. "Over and over again, I guess. That woman makes me so damn mad! She didn't even care about the Mohawk, but get her precious friends and business associates in the vicinity, and she suddenly cares *very much* what I look like." She lit the joint and inhaled deeply. "Here." She handed it to Annie.

Another one of Carla's very bad ideas. For all they knew, the Chief of Police could be downstairs right now, chowing down on shrimp and caviar. (Annie had put a dollop of caviar on her plate—china of course, not paper like her mom would use—expecting it to be the most delicious thing she had ever tasted. It wasn't. It tasted like salty mush, and that's when Carla told her she was eating fish eggs!) However, the champagne had gone straight to her head, so she wasn't going to once again point out the obvious to Carla, who wouldn't listen anyway. She took a hit off the joint and started rifling through Carla's closet. Carla had some beautiful clothes, most of them with price tags still on them. Mrs. Goldleib, of course, had picked these out.

"This one's nice." Annie handed Carla a blue silk sheath—plain, yet elegant. The label said Valentino. She gasped at the price tag, $2,000. She didn't spend a quarter of that on her entire wardrobe.

"Fine." Carla was still puffing away.

Annie was pretty sure that none of Carla's clothes were going to fit her. "I think I'll stay up here while you go down and make your appearance. They don't want to see me anyway." For some strange reason—maybe it was the pot on top of the champagne—she suddenly wanted very much to go to the party.

"Over my dead body. We can find something for you to wear." Carla took her turn looking through the clothes. "Maybe not," she conceded. "But I have an idea. Follow me."

She led Annie to her mother's closet where they had been once before, an hour of ripping off buttons and putting wadded up tissues in all the handbags. "Now I don't want to hurt your feelings," Carla said as she went to the very back of the cavernous closet and pressed a button on a huge mirror, which slid to the side, revealing yet another closet. "But Marge used to be fatter—I mean larger, I mean more *normal*—before she quit eating and before she vacuumed every speck of fat from her body. She kept some of the clothes to remind herself, as she puts it, of her *hideous phase*." Carla found a red linen Chanel dress. "This should do the trick."

They put on their dresses in Marge's closet and admired themselves in the mirrors. "I think we look nice," Annie said, admiring herself from all angles. She didn't think she looked fat at all.

"We clean up pretty good." Carla started to giggle uncontrollably. "But why stop at this?" At the back of the hidden closet, behind a shelf filled with handbags, was a safe. Carla knew the combination. "*Voila!*"

The open safe revealed, in Annie's opinion, a small mountain of gold and glittering gems. "We will get in such trouble." She was really flying high now. That pot had been way strong.

"Not in front of the precious friends and the dear business associates, and especially not in front of the Governor. Trust me. I can deal with Marge after the fact. Let's *adorn* ourselves, shall we?"

In addition to putting a ring on every finger, two necklaces apiece, and bracelets up and down their arms, they each picked out a pair of shoes. Miraculously, all three of them wore a size eight, so Annie took that to mean that at least her feet couldn't be considered fat. As the finishing touch, Carla put on a ruby and sapphire encrusted tiara that Marge had worn when the Goldleibs met the Sultan of Brunei. (Again, Annie was struck speechless at Carla's casual name dropping.) Giggling, caught up in the moment, caught up in their euphoric high, they were ready to make their grand entrance.

They stood at the top of the curving staircase, holding hands, holding each other up. The party spread out below them, the well-dressed men and women holding drinks and plates of food, talking in groups, laughing. A harpist and violinist were now in the center of the room, playing classy versions of all the Christmas carols that her mother had been playing for the last long month. They sure don't sound like Elvis singing "Blue Christmas" or Eartha Kitt sexily singing "Santa Baby" she wanted to say to Carla, but she couldn't form the words. She giggled, which caused Carla to go into another fit.

When Carla finally composed herself, she said, "Are you ready, mademoiselle?"

"Si, senorita," Annie answered, which started them all over again. Tears ran down both their faces.

"Time to *en-trance*," Carla said as regally as she could.

They started slowly down the stairs. Annie clutched the banister. She wasn't used to high heels, and it was hard to keep her balance. Her legs felt all rubbery.

"Let go," Carla said. "You're ruining the *effect*."

Annie let go. They descended even more slowly, right foot, then left foot, step by step. They were almost to the bottom, another four or five steps to go on the staircase, when Annie's heel caught at the hem of her dress. She clutched at Carla to regain her balance. "Sorry," she whispered to Carla.

"That was a close one."

They took another step, and neither could later remember whose ankle turned or whose toe stubbed or who initiated the tumble down the stairs. Later, it would seem to Annie that the whole thing was in slow motion, the two of them hitting each step, her wondering if her underwear was showing, Carla's nails clawing into her hand. They landed in a heap at the bottom of the steps, legs and arms askew, Carla's tiara slipping from her head.

The noisy party silenced abruptly. All eyes were upon them, and as Carla would later point out, they had finally been *noticed*. They sure had.

Marge Goldleib screamed and ran to them. Annie, on the floor, noticed that she was very adept at moving in high heels. "What in the world are you two doing?"

She didn't ask if they were all right or if anything was broken, nothing like that. To Carla, she hissed, "You're making a spectacle. Are you trying to ruin my party?"

Carla started to laugh, and Annie joined in, mostly because she couldn't think of anything else to do in this situation.

Ron Goldleib had appeared. "Dr. Sorenson is here. I'll have him take a look at them."

"They're fine," Marge snapped, trying to hoist Carla to her feet, but Carla wasn't budging.

"We're fine," Carla agreed. And then loudly, making sure the entire room could hear, she added: "We're just shit-faced!"

8

CHAPTER EIGHT

She hated this bed. She now hated this room, this room that she had so lovingly decorated only two years before with sky blue walls, blue and yellow sheer curtains at the window that overlooked the street, a white vanity with its oval mirror and her assortment of wrinkle erasing creams, none of which seemed to deliver what they promised, lined up neatly. Alex was nearing the end of her two-week mandatory bed rest, and she was going stir crazy. She couldn't bear to watch any more episodes of *Maury*—although she now certainly knew what Sam was talking about when she talked about a Baby Daddy and a Baby Mama—or one more Lifetime movie about a husband's infidelity and a wife who then murders him because he deserved to be punished because he was unfaithful. Nor could she bring herself to thumb through any more women's magazines that promised new ways to cook chicken, new ways to stretch your dollar, new ways to lose weight without dieting or exercise.

Alex was bored beyond belief. Used to constantly doing something—cooking, cleaning, laundry, shopping—she was amazed at how long the days could be when you did absolutely nothing. She had heard stories of women suffering from depression who took to their beds for weeks on end. How did they do that? It seemed to Alex that it would worsen the depression. The inertia, the stagnation, the lack of external stimulation only gave you more time to think about everything that was wrong in your life. And that was something that Alex certainly did not want to do. Thank

God for Sam's reliable nosiness and undivided attention. She would have gone crazy without her daily long visits.

"That was a close call," Sam had said on her first visit, the day after the night in the emergency room. "You're an amazing woman, Alex." She had brought magazines, chocolate-covered cherries, and an armful of red roses.

It had been a close call, or maybe it had been the shrimp dip. Alex had quit bleeding by the time she got to the hospital, and the ultrasound had not revealed any abnormalities. Sam, by her side viewing the screen, had said with tearful relief, "He's perfect."

She's perfect, Alex had thought, crying with relief, too. She and Sam, right there and then, decided against getting the amniocentesis test scheduled at eighteen weeks. It no longer mattered. They were going to keep this precious baby; they had known it all along. This scare, this false alarm, had cemented that vow. "Our baby *will* be perfect," she had said. The doctor recommended two weeks of bed rest, just to be on the safe side.

Jack had not shown up at the hospital.

"I called him and told him everything was fine," Sam had said.

Alex knew this was not true because Sam, unlike Jack, had not left her side the entire time.

Sam caught her mistake. "I mean, Chris called him."

That might be true.

Then Sam went too far. "Jack said he was relieved and would be waiting for you when you get home."

So not true. Her husband was passed out on the family room couch when they got home and didn't even stir when Sam helped her up to bed and settled her in with a pitcher of water and the sedatives the doctor said she could take. Too physically and emotionally exhausted to do anything about the situation, Alex fell into a deep sleep.

Jack had been sleeping on the couch or the reclining chair in the den ever since. For the first time in their long marriage, she and Jack were not sleeping in the same bed. She understood his reasoning, in a way. She was convalescing, and he had never seen her infirm before. Possibly, it frightened him, seeing his wife bedridden and rather helpless. He had been conciliatory, perhaps even embarrassed, and frequently popped his head into the room to ask if she needed anything, anything at all. At times, she had asked for a sandwich, or some orange juice, or a yogurt. Once, jokingly, she had asked for pickles and ice cream, and he had brought a bowl of each on a tray.

"I was joking," she had said.

"Funny," he answered, awkwardly holding the tray.

They stared at each other for a long moment.

"Do you want this or not?" he asked.

"That's not what I want at all," she had said, on the verge of anger.

"Fine. I'll give it to the dog." He turned to go.

"We don't have a dog."

"I was joking."

"Funny." She watched him leave.

No, she did not understand him at all.

Mostly, Jack sent the kids to see if she needed anything. Nick had sat on the chair by the bed and watched an episode of *Law & Order* with her. He had offered to make her one of his "mean" grilled cheese sandwiches, two pieces of white bread with four slices of Kraft American cheese. She had accepted, and they had munched on the sandwiches in companionable silence. Nick seemed different to her, somehow more self-possessed, more confident.

"Anything new with you?" she'd finally asked.

He mumbled something unintelligible around the food in his mouth.

"The winter dance is coming up soon. Maybe you'll ask someone this year?" She really hoped he would. It was about time he took an interest in girls, although she knew he was a late bloomer, and that was okay, too.

He blushed clear to his hairline. "Maybe I will, this time."

Alex sat up straighter on her mound of pillows. "Really? That's terrific, Nick! Who? Anyone I know?" To her, this was exciting news, but she should tone down her exuberance, not scare him off.

"I haven't decided yet. It's no big deal, you know?" He stuffed the last, large bit of sandwich in his mouth.

"I think it's a very big deal," she said happily. "Do I know the family?"

He shook his head, his mouth still full.

"Maybe I could meet her sometime. You could bring her over for dinner."

He shook his head again, and his mouth was not full.

She had overreacted. She knew that. "Well, when you're ready—maybe?"

He gathered their plates. "Sure, Mom, but you know, I'm just thinking about it."

Her longest conversation with Annie had been equally unenlightening. Her daughter had brought her a cup of herbal tea and a stale leftover Christmas cookie that Alex forced herself to eat. Annie couldn't sit still. She kept jumping up to change the volume on the TV, even though the remote was next to Alex on the bed, or close the window, even though the room was stifling.

"What have you and Carla been up to lately?" Alex knew that Annie had not stopped seeing Carla, although she had asked her to weeks before. Alex reasoned that she probably needed Carla with all that was going on around here.

"Same old, same old," Annie said. She had gone to the vanity and was opening and smelling the jars and bottles of cream. "Does this stuff really work?"

"Only in my imagination," Alex had said. "What's 'same old, same old'?"

"We hang out, watch movies, listen to music, all the stuff teenagers are supposed to do." She rubbed some cream into her cheek.

Alex wasn't sure how to broach the next question that had been on her mind lately. "I was watching an episode of *Oprah* yesterday about teenagers and drugs and peer pressure."

"What about it?" Annie asked. She sounded bored.

Alex hesitated. "I know SCDS is a rich school, and there is probably access to those kinds of things—"

"Carla and I don't have peer pressure because our peers don't like us." Annie closed the jar with a vicious twist.

"Oh, Annie," Alex said sadly.

"It's true. I've told you that before."

"I just want you to know that you can tell me anything, anything at all." Alex had told her this before, too, and she wished Annie would come to the bed so that she could hug her. As she always did.

But she didn't. "There's nothing to tell." And Annie left.

They were all leaving her these days, stranded as she was on this straightjacket of a bed. She could vaguely hear their comings and goings, their muted conversations or the squawk of the TV. But she was not a part of it, and it hurt her deeply. She had had the past two weeks to think and rethink about what was going on in her home, and she had come up with a truth. She didn't like any of it.

So now, as Jack brought in her dinner tray—the kids must not be around, or else he would have corralled them into the chore—she said unceremoniously, "Sit down."

"I don't have time," he said.

"Make the time." Where was he going almost every night? Oh, yes, he always had an excuse: practice, game, board meeting, buddy bonding, golfing, working on the damn cars. Anything to avoid her.

He sat down stiffly, not on the bed next to her but on the chair.

"How long are we going to do this?" she asked. It was ridiculous. This pregnancy was a fact, and he had, albeit reluctantly, agreed.

"I don't know," he said miserably. "I just don't know."

"We need to get over this, for the sake of *us*. Our marriage is a strong one, and what we're doing here is not terrible. In fact, it's a good thing, a very good thing. We're giving Sam a chance to have a baby." She tried unsuccessfully to keep the pleading out of her voice.

"I'm not handling it well. I know that, but I can't help how I feel." He didn't move closer or take her hand.

He needed a haircut. Before, she had always been the one to remind him of this. His dark hair curled over the collar of his sports shirt, and she noticed there was more gray. She felt a rush of tenderness wash over her. "How, exactly, do you feel?"

Silence.

"Come on, honey, we need to talk about this."

He finally looked directly at her face. His eyes were moist, bloodshot. "Guilty, ashamed, but mostly, madder than hell." He jumped to his feet. "Are you happy now, Alex, are you?" he exploded.

She was taken aback. "There's no need to yell, Jack. I'm trying to have a conversation with you, husband and wife."

"That's exactly it. Husband and wife." When he left, he slammed the door so hard the window rattled.

Alex leaned back into the mound of pillows, exhausted. Every time she tried to talk to her family, they left. Nick left. Annie left. Jack left. Everything was unraveling, and it was all because of this baby. How in the world was she going to make it better? She was going to be out of bed in two more days, and some way, somehow, she would fix things. She didn't know what she would do, but she would do anything in her power to heal the rifts that were threatening to break them all apart.

She started to cry, a sad, silent weeping. And that's when the baby decided to make herself known with her first fluttering kick/kiss deep inside her. Alex's tears stopped abruptly, and she put her hand on her slightly swollen abdomen and waited. The kick/kiss came again, the quickening of life.

And even though the rest of her family wasn't in her room, or even in the house, she whispered, "We have each other, don't we, baby?"

Jack's head pounded, his mouth was bone dry, and his stomach was queasy. He was drinking too damn much. He knew that, but he didn't seem able to stop himself. Every day when he woke up feeling hungover, he vowed that he wouldn't touch a drop on that day, that he absolutely would not take one drink. Then, inevitably, something would happen. He would look at his wife (who was pregnant with another man's child), or his son (who had not acknowledged the U of A acceptance), or his daughter (who was becoming the definition of a rebel without a cause), or his sister-in-law (who was the cause of everything), or his brother-in-law (who he now despised for sleeping with his wife), and he would allow himself one drink, telling himself that he deserved it with everything going on in his life. Then that drink would lead to three, five, or seven more.

What in the hell was the matter with him? He used to be a star athlete for Christ's sake. So what in the hell was the matter with him?

He didn't want to answer his own question because he knew the answer. When he looked at those closest to him in his life, especially his own family, he saw his own failure as a husband, a father, a person. And he reached for the flask that he now kept hidden in his desk drawer and took a quick drink. He needed it; he really needed it.

She knocked on his office door. Jack looked at his watch, and wonders of wonders, she was on time. He quickly tucked the flask back into the drawer. "Come in," he said.

Annie slouched into the seat in front of him and dropped her heavy backpack to the floor with a thud. "You rang, sir?" she said with more than a hint of sarcasm.

His daughter. Despite the pink stubbly hair and the heavy eye makeup that made her look somewhat like a raccoon, he could still see the cute, sweet little girl who would throw her arms around his legs when he came home from work, the little girl who thought the world revolved around her daddy. The nostalgia for those days felt like a sharp pain in the very center of his queasy stomach.

"You know why you're here, Annie. Let's not beat around the bush." Jack leaned back in his chair, feigning a nonchalance he didn't feel at all.

"I have no idea what that archaic expression means." She bit at her thumbnail.

He wanted to tell her to stop doing that, that she had pretty hands and there was no need to mutilate those, too, but he needed, first and foremost, to be a guidance counselor here, not her dad. "It means, let's get to the point."

"Fine with me. This is cutting into my lunch time, and I'm starving."

"You can eat in here."

"I'm supposed to eat with Carla."

"Oh, yes, the infamous Carla."

"What's that supposed to mean?" she asked sharply. "You know she's my best friend."

Of course he knew that. In fact, Annie and Carla barely spoke with anyone else on campus. He didn't like that she didn't socialize more with others, but he was still sticking with his theory that Annie was only going through a phase. But it was becoming a fucking long and worrisome phase. He was only going to give it until the end of the school year before he took matters into his own hands. It might be that Annie would benefit from professional counseling, but Jack hoped they wouldn't have to go that route.

"You're flunking Algebra II," he said.

"You know I hate math. I always have. Besides, when am I ever going to need those insane equations during my life? They're absolutely *useless*." Annie sat up straighter in her chair and shifted nervously, as if now she was ready for the inquisition.

"Math might not be your strong suit," he agreed.

"No, it's not." She seemed to relax a little, as if they agreed on the irrelevant issue of her flunking the course.

"You're also flunking English II. Do you think it's useless to learn how to write?"

He had to admit to himself that he had not been overly surprised about algebra. Disappointed, yes, but not surprised. He had talked to her teacher, and they had agreed that Annie could do some extra credit to get her grade up, and the teacher, Ms. Ellis, had agreed to tutor Annie after school. However, when Annie's English teacher, Mrs. Costello, had approached him with the news of Annie's grade, he had been speechless. English had always been her strongest subject. It wasn't as if Annie couldn't do the work, Mrs. Costello had explained, it's that she wasn't doing it. She hadn't turned in the last three papers. So, what was Annie really doing in her room every night when she said she was doing homework?

Annie stared at her scruffy red Converse tennis shoes.

"Why aren't you doing your work, Annie?" He was proud at the calmness of his voice, the reasonableness of the conversation so far, when what he really wanted to do was put her over his knee and spank her, good and hard. He had never, ever done that before, but right now, it's exactly what he wanted to do. "Annie," he said, slightly louder, "why aren't you writing your papers?"

"I am writing the papers. I'm just not turning them in," Annie said to her scruffy red tennis shoes.

He was absolutely not going to let his exasperation show. He was not going to explode. Where had that gotten him with the Mohawk? Nowhere. "And why not?"

"They're personal."

Okay. She was really testing his patience now. He took a deep breath. "This is what you're going to do." He told her about the tutoring and extra credit in algebra and then told her to turn in what she had written, or if she thought it was too *personal*, she should write something else. She had two weeks before the end of the semester, which meant this: She. Would. Do. It. Now.

"Are we clear?" he asked her.

"Crystal."

She hoisted the heavy backpack to her shoulder, and the weight of it, the effort of her lifting the heavy vinyl bag stuffed with thick overpriced textbooks, made his heart go out to her. She was so young, so vulnerable. He hoped that some boy would never break her heart, but it was bound to happen, and it made him ache for her.

"I'm not going to tell your mother," he said as a kind of amends. "You have two weeks to make things happen, and I know you will."

She was already out the door, but he still heard her say, "So when did you start talking to Mom again?"

So she had noticed. Shit, who could not help but notice that he went out of his way to avoid talking to his wife these days, especially since she had been bedridden? Their conversation last night, when Alex had tried to pry out of him how he really felt, had put him over the edge. Completely and unreasonably over the edge.

He had gone to the casino. He had lost two hundred dollars in a matter of thirty minutes. He had gone to the bar to do some serious, furious, shameful drinking, where Cookie had found him a short time later.

"You look a little down." She took the seat next to him.

He was down, broke and depressed. He didn't know how they would make it until Chris gave him the next needed, fucking check.

"Do you want to talk about it?" Cookie had her blonde hair piled on top of her head. She looked almost pretty in her hard biker chick way.

"No," he said.

"You're right. We should leave our personal lives outside of the casino. It's better that way."

They talked for three hours about everything and nothing in particular, and Jack, with the alcohol and conversation, felt better than he had in quite some time. When she asked him to walk her to her car, he readily agreed. No woman should be alone in the parking lot at that time of night.

Rather drunkenly, he put his arm around her shoulders as he walked her to the car.

Rather drunkenly, he gave her a long kiss good night.

The phone call came in the middle of the night, as phone calls bearing bad news generally do. Chris was awake immediately, his heart racing. Who could be calling at this hour? Sam was safely beside him, snoring softly, and if she was all right, nothing could be disastrously wrong in his life. If it was Jack, and if he was in trouble—a DUI, which he probably deserved—Chris was not going to get out of bed at 2:00 a.m. and bail him out. The guy was behaving like a first-class jackass these days.

It was a Doctor Somebody, Chris could not make out the name in the thickness of the man's Indian accent, informing him that Louise had had a heart attack.

"Oh, my God," Chris said, "is she . . . all right?" He couldn't bring himself to ask if she was dead. Even though his relationship with his mother had always been strained, he felt a fearful panic.

"It was a mild episode. She will recover," Doctor Somebody said.

"Is there anything I can do?" Chris had a fleeting moment of relief before the dread set in. He knew what was coming next.

"She is asking for you." Doctor Somebody paused. "I think it would help her recovery if you were here. Mrs. Connor is a somewhat . . . recalcitrant patient."

Of course she would be. After all these years of imaginary illnesses, Louise was probably madder than hell that she hadn't seen this one coming. "I'll catch the first plane out this morning," Chris said, already making a mental list of everything he needed to do.

He woke Sam and told her what was going on. "You should start packing," he said to her.

"I'm not going. You said it was a mild heart attack, and besides, the bitch hates me." Sam yawned.

"No, she doesn't." Chris was trying to find the Southwest Airlines number on his phone.

"Fine. She dislikes me intensely."

"She dislikes everyone intensely, but going to see her is the right thing to do. I'm her only son, and you're her only daughter-in-law. We're going."

Sam grumbled as she packed. She grumbled about how she shouldn't be leaving Alex now that she was up and about again. Chris told her Alex would be fine. She complained about how rotten the weather was going to be in Chicago in January. Chris told her to pack her fur-lined leather gloves. She bitched about how much she hated hospitals—the smell, the lack of privacy, the sickness of it all. Chris ignored this tirade completely.

They landed at Midway at ten o'clock and took a taxi downtown to Memorial Hospital. It was indeed typical Chicago winter weather: low gray clouds, twenty-two degrees, dirty snow piled along the roadways. Sam stared out the taxi's window, and uncharacteristically, she didn't say a word. Probably, Chris thought, she was bracing herself for her face-to-face with Louise. It was certainly what he was doing.

They could hear her before they got to her room. "Jell-O is not a food group. It is not dairy, nor meat, nor vegetable, nor fruit. In fact, it is a nothing food. It is a waste of swallowing. I want this lime green wriggling mass of a nothing food off my tray this instance. Don't look at me like that, young lady! I am a patient here, I had a heart attack, and I deserve to be treated with some respect!"

In her haste to get out of Louise's room, the young girl carrying the tray almost ran into Chris and Sam. Sam took a deep breath. "Welcome to Louise World."

"I heard that, Samantha! I'm not deaf. I had a heart attack," Louise barked.

Sam looked at Chris and mouthed: "See? The bitch hates me."

They entered the room, and Chris walked over to kiss his mother's cheek. She had the bed adjusted to a sitting position, and her white hair was combed. Her color was surprisingly good—a touch of pink in her cheeks, maybe rouge?—and he told her so.

"No, I do not look good," Louise disagreed. "I had a heart attack. I am a very ill woman."

"The doctor thinks you'll make a full recovery, Mother," Chris said. He had called the doctor back at the airport to get more details about Louise's condition.

"What do doctors know?" Louise sniffed. "I think it will take me weeks to regain my strength, and I'm going to need you to help me resettle into Golden Manor. I might not be able to do it on my own. Maybe I should come out and stay with you during my convalescence?"

Sam gasped.

"Well!" Louise said.

"Of course you're welcome to come and stay with us, Mother." He looked pointedly at Sam. "Right, honey?"

"Why don't we take things one day at a time?" Sam stood up. "I think I need a breath of fresh air." She looked a little green.

"You just got here, Samantha. Sit down. I want to talk about this baby business that you talked Christopher into—at his age!"

Not only was Louise not deaf, she wasn't senile either. All her insinuations about Alzheimer's and other illnesses were just smoke screens, a need to get attention. And now she had had a heart attack. She had everyone's attention now. She had an audience. She was probably in Louise Heaven. She was a piece of work, his mother. She really was.

"Like Chris told you, we're having a baby. Alex is our surrogate." Sam remained standing, probably ready to flee at the first opportunity.

"It is ridiculous, simply ridiculous. I know this was all your idea, Samantha, and I'm telling you, you need to let go of the past."

Sam, through clenched teeth, answered, "I have let go of the past, Louise. What I'm doing is planning a future for us, a wonderful future with a baby."

Louise snorted. "You are both too old to bring a baby into this world. It's selfish of you."

"If it's selfish to love a baby, then I'll admit it. I'm selfish."

Chris was proud of Sam's self-control so far, but he knew he needed to change the conversational path before Sam lost her cool. "It's already done, Mother."

"Don't count on me to babysit!"

"We wouldn't *dream* of asking you," Sam said more loudly.

Thankfully, Doctor Somebody walked into the room just then. "How is the patient doing?" he asked in a formal, clipped tone.

"I had a heart attack. How do you think I'm doing?" Louise asked snidely.

Chris introduced himself and Sam to the doctor, but what he really wanted to do was apologize for his mother's behavior.

The doctor didn't acknowledge Louise's rudeness. He looked through her file. "I think we will be able to release you tomorrow. All the tests have shown that it was a very mild heart attack, and there is no need for surgery at this point."

"Tomorrow?" Louise protested. "I think I need at least a week to make a full recovery. I am not a young woman anymore. I wouldn't say I was old, but I am not exactly youthful."

"You're eighty-five, Louise. That's old." Sam had obviously spent all her good behavior.

"Well!" Louise said.

"No, tomorrow you will be released," the doctor said as he closed her file. He turned to go, saying, "Although, I would advise you to abstain from sexual activity until your next check-up."

Chris was stunned. What? Had his mother been having sex when she had a heart attack? Did eighty-five-year-olds still have sex? And even more implausibly, who would want to have sex with a grouchy hypochondriac like Louise? "Mother?"

She was blushing, and Chris had never seen his mother blush before. She folded her arms staunchly across her chest and stared straight ahead.

Sam, of course, started to laugh. "I can't believe it!" she said. "You have a boyfriend!"

Louise continued to stare straight ahead.

Really, Sam's laughter was out of control. Soon she would be rolling on the floor. "Sam," he admonished, "it's not funny if Mother has a boyfriend." Although it was funny. It was hysterical. He hoped he could keep a straight face.

Louise snapped. "My personal life is none of your business, and he is not my boyfriend. He is my male companion. It is a very important distinction."

"Who is he?" Chris couldn't help himself from asking the question.

"None of your business."

"Is it Mr. Peterson?" Chris persisted.

"Who's Mr. Peterson?" Sam asked.

"According to Mother, an old coot who takes out his dentures at the dinner table."

"I think you should go now," Louise said.

"We'll be back tomorrow to take you to Golden Manor and help you get settled."

"There's no need," Louise said firmly. "I'll be fine. Mr. Peterson is still able to drive." There was a touch of pride in her voice. "The staff tries to discourage him, but he does it anyway."

"What about coming to stay with us in Arizona?" Chris asked. He was actually starting to enjoy himself now that Louise no longer had the upper hand.

Sam shot him a murderous look, but he knew they were in the clear.

"I've changed my mind. I'm feeling stronger by the minute."

"But you had a heart attack." He was loving this.

"Didn't you hear the doctor?" Louise said. "It was a mild attack. I'm a healthy woman. You two go back to Arizona. Go on."

"If you're sure—"

311

"I'm sure."

He and Sam said their farewells. He kissed Louise's cheek; Sam didn't. If Louise were able, she would have pushed them out the door, and they knew why as soon as they were in the hallway. A wizened bald man was coming toward them, a big bouquet of flowers in his hands, an excited smile on his face. He and Sam stopped in their tracks and stared after him as he went into Louise's room.

"Hello, you old coot," they heard her say.

To Chris, it sounded as if Louise had almost, finally, uttered an endearment.

The acting business was much harder than Nick thought it would be. Realizing that at some point he would have to acknowledge the big white envelope from U of A— and his dad's reproachful looks were getting very hard to ignore—Nick finally brought it down from his room and opened it in the presence of his parents. He read the acceptance out loud, his mom cried and hugged him, and his dad gave him a congratulatory slap on his back saying, "Way to go, Wildcat!" Then his dad immediately wrote out a check for the deposit on a dorm room and watched as Nick signed the acceptance form. His mom produced a stamp from the recesses of her desk drawer, which was unbelievable because she usually couldn't find anything in that mess. It was almost a surprise that they didn't fight over who got to lick the stamp or seal the envelope. "I'll take it to the post office," he'd said, and it was really a huge shocker that they didn't follow him out the door.

Nick didn't go to the post office.

But he didn't do what he had originally planned on doing, which was to tear the letter into microscopic pieces and throw it away. He was standing in front of the trash can in Fry's break room, letter in hand, when Loretta came up behind him.

"What've you got there, baby boy? Looks important."

He told her what it was, and she congratulated him. They stood in front of the trash can for some moments. He was waiting for Loretta to leave, but good old Loretta could smell that something was up. And she wasn't going to budge an inch.

Loretta, who didn't understand the concept of silence, spoke again. "Why're you thinking of throwing it away, sugar?"

"I don't want to go to college. I want to join the Marines."

She whistled. "I imagine your parents are going to have a conniption fit about that idea."

"They already have."

She took the letter from his hands with her long crimson nails. "Listen, sweetie, I don't mean to butt in. Well, yes, I guess I do. I'm always sticking my big nose in other people's business, my nature, I guess, but you might want to think this thing through a little bit more. 'Don't burn any bridges behind you,' I tell you, that's my philosophy. And it works pretty good, too—well, except for that sorry excuse of a second husband. I burned that bridge, and I'd burn his bony little ass if I didn't mind going to prison. But I'm not the prison type. I gotta tell you, I think dykes are scary people. I doubt if they're even real women. Now, I know I'm not what you would call politically correct . . ."

He listened to her ramble on for the rest of the break. As long as she was on the subject of herself (and her scumbag husband number two), she wouldn't be asking him questions about Jennifer and how their *little romance* was coming along. Which was a good thing. He was afraid that he would break down under Loretta's relentless questioning: Have you made it to second base yet, sweetie pie? What would he say to her? Loretta, we skipped the bases all together and went directly to home plate? No, he would rather listen to Loretta talk about Loretta and keep his *little romance* with Jennifer to himself.

The letter was now safely buried in the box in his closet that contained all the other ill-gotten and unfortunate belongings of his pre-Jennifer life, the things he no longer wished or cared to think about. However, he couldn't think of a good excuse to get out of this trip to Tucson to visit the U of A campus. His dad was all gung-ho and wanted Nick to get a *feel* for the campus, to see which dorm he might want to put in as a preference, to possibly meet the cross-country coach. The list went on and on. He tried to tell his dad that he was perfectly capable of driving to Tucson by himself, but Dad would have none of it. He wanted to share in the excitement of this new experience with his son.

Nick had brought Dylan along as reinforcement, but he sat in the back of the Lexus while Nick was held captive in the front with his dad and unable to make eye contact with Dylan, to roll his eyes with the stupidity of this whole embarrassing incident. Dylan was such a good guy. He hadn't even balked when Nick asked (begged) him to go. His response had been a simple *why not?*

"This is Speedway Boulevard we're driving on now, Nick. Isn't this a beautiful campus?" his dad asked.

"Sure is." It was getting harder and harder to feign any kind of enthusiasm. The trip down had worn him out.

"What do you think, Dylan?" Dad looked at Dylan in the rearview mirror.

"Nice grass," Dylan said.

Dad laughed, and then he rolled down his window and yelled, "Go, Wildcats!"

Nick wanted to sink down in the seat. No, he wanted to disappear altogether. "Yay, team," he said weakly.

"Rah," Dylan said from the backseat.

His dad found a parking space in a garage, and they got out of the car. He had with him a sheaf of papers that he had printed from the U of A website. "I thought we'd start off with a walking tour of the campus. What do you say, guys?"

"Sounds good." Nick was planning on walking fast, very fast. He wished he could take off running, in fact.

Nick and Dylan dutifully followed Dad around campus, passing by Old Main, ILC and Bear Down Gym, Steward Observatory, Stein Eller Dance Theater, Hillenbrand Aquatic Center, Biosciences East, Herring Hall, dorms, and other buildings that didn't register in Nick's brain at all. The more he saw, the blurrier everything became. He and Dylan said the occasional "very cool," "wow," "impressive building." And Dylan kept repeating, "Nice grass."

Dad was disappointed when the cross-country coach wasn't in his office, but Nick was relieved. (It was Saturday. What had his dad been expecting?) Finally, Dad looked at his watch. "I made an appointment with an old golfing buddy of mine, Ed. How about if I let you boys explore on your own for about an hour?"

Nick's response this time wasn't feigned. "That would be great!" Being around his dad in this upbeat—too upbeat—mood was suffocating. He and Dylan needed time to commiserate, alone.

They went back to Old Main and plopped down in the grass in front of the building. It was a warm January day, in the low 70s, and there were plenty of other students walking through campus or studying on benches or talking and laughing in groups. It looked kind of phony to Nick, like some scene out of a movie. It further convinced him that campus life wasn't real life, and it certainly wouldn't be the life-altering experience that war would be.

"I hate this," Nick said. "It's hard to fake being happy, you know?"

"Yeah, but it makes your dad positively giddy. We only have a few more months." Dylan stretched out on the lawn. "I really do like this grass."

"Enough about the grass, please?"

"Okay. They have some pretty chicks here."

"I hadn't noticed." Really, he only had eyes for Jennifer. He hadn't known that sex could really seal the deal in a relationship—how could he possibly have known?—but now that they were having sex frequently, it had made them, in his mind, into a fully mature couple. Oddly enough, it was Jennifer, as she had the first time, who usually initiated making love. That was fine with Nick. He didn't want to act like a sex maniac and scare her off.

"I think I'm going to break up with Melissa," Dylan said.

"What? Why would you do that?" According to Jennifer, Melissa was crazy about Dylan.

"I've been thinking. What are we going to do with our women when we go off to basic training, and then hopefully, Iraq or Afghanistan?" Dylan rolled to his side and propped his head up on his hand. "We can't ask them to wait for us."

"Why not?" And why, Nick wondered silently, hadn't he thought about this before? He'd been living in the moment, caught up in his love affair with Jennifer, who was going to go to Stanford. Would she want to wait for him, or would she hook up with some pre-med student who could give her a better life than he could? The thought made him feel sick.

"Well, I don't want Melissa to wait for me. She's a cool chick and all that, but think of the other women we would be missing out on. We're young, dude, young and virile. I'm not ready to settle down." Dylan spoke earnestly (for Dylan), as if he had given the matter a lot of thought.

"But I love Jennifer." That was the important fact to Nick.

"Dude, we have our whole lives ahead of us to fall in love. We need to go and be soldiers first. And remember, our number one love is the good old USA. We need to cut the cord, my friend, be free."

Maybe Dylan did have a point. He wanted above all to be fair to Jennifer, but he couldn't digest it all just yet. He was going to have to think this over carefully. "I don't know," he said.

Dylan sat up and pulled the "nice grass" from his ponytail. "Dude, we need to break up with our girlfriends."

It was Annie's idea for a change. "We should go to this party, Carla. They're having a big bonfire in the desert and kegs of beer, and there might even be live music. It sounds great, doesn't it?" She had overheard some girls talking about it in the bathroom, and it sounded like an open party—no invitation required, the more the merrier. She had felt a tingle of excitement as she waited in the stall, not wanting that group of popular girls, including Nina, to know she was eavesdropping. She couldn't wait to tell Carla about it.

But for once, Carla was the one who was reluctant. "I don't know. I hear those parties get pretty wild."

Annie stared at her in amazement. "You, of all people, don't want to go to a wild party? Knock, knock." She rapped lightly on Carla's forehead. (Today, she wore a black and red checked fedora). "Will the real Carla Goldleib please come out?"

Carla grinned. "You know I've been toeing the line since the parental unit's Christmas party." She emphasized this point by drawing a line in the dirt with her pointed cowboy boot. "I've been punished, as you know. My wheels are in storage until further negotiations."

Annie did know this, of course. Carla's parents had told her she couldn't drive her BMW for a while, and they were pretty vague about how long that would be. But the funny thing about it was how happy this punishment seemed to make Carla. Her parents had finally noticed her, she said, and she had seemed a little calmer since the tumble down the stairs.

To Annie's great relief, the Goldleibs had not called her parents. In fact, they seemed to not have noticed her at the bottom of the stairs at all. "Simple fact," Carla had said. "They probably don't remember your name. No offense."

However, Annie was certain that Carla recognized the irony of the situation. Carla couldn't drive the BMW, but she had the family's town car at her disposal. What kind of *punishment* was that? Also, the Goldleibs' notice of their daughter had been short-lived. They had been out of the country for three weeks now. From them, Carla had received one phone call (ignored, straight to voicemail), one email (unread, deleted), and one text (ignored, discarded).

"We could take the town car," Annie said.

"I know that." They were in the parking lot of SCDS walking toward that car at that particular moment.

"So why don't you want to go?"

"Why is it that you want to go so much?"

"I just think it would be fun, a good time, you know?"

"Guess again." Carla opened the door and slid into the Lincoln's plush back seat.

Annie slid in beside her. She fumbled in her backpack, trying to avoid the question.

Carla would have none of that. "Because Walter, in all probability, will be there. It's his group having the party. I heard about it, too. It's all over school. It's the party of the year. No, it's the party of the decade. No—I got it wrong—it's the party of the *century*."

Annie didn't answer her. She vowed that she would remain silent the entire way to Carla's house.

"Home, James," Carla said to Tom, the driver.

Annie's vow of silence lasted approximately thirty seconds. "Okay, that's the reason I want to go. Satisfied?" She still held onto the belief that, if she and Walter could have a real conversation, he would realize that they had a lot more in common than he could ever have *dreamed* of.

Carla put a piece of Nicorette gum in her mouth. "If they really wanted people to quit smoking, why do they make this gum taste like shit?"

"If you're going to be such a bitch about it, I'll find another way to get there," Annie said sulkily. She couldn't think of any other way to get there, none at all. Like she could go up to her dad and say, "Hey, Dad, want to drive me to a big bonfire party in the desert where the kids get totally wasted?" And he would answer, "Sure thing, kiddo! Why'd it take you so long to ask?" Yeah, right.

"Oh, Annie, Annie, Annie," Carla said. "You know I'll go with you. God knows you've gone along with my plans often enough. But this Walter thing. Don't you think you should let it go?"

"I don't want to talk about it." She knew this hope she had for Walter was tinged with a little bit of unreality—okay, an impressive *ton* of *impossibility*—but she couldn't help herself. The "all boys are pigs" motto, although true, didn't seem to include him, or else why would her heart start to pound every time she caught a glimpse of him? She couldn't explain it.

"Okay, we won't talk about it. But I want you to know that I am on your side, even when I sound like I'm not."

Carla really was a good friend, and when they dressed later in Carla's room, she started getting excited about the party, but that was probably due in large part to the joint they smoked. They chose their outfits carefully: tight jeans, tight halter tops covered with jean jackets, and stiletto heels. Even though Annie was again reduced to raiding Mrs. Goldleib's fat wardrobe, she didn't mind. It was much nicer stuff than she had at home anyway. After much deliberation, they decided to cover their short hair with stocking caps, but they were kind of dressy because they were silk, courtesy of Mrs. Goldleib. Lots of eye makeup completed the ensemble, and in their collective opinion, they looked *hot*.

It wasn't easy to find the party. It seemed to Annie like it took a long time of bouncing over rutted desert roads before they came upon a haphazard grouping of cars, a lot of cars. "This must be it," she said.

Carla took a deep breath. "Let the fun times begin." To Tom, she said, "Wait here for us, James. I'm not sure how long we'll be, but you better be here when we get back."

"Don't have anything better to do," he said, already reclining his seat.

"Why are you so mean to him?" Annie asked as they walked toward the distant sound of laughter. "We don't want him to ditch us. We'd be in deep shit then." Another thought occurred to her. "And we don't want him to tell either."

"He's not going to do either. My parents pay him $200,000 a year, plus a Christmas bonus. He's not going anywhere."

It was another Goldleib *wow* moment, but Annie didn't say it aloud. Her father probably didn't make half that much (she would never have dreamed of asking him), and in Annie's opinion, he had a much tougher job. Hanging around with Carla for the last year had certainly been eye-opening for Annie. It wasn't that Carla really flaunted her family's wealth, at least not as much as some of the other SCDS kids. She just took it as an indisputable truth. She could matter-of-factly state her town car driver's salary and then shrug her shoulders as if it meant nothing at all.

Neither one of them mentioned how nervous they were as they drew close to the party. The sounds of talking, teasing, laughing, and the occasional high-pitched girlish shriek grew louder. The bonfire, in Annie's opinion, was disappointedly small. She had imagined some towering inferno kind of thing. This fire was about twice the size of a normal campfire, so as usual, reality did not meet her expectations. Not that it really mattered. There were so many people hanging around or lounging on blankets or lawn chairs that she wouldn't even get close enough to feel its meager warmth. She shivered in her halter top and jean jacket. Fuck fashion. The desert night was cold, and she wished she had on her winter coat and knock-off UGGs. She was starting to wish she hadn't come.

"It looks like the entire school is here," Carla said. She, too, was shivering. "And about a hundred other people."

"This is impossible," Annie said. She would never get close to Walter in this teeming sea of teenaged, hormone-spouting bodies. What had she been thinking? She hadn't been thinking. She was an idiot.

Carla took pity on her disappointment. "We can have a good time. You and I always have a good time together, don't we?" She fished around in her tight jeans pocket and pulled out two Ecstasy tablets. "I came prepared like a good girl scout. We'll take these, and then we'll get as drunk as we possibly can. That's the plan. Are you in?"

Annie nodded and gratefully swallowed the pill. She felt immediately better, knowing that the drug would soon make her more relaxed and less inhibited and less intimidated. "Let's do this."

They had to wait in line at the keg for a long time, so when she and Carla made it to the front of the line, they did what everyone else was doing. They downed three beers and then poured a fourth to carry around with them. And it wasn't so bad. They were certainly not the center of attention, but people weren't ignoring them either. Even Nina stopped and said hello, and Annie, now thoroughly high, asked her where Walter was.

"I think he's over there puking under a tree," Nina said. She pointed vaguely past the campfire, unable to focus her eyes. "I am so over him," she said.

"Men are pigs," Carla offered.

"Yes!" Nina nodded emphatically. "But I wouldn't call him a man. He's a child."

"All men are *childish* pigs," Carla said. Maybe it was from all her practice, but Carla was holding her liquor extremely well.

"Yes!"

Carla nodded her head toward the vague tree and mouthed *go* to Annie.

Annie started off. She was confident, and she would not be deterred. She would finally get her man. No, she would get her *childish pig*. But that didn't sound right. Her brain was a little muddled.

She must have had some homing device going—it certainly wasn't luck, she wasn't a lucky person—because she found Walter right away, leaning against the trunk of a tree. Brazenly, not letting herself think, she plopped down next to him on the hard ground. "Hi," she said.

"I am so wasted," he said. He looked at Annie with blurry eyes. "Who are you?"

This did hurt, a little. "It's Annie."

"Oh, yeah, sorry. It's frigging dark out here. I'm glad you came, Annie." His golden hair was disheveled.

"Me, too." She was now very happy that she had come to this desert party. At long last, she was alone with Walter.

"Nina dumped me," he said.

"I heard."

He reached out and grabbed her hand. "You would never dump me, would you, Annie? You're a nice girl. You're not anything like that Nina bitch."

"I would never dump you, Walter," she said solemnly. This was going so well!

"No, you wouldn't," he agreed. "You are a very nice and caring person."

"Yes, I am." Annie hoped this didn't sound too conceited, but at this very moment, she believed it with all her heart.

"Would you help me find my car? I need to lie down."

"Sure, Walter." She helped him up and slung his arm around her shoulders. He didn't seem that drunk to her. He wasn't dead weight sagging against her, dragging her down. He stumbled some (she did, too), but at his direction, they found his Range Rover.

He climbed into the backseat. "It's cold in here. Do you want to come and keep me warm?"

She didn't hesitate even a heartbeat, never mind that he could have started the car and turned on the heater. "Anything for you, Walter." She stretched out next to him on the seat.

And then he was on top of her, kissing her. He probably should have tasted like vomit, but he didn't to Annie. He tasted almost sweet. So, this was what kissing was supposed to feel like! She felt warm throughout her body, a tingling sensation in the pit of her stomach. This was heaven to her. She was kissing Walter!

They stopped a moment to catch their breath. "Did you really mean anything?" he asked.

Alex seemed different to Sam. Since Alex had finished the medically recommended stint in bed, she seemed somehow more distant. It wasn't really anything overt, or one thing in particular, yet Sam, who knew her sister like she knew herself, felt that something had shifted. It must have happened when Sam and Chris went to Chicago. They had only been gone for a little more than twenty-four hours, but when she got back, something had changed.

Sam ran the pool net over the surface of the water, skimming off the leaves. Since she and Chris were economizing, they no longer had a cleaning lady, a landscaper, or a pool guy. So Sam had willingly volunteered to take over the duty of keeping the pool clean. Of course she would do her part! She had researched chemical balances and Ph levels. She faithfully fished out leaves. She absolutely despised this job.

And she suddenly knew. "The baby's first kick," she said aloud. Alex had been practically glowing, despite her recent breakout of hormonal acne, when she told Sam about it. Sam was equally excited, but she had to admit, also jealous. She had missed her baby's first kick! (Damn that grouchy old Louise, who ignored a heart attack and *refused* to die.) Sam had placed her hand on Alex's belly for some time, but nothing happened.

"I guess she's sleeping," Alex had said.

"I guess he's not in the mood," Sam had countered.

"Next time, I'll call you the minute it happens."

Alex hadn't called, and it had been more than a week.

"Shit!" Sam dropped the pool net and marched across the street. She was going to nip this in the bud. She remembered all too well the first time she felt Grace kick and the overwhelming flood of love she had had for her unborn child. It would make sense that Alex would feel this. It was probably inevitable that she would, but this kind of thing needed to be discussed, needed to be aired out. In short, Alex needed to be reminded whose baby this was.

But it had to be done delicately, which was not Sam's strong suit, not even close. She made sure she wasn't stomping by the time she entered Alex's house, and she rearranged her face into a smile that felt like she was stretching her lips like a rubber band. "Anyone home?" she called.

"In here," Alex called from the kitchen. Her Avon sample bag had arrived, and samples were spread out all over the table. "Smell this," Alex said as she thrust a jar of night cream under Sam's nose.

"It brings back memories."

"I know. Mother always wore Avon products when we were growing up."

"I wonder if she still does?" Sam picked up a tube of lipstick.

"It's a shame we don't know that," Alex said.

"I don't remember smelling her at Christmas time."

"I don't mean that we should have gone around her sniffing like dogs. I just mean that we should know whether or not she still wears Avon."

Did Alex suddenly think she was an expert on smell? She hadn't even started to sell the damn products yet. "Uh huh," Sam said.

"Do you want to try that lipstick? I think it would be a good shade on you."

Sam wanted to shout: No, I don't want to try on the fucking lipstick, Ding Dong Lady! I want to talk about important matters—i.e., my baby. "Sure."

Alex held up a mirror while Sam tried on the lipstick, Fuchsia Forever. "See? I told you."

It did look pretty good. "Fine. I'll buy it."

"This is exciting. You're my first sale, Sam." Alex beamed, and really did look glowing. "I think I'm going to be good at this. I know that people can buy everything on the internet now, but I still think it's important for that human interaction, don't you? Even when I pass through the cosmetics section in Macy's, which is not often these days, I always stop and try the free samples. Those poor saleswomen stand there all day and repeatedly get the brush-off from women who have nothing better to do than shop from morning until night. It's basic human kindness to acknowledge someone else, right? We need to show respect for one another as human beings."

Sam wasn't sure how to respond to this unexpected tangent. "Yes, we should show respect for one another."

"Damn right." Alex started to pack up her bag. "Did you want something?"

"Do you mean something else other than the lipstick?"

Alex smiled. It was a rather secretive smile, Sam thought. "No, sister. You must have missed my skip in the conversational plane here. Boy, that psych experiment in college when they taped us finishing each other's thoughts, even as we jumped from topic to topic, was long ago. I meant, is there a specific reason why you're here?"

Now was Sam's chance to say: You haven't forgotten that you're carrying *my* baby, have you? But she reminded herself that she was going to be delicate about this topic. "How are you feeling?"

"Much better now that I'm out of that damn bed." Alex started to pack up her samples. "If it wasn't for you, I think I might have gone crazy."

"I liked keeping you company."

"You're the only one around here who did," Alex said grimly.

Amazingly, the topic of Alex's family was a subject that they no longer talked about directly. Instead, they just alluded to *slight problems*. It was no secret how Jack felt and how poorly he was handling the pregnancy, but no one, as far as Sam knew, had confronted him directly. And Annie was another story. Sam still felt very guilty about keeping Annie's secrets from Alex. Nick, for some reason, never seemed to be at home anymore, and Sam had no idea what kind of secrets he was keeping. It was becoming an increasingly tangled web around the Carissa household, and Sam knew she played a part in it. In fact, she could be considered the spider who created the web, but she didn't want to believe it. Jack had a drinking problem. Annie was drinking and taking drugs. Nick was just acting weird like all seniors. Period.

She changed the subject. "Has the baby kicked again?"

"Oh, yes, I meant to tell you. The baby kicked this morning."

Disappointment washed over her. "You were supposed to call!" Sam couldn't stop her accusing tone.

"I was at the grocery store, Sam. Would you really drop what you were doing and run to the produce section of Fry's?"

"Yes." That's exactly what she would have done.

Alex sighed. "The baby is going to kick many, many more times. It's impossible that you're going to be around for all of them."

"I know, but—"

"Do you remember when Mom used to make pigs in the blanket?"

What in the hell was Alex talking about? Undoubtedly, she was changing the subject, but why? Fine. They would talk about pigs in the blanket now, but Sam was still going to delicately remind Alex that this baby was hers. "I thought they were the best food in the world when I was ten, but now they sound disgusting."

"It's what we're having for dinner."

"Oh." Maybe Alex had a craving?

Alex got the ingredients out of the refrigerator: hot dogs, crescent rolls, and Velveeta cheese. Sam watched her as she made a slit in each hot dog, filled it with two pieces of cheese (or whatever it was that Velveeta was actually made of), and rolled it into the crescent roll. She put the hot dogs on a cookie sheet and pushed it into the oven.

"I know it's not the healthiest choice for a pregnant woman to make."

It sure as hell wasn't, but Sam said, "If that's what you're craving, then that's what you're craving."

And Alex simply said, "It's the end of the month."

It took Sam a second to realize the full implication of that sentence. Alex's money situation was even worse than she thought, but she didn't want to insult her by asking how hard up they really were. "This recession has hit everyone hard."

"It sure has." Alex sat down heavily at the table.

Sam joined her. "Can I look at your Avon book?"

"You've already bought the lipstick. You don't have to buy anything else."

"Who said anything about buying? I'm just interested in what kinds of products Avon has these days."

By the time the pigs in the blanket were done, Sam had not mentioned the baby and had spent way more money than she should have on products that she didn't really want or need. The smell of the baking hot dogs and crescent rolls made her mouth water, and she ended up eating one before she left.

It was delicious.

Chris disliked the occasional department happy hour, but he knew it was obligatory. It was necessary to catch up with Dr. Smith's latest publication in the MLA or the latest panel Dr. Jones had chaired at a conference in Denver or Wichita. He didn't especially relish the mingling and drinking with his colleagues in the English department, and the fact of the matter was that he hadn't really connected with anyone in the few months he'd been at ASU. He suspected that they thought he was rather standoffish, possibly even anti-social, which he had been. They had no idea what he was going through at home with Sam, his in-laws, and the economic pressure this coming baby was putting on him. They had no idea at all.

However, he was here at a place called Roundabout, a sports bar on Scottsdale Road, with a drink in his hand and a somewhat forced smile on his face. The bar seemed like an odd choice for a professorial happy hour. Chris had counted twenty-one televisions with a sports game, a race, or a golf tournament on every one. And it was loud and crowded with a youngish group of people drinking beer and eating nachos and wings. He had a hard time hearing what was being said to him and had spent most of the last hour nodding agreeably. He would finish this drink, and then he would leave.

Renee Rosewall tapped his arm. "Isn't this place great?" she asked loudly. She was a dark-haired, plumpish woman in her late thirties, one of the foremost Shakespeare scholars in the country.

Chris nodded agreeably.

"I'm the one who suggested it. I heard about it from some friends of mine and have been dying to try it. My nights out are few and far between with a one-year-old at home!" She laughed gaily.

Chris nodded agreeably, the forced smile still on his face.

"Do you have children?" Renee asked.

How should he answer that? His smile disappeared. "Not yet," he said.

Renee put her hand sympathetically on his arm. "Oh, I'm sorry. Did I ask a nosy question?"

He really wanted to go home now. "No, it's fine. My wife and I are still . . . waiting."

"I'm sure it will happen for you." She squeezed his arm with even more excess sympathy, and then as a sort of apology, she offered to buy him a drink.

"Let me buy you one," he said, anxious to escape her hand. "I'll go to the bar and order. It'll be faster than waiting for one of the overworked servers."

With some effort, he managed to squeeze up to the bar, flag down the harried bartender, and order Renee's gin and tonic. While he waited, he gave a cursory glance down the bar. The dark-haired man deep in conversation with an aging blonde caught his attention. The man looked like Jack. At that moment, the man looked up and saw Chris.

It was Jack. And the expression on his face was that of a deer caught in the headlights. Chris knew that look because he had hit a deer once, years before. It seemed like the buck came out of nowhere, was simply plopped down in front of his car, and the look of sheer panic in the deer's eyes before impact would stay with Chris forever.

Chris didn't know what to do, so he nodded, took the drink, and hurried back to Renee. He made some feeble excuse about having to leave because his wife had just called, a pipe had just burst and was flooding the kitchen—it sounded unbelievable, even to him—and he had to leave right now. And all the while, he was thinking that the asshole was having an affair. He had just reached his car when Jack caught up with him.

"It's not what you think," he said.

Chris unlocked his car. "How do you know what I'm thinking?"

"That woman in there. She's just a friend."

"It's none of my business." Chris didn't believe him, not for a second.

"No, it's not," Jack said angrily.

It was so like Jack to get caught having an affair and then be defensive about it. The jerk. "Let me repeat myself. It's none of my business."

"Cookie's just a friend," Jack insisted.

"Her name's Cookie? How appropriate."

Jack's face grew red, which probably meant that he wanted to hit Chris. Let him. Chris was not a fighter and had never been in a fight before, but for the first time in his life, he felt like throwing a punch. Maybe it would clear the air between them, which would greatly please their wives. Maybe they would never speak to each other again, which would greatly please both of them.

Jack didn't hit him. "Cookie's a friend. She's having some marital problems, and I'm her . . . sounding board."

Wasn't that how most affairs began, with the admission from one, then both parties, that there was marital discord? Chris was sure that he had read that somewhere before. "Sure," he said.

"I'm telling you the truth. Nothing has happened between us."

Yet. Jack probably meant that nothing had happened between them *yet*. They had looked very cozy in the bar.

"And I need someone to talk to, too." The anger was gone, and Jack's voice had a subtle pleading quality to it. "Everything's going to hell in a handbasket."

The self-pitying fool. Jack was the one who was behaving like a jerk, drinking excessively and doing who knew what with this Cookie person. "You might want to take some responsibility for what's going on in your life, Jack."

"I do. I take responsibility. But you have to admit that most of what's going on is Sam's fault."

"We all agreed," Chris said. Jack had a point. Sam had started this whole thing with her obsessive desire to have a baby, but the overwhelming point was that all four of them had agreed. And furthermore, Jack seemed to have no problem with taking Chris and Sam's money. The checks had been cashed.

"Yes, you've reminded me of that before, but it doesn't make me feel any better about any of this."

"Well, I guess that's up to you." Chris got into his car, tired of the conversation and tired of Jack's whining.

Jack held the door so Chris couldn't close it. "Let's be clear. I am not having an affair with Cookie."

"Good. Great. I would hope that if you were having an affair, you would pick someone with a name that does not have connotations of chocolate chip or oatmeal raisin." Chris tugged at the door. It didn't budge.

"Very funny, you professorial prick."

"Let go of the door, you self-pitying jerk." There. He had finally called Jack a jerk to his face. It was long overdue.

Jack let go of the door, and Chris slammed it shut, but then thought of one more thing to say. He rolled down his window. "Let me be clear, Jack. You're treading on dangerous ground here."

"Don't I know it," Jack said sadly, all anger gone. "Don't I know it."

Dylan did it. He broke up with Melissa on a Saturday night, right after they had had sex in his truck (which Nick thought was in extremely poor taste). Melissa did not take it well.

"I just had to get it over with, dude. I couldn't keep stringing her along when I know that I'll be leaving in a few months," Dylan told Nick. "Besides, I know she's not The One."

"How do you know she's not The One?" Nick asked.

"I just know."

"But how do you know?" Nick persisted. Was there some kind of warning bell that went off in your emotional psyche?

"I just know, man. I can't explain it any better than that. This love thing is a pretty complicated business."

Naturally, this lack of specific information about The One prompted another Loretta lesson. Once again, he couldn't ask his mom. The very mention of a possible date for the winter dance had about sent her into orbit with joy. And what did parents who had been married for almost two decades remember about love anyway?

The late January day was warm, and Loretta had opted to take her break on a bench outside Fry's. Nick followed her.

"Can I ask you something, Loretta?"

"Sure, sweetie." Loretta took a long drag on her Camel cigarette. Today, her nails were bright orange.

Nick had rehearsed what he was going to say, and he had decided to get right to the point. "How do you know when it's The One?"

"The one what?" Loretta asked distractedly.

He thought she would know what he was talking about, what with all her advice about romance, etcetera. "You know, The One for you?"

"Are you talking about a person, place, or thing?"

"Loretta, I'm talking about Jennifer!"

"Oh, sorry, honey." Loretta shook her head to snap herself out of her reverie. "I was thinking about buying a new sofa, and I'm kind of torn between this green plaid one at Sears and a red leather one I saw on Craigslist. I think I'm leaning toward the green plaid one, which they would deliver, but the red leather one is cheaper, but I'd have to go get it myself, which means I'd have to borrow my cousin's pickup truck, which would be kind of awkward because we are not on good terms at this particular moment in time."

Nick sighed. Sometimes it was such an effort to keep Loretta on track. However, he really valued her advice. And lucky for him, he had a lot of patience.

"I'm all ears now, honey. We're talking about love."

"Yes." Despite himself, he felt his face grow warm. He was such a novice at this. Just a few months ago, he thought he didn't like girls at all, and now he was asking Loretta about *love*.

Loretta exhaled an impressive plume of smoke. "Let's see. How do you know if someone is The One, your forever after, your soul mate? You know that I consider myself somewhat an expert on this subject, what with three husbands and a lot of men—I mean boyfriends—in between, but I got to tell you, that is one tough question. Yes, siree, it's a question for the ages."

He thought she would have a ready answer. "So you don't know?"

"Now, honey, wipe that hangdog look off your face. That doesn't mean that old Loretta won't take a stab at answering your question." She lit another cigarette, buying time.

He waited.

"I think you just know," she said.

Oh, brother. This was no more informative than what Dylan had said.

"It's a feeling in your heart, I think, and a feeling in your gut, a feeling of rightness maybe, a feeling that you can't live without that person in your life. Hawks mate for life, did you know? And so do ravens."

He waited patiently, hoping she wouldn't get sidetracked with other birds.

"But some people think they find their soul mate," Loretta continued, concentrating hard, "and then they get divorced when things get tough, like when the husband is a drunk or a meth addict and can't keep a decent job to save his sorry ass, and on top of that he's whoring around, or they fall out of love, or maybe they really weren't in love to begin with."

She took a deep drag on her cigarette. "And some people never find their soul mate, and some people just settle so they don't have to eat supper alone every night, or they need someone to help with the electric bill, or they really want to have kids."

She was on a roll now. "But there are some people who fall in love and work at it and make it through the hard times because they care—or they could be Catholic or Mormon, I suppose—and stay married despite the odds. Ain't nothing so lovely as seeing an old wrinkled couple walking around holding hands, don't you think?"

Nick's head was whirring, and he was thinking about his parents and whether they were soul mates. "Yes, but, initially—"

"It's a special thing to find The One, but then you got to work at it," Loretta finished. She took a deep breath, looking pleased with herself, then she coughed. "Damn cigarettes," she said.

"Well, thanks, Loretta," Nick said hesitantly. He didn't think she had answered his question, but then, maybe no one could. Maybe it was just a personal thing, the feeling of *rightness*, as Loretta had said.

"My pleasure," she said and started to laugh. "Now, in my case, I thought I'd found my soul mate too many times to count, so maybe those scumbags weren't really my soul mate after all, but then, as you know, I'm a hopeless romantic, and I just jump in feet first time and time again . . ."

Nick pondered what Loretta had said for the rest of his shift, and when he met Jennifer at Starbucks, he still didn't have a clue. Was she The One? Were they too young? What if Dylan was right and the military should come first? It was all terribly confusing.

"Dylan broke Melissa's heart," she said, accusation in her voice. Jennifer took a sip of her jumbo, wasteful latte. "He behaved like a total jerk, and she's so depressed she can't even eat."

Because of Melissa's weight problem, Nick didn't think this was such a terrible thing. It wasn't the best diet in the world, but still. "I'm sorry she's taking it so hard."

"She loved him," Jennifer said. She looked especially pretty sitting there in a dark green sweater, her long silky black hair tied back in a matching ribbon.

"Yes."

"And he dumped her."

"Yes."

"What are you going to do about it?"

"Me? Dylan is the one who broke up with her, not me."

"But he's your best friend and Melissa's mine. You could talk to him. Tell him how much he's hurt her. Tell him that he is making a huge mistake." Jennifer, usually so calm, was agitated.

"I'm not going to do that." He knew Dylan's reasoning, and he knew that Dylan wasn't going to change his mind. "Really, Jennifer, it's not our business."

"But they're our best friends!" She was close to tears.

"I know, but maybe these things happen for a reason. Maybe it'll be a good thing in the long run."

"How can you say that? You act like you don't even care!"

"Of course I care." Why was she being so unreasonable? He hadn't done anything wrong.

"Is this what the two of you had planned all along, to have sex with us and then dump us? Is that it?"

"Absolutely not." He was shocked, and if he remembered correctly— and he remembered vividly—Jennifer was the one who had initiated sex with him, not the other way around.

"Are you thinking of breaking up with me?" Two silent tears slid down her cheeks in a perfect parallel. Even Jennifer's tears were pretty.

"No," he stuttered, because vaguely, after Dylan had said they should break up with their girlfriends, he had thought about it. But only briefly. But not really.

"I can understand the reasoning. I mean, we'll be graduating soon, and I'm supposed to go to Stanford, and you think you're going to join the Marines." Jennifer's voice was very quiet. "The logistics would be dif- ficult, to say the least."

"I don't want to break up with you, Jennifer." And suddenly, he didn't want that at all. It was the last thing he wanted.

"Why haven't you told your parents we're dating? Why do we have to sneak around at school so no one knows we're a couple? It's been bother- ing me for awhile now.

"I don't—I didn't—think the time was right."

"Are you ashamed of me?"

"No!"

"Then why?"

He didn't say anything. Telling her that his mother would smother them with kindness seemed like a stupid excuse now. Telling her that, for some misguided reason, he thought secrecy made their relationship more special seemed equally stupid. And selfish. He had been selfish.

"I think we should have a trial separation," she said. "We might have started off slow, but we've been moving very fast lately, very fast." She blushed. "Maybe some time apart would give us time to think more clearly and help us decide if we really want to be together."

It was one of the things he liked about her, her level-headedness. He didn't like it now. "I don't want to do that."

"I think it would be for the best." Two more perfect, parallel tears.

"Jennifer," he pleaded.

"I think it would be for the best," she repeated.

"For how long?" He felt like crying, like bawling like a baby.

She hesitated, thinking. "Two months."

"Two months!" It seemed like an endless amount of time.

"Two months," she stated firmly. "No dating, no calling, no emailing, no texting." She gathered her books together and left without a backward glance, without a waver in her step.

He got out of Starbucks before the tears started to fall, and he started to run. He was going to run and never stop. He had been so stupid. Stupid and selfish. He had thought he could nonchalantly consider breaking up with Jennifer when he didn't want to at all. She knew him so well and had sensed his fleeting, miniscule doubt and declared a trial separation. She was so much smarter than him, so much better. She'd probably find someone else.

He ran hard, pounding on the fear that he had just lost The One.

Walter didn't come to school on the Monday after the bonfire. He didn't come to school on Tuesday either. "Do you think I should call him?" Annie asked Carla for the hundredth time. "Maybe he's sick."

"Call him," Carla said, bored.

"But I don't know what to say."

"Then don't call him."

"Maybe I should text him. That would be easier."

"Then text him."

"But I don't know what to say."

"Enough already! For the love of God, Annie, shit or get off the pot."

"You're not helping," Annie said, hurt. She threw her backpack into the back of Carla's car. Just as suddenly as her parents had taken away the BMW, they had given it back. Annie had to agree with Carla that her parents were inconsistent.

Carla sighed and lit a cigarette. "We've been through this a *gazillion* times, Annie. Number one, you're assuming he remembers what happened, and number two, you're assuming that it meant something."

"He wasn't that drunk, and of course it meant something. People don't just have random sex." As soon as the words were out of her mouth, Annie knew how stupid that sounded, that Carla would have a field day with this one.

She was right. Carla rolled her eyes and laughed. "Are you living in the fifties, Annie? Have you seen too many reruns of *Happy Days*? Get real. You know as well as I do that people hook up all the time, and it doesn't mean anything. We, the so-called Entitlement Generation, have been bombarded with so much sex and violence on TV, in movies, and in video games that we are *immune*."

Carla thought she was so smart all the time. It was maddening. "Immune to what?" she snapped.

"You know."

"No, I don't."

"Well," Carla faltered a bit, which had to be a first. "Feelings, making real connections with people. We text instead of talk. We type on people's Facebook walls instead of having a face-to-face conversation. We are becoming anti-social beings!" she finished triumphantly.

"You're making this up," Annie said.

"No, I saw this program on TV. I think it was Oprah." Carla was driving too fast, as usual.

"Oh then, it must be true." Annie hoped her voice was dripping with sarcasm.

"Hey, don't knock Oprah. She's a guru, didn't you know that?"

"It meant something," Annie said stubbornly. Walter was different. He wasn't like some boys who would go around school bragging that they had banged a girl like it was a big joke. At least she hoped he wasn't like that. No, she was *sure* he wasn't. And he certainly was not anything at all like that boy on the cruise ship, that Adam. She shuddered just thinking the name, and the familiar bile rose in her throat.

"Do you want to drive by his house?"

"Whose house?" Annie was still shuddering.

"Geez, Annie. Walter's house."

"That would be like stalking him, wouldn't it?" she said, although the mere possibility of catching a glimpse of him made her heart beat faster.

"No, we're just concerned classmates, making sure that Walter is okay, checking to see if there are any paramedics in the driveway."

"You think you're so funny."

"No, I think I'm *witty*, which is way better than being funny."

They drove slowly by Walter's house on Mockingbird Lane, which had a big iron gate and massive oleanders towering over the walls that surrounded the property. They couldn't see anything at all. "I guess they like their privacy," Carla said.

And Annie couldn't believe how disappointed she felt. It was stupid, really, to feel as if Walter was somehow trying to hide from her. They had a *connection* now. They had had sex. No, they had made love. That's what it had felt like to Annie in the cold, cold back seat of Walter's black Range Rover.

Walter came to school on Wednesday, and even from a distance, he looked pale to Annie. Since they didn't have any classes together—number one, he was a senior and she was a sophomore, and number two, he was in all AP courses and she would never be—she searched for his face between classes. When she did spot him (three sightings, to be exact), he didn't have his usual smile on his face, he wasn't joking around with his friends, and he walked quickly to his next class, head down.

The big question was this: How was she going to get near enough to talk to him? And even if she did get close to him, how was she going to get him alone without all his jackass friends hanging around? Walter was very sociable.

She conferred with Carla about this as they walked to seventh-period study hall. "This is hopeless," she said.

"Just walk up to him and say, 'Hi, Walter, how's it hanging?'" Carla didn't carry her backpack. She was planning on doing her nails during study hall, which meant that for the fourth time she would have her nail paraphernalia taken away by grouchy Miss Barry. For some reason, this really delighted Carla.

"That's crude."

"I didn't mean that you literally had to say that. I meant that you could say something, anything. This indecision is killing you—and me."

"Easier said than done." It was important to Annie that she talked to Walter today, kind of like a follow-up to Saturday night, or maybe she thought of it as more of an *acknowledgment* that Saturday night with Walter had actually happened? Whatever it was, she felt a strong need to speak to him today.

"I don't suppose you ever considered the possibility that maybe he should be the one who seeks you out? You know, after what happened?"

Annie had not considered this possibility, not at all.

"Never mind," Carla said quickly. "It's not going to happen, not with all his buffoons around. Don't look like that, Annie."

Annie was close to tears. She knew what Carla was implying, that if Walter had any respect for her, he would come to her. And there was virtually no chance of that.

Carla took hold of her arm. "Listen, Annie, we can make this work, and I just had a great idea. I could pose a distraction, get everyone's attention, and then you can talk to Walter."

"What kind of distraction?"

"Leave that to me."

Well, if there was one thing Carla was good at, very good at, it was forming a distraction. When the final bell rang, Annie was waiting a few lockers down from Walter's when Carla's commotion started. There was yelling and shouting, and it seemed as if everyone at SCDS moved towards the center quad. Later, Annie would learn that Carla had stood up on one of the picnic tables and flashed the crowd. Luckily, she didn't get caught.

Walter, unlike the others, did not move from his locker. He continued to stuff books into his backpack.

Annie approached. "Hi, Walter. Are you feeling better?" This had seemed like a good introduction a few seconds ago, but he looked confused.

"Better than what?"

"You missed a couple of days of school, and . . ." Annie cleared her throat. "I thought you were sick."

Walter—her sweet Walter—gave a bitter laugh. "I wish! I wish I'd had the flu. I wish I had West Nile's disease. Hell, I wish I had been hit by a car." He shook his head. "No, it's much worse than that."

It was Annie's turn to look confused.

"I guess you're the only one in school who hasn't heard." Walter slammed his locker and turned to her. "I didn't get into Harvard. My dad went to Harvard, both my brothers went to Harvard, and me, a legacy, didn't make the grade." He pronounced *Hah-vaad* with a mocking, East Coast accent.

"I'm sure you'll get into another great school!" Annie said brightly.

Walter shook his head. "No, you don't understand. Harvard is it for my parents. There are no other colleges worth bothering about. I didn't even apply anywhere else because we were all positive that Walter would make the grade. My parents have spent the last few days trying to decide what to do about Walter's problem, Walter's failure, Walter's catastrophe."

"I'm sorry."

Walter struck his fist against his gray metal locker. "No, I'm the sorry one."

It was not a good time to ask him about Saturday night. "I'll walk with you to your car," Annie said, trying to buy some more time with him.

"Thanks, but no. As you can see, I'm rotten company right now, and I just want to get the hell out of here."

Annie so desperately wanted some kind of acknowledgment from him that she could practically taste it. "About Saturday," she began.

"Yeah, Saturday, the day that ruined my life. Harvard bonged me, Nina dumped me, and I got drunk off my ass. You were at the party, weren't you? I vaguely remember you being there."

"I was there," Annie said softly.

"I hope I didn't make an ass out of myself."

"No."

"Good." He gave her a small smile, a ghost of Walter's real smile. "I'll see you around."

And he was gone.

As it turned out, Alex wasn't really cut out to be a saleswoman. She had tried calling on every woman in the neighborhood who she thought might be receptive to the idea of Avon beauty products, she had left countless shiny brochures tucked inside screen doors, and in desperation, she had even knocked on Amanda Williams' front door. She had endured an endless hour of Amanda's snobbish gossip, and the bitch didn't even end up buying anything. ("I only wear Estee Lauder," she had said in a voice that was entirely too haughty for their middle-class neighborhood.) The other women's excuses followed the same themes, either they were too busy to take the time to sit down with her or even read the damn brochure, or they weren't spending money on "extras" because of the economy. From Amanda, she had learned that the Udalls and the Westmores were in danger of losing their homes; foreclosure was expected any day. It was a grim situation.

At first, Alex wondered if her role as a surrogate for Sam might have something to do with the women's attitudes. To her face, they gushed congratulations and good wishes, but she knew how these women could be when they talked behind someone's back. The Bunco parties she had attended in this neighborhood had very little to do with rolling the dice and everything to do with talking about the people who hadn't shown up. Truly, the women were ruthless about speculating on the absent person's weight, possible affairs, financial woes, and wayward children. And Alex was ashamed to admit that she, too, had participated in these discussions in the past. However, she didn't think her pregnancy was the reason the women weren't buying. It was the recession, and it was a grim situation.

So, Alex had been home all afternoon, and instead of doing something useful—folding laundry, mopping the floor, scrubbing toilets—she was sitting in front of the TV. It was strange. Now that she was no longer on doctor-advised bed rest, which she had hated at the time, all she wanted to do was crawl in that bed and stay there for the next five months. But she wouldn't let herself do it. Oh, no, she was doing something much more productive! She had been watching Game Show Network for the last three hours: *Lingo, Deal or No Deal, Family Feud, Password, Chain Reaction*. She would probably be feeling very guilty about her laziness if her mind hadn't gone so numb, the dazed neurons—or were they synapses?—blocking all thoughts and feelings.

She deserved this afternoon off, this brief respite from her daily life, she told herself. She was pregnant, after all, and everyone knew that pregnant women needed some pampering. And God knew that she wasn't getting it from anyone else. She was Alex, the rock, the steady center of her whirlwind family, and no one was going out of his or her way to lug in the heavy groceries from the car, or mow the back yard, or get on a ladder and swipe at the spider webs with a broom, or heave the broken vacuum cleaner into the trunk of the car to take to the repair shop. No one.

She deserved to sit and watch mindless TV in the middle of the day. She deserved to eat a quart of chocolate mint chip ice cream directly out of the carton with a spoon. She deserved to paint her toenails rosy pink during the commercials. She deserved to tell everyone in the house that she was not going to cook dinner that night, that they could either make themselves a sandwich or go to hell.

Maybe not.

It started with the phone call from the bank. She had thought about not answering it, but she was up anyway, throwing away the empty, leaking carton of ice cream. So she answered it, and was informed that the last two checks she had written had bounced, one for $72.68 to Fry's for groceries and one for $103.39 to Target for maternity clothes.

"There must be some mistake," she stammered. She was mortified. She had never bounced a check before. In fact, the only reason she had written those two was that Jack had canceled all but one of their credit cards, despite her protests. ("I handle the finances," he had always said. "Trust me." And she had, for years and years.)

But there was no mistake. "Your account is overdrawn," the anonymous bank person said.

"I'll be there first thing in the morning to add to the account," she said, hanging up the phone. She was not going to listen to any more of her failings from someone with a high squeaky voice who sounded like she was twelve.

Jack arrived home five minutes later, so she was not angry, not yet. She was still embarrassed when she told him about the bounced checks. "How can that be?" she asked. "I've been sticking to our budget. I don't overspend."

He became immediately defensive, his response to everything these days. "What? Do you think I overspend?"

"Knock it off, Jack. I'm not blaming anyone. I only want to know why we've run out of money this month. For crying out loud, we've had hot dogs or hamburger every night this week."

Jack was nothing if not predictable. After going into defense mode, he usually poured a drink. He did. "You know we've had a lot of extra expenses this month. That damn water heater was three hundred dollars. You do the math."

She had forgotten about the water heater at the beginning of the month. He was right. There had been a lot of extra expenses this month. These things happened to everyone, and it was really nothing to get upset about. However, that didn't solve the immediate problem. "Where am I going to get the extra two hundred dollars to cover the overdrawn amount? I can't write a check from the account to cover the money. I would be writing a soon-to-be bounced check to cover two already bounced checks. You do the math."

Jack thought a moment before he reached into his pants pocket and pulled out a folded stack of bills. "Here," he said.

Alex counted the money. There were seven one-hundred-dollar bills. Where had he gotten so much money? But the most important question was, why hadn't he told her?

Jack knew her well. "I played poker with the guys the other night. I didn't tell you because I know how much you hate gambling."

"I do hate gambling. You might as well flush money down the toilet. But were you just going to keep the money for yourself?" There was something sneaky about all of this, and the ice cream in Alex's stomach churned uncomfortably. The baby kicked.

"No, no, no. I just forgot. I've been busy lately, as you know."

No, she didn't know. They didn't talk anymore, as *he* knew.

"Look, I'm giving it to you now, so what's the difference? Go to the bank tomorrow and deposit it, and then maybe you could go to Fry's and bypass the Hamburger Helper aisle and go straight for the meat department." He smiled crookedly.

The anger was growing. When she went to the bank in the morning, she was going to ask for a copy of their monthly statement. No, she was going to ask to see all the statements from the last six months. She pocketed the money, and they stood there, once again, staring at each other, saying nothing that needed to be said.

The door slammed. Annie stomped into the kitchen and threw her backpack to the ground. "I hate school!"

Jack looked at his watch. "You're supposed to be at your tutoring session."

"What tutoring session?" Once again, they were leaving her out of the loop, and Alex was sick of it. "What's going on at school?"

"I'm flunking Algebra II and English," Annie snarled.

"Why didn't you tell me?" Alex's stomach churned. The baby kicked.

"We didn't want to upset you," Jack said as he glared at his daughter.

"It upsets me more when you don't tell me what's going on in my own family! I'm the mother here. Don't I get an opinion?"

"It doesn't matter now. I am not going back there. I hate that place, and I hate everyone in it, except for Carla. She's the only decent person in a sea of morons. They all deserve to *die!*" Annie was becoming hysterical, even for Annie.

Alex moved toward her, but Jack stepped between them. It was the first time she had ever wanted to hit her husband.

"Listen here, Annie," Jack said, his voice his guidance counselor tone. "You need to calm down. Everyone has a bad day, and a fifteen-year-old often overreacts to the simplest things. Of course you're going back to school, and of course you're going to pass those classes, and of course you don't want everyone to die. Why don't you tell us what's upsetting you?"

"My *life* is upsetting me. It's *horrible.*" Annie's face was streaked and smudged with black tears.

"What's going on here?" No one had heard Nick come into the kitchen.

He looked thinner to Alex, and his eyes were bloodshot. Oh my God, Alex thought, is he doing drugs? She was going to be sick.

"This doesn't concern you, son," Jack said.

"Get out of here!" Annie screamed. "You're as bad as the rest of them."

Nick walked calmly toward the pantry. "I'm getting a snack. The last I heard, this was my kitchen, too."

Jack's cell rang, and he fumbled for it in his pocket. "Carissa here," he answered. As he listened to the caller, his face grew pale. "That's terrible," he choked. "I'll do whatever I can. We're going to need support people." He clicked his phone shut and looked at all of them.

"What is it, Jack?" Alex asked, alarmed by the look on his face.

When he told them, Annie let out a scream and fainted. Nick sunk to his knees, the dropped potato chips scattering the floor, and Alex ran to the bathroom and vomited.

What Jack said, with tears in his eyes, was this: "Walter Caldwell has committed suicide."

9

CHAPTER NINE

It had to be the most terrible thing a person could experience in this life, the loss of a child. Alex, like all mothers, feared for her children. She feared a phone call in the middle of the night telling her that one of her children had been in a car accident. She feared that they would be stricken with meningitis or leukemia or any number of rare and fatal diseases. She feared that one morning, for no reason at all, they would not wake up. As a young mother, she had completely identified with the opening scene in *Terms of Endearment* when the mother crawled into her baby's crib to see if she was breathing. Alex had come close to doing that very thing. She couldn't begin to guess how many hours she had sat by Nick's crib, then Annie's, watching them breathe. She had told Jack that baby monitors were unreliable when he had tried to persuade her to go to bed. He had shaken his head, smiled, and left her watching her children in the moonlight.

Yes, Alex had always known that it would be devastating—no, it would be unendurable—to lose a child. Thankfully, her children had survived infancy and childhood to arrive awkwardly at the challenges of adolescence, but then there had been Grace. She thought she had experienced the pain of that loss with Sam, but she hadn't, not really. She hadn't been with Sam for day after dreadful day after the funeral, when Sam couldn't get out of bed, couldn't eat, couldn't sleep, couldn't function. She had consoled her over the phone as best as she could, but that must have been weak solace to Sam. Even as she cried with Sam, there was always an underlying relief that she was ashamed of. Thankfully, her children were alive.

Walter Caldwell's funeral was heartbreaking. Not only was a bright, promising young man gone from this world, but what made it even worse was that he had died by his own hand. Alex knew, of course, the staggeringly high number of teenage suicides, but this was the first one that had occurred in this school, which was small and close-knit. Every SCDS student was present, along with most of their parents. The Episcopal Church was packed with weeping teenagers and moist-eyed adults. The senior class, Nick among them, occupied the front pews, and Alex cried for them. They were too young to have to experience this, too young to have to give eulogies talking about Walter's virtues, too young to ponder the question of why this had happened. It was a question that had no answer.

Jack sat beside Alex, his back ramrod stiff, and his gaze locked directly ahead. He had taken it hard, and Alex guessed that he felt somehow responsible because he was the school's guidance counselor. He had spent countless hours at the school arranging for grief counselors for the students, as if he were trying to make amends for something that he had had no control over. Alex didn't know where Annie was sitting. She had barely spoken since they heard the news. But then again, no one in their home was speaking much. No, in the Carissa home they were not grieving collectively, like in this church, and Alex couldn't seem to muster the strength to bring them together. Instead, they each walked around in their own halo of grief that Walter's suicide had bestowed upon them.

After the funeral, at the somber reception in the Fellowship Hall, Alex and Jack made polite conversation with other shell-shocked parents. In hushed tones, in all the groups, the same things were said:

"But why? He was the most popular kid in the school."

"Do you think it was drugs?"

"His poor parents."

"It's this generation of kids. They've had every technological advantage handed to them, and they don't know how to cope. We parents, by trying to give them everything, have handicapped them."

"It's no wonder they're called the Entitlement Generation."

"I don't know about you, but I'm going to watch my kid like a hawk. If this could happen to the Caldwell boy, it could happen to anybody. I'm not taking any chances."

It *could* happen to anybody, Alex thought. On the way home, she asked Jack, "Do you think we should be worried more about Nick and Annie? I know you keep telling me that she's going through a phase, but she's not happy, Jack. And what about Nick? He's been acting strange lately. He's not eating much these days, and that is certainly not like him."

"I don't think you could worry any more about them than you already do, Alex."

"We've been giving them a lot of privacy over the last few months. I think we should start asking more questions."

Jack still didn't look at her, not a glance. "What do you want to do, detective, search their rooms, hack into their computers, check their text messages?"

That was exactly what she wanted to do, so she said nothing.

Jack, for the first time in months, reached over and took her hand. "Look, Alex, Walter's suicide is a terrible thing, but we don't need to go and project our own fears onto our children. We have good kids. You've been a good mother."

She wanted to squeeze his hand so tightly that he would never let go. "Thank you. You've been a good father."

Jack continued as if she had not spoken. "Besides, we want our kids to trust us, and they certainly wouldn't if we invaded their privacy. Didn't you tell me once that Emily searched your and Sam's room when you were in high school?"

"She did." Alex had forgotten all about that.

"And how did that make you feel?"

"Furious. We were still sleeping on a Saturday morning, and Mother came stomping up the stairs dangling a cigarette, demanding to know if we smoked. We were caught off guard, still half asleep, so we didn't answer right away. She pounced on us with the question: 'Is this yours?' Sam and I answered that it wasn't. When Mother had gone back down the stairs, Sam looked at me and said, 'We didn't tell a lie. That's not our brand.' We never could figure out where that Marlboro came from and eventually decided that Mother was trying to trap us." She and Sam had resented their mother for months after.

"You don't want Nick and Annie to feel that way towards you, do you?" Jack asked.

"No." But she still wanted to check out their rooms.

"That's settled, then." Jack withdrew his hand as they turned into the driveway. "I'm going to drop you off and head back toward the school. We have a teachers' meeting to discuss the coming week and how we can help the kids cope."

"But Jack—" She wanted him here, with her. Together, they could work through this tragedy and its impact on their family. In the past, they had been a team. But that was the past.

"I won't be long."

Alex entered the empty house and went upstairs. She changed into a ratty old sweat suit. She would find an old movie on Turner Classic Movie channel, or maybe she would take a nap. She would get that big box out of the closet and finally sort through the assortment of pictures that she had never gotten around to putting in albums, or maybe she would organize her underwear drawer. No, she would go downstairs and make a healthy snack of steamed broccoli, or maybe she'd allow herself one Oreo.

She went into Annie's room. And she felt like a thief, although a thief would know where to start looking for valuables, where most people kept hidden money or jewelry. However, she was looking for something entirely different and was hoping she wouldn't find anything. She stood in the middle of the room, surveying the pile of clothes on the floor and the unmade bed. She took a deep breath and opened a dresser drawer.

She was thorough. She went through every drawer, even every individual sock, every piece of clothing in Annie's closet and on the floor, rifled every page in every book, checked under the mattress, and opened every CD container. She found nothing—not even a joint—and she was elated. Annie was all right; her daughter was not on drugs. She was about to go into Nick's room when she heard the door slam downstairs and Sam calling for her. Nick's room would have to wait, although there was probably no need to go through his things. Alex suspected that Nick's recent moodiness probably had to do with the girl he had not taken to the Winter Dance. He hadn't gone to the dance at all.

Sam was stirring a big pot on the stove. "I brought over some vegetable soup. I didn't think you'd be in the mood to cook tonight."

"You made soup?" Sam didn't usually have the patience for all the chopping that vegetable soup required.

"No, I brought it over. Chris made the soup." She turned from the stove. "Are you all right?"

"It was heartbreaking." Alex told her the details of the funeral.

"Life doesn't make sense." Sam, who had never met Walter, was crying.

"It sure doesn't."

"I hate feeling sad." Sam went back to the stove to stir the soup.

"I did something I'm not proud of today, but the results were good." Alex told Sam about searching Annie's room and finding nothing. "So I'm not dealing with a drugged-out daughter. I'm only dealing with a depressed one."

"Hooray for depression."

"You don't sound convinced that Annie's not doing drugs." Sam was being like everyone else who didn't give Annie the benefit of the doubt. No wonder Annie was depressed.

Sam didn't turn from the stove. "I'm certainly no expert on teenage girls, but did you consider that, if she was doing drugs or maybe drinking, she could possibly keep those things somewhere else, like at someone else's house or car?"

Carla. Alex's elation deflated like a pin-pricked balloon. Why hadn't she thought of that? Maybe she gave Annie too much benefit of the doubt. "Do you know something I don't know?"

"Of course not. I watch too many Lifetime movies. You know that."

"Look at me, Sam. Turn around." Alex's suspicion was growing. Sam knew something.

"No."

"Turn around."

"No. I plead the Fifth."

Alex's phone rang, and she only answered because it was Annie. "Mom," came Annie's wobbly voice. "Could you come get me? Carla's too upset to drive. I'll wait at the bottom of her driveway."

"I'll be right there." To Sam, she said, "You lucked out. This time."

Annie wished she could cry. Her eyes ached to cry, but she could not. Carla could. Oh boy, could she *cry*, howling like a wounded animal. Carla, who did not even particularly like Walter, was a perpetual fountain of tears, walking around campus with a box of tissues, drawing attention to herself: "Look at me," she seemed to be saying, "I am in *mourning*." Someone who didn't know any better would have thought that Carla had been Walter's girlfriend. The only crack in the numbness that was now the essence of Annie's existence was the irritation she felt towards Carla.

Annie wished she could cry.

Instead, she relived every smile Walter had ever given her, every conversation she had ever had with him (all four of them), and of course, that Saturday night at the bonfire. It was a continuous loop running in her head, and at the end of the loop, before it would mercilessly start again, was the image of her standing in her kitchen wishing that everyone at SCDS would die. It was like she had *willed* him to die, but she hadn't meant it, not really. And now he wasn't here.

She had never told him that she loved him.

It probably would not have made a difference, but maybe it would have. It was possible that he had loved her all along and just never had the chance to tell her. It happened in the movies all the time. People thought they were only friends, but over time and circumstance, they come to realize that they are in love. It takes something to hit them over the head, something that makes them come to their senses. They are hit over the head. Not. Dead.

The rumors swirled at school. Walter had taken an Ecstasy tablet and then hung himself in his parents' closet. Walter had put a shotgun in his mouth and blown his brains out. Walter had drunk the entire contents of his parents' liquor cabinet and then suffocated in his own vomit. Walter had left his car running in the closed garage and died of carbon monoxide poisoning. Walter had weighted himself with rocks and drowned in his swimming pool. She wanted these people to stop talking, wanted to put her hands over her ears and scream that they were NOT TRUE! These people were hideous, talking about Walter like that. *Her Walter.*

Maybe he was still alive. They said he had been cremated, but there had been no body at the funeral. It was possible that he had decided to run away. He could have enlisted in the military, or decided to backpack across Europe or sail a boat in the Bahamas or hitchhike from coast to coast. There were so many possibilities of where Walter could have run. So many.

So she walked through her days like a zombie, waiting for Walter to contact her. She knew she would feel it if he were truly dead. They had shared a magical night, they had a connection, and she would know if he were truly dead. Eighteen-year-old boys did not just vanish off the face of this earth. It was inherently wrong. It was a sin.

She went to school. She went to her tutoring sessions. One step in front of the other. It was preferable to staying at home and being bombarded by her mother's ever-escalating, prying questions: What did you do at school today? (Nothing.) What do you do at Carla's house? (Nothing.) Do you drink? (No.) Do you smoke? (No.) Do you smoke pot? (No.) Are Carla's parents usually home when you go over there? (No.) That last rote "no" was a mistake. She would no longer be allowed to spend the night at Carla's house if Carla's parents were not there.

"No problem," Carla said. She coached Rita to answer the phone saying she was Mrs. Goldleib, and she would be delighted if Annie could spend the night. There was barely a trace of an accent when Carla got through with Rita.

But her mother detected it. "Is Mrs. Goldleib Latina?" she asked. "Carla certainly doesn't look like she has Latin blood. She has such fair skin."

Carla had coached Annie, too. "Her mother's half Venezuelan. Carla takes after her dad, who is German."

It was so easy to lie to her mother these days. She had been doing it for a while now. She was practically a pro.

The one truly bad thing about being in a perpetual zombie state was that it was her 16th birthday a week or so after Walter's fake funeral. (She couldn't remember the date of the fake funeral; time in Zombieland was not strictly chronological.) It was the day she had been waiting for anxiously her entire life. She would get a driver's license. She would be free, free, free at last.

Except that she didn't want to go. She wasn't ready. Everyone in the whole wide world knew that she wasn't ready. She still ran off the road on occasion, and she hadn't been practicing much because everyone she knew, including Carla, was afraid to drive with her. Uncle Chris, who had the most patience of everybody, gave up on her after she hit their mailbox. Which was not her fault. Mailboxes shouldn't be placed at the foot of driveways because they were a menace. But her mother talked her into going to the MVD, telling her that she would be fine, that she was better than she thought she was.

Mothers lied, too. It was a disaster. She ran off the road three times and even managed to get a speeding ticket for going 21 mph in a 15-mph school zone. Her stupid instructor hadn't warned her to slow down and told her that she should have seen the flashing yellow light at the beginning of the zone. She had always thought that yellow simply meant that the light hadn't turned red yet, so she gunned it a tad.

After the test, which she failed, naturally, she walked into the MVD and dropped the keys at her mother's feet. "I failed. My life is over."

"Oh, honey," her mother said, all wishy-washy concerned. "A lot of people don't pass on the first try. You can take it again later."

"I'd make it a lot later," the stupid driving instructor said. "This young lady has a way to go before she's ready."

"I don't care," Annie said. "I can learn the bus routes and take a bus with all the underpaid Mexican maids who work in Scottsdale."

"Annie!" her mom said before she rushed her out of the MVD.

The stupid driving instructor was Mexican.

Annie really didn't care. She could always get a ride with Carla, even though Carla irritated her *zombiness*, carrying around her box of tissues. She brought four boxes a day to school, and she didn't share them either. She walked around, saying nonsense like, "Poor Walter is dead. He was such a gifted young man." It was such bullshit. All of it was bullshit.

She could always get a ride with Walter, when he contacted her. They could go out together in his black Range Rover. He could pick her up and take her to school every day, and then everyone would know that they were a couple. And then everyone would know the truth about Walter: Not. Dead.

Nick was truly sorry that his classmate was dead. He and Walter had never been friends, not exactly, but it was a small school, so they couldn't help but know of each other. Walter, of course, was a popular kid. Nick was not. Yet Walter had always seemed like a nice enough guy, someone who would smile at you or nod hello. He wasn't like some of the other snobby rich kids who wouldn't be caught dead smiling at you, even though Walter's family was rumored to be very, very rich. No, Walter had been a good guy.

But Nick would always be eternally grateful that he was dead. He felt guilty about this because no one should be dead at eighteen, and no one should commit suicide. Nick wasn't sure if he believed that Walter had committed suicide because why would someone who had everything want to die? It didn't make sense. However, he still felt grateful because Walter's death had brought Jennifer back to him.

It had been terrible without Jennifer. Nick couldn't eat, sleep, do homework, or even run. He had followed Jennifer's rules. He didn't email, text, or phone her. Well, he had emailed and texted her, but he had not sent them, and that took a great deal of willpower. At school, even though he knew her schedule, he didn't wait outside of class for her. Actually, he had never waited outside of class for her before their break-up because he had been so adamant that his dad not know they were seeing each other. He had been so stupid. Now, he wanted to wait outside her classroom and help her carry her massive backpack. He wanted everyone at school to know that they were a couple. He didn't even care if his dad found out, and if his dad found out, he would tell Mom. Nick didn't care about any of that anymore.

He only wanted to have Jennifer back. He knew, instinctively, that the only chance he might have of getting her back would be to respect her rules. But it had been so hard. He had felt sick to the core of his being, literally sick on many occasions, the worst time being when he had thrown up the birthday cake his mom had made for his 18th birthday. It was the day he had been waiting for his entire life. He was legally an adult. And he didn't care. He was now convinced that Jennifer had been The One, and he had blown it. Big time.

Jennifer called him a couple of nights after Walter's funeral and asked to meet at Starbucks. She was sitting at their usual table when he arrived, and he was ten minutes early. And she wasn't drinking her predictable, wasteful giant latte, which he always teased/goaded her about. She was drinking water. She looked like she was in the same shape he was in: thinner, dark circles under her brown eyes, sad. Nick thought she had never looked so beautiful.

"I miss you," she said.

"I miss you so much," he said. He was overjoyed when she started to cry. It didn't look so bad that he was trying not to bawl like a baby.

"Three weeks, four days, twelve hours," she looked at her watch, "and forty-seven minutes is a long time to be away from the person you love."

So she had been counting the minutes, too. "I'm so sorry if I said or did anything to hurt you. I just want you back." He wondered if he dared to touch her.

As it should be, Jennifer was one step ahead of him. She scooted her chair around next to his and leaned her head on his shoulder. "I'm sorry, too. I was in an emotional state about Dylan and Melissa breaking up, and I was unreasonable. They shouldn't have anything to do with us. And then when Walter—" She reached for a napkin to dab her eyes. "It made me realize that life is too short to not be with the one you love."

He wanted to make sure he got this right. "So, are we back together?"

She tilted up her head to look at him. Her eyes bore into his heart. "Is that what you want?"

"It's *definitely* what I want. I couldn't want anything more." He needed to stop himself from babbling. "Is it what you want?"

"Oh, yes! I love you, Nick."

"I love you, too." And then he kissed her, right in the middle of a public place. From now on, everyone was going to know that he went out with Jennifer Sang.

Dylan was not enthusiastic about the news. After Nick followed Jennifer to her house and said hello to her parents—it seemed like the right thing to do, to let her parents know that he was dating their daughter again—he went straight to Dylan's house and told him the happy news.

"That's going to mess up the plan, dude." Dylan was lounging on the living room couch, watching The Military Channel. The house, although never clean, had a different peculiar smell. Dylan noticed Nick's expression. "Mom decided to make a vegetarian goulash. Not only did she try to substitute ingredients, but she also burned the crap out of it. My man, you are sniffing scorched garbanzo, pinto, and Busch's baked beans topped with cabbage and bleu cheese. Yum."

"You didn't eat that, did you?"

"Well, yeah. I was starving." He burped. "Kind of feeling the effects now, though." Dylan had a cast iron stomach.

"K rations will be gourmet," Nick said.

"Back to the main subject. Do you really expect a girl like Jennifer to wait for you?"

"We're just going to take it one day at a time." This is what they had discussed after the kiss. They were going to be totally honest with each other, trust each other, and see what happened. To Jennifer, this was a logical plan, and Jennifer was very logical. Nick had agreed, and they had sealed the deal with another public kiss. It was great being so open about being in love. Nick would bet that everyone else in the place was jealous. At least he hoped they were.

"I have my doubts about this, bro. Chicks just complicate matters." His phone rang. Dylan looked at the caller ID and snapped it shut.

Nick knew it wasn't polite, but he asked anyway. "Who was that?"

Dylan pulled nervously at his ponytail. "Uh, it was Melissa."

"Melissa?" What was going on here? It wasn't like Dylan to hold out on him.

"Yeah, dude. Melissa. I did something a couple of nights ago that I probably shouldn't have done. You weren't around, and I was a little bored, so I, uh, made a booty call. You know what that means, don't you?"

Nick did know what that meant. He must have seen it in a movie or something. "Not cool, Dylan. You probably got her hopes up that you were getting back together."

"That's exactly what happened. She keeps calling and texting me."

"It really is a mean thing to do to a girl." And it was ungentlemanly, and it was downright lousy.

Dylan sighed. "I know, bro, I know. I explained to her why I was over there, and she said she understood and everything, and now it's like she's stalking me. I'm in a *quandary.*"

"Good vocab word."

"Yeah, sometimes I surprise myself. Sometimes I actually learn something at school."

"You're going to have to fix this situation." Nick was starting to get a little mad at Dylan, which was a first. Again, he was not treating Melissa well. First, he dumped her, and then he reignited the whole thing again.

"I know. I need to make it up to her somehow. You got any ideas, dude?"

And just as quickly, he wasn't mad at Dylan anymore. Dylan, during Nick's three-week, four-day, twelve-hour, and forty-seven-minute breakup with Jennifer, had tried to be helpful. He didn't really understand what Nick was going through—because Dylan thought *chicks* were complicated, because he hadn't found The One—but he had tried to get Nick's mind on other things. They had gone to the shooting range, they had watched *Apocalypse Now, Hamburger Hill,* and *Platoon* multiple times, and they had played Battleship, a game they were too old for but still loved, seven times in one evening. They had been like brothers since kindergarten when they sat next to each other. Both had brought green plastic army men for the first show and tell. And that had sealed that deal. They would be best friends for life.

"We'll come up with something," Nick said. He would try to help Dylan. He would try very hard to help his friend.

"Thanks, dude, you're the best."

They sat in companionable silence for a few minutes as they watched the ending of the show. Dylan went and got a bag of Fritos, and when he came back, he said, "I do really think that chicks—girls, I know you hate that word—complicate things, but I think I've figured out what's really bothering me. I'm afraid you won't join the Marines with me. There it is, dude, on a silver platter. I'm afraid you'll choose Jennifer over me."

Nick's heart felt like a falling meteor. He knew he could never make that choice. It would be impossible.

Walter's death affected Jack deeply. The small SCDS community had suffered a blow with the suicide of the most popular kid in school, and everyone was shell-shocked, both students and faculty. Jack had spoken to him the day before he died. Walter had come into his office and told him about not getting into Harvard, the alma mater of his entire family, and Jack had tried to console him.

"You can get into another good school, Walter. Your record is outstanding," he had said.

"There are no other schools," Walter had said. "I didn't apply anywhere else."

This was exactly what he told his students not to do, to put all their eggs in one basket, but he wasn't going to lecture the kid now. "I could make a phone call to the head of admissions at Barrett Honors College at ASU. They have excellent programs, an amazing faculty, and distinguished guest lecturers from all over the world."

"My parents would have to quit all their social clubs if I did that. They'd die of embarrassment if their son was going to a state school."

It was a dilemma. It was past the application deadline for most universities. And damn these wealthy parents who looked down their noses at perfectly acceptable state schools. "Why don't you talk to your parents and get back to me?"

"Sure," Walter said numbly.

"It's not the end of the world," he had said to Walter.

"Right."

But for Walter, it had been the end of the world. It was the perpetual problem for teenagers; they couldn't see a long-range plan. No, everything was immediate, every feeling magnified, every disappointment catastrophic—until the next day when it all started over again. Jack ached for Walter and the senselessness of the loss.

He should have done more. But what could he have done? He should have immediately called the parents and tried to reason with them. No, he should have marched himself over to their house and slapped some sense into them. He would never literally do that, but it was a comforting thought to imagine that scene.

His rage was out of control, and it wasn't only because of Walter. It was directed at his life and what he was letting himself become. Jack had an uncle, his father's brother, who was a raging alcoholic. At every family get together, he would get drunk on cheap bourbon. First, he would be charming and tell jokes. Next, his voice would get louder, and his comments would have innuendoes of insult. Then he would get belligerent and rage against the United States government. (At that point, the gun in his truck would be procured and hidden.) Finally, he would be sitting at the kitchen table, crying into his drink about all the lost opportunities in his life. He wasn't a good drunk.

Jack wasn't either. That much was clear.

He had been trying to control himself lately, but it wasn't easy. He had been trying to stay away from the casino, but that wasn't easy either. He had been trying to avoid Cookie, too, but she was the one who was making that difficult. When Chris, that nosy son-of-a-bitch, had seen them at the sports bar, Jack had been trying to tell Cookie that they were in serious danger of crossing the line, reinforcing the fact that he was a married man and that he didn't make a habit—had never, in fact—had an affair.

Cookie had said, "I'm married, too, but it's not a happy marriage. Is your marriage happy, Jack? You spend a lot of nights out at the casino alone, which doesn't paint a very rosy picture of a blissful union at home."

He had not known how to answer her. He should have said an immediate *yes*, but that hadn't happened. He could have also said that his marriage was not currently in a happy state because of unusual circumstances, but that hadn't happened either. He said nothing.

"I thought so," Cookie had said.

His hesitation to answer her question, in Cookie's mind, gave her free rein to pursue him. She called him three times a day, at least. Jack did not remember giving her his number, so it must have been on one of the many nights when he had too much to drink. He tried to go to the casino on nights she wasn't there. On Tuesdays, she had her bowling league; on Thursdays, she had a pottery class. And he knew more about her than that. It was her second marriage, she had two grown children, and she worked part-time at Sears. He should not know these facts of her life, but he did. And his guilt grew.

It was only a matter of time before she would call when he was in the same room with Alex, and of course, it happened. He was in the bedroom, changing into his pajamas before going downstairs and falling asleep in front of the television again. Alex came out of the bathroom. She had just showered and was wrapped in a towel. Unselfconsciously, she dropped the towel and started to rub Gold Bond lotion on her body. Her stomach was rounding, her breasts fuller, and he remembered with a sharp pang of longing how beautiful he had always thought her body was in the early months of pregnancy, how they had made love almost every night when she was pregnant with their children. For the first time in months, he felt a deep sexual pull toward her.

Alex looked up and saw him staring at her. She smiled shyly. "Would you mind putting lotion on my back?"

He rubbed the thick lotion on her back, her skin warm beneath his hand. He grew hard immediately.

"Um, that feels good," she said.

He wanted to make love to her and wondered if she would be receptive to the idea. He could ask her, or he could just start kissing her. He would start kissing her.

His damn phone rang, but he would ignore it and kiss his wife.

"You better get that, Jack. Since Walter, you've had a lot of emergencies to take care of."

"It's late. I can take care of anything that needs to be taken care of tomorrow." He bent his lips to her bare shoulder.

"I'll get it then." She slipped out of his hands before he could stop her. She picked up his phone from the nightstand. "Hello?" She paused. "Who is this?"

By the startled look on her face, he knew who it was. Cookie.

Alex handed the phone to him with the startled look still on her face. "She wants to talk to you."

"Hello." He said brusquely.

"That must be the lovely wife," Cookie said. She sounded drunk. "Come on out to the casino, honey. The tables are hot."

"I'll take care of it tomorrow," he said, trying to keep his voice neutral.

"I'm going to need you here to fold me into a taxi. Maybe this time I can persuade you to come home with me."

Cookie's husband worked the night shift at Honeywell. Damn it, he knew that, too. "Tomorrow is soon enough," he said, and snapped his phone shut.

"Who's Cookie?" Alex didn't seem too suspicious, just curious. She yawned.

He thought quickly. "She's the substitute secretary filling in for Sharon. Sharon's had the flu all week."

"She's calling awfully late, isn't she?"

He tried to make his voice playful. "You know how tough it is to get a job these days. She must have taken some files home. Maybe she's trying to impress me." Once the lies started, they multiplied like rabbits.

"You'd never replace Sharon, Jack. She's a lovely woman and very loyal to you after so many years."

"No, of course not."

Alex yawned. "I'm beat." She crawled into bed and pulled the covers up to her chin. She turned out the light on the nightstand. "Good night, Jack."

She didn't ask him to join her, and that was his fault, too. He had absurdly, unreasonably said he would not make love to her until after the baby was born. Alex was hurt, he knew, but she was a patient woman. She understood, she told him. *Patient* and *loyal* and *trusting* were words that described his wife. She had not suspected an affair like many wives would have. Not that he was having an affair. Not yet.

It had taken many hours at Home Depot and many sample swaths of paint before Sam decided on what color to paint the nursery. She felt that the baby was a boy, but she didn't want to go so far as to paint the nursery blue. She chose a light, soft yellow called Butter Crème, and she was pleased with the results, even though it had taken her days to complete the project. It had been hard to find the patience to tape the edges of the walls and baseboards, then spread the paint evenly, but she wanted to do it herself. She owed it to her baby to create a warm, inviting atmosphere, and she was off to a good start, she thought, as she stood in the center of the room and surveyed her handiwork in her paint-splattered clothes.

Plus, spending days on this painting project had given her a good excuse to avoid Alex, who wanted to finish their conversation about Annie. Sam didn't want to finish that conversation, which would entail telling her sister about Annie taking the van when she was grounded and probably high on something. And she didn't want to tell Alex about her suspicion that Annie had stolen Valium and Xanax from her medicine cabinet. Sam loved her sister and niece, but she didn't want to become entangled in their mom/teenage daughter drama. It wasn't any of her business, not really, and God knew that she had probably already butted her nose into their affairs more than she should have.

She was going to have a fast, furious cigarette on her back patio before she showered, and since it was five o'clock, she poured herself a glass of chardonnay as well. She settled herself on the chaise lounge with an ashtray, cigarettes, wine, and book and felt extremely content. She could finally understand why people lived in Arizona. February, and the weather was in the mid-70s during the day and the 50s at night. Back in Illinois, they had just had the worst snowstorm in ten years, and The Weather Channel showed people digging their cars out of snowdrifts and downed power lines. No, Sam didn't miss the cold weather at all.

The side gate in the backyard wall creaked open, and Alex walked in. "I thought I'd find you here."

Damn. Sam felt trapped, all her defenses down. She needed more time to prepare her answers to Alex's questions. "How's that?"

"It's happy hour." Alex lowered herself gingerly in the other chaise. "Oh, the good old days. I miss wine. I miss cigarettes."

Sam was doing a poor job of abstaining to show solidarity with her pregnant sister. "I'll take this stuff inside."

"No, it's okay. I didn't expect you to go the distance with me."

That hurt. Sam hadn't really expected to give up her vices for the entire nine months, but still, it would have been better if Alex had not pointed this out. "I'm certainly going the distance emotionally." She took a large sip of wine.

"Are you?"

"Yes, I am. This baby is all I think about." The baby was actually what she was *living* for. Alex was halfway through the pregnancy, and Sam counted the days until her child was born. Literally, she crossed off the days on a calendar in her office like a child anxiously waiting for Christmas Day.

"I wish the baby was all I had to think about," Alex said snidely.

"Why are you being such a bitch?"

"I'm going to blame it on the hormones."

"Fine. Why don't you take your hormones home? I need to shower." She knew that Alex was under a lot of pressure, and she felt for her, but Sam had just spent a long day painting and wanted a little peace and quiet, a couple of cigarettes, and some wine. This would not be a good time to talk about Annie.

"Tell me what you know about Annie." Alex stretched out on the chaise and closed her eyes. "I can take it. And by the way, I know I'm being a bitch, but it's because I'm worried sick."

"Do you want a bottle of water? Some cheese and crackers?" She was tempted to go inside and lock the door. She would do anything to avoid telling Alex what little she did know. It was only going to make things worse for her.

"Sam."

So she told her about Annie driving alone when she was only fifteen and how she had acted like she might be on something. And then she told her about the haircut and that she suspected—*only suspected*—that Annie might have taken some of her pills. The words tumbled out. It was a relief to finally tell her sister these things that she had kept bottled up inside. And she kept repeating that these were suspicions only, that she wasn't sure, that she could be wrong. They were only *suspicions*.

Alex's eyes were still closed. "And do you think you could enlighten me on why you didn't tell me before about all of your *suspicions*?" Her voice was cold.

"I wanted to. I did."

"But you didn't."

"No."

"Damn it, Sam, you should have told me." Alex sat up slowly.

Sam felt a rising panic. "I know I should have told you, but first I felt like I had to protect Annie, and then I thought I should protect you, and then I thought all of you would think I was meddling, and then I thought you'd be angry at me. Really, though, now that I think about it, I wanted to protect you."

"You wanted to protect me from my own daughter?"

When it was put like that, it didn't make any sense at all. "Yes. No."

"Well, I think we've clarified who the real bitch is here."

Alex had never looked at her like that, with such coldness. Sam was now on the brink of a full-blown panic attack. "Please forgive me, Alex. I realize now that I made the wrong choice." She had been on the verge of telling Alex so many times. Why hadn't she told her before? Because of Alex's reaction. She knew that Alex would be angry at her one way or the other. It was a Catch 22 situation, her knowing these things about Annie.

"Annie could have hurt herself. If you knew she was acting dangerously, you should have told me."

"But she didn't hurt herself." Thank God.

"I'm exhausted." Alex stood up.

It was definitely a panic attack now. Sam's heart hammered in her chest, and her hands shook violently. "Don't go yet. Please stay until we clear this up, and you're not mad at me."

"I don't have time to stay here that long, which I figure will be sometime next *year*."

Was she making a joke? Maybe there was hope after all. "Again, I'm sorry," Sam choked. She was going to have to think of something, something huge, to make this up to Alex.

Alex turned back at the gate. "The baby just kicked."

"Oh! Can I—"

But Alex just walked on through the back gate.

Chris was exhausted from trying to console Sam. Finally, after she had taken a sleeping pill and downed two large snifters of brandy, she was asleep in their bed. She was probably more passed out than asleep, and for once, he didn't care about that. He just wanted her to find an escape from the real world. He was drinking brandy, too, because the way she was acting—a kind of hysterical grief—brought back all the memories of the days, weeks, and months after Grace had died.

She refused to listen to reason. "Alex is just having a bad day," Chris told Sam.

"No, it's more than that. I can feel it."

"It's got to be hurtful to find out that your daughter is behaving inappropriately, and that she had no clue." Chris, being a constant observer, wondered how Alex and Jack could not see the signs. Jack was a high school guidance counselor, for God's sake. But then again, Jack had his head so far up his ass these days that he couldn't possibly have a true grip on reality.

"I should have told her." Sam's eyes were almost swollen shut from crying.

"I don't know that it would have made any difference. If you blindsided Alex with that information, she would have been furious with you then, too."

"I know, but she's furious with me now. And the baby's kicking." Sam started to cry all over again.

It had become Sam's constant mantra: the baby's kicking, the baby's kicking. She said it with such hope and pride that it made his heart ache for her. He was glad, of course, that the baby seemed to be thriving. But at this point, he did not feel any strong connection to the child. The kid wasn't even born yet, and it was a financial drain.

He would be seventy-one when the kid left for college.

He poured her the second brandy then. "Why don't you call her, if it will make you feel better?"

"Do you think I haven't called? I've called four times. She's not going to answer, and among other things, I am now an annoying nuisance. I'm a *stalker!*" She was starting to feel the effects of the brandy, and her words were slightly slurred.

He caressed her shoulder. "Just give it some time, Sam. Alex will come around. She's having a difficult time right now, but you know that she loves you very much. Things will work out."

"I just have a terrible feeling. You have to believe me, Chris. You do believe me, don't you?"

"I believe you."

"What do you think this terrible feeling means? Is it a premonition that something horrible is going to happen?" she asked fearfully.

She passed out before he could answer, and he carried her up to bed and tucked her in. He would not have known how to answer that question because he, too, had a feeling that things were not in balance. It had bothered him from the very beginning that they didn't have a written contract about this whole arrangement. "Oh, no, Chris!" his wife and her twin sister had said. "We're family, we all trust each other, and everything is going to work out perfectly."

There was no such thing as perfection. He should have insisted—no, he should have demanded—that they have a written agreement. With the way things were going, it would have offered a safeguard for all of them involved. The old adage of never doing business with friends or family had been proven countless times over the course of history. And this was definitely a business arrangement, as far as he was concerned. And they should have all signed a written contract. Forget perfection. He and Sam needed protection.

He had locked himself into his office on the very slim chance that Sam would wake up, although that was highly improbable, and tried to distract himself with various porn sites. It made him feel even guiltier than usual. He didn't think there was any harm in looking at naked, lewd women on the internet. Millions of men did it, but he knew it upset Sam, which is why he felt guilty. She was upset enough.

He did a complete turnabout and started to research Arizona surrogacy and adoption laws. After an hour of this, he could say in all honesty that he, too, had a terrible feeling in the pit of his gut. According to Arizona Revised Statutes, Title 25, Section 218, Arizona prohibited all surrogacy contracts, whether paid or unpaid, declared the surrogate as the legal mother and entitled to custody of the child, and established a rebuttable presumption that the surrogate's husband, if she was married, was the father. According to Arizona law, the birth mother is listed on the birth certificate, even if it is a surrogate.

They had all four been such idiots, and Chris held himself accountable most of all. He was a scholar, and he had not had the foresight to research Arizona surrogacy law before they started this mess. He had thought a written contract would solve all the problems, when in fact, the whole arrangement was not even legal. What were they going to do now?

He plodded on. In a 1994 case, *Soos v. Superior Court ex rel. County of Maricopa*, a couple, using their own eggs and sperm, entered into a gestational surrogacy agreement, but filed for divorce before the triplets were born. The wife sought custody of the unborn children, but the husband argued that he was the biological father, and because of Arizona law, the surrogate was the biological mother. Chris felt a glimmer of hope when he read that the trial court found that the provision automatically conferring legal-mother status to the surrogate was unconstitutional, and an Arizona Court of Appeals upheld that decision. His rising hope was short-lived. The Arizona Supreme Court chose not to review the case, so the exact extent of the law prohibiting surrogacy agreements remained unclear. All that was established was that the intended mother was entitled to *rebut* the presumption that a surrogate was the legal mother.

To make matters worse, in the *Soos* case, the intended mother had donated the eggs. In their case, Sam had not.

And the basic, glaring fact of the matter was this. According to Arizona law, Alex and Jack were the parents of his and Sam's child.

He was going to have to hire a lawyer. It seemed like their only legal hope would be to have the lawyer seek a court order to list he and Sam on the birth certificate (not very probable), or to have no birth mother listed. But it was becoming more and more clear to Chris that he and Sam would have to adopt their own baby. They would have to face a state social worker and answer all kinds of questions, about their family, their history, their home. Basically, they would have to be interrogated to see if they were fit to adopt their child.

So many things ran through his head: Sam's prescription use, their drinking habits, Sam's failed therapy. But they would have to be interviewed, of course.

Or was there another way around it? What if he didn't even mention this to the others? The naiveté of this group was a palpable thing, and chances were good that the other three would not bother to research this subject. Besides, Alex was so concerned with her two children, and Jack was so involved in whatever nefarious thing he was currently doing, that it was unlikely they would take the time to consult Arizona surrogacy and adoption laws. When the time came, when the baby was born, everyone might find out the true facts, but he would have already hired a lawyer.

This was going to be one expensive baby.

He would be seventy-one when the kid left for college.

"You have to come home right now. I need to talk to you," Alex said to Annie over the phone. She had left Sam's house seething, and the first thing she did when she got home was call her daughter. She was going to get the truth out of Annie, even if she had to shake it out of her. She had never dreamed of hitting either one of her children, but she was that angry now.

"I'm spending the night at Carla's. You said I could. Can't this talk wait until the morning?"

"No, it can't." When had she said that Annie could spend the night at Carla's? Had she been distracted this morning and given an absent *yes* when Annie asked? She couldn't remember, but it was distinctly possible that Annie had not asked at all.

"You know I can't drive, Mother."

There is was, that insolent, disrespectful tone that Annie had been using towards her for months. And she had tolerated it. "From what I've just heard, that hasn't stopped you before."

Silence.

"Are you still there?" Alex couldn't even hear Annie breathing. Then she heard the phone click.

Her daughter had hung up on her. *Her daughter had hung up on her!*

That was it. She wasn't going to be a doormat any longer, the kind and loving wife and mother she had always been. For once, she was going to have to be very strong about this. She realized then that she had not gone to the bank to check on their financial statements, and she had not questioned Jack further about the money. She had been too preoccupied with Walter's suicide and its aftermath. All of this was going to change. Starting with Annie, she was going to take charge. She grabbed her purse and drove to the Goldleib's house.

The gate before the long, steep driveway was closed. She slapped her palms against the steering wheel in frustration. Damn it. She obviously couldn't call Annie to get the code. She had to think. The only option she had was to wait. Maybe a UPS truck would make a delivery. Maybe Mr. Goldleib would be coming home from work soon. She had never asked Annie what he did for a living. She had never asked her daughter many things in the past few months. Since Sam had moved to town, and since she had become pregnant, Alex had been in a kind of self-centered fog. No more.

She was lucky. She had only waited for five minutes before a black town car came down the driveway, which automatically opened the gate. It turned in the opposite direction of her parked car, and she had just enough time to squeeze through before the gate doors swung shut. She drove up the winding, cobblestoned driveway and parked the car. She had no idea what she was going to say to the Goldleibs or her daughter.

She rang the bell, and a Mexican maid answered. A warning bell in her head told her that this was probably who had been answering the phone when she called to see if the Goldleibs were home. Alex introduced herself. "I'm here to get my daughter."

The maid smelled like tequila. "She no here."

In the distance, Alex could hear a Mexican soap opera playing on TV. "Then where is she?" She supposed it was possible that the girls had gone to the mall or gone out for a bite, but every instinct vibrating in full-mother-mode told her differently.

The maid shrugged.

Alex crossed her arms and bore her eyes into the maid's. "Is Carla here?"

The maid seemed indecisive on this point. "Miss Carla do not like to be disturb when she in her room."

"Disturb her. Now. Or I will search this house myself."

The maid took a step back, then turned and walked quickly up the grand staircase. Now that Alex took a minute to notice her surroundings—she had never been inside before—she was amazed at the opulence. Original oil paintings decorated each wall, and the worth of the furniture alone could keep her family fed for the next twenty years. This is where Annie spent most of her time when she wasn't in school, a place that defied middle-class values and morals, hopes and dreams. A small part of her couldn't blame Annie for wanting to escape here. However, her daughter had been raised right, hadn't she? And she should respect what her hard-working parents had provided for her, shouldn't she?

Another warning bell. If a child was accustomed to this kind of opulent excess, she would probably have a lot of money to buy drugs.

Carla descended the stairs with a too bright smile. "Hey, Mrs. C.! What are you doing here?"

"I think it's fairly obvious, Carla, that I'm not here to make a social call. I'm here to take Annie home." Carla had to know that. What kind of a game was she playing?

"Oh, I'm sorry, Mrs. C., but you just missed her."

"Don't tell me that she hitchhiked home!" Alex felt a jolt of fear. Surely, Annie wasn't so far over the edge that she would feel the need to further defy her mother by getting in a car with strangers.

Carla's laugh was too bright, like her smile. "Don't be silly, Mrs. C.! I have a town car at my disposal."

It was entirely possible that Annie had been in the car that came out of the gate. But Alex didn't think so. Annie was here. She felt it. "Why didn't she call to let me know?"

"She must have forgotten. You know us teenagers! We get involved in something and *forget* to do what we're supposed to do. It happens all the time. We are a *thoughtless* sector of society!" Carla nodded her head emphatically, pleased with the power of her deductions.

This girl was a little shit, a spoiled little shit, and Alex didn't believe a word coming out of her spoiled little mouth. "Are your parents home?" she asked.

A curtain seemed to drop over Carla's face. "They're out to dinner."

Alex didn't think that people like Carla's parents would *dine* at 6:00. They probably made reservations for eight or nine. "What restaurant?"

"I don't know. I'm not their concierge."

Alex wanted to say to her, rudely, "You are not many things," but she was supposed to be the adult here. "Why don't you give me your mother's phone number? I've been meaning to get acquainted with her for some time now. But you know us parents! We get involved in something and *forget* to do what we're supposed to do!"

For the first time, Carla looked uneasy. Alex could almost see her ticking off the possible lies in her head. She might have chosen the truth. "Marge and Ron are in Rome."

"So you lied to me." And she called her parents by their first names, which demonstrated a lack of respect to Alex. It was becoming clear that Annie had been taking lessons from the master.

"Not technically. You asked me if they were home, and I said they were out to dinner. They very well could be out to dinner in Rome."

She was a little shit, a spoiled, *exasperating* little shit. "I don't want to argue time zones with you, Carla."

Carla changed tactics, becoming almost tearful. "I don't want to argue anything with you, Mrs. C. I really like you, and I think Annie is lucky to have you for a mother. I tell her that all the time."

She certainly had a lot of tricks up her sleeve, this one. "Are you telling me the truth about Annie? Did she really go home?"

Carla waved her arm expansively. "You can take a look around if you want to, search every nook and cranny. I want you to, if it will make you feel better."

"That won't be necessary." This girl was making her paranoid. Alex turned and walked out the door, but before she got to her car, she turned and went back. It was the things that Carla omitted that were the most telling. She hadn't answered Alex directly whether Annie was there. She had just told her to take a look around, suspecting that Alex wouldn't go that far. She was wrong.

Alex walked in without knocking. Carla was halfway up the stairs and turned, disbelief quickly turning to panic. "I think I will take you up on that offer. Please lead the way to your bedroom. I'm sure it's lovely."

"It's a mess. I'd be ashamed to show it to you."

"Cut the crap, Carla. I know she's here."

Carla's quickly ticking brain couldn't come up with anything. She stood stock still as Alex passed her. Then she followed.

Alex didn't need directions to Carla's bedroom. She could smell the reek of pot at the top of the stairs. She followed the scent hound dog-like to a room at the end of the hall and flung open the door.

In the pretty pink princess bedroom, there was Annie sprawled on the bed, a joint in her hand and a bottle of vodka on the nightstand.

"OMG!" her daughter said.

"I'm sorry!" Carla cried. "I tried to stop her."

Annie struggled to her feet but couldn't quite manage it. She fell back on the bed and started to giggle hysterically. "I'm so wasted."

"The jig is up," Alex said.

This was a nightmare. Since the *incident,* as her mom referred to it, Annie had been under close—make that *microscopic*—scrutiny. They should have just attached a ball and chain to her ankle, or better yet, they could tie her to her bed and station a guard outside her door. Months before when she had been grounded, she thought that was bad. *But she hadn't seen nothin' yet.* This was ten times, a hundred times, a thousand times worse than before. Basically, she had to ask permission to breathe. It was a nightmare.

Mom and Dad hadn't screamed and thrown things. No, they were stealthy in their punishment options. They kept telling her how *disappointed* they were in her. They were *disappointed* in her choices of pretty much everything: her friend(s), her schoolwork, her hair, her clothing, her decision to drive illegally, to drink and smoke pot.

When they asked her about taking drugs from Aunt Sam, she had said she didn't even know that Aunt Sam had drugs. She really couldn't bear to see the *disappointment* that one would have generated if she had told the truth. The air around Annie already reeked with *disappointment.*

There were many rules in this nightmare. Dad drove her directly to and from school. After school, she had to sit at her desk until her homework was finished and then rechecked. Her cell phone had been taken away, so she was now the only teenager in the universe who didn't have a phone! No computer privileges, unless supervised, which meant that Facebook was pretty much out of the question. She might as well be dead.

Walter still hadn't contacted her.

She wasn't supposed to have any contact with Carla. None. Whatsoever.

Well, Dad couldn't follow her into the school bathroom, could he? She and Carla—they were geniuses—had gone the old-fashioned route and were now passing notes, which mostly consisted of "Meet me in the toilet after second period."

"How long is this going to go on?" Carla asked at the end of the first week.

She gave her the answer she had been given. "Indefinitely."

"It's inhumane." For Carla, too. She hated walking around campus and eating lunch alone.

"Totally."

"Do you think that your mom is actually going to call my parents?"

"I'm sure she would, if she had the number. It's a good thing they didn't list their number in the SCDS Directory."

"I hate to say it, but sometimes their lack of interest in me can be a blessing in disguise."

The secret, brief meetings with Carla were all that she had to look forward to. It was a pathetic existence, and she was beginning to understand how prisoners of war made it through. One day at a time. Autopilot. It was a good thing she was still pretty much in Zombieland. If she allowed herself to really think or feel about her situation, she would go *absolutely bonkers*.

Where in the world was Walter?

Her period was late.

She didn't mind so much going to the counselor. Her dad knew a friend of a friend of a friend who would see her at a reduced rate. (Because her parents were middle-class people with middle-class values—i.e., they were poor.) She was a young, pretty, blonde woman named Georgia who wore jeans and sat on the couch in her office with Annie and just let her talk. Not that Annie was talking much. She had nothing to say, but this seemed to be all right with Georgia. The first two sessions went something like this:

Georgia: "What are you feeling, Annie?"

Annie: "Nothing, really."

Georgia: "Are you more sad or angry at this point?"

Annie: "None of the above." (What a stupid question!)

Georgia: "Is there anything specific you would like to talk about?"

Annie: "How about those Sun Devils!" Georgia was an avid NBA fan, and this was a good way to fill up the rest of the hour. Another good way was to get her to talk about Buddhism.

It was kind of funny. Her Nazi parents were obviously scared shitless that she was a drug addict or a drunk. Like her dad could talk, or her mom, too, before she got pregnant. They could both put away the booze to ease *disappointment*, to celebrate. If she really wanted to, Annie could sneak a shot of scotch when her dad was passed out on the couch, and her mom was upstairs in bed gestating that baby. But the funny thing was that she had no desire to do that. Absolutely none. Out of sight, out of mind, that kind of thing. She was not an addict.

She was starting to get a little pissed at Walter.

On day ten of her incarceration, she woke up feeling ill and vomited. The flu was going around school, and she asked her mom if she could stay home. Mom was skeptical. "Do you want me to show you the puke?" Annie asked. Then she immediately apologized. It was this kind of attitude that kept getting her in trouble, and she was learning that, if she ever wanted to get out of this prison, she was going to have to watch her big, fat mouth. By noon she felt okay, but then she had to spend the rest of the day in bed, pretending to be sick, which turned out to be a super boring drag.

She woke up vomiting again the next morning. Annie didn't want to see the dawning light. But her period was late. Her period was often late. She was irregular. She was an *irregular girl*.

She told Carla in the bathroom between third and fourth periods, and Carla brought an EPT pregnancy test the next day. "It only takes three minutes," she said. Carla, being such a good friend, was all sympathy and support.

"I don't think I can do this now." She only had unprotected sex one time (one time when she was fully conscious, but she wouldn't go there). She could not be that unlucky. She was just an *irregular girl*.

The next day, she said to Carla, "I can't do it here, in a public place."

"Well, you can't take it home with you."

This was true. The Nazis at home were probably going through the trash. "I just need more time. It'll come. I'm pretty sure I'm starting to feel crampy."

"We'll figure something out." Carla patted the top of Annie's head like she was a beloved puppy.

That afternoon, she had another session with Georgia. Georgia didn't want to talk about the Sun Devils or Buddhism. Georgia did not want to be deterred. "I believe there was a boy at your school who committed suicide. Do you want to talk about that, Annie?"

It sounded to Annie like Georgia said, "I believe in suicide."

"Annie?" Georgia gently coaxed.

Annie wanted to give her usual response: "I don't want to talk about it." But there was a sudden roaring in her ears, and it was growing louder.

"I know this is a painful subject, but it might help to talk about it. Was this boy a friend of yours?" Georgia, who was usually so chummy, was turning on Annie.

Annie shook her head. No, she didn't want to talk about her beloved Walter, and she didn't want to talk about why he hadn't yet come to take her away from all this crap.

She was very pissed at Walter.

Her period was late.

"Dealing with death is a part of life," Georgia, the monster, said.

The roaring grew louder, became unbearable. Walter was never going to come for her. Never. Walter was dead. Walter. Was. Dead.

She didn't cry then. No, it was more like the floodgates had finally been wrenched open.

Sam was not seeing any happy faces at the house across the street. When she had last called Alex—again, to apologize—Alex had briefly told her what was going on with Annie and what they were doing to remedy the situation. It was understandable that the Carissa family was closing ranks. It was understandable that Sam had no business intruding on them at this time. However, her baby was in the midst of their ranks, and she still had not felt him kick. She felt isolated and lonely. She missed her sister.

"You need to get out of the house more," Chris said to her. "Why don't you volunteer? Renee Rosewall is always talking about the Crisis Nursery. It's a shelter designed to stop the cycle of child abuse."

The last thing she needed was to see an abused child. It would simply break her heart, and as she knew from experience, it was excruciating to live with a broken heart.

"You could rock babies or something like that."

"I'm afraid I'd become attached. Once they put a baby in my arms, I would be extremely reluctant to give it back."

"You have a point there," Chris said.

She knew she had a very good point. However, she did get on the Crisis Nursery website and read the guidelines for becoming a volunteer. Among other requirements, she would have to get fingerprinted, which of course was a good thing, but now that Chris had planted the seed in her head, she really wanted to rock some babies. She wondered if she could just show up at Children's Hospital and say something along the lines of: "I have a few hours on my hands. Do you mind if I rock a few newborns?" They would probably think she was crazy. Maybe she was going crazy with the waiting. Nine months was a long time to wait for a baby when you weren't experiencing the physical and emotional changes along the way.

It was one of the reasons she and Chris had never tried to adopt. The waiting would have been unbearable, and then if the deal fell through and there was no baby on the appointed day (a baby she could rock endlessly), the disappointment would have driven her right back to the solitary confinement of her bed. She could not, would not, live through that torture again. She didn't have the emotional strength; Grace's loss had made her into an emotional cripple. She knew that. Thank God for Valium.

She missed her sister.

Her dear, patient husband finally said to her, "Get away from that damn window, Sam, or I'm going to board it up. And I'm not kidding."

She knew she had to do something. In desperation, she called up Amanda Williams and invited her to lunch. Now, she didn't even remotely like Amanda, the epitome of the Scottsdale Barbie, but because she was so oblivious of her own stereotype, Sam thought Amanda might be good for a laugh or two. And maybe she could even get an article out of this, although she certainly wouldn't be able to sell it to *So Scottsdale!,* or any other local magazine.

She had let Amanda select the restaurant, which was her first mistake. They were seated on an outdoor patio at the newest, trendiest restaurant on the downtown so-called Waterfront. In reality, the "waterfront" was a canal where developers had built crazily expensive condos, shops and restaurants—which were now in serious economic trouble. To add further ambiance to the overpriced restaurant was the smell. It stank like a sewer.

Amanda surveyed the menu with pursed lips, and Sam soon realized that Amanda's over-collagenous lips were always in a fish-like pout. "I've been dying to try this place," Amanda said. "Everything sounds so yummy."

Determined to be on her best behavior, Sam said, "It sure does. Yummy." She probably hadn't used the word *yummy* since she was six.

"It's so nice to go out and do something with another gal. You know, have some girl time?"

It was another word that drove Sam up the wall, *gal.* It made her feel like she should be wearing cowboy boots, a Stetson, and carrying a lasso. "It's nice to get out of the house," Sam said. She was trying to breathe, unobtrusively, through her mouth. The canal really, really stank.

Amanda's smile was creepy. Nothing on her face moved. "I just can't decide what to get!" She motioned to a waiter carrying a tray full of plates he was taking to his table. "What's that?" Amanda pointed at what looked like a tower of fish. "And what's that?" She pointed to a large salad.

To his credit, the waiter politely answered her questions and then hurried to deliver the food.

"That didn't help at all! Everything looks so *yummy!*"

Their waiter came to tell them about the daily specials. Sam held up her hand to stop him. "That's fine," she said. "We already have enough choices to boggle our little minds." If Amanda realized that Sam was referring to her, she didn't let on. Sam pushed her iced tea to the side. "Please bring me a glass of wine."

"I'll go get the wine list," the waiter said.

"No! Anything will do."

"Oh!" Amanda giggled. "Are we going to drink during the day?"

"I am," Sam said.

"Okay! I'll be naughty, too! I'll take a margarita."

Naughty? She probably liked to be spanked, Sam thought. What had she been thinking when she invited Amanda to lunch? Sam needed to guide this conversation into something—anything—more interesting, or she might need a *transfusion* of wine to get through the next hour. "So, Amanda, what are your interests? Do you have any hobbies?"

"My husband and my children are my interests. Oh, and of course my home. I like to create an enchanting environment for my family."

Jesus. The woman was living in the fifties. And then Sam remembered the holiday party and the puke green wall. She really should have thought through this lunch date idea. "So, what does Curtis do?"

Amanda waved her hand airily. "Oh, you know—investments."

"How's he doing in this economy?"

"He's doing brilliantly. He's a brilliant man."

The waiter brought their drinks, and Sam downed half a glass and ordered another. The fool probably didn't even know what her husband did for a living. They ordered food, and Sam listened to Amanda talk about her favorite subject, herself. Occasionally, Sam would grunt an acknowledgment, but it didn't matter. Amanda would be happiest talking to herself in a mirror. Sam was going to have to get her drunk to get Amanda started on her second favorite subject, the neighborhood gossip.

Fortunately, it only took two margaritas to get her to loosen up. It was an amazing transformation to witness. The girly voice was gone, replaced by a condescending, knowing tone. Amanda leaned forward conspiratorially and stage-whispered, "Did you know that the Westmores' house was foreclosed on last week? They're moving out, to *an apartment.*"

"That's terrible," Sam said, although she wasn't sure who the Westmores were. Maybe Alex was right. She should get to know her neighbors.

"Not so much. That Betsy Westmore is hell on heels. She always thought she was so much better than everyone else. It just goes to show." The irony of that statement was lost on Amanda.

"What other gossip have you heard?" Sam asked. She hoped that Amanda had had enough to drink that she might slip up and tell her what the neighborhood was saying about Alex being a surrogate for Sam's baby.

"I don't gossip! I merely relate the facts. It's important to know what's going on with your neighbors. It's the neighborly thing to do, in fact, to keep up with the community business."

Sam nodded. "Yes, it's very important to keep up with the Joneses."

"Who are the Joneses? When did they move in?"

Oh, brother. Sam quickly changed the subject, not wanting to explain the meaning of sarcasm to this fickle woman. "Does Annie still babysit for you?"

Amanda looked down at her lap and fiddled with her napkin. "Not so much."

"Why not? I thought your kids really liked her."

"They do, but things change. Really, the ideal babysitter is twelve or thirteen, you know, before they get *exposed* to certain things."

"Like what?" Sam wondered what kinds of rumors were floating around about Annie and how they could have gotten started.

"Look, Sam, I know she's your niece, so I'll be honest with you."

That would be a first, Sam thought.

"I didn't like the Mohawk. It wasn't appropriate. When my kids saw it, and mind you, they're only six and eight, they couldn't stop talking about Annie's hair."

"It's only hair," Sam chorused as she had done so many times before to Alex.

Amanda's hand automatically went to smooth her long, blonde tresses. "Hair is very important to a person's appearance."

The waiter came and asked if they wanted dessert. "I really shouldn't," Amanda said. "I gained a half pound last week!" She emphasized the point by patting her concave stomach.

Then she ordered the most expensive dessert on the menu, something called Decadent Extraordinaire that was made with 100-year-old cognac.

Sam ordered a third glass of wine. Right then, she wanted three things: this lunch to be over, this fool to shut up, and to know what the neighborhood was saying about the baby.

The baby won. As Amanda dug into the dessert, Sam asked, "Do you think I should give Alex a baby shower?"

"I love baby showers. I could be in charge of the games. I love the one where you guess how many sheets of toilet paper it takes to wrap around the mommy's belly. That's a good one."

This woman needed to be led like a blind mule. "Obviously, I couldn't give a shower where everyone brought a baby gift. Since it's *my* baby, it would almost look like I was giving *myself* a baby shower. Get it? I was thinking more along the lines of a shower for Alex where people bring things like sexy lingerie, or better yet, brought gifts like cookbooks and kitchen appliances. Alex would love that."

"Oh, that's right," Amanda said. She licked the spoon. "I think this Decadent Extraordinaire is making me a little tipsy." She giggled.

"What's right?"

"I keep forgetting the baby is yours."

Sam felt the heat rising in her face. "It is my baby."

"Yes, yes. It's just that Alex is the one walking around in maternity clothes, and you know, it's easy to forget that she doesn't keep the baby. It's no big deal."

To Sam, it was *the biggest* deal.

"Would you look at the time? I have to go pick up the little ones from school." She reached for her Prada bag and stood up. "I am so bloated! If I still purged, I'd walk into that bathroom on the way out and relieve myself of all these fattening calories. Haha. But I'm way past that. See you soon."

She did walk into the bathroom on her way out, leaving Sam with a two-hundred-dollar bill to pay and the beginnings of yet another panic attack.

There was no way he could bring Jennifer home to meet his mom right now. Absolutely no way. She walked around with a mad/sad look on her face all the time, and it was all about Annie, Annie, Annie. Mom didn't even cook dinner anymore, which is what had the biggest impact on Nick. He tried to explain to Jennifer what was going on, not that he exactly knew. It was more of what he had overheard: Carla, drinking, smoking pot, but he didn't know the details of where and when. Jennifer said she understood, but he doubted that she did. Even he didn't understand. Everyone in his family was totally miserable, yet he was the happiest he had ever been.

Dad wasn't acting much better than Mom. He watched Annie like a hawk all day long at school, and if he noticed that his son was now walking around with a girl, he didn't let on. Mom didn't cook; Dad didn't shave. He had perpetual graying stubble that shadowed his cheeks, and he had always been such a stickler about shaving. Annie had turned their world upside down. Annie, Annie, Annie. Really. It was about time they caught on. He, of course, hadn't said a word about what he knew about the cruise ship or the party Annie had thrown at their house, nor would he. As much of a dope as he thought Annie was, he still would not betray her. He was her brother.

Still, he felt that he owed it to Jennifer to introduce her to someone. When he talked about this with Loretta, she said, "Well, hell, babycakes, you can introduce her to me. I'll have you over for some orr-durves." She said the last with a fake French accent, her cigarette held at that funny high angle that rich women did in old movies.

"You already met her in the grocery store."

"I scanned a candy bar for the girl. I wouldn't call that a proper introduction. Haven't I taught you anything yet, honeybunch?"

They went over to Loretta's trailer on a Saturday afternoon. Nick had never been there before, and he was a little apprehensive because Jennifer was allergic to smoke. But Loretta had sprayed the place with Febreze (she told him that later) and didn't smoke one cigarette the whole hour they were there. She served them Ritz crackers and cheddar cheese and Genoa salami on a pretty plate (all on sale that week at Fry's, including the plate, she told him later).

"You are the prettiest little thing," Loretta said to Jennifer.

Naturally, Jennifer blushed. "Thank you, Miss Loretta." Nick had forgotten to tell Jennifer Loretta's last name, Wilbur.

"Why, don't I feel like a lady in the South! Miss Loretta! I like it, honey."

Loretta was even on her best behavior, conversationally speaking. She only came close to messing up once when Jennifer asked her, "Are you married, Miss Loretta?"

Nick groaned inwardly. Please *no*, he thought.

"I've had three husbands, the present one being in jail at the moment, but the second was the all-time, worldwide, international, prize-winning bast—"

Nick coughed.

Loretta hesitated, then finished proudly, "basting champion."

"Basting champion?" Jennifer, along with everyone else in the world, would not have heard of this nonexistent title.

"Long story." Loretta winked at him. "Another cracker, honey?"

And Loretta didn't call him babycakes once. He was grateful to her and proud of her, all rolled into one.

Still, it didn't seem enough. He felt like he needed to introduce Jennifer to *family*. He had already met Jennifer's parents, grandparents, and assorted aunts, uncles, and cousins during the months they had been dating, and he had promised her when they got back together that he would prove how proud of her he was by introducing her to his family. That left only one option—Aunt Sam and Uncle Chris. He didn't give much thought to the fact that he would be introducing Jennifer to his aunt and uncle before his own parents. Given the situation at home, it seemed like a good solution to the family introduction conundrum.

Aunt Sam wasn't so sure. "Your mother hasn't met this girl?"

"No, but Dad has. He's her guidance counselor, after all."

"I'd love to meet her, Nick, but I really think your mom should meet her first. That kind of thing is important to mothers." Aunt Sam was on a ladder in the nursery, adding finishing touches to the angel border. She took a wobbly step up to the next highest rung. The paint on the ladder platform sloshed.

Nick reached to steady the ladder. "I could do that for you, Aunt Sam. You're making me a little nervous."

"You're a sweetheart, Nick, but I need to do this all by myself."

"So, can I bring her over?"

"I really think your mom should meet her first."

Nick was not averse to begging on this issue. "Please, Aunt Sam. You know that people at my house are not very happy right now, and basically, when Jennifer and I got back together, and it was terrible when we broke up, I promised her that I would introduce her to my family, she's Korean, and family is very important to her—"

"Okay, okay," Aunt Sam said, laughing. "I can see you're in a bind here, and because you're my nephew, and because I love you to death, I will be happy to have you and Jennifer over for dinner. How about Saturday?"

"Saturday would be great!" He would have hugged her legs, but he was afraid he'd knock her off the ladder. "Thanks, Aunt Sam."

On Saturday, he brought Jennifer over to Aunt Sam's house promptly at 7:00. And it did feel kind of weird to ring the doorbell instead of just walking in like he usually did. And it did feel kind of weird to know that his mother was right across the street and hadn't met the girl he was introducing to his aunt and uncle. However, Aunt Sam and Uncle Chris acted like everything was no big deal, like they did this kind of thing all the time. Jennifer, thoughtfully, brought a bouquet of flowers, which Aunt Sam exclaimed over and then put them in a vase in the center of the patio table.

"This is terrific," Aunt Sam said. "I needed a centerpiece for the table. What can I get you to drink?"

He had a Coke, and Jennifer had a diet Coke. Aunt Sam and Uncle Chris drank wine, naturally, but not too much. They talked at the patio table while Uncle Chris grilled hamburgers, and he felt very grown up and very proud of Jennifer. Aunt Sam asked all the usual questions: How do you like school? Where are you planning on going to college? What are your hobbies? Jennifer responded: Very much. I've been accepted at Stanford. Photography. Uncle Chris told a couple of funny jokes (amazing, since he wasn't usually very witty), and the hamburgers were delicious. Nick ate three.

As they were getting ready to leave, Jennifer, blushing, excused herself to go to the bathroom, and Aunt Sam said to him, "Jennifer's adorable, Nick."

"I know." His pride in her kept growing.

"I think she's a keeper."

"I hope so." He fervently hoped so.

"I'll walk you guys to your car."

And that's when the evening pretty much fell apart. What were the odds that his mom, across the street, would pick that exact moment to wheel the trash can to the curb? What were the odds that his normally pretty mother would look like a bag lady with stringy, uncombed hair and wearing a tattered sweat suit that should have been placed *in* the trash can she was wheeling? They had driven over in Jennifer's car, and it was pretty dark, so maybe his mom wouldn't know it was her son across the street.

No such luck. "Nick, is that you?" she called. "What are you doing over at Aunt Sam's? I thought you were at the movies?"

It was not a lie that he had told her, not really. He and Jennifer were going to watch a movie at her house next. "Yeah, it's me." Instinctively, he reached for Jennifer's small, soft hand.

"He came over for dinner," Aunt Sam said. "He's just leaving."

"Whose car is that?" His mom started across the street.

"Oh, boy," Aunt Sam said under her breath.

"It looks like you're going to meet my mom now," he said to Jennifer.

His mom looked even worse when she came under the glow of Aunt Sam's front porch light. She had tiny pimples across her forehead, and even in the baggy sweatshirt, it was obvious she was pregnant. Nick had told Jennifer all about his mom being a surrogate for Aunt Sam, but the sight of her protruding belly thoroughly embarrassed him. And her eyes were pink and swollen, as if she had been crying.

He had no other choice but to jump right in. "Mom, this is Jennifer Sang. My girlfriend."

Jennifer extended her hand. "How do you do, Mrs. Carissa? I've wanted to meet you for quite a while now."

His mom looked dazed and confused, but she did shake Jennifer's hand. "Nick's girlfriend?"

"My girlfriend," Nick affirmed, squeezing Jennifer's hand harder, hoping he didn't break any of her tiny bones.

"What are you doing here?" Mom looked like things were not computing. Really, she looked like she was on drugs or something.

"We had a delicious dinner. Thank you again, Mrs. Connor," Jennifer said.

Aunt Sam had a guilty look on her face. "Lipton onion soup," she said.

"What?" Jennifer said.

"In the ground beef." Aunt Sam put her hand on Mom's arm. "Alex—"

"No one tells me anything anymore," his mom muttered, shaking off Aunt Sam. She turned and walked slowly, hunch-shouldered across the street. All that was missing was the shopping cart piled high with someone else's cast-offs.

"Well, Jennifer," he said. "You've finally met my mother."

Chris heard the crash and the pain-soaked "Shit!" He ran up the stairs and found Sam lying on the floor on her right side, the ladder splayed next to her, paint splattering the carpet. He had told her again and again that he didn't like her on that ladder, that he was afraid she would fall and hurt herself.

"I fell," Sam said, needlessly.

He knelt beside her. "Are you hurt?"

"I've fallen, and I can't get up." She mimicked the slogan from the Life Alert commercial, but they both knew it wasn't funny. "I've never broken a bone before, but I think I've broken my arm. I can't move it."

He helped her up and took her to the emergency room. After waiting for two hours in the ER, the doctor confirmed it. Sam had a fractured humerus. She would be in a cast for six to eight weeks, followed by weeks of physical therapy. All of this was glum news to Sam—except for the prescription for Percocet. Chris thought that was the last thing she needed right now, but he knew he would continue to refill it for her.

"I guess I won't be rocking any babies in the near future," Sam said after they got back home.

To Chris, in her cast and sling, Sam looked like a fragile bird with a broken wing. "You have plenty of time to heal before the baby gets here." He hadn't said a word to her about the possible legal complications with the baby, and the lawyer he had spoken to had not been encouraging. What it boiled down to was that they were going to have to trust Alex to honor their verbal agreement and give the baby, who was legally hers, to them.

"This really sucks. I'm right-handed, Chris. Do you know what this means? How am I going to write? How am I going to be able to do anything around the house? How am I going to shower and dress myself?" Her voice was growing more hysterical. "How am I going to put on *makeup*?"

He gave her a Percocet. Indeed, this was bad timing. He had midterms coming up and hiring someone to take care of Sam was out of the question. There was only one recourse. He called Alex and informed her of the situation. "Would you be willing to come over for a couple of hours a day, Alex? Once she gets used to the cast, she'll be more mobile, but right now she needs some help."

"I'm busy," Alex said.

"I don't mean that it has to be right this minute. I'll be on campus tomorrow from ten until three. Maybe you could come over for an hour or so then?"

"I'll be busy then, too."

Oh, come on, Chris thought. The woman didn't even have a job. "What is so important that you can't come over and help your sister out?" he said icily.

"If you must know, I have some Avon appointments."

"I thought you gave that up." As far as Chris knew, she had not yet broken even from her initial investment in the products. Both Alex and jackass Jack, apparently, were bad business people.

Alex was silent.

"Your sister needs you."

Again, silence.

He was starting to get it. Alex was mad this time about the dinner they had for Nick and his girlfriend. It was tiresome, really, the constant, petty squabbles she and Sam created. They were so close that they guaranteed a generated friction. Then they would make up and profess undying love and loyalty. Then some little thing would start the cycle all over again. "She would be there for you," he said.

"I think I'm holding up my part of the bargain here."

Meaning the pregnancy. Obviously. "Fine," he sighed. "Gestate your current grievance, Alex, whatever makes you happy."

There was another long pause. "On second thought, I think I will come over. I have a few things I'd like to say to your wife."

So now, Sam was *your wife*. Not a good sign. The last thing Sam needed was a berating on one of her many so-called failures as a sister. "On third thought, *don't* come over now. We will manage just fine."

"Too late." Alex walked in the front door, phone in hand. "Where's the patient?"

"Asleep," he said, hoping that the Percocet had knocked her out.

"Is that you, Alex?" Sam called woozily from the living room couch. "I'm in here."

Alex shot him a smug look and marched into the living room. Which meant that he was going to have to follow her. Which meant that he was going to have to referee. He had too much to do to bother with this nonsense.

"I really did it this time," Sam said.

"Yep." Alex remained standing.

"This is what I get for trying to do things my way. Chris and Nick offered to help, but I said, 'No, no, no. I can do this all by myself.' I guess I have a habit of trying to take control."

"Yep."

"It's silly of me, I know. I get these ideas in my head, and I let them run away like a herd of wild mustangs stampeding across the desert."

"Yep."

"Not that I know anything about wild mustangs. Except for that movie with Robert Redford and Jane Fonda. What was it called? Was it *The Electric Horseman?*"

"Yep."

"I loved that movie." Sam yawned.

The Percocet was starting to take effect, and if Chris hurried, he might be able to get her up to bed before Alex could inflict any emotional damage. "Why don't I—"

"I think we need to take a break from each other," Alex said.

He was too late.

"What are you talking about?" Sam's eyes were beginning to droop.

"I, for one, need a little space. Ever since you moved across the street from us, it's been one drama scene after another. I need to get my family back on track."

"Your family issues are not my . . . doing. They're not my fault."

Good for you, Sam, Chris thought. He had been about to point out the same thing. How dare Alex blame Sam for Annie's behavior, or Jack's, or Nick's! Alex had been taking care of her family long before they moved to Arizona. Very likely, there had been underlying issues before they embarked on this baby project.

"Maybe not," Alex conceded. "However, things in my life have certainly seemed to go south in the last seven months."

Sam was fighting the Percocet to understand. "Are you blaming me?"

"That's absurd," Chris interjected.

"It may be unreasonable," Alex glared at him, "and it may be *absurd*, but it's how I feel. I need some time away from you to sort things out. Let me emphasize this. I need to get my family back on track."

"Like a choo choo. Chug a chug a chug a chug a *choo choo.*" Sam was definitely losing the battle with the big P.

"What is the matter with you?"

"Amtrak trains. The Spirit of New Orleans. The Saluki. The Illini Express."

"What is the *matter* with her?" Alex directed the question at Chris.

"She's naming the Amtrak lines that travel across Illinois." Chris was not inclined to enlighten Alex about the pain meds.

"It just figures. I come over to have a serious conversation with her, and she goes wacko on me. It just figures."

"I think it would be fair under the circumstances to say that Sam has not had a very good day. Falling off a ladder and breaking your arm—I may be going out on a limb here, and yes, the pun is intended—is probably not on anyone's Top Ten list of things to do on a Tuesday."

Alex looked at Sam slumped on the couch, her eyes mere slits and her mouth slightly ajar and briefly, very briefly, her face softened. "You better take my wacko twin sister upstairs to bed."

"Yep," he said.

Jack felt sick and tired. To be more specific, Jack felt sick and tired of *himself*. When, exactly, had he stopped coping? When had he become a barely functioning, dysfunctional wreck of a man? Well, he knew the specific answer to that one. But what he couldn't quite figure out was when he developed this useless, raging pride that clouded every waking thought and cluttered every waking action, which consequently, caused everything to go spiraling downward into a black hole of seething resentment? He wanted to copy Rodin's posture of *The Thinker*, burying his face in his hand for all eternity. He wouldn't be lost in thought, though. He would be lost in despair.

But he would not. When his wife had said to him that she refused to be in the dark about their children any more, he had wholeheartedly agreed. They were going to: (a) ask more probing questions, (b) stop burying their heads in the sand, and (c) take nothing for granted. This approach to parenting, while good in theory, was leaving a bad taste in his mouth and a household cloaked in suspicion. He couldn't remember the last time anyone in his family had laughed. It seemed they were all just going through the motions. When was this going to end—when Annie was considered cured, when Nick went off to college, when the baby was born?

"Things will get better soon," his wife said with a confidence that rang falsely.

"Georgia said that Annie is making progress," he added to the forced bravado. Georgia, because of counselor/patient confidentiality, could not give specific information about what kind of progress, which was frustrating. To Jack, Annie seemed even more, and he now had to admit the word, *depressed* than before.

"We're doing the right thing," his wife said.

"If you say so." He had his doubts. Keeping such a close watch on Annie was stifling everybody.

"What? Do you have a better suggestion?" his wife said sharply.

"Not at the present time."

"Well, when you do come up with a better suggestion in the future, will you be sure to let me know?"

"Our daughter didn't come with a manual," he said.

"How original," his wife said. And then the zinger, and he was sure she had been waiting days for this moment. "How in the world could you not notice that Nick had a girlfriend? You supposedly—and I quote—'know everything that goes on at SCDS.'"

The valid question filled him with that shame-inducing, raging, useless pride. "I guess it's because I was so busy, as per your instructions, trailing Annie that I didn't notice another new transitory couple at the high school walking arm in arm."

"He's your *son*."

Jack should have known.

"And I didn't say to trail Annie. I said—and I quote—'keep an eye on her.'"

"You have a mind like a steel trap these days, all these quotes. Really, you're the sharpest you've ever been. You should go on *Who Wants to Be a Millionaire?* I'm not kidding. You are really on the ball." She thought he didn't know that she was spending more and more time in the afternoons watching game shows instead of trying to sell Avon. But he knew.

She threw a pillow at him. They were in the family room and not the kitchen where she could reach something breakable or sharp. "Why don't you go pour yourself another drink?"

He rattled the cubes in his scotch-empty glass. So far, he had only had one this evening, and he really needed another. But he wasn't going to give her the satisfaction. No sirree. He was going to cut off his nose to spite his face. He got up. "I'm going out."

His wife turned her face away from him, towards the blank screen of the television. "What a novel suggestion, coming from you."

He drove to the casino. He hadn't been there in a week, but he wasn't going there to gamble tonight. No, he was going to take care of the Cookie business once and for all. Her calls were escalating in frequency and hysteria. Today, while he was in a teacher's meeting, she had called seven times in five minutes. He kept reaching in his pocket to shut off the vibrating, quivering machine, which had obviously been noticed by everyone sitting around the oval conference table.

"Maybe you should take that call," Martin, the principal, had said pointedly.

"Maybe I better." So Jack had no choice but to go outside and pretend he was listening to the nonexistent person on the other end, nodding and affirming at appropriate intervals. It just figured that Cookie would have given up by then, not that he would ever talk to her on school grounds. That would be entirely inappropriate.

He had considered changing his phone number, but how would he explain that to his family? He could say something along the lines of, "I keep getting these crank calls," or "I must have gotten on some sort of universal telemarketing list," or "I need a change in my life and changing my telephone number is just the ticket!" No, it would be better to go to the source, Cookie, and tell her, once and for all, to *knock it off.*

Nick entered the smoky casino and scanned the crowded poker room. He recognized many of the regulars, but he didn't see Cookie. This was one of her regular poker nights, so that meant that she must be taking a break and was at the back bar. Sure enough, she sat on a stool in front of a video poker machine, drinking a vodka tonic and smoking a cigarette. She looked especially brittle tonight. Her dyed, teased blonde hair looked like it would snap at the slightest touch, and Jack had a stabbing realization that he had never been attracted to her. How could he have been? She looked like she had lived a hard life in an arid, unforgiving climate. Unfortunately, he knew this about her, too. Cookie was a rare breed, a native Arizonian.

"Hey, Cookie," he said, taking the empty seat next to her and ordering a scotch.

"Jack! Where've you been? I've been calling and calling you. I think your phone must be broken." It was obviously not Cookie's first drink of the night.

"It's not broken."

"You lost it somewhere?"

"No." He pulled the offending machine from his pocket and held it up. "Right here."

"Then," and it was like a light went on behind her metallic blue eyelids, "you're ignoring my calls."

Jack wanted to take his drink in a single gulp, but he forced himself to nurse it. "Cookie, you have to stop calling me."

"But we're such good friends. Good friends call each other."

"We're what you could call casino friends, but that's it. We talked about this before when we met at Roundabout. We're both married to other people, and there is never going to be more between us than being casino friends." Without thinking, he downed his drink. Shit.

"You kissed me." She puckered her red lips as if she wanted another, right then.

"That was a mistake, a drunken mistake." He ordered them each another drink. He silently vowed that it would be his last.

"So now I'm a drunken mistake?"

Today, his batting average for offending women was on a hot streak. "What I meant to say is that it shouldn't have happened."

"You initiated it," Cookie insisted, lighting another cigarette from the smoldering butt of the first. "You acted like you wanted me."

Had he? Looking at her now, he didn't see how he could have possibly sent out the strong signals she was suggesting. She wasn't even remotely his type. His wife was his type, not that he was currently doing so well in that department. He had been lonely, he knew, and feeling sorry for himself. "I apologize if I gave you the wrong impression."

"All those long conversations. I really felt as if we had a bond."

He had to give her that. They had had a bond, The Lonely-Hearts Club. "We were only casino friends," he said again.

"I really liked you, Jack." Cookie stirred her drink with her ringed forefinger. "I really did."

"I'm really sorry."

She lifted her glass. "But now I realize you're like all the others, just a regular, run-of-the-mill asshole." She emptied the gin and tonic on his lap. "We're through," she said as she staggered away.

Through? The crazy bitch. They hadn't even started anything. A drunken kiss didn't count. Jack ignored the stares directed at his wet crotch as he left the casino. It was clear that he shouldn't come back here again, that he was leaving this money-sucking, loved, abusive friend. It was the end of an era, a bad era of his life. All he wanted was to get home.

But he had only driven a mile in his alcohol-reeking Jeep before he heard the siren and saw the squad car's blinking lights in his rearview mirror.

10

CHAPTER TEN

Alex was six months pregnant, and she was feeling surprisingly good, better than she had in weeks. She had thrown her ratty sweat suit away, and finally, her skin had cleared up. Its unexpected, betraying eruptions from the months before had vanished, and when she looked in a mirror, even she had to admit that she had a maternal, healthy glow. It was about time. The twenty-two pounds she had gained had settled nicely on her belly. Her hips and behind weren't spreading yet, and she did not have cellulite or varicose veins either. She did have to admit, though, that being pregnant in her forties was not the same as being pregnant in her twenties. She didn't move as fast, she needed more sleep, and she had to pay more attention to her diet. But as Dr. Weinstein said, things were progressing *nicely*.

Alex thought things were progressing nicely all the way around. Maybe *nicely* was more optimistic than factual, but there hadn't been any major dramas in the past three weeks. She had started to cook again, and on some nights, they all ate dinner together around the kitchen table like they used to. They didn't laugh and joke around like in the good old days (and she was beginning to wonder if the "good old days" had really been more her imaginary longing than actuality). And for the most part, the meals were hurried affairs with no dawdling. But it was a start. Each member of her family was sitting in his or her designated seat at the designated time.

Yet in the middle of all this *niceness*, Alex often felt lonely. Her family was around her slightly more than before, and it seemed like they were all making a genuine effort at this. However, it didn't seem as if they were genuinely connecting. Each person had his or her own pursuits and agenda. Unfortunately, she was the one with the least outside interests. Funny how it had never bothered her before. But it bothered her now. Maybe she should get a job, although if her lack of success as an Avon representative indicated any level of competence, she would have to grade herself a big, fat zero. She had waited too long, she had no marketable skills, and she was a computer illiterate. However, when the baby was born, she would have more than enough to do. That job would be the most important one of all.

Luckily, Annie and Carla walked into the kitchen, interrupting Alex's reverie. Georgia had ambiguously told her and Jack that Annie had a *breakthrough* during a therapy session, and at her suggestion, she and Jack had given back most of Annie's privileges. Carla was one of them. Alex still had her suspicions about Carla's motivations and influence on Annie—plus the girl had flat-out lied to her—but after finally talking to Mrs. Goldleib, she had to say that she felt sympathy for the girl. What a cold bitch her mother was! When Alex had described the drunken, pot smoking scene to the woman, the woman's response had basically been, "So what?"

"Our daughters are drinking and doing drugs," Alex had emphasized again.

"All children experiment," she had countered.

"I think they're doing more than experimenting."

"Would it make you happy if I had the surveillance cameras reinstalled? Is that what you're asking me to do?"

"I have no idea what you're talking about." Surveillance cameras in a home?

"I suggest that you mind your daughter, and I will mind mine."

"Fine." Bitch. Even over the phone, Alex could imagine her perfectly, a tall, blonde, thin ice queen.

So, Carla was back in the equation, but within a supervised setting—i.e., she could come to their house, but Annie could not go to hers. And Alex had to admit that Annie seemed happier when Carla was around, although *happier* was a relative term when it came to Annie these days. She still acted like a sixteen-year-old girl who carried the weight of the world on her small shoulders.

"Hi, Mrs. Carissa," Carla said. She didn't say much to Alex since the *incident.*

"We're going up to my room to study. Is that okay, Mom?" Annie asked for permission for *everything* now. To Alex, it was becoming increasingly annoying.

"Do you want a snack? I baked some chocolate chip cookies this morning." If Annie could read the subtext of this, she would know that Alex meant: Please sit down and talk to me.

"Milk and cookies. Yum," Carla said.

Alex flushed. She had to stop being a June Cleaver.

"No, thanks, Mom." Annie ignored the subtext altogether.

Do not beg, Alex told herself. "Maybe later?"

"Maybe."

Maybe not. They wouldn't come down later. They never did. They would stay ensconced in Annie's room—talking, conspiring?—until Carla left. It was all right. They weren't drinking and doing drugs.

Jack came home from work then, and he didn't pour himself a drink. Alex had not seen him pour a drink in two weeks. He didn't give any explanation, and she didn't ask for fear that it would "rock the boat" on his neonatal sobriety. He still slept on the couch, though, which was more hurtful to her. He wasn't sleeping on the couch because he had passed out there. No, he was making a conscious decision to avoid her. He was certainly keeping his vow to not sleep with her until the baby was born. Three more months to go. She could take it.

"How was your day?" he asked politely.

"Fine. Yours?"

"Fine. I think I'll go for a run. What time is dinner?"

"Six." Dinner was always at six, and he knew it. Could their conversation be any more superficial?

"Good. I'll look forward to it."

Yes, it could be more superficial. "You do that."

This was how it had been going with her husband, and yes, she could take it. She had, finally, gone to the bank and asked for back copies of their monthly statements. She didn't find anything out of the ordinary, no huge withdrawals, no suspicious checks written. She hadn't seen the monthly credit card statement yet, but since they had canceled most of their cards, she doubted that anything would be amiss there. Possibly, she had to concede that Jack really did get that stack of one-hundred-dollar bills from a poker game with his buddies from work and golf. It was beginning to look like that was the case, and she couldn't help but feel ashamed that she had been so suspicious of him. "It's the hormones," she wanted to say to him. "I'm not myself." But then he would say something, with bitterness, along the lines of, "And whose fault is that?"

Jack finished his glass of milk. "Well, I'm going up to get changed now."

"Good idea."

Alex sighed as she got the chicken out of the refrigerator. Yes, things were going *nicely*. They were killing each other with *niceness*. It had to be better than the alternatives, the constant fighting, or worse, the demoralizing silences. She couldn't stand either of those, not with her husband, not with her children, and not with Sam. It was Alex, the initiator of the "break," who called Sam after three days apart. Three long, long days of absence.

"I was unreasonable," Alex said. And she had been. It was stupid and selfish to be jealous of her children's relationship with their aunt.

"I don't blame you," Sam said.

"Truce?"

"Absolutely."

"From now on, we're going to be completely honest with each other. We should tell each other everything, just like we used to."

"From now on," Sam repeated quietly.

And so the *niceness* had been extended to Sam, and she, in turn, was extending it back. Every day, Alex, Nick, or Annie would go over to Sam's and help her out for an hour or so. They'd take over a casserole, or do a load of laundry, or empty the dishwasher, or vacuum—Alex had even washed Sam's hair—anything she needed, although she didn't ask for much. She was trying to be independent, she told them all, she only needed a little help.

"Alex," Jack called from the top of the stairs. "Do you know where Nick keeps

his running shoes?"

"They're in his bedroom somewhere," she called back.

"Could you find them for me? I've got to make a call."

"And you can't do both at the same time?" Really. He was literally ten steps from Nick's room, and he wanted her to go up and find them?

"I have no idea where to look."

She had heard that all men were like this. Basically, as they were opening the refrigerator door, they would ask their wives, "Where's the ketchup?" And the ketchup, of course, was right in front of them, on the refrigerator door. Alex sighed. She probably could find the shoes faster.

Nick, unlike Annie, was fastidious about his room. Nothing littered the floor, and nothing was stashed/hidden under the bed. (She had once found an empty cereal bowl and spoon under Annie's.) Knowing Nick, his clothes and shoes would be in his closet where they should be. She scanned the neat row of shoes on the plastic rack at the bottom of the closet. Strangely, there were no running shoes, and she didn't see his cross-country jersey, either.

And then she spied the footlocker in the corner of the small closet. She pulled it out. The shoes must be in there, but it was easier said than done. The chest was locked, and the strangeness of that sent up a red flag in her brain. Why would Nick lock up his running shoes?

What else was in there?

He had never been so terrified in his life. The siren, the blinking red lights, and the bottom of his stomach dropped to his knees. Once, when Nick was six and had fallen out of the tree in their back yard, when Jack had heard the cry and run to see his boy lying misshapen on the ground, he had felt such an acute fear. But then, the fear was mixed with adrenaline, the need to scoop up his son and the need to *take action.* This fear was different, built as it was on shame and dread. He gripped the steering wheel hard to quiet the quaking in his hands as he pulled over to the side of the road. He hadn't had much to drink, had he? One drink or three? He weighed one hundred and seventy-five pounds. He could not be legally drunk. But he had not eaten anything since lunchtime, his pants were soaked with gin, and the car reeked like a rowdy bar on Sunday morning.

He might be legally drunk!

Everyone in Arizona knew that you didn't mess with Sheriff Joe, the self-proclaimed Toughest Sheriff in America. He was the one who had established Tent City where inmates were housed outdoors during the blazing summers and coldest winter nights. He was the one who fed inmates green bologna. He was the one who forced inmates to wear pink underwear. He was the one who brought back chain gangs. He was the one who enforced some of the strictest drunk driving laws in the country.

Even first-time offenders went to jail.

Oh, God, this can't be happening, Jack thought. What had he done to get pulled over? He wasn't driving too fast. He wasn't driving too slowly, or had he been a tad under the speed limit? He was in his lane. He had not forgotten to turn on his lights. His lost reputation flashed before his mind like a dying man's life: the legal fees, the probable loss of his job, the humiliation of his family, the disgrace of the truth.

In his rearview mirror, Jack watched the young-looking officer walk toward him.

Each slow-motion step painfully trampled his heart. He deserved this—he knew he did—but now that it was happening, he wanted to take back his behavior of the last months, he wanted to pretend that he hadn't done all the shameful things he had done, but most of all, he wanted to fling open the car door and run away—fast.

He rolled down the car window. "What seems to be the problem, officer?" Wasn't that the line asked innocently, by characters trying not to get caught, in all the action movies and comedies?

The officer had his hat pulled low. His gun rested easily, cockily on his hip. "License please."

Jack fumbled for his frayed wallet and pulled it out. "What seems to be the problem, officer?" he asked again. He smiled, demonstrating that he was confident of his innocence. "Nice night," he almost said, but stopped himself just in time.

The officer beamed his flashlight over the license and then into Jack's face. "Mr. Carissa? The guidance counselor at SCDS? Is that you?"

Even worse luck. Was this some parent who, before school started in the morning, would have alerted the entire school of Jack Carissa's fall from grace? "Yes, sir, that's me. What seems to be the problem?" This time, he asked the question desperately.

"Don't you remember me? I'm Brett Sommers, class of '02." He lifted his cap.

Jack's mind went into memory recall overdrive. He had had so many students. The guy standing in front of him would be twenty-four or twenty-five, but he didn't look like a kid anymore. Already, his hair was thinning. Stalling for time, Jack said, "Of course I remember you. How have you been?"

"I moved back from Boulder a year and a half ago. I loved going to school there and wanted to stay, but there weren't any openings for high school P.E. teachers." He barked a laugh, waved a hand over his uniform. "Of course—surprise, surprise—there weren't any openings here either."

University of Colorado at Boulder. Athletics. And then it clicked. Brett Sommers, a solid B/C student who had scored middling on the SAT exam and who had been a star on the basketball team. With relief, Jack said, "It's a tough time for young college graduates to be looking for jobs in this rotten economy."

"It sure is. But I like this job so far. I've only been on active patrol for a week now."

Maybe he was lucky after all. Maybe a rookie would be more lenient. "Are you still playing basketball?" he said to show Brett that he did, in fact, remember him.

"Not so much. I'm married now. My first kid is on the way."

"Congratulations!"

"Thanks."

"I mean, I think it's really great that you're married at your age. I married young, too, and believe me, Brett, it was the right decision. Young people these days are waiting for the right time to get married, but I've got to tell you, there is no *right time*. You've just got to jump in with two feet!" He needed to stop talking but he couldn't seem to control his tongue.

"Are you expecting a girl or boy, or do you not know? Personally, I think it's better not to know. The element of surprise, you know?"

Brett looked back down at the license. "Mr. Carissa, I stopped you because you have an expired registration, and I'm going to have to issue you a ticket for that."

"Yes. Sure. By all means. I can't believe I forgot to renew it last month."

"It expired four months ago."

"It always comes up for renewal during my seniors' college application process. I can't believe I forgot it this year. I'll take care of it first thing tomorrow."

"Mr. Carissa, I stopped you for the expired registration, but I'm afraid I'm going to have to investigate the smell that is emanating from your car. It smells like alcohol, sir." His voice was apologetic yet determined.

Not so lucky after all. Time to face the music. "I was at the casino, and a drink was inadvertently dropped in my lap. Obviously, I didn't have a change of clothes with me." Jack gave a dry laugh. "I'm afraid that the lady who spilled it was quite intoxicated. I hope she's not driving tonight. Haha."

"Do you consent to a field sobriety test?"

What choice did he have? He got out of the car and walked the line, touched his nose, and blew into the breathalyzer. He was probably more surprised than Officer Brett Sommers that his alcohol level was only .06, slightly below the legal limit. By this time, he was sweating copiously.

"I could still take you in, even though you're below the legal limit, Mr. Carissa."

"Why would you do that? I *am* below the legal limit, and I'm perfectly able to drive." He had passed the test. This snot-nosed rookie better not take him in. Please, please, please, do not take him in.

"I'm not going to take you in, Mr. Carissa. However, I suggest you call someone to pick you up and take you home. I'll wait here until they arrive."

"Fine . . . thanks." He would call Bob to come and get him, certainly not Alex or Nick, and certainly, certainly not his anal brother-in-law.

"I always liked you, Mr. Carissa. You were a good guidance counselor, helped me make one of the most important decisions of my life."

"I'm glad to hear that, Brett." He was exhausted, suddenly and completely.

"And I wouldn't want you to be my first DUI arrest."

"I wouldn't want that either."

His headache grew as they waited for Bob to arrive, and by the time he finally did arrive, Jack considered that perhaps his greatest punishment of the evening was to listen to rookie officer Brett Sommers spout off his version of the meaning of life, which was woefully young and naive. But it could have been worse, much worse.

Yes, he had finally been lucky.

He was never going to drink again.

For once, Annie was not the shit hitting the fan. Unbelievably, it was her "perfect" brother who had messed up, who was in the doghouse, who was up the creek without a paddle. It was her brother who was in Trouble with a capital T. He was the one standing defendant before the parent jury, head hung low, mumbling unintelligible excuses.

"Nick, can you explain where these items came from?" Mom held up a gold cross from a footlocker spread open on the kitchen table. From where Annie stood, it looked like the lock had been smashed in with a hammer.

"I'm sure you have a good explanation for these," Dad said reasonably, although it looked like someone had punched him in the stomach.

"As I recall, there were items stolen from the boys' locker room a while back." Mom's voice shook.

"The janitor was charged with that," Dad said.

Mom started to grasp at straws. "Maybe you're holding these for some-one else, someone you don't want to get in trouble, like Dylan?"

Boy, was Nick inexperienced in this Trouble department. He should have grabbed at that one and run with it. He should have said, "Yeah, that's it! They're Dylan's, and I didn't want to get him in trouble."

"They're not Dylan's," Nick mumbled.

Dad tried to give him an out next because he would not, could not begin to comprehend what was happening. "Someone at SCDS then. One of the boys was doing a prank and got you involved against your will. That jackass Corey Grosman is just the kind of kid who would pull a stunt like this, taking things that didn't belong to him just for the hell of it."

"Corey didn't take these things," Nick said. He was still staring at the top of his

shoes, and his ears were very pink.

"Someone at work," Mom suggested.

Nick shook his head.

"If not Corey, then someone else on the cross-country team," Dad suggested.

Nick shook his head.

Man, Nick, you are bad at this, Annie thought. Don't be such a dumbass. They're offering you every out they can think of, and you're acting like you just took some kind of truth serum. Come on, Annie silently rooted, say they belong to someone else. She found it hard to believe, but there it was. She felt sorry for her brother.

Dad finally noticed that she was sitting on the kitchen counter. "Go upstairs, Annie. This doesn't involve you." It was the line he usually delivered to Nick when she was in trouble. Boy, were the tables turned now.

"She can stay," Nick said. He had lifted his head and now stared straight ahead, at attention, like someone in the military being addressed by a senior officer.

Mom gave it one more final, weak try. "You bought these things?"

"He bought credit cards with someone else's name on them?" The words had popped out. She clamped her hand over her mouth, but it didn't matter. They were deaf to her right now. All their attention was focused on Nick who would not—could not possibly—steal. Their perfect son was not a thief.

"I stole these things months ago," Nick said. "I haven't stolen anything since, and I'm very sorry that I did it, and I'm very sorry that a janitor got fired because of me."

"But why?" Tears rolled down Mom's face.

"I don't know."

"You had to have had a reason." Tears rolled down Dad's face, too.

"I have no explanation." Nick's voice was deep, crisp.

Annie had to hand it to him. He was acting very . . . *professional* about the whole thing. She would have dissolved into a teary mess ages ago. It was like watching a movie, and he was the lead actor who, for noble reasons, was going to be thrown into solitary confinement but would be brave until the end.

"We're just *crushed*, Nick." Mom buried her face in her hands and started to sob.

Annie pushed herself off the counter then and went upstairs. It just showed how much more they loved him than her. She got *disappointed.* Nick got *crushed.*

Oh, hell. Annie heard Georgia's voice in her head telling her that that wasn't true, and she knew it. According to her past behavioral patterns, they would be surprised when she got in trouble but not shocked. Hence, they were *disappointed.* With Nick's past behavioral patterns, which were pretty damn perfect, they were shocked when he got in Trouble with a capital T. Hence, they were *crushed.*

And they ain't seen nothin' yet! She flopped down on her bed and stared at her ceiling at the poster of Black Sabbath. She didn't know the band, didn't know their music, but she had found the poster at the mall and bought it because of the name Black Sabbath. It had a satisfying, unholy ring to it. It suited her personality, she thought. She was satisfyingly unholy.

Walter was dead. She knew that now. Georgia had made her *talk* through her *feelings.* Georgia had told her that she was frightened about her feelings, and she had said to Georgia, "If you had my feelings, you'd be scared shitless, too." And then she had started to wail about her feelings until her face looked like a swollen red balloon.

Georgia said: You've had a breakthrough.

Annie said: I'd like to break *something.*

Georgia, smiling, said: That's good.

Annie said: Hey, how about those Sun Devils!

Georgia said: Oh, Annie. That's enough for today.

Annie liked Georgia, she really did, but the twice-weekly sessions were becoming more and more uncomfortable. Georgia was asking more and more questions, trying to unlock something that Annie never wanted to revisit mentally, let alone talk about. (It was a good thing Georgia couldn't take a hammer and smash that lock, like her mom had done to Nick's foot locker.) Annie sometimes wished her parents had hired someone incompetent. A lousy shrink would have been a lot easier to lie to. When she tried to lie to Georgia, Georgia would fold her arms and say, "I'll wait, Annie."

What, exactly, was Georgia waiting for? A better question was this: How could she possibly know that Annie was hiding something? Maybe she really did have a brand on her forehead? Maybe she had a funny smell, a kind of loser B.O.?

Walter was dead. She knew that now. But the scary thing was that she could sometimes understand why Walter had done it. Sometimes, she was a little jealous of Walter.

Oh hell. Georgia's voice: You don't really mean that, Annie.

A: Walter doesn't have any problems anymore.

G: Walter is dead.

A: Yeah, I guess that's the *unfortunate* part of suicide.

Carla walked into her bedroom and threw her heavy backpack on the floor. The

backpack was for show; they didn't do much studying in this room. "Holy shit! What's going on downstairs? Your parents look as if they've just seen a train wreck."

"I guess you could say they have." She told Carla about Nick's footlocker with the stolen wallets, watches, and gold cross.

Carla gave a long whistle. "I didn't know he had it in him."

"Me neither."

"He's kind of like Robin Hood." Carla popped a Nicorette tablet, since they obviously couldn't smoke in Annie's room.

"Except that he didn't give to the poor," Annie pointed out.

"Did he use any of the credit cards?"

"I don't think so." Annie couldn't recall Nick having any new electronics or a new phone or new video games. In fact, she didn't think he had even bought a new pair of jeans in quite a while. "He didn't even spend the cash in the wallets."

"Then I would say that robbing from those fucking rich assholes qualifies him for Robin Hood status. Most of them probably didn't even miss the stuff. All they'd have to do is tell Mommy and Daddy that they lost their wallets. And voila! Mommy and Daddy immediately—after saying, 'you poor thing'—replaced everything."

Annie suddenly had a thought, and it made her feel terrified for her brother.

"What if he gets expelled?"

"Maybe your parents aren't going to tell? I know mine wouldn't." Carla's mother had not even mentioned Annie's mom's phone call to Carla, a fact that had infuriated her. She had, as she put it, "been up for a rootin', tootin' showdown."

Maybe they wouldn't, but Annie suspected that her parents would *do the right thing*. "I guess it's not my problem," she said.

"Nope," Carla said as she rummaged through her big purse and produced the EPT

box. "It's really time that you peed on this stick."

For days and days and days, Carla had been repeating this mantra, and Annie had

resisted, resisted, resisted. She still held out the hope (a microscopic glimmer) that it wasn't true. Her period would come any day. She had been under enormous stress. Her hormones were fucked up. She was an *irregular girl.*

"We need to do this before it's too late."

Before it was too late. An unwed, knocked up, underage girl needed to have an

abortion in the first three months. Damn that health class that had shown a movie about the *fetus's* development. She wished she hadn't paid such close, fascinated attention to it. Oddly, though, she hadn't thought about it in relation to her own "with child" mother.

"We need to make plans," Carla said. "I still think that running away, I mean, *moving away* is a good idea." Carla corrected herself because Annie had finally told her that *running away* sounded kind of cowardly. "Just pee on the damn stick."

"Tomorrow," Annie said.

"Today," Carla said firmly.

"In a minute," Annie said, stalling.

"Now," Carla said as she practically dragged Annie to the door, opened it and checked if the coast was clear, and then dragged/shoved her to the bathroom. She pushed a trash bag—a very large bag, for some reason, instead of a small one like one from the grocery store—into Annie's hand. "Put everything in here when you're done. I'll stand guard. Should we agree on a secret knock?"

"A knock for being knocked up?" Annie tried to sound sarcastic, even though she

was scared to death.

"I'm glad to see your sense of humor is back."

"Fuck you," Annie hissed. She shut the door as quietly as she could, read the directions three times, followed the instructions, and walked back to her room.

"Well?" Carla said when the desk chair was safely placed under the doorknob.

The lock on her door was a privilege that had yet to be returned.

"I am *positively* screwed."

Sam watched Nick clean the pool through her kitchen window. He cleaned it methodically, resolutely, his face blank. She didn't know what to say to him, not after Alex's hysterical rendition of the footlocker filled with stolen goods.

"I don't understand. I don't understand," she kept repeating.

"This happened—when? One, two years ago?" Sam had asked.

"It doesn't matter when it happened. Nick stole those things, and an honest man lost his job because of it." Alex's Kleenex was a stringy pulp.

"But he hasn't stolen anything lately." To Sam, it looked like Nick must have tried to reform himself, probably out of self-imposed guilt. And it was curious that he had never used the stolen credit cards, spent the money, or worn the watches or jewelry. It seemed to her that he might have stolen those things because of some misguided principle. Perhaps the "victims" had been cruel to him. Perhaps the "victims" had deserved it.

"He's jeopardized his entire future. The school will probably expel him three months before graduation! His life is ruined!"

"Look, the kids he stole from have already graduated, right? They've probably forgotten all about it as they party their brains out at their Ivy League schools." She pried the soggy tissue out of Alex's clenched fist and handed her a new one.

"What are you saying?"

"Let bygones be bygones? Forget the past? Move on? Don't tell the school."

Alex stared at her, shocked. "We have to tell the school."

"Why?"

"Because it's the right thing to do," Alex stammered. "What kind of example for our son would we be setting if we let this slide, if we lie by omission?"

Sam didn't believe that "lying by omission" was, in fact, a "lie" by definition. "So, it's better if you do the *right* thing and ruin his life?"

Alex arched her brows even higher. "Are you saying that, if this were your child, you wouldn't tell the school?"

"That's what I'm saying."

"I sometimes worry about your morals," Alex said in a stern, preachy voice.

Sam sometimes worried about her morals, too, but not at this moment. "You sound just like Mother."

"Thanks for adding insult to injury."

"I'm not trying to tell you what to do. Obviously, I've never been in this predicament. But you keep talking about telling the school. Wouldn't the school notify the police?"

"Shit," Alex said. "Jack and I haven't even gotten that far yet. We're both so *crushed* that we're not really thinking clearly."

Sam wanted to be helpful. "When Nick comes over later to clean the pool, do you want me to talk to him? You know, an aunt could be more objective about—"

"No! I do not want you to say a word to him. We're not going through this again. I mean it, Sam, do not get in the middle of this."

Sam put up her one good hand in surrender. "I won't. I promise on our sisterhood." Alex was always doing this to her, dumping all her problems and worries in Sam's lap and then demanding that she not do anything about it. It was frustrating.

"Oh, grow up," Alex snapped as she left.

So now, she was looking at her nephew out the window, and her heart went out to him. He had always been such a good kid; he was still a good kid. What could she do to help him? She had tried before to give him money for the odd jobs he'd been doing for her around the house—strictly against Alex's instructions—but he wouldn't take it. Annie, on the other hand, had taken the occasional five or ten that Sam had offered. Alex, in fact, had set up land mines of rules for Sam concerning her children. Most were so petty that she had not bothered to remember them. Why did she even listen to Alex? Oh, right. Alex was carrying her baby, and Sam was therefore *beholden* to her.

She dug into the junk drawer for a ruler and stuck it into the cast. Her arm had been itching mercilessly all day long. Only four weeks to go. Four long, long weeks. The cast already looked dirty, and now she understood why people with broken bones had people sign their casts—to hide the filth. It was already disgusting enough that she hated to go out in public, which only increased the frequency of Chris's mantra that she needed to get out of the house more.

"Do you want me to drive with one hand, my left, non-dominant hand? I'm not that great of driver to begin with." Sam had often wondered if it could it be possible that Annie had inherited her aunt's lousy driving skills. She, like Annie, was a careless driver.

"Point duly noted," Chris had said. "However, you could take the occasional walk around the neighborhood."

She was going to do no such thing, so she pretended not to have heard. "I'm a disaster waiting to happen."

"I give up." Chris literally threw his hands up in the air. "You win."

It was a small, temporary, unsatisfactory victory because Chris then refused to go pick up the refill for the Percocet that she had called into the pharmacy. She then had to pretend that she didn't crave them. He then had to pretend that she wasn't a raging bitch for that first week. She now had to pretend that she was perfectly content to take Tylenol PM before bed each night, even though it was a piss-poor substitute for the P. It wasn't even close. Not at all.

She abandoned the unwieldy ruler and got a knife out of the silverware drawer, but it wasn't long enough to reach the itch that was driving her crazy. She threw it into the sink. Being so dependent on others was growing old. Not being able to work was causing her mind to atrophy. Dressing herself was such an effort that she spent most of her days wearing pajama bottoms and an old poncho she had found in the back of her closet, a leftover from a sixties party she had gone to years before. She had no idea why she had saved the hideous thing.

She was too damn old for this shit!

Nick had finished cleaning the pool and stuck his head through the back door. "All done, Aunt Sam. I'll be back in a couple of days."

"Do you want to come all the way in and have a Coke?"

"I've got to get to work. But thanks."

"Here, let me—" Her purse was on the counter and she dug into it with her left hand, groping for a bill, any bill in its murky mess.

"No, Aunt Sam, I can't take your money."

"I insist." It seemed like the least she could do for the poor kid.

His face turned scarlet. "I really can't." He hurried out the back gate.

Well, shit. He probably knew that she knew. *I can't take your money.* She had embarrassed him when she had only feebly tried to help. The fact of the matter, if he only knew, was that she was the embarrassed one. She was willing to bribe her own nephew, offer him anything, for a few minutes of his company. How pathetic was that? Very. She was too damn old to be this lonely. Sam sunk in a kitchen chair and put her head in her left hand. When the baby came, everything would change. Everything would be right. Everything would be perfect.

"This is so lame," Annie said as she banged open the back door. "Mom sent me over to borrow a cup of sugar. And she even made me bring the *cup.*" The offensive cup dangled from her finger.

She was so happy to see her niece that it was embarrassing. "I'm sure I've got some around here somewhere." She jumped up and opened a cabinet. "What's she making?"

Annie shrugged. "I don't know. She seems to be baking a lot lately." Her hair had grown out and the heavy eyeliner was gone. She looked young and cute. She looked *normal.* "Hormones, probably. She blames everything on hormones. Do all pregnant women act weird?"

Sam laughed. "Pretty much. It's probably how that pickles and ice cream thing got started." She was taking her time looking for the sugar, prolonging things, although she really didn't have a clue where Chris kept it.

"So, you can tell if someone is pregnant by the way they act?" Annie asked nonchalantly.

"No, you can tell if someone is pregnant when it looks like they have a beach ball in their belly." She opened another cabinet.

Annie cleared her throat. "I need to ask you something."

"Sure. Anything."

"Do you know anything about Planned Parenthood?"

"What?" Sam turned around so fast that her cast bumped the counter. She ignored the pain.

"It's for school. A paper. I'm writing a paper on Planned Parenthood. I've done research, but I thought you might know something about it, or know someone who knew something about it, you know, a personal source, or something like that . . ." Annie's voice trailed off.

The only time Sam had been to Planned Parenthood was with Alex. Did Annie suspect something? "No, I really don't know anything about it. My problem was on the opposite spectrum of things. I really wanted to get pregnant but couldn't." This had to be old news for Annie.

She nodded. "Funny how that works, isn't it?"

"Yeah. Funny." Sam didn't think it was funny at all. Teenagers could get pregnant at the drop of a hat, and she had spent most of her adult life trying to have a baby. *Funny* wasn't the word for it.

"I bet a lot of those girls would like to give their baby to someone who really wanted it, someone who would give it a good home. Someone like you, maybe?"

"Sign me up. I'll take all I can get." Why didn't Annie just go and interview someone at Planned Parenthood?

"Really?" Annie's eyes were wide, almost pleading.

"In theory, yes, but it's much more complicated than that. You can't just give a baby away." God knew that she had wished that thousands of times in the past. "I don't know where Chris keeps the damn sugar."

"It's in the second canister to the right of the stove." Annie pointed with the cup.

"Why didn't you tell me that sooner?" She was glad that Annie hadn't, but it seemed odd. In fact, this whole conversation was odd.

"I just remembered."

As she carried the canister to the kitchen table, the thought came with sudden clarity. Annie must know someone who was pregnant—maybe Carla? It couldn't, of course, be Annie. According to Alex, Annie didn't have a boyfriend. In fact, she hadn't even had a date in months. Delicately, she said, "I don't want to pry, but do you have a friend in . . . trouble?"

Annie kept her head down as she scooped a heaping cup of sugar. "No, no, no. It's a term paper. It's only a paper. Mom probably needed this sugar *yesterday*. I better run. Thanks for your help."

Annie was in such a hurry to leave that she left a trail of sugar from Sam's kitchen to her own house across the street.

"Whoa, dude. It's like the Don't Ask, Don't Tell policy in the military. Which is totally bogus anyway. Everyone knows who's gay and who's not." Dylan maneuvered his truck to the back of the long line at the drive-thru lane at McDonald's. "Look at all these lazy people who can't be bothered to get out of their car to order a burger. It's no wonder that fifty percent of Americans are obese."

"We're in line," Nick pointed out.

"Yeah, but we're talking, bro. You've got some heavy shit going down."

Dylan rarely swore, and it made Nick cringe. Yes indeed, he had some heavy *shit* going down. "I don't know why I took that stuff. I didn't even want it. The guys in the locker room were so careless with their stuff. They'd just leave their wallets laying on the bench in front of the lockers."

"So, like, the wallets were begging to be swiped?" Dylan offered.

He hadn't even acted all that surprised when Nick told him the story, when Nick had choked out the story through embarrassing tears. And Dylan, being his best friend, had not interrupted, had not said anything negative, had not passed judgment. Really, it was a little bit weird the way that Dylan had acted, kind of like he had suspected this all along, or that this kind of thing happened every day. But this kind of thing *did not* happen every day. This kind of thing was illegal, a misdemeanor or a felony or something like that. Nick had been *wrong* to steal. He knew it even as he did it again and again.

"I kind of went into auto zone. It was like my brain shut off, and my hand reached out." This was the only way he knew how to explain it, and it had become such a vague memory that he wasn't even sure that this was right. In his fuzzy recollection, it was like he was watching himself steal the wallets, the watches, and the gold cross. It was the cross that caused him the most guilt. He should not have taken a sacred symbol, although oddly, it had belonged to a Jewish kid.

Dylan crept the truck up another car length in line. "If it had been me, I probably would have done the same thing."

He was such a good friend. "No, you wouldn't have, Dylan."

"You never know. I don't hang around with rich kids, and a man never knows what he will do when faced with temptation. I'm only human."

Nick tried to hide a small smile, his first in days. Dylan, although he was trying to gain weight, still looked more like a skinny boy than a man. "Thanks, Dylan."

"Don't mention it, dude. So, you can forget the whole thing, right? Since you're so close to graduation and the *alleged* incidents happened a couple of years ago, your parents have decided not to tell the Dean of the school."

"Nice vocab word." He usually thought it was hilarious when Dylan popped out a word you wouldn't expect him to know, but not this time. The incidents were not alleged. He had *committed* them.

"Why is this line moving so slowly? Do they have a trainee in there or something? Are all these fat people ordering twenty Big Macs?" Dylan honked his horn.

"That's not going to do any good."

"I know, but it makes me feel better."

Nick wished that something, anything would make him feel better. He should have been relieved that his parents were going to protect him, but this only added to his mountain of guilt. They were going against their principles, as his dad had said repeatedly, to make sure that Nick graduated, to make sure that Nick's future would not be ruined. His mom, over and over and over, had said that they were just *crushed* that their son could make such poor choices. In scenes like this with the parents, Annie would just roll her eyes or cry until they felt sorry enough for her to let her escape. For Nick, these scenes felt like a punch in the gut. The stricken looks on his parents' face turned him inside out.

He wanted, *needed* to be punished, but his parents were at a loss to find a punishment that fit this level of *crime* (literally). So far, they had decided that he needed to do volunteer work, which is something he would like to do anyway, but they hadn't even been specific about that—St. Vincent de Paul, St. Mary's Food Bank, the Salvation Army, Phoenix Rescue Mission? The discussions always petered out, and everyone went to his or her separate corners to seethe/grieve (Dad) to cry/grieve (Mom) to throw up/grieve (guilty, sorry, guilty, sorry Nick).

"I think I should tell the Dean," Nick said.

"Are you crazy, dude?"

"It's the right thing to do." It was, and it was the only thing that could put this whole thing behind him. He had sinned, and he should pay the price.

"Are you crazy, dude?" Dylan repeated with rising panic. "If the Dean tells the cops, and the cops arrest you or whatever after all this time—maybe the statue of limitations is up—then what do you think will happen?"

"Statute of limitations."

"Whatever. The Marines probably won't want you. They don't just take anyone, you know. The Marines are an *elite organization*," Dylan said passionately.

It was the most emotion Dylan had ever displayed in a speech, and it brought Nick up short. He hadn't even considered that the Marines would not want him. It would be, truly, the end of the life he had been dreaming about with Dylan since the seventh grade. He buried his face in his hands. "What am I going to do?"

"You're going to join the Marines with me, right?"

"Yes."

"Then you know what you're going to do, or rather, what you're not going to do. I vote with your parents on this one."

Nick had created a complicated mess.

Why, why, why had he not given those things away? He had planned to get rid of everything in his footlocker for months now. He had thought about cutting up all the credit cards and disposing them in the large dumpster behind Fry's—after soaking them in acid to remove any trace of the numbers to protect their former owners from identity theft. He had looked up the nearest Goodwill where he could donate the wallets and the watches. Wouldn't poor people applying for jobs need a good wallet and watch? He thought he could take the cross to a jewelry exchange, and with the money he got from selling that, he could put it in the collection plate at the pretty Christian church on Lincoln Avenue, the one with the stained-glass windows that lifted his spirits every time he drove by there on the way to SCDS.

He had done none of those things.

"Shit, there's Melissa." Dylan slid down in his seat. "Duck!"

Nick did. "Why are we doing this?" he whispered, since the situation seemed to call for it.

"I don't want her to see me," Dylan whispered back.

"Why not?"

"It's complicated."

"I thought you broke up with her for good a few weeks ago?"

"Easier said than done. Every time I go over there to break up with her, we end up having sex, and then she gets her hopes up all over again. It's a mess. I still like her a lot, but I don't want to be tied down when we enlist."

Nick did want to be tied down, with Jennifer. However, after he told her what he'd done, he doubted that she would ever want to see him again. He mentioned this to Dylan.

"Are you crazy, dude?"

"I'm getting a little tired of you calling me crazy," Nick said.

"Sorry, man, but sometimes, you know, you're too honest. You're a very honest person."

"Except for the stealing."

"Yeah, aside from that." Dylan grinned. He slid slowly up and peeked out the window. "The coast is clear."

By the time they finally got their food—indeed it was a trainee working the drive-thru window—Nick was no longer hungry. He was going to have to tell Jennifer. They had vowed to be totally honest with each other after their miserable three-week breakup. The more he thought about it, the more he wanted to get it over with, and the sooner the better. "Would you drop me off at Jennifer's?" he asked Dylan.

Dylan cast him a sidelong glance. "You sure, dude?"

"I'm sure," he said. In fact, he wasn't sure of anything these days.

When Jennifer opened her front door, her pleased look of surprise vanished when she looked into his face. "What's wrong?"

"I need to talk to you." He was so nervous that his hands were shaking. He thrust them into his pockets. "Would you take a walk with me?"

Always practical, Jennifer said, "It looks like it's going to rain. Let me get an umbrella."

After she found an umbrella, which seemed to Nick like it took hours, and they had walked down her sidewalk, she said, "So, are you finally going to tell me what's been bothering you for the last few days?"

He told her everything, every agonizing, shameful detail. Like Dylan, she did not interrupt him. "I can totally understand if you don't want to be with me anymore," he finished, close to tears.

"You were trying to put Corey's ring *back*?" she said.

"Yes."

"You stole all those things before you knew me?" she said.

"Way before. I wanted to be a better person after I got to know you."

Jennifer raised her eyebrows at that sappy sentiment. "Now that you've told me everything," she looked to Nick for confirmation and he nodded, "does this mean that I'm an accessory to a crime?"

Nick said he didn't know.

"Why did you tell me?"

"Because I wanted to be totally honest with you."

"*Honest?*"

He felt a deep, reddening blush. "With you."

"I don't know what to do with this information," she said.

"I'm so sorry," he said, which was the understatement of his life.

It started to sprinkle, and Jennifer opened the umbrella. "Move closer to me, Nick. You don't want to get wet."

He was grateful for her small gesture of kindness. "Do you want me to leave you alone for a little while?"

"No."

"Do you want me to leave you alone . . . forever?" he choked out.

"No."

He was relieved but confused. "What do you want to do?"

"I wish you'd never done those things."

"Me, too."

"But you did."

"Yes."

"However, you would never even *think* about stealing anything ever again, right?"

"Never!"

"I do have to tell you that I'm disappointed in you."

"You should be."

"But I'll get over it."

"Thank you." He was overwhelmed with relief. He took her hand. "Thank you."

"I was way off," she said. "I knew something was bothering you, but I had convinced myself that you were fretting about giving me a promise ring, that you were afraid to give it to me. How silly of me."

He squeezed her tiny hand. "I'll give you a promise ring." He would give her anything she wanted. He wasn't exactly sure what a promise ring *promised*, but he could always ask Loretta.

"What in the hell is she doing here?" Sam said as Chris drove to the Biltmore Hotel.

"I told you everything I know. She's staying one night, then she's off to Vegas." Chris wondered how Louise could afford such an expensive hotel and vacation. Since she said she had given most of her money to Dorothy's delinquent grandson, how in the world could she afford this?

"She made a miraculous recovery from her heart attack," Sam said sarcastically. "She sure is one tough old broad." This she said with a very slight hint of admiration.

"Louise will live to be two hundred."

"Out of spite," Sam said. She shifted uncomfortably on the seat. She had tried to hide her grimy cast with a rainbow-colored sling.

"Look at the bright side," he said, turning into the parking lot because there was no way he was going to pay for a valet, "she's not staying the night with us."

"Thank God."

He, too, was thankful that Louise wasn't staying with them. However, it did sting a little that she didn't want to see where her only son, her only child, lived. In fact, she hadn't even mentioned coming to their house at all. Wouldn't a normal mother want to see where her child lived, even if that child was in his fifties? "I just remembered something else she said. She said she had a surprise for us."

Sam perked up at this. "Do you think that Louise is actually going to give us a gift?" She shook her head. "That doesn't sound like Louise at all."

"No, it doesn't," he agreed. Louise had never been, nor would ever be, a gift-giver. "We can do this with a smile on our faces. It's only cocktails."

"Only cocktails. The old bitch is too cheap to buy us dinner."

"You and Louise are not capable of sitting at the same table for the duration of a meal," he said. They had proven this in the past. The two women in his life either screamed at or completely ignored each other. Either way, it was a painful process. He would try his best to mediate, but ultimately, each woman would want him to choose her side. Ninety percent of the time, he had sided with his wife, which infuriated his mother. It was a lose/lose situation.

They made their way through the opulent hotel, whose claim to fame was that it had accommodated numerous presidents, and arrived at the back bar. It was dim, but he could make out his mother at a small table near the window. She sat in a velvet maroon wing chair, white hair perfectly styled, regal as a queen. He walked over to her, bent down, and kissed her cheek. "Hello, Mother."

"You're late," Louise said.

"We're right on time," Sam said, perching herself on the edge of the seat of a facing chair. She was probably posing herself for a quick escape, as she always did when she was around Louise.

Louise looked at her gold watch. "I said 5:00. It's 5:03."

The watch looked expensive and new. "We're sorry, Mother."

"Three minutes is hardly late," Sam said.

Louise sniffed. "In my day, people were punctual." She pointed to Sam's cast. "What have you done now, Samantha?"

"I had a motorcycle accident," Sam said.

Chris laughed hollowly. "She's joking, Mother."

"People on motorcycles drive like maniacs," Louise said. "And most of them don't even wear helmets. In my opinion, they deserve to be hit."

"That's a terrible thing to say," Sam said.

"Mother, Sam did not have a motorcycle accident," Chris quickly interjected. "We don't even, and have never, owned a motorcycle. She fell off a ladder while painting the nursery."

Louise rolled her eyes. "That baby thing."

The cocktail waitress arrived to take their drink order It was perfect timing in Chris's opinion. Sam ordered her usual chardonnay, he ordered a scotch and soda, and Louise ordered a vodka martini. This, too, was new.

"Make that two vodka martinis," she said before the waitress left.

"Two, mother?" He had never seen his mother have more than one drink during "cocktail hour," as she called it.

"Are we becoming a bit of a lush, Louise?" Sam, of course, had to say that.

"I'll ignore that remark, Samantha," Louise said sternly. "I have a perfectly good reason for ordering two martinis. We have another guest joining us."

His mother did usually travel to Vegas with another woman—what was her name? Gilda? Really, she was getting too old to do this. He had pointed this out to her for years now, and her response was always the same: "I'm not dead yet." What he did not point out to her was the irony of the whole thing. His mother, the paragon of frugality, liked to vacation in Las Vegas. It made no sense whatsoever, but then again, Louise was a maddening woman of contradictions.

"Here he is," Louise said brightly. She sounded almost, but not quite, girlish.

Chris looked up to see the small, bald man from the hospital shuffling towards them. Mr. Peterson. His mother's boyfriend. He looked over at Sam, who was trying hard not to giggle. She arched her eyebrows at him and mouthed, "I'll be damned."

No kidding. He stood up to shake the old man's hand and introduce himself and Sam.

"This is Mr. Peterson," Louise said.

"You can call me Jimmy," the old man said. He had youthful eyes in his heavily wrinkled face.

"You can call him Mr. Peterson," Louise said firmly. "Sit down, James."

He obeyed. "Forgive me for being tardy," he said. "I had to phone my daughter to tell her the news. She lives in Atlanta. She has two boys. They just bought a new Chevrolet, and boy, did she hear it from me! I'm a Ford man myself."

"We have an old Saab," Sam said, smiling. She was going to thoroughly enjoy this whole scenario, Chris knew.

"No offense, Miss Samantha, but it is much better to buy American. Americans should buy American. That's what I say."

"Yes, sir, support America. That's what I'm going to do from now on. And I promise you, Mr. Peterson, that the next car I buy will be a Ford Taurus." Sam's smile had grown even wider.

"That a girl!" He took a drink of his martini. "I like this one," he said to Louise.

Louise sniffed.

"What did you do for a living?" Chris asked. The old man was likable. What did he see in his mother?

Mr. Peterson gave a rambling story of serving in the military, the odd jobs he had held (including as a train conductor, in his youth), and how he had finally ended up owning a hardware store in Chicago, eventually expanding it to twenty hardware stores across the metropolitan area. This explained the Biltmore and his mother's new watch. The old man must have money, and this was probably his mother's attraction to him.

"Mr. Peterson and I have an announcement to make," Louise said finally.

"The surprise," Sam said, nodding.

"It's a humdinger." Mr. Peterson reached for the nut bowl on the center of the small table. "A real humdinger."

Chris suspected what the announcement was going to be, but he couldn't believe it. His mother was eighty-five!

Mr. Peterson held a handful of nuts and reached for his mouth with his other hand.

Louise leaned towards him and hissed, "Do not dare to take out your teeth, James. We are in public."

"Yes, dear." He patted her hand.

Louise straightened up. "Mr. Peterson and I are going to Las Vegas to get married. We are eloping at the Little White Chapel of the Dessert tomorrow evening at six o'clock sharp. We thought you should know."

Sam couldn't stifle her laughter any longer. "Congratulations!" she sputtered. "That's wonderful news. We could drive up to Vegas tomorrow and be there."

"We are eloping, Samantha. There will be no guests."

"You two make a lovely couple," Sam, of course, could not resist saying.

"Elvis is officiating at the ceremony," Mr. Peterson said.

"That's enough, James."

"It was my idea. I always liked Elvis. I visited Graceland in the summer of '83, or was it '84? Elvis was a true American—until he got abducted by aliens."

"That's enough, James."

Chris got up and gave his mother his dutiful son peck on the cheek. "Congratulations, Mother. I hope the two of you will be very happy." The old man probably wasn't lucid enough to know what he was getting into, but what the hell? Maybe he could make Louise happy in her final years. (It would be a first.) Maybe Louise wouldn't steamroll over him. (It was doubtful.)

"That was fabulous," Sam said in the car on the way home. "I can't believe that Louise found someone to marry her at her age. Actually, I can't believe that anyone would marry Louise at any age."

"People get lonely," he said in a feeble attempt to be loyal to his mother. "Even Louise."

"I guess so." Sam started to giggle yet again. "You're going to have a new step daddy, honey! Maybe he'll take you fishing, or to a ballgame."

Chris couldn't help himself any longer. He started to grin. "Maybe my new step daddy will help me with my stamp collection."

Sam held out her left hand and started to shake it in imitation of the old man's palsy. "He could help you build model cars."

"Maybe my new step daddy will leave me money in his will."

"Maybe so, if you're nice to him!"

"But I doubt it," Chris said as he turned into their driveway. "He'll probably leave his money to be used as ransom to the aliens. He'll bring Elvis back!"

That one really cracked up Sam.

It was his first drink in twenty-three days, and it burned going down, burned with rage and bitterness and disappointment. How could things get any worse?

"I thought you knew," Chuck Cornwall, his friend in the U of A admissions department said. "I assumed that Nick decided to go to another university when he didn't send in his acceptance form. As you know, that happens all the time."

"Right," Jack said. It was becoming increasingly clear to him that he didn't know jack shit about his son. First, about the stealing. Second, about this. Really, how could things get any worse?

He and Chuck sat in the bar at the Mountain Shadows Golf Club, surrounded by other soggy golfers who had been forced off the course by a sudden, freakish thunderstorm. Jack was glad for the rain, for the interruption. His golf game had gone to hell after Chuck had said casually, "So, Nick decided to go to another school? I thought he was one hundred percent on Arizona."

There was no way that Jack could hide his astonishment. He had seen his son mail in the acceptance form, hadn't he? He had been right beside his son as they stood in front of the mailbox and ceremoniously dropped the letter in the slot, hadn't he? They had gone out for a celebratory lunch of burgers and fries and talked about what curriculum Nick should pursue and about the cross-country team and Nick had been smiling and enthusiastic . . .

No, none of that had happened. It was the scenario he had wished for and dreamed of, but it had not happened. Nick had said that he would take care of mailing in the form, and he had trusted his son—he had no reason not to, at that time—and he had been thrilled that Nick had finally given up on the idea of joining the Marines. He had only seen what he wanted to see. He had only believed what he desperately wanted to believe. He had been a fool, and it was too late for Nick to apply anywhere else. Jack had only had his son apply to one school, exactly what he told his students not to do, exactly what Walter had done. No, Jack wasn't a fool; he was a raging idiot.

"Where's Nick planning to go?" Chuck asked.

Jack shrugged. "You know."

"A lot of choices, huh? Good for him."

"Yes," Jack said. He and Chuck were reasonably good friends, but there was no way he was going to tell him that Nick, the son of a guidance counselor, a student at a prestigious college prep school, wanted to join the Marines. There was no way in hell.

"Did I mention that my younger daughter got accepted at University of Chicago Law School?"

Chuck had mentioned this at least ten times that afternoon. "Congratulations," Jack said. He was going to need another drink. "Let's get another round."

"No, not for me." Chuck finished his beer and pushed away from the bar. "I've got to make the most of my time with my grandson while I'm in town. Did I mention that he's walking, and he's only eight months old! He's going to be a corker, that one. I see a future Wildcat sprinter in his future."

"You can tell he'll be a future sprinter at eight months?" Jack said drily.

Chuck's hearty laugh shook his large belly. "I dote on that boy, I really do. Just wait until you're a grandparent. You'll know what I mean then. There's nothing else like it." Chuck seemed to have forgotten the fact that Jack's children were only eighteen and sixteen.

"For the time being, I'm going to have to take your word on it." Jack usually liked being around jovial Chuck, but not today. Today, Chuck had been the bearer of extraordinarily bad news. Chuck had enlightened him to the fact that, in all probability, his son would not be going to a four-year college in the fall.

"Tell Nick no hard feelings on his choice of schools, although tell him he made the wrong one. Haha."

"Sure will," Jack said.

Chuck laid a twenty on the bar. "I'll buy, just to show you there are no hard feelings. Haha."

"Haha," Jack echoed weakly as Chuck left the bar.

He started to signal the bartender for another drink, but then thought better of it. He didn't need another drink. He wanted one, but he didn't need it. He was stronger than that. He didn't need AA; he could do this on his own. He had, though, looked up nearby AA meetings. He had even driven past the one at the church on Shea Boulevard just as it was convening, the parking lot crowded with cars. At the last minute, he had decided not to go. What if he thought it was bogus, a waste of time? What if he ran into someone he knew?

When he got home, Alex was lying in bed, reading a book that was propped up on her burgeoning belly. He told her that Nick had not sent in his acceptance form to Arizona, that it looked like their son had no chance of going to a four-year university in the fall. He paced back and forth at the foot of the bed, waiting for the anger to build, waiting for the emotion that had been his constant companion for the last six months to course through his veins. It didn't come.

"It's not the end of the world," Alex said calmly.

He had expected her to burst into tears.

"There's always the possibility that he could apply in the spring. He could work more hours and save some money. Maybe he isn't ready. Maybe it would be a good thing for him to wait."

He sagged onto the edge of the bed and took her hand. "We planned on him going in the fall, just like all the other SCDS students." He felt exhausted, drained. Is that what happened when rage burned out, when you had been misguided by the wrong feeling, when you had wasted too much time embracing hostility?

"I know, but it's obviously not what Nick wants."

"He doesn't know what he wants."

"He thinks he does."

"He's only eighteen."

"Didn't you think you knew what you wanted when you were eighteen?"

Of course he had. He had wanted to go to college to escape his small town. He had wanted to get the hell out of Dodge and do something useful with his life. "Things were different then." Somehow, at eighteen he had been so much more mature than kids at eighteen were now.

"Not really."

She wasn't behaving like she formerly would have in this situation. Perhaps it was the baby that had transformed her into this Madonna role. Perhaps it was something else. "Have you been talking to Sam?" Even with the mention of her name, he couldn't arouse the familiar anger.

She ignored that, probably because it was so obvious that she always talked to Sam. "I've been thinking. Maybe we wanted him to go directly to college because it would be safe for him. Maybe we wanted him, theoretically, to be safe for a little while longer. Even though there's no guarantee of that. Unfortunately."

"Unfortunately." Ideally, he and Alex had wanted to keep their children safe forever. They were like all parents in that respect, and what was wrong with that? Nothing. Nothing, except for the fact that it was impossible.

Alex reached up tentatively and stroked his cheek. "Our problem is that we're already having a hard time letting him go."

Her touch felt so familiar, so dear, even after all these months. "He has three months before he graduates, and we're having premature, letting-go issues." He nestled his cheek into her palm. She was right. Their first-born wasn't a little kid anymore. He had been wrong to treat Nick like he was too young to make his own decisions, and he had been wrong to try to strong-arm his own opinions onto his son. And he was sick and tired of the fighting, both verbal and internal, the impasses, the effort of trying to hold onto—what? His stubbornness? His damaged pride? He didn't have the energy to keep going in his solitary, possibly misguided, direction. He needed to *let go*.

"About the stealing," he said. He didn't want to bring it up, but they might as well get everything out in the open.

"I hate the thought of it. I hate the fact of it. But I've decided to trust Nick—"

"To do the right thing," he finished.

"Yes."

Everything she said made sense. Without thinking, he climbed in next to her and took her in his arms. He felt a tranquility settle over him that had been gone for too long.

"I've missed you," he said, holding her tighter, "and I will always be in love with you, no matter what." That, too, made perfect sense.

"Here," Carla said as she pointed the flask toward Annie. "Take a sip."

"I can't drink. I'm pregnant." And she already felt like she was going to puke. Really, she could taste the vomit at the back of her throat.

"I'd say there's a touch of irony in this situation, considering as how we're sitting in my Beamer in front of an abortion clinic."

"Planned Parenthood."

"Well, according to the protesters, this is an abortion clinic." Carla waved the flask in the direction of the placard-carrying group milling around the front door: Abortion Is Murder, A Fetus Is Human, God's Will Be Done. "You need a drink to calm your nerves. Hell, I need a drink to calm my nerves." She took another gulp from the flask and handed it over.

Annie obliged. What did it matter at this point? She was going to walk through that mob and be jeered at, be judged. Would they throw tomatoes or Bibles at her? Would they tear at her hair and clothes? Would they curse her into eternal damnation? Was Walter in eternal damnation because he had committed suicide?

Abortion Is Murder.

(She wondered what Georgia would say about this. She wondered if Georgia had ever had an abortion.)

She was barely sixteen, and apparently, extremely unlucky. She didn't even have her driver's license yet. She couldn't have a baby!

"I can't go through with this," she said. "I can't walk through that mob."

"That mob is four elderly women who have nothing better to do on a Saturday morning. The two of us could take them on if we had to." Carla took another drink. "Which we won't," she added.

Funny. It looked to her like there were four *hundred* of them. "I'm scared." That was the understatement of the year. She was scared to *death* and had been ever since she peed on that damn stick. If she hadn't, maybe the whole thing would have just gone away, although Carla had pointed out many times how absurd that thinking was.

"You can do this, Annie. You *have* to do this." Carla was being her supportive self, the role she had adopted since the beginning of the *fiasco*, as they called it.

"I'm starting to understand that whole coat hanger thing," she said, shuddering.

Carla shuddered, too. "Annie, that is just *gross*. Women do this every day. It's legal. It's a woman's right to choose."

"That's just it. I'm not a woman. I'm a knocked up sixteen-year-old *child*." A child who did not want her mother with her at this particular moment. A child whose mother would not be disappointed, would not be crushed. A child whose mother would be DEVASTATED at this *fiasco*.

"Twelve-year-old girls in Appalachia have children every day. Hell, in polygamist sects in Utah, men impregnate their twelve-year-old *daughters*," Carla said with shaky authority.

Annie frowned at her. "Why are you talking about twelve-year-olds?"

"Sorry. I guess I'm getting off track. The truth of the matter is that I'm scared, too. Fucking terrified. But what other choice do you have?"

None. Nada. Zilch. Except for that fleeting, insane notion that maybe she could give the baby to her aunt Sam, she could not think of any other option, since there was no way ever that she would tell her parents about this. No. Way. Ever.

They would be DEVASTATED!

"Let's go over your story one more time."

Annie drew a trembling breath. Carla, through Tom her driver, had somehow managed to come up with a fake ID. "My name is Jackie Drewer. I live at 5908 E. Cholla Lane, Scottsdale, AZ. My birthdate is 01-23-91, which means that I am eighteen. I am eighteen and am legally entitled to an abortion, so here I am."

"Don't say that last part," Carla advised.

"Right. I won't say that 'legally entitled' stuff."

"Actually, why don't you let me do the talking? I'm a much better bullshitter than you. I've had a lot of practice with the parental unit, as you well know."

"That's just stupid, Carla. Why would my sister do all the talking? And that's another thing that's bothering me. We don't look anything alike. Won't that make them suspicious?" She was stalling. It was almost one o'clock, time for her appointment, and she did not want to go in there.

"Good point. I can be your cousin from Connecticut. I did used to live there, after all." Carla applied lip gloss.

This was a new, irritating habit of hers. She applied lip gloss a hundred times a day with methodical strokes, as if lip gloss were important. Who the hell cared about lip gloss—the brand, the color, the shimmer of it—when there was war and famine in the world? Who should give a shit about lip gloss when your best friend was miserable and pregnant and scared to *death*?

"I know. I can be your step-sister. That would work. I'm Rachel Carns, your step-sister."

"I think I should do my own talking." She really didn't want to have to say anything at all, but the seconds were ticking rapidly toward her appointment time, and she did not want to get out of this car. She wished she was superglued to the seat. She wished that Walter would magically show up and whisk her away (if he wasn't eternally damned, and she really hoped he wasn't).

Carla looked at her slyly, smiling. "We can say you're a mute."

"How humorous of you." She was going to throw up; she just knew it.

"I'm trying to lighten the mood here, but I guess that's irrelevant, isn't it? If you get stuck, Annie, just stand there and cry."

"That shouldn't be any problem." She tasted bile, and the tears were there, on the verge of falling. She blinked rapidly.

"We need to go in now," Carla said gently.

Annie didn't move.

"I'll come around and get you, and I'll hold your hand." Carla got out of the driver's side and walked around to open the passenger door. She reached for Annie and pulled her with force to her feet. "You can do this. You can do this."

No, I can't. No, I can't. But she let Carla lead her to the door. The angry mob of four parted, but a gray-haired lady, the one carrying the placard with *Abortion is Murder*, hissed, "You will be sorry, young lady. You will be very, very sorry."

"Shut up, you old bitch," Carla said.

She propelled Annie through the door, and they landed in a silent waiting room dotted with women of all ages and all shapes and all sizes. In unison, or so it seemed to Annie, they all looked up at her with wide, tired eyes, then they returned to their magazines, their books, their phones, their knitting. Annie stared at the knitting woman. It looked like she was knitting baby booties, but that could not be possible, could it? That would just be too . . . *surreal.*

Carla led Annie to the front desk. "This is my step-sister, Jackie Drewer. She has a one o'clock appointment," she said to the large, redheaded woman seated there.

She looked at them with a bored, knowing glance. "Fill out this medical history." She handed Carla a clipboard and pen. "Have a seat. I'll call you when the counselor is ready to see her." She gave Annie another once-over, then went back to her computer.

Carla led Annie to a seat by the window. "So far, so good."

"I have to see a counselor?" Annie whispered.

"Did I forget to tell you that?"

"Yes." It was, of course, Carla who had made the appointment, Carla who had gotten the fake IDs. Where would she be without Carla? Well, for one thing, she wouldn't be *here*, and she didn't know whether it was a good thing or a bad thing. "I don't know if I can face a counselor. If she's anything like Georgia, I'm afraid I'll cave. I'm afraid I'll tell her everything." (Not everything. Never *everything*.)

"No, you won't. It's just a formality. They want to make sure you're not psycho or mentally unstable or something along those lines. At least that's the impression I got when I made the appointment." Carla bent over the clipboard. "When was your last tetanus shot?"

Psycho? Annie sometimes thought she was. The *mentally unstable* part was all that Annie's bile needed. "I need to use the restroom." She barely made it into the stall before the onslaught. She heaved and heaved and heaved until there was nothing left. And yet she still felt nauseated.

She was at the sink, rinsing her face —no need for makeup when you're getting an abortion!—when the slender blonde walked in. She looked to be in her early twenties, stylishly dressed in Seven jeans and black stilettos. Her tan arms were covered from wrist to elbow in gold bangles.

She gave Annie a sympathetic look. "The first one is the hardest."

"First one?" What did she mean?

"Yeah, it can be pretty rough. But then you know what you're in for when you put your feet in the stirrups. You know what I mean?"

Annie was finding it hard to breathe. "So, you've had more . . . been here before?"

The girl was staring at herself in the mirror, pulling her waist-length hair into a ponytail. "This is my fourth, and I swear that it's my last." She gave a rueful laugh. "I swear. Alcohol trumps condoms every time I go to Minx, the nightclub in Old Town. You ever been there?"

That was the last straw for Annie. She didn't want to be pregnant, and she certainly didn't want to have a baby, but being here was Wrong with a capital W. She could not go through with it. She. Could. Not.

As she dashed through the waiting room, a nurse was calling for Jackie Drewer. "We're leaving," she said to Carla, and she didn't pause until she was at the Beamer.

"But Annie, this is your only—"

"Please!" Annie yanked on the locked door.

"Okay, okay." Carla unlocked the door and got in.

Annie got in and slammed the door. Not only was she crying, but her nose was running. Her entire face was an unsightly water feature.

"Where do you want to go?"

"I don't care. Just drive."

"We could . . ." For once, Carla seemed to be at a loss for words. "We could go get a pizza or something." She started the car and squealed out of the parking lot, barely missing a pedestrian, a mother pushing a stroller.

It was one more thing to put Annie over the edge, the sight of the young mother and the baby with its chubby legs. "I don't want food. I want to drive away from this *fiasco*!"

Carla was driving fast. She liked to drive fast; she always drove too fast. She had already accumulated several photo radar tickets for speeding. "You mean," she looked at Annie, "you want to do what we've talked about?"

"That's right," Annie said. She was still hopelessly crying. "Thelma and Louise."

"Surprise!" Sam's voice was the loudest of all the neighborhood women she had gathered in her family room. And it was a surprise. She had managed—against all odds—to keep this surprise baby shower a secret from Alex. It hadn't been easy either. She had been so excited to do something nice for her sister that she could barely contain herself. Even when Alex had been rather bitchy towards her two days ago when she said that Sam needed to quit putting her hands all over her belly, Sam hadn't retaliated by saying, "You're going to feel terrible when you find out that I have planned a party in your honor, you bitch." No, she had refrained from saying anything that would give away this surprise.

Alex didn't look surprised, and the expression on her face could best be described as irritably pissed off. "What's going on here?" And then she saw the "Baby Shower" banner and the pink and blue balloons and the mound of presents on the coffee table. "Oh, it's a baby shower." She smiled weakly. "Really, you shouldn't have."

"Who needs more wine?" Sam said with enough enthusiasm to cover for Alex's lack.

"I'll take another glass, although I probably shouldn't," said Amanda Williams.

"I'll open another bottle," Sam said. It would be Amanda's third drink, and Sam was beginning to think she was something of a lush. This new discovery made Sam like her better, or rather, it made her tolerate her better.

Alex followed her into the kitchen. "Sam, I mean, really, you shouldn't have."

"Isn't this great?" Sam got another bottle of La Crema chardonnay out of the refrigerator. Chris had thoughtfully opened the bottles before he escaped the house, since she wouldn't get her cast off for another week. He was not going to be happy when he got the credit card bill from Bev Mo, but she had thought, what the hell, it's a special occasion, a baby shower for a woman who was carrying a baby for her twin sister. It was indeed a cause for celebration!

"Really, Sam, you *shouldn't* have," Alex repeated.

Sam thought she knew what Alex was getting at. "Don't worry. It wasn't any trouble at all. I enjoyed planning this shower. Can you believe it? I usually abhor doing things like planning a party, but not this time. It's something I really wanted to do for you. And believe me, it was murder trying to keep it a secret! You know what a blabbermouth I am." She lowered her voice, just in case the women in the other room were listening. "And I practically had to bribe Amanda to keep this secret. She is the worst gossip I have ever met!"

"There is no need—"

"I know you hate surprises as much as I do, but this really is a noteworthy event in both our lives, don't you think?" She took in Alex's slacks and maternity top. Thankfully, she had on a decent one today, even though it had an old-fashioned Peter Pan collar. "And don't worry about how you look either. You look *fine.*"

"Sam—"

"Let's go join the party. Everyone I invited came. Can you believe that?" Technically, Sam had asked Amanda to invite the other women, since she didn't know their street addresses, their telephone numbers, or their email addresses. But that was a minor point. "I think these women really like you, Alex, and I—"

"Sam! Would you let me get a word in edgewise? What I'm trying to say is . . . don't you think this situation is a little . . . awkward? In a sense, you're giving *yourself* a baby shower. Am I supposed to open the presents and then hand them to you?"

Sam laughed gaily. She had only had one glass of wine, but it had gone straight to her head. "Of course I thought of that! Once again, stop worrying! Wait until you see how I took care of the situation. Believe me, honey, this shower is for *you!*"

"You look great, Alex!" said Rosemary Carter. "You haven't gained much weight. When I was pregnant with Raymond, I was a horse! Gained sixty pounds! Do you know if it's a girl or a boy?

"No—"

"It's so nice to have something to celebrate in the gloom and doom of this economy, isn't it?"

Since Sam knew—via gossip whore Amanda—that the Carters were losing their home to foreclosure, she wanted to steer the subject back to the matter at hand, the party. "You need more wine, Rosemary!"

"I'd like to thank everyone for coming," Alex said. "This is very nice of you."

Good, Sam thought. Alex was going to *do the right thing*, the phrase she was so fond of these days, and be gracious.

"When's your baby due?" gossip whore Amanda asked.

"*My* baby," Sam said. The next time she filled Amanda's glass, she would give her the cheap wine from the box in the refrigerator.

"June 6th."

"Have you picked out names for the baby?" Greta Udall asked Alex.

"*My* baby," Sam said. "And I'm leaning towards Jordan and Madeline."

"I love the way babies smell," Crystal Walker said dreamily.

All the women concurred: The baby smell was the pinnacle of happiness! And then there were their baby stories, each and every woman there, each and every baby they had borne. It went on and on.

It was no wonder that she didn't hang out with these women, Sam thought, as she passed around the miniature quiches and stuffed jalapeño peppers and Chinese spring rolls that she had bought from Costco. They had absolutely nothing interesting to say. Even she—who talked, thought, and slept babies—was practically yawning with boredom. A person could stand only so many labor stories laced with vaginal tears and epidurals.

However, and Sam felt a little twinge at the realization, all the women seemed happy as they enjoyed each other's company. For this particular afternoon, they were all on the same page. She had never experienced anything like it in her own social situations, and she wondered how this personality deficit could happen to her and not to Alex, her identical twin sister. In Champaign, she had had acquaintances, but most of those had been either a colleague or the spouse of a colleague of Chris's. Her "best friend," if she used that term loosely, was their gay florist with whom she went shopping on occasion. She had dressed better back then, with his help, but the shopping expeditions had been erratic, maybe once every three months, and then he and his partner moved to Key West. She had been sad, but not all that sad. She hadn't bothered to replace him with another "best friend."

Come to think of it, it had always been like that. Even though most people would view Sam as the "stronger" twin—perhaps because she was louder, or bossier, or less nice, whatever—that wasn't necessarily true. When she and Alex were children, it had been Alex who would make an overture to a new girl in their class. It had been Alex who would invite friends over for sleepovers and afternoon sessions on their backyard swing set. In high school, it had been Alex who made arrangements to go to the mall with other girls, and in college, it had been Alex who insisted they go to frat parties and bars to meet people. She had wanted to go to these parties, too, but she would have been content to drink beer and stand in a corner with Alex. But with Alex, they had become the boogie-woogie twins, dancing on tables and livening up a party. It had always been *with* Alex. Together, they were an invincible team.

And then Alex had gotten married. She had really tried to be happy for her sister, but to her, it was more like a painful divorce. They had to decide who got the electric rollers, the curling iron, the blue turtleneck they both adored, who got the wok, the silverware, the space heater, the hamper from the furnished apartment they shared. Perhaps out of pity, Alex let her keep the framed picture of their childhood dog, Zigzag. It hadn't helped, not at all. After Alex pulled away from their apartment with Jack, their rented van loaded to the ceiling with all the crappy collegiate possessions they owned, Sam had cried on and off for weeks. She could still remember the pain and panic of feeling so utterly abandoned and alone.

"You'll find your own man," Mother had said, which is not what Sam wanted to hear at that point. Eventually, of course, she found the right man, but still . . .

"I feel the same way," Alex had said during a tearful phone call one night at the beginning of their separation. "I miss you terribly!"

But Alex could never understand. Alex had been the one to leave.

No one at the baby shower seemed to notice that she had been silent for quite some time. Not only did they not know her, but also, she got the feeling that they didn't much care for her. Well, that was all right. She didn't much care for them either. Besides, at forty, it was just too exhausting to try to make friends, to go through past history, to have to listen to recollections of childhoods, schooling, jobs, lovers, and families, and then be expected to share the same. It was hard to find the energy for that routine, and now that Alex lived across the street, she didn't have to. She could "know" these women through association with Alex.

"It's present time!" she finally said. The presents were the point of the party, after all, and she was going to have to shake off the gloomy reverie she had fallen into. This party was to celebrate the baby. This party was to celebrate Alex, her twin sister, who had come back to her in the most generous way possible. Together, they would have a fresh start, a new beginning.

"Open mine first." Amanda thrust a silver-wrapped package at Alex. "I just adore what I got you. I thought about keeping it for myself, and we all know that means it's a good present!"

The other women laughed appreciatively, too loudly.

Sam was thinking that last call should have been about an hour ago.

"This is too much!" Alex carefully unwrapped the gift, sliding her finger under the tape slowly in order to not rip the paper, in order to save it for some future gift, just as their mother used to do.

It was maddening. At this rate, they would be here—these *neighbors*—would be here for hours. "Just rip the damn thing open," Sam said.

"Let her take her time," Greta said sloppily. "I, for one, am in no hurry to get home and start dinner."

The sentiment was chorused by the others.

The wrapping paper finally released from the gift, Alex held what appeared to be a shoebox on her lap. She opened the lid and drew out a stiletto sandal with pink pom-pons on its bridge. It looked like something that Zsa Zsa Gabor would wear in the fifties with her expensive dressing gown, or perhaps, what a man's fantasy mistress would wear as she waited for him in the condo he'd bought for her. "Wow," Alex said.

"Are you kidding?" Sam said. What the fuck was that nincompoop Amanda thinking? A feeling of dread washed over her. She should never have trusted that stupid woman to take care of the invitations.

"I had to ask Jack what size shoe you wore. The other day, when he was trimming your front bushes. He looked at me like I was crazy, but of course I couldn't ruin the surprise. A size seven, right?" Amanda looked like she wanted to snatch the shoes out of Alex's hand and parade around the room in them.

"A size seven. Right." Alex looked at the shoe like it was a foreign object. She had never worn anything like it in her life. "I'm sure Jack will like these." Jack would think they were as ridiculous as she did.

"That's the idea! Just wait until after the baby is born and you have your figure back. Aren't they a hoot?"

"Amanda," Sam said, trying to remain calm. "I said *cookware*, not *footwear*."

"Ahh . . ." It was the sigh of dawning recognition from all the women in the room.

"I did think it was a little odd that we were supposed to bring shoes," Rosemary said. "But then, it's quite a unique situation here. I've never been to a party for a surrogate mother before, so I thought maybe shoes were an appropriate gift."

"I thought maybe it was a fetish party." Greta hiccupped. She noticed the others staring at her. "Not that I've ever been to one of those before," she added hastily.

"Who wants a bunch of pots and pans?" Amanda said. "I could spend my life shopping for shoes."

A smile twitched at the corner of Alex's mouth. "I think shoes are a perfect gift. A woman can never have too many!"

And so it went. Ten pairs of shoes were opened: running shoes, slippers, flip flops, ballet flats, etc., *ad nauseam.* Amanda had done an excellent job of spreading the word *footwear.* From Sam, Alex opened a black Cuisinart blender, and Sam was gratified when Alex's "wow" was heartfelt.

Really, she later told Alex, she had specifically said *cookware,* and Amanda knew it, which meant that Amanda Williams was a siliconed, collagenous, dyed, bulimic, botoxed bitch.

Nick, Jennifer, Dylan, and Melissa sat on the topmost bleacher in the SCDS gym, but they weren't really watching the basketball game below.

"You guys don't need to be here," Nick said. It was hot in the gym, but that was not why he was sweating.

"How many times do I have to tell you, dude? We're your backup, your reinforcements, your buds. But dude, I hope you're not making a tactical error." Dylan sat on his right side.

Tactical error. It seemed like Dylan, suddenly, for no explicable reason, was getting smart, or at the very least, his vocab was improving. It was scary; Dylan might be right. However, Nick's mind was made up. He couldn't sleep at night, and he knew he didn't want to live with a bruised, rotting spot on his conscience.

Sitting on his left side, Jennifer said, "We support your decision." But she, too, had expressed doubts. She didn't want Nick to get kicked out of school.

He didn't want that either, but a person needed to own up to his actions, take responsibility, and so forth and so forth. Hadn't his parents drilled that into him from the time he was born? Wasn't that *the right thing* to do? And yet, his parents were retreating from this whole thing, acting like it never happened. He knew they didn't want to tell the school about his stealing because they were protecting him, but that was not a good enough reason for Nick. In fact, their protection of him was rapidly becoming a disappointment to him. And it was a sad thing, to be disappointed in your parents. And it was a sadder thing because it was his fault. (Guilt, guilt, guilt. It could eat a person alive.)

"I'm hungry." Melissa sat on the other side of Dylan.

Dylan sighed. He hadn't wanted to bring Melissa, but he hadn't been able to "shake her off," as he told Nick. Dylan was still having a very hard time "shaking off" Melissa. "Why don't you go get some popcorn?"

"I can't. I'm on a diet," Melissa said. Melissa was always on a diet—not that you could tell. Still, she had a pretty face.

"Go, Eagles," Dylan said without enthusiasm. "Dude, your team sucks."

"We never have a very good basketball team," Nick said. "They try, though."

"All brains and no brawn."

"Look who's talking," Nick said. Dylan—the polar opposite of Melissa—was having a lot of trouble gaining weight.

"It's my metabolism. I think I'm hyperallergenic or something."

Just when he thought Dylan was getting smart . . . Somehow, this made him feel better, like things could get back to normal, be like they used to be.

"Maybe you have a hyperactive thyroid," Jennifer offered, "although I think you might be too young for that. I can ask my dad if you want me to."

Dylan stared at her blankly before saying, "Nah, it's okay."

"I really am hungry," Melissa said.

"I'll go with you to the snack bar." Jennifer stood up. "I'm too nervous to just sit here anyway, waiting for Dean Whittaker to show up. Come on, Melissa, maybe they have something healthy, like an apple or carrot sticks."

"I really want popcorn." Melissa followed her down the bleachers.

"Dude." Dylan shook his head as he watched Jennifer's petite form being followed by Melissa's, which was—not. "Dude," he repeated.

"I wonder why he's not here yet." Nick craned his neck to the spot where Dean Whittaker always sat, on the first bleacher, just to the right of the team bench. It was empty, reserved for him.

"Maybe he's not coming, and we can forget the whole thing," Dylan said hopefully. His greatest fear was still the impact that Nick's confession would have on his ability to join the Marines. "It's in the past, dude. Give the stuff to charity like you were going to do anyway, and call it a day." This was his familiar refrain.

Nick was not going to do that. What if some of the guys he stole from wanted their stuff back? It only seemed fair to give them first option on their own belongings. "He'll be here. He comes to every game. His son is the point guard." Nick nodded toward the frail blonde dribbling the ball.

"He's missed every shot. I'm beginning to wonder if he can even *see* the hoop."

"He's going to Stanford in the fall," Nick said, as if that explained something.

"Big deal." Dylan yawned.

"It is around here, Dylan. You know that. It's like my dad's crowning achievement to get a couple of kids into Stanford, or Harvard, or Yale, or any Ivy League school each year. You *know* that." His voice was sharper than he had intended.

Dylan looked at him. "Sorry, man. Sensitive subject." He went back to watching the game for a few moments, then said nonchalantly, "Still no Big Discussion?"

"I don't think there's going to be one." It was eerie, really. His dad had said to him a few days ago that he had golfed with the admissions director at U of A. Nick's heart had dropped to the floor, expecting the worse. His dad looked at him a long time and said, "Your mom and I know," and then he walked away. It was as simple as that—no argument (Dad), no crying (Mom), no pleading (both). Nothing. For a couple of days, he had waited for the bomb—The Big Discussion—to happen. He hadn't tried to avoid it, not at all. He hadn't tried to stay away from the house by going to Dylan's or Jennifer's or trying to get more hours at work. He prepared himself to take his punishment like a man, but there was nothing, no hint, no out-and-out confrontation, no reproach. Nothing.

In a very, *very* weird way, this was disappointing, too. Didn't they care anymore? Of course they did. He knew that. But it seemed to him that they were way too old to change their parenting patterns now. So what had changed? Well, for one, his mom and dad seemed to be talking to each other now, which was good. His dad wasn't drinking, which was good. And his dad was no longer sleeping on the couch. (Good, but he didn't want his mind to go there).

The girls came back with popcorn. "Don't you say a word," Melissa said to Dylan. "Not one word."

Dylan threw his hands up in the air. "I surrender!"

Jennifer offered Nick some popcorn. "He's still not here, and it's almost halftime. Maybe you should take that as a sign? I still don't think it's right to tell him about this at a basketball game. It seems inappropriate."

"I don't want Dad to know, so I thought this was my best chance." The offices of his dad, the head of the upper school, and the dean were all in the same wing of the administration building. Say he was sitting in a chair outside the dean's office, waiting for his appointment to tell the dean, and his dad came out of his office, which was right across the hall. What would happen? His dad would know immediately why he was there because why else would he want to talk to the dean? Then his dad would probably try to dissuade him from doing it. It had been stated by his parents more than once that they did not want Nick to leave SCDS with a *tarnished* reputation.

"Why don't you text the man, dude? It's a great way to get things out in the open without having to do a face-to-face. Know what I mean?"

"Yeah, it's a great way to communicate—if you're a chicken." Melissa looked pointedly at Dylan, who was always "breaking up" with her via text.

"That, too, would be inappropriate," Jennifer said. "Besides, old people aren't very good at texting. They would rather you call them."

Before Nick could respond—he wasn't going to either text or call—the buzzer rang for halftime, and Dean Whittaker walked into the gym. Nick's mouth went as dry as a cotton ball, while at the same time his underarms did double duty in the sweat department. (There was absolutely no balance to his bodily secretions at this moment.) "He's here." His eyes followed the dean as he made his way to his seat, said a brief hello to the coach and team, and sat down.

"What now?" Dylan asked.

Nick had no idea. Oh sure, he had rehearsed what he was going to say: "Dean Whittaker, I have a confession to make. Do you remember the stolen items from the locker room awhile back? Well, that was me. I am very ashamed and penitent for what I have done, and I would like to make restitution to the—he exchanged "victims" to "fellow athletes"—and the janitor who was fired because of my inappropriate behavior." It had taken him hours to come up with this statement, which he thought was concise, to the point, brief. But looking at the man, the head honcho of SCDS, who was actually slightly built, like his son, and seemed friendly enough, the words lodged in his esophagus. How could he go through with this? He could jeopardize his entire future, he could ruin his life, and he could hurt his father's reputation.

But he *had* been a thief. He stood up.

"You going in, dude?"

Nick nodded and swallowed (tried to—his throat was so dry it was more like a paroxysm of the larynx).

"Remember, we've got your back."

"Good luck." Jennifer looked close to tears. "I love you." She squeezed his hand. "I'll be waiting for you when you've done what you have to do."

This was a battle he had to endure. He wished he could march down the bleachers, but his legs had a mind of their own. They transported him down the metal bleachers slowly, one painful row at a time. It seemed to take an eternity to get down to the gym level, but unfortunately, he was eventually standing in front of Dean Whittaker.

"Dean Whittaker, can I speak with you for a second?"

"Nick! How's it going with you?"

The seat was empty next to the Dean. "May I sit down, sir?" It was part of his strategy to be polite, polite, *polite* to show that he was a *reformed* thief.

"Sure, sure." He patted the seat.

Nick sat. "Sir, I have—" What was the first sentence of his speech? It had been a good one; he knew that much.

"Are you still running?" the Dean prided himself on not only knowing every student on campus, but also knowing a little something about them.

"Yes, sir. I mean, the season is over, but I still run to work and things like that."

"It's difficult to believe that graduation is just around the corner. Where are you going to school next year?"

"Well—"

The band chose that moment to begin the school song. The band always played at halftime—he knew that—but Nick had been too preoccupied to notice them in their regular section of the bleachers.

"I'm sorry. I couldn't hear you. That Delvin Mitchell is a fine trumpet player, but a little *loud*." He leaned closer to Nick.

The Eagles and the opposing Trojans chose *that* moment to run back onto the court, thundering the gym with bouncing basketballs.

"Dean Whittaker, I have a confession to make." Yes! That was it.

"You're going to Kansas State?"

"No, I have a *confession* to make!"

"And where is that?" the Dean yelled.

Maybe he would have better luck if he soldiered on to the next sentence. "Do you remember the stolen items from the locker room awhile back?" he shouted into the man's ear. Someone was testing the P.A. system: "Testing, one, two, three."

"I'm having a hard time hearing you, Nick. I'm just getting over a cold, and my ears are blocked up!"

"It was me! I stole those things!" And it was at *that* moment the band ended its rousing, raucous rendition of "Hail to the Alma Mater."

Jack wasn't much of a cook, but he was doing his best. He had a couple of chicken breasts and potatoes baking in the oven, and he had made a rather anemic salad from what was in the refrigerator—a half head of lettuce, a stalk of celery, one tomato, an onion. To cloak his feeble attempt at dinner, he had set the table with the good china and found a couple of candlesticks in the back of the pantry. The candles were another matter. Finally, after searching and searching, he had found two stumps in the junk drawer, one green and one white, and plopped them in the candlesticks. He wondered why Alex hadn't tossed them away, but he was glad she had not. Maybe it was a sign? He fervently hoped so.

Jack was nervous as hell. Things had been going so well between them the last week, and he was grateful to have her back. After the way he had behaved, he didn't deserve her, but that was Alex: forgive and forget. At least he hoped that would be the case tonight. He *fervently* hoped so.

He had decided to tell her, to come clean. After all these years of living with the guilt, it was time to let go, to wipe the slate of smudges. It had happened so long ago, and maybe it wasn't really a big deal at all. Maybe she would even think it was funny. But Jack didn't want any more secrets between them. He would tell her it was because of that event (meaningless, really) that he had *reluctantly* agreed to this absurd surrogacy plan. He would make her see that, in a way, it was an exchange of what—foibles? Two rights make a wrong, that kind of thing.

So, he would start with that incident and then tell her about the casino, kissing Cookie, and the financial mess they were in. The economy was to blame for some of it, but it was mostly his fault. He could probably rush through this part (meaningless, really), but he would underscore how everything was related, the result of wrong decisions made hastily and drunkenly. He was going to tell her everything. He owed it to her. She would understand, and they could go on without secrets or blame.

He really wanted a drink. The half-empty bottle of scotch was still in the pantry. He knew he should throw it out, but it was comforting to have that safety net. And he had been sorely tempted after finding out about Nick not sending in his acceptance form to U of A, so tempted that he had actually gone to an AA meeting and sat through the stories of hitting rock bottom: waking up and not knowing who you were in bed with, leaving your children in the car while you drank in the bar, falling drunk down a stairway and breaking both legs. He wasn't *that* bad, he thought, although he had to admit that the meeting had helped. He had not poured a drink. One day at a time.

He heard the front door open, and it was Alex. "Yoo-hoo! Anyone home?" she called out gaily.

Show time. "In the kitchen," he said. She sounded like she was in a good mood, which was definitely in his favor.

She carried two shopping bags. He thought she had gone over to Sam's. "You went shopping?" How could that be? Both credit cards were maxed out.

"No, Sam gave me a surprise baby shower! It was really great. All the old Bunco gang was there."

His confusion must have shown on his face.

She laughed. "It's not what you're thinking. They didn't give me—or Sam, I guess—baby things. They gave me *shoes*. It's funny when you think about it. Sam told everyone to give me cookware, and Amanda told everyone to bring footwear. Isn't that a riot?"

That would explain why Amanda had asked him Alex's shoe size. He had so much on his mind that he had immediately forgotten all about it.

Alex saw the set table, the stumpy candles. "Oh, Jack! You fixed dinner? What a perfect ending to this day. I love it."

"I thought we could have a romantic dinner. It's been a long time." So far, the evening was going just as he had planned.

"Where are the kids?" Always, Alex was in automatic mother mode.

"Nick's at a basketball game. Annie went to the mall with Carla."

"You let her go to the mall with Carla?" Alex's voice had more than a hint of reproach.

"She's been cooped up in this house for weeks now, she's going to therapy, and her teachers told me that her grades are improving. Come on, Alex. We have to cut her some slack every once in a while. She's just a kid." He refused to get defensive and spoil the mood. Annie had been following the rules to a T. She needed a break. "She even called and said they'd decided to see a movie. She'll be home at nine."

"Well, okay," Alex said slowly. Then she brightened again. "Should I dress for dinner?"

"My lady can do anything she wants to do, but her dining companion is wearing what he has on." He gestured grandly at his jeans, then wondered if he should have put on a nicer shirt. "We're only having chicken," he added. "I am not a formally trained chef, madam."

"You can make up for that in other ways," she said, smiling.

Oh, did he love her!

She rummaged in a shopping bag and produced a pair of silver stilettos with pink pom-pons. "Courtesy of Amanda."

"No surprise there," he said.

Alex tried to bend down and put them on, but she couldn't get past her belly. She waddled to the kitchen table. "So much for the sexy/slutty effect. I'll have to sit down to put these on."

She had gotten suddenly so much bigger in the last week or so. It had happened like that with Nick and Annie, too. Of course, this wasn't his child. But he was not going to go there, not anymore. "Dinner is served," he said.

They toasted their meal with sparkling apple cider, and Alex raved compliments about the barely adequate meal that was absolutely tasteless. They chatted about inconsequential things—should they paint the powder room?—and Jack tried to gather his courage to say what he had to say. How could he bring the subject nearer to what he must say? Blue versus beige paint was nowhere close.

They were almost done when he had an idea. "What should we do for our anniversary this year?" It was in May, only six weeks away, so it seemed like a plausible question.

"I haven't even begun to think about it yet." She smiled and squeezed his hand. "How about Mary Elizabeth's at the Phoenician? I hear it has wonderful cuisine and a fabulous view. I could wear my pearls and tiara."

She was joking, of course. It was one of the most expensive restaurants in town, and the bit about the pearls and tiara . . . It almost brought tears to his eyes, and he choked on his last bite of dried chicken. He would probably never be able to afford an inferior strand of pearls. She deserved more.

"Hey, you were supposed to laugh." She squeezed his hand again. "A repeat of tonight would be perfect."

A repeat of tonight. She had no idea. He swallowed hard. He didn't really have to do this. It could stay buried forever. That would be the easy way out. However, she needed to understand why he had allowed her to sleep with another man to have her sister's baby, even though it knifed him through his heart. She needed to understand why he had behaved as he did. *She needed to understand his shame.*

"Maybe we could celebrate it later, after the baby's born?" Alex said. "We could go camping or something."

Now was the time. "Do you remember your parents' twentieth-fifth wedding anniversary?" His voice was a croak.

"Of course I remember! What a party that was. I think everybody in Fairview was at the American Legion that night. Mother almost had a fit that alcohol was served, but then again, she had no say in the matter because Daddy's golfing buddies threw the party." Alex giggled at the memory.

"There was a lot of alcohol," he said. Way too much. All the warning signs had been there.

"As I recall—and I can't really recall everything—you, Sam, and I were no slouches. We were only a year out of college, and we still drank like college students. I had the worst hangover of my life the day after the party."

"We were all really drunk."

"*Wasted,* as our daughter would say," Alex said dryly.

"Something happened that night." He just had to get it out, fast, before he lost his nerve, before he let the fear of what he would see in his wife's eyes stop him. "You wanted to go home, demanded to go home, and I went in the coat room to get our coats. Sam was already in there—just as drunk as the two of us—and something happened. I don't know how it started, or who started it."

"Started what?" Alex had gone very still. She was breathing shallowly.

"Kissing."

"You and Sam made out at our parents' anniversary? We were *married.*"

He didn't look into her eyes when he continued. "Yes. But it was more than that. One thing led to another . . . groping . . . fumbling . . . she gave me . . . oral sex."

Alex spoke slowly. "You got a blow job from Sam, at my parents' anniversary, after we were married?"

"Yes."

"And the two of you have kept this from me all these years?" She stood up. "You always told me that you've never cheated on me." Her voice was still deathly calm.

"I didn't count that as cheating. It was your sister—"

"Which makes it worse."

"And we were drunk—"

"No excuse."

He finally looked into her eyes and saw what he had so feared: a hollow haunting of disbelief, the beginning of betrayed trust, the reflection of his shame.

His stuttered words tumbled out. "I am so sorry, Alex. I wanted to tell you years ago, and then I didn't, and then time passed, but then with this surrogacy thing and you sleeping with Chris. I thought maybe it would make up for—compensate for—what I had done." He wished she would throw one of those pointy-heeled shoes right at his forehead.

She just stood there, staring at him.

The phone rang, and he jumped up. He had to get away from those hollow, haunting, betrayed eyes. "I'll get that," he said.

"You do that." Alex turned toward the stairs. "And then *get out*."

11

CHAPTER ELEVEN

Shock. Alex had been walking through the last couple of weeks in a hazy, bitter cocoon of shock. In a way, it was comforting, this isolating cocoon. Without daring to think about the recent turn of events, she could just put one foot in front of the other and waddle toward the next task. And she was waddling, no doubt about that. At the seventh-month mark, she had instantaneously *inflated*. She could be the model for a poster advertising the whale exhibit at Sea World. Or a hot air balloon ride. Or a Sumo wrestling match. Or she could be the Fat Lady at the carnival: Come one, come all! Make fun of obesity and human deformity. It's entertainment, folks!

She could be a poster woman for what she actually was: a betrayed wife, mother, and sister, a stupid, blind-sided idiot who had given everyone she loved the benefit of the doubt over and over and over and over again. And what had that gotten her? Loved ones who carried on behind her back; loved ones with more secrets than the CIA; loved ones who obviously thought she was not caring enough or intelligent enough or *worthy* enough to share in their lives. What had Annie called her a few months back—it seemed like a lifetime—a Pollyanna? Well, that was what she was. Let's call a spade a spade. (Was that a racist expression, or did it refer to cards these days? You couldn't flip through the TV channels without seeing some damn poker game.) Let's face facts. Let's get down to brass tacks. She was a betrayed, stupid, blind-sided, idiotic *Pollyanna*.

Look at the bright side, Alex, she told herself. The kick-in-the-gut revelations had been swift, delivered in one-two-three-pointed cowboy boot jabs. First was Jack's confession that her twin sister had given him a blow job. (Actually, that should count as two kicks, shouldn't it?) The next was that the ringing phone had delivered the news that their daughter had been in an accident and was at the ER at Scottsdale North. The third was that Nick had walked in just as they were rushing out the door and delivered the news, as the three of them sped to the hospital, that he had been suspended from school. Perfect timing—no, make that *impeccable* timing—all three revelations had pummeled her within five minutes. Her family scored! They rocked! They pulled the proverbial rug out from under her feet in five minutes flat. They turned her world upside down. And it was only the beginning.

She, Jack, and Nick rushed through the doors of the ER. "My daughter, my daughter," was all she could gasp.

Jack supplied Annie's name. Nick took her arm and led her to a sickly green plastic seat. She had no idea how long it was before a nurse led them to a curtained cubicle. There she was, her beloved daughter, a bandage over her swollen, blackened right eye, a morphine drip attached to her child's thin wrist. She looked impossibly young and small and still under the blanket.

"Annie," she said. "Can you hear me?"

"How did this happen? Where did this accident happen?" Jack seemed to be having a hard time looking at Annie or comprehending the situation. He concentrated his gaze on the heavy-set nurse.

"I don't know the details about the accident, Mr. Carissa, but the doctor will be in soon to update you on her condition. And then I believe that the police would like to have a word with you."

"I think that's normal," Nick said. He stood at the end of the bed, staring at his sister. "The police, I mean. The police always go and question people in the hospital on *Law and Order.*"

"Can she hear me?" Alex said.

"She's sedated, ma'am." The nurse swished out.

She knew her daughter was sedated. Of course she knew that. It was obvious. All she wanted to know was if her daughter could *hear* her.

Minutes . . . hours . . . and the doctor pulled the curtain and walked in. He, too, looked impossibly young, no more than late twenties. When, exactly, had people in authority positions become younger than her? When had that happened?

He was curt, brief, obviously a man in a hurry. (Alex resented this.) Her daughter should take precedence over the other patients. Her daughter was special. Her daughter should be given the best care the hospital could give, damn it!

"She has a mild concussion and some bruised ribs. We would like to keep her overnight for observation," the hurried young man said.

"She's going to be all right?" Jack asked in a strangled voice. (Alex could not, would not, look at him.) "She'll be fine?"

"She'll be fine—sore for a couple of weeks and some swelling on the face, but she will make a full recovery. She's young."

Relief flooded Alex. *Everything would be all right!* She still believed that at the time, good old Pollyanna Alex.

"However," the doctor looked at his clipboard, "about the baby—"

The baby? Why would he be asking about the baby? Alex was emotionally battered at the moment, unquestionably, but the baby was fine. As if to prove the point, the baby gave a rousing kick. "I'm fine," she said to reassure the doctor. She patted her gigantic belly. "I'm fine."

The doctor seemed to notice her for the first time and took in her condition. "I mean," he looked again at his clipboard. "Annie. She lost the baby." He put the damn impersonal clipboard in the pocket hanging at the foot of the bed, done, prepared to leave this patient and go on to the next.

"Wait a minute," Jack's voice was now hoarse. "Do you mean to say that Annie was *pregnant*? That's not possible."

The young doctor looked at him quizzically, or was it with a touch of pity? "Indeed it is—was possible." He had to retrieve the clipboard once again to ascertain who he was speaking to. "Mr. Carissa."

Stricken. That was the word that would describe Alex at that point. *Stricken.* Was that the exact moment when the numbing, bitter shock took effect, when the synapses of her brain went into premature menopause so that she no longer had the will to comprehend the full extent of everything that was going on around her?

Possibly, but there was more to come, much more.

The next day, they brought Annie home and settled her in her room. She wasn't talking and wouldn't respond to questions. Why didn't you tell us you were pregnant? Who was the father? What were you doing with Carla on I-57 headed towards Flagstaff? Why were you driving the car? Jack had found out from the police that Annie had been driving. She was ticketed for driving without a license. Carla was ticketed for underage drinking. Of course.

Through the interrogation, Annie remained mute. (Shock? Probably. Join the club. It was *the* happening scene right now in Alex's familial sphere.)

"I'm calling Georgia," Jack said. "And then I'm going to kill the little prick who got her, got her—" He couldn't spit out the word.

"Good. Fine. And then you can *leave*." Calling Georgia was the best idea she could come up with, too, and personally, she wouldn't mind if he strangled the little prick who had taken advantage of their sixteen-year-old daughter. It had to be something like that. Annie had been taken advantage of. After all, she didn't even have a boyfriend!

"I'm not leaving now, Alex. Now, more than ever, we have to stick together as a family, and we are going to stick together as a family." The couch in the den was again his bed.

The day after they brought Annie home from the hospital, Nick further explained his situation: "I went to the Dean and told him everything because it's the right thing to do." (There was going to be no reprieve from the escalating shock.)

Yes. But.

"Dean Whittaker suspended me for ten days. I guess that's two weeks of school, which we both thought was pretty fair. Dean Whittaker's a fair guy."

Yes. But.

"And I need to make restitution to the guys I stole from, notify them and apologize and everything—they're kind of spread out across the country—and then I need to apologize to the janitor. Dean Whittaker pointed out that there was no way I could personally compensate him for his lost wages, so I asked the Dean if he'd hire old Mr. Kowolski back, and he said he would. I think that's the best part of the whole deal. Mr. Kowolski gets his job back. I'm going to help him out for the rest of the school year, cleaning classrooms after school and things like that, which I also happen to think is extremely fair."

Yes. But.

"I guess I have to tell you the downside, Mom and Dad." Nick took an excruciatingly long breath. "During the weeks I'm suspended, I'm going to miss some major exams in all five of my classes. That means I'm going to have to do really well the rest of the semester—I mean, *ace* the finals—in order to graduate in May."

Oh. *No!*

"Jennifer has already said that she'd tutor me, and she's a really smart girl She takes all AP classes, so I'm hoping I can pull this off." Nick looked from his dad to his mom. "You guys are creeping me out, just staring at me like that. Aren't you going to say anything?"

"What happens," Jack cleared his throat, "if you don't ace the finals?" He did not mention the rest—and don't graduate. And he did not mention the fact that Nick was a solid B/C student.

"Well, the way I see it, I could always take the GED."

Alex gasped. Her son might not graduate from high school? He didn't want to go to college right away, she had come to terms with that, far more so than Jack, but she had never considered that he might not graduate from high school. It was unthinkable.

"Or I could go to summer school," Nick added quickly. "That's probably what I would do, go to summer school. Right?" He looked back and forth at the two of them and shifted his feet. Was he looking for some type of approval?

It was too late for that. Even though she knew that he had done the right thing, as she had hoped he would, she couldn't feel any pride in the situation. How many people at SCDS already knew that dependable, responsible Nick Carissa was a thief? Unsavory gossip traveled at the speed of light at the school, and the faculty was just as bad as the student body in circulating trash. Would Jack feel as if he had to resign because of embarrassment? Well, who the hell cared what Jack did anymore?

"Uh, Dad, I have some money saved from working, but I might need to borrow a little to pay everyone back. I want to do it as soon as possible. Dean Whittaker said the sooner I could put this behind me, the better. He really is a nice guy—I mean, man."

"How much?" Jack asked warily.

"I'm only short about eighty dollars. I thought it would be a good idea to pay for the price of the wallets, and watches, and cross, with interest. You know, punitive damages, or something like that. Dean Whittaker agreed."

The amount didn't sound unreasonable to Alex, and Dean Whittaker had made an excellent point. They needed to put this whole thing behind them. "That sounds—"

"We'll talk about this more later," Jack interrupted. "Alex, can you come with me?" He nodded toward the den.

She was not going to go anywhere he went, not if she could help it. "No, I've got laundry to fold."

"Alex."

"No."

"Alex, please, this is important."

His face was flushed, and he had a film of sweat on his forehead. Was he having a heart attack or something? (Remember, Alex, she reminded herself, you don't give a damn anymore.) She hesitated.

"Alex, I wouldn't, at this particular point in time, ask you if it wasn't extremely important. Please."

"Two minutes," she said as she led the way to the den. What the hell. The way things were going, they couldn't possibly get any worse. As usual—as was becoming the norm—she was dead wrong.

Jack closed the door and went to his desk. He pulled out a stack of papers and waved them before her face. "These are our credit card statements from the last six months."

"Are you accusing me of spending too much money?" That was laughable. She'd done her best to stretch the stingy budget he had put them on. She scoured the grocery store ads for the best deals on everything, and last week, she had gone grocery shopping at the Walmart Supercenter. You couldn't get any cheaper than that. Thanks to Jack, she had become a professional cheapskate, the queen of the bargain basement.

"No, I'm accusing myself." He handed Alex the stack of papers.

She glanced down, and her heart started to pound erratically. In stark black and white, she saw cash withdrawal after cash withdrawal—$200, $400, $200, $500—from the same place: Casino Arizona. She rifled through the papers, and they were all the same. Her husband had thrown away thousands of dollars gambling. All those nights that he had told her he was going to a board meeting, or to a school function, or to play poker with the "guys," he had been out at the filthy casino wasting their money.

"You piece of shit," she said flatly.

"Yes," he said.

"How much credit card debt?" Why had she not paid more attention to their finances? Because she had *trusted* this piece of shit for almost twenty years. She didn't even know where to look on the statement to see the final, awful number.

"$20,000." He couldn't look her in the eye when he said that.

$20,000. It was impossible that they could be in that much debt. What had happened to the money from Sam and Chris? She started to ask but stopped. She already knew, didn't she? Some went to the Lexus that was too extravagant for them, and the rest went into the ravenous gullet of some fucking slot machine.

"Is there anything else you feel the need to share with me, since you seem to be on a mission to *clear Jack's conscience?*" Her voice still sounded flat, remote. She was still as a stone, except for her womb. The baby had the hiccups.

Oh, yes, there was more. Why should she be surprised? He told her about a woman poker player with the idiotic name of Cookie. He had kissed Cookie on one drunken night, but it didn't mean anything. She had gotten the wrong impression from that kiss and had called him repeatedly—remember that phone call in the bedroom?—but he had ended it. It meant *absolutely nothing.*

By the end of this confession, Jack was sobbing, sobbing, sobbing in a very unmanly way. "I'm so sorry, Alex. I'm so sorry about everything."

She wanted to cry, her eyes ached to shed tears, but she could not. She was too devastated; no, she was too *tired.* Her daughter, the former *druggie,* had been in a car accident and had lost a *baby,* her son was a *thief* and had been suspended from school, and her husband was addicted to *gambling* and *drinking* (why not throw that in too?) and messed around with other women, including her *twin sister,* every nineteen years or so. Yes, that pretty much summed things up.

Except there was more. Sam was sitting at her kitchen table. She should never have given her a damn key. "What do you want?" Alex said curtly.

"Hello to you, too, sister. You've ignored my phone calls and texts for the last two days. What in the hell is going on around here?"

Alex put her hands on her hips—what little hips she had left—and said, "You want to know what the hell is going on around here? I'll tell you what's going on around here. *Hell* is going on around here. Annie was in a car accident."

"Oh, my God!" Sam's hand flew to her throat.

"And she lost her baby."

"She lost her—" And then the realization hit Sam. "Oh, my God!"

"Nick went to the Dean and told him everything, and he is suspended from school, which means he might not graduate in June." She was firing off these horrific facts calmly, as if she were reading from the parents' manual entitled "How NOT to Raise Your Child."

"Oh, my—"

"Knock it off. I'm not done yet. My husband has gambled away all our money, and then some, and apparently, you treated him to a blow job at our parents' twenty-fifth wedding anniversary."

The color drained from Sam's face. "Oh, Alex, that was so long ago, and we were both drunk, and I wanted to tell you so many times, but I was ashamed and afraid that you would never speak to me again." She gulped for air.

"I'm getting fucking tired of people being afraid to tell me things." She was getting used to this flat-toned voice that sounded as if it belonged to someone else. "And apparently, you should be glad it happened. It's the reason why Jack *allowed* me to fuck your husband and become pregnant with this child. Don't you see? It was karma; it was fate; it was the most perfect blow job in the world."

"Oh, Alex." It was Sam's turn to cry.

Really, when Alex thought about it, Sam cried *a lot*. She cried more than enough for the two of them. "Go home, Sam. The sympathy department formerly known as Alex has shut down for the day."

And it had been shut down since then, shocked into this hazy, bitter cocoon. She put one swollen foot in front of the other as she did what she was supposed to do. She mechanically cared for her daughter and son, ignored her husband as best as she could, and slogged through the remains of her life. She did, however, take time out to hold a brief funeral for Pollyanna.

There were no mourners.

The Thelma and Louise adventure had started with high hopes, but inevitably, it had been doomed from the start. The adrenaline rush of leaving town, of going somewhere, of being *free*, had been curtailed by nature.

They made it a mile from Planned Parenthood before Annie said, "I have to pee."

"Again? You just went back there."

"I threw up back there. Now I have to pee." It was a symptom of pregnancy, she had read, the constant urge to urinate.

"Well, okay. We need some gas, and I need to get some money out of an ATM." Carla ran over the curb as she turned too early into the Shell station.

Annie had to get a key from the attendant inside for the privilege of using the filthy, paper towel-strewn restroom. When she returned, Carla was staring at the pump. "Do you know to work these things?" Carla asked. "I always have James fill up my car."

"Your town car driver's name is Tom, Carla." It was a miracle, really, that Tom hadn't slapped Carla around by now. She treated him like shit most of the time.

"Whatever," Carla said, still staring at the pump with a look of total perplexity.

Annie took the credit card from Carla's hand, swiped it, pressed the appropriate buttons, and began fueling the car. "Even I know how to pump gas, Carla." Nick had shown her how on one of their first excursions—before he flatly refused to ride with her. "There's an ATM inside."

Annie was sitting in the car when Carla returned with bags of candy and chips and a map. "Sustenance," she said, tossing the bags in the backseat. She spread the map out over the steering wheel. "Where shall we go on our excellent adventure?"

"I kind of thought we'd just drive, you know, and see where we end up?" Thelma and Louise hadn't had a destination, had they? And then she remembered that they had. They were trying to get to Mexico without going through Texas, or something like that. "Let's just get moving." Already, her resolve was weakening, just a little. She was still pregnant, but she didn't want to dwell on that. She wanted to get going, roll down the windows, and let the breeze blow through her hair. She actually had hair now, though it was very short, the same as Carla's.

"Why don't we head up to the Grand Canyon? I've never seen it, have you?"

"Yes. It looks just like every picture you've ever seen of it. It's very photogenic." She had seen it every time her family went camping up north, and frankly, she thought it was a little on the boring side. You stared at it awhile, oohed and ahhed, and then you were done.

"Well, I'd like to see it," Carla pouted. "It's one of the seven natural wonders of the world."

"What are the other six?"

"How the fuck do I know?" She took a sip from her flask. "Damn. That's the last of it. Maybe we should go by my house and pick up some more?"

"Let's just get *going*." If adventures were supposed to be spontaneous, they were already messing up this one.

"Okay, okay, but I'm driving to the Grand Canyon."

"That's what Thelma and Louise did, and you know how *that* turned out." In the final, vivid scene, trapped by a multitude of cops, they made a pact that they would not go back, held hands, Louise floored it, and they careened (well, it was in slow motion) over the side of the Grand Canyon.

"Good point," Carla said. She folded the map. "But let's head north anyway."

"Yeah, Flagstaff is a neat town, sort of bohemian." She had an idea. "We could go up there and take Route 66, you know, that historic road."

"Where does it go to?"

About this, she had no idea. "Across the country, the heartland—is that what it's called?—I think."

"Good enough for me. Let's roll!" Carla started the car and revved the engine, which caused them both to giggle uncontrollably.

They weren't laughing five minutes later when it was apparent to both of them that Carla wasn't in any great shape to drive. After she ran her second red light, Annie said, "I would prefer it if you didn't kill me before we've even gotten out of town."

"Sorry about that," Carla said. "It's like that last drop of vodka sent me over the edge or something. I'll stop at a convenience store and get a Red Bull to sober me up." She saw a 7-11 store a half block away and veered across two lanes of traffic, amidst a cacophony of honking, to pull into the parking lot. She was sweating. "Um, Annie, on second thought, I think you better drive."

"But I don't have a license!" She hadn't had the nerve to even *try* to drive since her failed driver's test. And then she found out she was pregnant, and getting a driver's license didn't seem too important in the grand scheme of things.

"I'm seeing double, Annie, which would be fucking fantastic under normal circumstances, but not such a good idea when you're driving in rush hour."

Rush hour. Just the thought of that made Annie's hands go clammy. She would have to get on the interstate, and she had never driven on the interstate. (As Nick had said once, "Annie, we value our lives too much to let you drive on the 101.") "Oh, God, Carla, I don't think I *can.*"

"Look, if you're old enough to get pregnant, you're old enough to drive. It's just a matter of confidence. I'll talk you through it, and you can go as slow as you want." Carla was already getting out of the car.

"I know it's a matter of confidence. And I don't have *any.*"

"Do you want to get out of town?"

"Yes." She couldn't go home now. She had crossed over some kind of *great divide,* and she couldn't go back. And she was still pregnant with Walter's baby!

"Then get behind the wheel." Carla, once again, had to practically drag her out of the car. It was *definitely* that kind of day. "Everything will be okay. Trust me."

With her hands clenching the steering wheel so hard that they hurt, she listened to Carla's directions and encouraging words: "You're doing a great job, Annie!" "Good peripheral vision!" "You're actually staying in your lane!" "That guy honked at you only because he's an asshole!" She was doing fine, she really was, until it was time to merge from the ramp onto the freeway.

"Okay, now you need to speed up a little to merge," Carla said soothingly. "If the other drivers are following the rules of the road—and if they're polite—they'll move over and let you in."

The other drivers were not polite. Annie wasn't sure what happened next, but she knew for a fact that she *freaked out.* The other car didn't move over, and there was another car behind her, and she slammed on her brakes, and they were knocked from behind, and spinning. And then everything went black . . .

The unfortunate part was that she eventually woke up, and then she had a lot of *explaining* to do. (She didn't mean "unfortunate," not exactly—she was glad she was still alive and all that—but how did they expect her to

answer all their questions when she couldn't explain most of it to *herself*?)
What were you doing driving on the freeway? Why didn't you come to us
when you found out you were in *trouble*? (Neither Mom nor Dad would
utter the word *pregnant*.) And of course, the real clincher question was:
Who got you in trouble? Both of her parents were under the assumption
that someone had taken *advantage* of her. She didn't dissuade them from
this notion. It was easier to melt into tears and shake her head mournfully.
This tactic, so far, had shut them up.

Really, she wanted them all to leave her alone, to stop hovering.

Yeah, right. Like that was going to happen.

Nick stuck his head into her room. "Let's go, kiddo."

"Don't call me that, moron." She was no longer a "kid." In fact, she
felt *ancient*. But Nick was the only one treating her with any normalcy, so
she should probably try to be nicer to him. "Thanks for offering to drive
me," she said.

"No problem."

In the car on the way to her appointment with Georgia, they couldn't
seem to find anything to say to each other. "You can change the channel
if you want," Nick said. He had on a country channel, which he knew she
despised.

"It's okay."

"Is it too cold in here for you? I could turn down the air."

"It's fine." She let her mind wander. What in the world was she going to say to Georgia? Georgia would want to know what she was *feeling*,
and she was doing her best to not have any *feelings* whatsoever. She wasn't
pregnant anymore, so there really wasn't any problem, was there?

"I guess we'll both be going back to school on Monday," Nick said.

"Ugh." She was trying her best not to think about that, too. How much
did everyone on that nosey campus know about her accident, about Nick's
suspension? (And Nick actually acted *cheerful* about going back to school.)
The only good thing about it would be that she would finally, after two long
weeks, see Carla. She knew that Carla was fine—her parents had told her
that much, at least—a few cuts and bruises but nothing serious. But she
hadn't talked to her since the accident. Somewhere along the way—the
accident, the hospital, her parents—Annie's phone had disappeared. She
knew instinctively that her parents didn't want her to talk to Carla; they
thought she was a bad influence on Annie. Little did they know: Annie

was a bad influence on *herself*. Maybe she could say that to Georgia, and they could spend the rest of the session dissecting that juicy morsel?

"Do you want to drive through Taco Bell?" Nick asked.

Just the thought of it made her mouth water. She adored Taco Bell, everything on the menu. When she had been—pregnant—she had tried to eat healthy foods, and it was boring as hell. Now she could eat anything she wanted! "That sounds great, but I don't have any money." She hadn't had a babysitting job in a long time. The word must be out in the neighborhood: Do not entrust your children to Annie Carissa. She's a *bona fide mess*.

"My treat."

"Why are you being so nice to me?" she asked. It was almost irritating, yet she was grateful, too. She liked her brother more now that he wasn't so seemingly damn perfect.

"Is there some kind of law against being nice to your sister?"

"Maybe there should be because if you're nice to me then I have to be nice to you." She couldn't help but smile at him. Nick also seemed to be better looking these days—almost handsome. Funny. She hadn't noticed that before.

Nick went through the drive-thru and they ate their tacos as they continued to Georgia's office. For some reason, the taco didn't taste as good as Annie remembered. In fact, she had a hard time swallowing the ground meat and cheese, which tasted something like mushy plastic. Maybe being—pregnant—had altered her taste buds? Hadn't she read that somewhere?

"When you were—laid up—I tried to think of a way to cheer you up," Nick finally said.

Annie didn't remember anything he had done that cheered her up while she was *laid up*. (Obviously, he was having a hard time with the "P" word, too.) He had brought her some hot chocolate once, and some Oreos.

"I went to see Carla. I thought maybe she would, I don't know, have a message for you or something like that."

"Really?" This news did cheer her up. "What did she have to say? Is she okay? Her parents are real nut cases, and it's hard telling what they will do—or probably *not* do—about her underage drinking ticket." She couldn't wait to hear Carla's version of what happened to her after the accident. She was probably livid because her parents went out and bought her a new BMW, or something like that.

"She wasn't there, Annie." Nick said quietly.

"Well, did you go back another time?"

"She wasn't there, Annie, because her parents took her to a boarding school in Switzerland. The maid told me, and I couldn't tell you when you were—laid up." He gave her a sympathetic glance.

"I don't believe it," Annie said. Carla couldn't have just vanished like that. There must be another explanation. Besides, and she knew this for a fact, Carla would never, ever leave her.

"That's what the maid said. I'm sorry."

"She'll be back," Annie said with confidence. "Carla will not put up with a bullshit boarding school—and that is a direct quote—for longer than ten minutes. I know she'll be back." After her session with Georgia, she would have Nick drive her to Carla's house. She would bet all her future earnings that Carla was already back home. She knew for a fact that Carla would never, ever leave her.

After a short, uncomfortable silence, Nick said, "So, we'll both be going back to school on Monday."

"You've already mentioned that sordid fact." She wrapped the rest of the taco in its paper sack. She no longer had any appetite. She was done with it.

"Yes, I know. It's taking me a while to spit out what I'm trying to say."

"Then just spit it out."

"Do you need any . . . help?" Nick was turning red around his ears.

She wasn't sure what he was getting at. "What kind of help?"

His blush was growing. "I mean, do you want me to talk to someone or do something else? Some guy . . ." Nick trailed off.

He couldn't be serious. "Are you asking if I want you to beat up—" She couldn't force herself to say the rest: *the father of my baby.*

"Yes." He was beet red.

"No." *Walter is dead. You can't beat up a dead person. And now his baby is dead, too.*

Nick cleared his throat. "Just thought I'd ask."

"Uh . . . thanks?" Annie wasn't sure if it was a situation that called for gratitude. She didn't like the picture that had come to her mind: Nick pounding Walter's urn (is that where his ashes were?) against a brick wall.

They arrived at Georgia's. "I'll wait for you out here," Nick said.

"You don't have to do that." A long walk home after talking to Georgia might be just what the doctor ordered. Haha.

"It's okay. My books are in the back. I'll use the time to study. As you know, I've got a lot of catching up to do." He smiled.

She gave him a shaky smile back. "I'll see you in an hour then." She was feeling jumpy and a little shell-shocked by their conversation, and she really didn't want to go in and face the all-seeing, all-knowing Georgia.

But there was no wait, no one in the reception area, so she went directly into Georgia's office and took her usual seat. "Hi, Georgia."

"Hi, Annie," Georgia said with a warm smile. "How are you today?"

Annie burst into tears. (Hadn't she known all along that she would do this very thing? Yes, yes, yes.) "Walter is dead. And now his baby is dead, too!"

Sam hated doing the exercises the physical therapist prescribed, but she did them diligently anyway. She had to get her arm strong enough to take care of the baby who would arrive in six weeks. Finally, after all the months—years, really—of waiting and hoping, she would hold her baby in her arms. She knew the baby was a boy, and she knew she should probably name him Christopher Junior, but she now had her heart set on a new name: Caleb. Caleb Connor. Maybe Caleb Christopher Connor? Yes, that was it, the perfect name for her perfect little boy.

Alex had not spoken to her in two weeks, the longest time they had ever gone without speaking. Alex was not just angry at her; Alex was livid at everyone, and it was understandable. Her daughter had been in a car accident and suffered a miscarriage, and Alex hadn't even known she was pregnant. Her son had been suspended from school for stealing, her husband had gambled away all their money, and then she found out about that long ago, drunken night at their parents' twenty-fifth anniversary. Alex had been bombarded with betrayal. Understandably, she was angry.

Well, Sam was angry, too—at herself. There had been so many times over the years that she had wanted to tell Alex about that night, but she was too ashamed of her guilt. Back then in the late 80s, she and Jack had had a flirtatious relationship. She had found him attractive and vice versa. Alex knew this and didn't mind; she certainly didn't want her twin sister to think she was dating an unattractive man. In college, if Sam didn't have a date, the three of them often went out together, usually to the campus bars. During the drunken walks home, Jack would walk between them with an arm flung over each of their shoulders. He would even kiss them both good night, quick pecks on the lips, and say how much he loved "his girls." It was all innocent fun, or so they thought. At the anniversary party, after Jack and Alex had been married and gone for a year in Arizona, they had pretended to have the same camaraderie, with the mutual flirting and sly glances. In the coat room, alone with Jack, Sam didn't remember how the kissing started, but she remembered Jack saying, "I want to make love to you." She wanted that, too, and she was ashamed to admit it, even now. Instead of doing the ultimate, unthinkable thing, she had given him a blow job.

It was so wrong on all levels. The only explanation she could come up with for her atrocious behavior was that she was jealous of Alex and Jack. That, combined with the horrible, lonely year alone she had just experienced, must have led her to that act on her knees. Oh, and the alcohol certainly escalated things to new deplorable heights. The next morning, all three of them staying at their parents' house, all three viciously hung over, she and Jack couldn't bear to look at one another because they were so guiltily ashamed. And things were never the same. She blamed Jack, and he blamed her, and now they could barely stand to be in the same room. They were civil to each other only for Alex's sake, only because she loved them both so much.

Or so she had.

Sam was at a loss. How was she going to make amends to her sister? How could she let Alex know how deeply sorry she was? And it seemed to Sam that she had spent a good part of her tenure in Arizona apologizing to Alex for one thing or another. Sam sent Alex an apology email. No response. She sent Alex flowers with an attached note saying, "So Sorry, Sam." No response. She sent Alex a long letter with multiple mea culpas. No response.

But two weeks was a long time to let something like this fester. Sam had tried to be patient, to give Alex space, to let Alex know that she, Sam, was wallowing in remorse. And she was wallowing. She woke up every day with a sickening dread in the pit of her stomach, a feeling that would not go away because things were not right with her sister. And along with the dread was a persistent, wretched anxiety. What if Alex was so angry with her that she wouldn't give her the baby?

That was impossible. She and Alex had made a pact, a promise, and they had never gone back on a promise made to each other. And they wouldn't this time either. However, her anxiety was not mollified when Chris said to her, "You need to go over to Alex's and get her to sign the contract I had a lawyer draw up." She hadn't known he had gone to see a lawyer, but she supposed it made sense in Chris's worldview. Everything was better if it was legally binding with a contract, etc., etc.

"Why?" she asked.

"I've done some research, Sam, and the laws in Arizona on surrogacy are strict. The birth mother is the one whose name is on the birth certificate and—"

She put her hands over her ears (literally, to hear no evil). "I don't care about the legalities! Alex and I made a promise, and we both know that it's my baby!" They had been going around and around about this for weeks now. Why didn't he just drop it? Why had he never tried to understand the bond she had with her sister?

"You're not being realistic, Sam."

"I've never been realistic. Why start now?" This might very well be the first time her husband had initiated one of her panic attacks.

Chris shook his head and tried another tactic. "Okay, how about this? *I* will feel better if we have Alex agree, in writing, to not sign the birth certificate."

"Well, I wouldn't. It would insult Alex." She knew Alex would be insulted because, if the tables were turned, she would be insulted.

"If you don't get her to sign this contract before the baby is born, I will."

"Don't you dare!" He had on the jacket that she absolutely could not stand, the brown corduroy with the elbow patches. He looked like the stereotypical college professor. No, he looked like the stereotypical college professor from the seventies. Her heart was pounding (breathe, breathe), and she needed to do something to divert him from the subject—throw something, feign a faint, ask him to go upstairs and make love, what did it matter? For someone who was supposedly brilliant in his field, he sure could be stupid about matters of the human heart. Specifically, her human heart.

"I'll do it later," she said when she got her breathing under control. She was going to take a Valium when this was over.

"The sooner, the better," her husband said. Of course.

"As you well know, she's not speaking to me right now." She had told him everything about the scene in Alex's kitchen. She had told him about the blow job years ago when they were dating, before he had even met Alex and Jack. He hadn't cared; it really didn't affect him at all.

"That fact underscores my point."

"I will ask her to sign the damn contract the minute—no, the second—she no longer wants to shoot me."

"Oh, Sam," Chris sighed as he picked up his briefcase. "Sometimes, you wear me out, you really do."

And she didn't say: And sometimes, you act like an old man, you really do.

"I'm only doing this for you." He didn't kiss her goodbye.

"Gotcha." She didn't want him to kiss her goodbye. But after he left, she wondered: Did he mean the contract, or did he mean the baby? The contract, she decided. He wanted Caleb as much as she did, and he better know it, damn it.

She had no intention of asking Alex to sign anything. In fact, she put it in her desk drawer and refused to think about it. When Chris asked her again, later, if the deed was done, she simply said, "I'll do it when the time is right. Trust me." He looked skeptical, but he wasn't pushing her, not yet. And really, he should know better than to push her after all these years together. It *never* worked.

She should be working. Now that the cast was off, she had a lot of catching up to do, but she had been staring at her computer screen for over an hour now. She couldn't concentrate on the pollution levels and particulates in the air in the Phoenix metropolitan area, the subject of her current article. Frankly, if people were so worried about the ill health effects caused by said pollution, they should wear a mask, stay indoors, or *move* for god's sake. There were so many more important things to think and/or worry about in the grand scheme of things.

Like Annie. She had been pregnant, and no one had known about it. How could Alex not have known? Why didn't Annie tell her parents? Who was the father? Sam recalled the conversation when Annie had come over to borrow sugar and asked about Planned Parenthood. She, too, had dismissed the possibility that Annie was talking about herself because Annie didn't have a boyfriend. Annie didn't even date. How blind they had all been! And there was this remembrance: Annie had said something about it being too bad that a person couldn't just give an unwanted baby to someone who really did want it, someone like *her*. Oh, Annie, Annie, Annie! She, her Aunt Sam, would have gladly taken the baby. Aunt Sam would have done anything in her power to help her frightened, sixteen-year-old, pregnant niece.

And why was it that all these teenagers could just—zap!—get pregnant without even trying?. All those episodes of *Maury*, all those young mothers, and all those possible baby daddies—but she didn't watch that program anymore. It was one addiction, the only one so far, that she had successfully weaned herself from. She would steer away from the TV when the clock hit ten; she would not allow herself to turn on channel twelve to watch the sobbing young mothers. ("He says the baby's not his, but look at this picture! He looks just like his daddy!") Ultimately, it had made her too sad. None of them realized the importance of having a child, of being a parent. She knew that she wasn't the only woman in the world who had struggled with infertility—there were way too many women in the same boat—but it seemed to her that the women who really longed to have babies were the ones who could not. It was so unfair.

The first miscarriage wasn't the hardest. All four of them had been equally devastating. Because of her endometriosis, she had been told that it would be difficult to get pregnant, but it had happened! At the time, she felt like the luckiest woman in the world. She had defied the odds; yes, she was going to be a mother! She miscarried at eight weeks. The second pregnancy, she lost the baby at seven weeks—the third at five, the fourth at three. It was as if she had a diminishing capacity to hold onto her children. She was a complete failure at having the one thing she really wanted in life. A complete failure.

Then there was Grace. Those three months had been the happiest time in Sam's life. Finally, she had held onto one of her babies, had nourished her into this world. Together, they had made it! She fed her, bathed her, rocked her, and loved her with all her being. She had a daughter. She had a family. There was a God.

And then the world went dark.

But she still had a twin sister, and Alex had saved her from complete self-destruction. All those late-night, booze-soaked conversations with her sister had kept her hanging on. Slowly, slowly, slowly, she got "better," or so everyone said. She still had her doubts about that. She was never going to *get over* the miscarriages and the loss of Grace. Never. But Alex had come through again, agreeing to be a surrogate for her. And what had Sam done for her? Cajoled, pled, begged, badgered, and harangued her, and on top of that, messed around with her husband.

What a *swell* sister she was! She deserved an award for Atrocious Sister of the Year—no, make that Atrocious Sister of the Decade—no, make that Atrocious Sister of Alex's Entire Life!

Alex had every right to shoot her.

Sam opened her desk drawer and pulled out the bottle of Valium, a new hiding place that Chris had not yet discovered. Another panic attack was coming. After everything she had done, what if Alex really didn't give her the baby? No, she wasn't going to think like that. Everything would go according to plan, and everything would be fine. They had made a promise, and they kept their promises. She loved her sister dearly, and her sister loved her.

Or so she had.

"You're not studying," Jennifer accused.

"Yes, I am," Nick said.

"No, you're not. You're staring at my breasts."

It was true, but she had been staring intently at her AP physics book, so how did she know? "Sorry," he said, although he wasn't sorry in the least. Jennifer had very pretty breasts, and the subject he was supposed to be studying, world history, did not interest him in the least. Jennifer was doing her best to tutor him, but he guessed she didn't realize how distracting she was as she sat across from him at his kitchen table. "Let's call it quits for the day, okay?" He slapped his book shut.

Jennifer opened the book to the exact page he had reread four times without comprehending what it said. "Let's not," she said.

"Slave driver," he said with affection.

Jennifer jabbed at the page. "I'm going to do whatever it takes to get you to graduate on time, with me."

"Do you want something to eat? I brought home some powdered sugar donuts from Fry's." Someone around his house had to bring food in. His mom, once again, was not cooking, his dad was hardly ever home and certainly didn't eat with them lately, and Annie didn't seem to care whether she ate and obviously couldn't drive to the store to get food. So that left him to do the grocery shopping. He'd been bringing home a lot of frozen pizzas.

"You're procrastinating," Jennifer said.

"I am world-famous for my procrastination techniques." He grinned endearingly (he hoped) at her.

"You will know Winston Churchill's foreign policy backward and forward before I'm through with you."

Is that what he'd been reading? It didn't ring a bell. She was right. He was going to be in serious hot water if he didn't get down to work, but she was so darn *distracting.* "Can't we please take a little break—five minutes? I need sustenance for my brain to work."

Jennifer sighed dramatically. "Okay. Fine. If you need a sugar rush, I'm not going to stop you." She smiled her pretty, white, white smile. "I wouldn't mind a donut myself."

Nick got the box of donuts from the pantry and poured them each a glass of milk. He brought home a lot of milk, too, mostly for his mom. If she, like Annie, didn't want to eat, he could at least count on the fact that she would drink a glass of milk. He was worried about her. She didn't seem to be eating much, yet she was getting enormous. Maybe she needed more exercise? She stayed holed up in her room most of the day, as did Annie. And with his dad gone most of the time, Nick pretty much had the house to himself, which is why he felt comfortable enough to invite Jennifer over to study. No one in his family was going to bother them.

"Where's your mom?" Jennifer asked. It was like she could read his mind.

"She's probably resting. She's pretty pregnant and all that." It was clear to Nick that his parents had had a major argument. So what else was new? They had been arguing for months now, about Aunt Sam's baby, about Annie, about money, about him (to his great shame), about Annie, about the baby, about *everything.* He shouldn't care—he would be gone in a couple of months—but he did care. He had decided to keep out of the fray, keep his head down, do what he was supposed to do, go to work, and study, study, study—if Jennifer just wasn't so *distracting*.

"This is the third time I've been here this week, and I haven't even seen her." Jennifer dabbed at the powdered sugar on her lips daintily with the paper towel/ napkin he had given to her.

"She probably doesn't feel well. She's pretty pregnant and all that." Jennifer was right, though, as usual. It did seem as if his mom could at least make some effort to get to know his girlfriend. He talked to Jennifer's parents, Mr. and Mrs. Sang, all the time. After the months of trying to avoid introducing Jennifer to his parents, he now wanted them to know her, and they were showing no interest. They weren't even around, not really. He was a little hurt by this, but then again, his parents were acting pretty crazy these days. He wouldn't want smart Jennifer to think it was *genetic* or something like that. And maybe he should never have her in the same room with Annie? He immediately buried that thought out of loyalty to his wacko sister.

"Being pregnant is not a state of illness," Jennifer said matter-of-factly.

"Sure." What else could he say? He knew the excuses he was making for his mom were weak, very weak. He felt a little stab of resentment at her for putting him in this situation.

"Maybe she doesn't like me?" Jennifer whispered.

"It's not that at all!" How could anyone in the whole wide world not like Jennifer? How could anyone in the whole wide world not *love* Jennifer? "She's just . . . hormonal?" He threw up his hands. "I don't know what's going on around here, Jennifer. I really don't."

He really didn't. He had contacted the guys he had stolen from, with the help of Dean Whittaker, and told them he had never used their credit cards, told them how much had been in their wallets, and then sent them twenty percent more than he had stolen. One of the guys, Derek, hadn't even remembered getting his wallet stolen, and the others hadn't given him a hard time either. Did his parents acknowledge that he had done the right thing? No, they did not. Well, maybe they had said something like "good job," but he couldn't remember if this was a fact or just wishful thinking on his part.

Now, he could understand that they were upset about Annie being *laid up*. He was upset about it, too. In fact, he wanted to pulverize the guy who had gotten her in trouble. But they couldn't do anything about it now, could they? Annie refused to tell them who the guy was, and he had overheard his parents talking—the last time they had spoken?—about how she would probably tell her therapist, and then they would know. Hello? Wake up, folks. There's this thing called doctor/patient confidentiality. (He had decided not to tell Jennifer about Annie. He just couldn't do it, despite their pledge of total honesty. The way he figured it, his sister's *mishaps* were not part of the equation.) In the meantime, all this moping around was a gigantic waste of time. People in this house needed to grow up. Possibly, all the people in this house should be seeing a therapist.

"I didn't mean to pry," Jennifer said. "I'm sorry if I said something I shouldn't have."

"You didn't say anything wrong, Jennifer. My family's just a little bit messed up right now. We'll get over it; we always do." He almost wanted to study again, just to change the subject.

"You shouldn't feel bad, Nick. All families are dysfunctional to some extent." She reached into her backpack and pulled out her psychology textbook. "In fact, I don't think there is a definition of a *normal* family. Let me look it up." She flipped through the pages of the obscenely heavy book.

He put his hand over her moving hand. "Let's not look it up." It didn't matter what any book said. He knew that what mattered was the process of living through disharmony one day at a time.

Jennifer closed the book and gave him one of her perfect smiles. "Okay."

"Do you want to make out?"

She blushed, giggled. "Here? What if your mother or father walked in?"

Fat chance of that. He kissed her, and he kept kissing her until Jennifer gently pushed him away. "Too much," she said in a slightly ragged breath.

"Too much what?" Would his mom even notice if he took Jennifer upstairs? It would probably be the exact moment she decided to *wake up*.

"Too much for *now*," Jennifer said as she smoothed her hair. "We need to get back to work." With a look of determination, she reopened her physics book.

Would she notice if he went upstairs and took a quick, icy cold shower? Yep. Not much got past Jennifer. "Slave driver," he said. He sighed and opened his book. He so very much wanted to tell her the secret, right then, at that moment, but it would ruin the *big ta-da*, as Loretta would say. "So, this Winston Churchill guy. Was he president of England or something?"

Jennifer rolled her dark, dark eyes. "Nick, baby cakes, we have a long way to go." Nick should never have told her the names Loretta called him.

The secret was this. He was meeting Loretta at the Kay's jewelers in Paradise Valley Mall the very next morning. He arrived on time and was waiting in front of the store when Loretta bustled in, dyed blonde hair piled on her head, the tops of her breasts bulging out of a pink tank top, and all manner of flesh bulging under her tight, tight jeans. So this is what Loretta looked like out in the "real world." He needed to remember that Loretta was not yet thirty-five, but when he had taken Jennifer to her trailer, she had worn a normal dress. He wanted to look away, seeing her like this, not in her Fry's uniform and apron, but in the flesh. And boy, there seemed to be a lot of *flesh* to Loretta.

"Sorry I'm late, baby cakes, but I spent all morning trying to find the damn thing." She smelled like a combination of Camel smoke and flowery perfume.

"What were you looking for?"

She searched in her overly large magenta purse and pulled out a Ziploc bag. "This. I thought you might want to have it, to save some money, you know?"

Nick couldn't see anything, so he leaned closer to the bag.

"In the corner," Loretta said. "It's an itty-bitty diamond ring." She shook the bag at him.

Nick could finally see the gold ring with the diamond the size of a pin head. "I appreciate it, Loretta, I really do, but I think—"

"I know, I know. I came to my senses on the way over here, sugar honey, and I said to myself—no, I think I actually said it out loud to myself in the car—that sweet boy is not going to want some cast-off ring from Loretta, although this happens to be my engagement ring from husband number one, who was not as bad as two and three—and you know number two was a prick bastard, pardon my French." She gave a raspy cough as she paused a moment to catch her breath. "So, anyway, I said to myself, 'that sweet cakes is going to want something new for his girl,' not some cast-off from Loretta, although I thought it might save you some money, you know, and everyone, God help us, could stand to save some money in this depression—or is it recession?—but it is not right for you and your love, sugar bunny, not at all. *It's too itty-bitty for the big ta-da!*"

"Thanks just the same, Loretta." Nick was touched that Loretta wanted to save him some money, and boy, he could really use it. He had never asked his dad to borrow money again because it was clear that his dad was either not capable of or not interested in giving him money. So after he gave back the money he had stolen, plus twenty percent, his own idea, he had asked to borrow money from Dylan. Now, Dylan usually had zero in his pockets, but surprise, surprise, he had managed to squirrel away one hundred dollars, which he took from under his mattress and handed to Nick. ("You sure you want to do this, dude? Jennifer's a nice girl and all that, but our destiny is to be *soldiers*, man.") Nick was sure. He hated borrowing the money from Dylan, but with his restitution and the months of taking Jennifer out on dates (gas was expensive), his meager savings account had been sadly depleted. He looked again at the forlorn ring in the Ziploc bag, but Loretta was right. Definitely too itty-bitty for the big ta-da.

Loretta led the way into the store. "This is much nicer than the jewelry store at Walmart where my exes shopped for me—well, technically number three is not an ex, but we'll see about that when he gets out of the slammer—very hoity-toity, I tell you, this place. I always knew you were a classy number, darling."

"How much do you think a classy ring will cost, Loretta?" He only had two hundred and fifty dollars.

"I don't have a clue, baby cakes. You're talking to the Walmart girl." She took Nick's arm. "Now don't you worry about a thing. We'll find something real nice for your little oriental girl."

"She's Korean, Loretta. We've talked about this before." He wasn't really offended by Loretta's remark. How could he be when she had helped him so much? And as she said repeatedly, she couldn't help being politically incorrect; she was an Arizona native. He didn't touch that one because he didn't know what it meant.

"That's right, baby, Korean. Those poor people with that awful war in their country and then all those hippie protesters over here with their long hair and bell bottoms. What were they called—draft dodgers, like the baseball team? You know, I think I would have made a good hippie. I just figured out my life! I was born in the wrong time!"

"I think you're talking about Vietnam," Nick said, although he wondered why he even bothered.

Loretta stared at him, eyebrows arched. "Say what?"

"But there was a war in Korea, too, earlier," he assured her.

"There you go!" She tugged him toward a counter in the back of the store. "Look, sweetheart, fifty percent off. Let's start there."

Later, after they picked out a ring in his price range, which wasn't much larger than Loretta's in the Ziploc bag, he bought her a coke at the food court, and they found the one table in the entire place that wasn't sticky or covered in crumbs. He took that as a lucky sign. "Thanks again for helping me, Loretta," he said.

"No problem at all, baby cakes, no problem at all." She drummed her metallic silver nails on the table. "Do you think people would notice if I smoked in here?"

"I think it's illegal, Loretta."

"I hate this new law. They treat smokers like criminals when they can't seem to catch the real criminals who are running around willy-nilly—unless of course you're my husband who will probably be my ex-husband as soon as they let his sorry ass out of jail. That 'life is a box of chocolates, and you never going to know what you're going to get' is a true statement. So true."

With Loretta, he certainly never knew what he was going to get, or what was going to come out of her mouth next. However, he had gotten pretty good at steering her back on track. "So, let's go over this one more time. A promise ring means that I'm making a promise to marry Jennifer, right?"

"That's the idea, honey." She patted his hand. "Now, I never got a promise ring. I just got knocked up instead, and my daddy—God rest his soul—when he found out—really did take a shotgun out of the closet and—"

"So that means she'll wait for me," he pressed on. As the time drew nearer for graduation—or maybe not, in his case—he and Jennifer were constantly thinking about, but not verbalizing, their dilemma. They didn't want to be apart, but how could that not happen if she was in Palo Alto, and he was—where? They were young, they knew that, but didn't people fall in love at *every* age? It's not like you could pick the exact moment in time when you would meet The One.

"That's the idea, honey. Okay," Loretta stood up, "I need a cigarette. Pronto. Slurp down that soda, sweetie, and let's go outside and stand in the designated patch of raggedy weeds where the *criminals* are allowed to *smoke*."

"But, Loretta—" He had so many other questions to ask. It's not as if Loretta had all the answers, but she certainly had more than he did.

"Don't you worry, Nicky baby, that little girl will wait for someone like you. Let's go outside and plan when you should give your girl the promise ring—and where. Maybe you could take her out to a nice dinner, or maybe you could take her to a park—no, no, you already did that one, didn't you? Hurry up, sweetheart. I think better when I smoke—don't you dare start smoking in the Marines!—I'll have a Camel, and together, we'll come up with the perfect time and place for you to give that little girl the ring— I'm good at this kind of thing, I think—we can concoct the *perfect ta-da!*"

Georgia did not seem happy to see him. "You know I can't answer your questions concerning what goes on in Annie's therapy sessions, Mr. Carissa." Her gaze was level on his.

"Yes. Doctor/patient confidentiality. Yes. I understand. However, Ms. Bell, don't you think there are extenuating circumstances in this case?" Try a pregnant sixteen-year-old. Try an unknown teenaged father. Try the sixteen-year-old's father who is going out of his mind with worry and incomprehension and grief. Jack wanted and needed answers to the sharply jagged, fragile puzzle that was his daughter.

"Since this is not a criminal investigation, Mr. Carissa, I will not answer your questions concerning what goes on in Annie's therapy sessions."

He wanted to beg. He wanted to say to her: This is my only hope of understanding my daughter. Please, please, please help. "I only want to help her." He wondered how much Annie had told Ms. Bell about what was going on in their household. It made him uncomfortable. Did she know about Alex being a surrogate for her twin sister, about his drinking, about his gambling, about Nick's stealing? Probably. He felt like squirming in embarrassment and failure.

Ms. Bell picked up a file from her desk. "I'm sorry, but I have another patient."

He just sat there, mute. If she didn't give him the answers, where would he go to find them?

Ms. Bell was young—she didn't look much older than his daughter— but she was insisting on being professional. "I have another patient," she said firmly.

He couldn't move.

Pretty, young Ms. Bell took some pity on him—and he knew he looked haggard, eyes bloodshot. "When Annie is ready to talk to you, she will. You need to give her time."

"How much time?" This was a crucial question for him.

She gave a slight smile. "We'll have to leave that up to Annie."

But he wanted to know *now*. How could he begin to fix things in his family if he didn't know the answers? These days, he wondered if he even knew the correct *questions*. He still couldn't move. He was a column of hopeless lead.

Even though Ms. Bell obviously wanted him gone, she maintained her cool composure. "Before you go, Mr. Carissa, may I offer a suggestion?"

"Yes, please." *Anything.*

"Perhaps you could offer to give Annie driving lessons?"

"Driving lessons?" This young woman had no idea what that involved. Everyone had tried to teach Annie to drive. It was like trying to teach a linebacker to limbo. He loved his daughter dearly—even as he was now angry, frustrated, hurt, and dumbfounded by her—but teach her to drive? She had just been driving unlawfully on the interstate and had caused an accident. It was a miracle that no one had been seriously hurt other than the . . . he couldn't even stand to *think* the word *baby*. One miracle in a succession of disasters. It was harsh to think that way, he knew, but for now, he was going to have to leave it at that.

"A metaphor, perhaps." Ms. Bell stood up and extended her hand. "Thank you for stopping by, Mr. Carissa."

He had no choice but to hoist up his leaden body and leave.

A metaphor, perhaps. Ms. Bell was suggesting that Annie needed to learn to drive as a metaphor for learning to navigate her own life. Which would lead to Annie finally developing confidence and self-esteem? Which would solve all her problems and cause her to become a happy, well-adjusted person? He had serious doubts that, at this point, things could be solved so simplistically.

For months, he had been insisting his daughter was only going through a phase.

For months, he had been a terrible father.

For months, he had been a terrible husband.

For months, he had been a pompous ass.

He really wanted a drink.

He hadn't been to Cochran's in weeks, and he could drive there on his way to—where? His wife had told him to get out, but it was not an easy feat. First of all, he didn't want to leave his wife and family; he wanted them to forgive him. Secondly, he couldn't afford to stay in a motel, not even a cheap one like Motel 8. One night, at Alex's suggestion—well, it was more like her insistence—he had stayed overnight on the couch at his friend Bob's apartment. It had been the most depressing night of his life. Bob's wife, too, had recently requested that he leave, and Bob had been living in the apartment for close to two months. Maybe *living* wasn't the appropriate word. Bob was *existing* in the midst of unpacked cartons, empty pizza boxes, countless empty beer bottles, and a clutter of regrets. For the first couple of hours, they pretended everything was fine. They watched a Suns game and drank some beers (he had had two, which he regretted; Bob had seven) and pretended that they weren't miserable. But it was only a matter of time before that façade crumbled, and Bob was crying about his wife being in love with another man and Jack was sobbing over Alex. They were a pitiful sight. In the morning, they again pretended that everything was fine, but they were broken men, and they both knew it. Jack didn't have the emotional stamina to go through that again.

One other night, he had slept in his Jeep. A Jeep was not the world's most comfortable car to begin with, and it didn't take Jack long to realize that sleeping in it was impossible. He had driven to South Mountain, thinking that if he was going to be homeless and sleep in his vehicle, he might as well have a nice view of the valley below. He was not the only one who thought South Mountain was a perfect parking spot. A lot of valley teenagers also thought South Mountain was a perfect parking spot. He had been surrounded by cars of kissing, groping teenagers. It hit too close to home. Was Nick having sex with Jennifer? Did they use protection? Where had Annie gotten pregnant, and by whom? If she decided to have sex at such a young age—and the thought turned his stomach inside out—why oh why hadn't she used *protection*? He spent the rest of the night driving aimlessly through town and went to work the next day without a shower and unshaven and didn't even care. He was a mess.

He deserved a drink. Why in the hell was he trying to stay sober? He was practically living in his vehicle, his wife despised him, his young daughter had been pregnant by an unknown, acne-prone, teenaged, aggressive, horny son of a bitch, as Jack imagined him. And his son had stolen from other students, and now everyone at his workplace knew it. Gary Whittaker had been grandiose about it to the point that it made Jack want to punch him. Gary called a faculty meeting and told everyone the story, ending with: "We abhor this kind of behavior at SCDS, but Nick Carissa eventually did the right thing. He has been suspended and is making recompense, and I felt no need to notify the authorities. We are a family at SCDS, and the punishment has fit the crime. We will relegate this instance to the past." Since then, Jack was having difficulty looking his colleagues in the eye. They, on the other hand, did their best to avoid him.

He deserved a drink. On top of everything else, his girls' soccer team had had a lousy year, 3-9, and they hadn't had a chance of making the state playoffs. The icing on the shit cake of this year. There was no doubt about it. He had lost his touch. He pulled into Cochran's and sat there awhile, debating. There was nothing to go home to, no welcoming family member waiting, but yet he had been so good at keeping his drinking under control. Plus, he hadn't gone to the casino once, *not once*, since he showed Alex the shameful credit card statements, and he hadn't gambled online either. In a way, it was a relief. For months, he had been robbing Peter to pay Paul, taking money out of their household account to pay the minimum on the credit card and telling Alex that she needed to budget, budget, budget. It was amazing he didn't have an ulcer. Maybe he did have an ulcer? His stomach burned, constant as a smoldering chunk of coal.

He got out of the Jeep and walked into the familiar bar. Rinaldo was at his usual stool by the waitress station. Jeremy sat morosely on the other side. In all the years Jack had been coming to Cochran's, he had never seen Jeremy smile. When Jack thought about it, none of the regulars ever smiled. This probably should have told him something months ago when he, too, had become an unsmiling regular. He should leave. He should stay. He had nothing to go home to. He sat.

"Hello, stranger." Mercy, the bartender, had on a too tight red tank that matched her flaming red hair. She could have been thirty. She might be sixty. Her thick makeup was burlesque, but she was always nice to the regulars. "Have Mercy on me," they all said to her, over and over again. Haha. She always laughed at their sophomoric, pathetic, drunken humor—all for their measly quarter tips. The poor woman. He should leave. He should stay. He had nothing to go home to. He sat.

"How's it going?" he said.

"The usual?"

It was one more depressing thing; he had a *usual* drink in this dark place that stank of old beer and wasted time. She would pour him a scotch-rocks if he barely nodded his head. It would be so easy. He took a deep breath. "I'll have an iced tea."

She cocked her head at him, waiting for the punch line. None of the regulars came into this bar and ordered iced tea.

"For now," he said, to placate her. He would drink his iced tea quickly—and he didn't even like iced tea—and leave. Cochran's would have helped him kill a whopping ten minutes, in and out the door.

"Do you mind if I sat here?" a woman over his left shoulder asked.

Of course he knew who it was. "It's open."

Sam sat down. "I'll have what he's having," she said to Mercy. "Make it a double."

"He's having iced tea," Mercy said. "You want me to give you a pitcher?"

"Oh. No. A glass of tea would be perfect."

Mercy brought their drinks.

"I hate iced tea." Sam moved the ice around with her straw.

"Me, too." He was too drained to work up any anger towards her right now. He was going to drink his drink and leave.

"I saw your Jeep in the parking lot." Sam continued stirring. "I thought I'd see how you're doing. How everyone's doing."

"Pretty much what you'd expect." He took a sip. The tea tasted like it was a week old and probably was. It reminded him why he didn't like the drink. His mother used to make sun tea in an old, stained glass jar. It stayed out in the sun, fermenting, then she would put the leftovers in the refrigerator until every drop was gone. Waste not, want not, she said. By the time that happened, it tasted like dirty, sludgy water.

"It's a mess," Sam said. She took a tissue from her purse. She was starting to sniffle. "I'm a mess."

"Join the club." He still wasn't angry at her, which was strange. It had been a habit for years for him to flare up every time he saw her or thought about her, and it all went back to that stupid, drunken, childish incident. Then, he had blamed her for starting this entire production with a baby and interfering with his family, but mostly—if he was truly honest with himself—he resented her spending time with Alex, for encroaching on his time with his wife. But she certainly could not be blamed for his or his family's mistakes since June. He suddenly felt very, very tired. His anger had been spent foolishly.

"I'm glad you told her about that . . . the twenty-fifth anniversary. I hated keeping it a secret from Alex all these years."

"I owed it to her. I've been a prick."

"I've been a bitch. We make a lovely pair."

That was pretty much it in a nutshell.

"Is she talking to you?" Sam asked. She finally stopped stirring her damn tea. "I just did it again—prying."

He was very, very tired. "She's not really talking to anyone." He paused. "I'm afraid to go home," he said. He was not going to get all mopey. He was not.

"I'm afraid to go outside," Sam said. "I'm afraid she'll be going out or coming in your house, and once again, she'll turn away from me."

"We probably need to give her time." That's what Georgia would say, right? And Georgia was the professional.

"How much time?"

The crucial question. "I have no idea."

They sat glumly, and they certainly belonged in the ranks of the un-smiling regulars. Mercy kept glancing his way, and he knew that all he had to do was give a slight nod of the head and the magical scotch-rocks would appear. One nod. That one day at a time motto was going to be excruciatingly tough.

Finally, Sam asked, "What can we do?"

He didn't have a fucking clue on that one either, but it was certainly going to be a *one day at a time* type of thing. "Between the five of us, we're going to teach Annie to drive."

Sam looked puzzled, but she was obviously grasping at straws, too, and she didn't ask him why. "I'm all in," she said.

All in. It was a poker term. When you were almost out of chips and down to your last hand, you pushed everything you had to the center of the table and waited for the cards to turn. You either lost everything, or you won the hand.

If you won the hand, you were still in the game.

Sam had been badgering him ever since she had finished painting the nursery to ask Renee for the baby furniture. "Time is running out," Sam said. "I need time to sand and repaint the furniture. What if Alex has the baby early? I don't want to be unprepared. Would you please ask Renee when we can pick up the *used* bassinet, crib, and changing table?" she said to remind him of the items he insisted she return to Overstock.com.

It was getting near the due date, so Chris reluctantly called Renee, rented a small U-Haul trailer, and arrived on her doorstep early on a Saturday morning. Inside, he could hear a child crying and a mother screaming. Not a good sign, but he needed to get this over with. He took a deep breath and knocked.

Renee, the renowned Shakespearean scholar, opened the door with the squalling baby on her hip and her dark hair a disheveled mess. She, too, looked as if she had been crying. "Oh," she said, "I didn't realize the time."

"I could come back later," Chris offered, although he wanted to get this over with, and he had only rented the U-Haul for the morning. Renee made him nervous. She was always dropping by his office to have a "chat," always standing too close to him when they happened to be in the elevator at the same time.

"No, no, you're here. Please come in." She stood aside to let him in, and he noticed that the sweat pants she had on were stained.

He entered a living room that looked like it had been hit by a small tornado, toys strewn everywhere, a lamp knocked from an end table. "Renee, if you just open your garage door, I could retrieve the furniture."

She saw Chris's involuntary shudder. "We've had a bit of a rough morning, haven't we, Franklin?" she cooed to the still crying child. "Mommy needs to talk to a grown-up now. Follow me, Chris. I made coffee." She headed toward what had to be her kitchen.

He didn't want to follow her. He wanted to pack the trailer and get home. The little boy must have been around eighteen or nineteen months old, and Chris wondered how such a little guy could: 1) create such havoc, 2) create such noise, and 3) create such a smell. The entire place smelled like dirty diapers and spit up peas.

Renee looked over her shoulder at him. "Come *on*, Chris."

He followed her, which begged the questions: Why was he always following women around? Furthermore, why was he always doing what women told him to do? He was no fool; he knew the answers to these questions.

His behavior had obviously been instilled by Louise, a cold, domineering, and demanding mother, and his father. His father had been forty-five years old when he was born, twelve years senior to Louise, and to Chris, he had always seemed like an old man. Play baseball with him? No, collect stamps. Take him to the park? No, build model trains. Chris had not questioned any of this, growing up. It was the way his family operated, and it was all he knew, his only frame of reference. However, he was questioning it now. Certainly, Sam was strong-willed, but he was going to give her the benefit of the doubt about her untested mothering skills. Because he would turn fifty-three shortly after the baby was born. He would be eight years older than his own father when he became a parent. He was going to be a very old father.

Renee plopped the baby down in a high chair streaked with something orange—Chris could not bear to look too closely—and poured some cheerios on the already messy tray. "Here, Franklin, sweetie," she said with forced cheer, "a little snack for the angel." The baby, mercifully, stopped crying. She got two cups from the cabinet. "Black, right?"

He liked cream in his coffee but wanted to hurry things along. "Perfect."

"Sit," she said, bringing the cups to the table, which was also dubiously clean.

He sat.

"Things aren't normally like this around here. We're having a bad day. I think Franklin's teething." She combed her fingers through her hair. The feeble attempt at grooming did not help.

"I'm sure some days are better than others." The coffee burned his tongue. It was too hot to chug and then bolt out the door.

"Absolutely. Some days are marvelous, such joy."

He noticed that her right cheek had a dried patch of the same orange color. Strained peaches?

"You have so much to look forward to." And Renee burst into tears.

Crying women were not his strong suit. "Renee?" What should he do? It wouldn't be appropriate to comfort her, to touch her. She was a colleague, not even someone he would call a friend.

"I'm sorry," Renee hiccupped between tears. "My husband is out of town, and I can't get in touch with the babysitter, and Franklin is behaving atrociously, and I am *terrible* at this motherhood business!"

"There, there," he said ineffectually, and tried another sip of the scald-ing coffee. Maybe he should ask her for some cream? He could pour enough into his coffee to cool it down and allow it to be drunk.

The baby started to whimper again, and Renee poured the rest of the Cheerios onto his tray. "I'm bribing my baby to shut the fuck up," she said. "And I don't even care God, this has been the longest day of my life!"

"Um, Renee, it's only 9:30." But he could see her point. He had only been in her house for about five minutes, and it seemed like hours.

"Do you think it's too early for a shot of brandy?" she asked. Her eyes were wild, pleading. "We could talk about the department, or anything else you want to talk about, as long as it's something *grown-up.*"

She was really starting to make him nervous. "I think it's a little too early for me," he said. He shouldn't have even let her talk him into the coffee.

"Oh, come on," she said. "I could really use the company. My husband's off on another business trip, or so he says, and I'm once again going to be alone for the entire weekend."

"I need to get the U-Haul back by noon, and by the time I pack and unpack the furniture—"

"Then we have time." Renee went to another cabinet, pulled out a bottle of E&J and poured it into two glasses—also dubiously clean—already sitting on the counter. She placed one in front of him. "Drink," she said.

He drank.

"That's better," Renee said. "Now what do you want to talk about?"

He tried to disentangle himself from Renee and her dirty kitchen for another hour, but Renee went on and on: "What are your hobbies, Chris? I know all about your brilliant dissertation on *All the King's Men* because I looked it up as soon as you came to the department. I've read every single paper you've ever published, Chris, every single one. I think you're brilliant, Chris, I really do." (This said after another two shots of brandy.) "Are you going to the MLA conference in June, Chris? I'm going, and I really think you should go, too. We could have a wonderful time."

And that was when he knew it was definitely time to leave. The poor baby was slumped over in his high chair, his head smashed into the remain-ing Cheerios, and Renee looked close to slumping, too. "I've got to go, Renee. It's going to be tight to get the trailer back by noon."

"What are you talking about?" Renee slowly enunciated every word.

473

"The baby furniture."

"Oh, that," she waved her hand dismissively. "Take anything you want. No more children for me. I have my little angel." She noticed her Cheerio-ravaged child. "Oh, dear. I need to get him to bed."

He had dawdled too long at Renee's, had let her persuade him to have two cups of coffee and two shots of brandy, and by the time he packed up the furniture, drove from Tempe to Scottsdale, unloaded the furniture and returned the trailer, he was late. He had to pay an exorbitant late fee, and he was, by his own meager standards, mad at women in general by the time he got home.

Sam stood waiting at the garage door, hands on hips in her familiar "I'm really, really pissed" stance, when he pulled in. Great, he thought. What was she going to do now—go off on a rant about how the furniture was used and not up to her standards? He really was not in the mood. He got out of the car and walked past her into the family room.

"Hey," she said, following him.

"The furniture is fine," he said, continuing into his office. He would shut the door decisively to let her know that she was not welcome. Perhaps he would lock his door against her, just to emphasize the point.

"I thought you'd quit," she said accusingly.

He knew as soon as he entered his office that she had been there, that she had been on his computer. However, he had changed the password many times since she had first discovered the kind of websites he looked at, so how could she know that he still frequented the Frolicking Threesomes and other porn websites? She couldn't.

"Lucky guess," she said. "Or maybe not. Everyone knows that the biggest porn flick in the late seventies was *Deep Throat*."

Life would have been so much easier if he had married a stupid woman.

"I can't understand why you look at pictures like that, Chris. They're disgusting."

"Why were you on my computer, Sam? I believe it's my private property." He was embarrassed, yes, but also angry. He couldn't explain what the compulsion was to go onto those websites. He didn't do it very often anymore, and he was convinced that millions of other men did the same thing. Would she prefer it if he went to a strip bar—a titty bar—in town and got lap dances for twenty dollars a shot? He asked her.

"No, I wouldn't want you to go to a live strip joint, and I was on your computer because mine crashed. It wasn't like I was being intentionally nosy."

"Are you saying that you were unintentionally nosy?" He was tired. His morning with Renee had wiped him out, and now this. He was not in the mood. This time, he was going to take Sam's self-righteousness and throw it right back at her.

"I probably shouldn't have looked, I know. I got curious."

"You should not have looked."

"However," she put her hands on her hips again, preparing for the attack, "those pictures are disgusting. And they're degrading to women."

"I'll concede that point."

"Oh." Sam's planned speech had been somewhat derailed. "Then why do you look at them?"

"I'm not sure." Maybe because strong women had overrun him all his life and when he looked at those pictures of naked, vulnerable women, he felt more in control? He hated to think that was true. But it probably was.

"I want you to quit looking at naked women. No, I *demand* that you quit looking at naked women." Sam looked as if she was about ready to stomp her foot.

It was comical, really, how Sam thought she could manipulate him. It was probably because he had spent the morning with a drunken Shakespeare scholar that the phrase *the taming of the shrew* came to mind. "You're demanding me?"

"That's right."

"You're demanding me to quit looking at pictures of naked women?"

"That's right."

"You're demanding me to quit looking at pictures of naked women in the privacy of my own home when it does not involve interacting with another person?"

"That's right." Sam's voice was not as sure as before.

"You're demanding me to quit looking at pictures of naked women in the privacy of my own home when it does not involve interacting with another person or having any actual physical, sexual relationship with said person?" He was watching her face closely.

She was smart; she got it. "That's a low blow," she gasped.

He waited patiently. That, he knew how to do well.

"We were not talking about me," she said finally.

"Why the hell not? It seems as if you are often—and I'm being gracious with the word *often*—the center of attention around here."

"Why are you being like this?" Sam asked. Her voice caught.

He was on a roll, and it felt good to be in control of the situation. "Did you have Alex sign the contract?" He knew full well that she had not.

She was silent (for once).

"Where is it?" He was going to march over there and have Alex sign the damn thing, even though he was feeling especially ambivalent about the whole situation after a morning with a sloppily depressed mother and an unhappy, smelly baby. However, the four of them had an agreement, and he was going to enforce the agreement and make it as legally binding as he could. Now.

"Please don't do this," Sam said quietly.

"I'll find it myself." He marched into her office. He knew all her hiding places, all of them. She thought he didn't know where she had recently taken to hiding her Valium when her desk had been the first place he had looked when they had disappeared from the kitchen silverware drawer (before that, the china cabinet, before that, her nightstand, before that, the medicine cabinet). He found the papers immediately as Sam watched from the doorway.

"Please don't ruin everything." Slow tears trickled down her cheeks.

The ultimate test: A crying woman. But for once, he was going to be strong. It was imminently possible that the whole surrogate plan had been doomed from the start, but he was going to make sure that didn't happen. "What I am doing, Sam, is trying to save everything."

"Alex and I made a promise." This was Sam's refrain.

"And I intend to make sure that promise is kept. Are you coming with me?"

Sam, weeping, shook her head.

"Fine." He marched out the house and across the street and rang the Carissa doorbell. He hoped that Jack wouldn't open the door, but if he did, Chris could take him on today, too.

"Hi, Chris." It was Alex who opened the door. Perfect.

The words rushed out. "I had a lawyer draw up a contract about the surrogacy. I'd like you to sign it. It would be better for all of us if our verbal contract was further enforced with a written contract."

"Interesting," Alex said. "I've been doing some research, too."

She was heavily, roundly pregnant, but she looked good to Chris: rested and peaceful—*serene*, he would say. After everything she had been through in the last couple of months, Chris thought she would look bedraggled or depressed or mad. If she had been those things—and according to his unintentionally nosy wife who continued to spy out the window, she had been—something had changed.

"I know that the surrogate mother is the name on the birth certificate." She smiled.

"Yes," he said. This was going to be much easier than he had thought. He had been with her so little since Vegas that it was surprising to him to see how much she looked like his wife. They were both beautiful women, one fertile, one infertile.

"I've also learned that identical twins, after years of separation, might no longer have identical DNA."

Chris's heart plummeted. He had not done any kind of DNA research. Could this be possible? Alex seemed to be one step ahead of him, and he felt himself falling back into his normal subjugated role with women. "The contract," he said, handing it to her.

Alex smiled sweetly, serenely. "I'm not signing any contract, Chris."

12

CHAPTER TWELVE

Annie knew that Carla would come back, and she did. On a warm mid-May afternoon, Annie was sitting at their usual place on the picnic table, eating lunch alone like she always did, when Carla suddenly appeared, slamming her backpack on the table and slipping onto the bench across from Annie.

"The prodigal daughter has returned," she said with a wide grin. "It took me longer than I expected, almost a month to get out of that place. The Swiss can be very stubborn people, but I have returned!"

"It's about time. I was beginning to think you'd lost your touch." Annie was also grinning from ear to ear. Even though they hadn't spoken to each other in the past long month, she knew deep down inside that Carla would never, ever leave her. (G: "You need to make new friends, Annie." A: "No, I don't. Carla will come back." G: "What if she doesn't?" A: "She will.") She couldn't wait to tell Georgia that, about this one thing, she was absolutely right.

"Oh, ye of little faith. But I am a pro. The place was strict—uniforms, no cell phones, no cigarettes, certainly no booze, blah, blah, blah—but I finally came up with the most perfectly brilliant idea." She fished a brown bag out of her backpack and unwrapped a large ham and cheese sandwich. She had gained some weight while she was away, and she looked better, almost healthy.

"Did you bribe someone to bring in a bottle of vodka?" That sounded to Annie like something Carla would successfully do.

"Too amateurish. No, I developed a mysterious allergy to the detergent they used, the food they served, for all they knew the damn air in Switzerland, everything. I sneezed and sneezed and sneezed, and my eyes watered, watered, watered, and they finally took pity on me and called Marge and Ron to come and get me. They feared for my health, they said. I distracted the other students, they said. Marge and Ron had no other choice but to bring me home." She took a huge bite of her sandwich. "American food is so delicious. I've been eating like a pig since I set foot on the homeland."

"So, what are you allergic to?" Annie was rather confused (so what else was new?). What was so brilliant about developing an allergy? It sounded pretty miserable.

"Oh, Annie, Annie, Annie. I wasn't really allergic to anything. I carried around a box of tissues that I sprinkled—more like doused—with red hot pepper flakes. Now *that* I had to bribe someone to bring in, and to tell you the truth, it got rather painful after a while. But I soldiered on, so I could come home to you. Of course, the parental unit insisted that we stop in NYC on the way home so that a specialist could check me out. And guess what? He couldn't figure out my mysterious allergy either, which by the way, was gone the minute I left Switzerland. I got home late last night, so I couldn't call. But voila! I'm here at last."

"I'm so happy to see you." Annie could cry she was so happy to see her best friend, but then again, she seemed to cry about almost everything.

"Same here. What's new around boring old SCDS?"

"Same old, same old." But Annie did tell Carla about Nick confessing to Dean Whittaker about stealing and then his suspension.

They then had to get a few things out of the way as quickly as possible:

"Is the P still a secret?" Carla asked.

Annie knew what she meant: Is the (lost) baby's paternity still a secret? "Yes."

"Okay," she said. "I'm in. We're both okay, right? No harm, no foul."

"We're both okay, yes. No harm, no foul." Translation: It was a stupid accident. Carla shouldn't have been drinking, and Annie shouldn't have been driving, but they didn't seriously injure themselves, they would not talk about the lost baby, and neither one had to say they were sorry. It was understood.

Annie watched in amazement as Carla *ate a candy bar!* It was like things were changing before her very eyes. If Carla could get over her eating disorder, then maybe Annie could get over . . . all her shit?

"Are you still seeing your shrink?"

Annie bristled, just a little. "Yes, and Georgia is a *therapist*, not a shrink."

Nothing was ever lost on Carla. "Sorry. Your *therapist*. The reason I asked is because I'm going to be seeing one, too.

"Why?" If her parents hadn't insisted, Annie would never have gone to get counseling, although she had to admit now that she was glad she did see Georgia. On second thought, though, it might be a good thing for Carla. She was a little crazy—okay, a lot crazy. It was part of the reason Annie loved her so much.

"Marge and Ron gave me a choice: go to rehab or see a shr—therapist. I thought it was the lesser of two evils." And then Carla *ate another candy bar!*

"It's not so bad." It had been at first, though. It had been pretty shitty.

"Good. We can be nut cases together."

"Fucked up friends forever."

Carla was delighted. "That's good, Annie. That's perfect. Carla and Annie, fucked up friends forever. I love it!"

They beamed at each other, completely happy, and then the stupid bell rang. They threw away their trash and started walking across campus.

"Chemistry," Carla groaned.

"Algebra II," Annie groaned. It felt wonderful to have someone to walk with again. It wasn't as if the other girls at school had completely ignored her while Carla was away. In fact, Nina had even asked her to eat lunch with her snotty group one day, but Annie had said *no*, secretly afraid that the subject of Walter would come up and she would stupidly spill her guts about *everything*. (Everything at SCDS still reminded her of Walter. Would that ever go away? G: "It will, Annie, in time.")

"Leave it to Marge and Ron to plop me back into SCDS right before finals."

"Parents don't know how to plop appropriately," Annie agreed.

"But you know what?" Carla continued thoughtfully. "Marge and Ron haven't been so bad lately. Even though they tried that old boarding school trick again, they did hire a lawyer to get me out of that underage drinking ticket and stopped at that specialist in NYC. They actually said they're going to stick around for a few weeks."

Wow. Carla was saying something nice about her parents? Things were definitely changing.

And then Carla said, "I think hell has frozen over."

Annie laughed. "Maybe so."

Just as they reached their classrooms, Carla asked, "So, is everything okay on your home front?"

It would take her about a week to describe what was going on. No, it wouldn't. It would be simple enough: "I don't know. First, Mom and Dad seemed happy again. Then they were in a huge fight. Now Dad was trying so hard to be nice, and Mom was completely ignoring him, going around the house fat and humming." But she didn't say that to Carla. For now, she would just stick with the factual. "Everyone is trying to teach me how to drive."

Carla kept a straight face before she darted into chemistry class. "You might let them know that your *merging* needs some work."

"My *everything* needs some work," Annie said. She was already dreading the driving lesson after school. When her dad had first said that everyone in the family was going to help her learn how to drive, she had been skeptical, and about that, too, she had been right. (G: "Maybe you should trust your instincts more, Annie?" A: "I think that would be premature, Georgia.")

It quickly became apparent to Annie that her family had concluded that *it would take a village* to teach her to drive. She couldn't really blame them for thinking that way. It was true. She was a menace to society when she was behind the wheel of an automobile. (Maybe she was a menace to society in general?) It was decided that she would learn how to drive in the van because it was a safer vehicle. Annie doubted this. No vehicle was safe in her hands.

Annie also suspected that they had drawn straws or something like that, the loser being the first to venture into a car with her. Poor Aunt Sam drew the short straw. She came over on the first driving lesson day with a brave smile on her face and in a cheerful mood that had to be Valium-enhanced. "Let's go, sweetheart," she said as she buckled herself in tightly. "I know you can do this."

Annie wanted to say, "You got any spare Valium on you?" But she didn't. Her heart was racing as she turned on the ignition. "Damn," she said when the notoriously unreliable heap of junk fired up on the first try. If she'd really wanted to go someplace, the stupid thing wouldn't have started in a million years.

"We need a destination," Aunt Sam said. "It's more fun to drive if we have a destination in mind."

What was with all the "we" stuff? It wasn't like she had a steering wheel and a brake on her side, although Annie was fairly sure Aunt Sam wished she did. "Okay. How about Cactus Park? It's not far, and I don't have to drive on any major roads."

"Perfect!" Aunt Sam was annoyingly enthusiastic. "We can go as slowly as you like."

"Well, I have to go the speed limit, don't I? I think you can get a ticket for going too much under."

"Can you? I never pay any attention to the speed limit."

And Aunt Sam was supposed to be teaching her how to drive? Just great. Annie sighed, then inched the crappy van backward down the driveway. She slammed on the brakes when she heard the sound of metal on metal. "What was that?"

"Um, just your mailbox. You need a new one anyway. Keep going."

She had hit the stupid mailbox *again*. (Why did they put them at the end of driveways anyway? They were annoying.) Annie wanted to cry in frustration. She would never get the hang of this. "Maybe we should call it a day?" she said.

"We haven't even made it out of the driveway yet. You're doing fine. Keep going."

Annie didn't want to. "I'm afraid of the other cars." She had been afraid of the other cars on the road before the accident—the car ahead, the car behind, the car in the next lane—and now, she was just deep down terrified.

"There's nothing to be afraid of," Aunt Sam said in a slightly wobbly voice. "Just don't pay any attention to the other cars."

This didn't sound right to Annie, but she focused, focused, focused, and they made it to the park and back in an hour, which must have been some kind of record. The park was only five miles away.

"Great job," Aunt Sam said when they made it safely home. "See? You can do this." She practically jumped out of the car before it even stopped. She immediately lit a cigarette and took a deep drag. "Don't pay attention to honking cars. I never do."

Maybe the next time I should go the speed limit, Annie thought.

Mom was next. "This is going to be fun, just like old times. Remember when we used to have our girl days, Annie?" She struggled to get the seatbelt around her gigantic beach ball belly. Annie had to look away. (G: "How does your mom's pregnancy make you feel, Annie?" A: "Duh.")

"Are you sure you're up for a trip to Target?" Her mom had mentioned that her ankles were swollen to the size of tree trunks. (Would hers have done that?)

"I need to get out of the house." Mom finally got the seatbelt clamped. "Relax, Annie. It looks like you're trying to strangle the steering wheel." She smiled. "The secret is to be aware of what's around you at all times."

Annie was getting contrary advice. "Aunt Sam said I shouldn't pay attention to the other cars."

"Forget what she said." Mom's smile vanished. "Your Aunt Sam is a terrible driver—really, really lousy. Extremely lousy. Just do what I say. Pay attention."

There was more traffic on the roads they took to Target than on the roads she had taken to Cactus Park. Again, she was a honking target. She accidentally ran a red light, forgot to use her turn signal, and she swerved into the other lane when she reached for her beeping cell phone.

"Don't ever talk on your phone when you're driving," Mom said sharply.

"I wasn't going to talk. It's just a text."

"Don't do that, *especially*," Mom said.

It was pretty tense for the next couple of minutes. Annie didn't feel like arguing the point that she wasn't going to text, of course not. She knew better than that. She only wanted to see who was texting her, which was also a lame excuse. It would probably be Carla, maybe Nick. And it still wasn't quite gone, the hope that Walter would, out of the blue, miraculously, text her and ask her out. (G: "Walter's dead, Annie." A: "That seems to be the popular opinion.")

Mom broke the silence. "How was school today?"

"I can't talk and drive at the same time," she snapped.

"I'm only trying to give you good advice," Mom snapped back.

"The phone point has been *duly noted*."

"The car in front of you has its brake lights on."

Annie slammed on the brakes, inches from the car. "I saw it."

"You did not. Your mind wasn't on the road. Your mind needs to always be on the road." Mom rubbed the place below her gigantic beach ball belly where the seatbelt had cut in during the lurching stop.

"I'm doing the best I can." Annie's voice was close to a wail.

"I know, honey. I know," Mom said soothingly. "You're doing fine."

They were both exhausted when they got to Target. They didn't go in.

Nick had the third shortest straw, and he was in a *jolly* mood. "What a great day!" he said when he got in the car and buckled up. "I'm starving."

"What's the matter with you?" Annie said suspiciously. He *hated* riding in a car with her, absolutely *hated* it.

"Nothing's the matter with me. Can't I be in a good mood?" He had a stupid grin on his face.

"Not when I'm driving."

"You're going to nail this, Annie, just nail it."

"That's it," she said. "Get out of the van. I don't trust anyone who is that happy when they get in a car with me."

He didn't move, and he still had on that stupid grin. "Adjust your mirrors, squirt."

Annie stared blankly at him.

"Your rearview, your side mirrors. It's very important that you *see*."

Whoops. She always forgot to do that, and she had to admit that it was probably very important to *see*. She adjusted the mirrors. "Are you going to tell me what makes you so stupidly jolly?"

"Nope."

"Then I'm not starting this busted down piece of crap."

"I'm starving."

"Tough."

Nick considered, still grinning. "Can you keep a secret?"

Annie considered. Now she really wanted to know what he was so happy about, but it was no reason to lie. As a child, everyone had called her the family blabbermouth. "You know very well that I'm lousy at keeping secrets, but I—" She stopped herself. Obviously, she wasn't *that* lousy. They still didn't know that Walter was—had been—the father of her—their—poor lost . . . baby. (G: "You might consider telling your family, Annie. It would help in the grieving process." A: "Over my dead body.")

Nick's mind didn't go in the same direction as hers; he was still wrapped up in his irritating happiness. "Then drive," he said.

She crossed her arms over her chest and just stared at him.

"Okay, okay, you win. I'll tell you when we're done with the lesson. Now drive to Taco Bell. All you have to do is get me there and back in one piece. You can do that. No problem, right?"

"Right," she said doubtfully. She started the van and backed down the driveway. It was a fucking miracle. The piece of crap started right up every time she had a driving lesson.

"Watch out for the mailbox." Nick had gone to Home Depot and gotten a new one that sat gleaming evilly on its post.

"Are you trying to be funny, or are you trying to make me mad, or are you trying to psyche me out?" She could see the malevolent, glowing box in her newly adjusted rearview mirror. She shuddered. She really, really hated mailboxes.

"None of the above. I moved the new one a little farther left of the driveway, so it'll be harder to hit—not that I think you will," he added. He was still grinning.

"Thanks." It was kind of a nice thing for him to do, but she couldn't dwell on that now. She had to focus. One piece, she thought, one piece. All I have to do is get him to Taco Bell and back in *one piece*. She would feel bad if she spoiled his insane good mood. "I have to warn you, Nick. A lot of cars honk at me."

"Not a problem. My middle finger could use a good workout." Nick flexed his middle finger.

She giggled. Nick would never in a million years flip anyone the "fuck you" finger, and they both knew it. He was too fucking nice. (Whoops. She needed to *focus*.)

"And don't forget, squirt. I'm a pretty good navigator."

Even though he had, once again, called her *squirt*, she had to admit that he was a good navigator. He calmly told her when to flip on her turn signal, when to slow down when the light was about to turn yellow, when to start braking at a red light, and on and on. It was a play-by-play driving experience as narrated by Nick. The only irritating part was when he pointed out that he had not had one traffic violation in over two years of driving. It was unspoken but there: She wasn't even legal, and she had already had one major traffic *violation*. But he made up for his gaffe by buying her lunch.

"We made it," she said when they pulled into their driveway. She felt a tiny stab of triumph. She had fulfilled her duty. She had gotten her happy, peppy brother back home in *one piece*. She was almost surprised that her mom wasn't staring out the window, waiting for them. After all, both of her children had been in a car driven by Annie—all her eggs in one basket, so to speak. And Annie hadn't messed it up!

"Only two cars honked at you, Annie." Nick didn't immediately jump out of the car like her mom and Aunt Sam had.

"That's, like, twenty less than yesterday." Unfortunately, she wasn't exaggerating the number at all.

"I'm proud of you. Good job." Nick gave her a thumbs up.

"Thanks, Nick." Annie smiled happily. But when he started to open the door, she remembered. "Wait a minute. A deal's a deal. What's up with you?"

If it could be possible, her brother was grinning even more widely. "Sucker," he said, with affection.

Uncle Chris was next. Annie had always loved her uncle, but the truth of the matter was that she had not, in her sixteen years, spent much "alone time" with him. Aunt Sam was the one who had always organized fun outings and played games and watched movies with Annie and Nick. Uncle Chris was usually in his office, working. And in the last couple of years, when Annie had come to realize how many academic awards her uncle had earned, as well as what a Doctorate actually was—she had been too embarrassed to let anyone know that she thought Uncle Chris was some kind of medical doctor, even though he didn't wear a white coat and a stethoscope—she had to admit that she felt a little intimidated around him. He was incredibly smart, and she was . . . *not*.

"It's a fine day for a drive," Uncle Chris said as he buckled up.

In Annie's opinion, it was never a fine day for a drive. "Sure is," she said. Then: "I mean, it certainly is a fine day for an automotive outing." She had decided that she would try to use good grammar and proper diction during this lesson in an attempt to sound smart—well, in an attempt to prove that her parents hadn't *totally* wasted their money sending her to a fancy, stuck-up private school (that she hated, but Uncle Chris didn't need to know that).

Uncle Chris almost succeeded in hiding his smile. Almost. "Yes. Well. Where are we off to on this fine *automotive outing*?

She felt herself reddening but continued on. "The possibilities are infinite. We could drive to numerous recreational or mercantile establishments."

"Yes indeed, but perhaps we could narrow our field of options? The theorem seems unduly complicated."

What in the fuck was a theorem? It sounded like something mathematical, and the *entire world* knew that she was hopeless at math. Ten seconds into this conversation, and she was already at a loss. "Yes. Indeed."

Uncle Chris was definitely smiling now. "I need to pick up something from my office. Why don't we drive to campus?"

No, no, no. That meant that they would be driving down busy Scottsdale Road. If you didn't count her major traffic *violation*, she had never driven that far on a major city street. "Certainly," she said. She turned the key, and wonders of wonders, the van sputtered and coughed and then petered out. "Sorry," she said. She tried again, pumping the gas, then again. Nothing. (There was a God!) She was so relieved that she forgot her grammatical aspirations. "It looks like we're shit out of luck," she said. "I mean, I think our automotive outing will have to be postponed."

"It does look as if we're shit out of luck," Uncle Chris agreed, "and I don't know much about cars, but I think the engine is flooded. Why don't we wait a few minutes and then try again? I've got time. I took the afternoon off for this driving lesson, and I've been looking forward to it."

Was he *mad*? He was putting his life in her hands, and the *entire world* knew that was a terrifying thing. "That's nice of you, but I really don't mind postponing the lesson. I've been out every day this week, and frankly, Uncle Chris, I find the tension *defribulating*." (The word didn't sound right to her, and only later, when she looked it up, did she realize she should have said *debilitating*. How mortifying!)

Uncle Chris didn't correct her. "Practice makes perfect, or so they say."

"Yeah, well, the people who say that don't know squat." So much for trying to sound smart. That, too, was *defribulating*.

Uncle Chris laughed. "What worries you most about driving, Annie?" He asked conversationally.

"Everything, although I have to admit that I did okay yesterday, with Nick. He's a pretty good teacher." Just great. Now that they had to sit here, did they have to have an actual conversation? Surely, he wasn't going to ask her about—everything? He wouldn't do that, would he? For the first time, she wished the pile of crap van had started and they were on the road

"See? Practice does make perfect."

"I'm unconvinced."

Uncle Chris laughed again, which was kind of unusual for him. He, unlike Nick, didn't seem like a very jolly fellow these days. Was he worried about the baby or something? People were hard to read, really, and you never knew what kind of secrets they carried around. Look at her. She was a case in point.

"Patience is an underrated virtue," Uncle Chris said elliptically.

Oh, brother. The stupid, stupid van. "Am I supposed to know who says all these idiotic quotes? Is this like a test or something?"

Uncle Chris laughed again. "No, no, Annie. This isn't a test. I'm suggesting that, when you drive, you use patience. You'll get there eventually."

"Not at this rate, I won't. Should I start the van again?"

"Be my guest."

It started, and for the first time, she was glad to be on the road. They couldn't *converse* if she was driving. However, she had to admit that Uncle Chris was as good of a teacher, if not better, than Nick. He gave her instructions calmly, told her to take her time, and then had her practice parking in the ASU parking garage. He didn't once raise his voice or admonish her or grab onto the dashboard when she came a little too close to the car in the next lane. "You're doing well," he kept saying, and she felt her confidence begin to grow. She would bet money—if she had any—that Uncle Chris had won a ton of teaching awards, too.

When they made it safely home, she gave him a big hug and thanked him.

"My pleasure," he said.

"You taught me a lot," she said, "and I quote: 'Practice makes perfect,' and 'Patience is an underrated virtue.'"

He laughed one more time. "Whatever," he said.

Dad was the last resident of Annie's village to get in the car with her, which made him the winner of the lottery, right? No matter. They all had to get in the car with her sooner or later. He looked tired. Annie noticed new tiny creases at the corners of his eyes, and it looked as if he had lost weight. His jeans bagged at his hips. Still, he tried to act cheerful. That annoying cheerfulness must have been part of their plan: They were going to *kill* her with *kindness.*

"Hey, kiddo, are you ready for our excellent adventure?" he said as he buckled in.

Even though she had gained some confidence in her last four lessons, being in the car with Dad was a different story altogether. Dad cared too much. Oh, she knew that everyone in her family wanted her to succeed—in this one thing, at least—but Dad, since the accident, had been looking at her with an expression that made her want to drop through a hidden trap door in the floor or run away and hide. How could she define that look? She tapped her fingers on the steering wheel, thinking. *Mourning,* that was the word. Dad looked at her with *mourning* in his eyes.

"Annie," Dad said gently. "Why don't you start up this decrepit excuse for a vehicle so we can chug on out of here?"

"It's not so bad," she said. Here she was, defending the vehicle she had been cursing for as long as she was allowed to get behind its wheel. What was up with that?

"I wish we could afford a better car for you to drive, one with air bags."

"It's not so bad," she repeated. Now she knew. She was defending the stupid van because she didn't want her dad to feel bad. (Man, his cheerfulness had lasted a whopping nanosecond.) "Where to, sir?" she said in a particularly bad English accent, trying to lighten the mood.

Dad was going to try. He replied in an equally bad English accent, "To the moon, Chester, and let's take the scenic route!"

"Aye, aye, sir!" (Whoops. That would be sailor-speak, not chauffeur-speak.)

"Chip, chip, cheerio," Dad said.

Annie started the van. "We should stop for tea and crumpets."

"We shall visit the queen!"

Annie put the van in gear, then put it back to park. "Uh, Dad," she dropped the phony accent, "I mean, really, like, where are we going?"

"Where would you like to go, Annie?"

The way he said it, looking directly at her, made her suspect that he wasn't just talking about this driving lesson. She squirmed. "I'd like to drive to SCDS. If I get my driver's license—"

"*When* you get your driver's license."

"*When* I get my driver's license," she repeated dutifully, "I'll be making that drive almost every day."

"Sounds like a good plan." Dad settled back in the seat.

"Off we go!" Annie remembered to adjust her mirrors, thanks to Nick, took a deep breath, and backed down the driveway, giving a mental finger to the evil mailbox.

She hadn't made it out of the cul-de-sac when Dad said, "Remember, Annie, you're driving a lethal weapon. A car driven recklessly is just as dangerous, if not more so, than a loaded gun."

Annie gasped and slammed on the brakes. "Gee thanks, Dad, are you trying to freak me out, or what?" A lethal weapon? What in the hell was she supposed to do with that information? It was bad enough that she had to remember to adjust her mirrors, and pay attention to other cars, and use patience, and forget everything that Aunt Sam had told her. Now, she was supposed to keep in mind that she was driving a *lethal weapon*?

She might as well throw in the towel right now. It was all too much.

"Calm down, Annie. I was only trying to point out that driving a car is a huge responsibility."

"I know that!" she wailed. *"It's why I suck at it!"* Damn it, she was going to cry.

"You don't suck at it. You need to develop your confidence."

(Carla had said that, and look where that had gotten them.)

"And practice."

That echoed Uncle Chris. (Were there some developing themes here?)

Dad unbuckled his seatbelt and scooted over. He took her in his arms and stroked her short curly hair. It had been a long time since he had done that, and just thinking about that made her cry harder. She cried for a long time—she didn't know how long—and Dad didn't say a word. He kept stroking her hair, and it felt so familiar, so safe. She had missed him, and she hadn't even known. For months, the only person she had cried this much in front of was Georgia. (G: "It's therapeutic to cry, Annie." A: "I hope you buy your tissues in bulk at Costco.")

When she finally shuddered to a stop, she said, "Is it okay if we don't do this today?"

"I think a drive would do us good." It looked as if Dad had been crying, too.

"I don't think I can." She was too numb to remember everything she was supposed to remember.

"How about if I drive first? If you feel like it, you can drive back."

She nodded. It sounded fair enough. They changed places.

Dad drove them to Bartlett Lake, a lake nine miles past Cave Creek, a forty-minute drive from home. It was a place they used to go to when Annie and Nick were young and their dad, on the spur of the moment on a Friday evening, would suggest a "mini-vacation." They would load up the van with their camping and fishing equipment and spend the rest of the weekend pretending they were "roughing it" in an exotic place much farther from home. On a table in the family room was a picture of Annie at age five running on the pebbly beach topless, with Nick chasing her with a fish he had caught. For some reason, her mom loved that picture.

Dad parked the van, and they walked to the water. Then he sat on the beach and took off his shoes and socks and rolled up his pants legs.

"What are you doing?" Annie asked, even though she had a good idea.

"It's a beautiful day. I'm going wading."

It was a beautiful May day, not too hot yet. Because it was a Tuesday afternoon, there were few people around, but it embarrassed her to see her dad slosh around like that with such a goofy grin on his face. He was too *old* to go wading.

He kicked a splash toward her, and she recoiled. "Stop it," she said.

"Come on in, Annie. The water's fine."

"I don't want to," she said. She still felt drained from crying, and she was in no mood to take a chance on cutting her foot on a rock.

"Ah," Dad said. "Youth is wasted on the young."

"What?"

"George Bernard Shaw."

Great. More quotes. It sounded like everyone over forty was getting senile this spring. "Shouldn't we be going?" She was supposed to spend the night at Carla's house. Now that Carla's parents were around, Mom and Dad allowed this.

"I'm not leaving until you go wading with me. The water's not just fine; it's g-r-r-r-eat!" Dad did the Tony Tiger imitation, and sloshed back and forth in front of her, the gray of his hair (when had that happened?) glistening. And he actually looked happy.

She had tried this very tactic with Nick, and it hadn't worked. She still didn't know his big secret. However, she was pretty sure her dad meant it. She shed her flip flops and went in.

Surprisingly, the water felt *delicious*, and the sand squished between her toes. "Not bad."

"It's g-r-r—"

"Don't do that again, okay?"

"Okay."

They sloshed back and forth a few times, side by side. "Sometimes, when you take a chance, things work out surprisingly well."

He was going for that *deeper meaning* again. "Uh huh," she said.

She drove back home from Bartlett Lake, and after that, Dad took on the sole responsibility of teaching her how to drive. Every day for a week, he took her some place new. She drove through town (no biggie), she drove through the airport (scary), she practiced parallel parking (amazingly, a piece of cake), and she drove on the interstate (terrifying), but he was right there, encouraging her every step of the way. "You're getting the hang of it," he said. "You've got the skills," he said. And then he said: "I think you're ready."

She passed the test! *She had her driver's license!*

Afterwards, she was on cloud nine. She could not believe that she had done it. She, Annie Carissa, could get behind the wheel of a car, no longer a lethal weapon in her hands, and drive. It was a big—no, it was a *humongous*—deal. When Dad asked where she wanted to go to celebrate, she knew where she wanted to go.

They picked up a small cake at Fry's—Nick gave her a high five when she told him the news—and drove to Bartlett lake. They went wading first, and then, because they had forgotten to bring plates, plastic silverware, and napkins, the kind of things her mom would have remembered, they sat on the sand and ate the cake with their bare hands.

"I'm so proud of you, honey," Dad said, wiping the icing from his mouth with the back of his hand.

"You know what?" She had sticky cake all over her face, and she didn't care. "I'm proud of me, too."

He smiled at her, and the *mournful* look was gone. "You know what? That is the important thing."

"Thanks for everything, Daddy." She hadn't called him Daddy in *forever*, but it felt right, right then. "I couldn't have done it without you."

"Yes," he said, nodding, "yes, you could have."

Maybe so. "I love you, Daddy."

"I love you, too, sweetheart." He gave her a sticky hug. "I would do anything for you."

She was starting to believe—to remember—that this was true. And because of this, and because their toes were in the sand and the sun was setting a vibrant palette of orange, pink, and lavender in front of them, she took a deep breath—and told him about Walter.

"I'm taking you out for dinner," he said.

"Where? McDonald's?" Alex regretted saying it the minute the words popped out of her mouth and she saw the hurt in his eyes. He had been so happy when he and Annie walked in the door, both beaming because she had finally passed her driver's test, both jabbering away in excitement. And she had deliberately hurt him. Again.

"Forget it," Jack said, turning away.

"Wait, Jack." The truth of the matter was that she was getting tired of ignoring him, of turning away from him day after day. She had made him suffer for weeks now, and she was tired of the whole scenario. Stoking the fires of anger and resentment was exhausting and futile work.

He looked at her, waiting.

"I'll go with you. I mean, I'd like to go out to dinner with you." She tried to smile, but it was weak. She was out of practice.

"Okay," he said.

She fixed her hair, the only good feature she had left, and put on makeup for the first time in months. She put on her prettiest maternity top, which wasn't pretty at all, an unflattering pattern of petunias, and tried to squeeze her swollen feet into a decent pair of pumps, but it was no use. Ratty old flip flops would have to do. Her reflection in the mirror made her want to cry. She was a beached whale, a small cargo ship, a fat walrus. The baby kicked just then, and she reflexively patted her belly. "Yes, I know," she said to the baby. "It's all worth it, but Mommy looks like shit right now."

The waitress at Denny's led them to a booth. The space between the table and the seat was not large enough, and she should have known better than to try and wedge herself in, yet she did. She got stuck, and Jack had to put both hands under her arms to hoist her out. She blushed furiously. "This isn't going to work," she said.

"We would prefer a table," Jack said to the waitress, acting like nothing was out of the ordinary. When they got to the table, he pulled out the chair for her.

"Thank you," she said, touched.

To cover up their awkwardness, they each studied the menu intently. This is insane, Alex thought. She'd been married to the man for almost two decades. In a few short months, how could they have lost the art of conversation?

"I think I'll get the Denver omelet," Jack said, putting down his menu. "The breakfast for dinner thing."

"Eggs give me gas these days."

"Good to know," Jack said.

Shit. She really needed to filter her thoughts more before they went flying out her mouth. She was beginning to be as bad as Sam. Sam. She had to admit it. She missed her terribly, and she was getting sick and tired of being mad at her, too. Something was going to have to give—and soon. Her baby was due in two weeks.

"You look pretty tonight." Jack smiled.

"Bullshit." She was doing it again. "Strike that last comment. What I meant to say was 'thank you.'" And she should probably thank him for getting her out of the house. She hadn't been out to dinner in a long time, and she didn't care that it was only Denny's. "It's good to be out," she said.

"It sure is."

"Are you going to get French fries or hash browns with your omelet?"

"Hash browns."

"Wheat or rye toast?"

"Wheat."

"Coffee or tea?"

"Coffee."

"Are we going to do this all night?" Alex said.

"God, I hope not."

Alex smiled at him, a genuine one this time, and he returned the favor. "It's sad that we've forgotten how to talk to each other."

"To quote our daughter: It sucks. We need more practice—a lot of practice, I hope."

Two women walked by their table, and Alex did not miss the fact that they checked out her husband, which made her proud *and* pissed. He was a dark-haired, handsome man with a trim, athletic body. (It was frightening how anger had clouded her vision and judgment.) She stared at him until she realized she was making him uncomfortable. She fiddled with her silverware. "It's amazing about Annie. You did a wonderful job teaching her how to drive. I'm afraid I didn't have the patience to properly teach her."

"I loved it," Jack said simply.

The waitress came and took their order. Alex didn't want to seem like a pig, but she was starving. "I'll take the country fried steak and mashed potatoes. Does that come with biscuits?" The waitress said yes. "Maybe I could have a side order of fries? And a strawberry milkshake."

To his credit, Jack didn't say a word.

"I'll have leftovers for lunch tomorrow," she said, but knew she was going to consume everything.

When the waitress left, Jack said, "Annie and I went to Bartlett Lake to celebrate after she passed her test. Remember all the good times we had there?"

Alex nodded. "Our mini-vacations." Things had been so much simpler back then when they could just pile in the van and go on a spur-of-the-moment camping adventure. Maybe she looked at the past through rose-colored glasses, but she was sure—*positive*—that they had all been happy in those days.

"I think the place made Annie feel comfortable, or it could have been the euphoria of passing her driver's test, I'm not sure, but she told me who the father of the baby was." Jack looked at Alex intently.

Alex's first thought was: Why not me? Why didn't she tell her *mother* first?

Jack knew her too well and could probably read every thought as it skittered across the screen of her face. "I don't think she intended to tell me at the lake, and I hope that she had planned to tell us, together, sometime in the future, but it was as if she couldn't keep the secret one second longer. Our daughter, as we both know, is spontaneous."

Alex's second, belated thought was: WHO?

"Walter Caldwell," Jack said quietly.

"Oh, my god," Alex whispered as the full impact hit her. Annie had been carrying a dead boy's baby, a boy who had committed suicide before he even graduated from high school. She had had to deal with the loss of Walter and then had probably found out she was pregnant shortly thereafter. How much was a sixteen-year-old expected to go through? "Why didn't she come to us for help?" she asked in a strangled voice.

"I think we know the answer to that," Jack said sadly.

"I would have been hysterical." Alex knew that she would have done some serious yelling and crying and hand-wringing.

"I would have blown my top. Look at how angry I got about her Mohawk." Jack shuddered at the memory.

"And it was only hair." Finally, she could see Sam's point. Well, almost.

"We would have told her how *disappointed* we were in her."

"I would have been—still am, in fact—disappointed."

"And hurt. We might as well throw that one into the mix, too."

"And confused. When, where, how, and why?"

Jack shook his head. "I don't know. Once she told me who the father was, she didn't go into specifics, and frankly, I don't think I could have taken the details of the situation. She's my daughter. I've been walking around with the idea that, when I found out who the fucking punk was, I would literally strangle him. I know how childish and immature that sounds, but I was carrying around so much anger. And then Annie tells me it's Walter Caldwell. It would be pretty tough to strangle him."

"Poor Annie," Alex said. Despite all the conflicting emotions she felt about the situation, her heart did ache for what Annie had gone through. But still. "How could she have been so stupid?"

"Why didn't she use protection?"

"Did she date Walter?"

"Did it happen at some party?"

The waitress brought their food, and they abruptly stopped talking.

Alex continued immediately after the waitress was out of earshot. "Did she consider an abortion?"

"Dear God."

"Should we tell the Caldwells?

"If you had lost a child, would you then want to know that you had also lost a grandchild?"

The gravy congealed on Alex's plate, and she no longer had any appetite whatsoever. "We lost a grandchild." The realization hit her suddenly, hard. She thought of the baby growing inside of her constantly, but up until this point, she had thought of Annie's condition—learned after the fact—an *unwanted pregnancy, a mistake.* If Annie had not been in the accident, she and Jack would have been grandparents. It was unbelievable. The tears started.

Jack's eyes were wet, too. "It wasn't meant to happen."

"She's so young." Alex used her napkin as a tissue.

"I know." Jack put his hand over hers.

She didn't shake him off. She was so very tired of fighting, of railing against all the elements of her life and getting nowhere. Her marriage was on rocky ground, to put it mildly. Her daughter had been using drugs, then had gotten pregnant, then had been involved in a car accident. And her son had stolen, been suspended from school, and instead of going to college, wanted to join the Marines and go to war. How had things veered so terribly out of control? The baby kicked. (Alex sent her a silent message: No, sweetheart, it's not your fault.) To Jack, she said, "We've really made a mess of things."

"That seems to be the case, but I am willing to do anything in my power to make things right again." He leaned closer across the table, his face earnest.

Did he think she wouldn't try as well? It was a small flare of anger, and she quickly tamped it down, but damn it, he read her like a book.

"I know you'll try, too," he quickly added, "but I have a lot more to atone for than you do. I don't know if you've noticed or not, but I've quit drinking. It seemed like the logical place to start."

She had noticed. As hard as she had tried to ignore him, it hadn't worked. She had been intensely aware of everything he did in the house, where he was at any given moment, what he ate for dinner, when he did his laundry and then folded the two baskets of clean clothes she had been too tired to contemplate. She knew he had not touched the bottle of scotch in the pantry or the beer in the refrigerator in the garage. She was proud of him, but it had to be easier for him to stop since she wasn't drinking, and unfortunately, she was really looking forward to that first post-pregnancy glass of wine—and the ones that would follow. What would he do then?

Jack continued to plead his case. "I've already consulted with a financial specialist, and we're working on a plan to consolidate our debts. We're not going to lose the house—"

"Whoa!" she said, her heart pounding. Lose their house? "What did you just say?"

"We're not going to lose the house," he said quietly. "I got us in deep, Alex, but I will get us out. I've got two extra jobs lined up for the summer, and I'll take a third or a fourth, if I have to."

What he had done to them financially still made her furious. Unlike dealing with living, breathing people, money was something they should have had control over. They had always been frugal, conscientious, and he had ruined it. "Every time I think about how you gambled away our money, our savings, I get so mad I want to slap you." Why had he even brought this up? The evening had started out so nicely, and he had to remind her that they were over their heads in debt.

He lifted himself out of his chair to lean closer. His face hung directly over her plate of stone-cold food. "Go ahead. I wish you would."

"We're in a restaurant, in case you haven't noticed," she hissed.

"I don't care. Take a chance, Alex."

Hadn't Sam said that to her a long time ago? *Sam.*

"Come on."

She slapped him, although his face was too close to get the leverage she wanted.

"Thank you." He sat back down. His cheek was only slightly pink.

"You're welcome."

"Do you feel better?"

She looked around. Their waitress had stopped dead in her tracks on her way to clear their plates, or offer doggie bags, or dessert, or whatever. She almost ran back to the waitress station. It was all so ridiculous; Alex stifled a giggle. "Maybe a little."

"Good." Jack looked relieved. "I think we both need to let go of our anger. I've been so mad at myself for the last few months—eleven months, to be specific—that I wasn't any good to anyone, not to you and not to the kids. So, I drank and gambled and railed, which filled me with self-loathing.

So, I drank and gambled and railed, which filled me with self-loathing. Talk about a vicious cycle."

In retrospect—perfect 20/20 hindsight—she could begin to understand his behavior. And what had she been doing during Jack's struggles? Excluding the disastrous attempt to sell Avon, she'd been completely consumed with being the Baby Mama. "I haven't been there for you," she finally said.

"I haven't been there for you," he echoed sadly.

Shame on both of us, Alex thought.

"Would you be willing to try marriage counseling?" Jack's voice was tentative.

"Not Georgia."

"God, no," he laughed nervously. "I don't want to imagine what Annie has said about us."

"A definite conflict of interest." Alex laughed nervously, too. She would never, ever have thought that she and Jack would need counseling. However, people and their lives and circumstances changed over the course of a long marriage. And look at the last year she and Jack had had. There had been a few major upheavals, to say the least.

"So, you're willing to go to counseling?" Jack's hand was back over Alex's.

She took a deep breath. "I think it's a very good idea, Jack."

"I know that I have fucked up royally, and I am deeply sorry."

She would not let herself cry.

"It means everything to me to try and save our marriage." Jack did let tears roll.

It was one of the things she had always loved about Jack, his willingness to be emotional, his ability to *feel*. She needed to remember positive things like this about her husband. "It's going to take some time—and work."

"I'm committed," he said. He kissed the wedding ring on her finger. "And once the baby is born, things will be easier."

"Are you kidding?" Had he forgotten how much work babies were? Had he forgotten the midnight feedings, the colic, and the sheer exhaustion of caring for an infant?

"After you give birth, and Sam and Chris take the baby, it will be easier to rebuild the pieces of our lives," Jack said slowly. He looked at her intently. "Right, Alex?"

She knew what she was supposed to say. Of course she did. He had no way of knowing the thoughts she had had during the past months and the feelings that had developed ever since the baby's first kick. "Right," she said. She averted her eyes, hoping it was not too late.

But it was.

"Oh, Alex," Jack said sadly, so sadly. "You're not thinking of keeping this baby, are you?"

Finally, she was summoned. After four weeks, two days, fourteen hours, and thirty-seven minutes (approximately), she was summoned.

Sam had waited patiently, which was not her forte. After Chris had come home from Alex's house with the unsigned contract in his hand, he paced the family room, shaking the paper like an accusation. "This is exactly what I was afraid of," he said. "She won't sign the contract."

"How many times do I have to say this, Chris? She doesn't need to." However, she didn't let him see how the glass of chardonnay shook in her hand as she brought it to her lips.

"Don't be obtuse," he snapped.

Chris had been in a very strange mood that day, after he had brought home the baby furniture, and after she had confronted him with the disgusting porn she had found on his computer. He should have been contrite or embarrassed, but instead, he was, for him, defiant. She didn't like it—not at all—but she had decided to play along with the peculiar role reversal. "Calm down, honey," she soothed. "Let me pour you a drink."

"Are you not understanding the magnitude of this, Sam? There is a distinct possibility that she will keep the baby. Legally, she has that right."

"Here you go, sweetheart." She handed him a brandy. Brandy always made him mellow. She poured the expensive Hennessy. She'd ply him with drink.

"She said she'd been doing research. She knows about the surrogacy laws in Arizona, and she said something strange about how DNA can change in identical twins after years of separation." He took a gulp of brandy.

"Nonsense. I took a course in genetics in college from a very well-respected doctor. He didn't mention anything about DNA changing in identical twins over time. The DNA is the same. Period. Honey," she remembered to add.

"Perhaps there has been some ground-breaking new research? Have you thought of that? You took that course twenty years ago."

Why did he always have to be the fucking academic? He was intentionally pushing her buttons, alluding to her so-called advanced age, but she would not be pushed. She'd make him see that she was right. She would win. "Maybe there has been some new research on DNA in identical twins. Perhaps they did a study on sociopaths raised in foster homes on different sides of the continent and concluded that, on extremely *rare* occasions, the DNA could be altered by diametrically opposed nurturing situations." She drained her glass. "Sweetheart."

"Are you going to have her sign this contract?" Chris enunciated every word.

"Are you enjoying your brandy?"

His voice rose. "Are you going to have her sign this contract?"

"I think I'll have a glass." She smiled sweetly while seething inside. How many times did she have to tell him? She and Alex had made a promise, and she knew that Alex would do the right thing and honor their verbal agreement. She would. It was a Murphy twin law.

"Sam!"

"What is it, darling?"

"I give up!" He stomped up the stairs.

She had won.

She waited patiently.

And then Alex finally called. "I've missed you," she said. "I'm sick and tired of being mad at you and Jack." Her voice quavered. "Even though what you did was disgusting."

"I know." Sam could barely breathe.

"Filthy."

"Yes."

"I threw away the flowers you sent."

"I don't blame you. They were a sorry excuse for the apology I need to give you." Sam was sorrier for that night than anything else she had done in her life. They had been young, stupid, and drunk—a lethal combination.

"Now I wish I hadn't tossed them into the trash. They were beautiful. I'm a sucker for roses, as you know."

"I do know." Sam tried to catch her breath. "I'm sorry from the bottom of my heart."

"Apology accepted. Forgive and forget, let bygones be bygones, and all that crap. I've really missed you. Can you come over?"

"Open your front door." Sam hadn't fully realized that she had been walking toward Alex's house from the minute she answered her phone, but here she was, on Alex's front porch.

Alex laughed. "Come on in. It's unlocked. I'm on the back patio."

Sam walked through the house, which was rather messy—clothes on the couch, magazines on the floor, and dirty dishes stacked in the sink. She spotted Alex through the back window. She was on a chaise by the pool, her belly resting heavily on her thighs, her hair in a ponytail. She looked beautiful. Sam joined her on the adjoining chaise. "When in the hell are you going to start locking your front door? This is not a small town, Alex."

"Gee. I was expecting a hug, not a lecture."

"I wanted to hug you, but I didn't know if we were ready for that yet."

"We're ready."

Sam jumped out of her chair.

Alex didn't move. "You're going to have to bend down. I don't think I can get out of this chair. It's starting to happen every time I sit down. I can't get back up. I'm starting to like it. Basically, it's a good excuse to not do anything."

That would explain the untidy house, not that it mattered. Sam bent down and gave her sister a heartfelt hug, and Alex hugged her back. "You look beautiful."

"You better be careful. The last person who told me that got slapped."

"What?"

Alex gave her a quick rundown of her Denny's dinner with Jack, concluding with, "We're going to try to work things out."

"That's wonderful. How's Annie?"

"She's driving; I'm terrified. How's work?"

"It's there, but I'm not. I haven't been able to focus lately. What's new with Nick?"

"We're waiting to see how he did on his finals. How's Chris?"

"Fussy."

They covered ground quickly in their familiar shorthand style, getting the preliminary topics out of the way before they zeroed in on what was really on their minds.

Alex looked at her phone. "It's five o'clock on a Friday afternoon."

"Happy hour," Sam said automatically, even though Alex, obviously, had not been drinking for almost nine months. "Do you want me to get you some juice?"

"Nope. I think I'll have a glass of chardonnay." Alex's smile was huge.

"But—" Sam would love to have a glass of wine with her, just like the old days, but would a glass of wine hurt the baby?"

Alex laughed. "Don't look so stricken, Sam. The doctor said it was all right. I've been having some mild contractions—don't get overly excited just yet, Sam, the baby hasn't even turned—and he suggested a glass of wine." She patted her belly. "At this point, I don't think we have to worry about the baby's development. To me, it feels as if the baby is fully grown."

Sam happily fetched the wine and settled back next to Alex. "We're almost there."

Alex knew what she meant. "June 6th, the same day as Nick's graduation, if he graduates. Mother and Dad might be coming."

"Nice of them to tell me." It stung. It was her baby, so why wouldn't they tell her they were coming to visit? It was a mystery. How could two such doting parents turn into such laissez-faire grandparents? Be fair, she chided herself. Paul and Emily had worked hard their entire lives to enjoy this retirement in their stupid RV that had the ridiculous name of Ginger.

"Don't be hurt. I invited them—once I finally got hold of Mother—and it's still iffy. They had planned on going to a big pinochle tournament in San Diego or San Pedro or San something." Alex closed her eyes and took a luxurious sip of wine. "Dear wine," she said. "I have missed you."

Sam took a drink and shuddered. "This wine sucks. How long has that box of Franzia been sitting in your refrigerator?" She didn't trust wine in a box on principle, but this stuff was downright putrid. It tasted faintly like turpentine.

"Is it bad? I'm so out of practice that I can't tell." Alex held her glass up to the light. It was the color of dark urine.

"Stay right here. I'll run across the street and get a decent bottle. I still have a bottle of La Crema left over from the baby shower."

"Fat chance that I'm going anywhere. I've become a Buddha."

Sam ran to her house to get the wine and was back in less than two minutes. Breathless, she opened the wine and poured. "If you can only have one glass of wine, you don't want to waste it on the cheap stuff."

"So true." Alex closed her eyes again and took a sip. "Dear *good* wine," she said. "I have missed you."

"To the baby." It was time to get to the heart of the matter and talk about her baby. Sam needed—no, she *ached*—for Alex to say that she was still going to give her the baby, that she would never go back on a promise made to her sister, no matter how wretched that sister had been in the past.

Alex still had her eyes closed. "The baby," she murmured.

"I know his name: Caleb Christopher Connor." By naming the baby aloud, Sam convinced herself that she was establishing her true role as his mother.

"That's nice, but I think it will cause some gender issues. I am almost positive that the baby is a girl. I've been talking to her for months now."

Sam felt sick with jealousy. What if it was true that babies could recognize voices in utero, and the baby already identified Alex as its mother? The quicker she could get the baby after it was born, the better. She had a lot of catching up to do.

"I like the name Sophie." Alex had a dreamy quality to her voice.

Be calm, Sam said to herself. She knew she was still walking on tentative ground with her sister. She had waited patiently for Alex to forgive her, and she would wait patiently until the baby was born. And she planned on being in the delivery room for the birth of her baby. Then she was going to be at the hospital every second, holding and feeding and changing the baby until she could bring him home. "Sophie Connor. It has a nice ring to it."

If it was a girl, Sam would name her Madeline.

"I've been doing some research." Alex's eyes were still closed, and she looked very peaceful reclined on the chaise.

Now they were getting to the heart of the matter. Sam's mouth went dry. She took a quick sip of wine, but it didn't help at all. Should she pretend that she didn't know about the Arizona surrogacy law that required the birth mother's name to be on the birth certificate? Should she pretend that she didn't know about Chris drawing up a contract? Unfortunately, she knew that she would have done that very thing a month ago in her desperation to keep her baby.

She was not going to do that now. "So you know about the birth certificate," Sam said flatly. "I will have to adopt my own baby."

"How do you feel about that?" Alex finally opened her eyes and looked
at Sam.

How in the hell did Alex think she felt about it? Lousy. Angry. Terrified.
"I'll do what I have to do to keep my baby." She poured another glass of
wine. "I'll do anything in my power to keep my baby." It was getting harder
and harder to keep her voice calm. What was Alex thinking? It took all
of Sam's minimal powers of self-control to not blurt out: *Are you going to
give me my baby or not?*

"I've also been doing some research on the DNA of identical twins."

Sam tried to take deep breaths. Was this going to be the bombshell?

"And I quote: 'Although identical twins have the same genotype or
DNA, they have different phenotypes, meaning that the same DNA is
expressed in different ways.'"

"I have no idea what that means." And she doubted that Alex did either.

She was right. "I'm not totally sure. It helps explain why one twin can
get Parkinson's disease or cancer and the other one doesn't. And it means
that we are not totally identical."

"I guess that explains why I had endometriosis and you didn't." Sam
drained her glass.

"Oh, Sam," Alex said sadly.

Are you going to give me my baby or not?

Alex watched as Sam poured her third glass of wine. "This baby is a
blessing."

To whom?

"I will do the right thing," Alex said with a Zen-like smile.

But before Sam could ask her what the hell that meant, they heard a
commotion in the house and then Nick was on the patio with Jennifer in
tow. They were both grinning, looking as if they had just won the lottery
or had been crowned prom king and queen.

"I have the best news in the world!" he shouted.

The suspense was killing him. Just killing him. Nick had finished his finals
last Friday, and today was Wednesday. Graduation—if he graduated—was
one week away. It was a tradition at SCDS that the seniors had the week

off before graduation and took a class trip together, either to Moab, UT, or a rafting excursion down the Colorado River. However, his class had unanimously voted to cancel the trip because it wouldn't seem right to celebrate their graduation (or maybe not, in his case) without their class president. Walter had been the class president.

Nick was glad—not about Walter, obviously—but glad that he wasn't going to be camping in another state with people he had spent the last four years with and still didn't really know. He'd much rather spend the time with Dylan and Melissa, who Dylan still hadn't committed to or broken up with, and Jennifer, but he couldn't move forward, it seemed, without confirmation of his graduation status. He couldn't buy a new tie and get a haircut. He couldn't pack up his locker. He couldn't quit his job at Fry's. He certainly couldn't do the *big ta-da*, which was killing Loretta. Just killing her.

"The suspense is killing me." Loretta was painting her nails a metallic green in the break room, which was against *all* the rules—and then some. Nick was pretty sure it posed some kind of health hazard. "Just ask her, sweet cakes. You've been carrying around that ring in your pocket for over a month now. It ain't about to jump out and attach itself to the finger of your little oriental girl."

"Korean," he said, pointlessly.

"She's got a good head on her shoulders, that one, and she can probably sniff that something's up. You tend to wear your heart on your sleeve, honeybunch." Loretta smiled fondly at him.

"Yeah, I think she does suspect something." Jennifer looked at him these days as if she was waiting for something. No, she looked at him as if she was *expecting* something. And why wouldn't she? He had never even heard of a promise ring before she brought it up, and he had basically *promised* her a promise ring, and now they were a week away from graduation—*if* he graduated. Jennifer had spent countless hours studying with him. She helped him make outlines and study guides, and she even gave him daily quizzes. ("You should be a teacher instead of a doctor," he had said to her. "We'll see," Jennifer had said.) *If* he graduated, he owed it all to her.

"Then ask her already." Loretta capped the nail polish and blew lovingly on her wet, long, green nails. "Time's a wastin'."

As if he didn't know that. "I'm waiting for the perfect time and place." He had already decided the where. He just didn't know the when.

"Now we tried that before, didn't we, with your first date? We came up with the idea of a romantic picnic, and you and your little girl end up upturning a canoe and getting soaking wet. That wasn't perfect, was it?"

"I guess not." Nick thought it had been pretty close.

"So, I'm saying that there's really no such thing, sweetheart. If my boyfriends had waited for the perfect time and place, well then, I might never have gotten married. Well, of course, the first time, I was knocked up"—she seemed to remember who she was talking to—"I mean, with child, but number two asked me when he was in the middle of a bar fight, and number three just drove me to Vegas without even mentioning the marrying part. I thought he was going to teach me to play craps. I always wanted to learn how to play craps like they do in the movies. It always looks so . . . *glamorous*." She smiled broadly as the word came to her.

"Uh huh." It was at times like these, when he was trying valiantly to follow Loretta's logic, that he would begin to feel the beginning of a headache behind his right eye. He always waited it out. If you gave Loretta enough time, she always, sooner or later, came to some point.

"So, as you can see, sugar, there is no such thing as the perfect time and place to pop the question. My exes and soon-to-be ex all . . ." Things were starting to come clear for Loretta.

Nick waited.

"Well, the trip to Vegas wasn't so bad, but I guess I have to admit that being asked by a drunk who just got his front teeth knocked out and his nose broken wasn't the most romantic thing in the world. I might have had a few too many beers myself, honeybunch, if I tell you the truth. And I always try to tell you the truth, my dear boy."

He knew that. It was a big part of why he liked Loretta so much.

Loretta blew on her nails again. "Let me start again. In my vast experience, no, wait. I don't really mean *vast*. It makes me sound kind of trashy or something, and I'm not trashy."

"I know you're not."

"Well," Loretta conceded. "I might be a *little* trashy, but that's not what we're talking about here."

"Right," Nick said.

"Looking back, my exes and soon-to-be ex, well, things didn't turn out so hot, did they? Maybe if they had asked me somewhere romantic—like if number three had asked me at a craps table in the Imperial Palace Casino—things might have been different. Gee, sweetie, that's food for thought, isn't it?"

"So what exactly are you saying?" Nick prompted.

"I'm saying you're right. There can be a perfect time and place. Boy, I almost lost my touch for a moment there, but if you knew the night I had last night. I was up until three a.m. with the baby because my daughter has hooked up with this low-life—"

She looked at Nick's worried face and stopped. "I do rattle on, don't I? You are absolutely, one hundred percent right that there can and will be a perfect place for your *big ta-da*, angel face. I *bona fide guarantee it,* love." She leaned over and gave him a hug.

As always, she did make him feel better. "Thanks, Loretta."

"So, when are you going to ask your little girl? The suspense is *killing* me."

Nick sighed. Back to square one. "I just can't, Loretta, not yet."

Loretta folded her arms over her ample chest. It was her turn to wait.

"I can't ask her until I know I'm going to graduate. It's like," he fumbled to say it right, "I wouldn't be good enough for her if I didn't graduate at the same time as her. She's so smart and talented, and I . . ." he trailed off.

"You're smart and talented, angel face," Loretta said with confidence.

"Not like her," he said, saying a silent prayer that Loretta wouldn't say something about how he shouldn't worry because all *orientals* valued education.

She didn't. "She's lucky to have you. Believe me, sugar, she's lucky to have a boy—man—like my Nick. You've just got to get on the horse and ride."

Easier said than done. Jennifer kept *looking* at him.

Dylan did his best to try to occupy Nick's time during this week of waiting and hoping and worrying. Dylan had graduated a week before from Horizon High School, but he didn't push Nick to go down to the Marine recruitment office and enlist. He knew all about Nick's sickening worry about graduation. "You gotta do what you gotta do, bro," Dylan said. The obvious fact—that Nick would not be in this situation if he hadn't stolen—was never mentioned.

"I can't do anything now. That's the problem." Dean Whittaker had said he was going to call, and he hadn't called. It was now Thursday.

"You either passed or you didn't." Dylan was lying on his bed, throwing a tennis ball against the wall.

"I'm aware of that, Dylan." Nick couldn't keep the sharp note of frustration out of his voice.

Dylan, being Dylan, didn't take offense. "It's only a little piece of paper. I already lost mine. I know it's in my truck somewhere. I think it's in my truck somewhere."

After all these years of knowing Dylan and his family, it still amazed Nick how little Dylan's parents seemed to care about his schooling. Unlike his. "My mom would have already had it framed and hung on the wall," Nick said. "She would probably have stood in the framer's shop and watched the diploma being matted and framed." Nick knew he was exaggerating, and being unfair to his mom, but the stress was making him think crazy thoughts.

"Dude, you need to chill."

Nick, for the third or fourth time that afternoon, continued repeating the litany of his worries. And Dylan patiently listened again and again. He was such a great friend. "I can't give Jennifer the promise ring until I know. I feel like time's running out." Or it was *a wastin'*, as Loretta would say.

"What's your hurry?" Dylan had given up on trying to talk Nick out of giving the ring to Jennifer. (His situation with Melissa was that they had an *understanding*. "What kind of understanding?" Nick had asked. "We both understand that we don't understand anything, and we're both cool with that." Great. Nick didn't *understand* it at all.)

"I've already told you. Jennifer's parents want her to take a course over the summer at Stanford. She leaves July 1st." Neither Jennifer nor Nick was happy with this new development in their summer plans. They had counted on having the entire summer together, but in their conversations, they had never gotten past the end of August. Nick supposed that they were both secretly hoping for a miracle solution to their impending separation. They had placed their bet on hope.

"The point is, what's your hurry? You have until July 1st."

Nick sighed. He wasn't going to try to explain it to Dylan again.

"You are seriously stressed out, dude."

"You think?" He might as well go home and stew on his own bed. The rhythmic thumping of the tennis ball was getting on his nerves.

"Do you want to go to the shooting range? That might let off some steam."

"No." Since buying the ring, he had been seriously short on cash, but it didn't bother him at all. "Do you want to go for a run?"

Dylan snorted. "It's frigging one hundred degrees outside." He sat up and adjusted his ponytail. "Do you want a beer?"

"We don't drink." In fact, years ago they had made a pact to not drink, to not get as stupid as everyone around them did at parties—not that they had been to many high school drinking parties.

"Speak for yourself, dude. I had a beer the night of graduation."

When had that happened? Nick, Jennifer, and Melissa had gone to Dylan's graduation in the cavernous Horizon gym. Dylan's parents and brother had not. They had gone to a horse show. "It's no big deal, bro," Dylan had said. Nick thought it was scandalous, but he hadn't said anything. (It occurred to him that he was his mother's son; she would have been appalled at Dylan's parents' absence from such a monumental moment in their son's life.)

"I had one after you and Jennifer dropped us off. Melissa had one, too. It tasted pretty rank, but it put us in a good mood, and one thing led to another, and we still didn't dump each other."

"It's ten o'clock in the morning," Nick pointed out.

"So what? You, my friend, are seriously stressed."

Nick followed him into the dirty kitchen. Dishes were piled haphazardly in the sink, and every available inch of counter space was occupied by something: horse magazines, newspapers, an empty peanut butter jar, a bridle, one boot, a cowboy hat, and on and on. The place looked more like a refuse depository than a kitchen, and Nick didn't look closely at the clutter for fear he would see a roach scuttling through the mess. It had gotten progressively worse over the years. It was as if Mrs. Taylor had gotten so far behind that she had just decided to give up completely.

Dylan didn't seem to notice the mess. "Here you go." He handed Nick a cold Budweiser. "The king of beers," he said. "I guess we'll just have to take their word for it, since we don't have anything to compare it to."

"I'd rather go for a run," Nick said.

"Yeah, I hear that heat stroke is a good stress reliever."

Dylan had a point, and Nick had to admit that he was getting desperate to relieve the gnawing panic in his gut. Reluctantly, he opened the beer. "Cheers," he said, and took a tentative sip. Dylan was right about that, too. It tasted rank.

Dylan smiled at the face Nick made. "Yummy, huh?"

"I don't get the attraction. Coke tastes way better than this."

Dylan took a sip and grimaced. "And the weird thing is that Coke is a stimulant and beer is a depressant, yet you see drunk people acting like they're wired, you know?"

Unfortunately, he did. "Yeah, they act like they're wired until they pass out." Nick was thankful that his dad wasn't drinking these days, but the jury was still out on that one. Nick had done some research on addiction; it wasn't easy to be "cured" of anything. He took another sip. It was awful. Maybe that was why his mother drank wine? Maybe it tasted better? Maybe, deep down, he was a wine drinker?

"You just got to stick with it. You can't taste it so much after a while." But the next sip still caused Dylan to shudder. "Hey, since this is our first drink together, we should probably make a toast or something."

"Why not?" Nick lifted his can. "To graduation. Let there be one for both of us."

"Right on, dude. Semper fi." He clinked his can to Nick's. "Maybe this would taste better if we put sugar in it?"

They didn't try the sugar, and it took them a couple of hours to finish one can each, but Nick had to admit that he did feel somewhat better. Maybe the stress was a fraction less severe. But when he got home and checked the messages on the home phone, there weren't any from Dean Whittaker. Older people still used land lines, but maybe the Dean had called the wrong number.

Annie walked into the kitchen and sniffed. "You smell like beer."

"You would know. You're the expert around here."

She grinned and hopped up on the counter. "Not anymore. I've mended my ways, turned my life around. I'm a changed woman!"

"It's funny how a driver's license can do that for you." He was sincerely glad that Annie had finally gotten her license. After the year she had had (and it gave him a physical pain in his chest when he thought about her getting caught with drugs and then being *laid up*), his sister needed something to cheer her up. It was about time she got a break.

"I'm just feeding you a load of bullshit. You know that, right?"

"You're the expert at that, too." Annie no longer wore that ghoulish eye makeup, and her hair, although still short, had grown in thick and curly. To Nick, she looked like she was about twelve.

"You still haven't heard?" she asked with what seemed like genuine sympathy.

"Nope." Nick went to the refrigerator and got out a carton of milk. He drank directly from the carton.

"Whoa, look at you! My brother is living on the wild side today—first beer, then milk directly from the carton. Did you bother with a glass? No, siree! You violated a rule!"

"Shut up, squirt," he said affectionately.

"That's tantamount to treason. *Tantamount.* It's a vocab word. English final tomorrow. Unlike you seniors, we sophomores are still in finals week. It sucks." She didn't look unhappy. In fact, she looked happier than she had in months.

"Maybe you better look up the word *treason*," he suggested.

"It's not going to be on the test."

Nick dug his phone out of his pocket and checked one more time. No missed calls. No messages because older people did not text.

"You're going to graduate. I know it."

"I wish I did." All those hours of studying had not been so bad. What he was really worried about was that he had wasted Jennifer's time. He couldn't stand to think that he had wasted her time.

"I do know. A little birdie told me." She reached for the milk carton and drank. I'm violating a rule," she said happily. "Par for the course for me."

He wanted to knock the carton out of her hand, not because he was angry or annoyed with her, but because she had just ignited the first flicker of hope he had felt in days. "What birdie? What do you know? Did Dean Whittaker tell Dad something? You've got to tell me, Annie. The suspense is killing me. Just killing me."

Annie widened her eyes and said in a phony, innocent Southern drawl. "I don't know what you're talking about, sir. My, my, but you do carry on."

"Cut it out, Annie. Tell me."

"I am no longer the family blabbermouth."

"Yes, you are. You better tell me." His heart was beating fast.

"I have officially resigned."

Mom walked in. "I thought I heard voices in here. Still no word?" She looked hopefully at Nick.

"Not yet, Mom." It was hard for him to look at her these days. His mother, who other guys on the track team had called a MILF—which had been excruciatingly embarrassing once he found out what it was—was so heavily, horribly pregnant that he almost didn't recognize her. It was too much. She looked so *ripe*.

She sighed. "Well, honey, keep me posted." She drifted out of the room in the dream-like state she had recently adopted.

Annie stared solemnly after her. "I wish she'd just have that kid. This is becoming *egregious*. Another vocab word."

Nick couldn't imagine how looking at their mother made Annie feel. He hoped she talked to her therapist about it, but as much as he loved both his sister and his mother, he could not, would not go there. His mother was enormously pregnant, and his kid sister had been pregnant at the same time. It was unnatural, unfair, cruel. It was, for lack of a better phrase, *totally fucked up.*

Annie jumped off the counter. "I've got to get back to studying."

"Not so fast." He grabbed her arm. "Tell me what you know."

"I can't. I promised Daddy. And I don't know everything. I mean, he doesn't know everything yet—"

"Spill it." When had she started calling him Daddy? It didn't matter. He had no time for that right now.

"Annie!"

His phone rang. He checked the screen but didn't recognize the number. "Hello?"

"Nick, it's Dean Whittaker here. Sorry to have kept you waiting for so long, but Mrs. Parsons is the school's slowest grader. I just got your final from her now."

"Yes?" Nick whispered, or thought he did.

"Let me be the first to congratulate you, son. You are officially part of the SCDS graduating class of 2009."

"Thank you, thank you, thank you, sir!" Later, he would not recall the rest of the conversation. He would only recall jumping up and down with Annie as they circled the kitchen, laughing and hugging. For some reason, his mother didn't hear them, and they were loud.

Immediately after that, he picked up Jennifer and drove her to Fountain Hills. He hadn't been there in a long time, even though it was only ten miles east on Shea Boulevard. It was a beautiful, master-planned community near the Yavapai Apache Reservation, and its claim to fame (other than its annual art festivals and hot air balloon festival) was the fountain in the park that went off every hour from a concrete lily pad base and could spew up to three hundred feet, or even higher when all the pumps were working. He had learned all of this as he was researching the time and place for the perfect big ta-da. It appealed to him because it reminded him of a man-made Old Faithful. And he didn't think they could swing driving all the way to Yellowstone Park to see a natural geyser.

When he told Jennifer he would be graduating, she said, "I didn't have any doubts, Nick. I knew you could do it." When he asked her to come for a ride with him, she didn't ask where they were going. That was how much she trusted him. Her faith in him was awesome, and he hoped against hope that he wouldn't ever let her down.

They parked the van and walked hand in hand toward the middle of the grassy park, toward the fountain. "I haven't been here in a long time," Jennifer said. "I always forget how pretty it is."

"It sure is."

"And peaceful."

Not for long. They had just settled themselves in the grass on the shore of the man-made lake when a busload of kids arrived. It must have been a year-end field trip because these kids—probably third-graders—were out of control, shouting and chasing each other around the lake. Their teacher and some volunteer moms and dads came after them, carrying picnic baskets and sacks of soft drinks. They made no effort to control the kids, and if Nick swore, he would have done it right then.

"They certainly have a lot of energy," Jennifer said.

That was an understatement. The kids acted like they were on speed (not that Nick knew what that was exactly). What was he going to do now—shout the words he had rehearsed? "Maybe we should go someplace else," he said, although he hadn't thought to come up with a Plan B.

"This is fine." Jennifer gave him her perfect white, white smile, and Nick would have to say that it was full of *expectation*.

How was he going to kiss her in front of all these people? He liked little kids—he generally liked them a lot—but this group was ruining his perfect big ta-da! What would Loretta do in this situation? Would she march over to the parents and tell them to make their screaming brats shut up?

He deflected a ball that was aimed at Jennifer's head. "Cut it out," he said to the smirking little boy.

"Is that your *girlfriend*?" he said in a whining voice. He badly needed a tissue.

"Yes," Jennifer said sweetly. "I'm his girlfriend. Now why don't you go ask one of the adults to administer your dose of Ritalin?"

The kid wiped his nose with his hand. "Okay," he said, and ran off.

The fountain erupted then, spewing water in a tall, straight column. It was the moment he had planned on producing the ring and saying, "Will you promise to be my wife some day?" But the screaming kids were now cheering and clapping, and the fountain was louder than he would have imagined. He wanted to yell in frustration, and he felt mortifyingly close to tears. He looked at Jennifer.

"This is fine," she mouthed.

So he took the ring out of his back pocket and opened the velvet box. She nodded, smiling.

So he put the ring on her finger and then—*what the hell?*—leaned over and kissed her.

Back in the van, he kissed her again, thoroughly. He didn't have much breath left to say, "I wanted this to be perfect."

"It was," she said.

"But the kids—"

"It was perfect because it was you who gave me the ring."

Aha! he thought. The time and place didn't really matter. It was the person, *The One*, who mattered. If you asked the right person, it was the perfect big ta-da. (He was going to have to share this piece of information with Loretta.) And just to clarify things further, he said, "So, we're promised to each other, right? We'll wait for each other, and then we'll get engaged, and then we'll get married, right?"

"That's what it's supposed to mean." Jennifer looked down at her ring.

"Supposed to mean?" He really wished he could have afforded a bigger diamond. Even though Jennifer's hand was small, the diamond was pathetically tiny.

Jennifer looked at him, her eyes moist with tears. "I love you so much, Nick."

"I love you, too."

"I don't want to wait."

He was confused. It wasn't as if they had waited to get married to have sex. "What do you mean?"

"I don't want to go to Stanford. I'd rather follow you to boot camp and then to Iraq and rent a one-room shack in a war-torn region, but I can't. My parents would die—not literally, of course—if I didn't follow their dream and go to Stanford, and so I will. I want to always be a good daughter to them, but I also want to be a good wife to you. I don't see why I can't be both."

Her excellent tutoring must have sharpened his mind, Nick thought, because he knew exactly what she meant. Probably, too, he had been thinking the same thoughts himself. "Will you marry me?" he asked.

"The sooner, the better," Jennifer said.

And so they were in a state of euphoria when they reached his house, bursting to share their news. "Mom! Dad! Annie!" he called as they ran from room to room. They found Mom on the patio with Aunt Sam. Dad and Annie followed them out.

It looked like he was interrupting a conversation between his mom and Aunt Sam, but he didn't care. His news had to be more important. "I have the best news in the world!" he shouted.

"You're going to graduate!" Mom said. She tried to rise from her chair but that proved to be impossible. "Help me up, Sam."

Unbelievably, he had almost forgotten about that. "Yes, but—"

"Congratulations, son. Dean Whittaker told me it was almost a sure thing, but now it's official. That's great!"

"Oh, Nick." Mom (kind of) hugged him. Because of her stomach, she could only put her arms around him halfway.

"Good going," Aunt Sam said.

"I already knew," Annie said.

"Now I can start planning a graduation party," Mom said. She would probably have liked to run up and down the street, telling everybody, but that, too, was impossible.

"That's not the best news," Nick said.

"What can be better than that?" Mom asked.

Nick put his arm around Jennifer and pulled her close. "We're engaged!"

The best news in the world was met with a stunned silence.

Practical, thorough Jennifer stepped up to the plate. "We were going to be promised to each other, but it seemed like an unnecessary step." She held out her hand to show them the ring. "We both know what we want, and it's each other." She looked up at Nick with love.

Dad looked at Mom, and Mom looked at Dad. How would Nick describe that look? Utter shock.

Dad said, "Why don't we concentrate on the graduation first, and then we can talk about this—development. You're both going in different directions and—"

"We know that," Nick interrupted. He didn't think he had ever interrupted his dad before, but on this subject, he was not going to be deterred. He was eighteen, legally an adult, and so was Jennifer.

"I haven't even met Jennifer's parents," his mom said weakly.

"Wow," Aunt Sam said.

"It's going to be a short engagement," Jennifer said.

Nick squeezed her shoulders. "It sure is. On Wednesday, right after graduation, we're going to Vegas!"

The only one who could manage any speech to that announcement was Annie. "Holy shit," she said.

13

CHAPTER THIRTEEN

It was mercilessly hot. Alex wondered yet again why SCDS tradition insisted on holding the high school graduation ceremony outside, in June, in the Arizona desert, when there was a perfectly accessible air-conditioned gym yards away. The sun, minutes before, had dropped below the distant mountains, and the sunset was a stunning striation of orange, red, and pink hues. However, the beauty of the sunset did not in any way mitigate her discomfort. Her pregnant bulk flared over the white, narrow, straight-backed chair, she was sweating profusely, and she had been feeling *funky* all day. It wasn't like she was having contractions, not really. She was fairly certain that she still remembered what contractions felt like. Even though the baby was due today, she would not be born. Both Nick and Annie had been one week late, and Alex was certain this was the case with Sophie. She would not enter the world on the night of Nick's graduation.

She would not enter the world on the night of Nick's *wedding.*

But that had been a close call.

Nick and Jennifer had firmly stood their ground. They were going to get married. Period. It had taken hours of persuasion from Jack, her, and Jennifer's parents, Cornelia and Charles, just to convince the young couple that they could at least wait until the end of July. Both sets of parents were trying to barter more time. Both sets of parents were probably thinking that maybe, just maybe, if they had more time, they could convince the young couple of the folly of their plan. But Nick and Jennifer stood before them, the parental firing squad, with hands held tightly, repeating, "No, we don't want to wait. We're in love."

The final thing that convinced them—the straw that broke their combined, stalwart resolution—was when Alex said, her voice choked with tears, "If you go to Vegas to get married on Wednesday, I won't be able to go. I can't travel when I'm this pregnant. Please, Nick, I'm your mother. Please wait until I can go to your wedding."

Nick was obviously torn, but he was her son. He looked at Jennifer and said, "I suppose we can wait a little bit. What do you think, Jennifer?" Jennifer said that she supposed a *little* wait would be acceptable.

Jennifer's parents had reluctantly given up on the summer course Jennifer was supposed to take, with a vow from Jennifer that she would go to school and she would graduate. So it was agreed that Nick would not enlist in the Marines, and Jennifer would not go to Stanford until August. Cornelia and Charles had not seemed as stunned by the announcement as Alex and Jack, and it became clear during those long hours of discussion that Nick had spent time with them and that they were quite fond of him.

On the other hand, she and Jack barely knew Jennifer at all. Whose fault was that? Hers and Jack's. They had been so caught up in their own contentiousness that they had not made any effort to know the pretty little girl who had sat diligently at their kitchen table for two weeks, tutoring their son, ensuring that he would graduate. Why had she never had the girl over for dinner? Even Sam had done that. However, already certain personality traits of Jennifer were starting to emerge. Cornelia, on her way out the door, said to Alex, "My daughter has a stubborn streak, and she always knows what she wants." Alex's response had been: "No kidding."

Alex was still having a hard time wrapping her mind around the facts that her son was going into military service and was also going to get married at the young age of eighteen. But after all the events of the last year, she and Jack had discovered during their first counseling session that they had no fight left in them. None. Not directed towards each other and not directed towards their children, and the revelation had been a relief. They had then resigned themselves to the "as long as they're happy" philosophy. Really, what else could they do? And there was still a chance, although it was starting to look like a long shot, that Nick would change his mind.

Things would have turned out differently if she had not agreed to be a surrogate for Sam. Alex knew this. She would have been paying more attention to her kids. She would have been as diligent as she had always been, right? She would have been happy, right? But the foundation of her supposed happiness had been growing increasingly flimsy. Even before Sam moved across the street and proposed this outlandish plan, she had felt as if things were starting to crumble around her, as if her children were leaving her before she was willing to let them go. Still, she might have been a better mother to them during their struggles the last year if she had not been absorbed with her pregnancy. She supposed the real question was this: Was she sorry?

No. She wanted this baby. After conceiving and carrying this child for nine months, she very much wanted this baby.

"Would you like another bottle of water?" Sam was sitting next to her, fanning herself with the program.

"I better not." Alex had already had two and hoped that she wouldn't have to get up in the middle of the ceremony to use the restroom. It would be the ultimate irony if she missed her son's graduation, the ceremony that she had put such emphasis on for years, because she had to pee.

"Do you feel all right?" Sam looked at her intently. She had been asking this question all day, following Alex around, driving her to her errands. She acted like the due date meant that this *was* the day the baby would be born.

"Why don't you put on a catcher's mitt, Sam? I'll tell you when the baby's coming, then I'll squat, and you can catch it. Would that work for you?" Alex said irritably.

"Actually, that's exactly what I want, Alex," Sam snapped back. "As a matter of fact, my catcher's mitt is in the trunk of the car. It was a great deal, too, for that Spaulding glove. Sports Authority was having quite the sale."

"As long as it's sterilized."

"I soaked it in iodine."

"The ceremony is about to start," Chris said, attempting to intervene in their bickering. He sat on the other side of Sam, then Jack, Annie, Carla, and Dylan. The grandparents had yet to appear.

"I know I'm getting on your nerves," Sam said, "but I'm only trying to be helpful. My baby could be born this very night."

"Let's concentrate on Nick's graduation." Alex shifted uncomfortably in the hard chair. Of course she hadn't told Sam how she had come to feel about this baby. Alex knew her sister well enough to know that Sam suspected something was up. Sam knew that corners had been turned when Alex found out Sam had kept secrets about Annie, and then of course, the icing on the cake, when Alex found out about the tryst at their parents' anniversary party. After their millions of conversations, at this pivotal time in their lives, neither one could bear to voice what they were both thinking. Alex might want the baby, too. Sam would be heartbroken. Promises would be broken. Their life as twin sisters would be irrevocably shattered.

Jack leaned forward in the narrow aisle. "Alex, Annie wants to know if you have any gum."

He should be sitting next to her, sharing in this moment of celebration, but they weren't there yet. They had been more than civil to each other— kind, in fact—but things were still a long way from where they used to be. The counseling was helping, but rebuilding on raw emotions was going to be very hard work. She dug in her purse and pulled out a misshapen, flinty piece of Juicy Fruit and passed it down. Alex heard a resounding "yuck!" from Annie, and then the ceremony started.

The high school band began playing *Pomp and Circumstance*, the audience stood, and the processional started down the aisle between the two sections of chairs—first the faculty, followed by the students in their navy-blue robes. Nick passed right by her, and Alex reached out, but she wasn't quite close enough to touch him. He gave her, and she supposed, the entire family, the "thumbs up" sign and a big grin as he continued down the aisle to his seat in front. Already, to Alex, he looked older. Already, to Alex, he was almost gone.

When the processional was done, the audience took its seat. Something was definitely *not right*. Alex gasped at the force of the spasm.

Sam noticed. "Alex?" Concern etched her face.

"It's nothing. These damn chairs are too hard." She would ignore whatever it was. The baby hadn't even turned yet and would not be born tonight. Tonight was Nick's, only his.

She was fine, she told herself, as she ignored the next spasm as best she could. She readjusted herself on the unforgiving chair. Sam kept sneaking looks at her, and Alex gave her a forced smile and a nod.

The boring ceremony—the one she had so longed for—droned on and on. The president of the school board gave a speech (who cared what he thought?), Dean Whittaker gave a speech (something about family and community), the class sponsor gave a speech (unintelligible), the salutatorian gave a speech (bright future before us, blah, blah, blah). The valedictorian, who was Jennifer, spoke next. As she shifted in her chair, Alex tried valiantly to pay attention to this bright girl who might soon be her daughter-in-law. The only part that came through the pain of Alex's intermittent spasms was something Jennifer said about destiny. At that point, she looked meaningfully at Nick. *She has already claimed him,* thought Alex, and tears welled.

"We need to take you to the hospital," Sam whispered. She knew.

"No, I'm fine." She wasn't. Oh, *come on,* she wanted to scream. *There are only sixty-three graduating students. Give them their damn diplomas and be done with it!*

The final speaker, the head of the upper school, gave a eulogy to Walter Caldwell, the class president, the captain of the lacrosse team, the epitome of all that was bright in the future of these young people. The audience sobbed. Alex barely had the presence of mind to take a quick peek at Annie. She stared stoically ahead. Alex, too, along with the SCDS community, had mourned the needless, horrific suicide of one of their own, but now, in the throes of another spasm—she might as well start calling them contractions— she was thinking along the lines of: *The kid committed a selfish act. The kid got my sixteen-year-old pregnant.* Hand out the damn diplomas!

Finally, they started to call out the names of the graduates. Each one walked across the stage, accepting the handshake of the school board president, the class sponsor, and Dean Whittaker. And dear Lord, each one milked it for all it was worth. They pranced, they beamed, they paraded across the stage. When it was Nick's turn, his row of family—Alex's row—stood up and cheered and clapped and stomped their feet, trying to make as much celebratory noise as possible.

That was when her water broke. She stood in the puddle, clapping and whistling with all her might. Her son was a high school graduate, and she was going to have a baby. Soon. She sat back down, trying not to pant. She would make it through the rest of the ceremony through sheer will.

"You're in labor," Sam said. "Let's go."

"I am going to stay until the end," Alex said. "The baby can wait."

"You might want to let the baby know that because it's looking as if he has other plans." Sam took hold of her arm.

"I want to stay and congratulate him. I want to take a picture of him in his robe. I bought him a cake!"

"I don't think you have much of a choice here, Alex." To the rest, she said, "I'm taking her to the hospital. She's in labor."

"Great timing, Mom," Annie said.

"I want to go," Carla said. "Come on, Annie, we could use some excitement after this boring thing. God, could they drag it out any longer?"

"Whoa, Mrs. C." Dylan turned a whiter shade of pale. "I think I'll pass."

"I'll drive." Chris stood up.

"I'm going, too," Jack said. He was immediately at Alex's side.

"I'm taking her," Sam said.

Alex was going to have to give in and let Sam take her to the hospital. This was her third baby, and the contractions were coming fast. "No, everybody needs to stay here. Jack, you have to stay. One of us needs to be here when it's over. One of us needs to congratulate him properly and take lots of pictures. Unfortunately, it won't be me. I'm having a baby."

"There are too many people in this room," Dr. Weinstein said as he tried to squeeze through the door. He had a point. All eight of them—Sam, Chris, Jack, Nick, Jennifer, Annie, Carla, and Dylan—were crowded into the small maternity room at Osborn North Hospital. Shortly after Sam had checked Alex in, they arrived *en masse.*

"I agree with the doctor, although I'm glad my family's here." Alex said, panting. "However, I don't need an audience right now. I've had much better hair days." Already, her hair was plastered to her forehead with sweat.

Sam agreed with the doctor, too. All these people—she didn't include herself—were sucking the oxygen out of the room, and Alex was gasping enough as it was.

"We're here to give you moral support," Carla said. She was eating a candy bar, acting like she was a spectator at some sporting event.

"Who are you?" the doctor asked.

Under the doctor's glare, Carla had the good sense to throw away the candy bar. "Well, I'm a family friend, or to be more precise, I'm the best friend of the patient's daughter."

"I invited her," Annie said sheepishly. "I'm the patient's daughter."

"I'm her son," Nick offered.

"I'm his fiancé," Jennifer said.

"I'm nobody," Dylan said. "They didn't want to take the time to drop me off at home."

"Out," the doctor said, not unkindly. "The waiting room is down the hall. We'll keep you posted." They left the room, and he said, "Five down, two to go. I understand your husband wanting to be here, Alex, but you two?"

"I'm the baby's mother, Dr. Weinstein, don't you remember?" Sam said quickly. "I came to Alex's first few doctor appointments." But she hadn't been to any in months. Alex had not invited her, saying that they were just routine. Sam felt a panic attack coming on. She should have insisted on going to every appointment. She should have driven herself to Walgreens to pick up Alex's prenatal vitamins. Should have, would have, could have. "Alex is my surrogate."

"Be that as it may—and I do remember, now that you've reminded me—it is Alex who is my patient. Alex is the one having a baby, and I need to do an examination to see where we are at this point."

Sam grabbed Chris's arm, presenting him to the doctor like a present. "This is the baby's father."

Chris was decidedly uncomfortable. He cleared his throat. "Sam."

"Go ahead, tell him who you are." Her heart was an injured bird, flapping uselessly. It was paramount that she establish the relationships now, here, in front of this doctor, in front of everybody in this room. She was the baby's mother, and Chris was the baby's father, and Alex was the vessel to bring their baby into the world. The *vessel*.

Jack, who had said little since arriving, who had sat by Alex's side, stroking her arm and feeding her ice chips, murmuring things that Sam could not hear, decided to assert his rightful position at this awful point. "Cut the crap, Sam. I'm Alex's husband, and *my wife* is having a baby. Get the hell out."

"She can stay," Alex said.

Sam was flooded with relief.

"We'll go get a cup of coffee," Chris said, taking Sam's arm.

"I'm staying here." She had the weirdest notion that, if she left, when she came back Alex and the baby would be gone, vanished, as if the entirety of the last year had been an unattainable dream.

"Let's give Alex some privacy," Chris said firmly. He gave her the look that said: I know you're having a panic attack, and you need to do something about it now.

She did need to do something about it. She knew that. She needed to pop a Valium and regain her self-control.

Alex groaned. She was now bathed in sweat.

"Remember our Lamaze classes with Nick and Annie, honey?" Jack said. He wiped her brow with a damp cloth. "Remember how we brought that ugly Cabbage Patch doll to the hospital for you to focus on?"

He was doing her job. She should be the one feeding Alex ice chips and wiping her brow. Should have, would have, could have. "We'll be back soon," she said. She couldn't look at the two of them like that, intimately together—against her? Alex was in pain, and he was the comforter. And she was the twin sister who had caused it to happen.

Alex was in pain because of *her*. Sam had brought her pain in too many ways. She did need to leave the room. Because she was crying. "I wish it were me," she said softly.

Alex heard her. "I know."

After Sam went into the restroom and took her pill, she stopped by the waiting room. The kids—she guessed they weren't really kids anymore—were playing poker.

Annie threw her cards on the table. "I suck at this game."

Carla had a pile of cotton balls in front of her. "You need to learn how to bluff, Annie."

"Oh, she knows how to bluff, all right." Nick's pile wasn't as fluffy as Carla's, and he was the dealer this round.

"I don't understand bluffing either. It seems to me it's a form of lying. Either you have the cards, or you don't. Why try to win if you don't have a good hand?" Jennifer delicately selected one card from her hand. "I'll take one, Nick."

He kissed the card before he handed it to her.

"That's just gross, Nick. Do you know how many people's hands have touched those things? They're a germ fest," Annie said.

"Great," Dylan said. "Now we know Jennifer's got a good hand." He turned his cards over. "I fold."

"Don't be a pussy, Dylan," Carla said.

They seemed so content, and she envied their calmness. This was one of the biggest days in her life, and they had the ability to play cards. (What if Alex didn't give her the baby? How could she go on?)

Annie saw her first. "What's going on with Mom, Aunt Sam?"

"The doctor's examining her."

"Exciting, huh?"

"Very."

Annie looked at her strangely. "Do you want to go to the cafeteria with me?"

"No, it's too far. What if your mom needs me?" Where in the hell was Chris? He probably had gone to the cafeteria for a cup of coffee. He was probably also having a piece of cherry pie *a la mode*. The shit.

"The vending machine is just at the end of the hall. Come on." Annie tugged Sam down the hall. "Everything is going to be all right, isn't it?"

"Of course it is, honey!" she said brightly, too brightly. She wasn't sure, exactly, what Annie was asking. Did she know that her mother had plans for keeping the baby, or perhaps—Sam's heart seized in her chest—did Annie have some weird idea that she should have the baby to replace the baby she had lost? That couldn't be it. That was not it. Sam knew she was going a little crazy from all the anxiety; the Valium had not fully kicked in.

"Having a baby is the most natural thing in the world!" She didn't really believe this, not at all. She had had a C-section, major surgery. And Alex had had two C-sections. Why oh why had she and Alex decided that she should have a natural childbirth with this baby? Because the decision had been made before Alex got pregnant on one of their three-bottles-of-wine nights. That's why.

Sam dug in her purse for some change. She didn't have any. She pulled out a twenty. "What do you want?" She inserted the bill into the machine and blindly started pushing buttons.

"I didn't really want anything, Aunt Sam, and I don't think that machine gives change for a twenty."

"We'll use it all up then. We'll buy junk food for everybody." She pushed buttons, packs were pushed off their rows and piled up in the tray below.

"I didn't know it would be like this. I've seen stuff on TV and in the movies, but I didn't know it would be like this. Seeing Mom . . . it's *intense*."

Annie was right. Sam hadn't dwelt on the physicality either. Theory was being put into practice, and she had to agree. It was *intense*.

"I am too young to have a baby," Annie said quietly.

Now they were getting to the heart of the matter. Sam stopped pushing buttons long enough to put her arm around her niece. "Yes, honey."

"But I was going to do it. I was going to have the baby and put it up for adoption. I was going to recommend you to be the mother, if they would have let me do that sort of thing. I had this fantasy I was working out right before we got into the accident that I could give the baby to you and visit it every day. Something like that. I hadn't figured it all out yet . . ." she trailed off.

What could Sam say to that? What did you say to a sixteen-year-old who had miscarried the baby of her dead boyfriend? Did you placate her with platitudes: everything happens for a reason, it's all for the best, it was not meant to be? Even a sixteen-year-old knew such hollow sentiments were total, utter bullshit. Sam hoped that Annie had been talking to her therapist about this because she was at a loss. "I'm so, so sorry," she finally managed to say. "So sorry."

Annie sniffled. "I'll be glad when this is over. It's all so . . . *painful*."

"Everything is going to turn out wonderfully, you'll see," Sam said in her bright, false voice. She wasn't doing a very good job of comforting her niece. She wasn't even sure if comfort was what Annie wanted or needed at this difficult moment.

"Yeah, sure." Annie scooped out the loot from the tray.

"I'll help you carry all the stuff. I didn't know a twenty could buy so much." Sam wished an all-knowing, benevolent voice would whisper in her ear and tell her what she should be saying to dear, sweet Annie. Granted, Annie had fucked up magnificently over the last year, but she was a teenager. Sam, too, hadn't been a model of good behavior over the past year. She was forty. What was *her* excuse? She needed an all-knowing giant hand to descend from heaven and slap some sense into her.

When she got back to the room, they were lifting Alex onto a gurney. "Is it time?" Why hadn't they called or texted? Were they going to leave her behind? She hadn't been gone more than five minutes.

"There's been a change of plans, Sam. Alex is going in for a C-section." Jack put his hand on her shoulder. Where in the hell was Chris?

Sam knew that the baby hadn't turned, but there was too much frenzy in the room, too many people, too many monitors. "What's wrong?"

"Everything's fine." Alex stifled a scream. "You can give me that epidural shot as soon as we get into the delivery room. Make it a double."

Sam didn't believe that everything was fine. "Jack? It's my baby!"

He hesitated, looked toward his wife. Alex shook her head.

"Tell me. Please." She could imagine so many awful things happening.

He must have felt pity for her. Quietly, he said, "The umbilical cord is wrapped around the baby's neck."

That was one of the awful things. The baby was not getting enough oxygen. How tightly was the cord wrapped around his neck? What if her baby suffered brain damage?

She would love him anyway. She would love him no matter what. She said a silent prayer. They had come so far. *They were this close.* Please, please, please God, let him live.

She and Jack followed the gurney out into the hall. One of the orderlies, the tall one who looked like a skinny version of Charles Barkley, said, "Which one of you is going into the delivery room?"

"I am," Sam said. She grabbed Alex's hand as they raced down the hall with the gurney carrying her sister and her baby. These guys were moving fast. She could smell their sense of urgency.

"We both are," Jack said. He grabbed Alex's other hand. He was in better shape than Sam. He wasn't even out of breath.

"Dr. Weinstein only allows one companion during a surgery," the orderly said. "It's his policy, and he's a stickler about it." They had reached the swinging door leading into the emergency room.

"I'm her husband," Jack said.

"I'm the baby's mother," Sam said.

"Alex," they both pleaded.

Alex's contraction had subsided. "I don't have time for *Sophie's Choice* now, you two. You're going to have to understand this, Jack, and I don't want you to say a word or argue or bring it up again later, but I want Sam in the delivery room with me."

"Here we go." The orderlies pushed open the door.

Sam didn't look back at Jack, and she didn't think about him as she washed up twice and changed into scrubs while Alex was getting the epidural. This is how she had imagined it: She and Alex in the delivery room, the baby being born, the baby being weighed and examined and found perfect, the baby being handed to her, the sense of accomplishment they both would feel, the sense of rightness.

She sat by Alex, holding her hand. The screen erected at Alex's chest prevented them from seeing the birth. It had been the same when she gave birth to Grace, and she knew that Alex was feeling a strong tugging sensation. "I'm so proud of you," she said to her sister. "Thank you."

"I'm glad we did this." Alex squeezed her hand. "No matter what."

Sam didn't have time to dwell on *no matter what* because the doctor was presenting the baby over the top of the screen, the tiny bottom resting in his hands, the baby's feet crossed, and its tiny belly sticking out. It looked like a miniature Buddha.

"You have a baby girl," he said, his voice muffled by his surgical mask.

"I knew it!" Alex said. "She and I have been talking about a lot of girl stuff these last few months."

"She's beautiful," Sam breathed. She was the most gorgeous thing— next to Grace—that she had ever seen. Perhaps, in her heart of hearts, she had pretended to want a boy because she was afraid, or felt that it would be disloyal, to want another girl, as if another girl would replace Grace. She knew the instant she saw this baby that it would never happen. She would always have the memory of Grace, distinct and loved, but this baby would be Madeline, another story to unfold, distinct and loved.

She cried.

Alex cried. "She's incredibly beautiful."

The baby was a healthy seven pounds, three ounces, and twenty inches long. Her Apgar score was nine (only doctors' babies received a perfect ten—an old delivery room joke), and then she was whisked away to recovery. Sam was disappointed, of course, she longed to hold this baby that she had dreamed about for so long, but Dr. Weinstein was a stickler about that, too; the baby was removed while he wrapped up the surgery.

Sam waited in the room with the others while Alex spent the required amount of time in recovery. She waited impatiently, euphorically for her baby girl. She's beautiful, she's incredible, she's perfect, Sam told the others. She recited the baby's statistics, told them about her thick black hair. Her eyes, of course, were blue. All baby's eyes were blue, but she already knew that Madeline's eyes would not change color. They would remain cornflower blue, and when she lost her newborn hair, it would grow in blonde and curly. She would wear smocked dresses and patent leather shoes, but she would also know how to throw a ball and climb trees. She could become a ballerina or a Nobel scientist or a lesbian. Sam didn't care. She would love her *no matter what.* Her little girl.

Such was her euphoria, it took her awhile to realize that Chris was not there. Where in the hell was he?

Finally, they wheeled in Alex and the baby. Alex was holding the baby, Sam's baby, wrapped in a pink blanket with a pink beanie on her head. Sam should have been the one to hold her first, but she would overlook this. Alex was the one who had carried the baby for nine months and then endured emergency surgery to give her birth. She was allowed to hold the baby for a few minutes. Two minutes.

Immediately, everyone crowded around, and again, there were too many people in the small place. (Where was Dr. Weinstein when you needed him?) Sam could barely get close enough to the bed to see her. If these people did not move soon, she would start elbowing her way to her baby.

Jack kissed Alex's cheek. "I'm glad you're all right. She is a beauty, isn't she?" The baby clasped his finger. Alex beamed.

"Wow," Annie said, "she's so tiny."

"She looks like a little doll." Even the cynical Carla had a sense of awe in her voice.

"She looks like a little pink doll, dude," said Dylan. "Why is she so pink?"

"All babies are pink, Dylan," Jennifer said with authority. Since Sam was standing behind them, she heard her whisper to Nick, "Our babies will be half Korean."

"Our babies will be beautiful," Nick whispered back.

Oh, knock it off, Sam wanted to scream. Everybody thinks everything is beautiful when you've been engaged for a whopping five days. Which reminded her. Where in the hell was Chris?

"She looks a lot like Annie," Jack said.

"I think so, too," Alex said as she gazed lovingly at *Sam's baby.*

That was enough. Sam did elbow her way to the bedside. "I need to hold my baby now." She held out her arms. Was it her imagination? Did she see the reluctance in Alex's eyes? No matter. Her baby was in her arms. Finally, her baby was in her arms, and she was never going to let her go. She would demand that they put a cot in this room, so she could spend the night next to her baby in her bassinet.

"I can't believe this," she said, tears streaming down her cheeks. "My baby is here." The baby fit perfectly in the curve of her arm. She would never be able to fully thank her sister for this gift of love. Alex had made it all possible. Alex had made all her dreams come true.

"What's her name, Aunt Sam?" Annie was right next to her, peering down at the pink bundle. She seemed incapable of tearing her eyes away from this perfect little girl.

Sam, too, had great difficulty tearing her eyes away from her baby. She looked at Alex and smiled. "Her name is Sophie."

Chris was in the cafeteria drinking a cup of black, bitter coffee and eating a piece of pie. He sat alone at a table in the corner. He was hiding.

He hated hospitals and had from the time that his dad died in Memorial Hospital in Wheaton, IL. It had been a year-long, painful battle with prostate cancer, and even now, years later, the smell of a hospital—antiseptic grief—made him feel as if he might faint. His dad was an old man at the time of his death. Granted, he had been old when Chris was born, but it had not made it any less heart-wrenching to see him lying helpless on the white, nondescript hospital bed, connected to a feeding tube and a morphine drip. He took so long to die that it almost seemed as if he had never been alive. His dying was the prominent image imprinted upon Chris's memory.

He was thinking about death, and it was supposed to be a joyful event, the birth of his and Sam's baby. Of course it all depended upon whether Alex actually gave them the baby. He had consulted his lawyer once again, and his lawyer had assured him that oral contracts were indeed binding. Right. Without any witnesses, it could rapidly disintegrate into a costly legal battle of he said/she said, he said/she said. He was exhausted from mulling all of this over so many times and not being able to come up with a definitive answer.

And he was exhausted from thinking about what no one else had seemed to consider. What if the baby wasn't his? What if the baby was Jack's? Neither he nor Sam had asked Alex, "Did you sleep with Jack that weekend?" So single-minded in her determination to get a baby, Sam had not even let herself imagine this possibility. And Chris thought it was a definite possibility. Jack seemed to him to be the kind of man who would have regular sex with his wife—at least before his wife got pregnant by another man, if that was indeed the case.

And most of all, he was exhausted from thinking about Sam. He had seen her in the depths of grief before when Grace died, and he did not think she could survive another bout with that kind of pain. The most frightening aspect—he could barely stand to think of it—was that he didn't think Sam would *want* to survive the enormity of the realization that she would never have a biological child. She had been fueled by hope, only by hope, for far too long.

He should have forced her to keep seeing a therapist, but he had not.

He should never have gone along with this plan, but he had.

He should go back up to the room and be with Sam as she watched her twin sister in labor, the labor she was incapable of having. He didn't want to go. Before, when they had all been crowded into that tiny hospital room, he had felt a curious sense of detachment. It wasn't his wife in labor, it might or might not be his child, and quite frankly, he was weary of the whole thing.

Or so he told himself. He would not let himself imagine seeing the child. He would not let his mind go there. He had been, and would continue to be, the practical one of the four in this tricky situation. However, and he hadn't told anyone this, not even Sam, he had received an unexpected royalty check from a book he had published a few years back. And he had opened a savings account, a college fund, for the child. No one else needed to know.

He pushed his half-eaten pie away. He should go back upstairs. This cafeteria was certainly no place for people watching. Too many people, like him, were sitting alone, hunched over their stringy stroganoff and dried hamburgers. Except for a group of young nurses—all overweight, all wearing unbecoming scrubs with bunnies or kittens—not one person smiled. Not one. Hospitals were horrible, depressing places. Except for the births. He should go back upstairs. His wife might need him.

His phone sat on the table, and it vibrated. He recognized the number of Golden Manor. He had not spoken to Louise since they had met at the Biltmore before her "elopement" to Mr. Peterson. She was his problem now, he had thought, and he wished the old man well. He stared at the vibrating phone, and his hand moved toward it. Instinct told him to answer it. "Yes, Mother," he said.

"Mr. Connor, this is Imogene Baker, the assistant director of Golden Manor," the woman said. "I'm afraid I have some bad news."

Leave it to Louise to have another fake heart attack on this of all days. He sighed, then went into polite-son mode. "Is my mother ill?"

"No, Mr. Connor, Louise is not ill." The woman cleared her throat.

"Well?" Now he wanted to go upstairs. Anything was preferable than dealing with Louise. What was she complaining about this time?

"I'm sorry to be the one to tell you this," and Imogene did sound genuinely sorry, "but your mother has been in an accident."

Louise didn't drive. Had the walker that she sometimes used, for effect, collided with a wheelchair? Had Mr. Peterson finally seen the light and gotten so fed up with her that he pushed her down a flight of stairs? Chris was going to be patient about this, but only to a point. He stood up. It was time to go upstairs. "What kind of accident?"

"A car accident."

"My mother does not drive," he told her. Then the obvious occurred. "Was Mr. Peterson driving?"

"No, your mother was driving."

Chris's mouth went dry. Louise, driving a car, was a disaster waiting to happen. She always confused the brake and gas pedals. He had made sure that her license was taken away ten years ago after she plowed into the side of a Jewel grocery store. "I don't understand."

Imogene quickly, somberly told him the details. Louise and Mr. Peterson had left a note saying that they were taking a weekend trip to the Wisconsin Dells. The note said that they would be back in two days. Under normal circumstances, Imogene told him, they would have had to ask permission, and of course, permission would not have been granted since Louise did not have a driver's license and Mr. Peterson had not passed his last driving test. They had run away, she said, and Golden Manor was not in any way responsible for what had occurred. She stressed this point. Golden Manor was *not responsible.*

Chris's mind was spinning in disbelief. Imogene didn't say it, but he knew. He knew by the surprising, shocking stab in his heart. "They're both dead."

"Yes. I'm so sorry."

He could not believe it. "They were married," he said, uselessly.

"Well." Imogene cleared her throat again. "I guess that's a matter of debate."

Suddenly, and for no reason, he felt heated about this point. "Yes, they were married. I saw them before they went to Vegas to get married."

"Yes. Well. If the marriage certificate signed by Elvis is—"

"Did she injure anyone else?" The cherry pie was rising in his throat. He imagined a school bus filled with kids.

"No, I suppose that's something to be thankful for under these dire circumstances, isn't it?" Imogene sounded almost hopeful. "She hit a tree. Unfortunately, they were not wearing seatbelts."

Mean-spirited, willful Louise had hit a tree. And she had died. And she had killed Mr. Peterson for good measure. She had not been kind towards people, except for Dorothy, the housekeeper she had given his inheritance to. She had never once told Chris, her only son, her only child, that she loved him.

She was the only mother he would ever have. Both of his parents were dead now. What did that make him? An orphan? No, it made him an old man. He realized he was crying.

"Mr. Connor, how soon do you think you can come to Illinois and make the necessary arrangements?"

He needed to go and bury his mother. "Tonight." His voice cracked. "I'll leave on the last plane tonight."

Imogene had to clear her throat again. "And I should probably let you know, Mr. Connor, that Mr. Peterson's family has some," she searched for the appropriate word, "issues."

"What kind of issues?"

"Well, there's the will, and—well, I think it would be better to discuss these things when you get here. I'm so sorry for your loss, Mr. Connor." Imogene hurried off the phone, her unpleasant task completed.

His loss. Louise, his mother, was dead. How many times had he thought that his life would be so much less complicated without her? How many times had he wanted her, not dead exactly, but out of his life? Too many times to count. And now she was dead, and he was surprised how much it hurt, surprised to find out at last how much he cared about Louise. She was the only mother he would ever have.

He lost track of time, sitting alone in that dreary, depressing cafeteria. He was in a daze, and it took a great deal of effort to rouse himself and go upstairs. He had a lot of preparations to make. He and Sam would be leaving tonight. She would not want to go, she would undoubtedly make a scene, but she would go. He needed her now more than he had ever needed anybody before.

When he got to the room, he was relieved to see that it contained only Sam, Alex, and Jack. He wouldn't have to deliver his unhappy announcement in front of the kids. Sam was holding a baby wrapped in pink. They had had a girl, and Sam, judging by her face, was already deeply, madly in love. "Look at our daughter," she said. "She's absolutely perfect."

Chris did not want to look. If he did, he would be truly lost.

"Where in the hell have you been?" Sam was not angry. She gazed at the baby. "You missed all the excitement. Alex had an emergency C-section, but everything turned out perfectly."

Chris looked over at Alex and Jack. They couldn't take their eyes off the baby either. Nothing had been decided. He could tell.

He felt more tears well up and fought for self-control. On principle, he was not a crying man, and he had already done all the meager crying for his mother he was going to do, alone, in the dreary cafeteria. His wife was holding the baby she had longed for, and his mother had hit a tree. He didn't know how else to handle the situation, so he blurted it out. "Louise is dead. Sam, we have to leave tonight."

Sam said nothing. She stared at the baby.

"I'm so sorry, Chris," Alex said. "I never met your mother, but I'm sure she was a lovely woman." Alex was trying to do the right thing, say the appropriate words of consolation.

"She wasn't a lovely woman. I've told you countless stories of how bitchy she was, Alex."

"I know, but you tend to exaggerate, Sam."

"My mother is—was—not a very nice woman. But she was my mother."

"I'm not leaving Sophie." Sam finally looked at him. "I'm not leaving our baby."

Sophie? The name was not one that he and Sam had discussed, but he had no time for that now. He allowed a quick glance at the baby, the rosebud mouth and the tiny fist against her cheek. Even that was too much.

"We have to do the right thing. We have to bury my mother."

"We just had a baby, Chris. Leave it to that vindictive bitch to go and die today on one of the happiest days of my life."

"I'll take care of Sophie until you get back," Alex interceded. She eagerly lifted her hands toward the baby.

It was a slight movement, but it was a protective one. Sam shifted ever so slightly away from her sister. "She could come with us."

"No," Chris, Jack, and Alex said. She's too young, a newborn. There are germs on the plane. There is too much baggage to pack—stroller, bassinet, diaper bag, bottles, etcetera. The trip would only be for three or four days. They wore Sam down. They reasoned with her. They argued with her. Still, she held the baby as if she would never let go.

Finally, exhausted, Chris said, "I need you to come with me, Sam. You're the only family I have left." His voice broke.

"I can take care of her for the three or four days," Alex said.

"You just had surgery," Sam whispered.

She was weakening. Chris knew that she didn't want to let go of the baby, not ever, but she also would never intentionally put the baby in harm's way.

"I'll help," Jack said. "I'm a pro at changing diapers."

"Please, Sam," Chris said quietly. "I've never asked you for anything before."

Sam gazed at the baby for a few, long moments before she said, "You're a good man, Chris." With sadness, with love, and reluctantly, very slowly, she handed the baby to Alex.

"Could you please watch the baby while we're gone? Dad and I have a meeting at the bank. It shouldn't take more than an hour, and Sophie should sleep the entire time. She just had a bottle." The baby had only been home for three days, and Mom was still wearing her maternity clothes. Because of the stitches, she walked tilting slightly forward, as if she were walking on thin ice.

"No problem," Carla said. "You can count on us. We won't even charge you!"

No, is what Annie wanted to say. So far, she had managed to keep her distance from the baby, watching from afar as someone else held her. Nick had managed to give her a bottle, Jennifer had taken a turn, and even her dad was pitching in. But not her. (G: Sooner or later, you will need to hold the baby. A: Later.)

"Well then, good." Mom obviously had not been planning on paying them anyway. "The baby monitor is on, so you girls can watch TV or something."

As soon as they left, Carla said, "Let's go check on the baby."

Annie picked up the baby monitor sitting on the kitchen counter. "She's not making any noise." She didn't want to look at the baby. She didn't even want to *think* about babies. Everyone around her had babies on the *brain.*

"Oh, come on," Carla said, starting up the stairs. "This is the first time I've ever gotten to babysit."

"We're not babysitting her. We're *listening.*" Annie picked up the monitor again.

Carla came back down the stairs. "Are you talking to Georgia about this?" Carla knew that Annie was having a hard time dealing with the baby.

Annie didn't answer.

"Good. That means *yes.* It's *essential* that we examine our feelings. I am, of course, quoting Raymundo."

"His name is Raymond, not Raymundo." Carla had been seeing her therapist for two weeks.

"He's half Hispanic, so I'm going to call him Raymundo. He doesn't seem to mind. In fact, I think he finds me quite entertaining." Carla put her ear to the monitor. "Are you sure this thing is on?"

"He thinks you're entertaining because you make up all kinds of shit to tell him. You told him you slept with the entire football team." Which was kind of funny. SCDS didn't have a football team.

Carla laughed. "I also told him I was incapable of orgasm. Raymundo can't decide if I'm promiscuous or frigid. Or a nympho. He thinks I might by a nympho."

It made Annie uncomfortable when Carla talked about sex so *specifically.* Annie still wasn't sure what an orgasm was, or a nympho—not that she would ever tell Carla. That one night, after she had been with Walter, Carla had asked her if she had had an orgasm. Annie had said yes. (She had talked about most things with Georgia by now, but the orgasm thing wasn't one of them. She would buy the next issue of *Cosmo,* just to be more informed if she ever broached the subject with her.)

"My next major project with Raymundo is to tell him that I'm falling in love with him. He's kind of cute in a thirtyish type of way. I'm going to develop a classic case of transference."

"Therapy is not going to help if you don't tell the truth." Annie blushed. Where was she getting off saying something like that? It had taken her a lot of sessions to get honest with Georgia, and she still hadn't told her *everything*.

"Oh, Annie, Annie, Annie. What's a girl got to do to have fun around here? We're not drinking, we're not doing drugs, although Raymundo said he would write me a prescription for another antidepressant if I want it, and I might take him up on it. I'm not even smoking." She held out her hands and made them tremble like falling leaves. "I'm in serious withdrawal. I thought having Ron and Marge around more often was what I wanted, but now I'm having serious doubts."

Mr. and Mrs. Goldleib had been in town for three weeks straight, a record. "You know you like having them home," Annie said.

"Be careful what you wish for."

"That's a stupid saying," Annie said, wondering what it was she should be careful to wish for. She wished she hadn't messed up, and she still had a summer job with the Williams kids. She wished that Walter hadn't died. She wished she had not been in the accident. She wished *that baby* was not upstairs. What, exactly, was she supposed to be *careful* about? (G: Don't wish for things you can't *undo*, Annie. A: Shut up, Georgia.)

"Let's go check on the baby, Annie."

"She's fine." She pointed to the monitor again. "It's *All Quiet on the Western Front*." She had had to read the book for her English final.

"Her name is Sophie, and it's time that you quit using avoidance as a tactic. It will do you good to be in the same room with her. It will be therapeutic."

Carla thought she was such an expert. Carla had been in therapy for two weeks.

"I'll see you up there." She went upstairs.

Annie was not going to succumb. She was not. She had no interest in this baby who was either her cousin or her half-sister, depending upon how you looked at it. Mom had said the baby was her cousin when she first got pregnant, but now that the baby was here, Mom did not refer to her as Annie's cousin, as in, "Why don't you hold your *cousin*, Annie?" When she thought about it—and she tried not to—it was all totally confusing. She probably was using *avoidance* as a *tactic*.

"I can't tell if she's breathing," Carla's whispered voice came from the monitor. "I'm not kidding."

She didn't think. In a heartbeat, she was in her parents' bedroom, staring down into the bassinet. The baby was lying on her back, dressed in a pink onesie, covered with a pink blanket. All the pink crap was part of the problem. Why not just give the kid a bath in Pepto-Bismol and call it a day? She was so still, so peaceful, her tiny little mouth slightly open, so helpless. The sight of her made Annie want to cry for a year or two.

A tiny spit bubble formed on the baby's miniature mouth. "She's breathing," Annie whispered. She didn't leave. She could not make herself leave.

"Thank God."

Annie stared at the baby. (Would Walter's baby have been a girl or a boy?)

"Look what I found on your mom's nightstand." Carla held out two 8" x 10" pictures of baby girls.

Annie recognized the one taken of this baby girl at the hospital. She looked closely at the other and gasped. "Wow."

Carla was excited at the discovery. "I know. It's unbelievable. It's uncanny. Sophie looks just like you. You could be twins. I mean, not twins—you were born sixteen years apart—but you look so much alike."

It was true. Annie had had more hair than this one lying in the crib, but still. She shivered.

"I wonder how it makes your mom feel?" Carla put Annie's baby picture next to the baby lying in the crib. "Unbelievable."

"What do you mean?" Annie couldn't help it. She was mesmerized as she made the feature by feature comparison—same nose, same mouth, same eyebrows.

"You know—"

"*Whisper!*" she hissed.

"*Sorry!*" Even Carla's whispering was loud. "Your mom has a baby girl, and sixteen years later, she gives birth to a baby girl as a surrogate for her twin sister, and the second baby girl could be the twin of the first one, her daughter. *Déjà vu*, right? It's both cool and creepy."

Annie agreed as she studied the pictures. It was both cool and creepy. (If Walter's baby had been a girl, would it have looked like this?)

The baby shifted slightly, and they both held their breath. Neither one of them would have the slightest idea what to do if she woke up.

"It must be the DNA thing. Identical twins have identical DNA. Mom said that's why she would be the perfect candidate as the surrogate for Aunt Sam's baby." It seemed so long ago—a lifetime—since her mom was explaining all of this to her. She wasn't sure if she was getting it exactly right.

"Umm," Carla said. "But your dad and uncle Chris don't look anything alike. Wouldn't that have something to do with the way the baby looked?"

She had a point. "You would think so." Annie's brain galloped ahead. "Are you saying, Carla, that maybe my dad is the father of this baby?" Which would make this baby her *sister*, not her half-sister, not her cousin. Which would change things entirely, and Annie wasn't sure if it would change things for the better or worse. Poor Aunt Sam would be devastated.

"I don't know. I'm just shooting my mouth off, but it's so weird." She looked from Annie's picture to the sleeping baby. "And I keep wondering how it must make your mom feel."

Carla thought she was such an expert. Carla had been in therapy for two weeks.

Annie needed to stop this nonsense; it was giving her a headache. "I think my mom would know who the father was, don't you?"

Carla sensed she had crossed a line. "Right. I'm being a fucking idiot, I know. And my mom says that babies change daily. She also says that all Jewish babies are adorable but look at how they turn out, especially the men!"

"Jesus, Carla."

"She can say that. She's Jewish. What was that?"

Annie also heard a tiny noise, like a squeak. The baby wrinkled up its face. "What's it doing?" she asked.

"It is a *she*. Say it." Carla's whispered command was forceful.

Annie suddenly decided to give in. What was the point of dwelling on things you could not change? The baby had been born. The baby was a girl. The baby was not hers. Her baby would never be born. (G: Excellent insights, Annie. A: Insights suck.)

"I don't know what *she's* doing. The Williams kids were older when I sat for them, definitely out of diapers."

Carla pondered the reddening face. "I think she's farting!"

"Can babies actually fart?" She seemed too doll-like to be capable of something so gross.

"I would venture to guess that it's an innate characteristic of the human species. We're probably born knowing how to fart." She stared at the baby. "Actually, apes probably fart."

"Dogs certainly do." She had a friend in grade school once, long before Carla, who had a one-hundred-pound Golden Retriever named Jesse. When that dog farted, it could clear a room.

"Okay. Let's leave it at this. All mammals fart."

"Why are we even talking about this?"

"I don't know about you, but I'm talking about farting to divert my attention away from the fact that this baby girl is pooping her diaper."

There was a definite stench in the air, and it emanated from the pink-clad, tiny baby who was now squirming and starting to whimper. "Maybe she'll fall back to sleep once she's done," Annie suggested hopefully.

"When's your mom due back?"

Annie glanced at the clock on the nightstand. "Another half hour or so."

"Just great," Carla said.

They waited for the inevitable, and it didn't take long. The baby started to cry, a soft mewling sound. "I still think she might fall back to sleep," Annie said, although she knew it wasn't going to happen.

"Would you like to be wallowing around in your own shit?"

The baby's cries escalated suddenly, dramatically.

"She certainly doesn't like it." Annie stared at the writhing baby. She was petrified.

"She's royally pissed off," Carla said. "What are we going to do?" She wrung her hands. "I suppose the good news is that we know she's breathing."

"We need to change her diaper."

"Okay."

Neither one moved, and the baby grew madder and madder.

"She has quite a temper, doesn't she?" Carla shouted over the baby's wails.

Annie wanted to cry, to join in the wails of her cousin, or half-sister, or sister, or whatever she was. She wanted to help her; she really did. But she was terrified of dropping her, or not holding her neck properly, or accidentally crushing the soft spot on the top of her skull. Babies were so complicated and so *fragile*.

It probably wasn't more than a couple of minutes—although a wailing baby could make time crawl like a *turtle*—before Annie took a deep breath and picked up the baby.

It was like a miracle. The baby stopped crying instantly, and Annie pressed her to her shoulder. She was so warm and surprisingly solid for such a little thing. She wasn't nearly as fragile as Annie had suspected, but she certainly did *stink*.

Annie patted the baby's back as she had seen her mom do. "There, there," she cooed to the baby.

"I think she likes you," Carla said.

"This isn't bad at all," Annie said.

"Why don't you just stay like that until your mom gets home? She seems happy enough now."

That would certainly be taking the easy way out, but Annie didn't want the baby to be uncomfortable. "How would you like to be wallowing around in your own shit?"

"Point taken, point taken."

They got the baby changed—even though they both gagged a lot—but then the baby seemed wide awake, her blue eyes alert. "I think I'll try rocking her," Annie said.

And that's how her mom found her a short time later, rocking Sophie.

Annie was rocking the baby.

For Jack, it was love at first sight. All those months of resenting the baby growing inside Alex had been a colossal waste of emotional energy. He had always known that subconsciously, yet he had persisted. What a fucking waste of time. The baby girl was beautiful, and her resemblance to Annie as a baby was uncanny. Looking at Sophie could easily transport Jack back sixteen years when he held his only daughter and dreamed of her bright future. Yes, Sophie deserved to be born, and Alex had done a fine and noble thing for her sister.

Except that Alex now wanted to keep the baby.

She had not overtly—not yet—said she wanted to keep the baby. However, when Jack would mention Sam coming home and taking the baby across the street, Alex would usually say, "We'll have to wait and see." A few times, she had said, "We have to do the right thing."

He agreed with her totally on that. They should *do the right thing*, and the right thing was to give the baby to Sam. He had taken money from Chris—after the conception, after the first trimester, and after the second—and only the final payment remained. What was he supposed to do? Give the money back and say to Sam and Chris: "Oops! Sorry, but we decided that we want to keep the baby for ourselves. After all, she is, biologically, half ours." Yeah, well, there was a big, fat problem with that. The money was gone—some of it for living expenses, most of it at the damn casino—and there was no way in hell that money was going to magically reproduce itself and come back. No way in hell.

He had agreed to go to the bank with Alex when she said she wanted to see if she could get a small business loan. The Avon thing had gone nowhere, she said, and she wanted to try something else. When he played along and asked her what she had in mind (knowing all the time exactly what she had in mind), she said she wanted to start hosting Pampered Chef parties, it was a good business, all she needed was a little "startup" money. She knew they were in debt, and she wanted to contribute her share to the family finances, blah, blah, blah.

Alex wanted to reimburse Sam and Chris. Alex wanted to *buy* the baby.

Short of him robbing a bank or selling a kidney, he didn't know how that would be possible.

On the way home from the bank, Alex said, out of the blue, in relation to nothing that had gone on conversationally before, "I didn't sign anything. I didn't sign the papers Chris brought over."

This was news to him, but when he thought about it, it made perfect sense. As oppositional as he and Chris had been toward each other over the last year—well, *antagonistic* might be a better word—Chris was not a stupid man. Of course he would want to leave nothing to chance, every i dotted and every T crossed. He would have done the same thing if he had been in Chris's position. It was clear to everyone that, as the pregnancy wore on, Alex was becoming more and more attached to the baby. He, unfortunately, had chosen to ignore that fact.

"And my name is on the birth certificate as Sophie's mother," Alex reminded him.

As if she needed to remind him of that. The nurse hadn't brought in the birth certificate until after Sam and Chris had left the hospital. He had watched, flabbergasted, as Alex signed her name next to MOTHER. "What are you doing?" he had asked. It was then that his wife explained the surrogacy laws, adding that he, as her husband, was legally the father of this baby. "Sign here," Alex pointed at the FATHER line. He would not. "It's not right, Alex, and you know it," he had said. "It's just a formality, Jack," she had said ambiguously. He had no idea what she meant by that.

They had reached their driveway. "Oral contracts are binding," he finally said. He had watched enough episodes of *Law and Order* to know that much, even though it was a weak argument in this case.

"Wouldn't they be difficult to prove?" she asked.

He didn't know the answer to that. But he did know the answer to this: They could never afford to hire an attorney.

"Did we shake hands? I don't remember shaking hands that night in the hot tub."

He didn't remember much about that night either. He had been drunk, drunk on scotch and disbelief at the scene that had unfolded in front of him. If he hadn't been drunk, would things have turned out differently?

He would never know.

They had had the baby for eight days now. Four or five times a day, they received frantic phone calls or emails from Sam asking about Sophie. She was stuck in Illinois, she said. There was a question of wrongful death because Louise had been driving the car while she was "suspiciously medicated." Mr. Peterson's family was contesting the will, which seemed to have left some money to Louise, or Chris, or Sam. There was a question of the validity of Louise's and Mr. Peterson's wedding, which had been performed by an Elvis impersonator in Vegas. There was a question of a storage locker that Louise had rented secretly for years. It was dragging on and on, and Sam knew that the longer Alex had the baby, the more attached she would become.

He was becoming attached, too. He was trying hard not to become attached, but she was a damn cute baby. And she looked so much like Annie. Until he became a father, he would never have imagined it, but it was a fact. He was a man who doted on babies.

He forced himself to remember the scene at the hospital when Sam, bawling her eyes out, handed the baby over to Alex. It was obvious that it took every ounce of her will to transfer the baby to Alex's outstretched arms. "Take good care of her, Alex," Sam had said.

Alex nodded.

"I will be back to get her."

"We need to go now," Chris had said for the tenth time, wearily. Jack had never seen him look so drawn, so old.

"I *will* be back to get her." Sam stroked Sophie's cheek.

Chris had had to literally carry Sam out of the room. He stood behind her, clasped his arms around her waist and hauled her away.

And now, day followed day, and Alex still had Sophie.

And he still had Sophie, too. Sometimes after he fed her, when he was rocking her to sleep—and he was almost asleep as well—he pretended that Sophie was his daughter. He would get to do everything all over again: the toddler years, the first day of school, the back-to-school nights of every grade, the band concerts, the birthday parties, the soccer games (this one, Sophie, would be athletic, like him), the Christmases, the summer camping trips, all of it. And he would get it right—not that he regretted decisions made with Nick and Annie—but this time, he would be older, wiser. He wouldn't sweat the small stuff. He would watch more vigilantly for the pitfalls. He would be a good father, all the way around.

It was crazy thinking. The baby belonged to Sam and Chris. Period.

But what was he going to do about Alex? They hadn't been to a counseling session since Sophie had been born (and only two before that), and he wanted things to be the way they used to be between them. He had fucked up, then apologized, apologized, apologized, and was now trying to be a better husband to her. Yet he still slept on the couch in the den, and he had not made love to his wife in nine months. The last time had been in the hot tub in Vegas. Before it happened.

If he sided with Alex about keeping the baby, would she come back to him? He didn't know the definitive answer to that question, but he could almost guarantee that it would help. She would love him like she used to. They would actually laugh again. Such a small thing to wish for, yet so much to hope for.

But they couldn't keep the baby. Alex had made a promise to her sister. It was time to tell her that, before it was too late.

He found her in their bedroom, rocking the baby. Of course. She had left the house once—the trip to the bank—since they brought Sophie home. His wife beamed at him when he walked through the door. She hadn't done that in a long, long time.

"She just dozed off. I know that babies aren't supposed to smile at this age, but look. She's smiling, isn't she?" Alex said.

It did look as if a smile was playing around the corners of Sophie's tiny mouth. "It's probably gas."

"No, it's a smile."

"Have you heard from Sam today?" he asked. If he could get her to focus on Sam, maybe she would remember whose baby she was holding.

"Multiple times." She stroked the baby's head.

"When are they coming home?"

"They're not sure," she said absently.

She looked at the baby with such love that Jack wanted to snatch her out of Alex's arms and say *no more*; this is not your baby. "How did Sam sound? She must be chomping at the bit to get out of there and come home to the baby." Come on, Alex, he silently coached, just say that Sophie is Sam's baby.

"She's Sam. She's hysterical. She said that if Louise weren't already dead, she'd strangle her, push her off a cliff, and then drop a bomb on her for good measure."

"Alex," he said gently. "You know that she will come home eventually."

"This baby is growing every day," Alex said.

"She will come home and—"

"Do you want to hold her?"

She was trying to divert him; they both knew it. And unfortunately, he would like to hold the sleeping child, nestle her in the crook of his arm. "She looks peaceful where she is," he said. It was a beautiful picture, his wife holding the baby, a thin stream of sunshine falling over the two of them.

"I'd forgotten how wonderful this feels." Alex sighed contentedly.

He hated to ruin her blissful moment, but he had to. "Alex, you have to acknowledge that Sam will come home, and she will—"

"I think we should make love tonight." She smiled at him.

She was good. He'd have to give her that. His beautiful wife was trying to blackmail him. She knew that he wanted to make love to her more than anything. "You're changing the subject," he stammered.

"I'm so happy." She gave him another beatific grin.

And then he couldn't tell her. "I'm going to get my camera," he said instead. He wanted and needed to take a picture of Alex and the baby, a picture he would always cherish.

"I don't want the damn money," Sam said for the thousandth time. She wanted to strangle the selfish, vindictive offspring of that sweet old man, Mr. Peterson, who according to his will, had taken an immediate liking to her the first and only time they met at the bar at the Biltmore Hotel. He had left her $50,000 in his will, and his children, Mallory and Duncan, were adamant that she not receive a dime.

She did not want the money. She wanted her baby. Alex had been bonding with Sophie for ten days now. Time was running out, and Sam knew it. She had to get home.

"There were no witnesses to the revised will," Mallory, a thin-lipped woman in her late forties, repeated.

"Right. No witnesses. Case closed." Sam stood up. She felt a little woozy and blamed the bottle of wine she had drunk before this, yet another tedious meeting, but even the wine flowing through her veins was not making this palatable.

"Sit down, Sam." Chris wanted the money. Mr. Peterson had not left any money to Louise or to Chris, only to Sam.

"Our father had not been in his right mind for quite some time," Duncan said. He was a fifty-year-old carbon copy of his wizened father.

"He suffered from dementia," Mallory added.

"I don't doubt that," Sam said, sitting down, sighing. "He must have been senile to marry Louise."

"I beg your pardon," Mallory said.

"Just keep the fucking money." Sam had had enough. Even though Mr. Peterson's finances had taken a dump like everyone else's in the past year, the amount his vindictive offspring would inherit was nothing to sneeze at. Yet they persisted in clamping their fists around the money Mr. Peterson had supposedly left to Sam. Sam did not want the money. She wanted her baby.

Chris wanted the money. "The will states that it was Mr. Peterson's wish to leave Sam $50,000."

"He must have been coerced," Mallory said.

"That's ridiculous," Chris said.

"Who cares?" Right now, Sam wouldn't mind strangling her husband, too.

"Louise was driving the car." Mallory kept returning to this point, kept insinuating that Louise was responsible for her father's death, kept insinuating that she would consider filing a lawsuit for wrongful death.

"Mr. Peterson was not wearing a seatbelt," Chris returned.

"Who cares?" Sam yelled.

The lawyer droned on and on about the process of contesting a will, probate, etcetera, etcetera. Sam tuned him out. To her, the only mildly interesting thing about the will was the fact that Mr. Peterson had not left any money to Louise, not one dime. Sam had a couple theories about that. Either he didn't think Louise would outlive him, or he didn't think Louise was a very good fuck. And what did it matter anyway? They were both dead, buried, gone. They had both been in their eighties.

Finally, the meeting was over, and once again, nothing had been accomplished. "I want to go home," Sam said to Chris as they walked to their rental car. She had said this so often during their stay in Illinois that Chris no longer acknowledged it with a reply. It was possible he no longer even heard her whining.

Chris had been focused on what had to be done to "lay Mother to rest." First, there was the funeral, which they held at Golden Manor; otherwise, no one would have come except them. Dorothy, the former housekeeper who had finagled money out of Louise to bail her delinquent grandson out of jail, was a no-show. It was a closed casket, and the old men and women who attended the service were confused. "Who is it this time?" one old man asked Sam. "Louise Connor," she said. "I don't really recall her," he said, "but we like our funerals at Golden Manor. They give us something to do."

Then Chris needed to "sort out Mother's possessions." She didn't leave a will, there were no secret bank accounts, stocks, or bonds, and apparently, she had cashed in her life insurance policy before her trip to Vegas. In a strange way, Sam was impressed by this. Louise must have wanted to pay her own way with every cent she had, and it didn't appear that she had taken any money from Mr. Peterson. "It's hard to believe but it looks like she married Mr. Peterson for love," Sam said to Chris. He just gave her a mournful look. It was glaringly clear that his mother had left him *nothing*.

Except for a storage unit filled with crap. She and Chris had spent days going through a pyramid of mildewed cardboard boxes, the drawers of an old roll-top desk, and the contents of an old wardrobe. Chris examined each item carefully. He turned the pages of old books and photo albums filled with sepia-tinted pictures that would crumble from age if touched. He searched the pockets of old housedresses and aprons. He stuck his hand into his father's old loafers. (Strangely, shoes were the only things that Louise had kept of her husband's.) He unfolded and refolded every item of clothing. He was searching, Sam knew, for something, anything that Louise had left behind for him.

On the third day in the storage unit, Chris found something that gave him a small moment of joy. A box filled with old model airplanes and trains made him weep. "Dad and I built these together. This is something I can keep."

"We can put them in Sophie's room." Their child did not have to have gender-specific toys. She could play with anything she wanted, even old, rickety, faded model airplanes. At that point, Sam was still trying to be loyal, patient, and supportive.

"This is really something," Chris said.

No, it wasn't, she wanted to say. Where was your baptismal gown, a lock of your baby hair, bronzed baby shoes, a silver spoon? Where were the pictures—many, many pictures—that they sent of Grace? They hadn't been saved as treasures; they didn't exist. It made Sam furious at Louise all over again. Did that woman not have a heart?

When Chris found Louise's old jewelry box, Sam thought he was going to turn cartwheels in happiness. "This is it," he said happily. "I know I can find something in here to remember her by."

Or to show that she thought of you at all, Sam seethed to herself. It was heartbreaking to watch her husband open each box with hope, only to discover nothing but junk, time and again.

Chris examined each costume piece carefully, the earrings, bracelets, necklaces, and brooches. There weren't many. Louise was not a jewelry kind of woman, and honestly, the pieces were ugly and cheap.

"Do you remember her wearing anything in there?" Sam prompted.

"No." Chris turned over an old watch. There was no engraving on the backside. "I think she must have worn these things before I was born."

"Is her wedding ring in there?" Sam knew that she had worn a thin gold band until Chris's father died. That would be something worthwhile for Chris to keep, since Mallory and Duncan had claimed the ring Mr. Peterson had given Louise. Although it had no sentimental value to Chris, he could have pawned it and at least gotten some cash. It might have made him happy.

"No, it's all junk," he said. He clamped down the lid. "All junk."

Now, on the tenth day of their Louise duty, after the funeral, after three futile meetings with the lawyer, after days in the dank, smelly storage locker, Sam had had enough. She had done her duty. She had gone beyond the call of duty. She was going to go home, with or without her husband.

The rented Honda smelled like wet dog. She rolled her window down, despite the air conditioning. Not even a year in Arizona, and she had forgotten how humid summers in the Midwest were. "When we get back to the room, I'm making flight arrangements. We're done here, and I want to see my baby."

Chris drove right past the Embassy Suites Hotel, their home away from home for the last long ten days. The only thing good about the place was that they had certainly gotten their money's worth at the free nightly happy hour. "Hey," Sam said.

"One more trip to the storage locker." Chris stared straight ahead, determined.

Sam groaned. "We've been through everything in that storage locker at least twice. There's nothing worth keeping. Tomorrow, the truck from St. Vincent de Paul will pick everything up and haul it away."

"I feel like I missed something."

He hadn't missed anything. Louise had been a cold-hearted mother. Louise was still being a bitch, even in her grave. During the days in the storage locker, Sam had even considered planting something for Chris to find—a love letter from Louise to Chris, for example. Something that would give Chris closure. Something that would give Chris peace.

They pulled into the parking lot of the U-Store-It, and Sam fished her phone out of her purse. "Five minutes, okay, Chris? I'm going to call Alex and give her the good news." She dialed Alex's home number.

The phone rang and rang and rang. As the days had passed, this had become a frequent occurrence. She's busy right now, Sam would tell herself. She's changing Sophie now, or giving her a bottle, or strolling her in the park. With a new baby, there were a million reasons why a mother couldn't answer the phone.

Alex also had caller ID. There was the possibility that Alex knew Sam was calling and was not answering on purpose.

Sam refused to believe that.

She tried Alex's cell phone and was relieved when she answered on the third ring. "Guess what?" Sam said. She didn't give Alex time to answer, or even say hello. "We're coming home tomorrow. Finally! I can't wait to see my baby! How is she?"

"I talked to you three hours ago, Sam. Sophie was fine then, and Sophie is fine now." There was a definite note of impatience in Alex's voice.

Sam ignored it. So what if she had been calling Alex five or six times a day? She was Sophie's mother. She had a right to know what was going on. Besides, Alex was probably cranky from lack of sleep. "Don't worry about packing up her things. I'll be glad to do it when I get there."

"I wasn't worried about packing up her things."

"Good. I'm doing it. You've already done more than enough. I can't tell you how grateful I am, knowing that she was in good hands with you. I've missed Sophie so much!"

"You don't even know her."

"What's that supposed to mean?" The bitch. It wasn't Sam's fault that she hadn't had time to bond with her baby. It was Louise's. The bitch.

"Nothing. I'm sorry. I didn't get a lot of sleep last night, and I'm a little cranky."

So, that was it. Alex had seemed so distant because she wasn't getting a lot of sleep. "Sophie had a rough night?"

"No, it wasn't that. I've been doing a lot of thinking . . ." Alex trailed off.

Red flag. Sam wanted to grow wings and fly home immediately. "I've been doing a lot of thinking, too." Chris had been offered a job at Wheaton College, and they had discussed the possibility of moving back to Illinois. It was there but unspoken between them: They could take the baby far away from Alex.

"We'll talk when you get here."

"You bet we will."

"Have a safe trip."

"Give Sophie a kiss for me."

"Believe me, Sophie gets plenty of kisses. I think I hear her now. Gotta go."

It was a completely unsatisfying call, but it didn't matter. She would soon be reunited with her baby. A lack of sleep could make anyone cranky, Sam reminded herself as she went to get Chris from the storage unit. Alex would probably be relieved when she could get a good night's sleep.

She found Chris sitting on the floor, next to the jewelry box. Tears streamed down his face. "Last night, I had a dream, or maybe it was a memory, of Mother showing me this jewelry box. I must have been two or three. We were at her vanity, and Mother pulled me into her lap to show me what she called her *secret heart.*"

It must have been a dream, Sam thought. She couldn't picture Louise pulling a child onto her lap, but she let Chris continue.

He opened the jewelry box and took everything out. In the bottom corner was a tiny flap. Chris pulled gently on it, and the bottom came up, exposing another layer. A heart-shaped locket lay nestled in faux satin. Chris lifted the locket and opened it.

Sam walked over. The locket contained the picture of a blond baby boy.

"It's me," Chris said. He was sobbing now. "She might not have overtly shown me love, but I was *in* Louise's secret heart."

Dylan was the most laid-back person Nick knew, but Dylan was losing patience with him. "The sooner we enlist, the sooner we can become recruits, dude, and go to basic training in San Diego. What are we waiting for? We're both eighteen, we're both high school graduates, so there should be nothing stopping us now."

Of course, there was something stopping Nick. He and Jennifer had promised their parents that they would wait until August, wait for him to enlist, wait for Jennifer to go to Stanford, wait for them to get married. He was regretting that promise now, all the way around. It was going to be a long summer of *suspension.* It had only been ten days since his high school graduation, and he was bored silly, restless. He wanted his life to *move on.*

Dylan turned into the parking lot of the shooting range. "Dude, my parents are no longer dropping subtle hints about me moving out. We're talking blatant. My mom went to Home Depot and bought paint—gallons of *buttercup*, man—and she's put tarps over everything in my room except the bed. She says she's going to make my room into a sewing room. And my mom doesn't know how to sew! You can't be more obvious than that, dude. One of these mornings I'm going to wake up under a tarp."

This made Nick feel even guiltier. "You could move in with me," he said, although he doubted that event would be greeted with applause at his house, not with the baby and all that.

"Not cool, dude."

He was right. Before the promise he had made to his parents, he had made one to Dylan. He and Dylan had made the commitment to join the Marines on the very day that they became blood brothers using Dylan's dad's rusty switchblade. They had been in the seventh grade. So he supposed it wouldn't hurt to go talk to a recruiter. It wasn't like they had to enlist today or anything like that, but it would make Dylan feel better to know that Nick was still *all in* on the plan. He would never tell Dylan that he did have a few doubts—not many, just a few—now that Jennifer was going to be in the picture for the rest of his life.

"Let's go to the recruitment office," he said. "We can at least talk to someone, you know, about the time frame and stuff like that."

"Seriously, dude?" Dylan's face was full of hope.

"Yeah."

"Okay then." Dylan backed up so fast that the tires spun in the loose gravel of the parking lot. "I know exactly where it is. I've been driving by it every day since I graduated, but I would never go in, not without you."

Nick was touched. "Thanks, Dylan."

"We're best buds, dude. We'll always have each other's backs, right? We'll be Marines, and it is an *elite organization*. Semper fi!"

Nick felt a surge of excitement. "We'll be soldiers!"

"Twelve glorious weeks of basic training, dude. Bayonets and pugil sticks."

"Rappelling and shooting," Nick added.

"We'll be so hot. Our bodies will be ripped." Dylan was bouncing on the truck's seat in excitement.

Nick looked at Dylan's stick-thin arms and hid a smile. It was hard to imagine Dylan with bulging biceps, but he'd carry Dylan through an obstacle course if he had to. They were blood brothers. "We'll be defending our country against terrorism," he shouted happily.

"We'll go to war," Dylan yelled back.

"We'll be honored on Veteran's Day!"

"That is so cool, dude! I never thought of that! Maybe we'll be in a parade one day! I always wanted to be in a parade!"

"We'll be marching in a parade!"

"*Marching*!"

They were buoyed by adrenaline, suffused with excitement, carried away by their bright dreams of becoming Marines when they pulled into the recruitment center. And it didn't go away when they sat in front of the smartly outfitted recruitment officer. *Officer,* Dylan mouthed to Nick. It was something more to aspire to.

They walked out two hours later as enlisted men. They had passed their physicals (even Dylan!), read the pamphlets, watched the video, and signed the paperwork. They would be going to Camp Pendleton. They were *exhilarated enlisted men*!

"You know what's next, right, dude?" Dylan's eyes shone.

"Great Clips, here we come."

"I was thinking more along the lines of a real barber. It's more manly, and we are Marines!"

"Good point," Nick said.

They stopped at the first one they saw. The place was empty, and there were two barbers on duty. They were dark, burly men—maybe Italian?—and Dylan's barber had a mermaid tattooed on his right forearm. Nick and Dylan sat side by side as the barbers draped plastic capes around their necks. They explained that they wanted authentic marine buzzes.

"I do have to admit something, dude," Dylan said as he fingered his thin, dirty- blonde ponytail. "I kinda hate to see this go."

"You can grow another one when we get out of the Marines." Nick swallowed. His dark brown curls would soon litter the floor. Jennifer always said how much she loved his hair. She would understand, though. He was doing this for the noblest of causes.

"Could you do me a favor?" Dylan asked his burly barber. "I'd like to donate it to Locks of Love, you know, that organization that makes wigs for kids with cancer and stuff."

The barber snorted. "We don't do that here, son."

"Oh," Dylan said, momentarily disappointed.

"I can put it in a plastic baggie for you, though," the barber offered.

Dylan immediately perked up. "That would be great, dude—I mean, sir. I can get the address from the web and send it to them." He closed his eyes as the barber snipped it off.

He was being shorn, Nick thought, like a lamb. But it was for the noblest of causes, he reminded himself. He thought of Annie coming home with a Mohawk and how his parents had totally freaked out. They had been so obsessed with what people would *think*. Looking back on it, Nick had to give Annie credit. In a way, it was a very brave thing to do—stupid too, maybe—but brave. Probably, it was Aunt Sam who had the right idea: It was only hair. It would grow back. (Until he was, like, forty and might start to lose it for no reason. He could always buy a toupee, or he could start a Locks of Love organization for balding men. Today, possibilities seemed infinite.)

When the barbers were done, Nick and Dylan stared at themselves in the mirror. Nick had thought that having Marine buzzes would make them look older. That was not the case. Dylan looked like he was about twelve, and he looked like he was maybe fourteen. Their eyes and ears looked bigger. It was strange that he had never noticed before how much Dylan's ears stood out from his head.

They left the barber and walked to the truck, rubbing their heads. "This feels so weird, man," Dylan said.

Nick could feel the sun beating down on his shorn scalp. "The sun feels hotter with no hair."

"Sure does. It's no wonder so many bald men wear baseball hats. I vote that we stop at Walmart and get baseball caps and then go tell the girls."

Nick's euphoria deflated, just a little. He was dying to share the news with Jennifer but wasn't sure how she would take it. He had "jumped the gun," and Jennifer was very particular about details. But she was also the one who had told him that joining the military seemed like it was his *destiny*. But then again, maybe she said that because she secretly hoped that he would change his mind and move up to Palo Alto to be near her? He was starting to get a headache—probably from the sun searing his scalp. He didn't want to believe, like Dylan, that girls—women—were so complicated. His Jennifer was a straightforward, practical person. She was a calm girl, reasonable. She would totally understand when he told her he was leaving for Camp Pendleton in two weeks.

Who was he kidding?

He could always blame Dylan. When the recruit officer had asked when they wanted to leave, Dylan had said, "Tomorrow!"

"I appreciate your enthusiasm," the officer said.

"The sooner, the better," Dylan said.

Nick should have told him to stop saying that, but did he? No, he did not. He was as excited as Dylan and so caught up in the moment that he would have left immediately. All rational thought had flown out the window.

"I can get you set up to leave two weeks from today," the officer said.

"We'll take it!" Dylan and he exclaimed. It was like the officer had just offered them a super-duper deal on a Lamborghini.

But now he had to tell Jennifer that he had cut short their summer, their precious time together, by two months. Would she still want to marry him? And if she did, when would they get married—at Christmas, after he completed basic training, before he was deployed overseas, or would they have to wait a year, two years, four years? He was starting to think that he had really messed things up. He didn't want to wait that long to marry Jennifer, and he had, for the past ten days, politely ignored his parents' voiced concerns. You're too young, Nick. Jennifer has four years of college ahead of her and possibly med school, Nick. Things might look differently to you now that you've graduated, Nick. In private, his mom said, "Jennifer is the only girl you've ever dated, honey. You don't want to rush into anything." In private, his dad said, "You don't have to be married to have sex, Nick, if that's what you're concerned about." Nick, face flaming, had left the room, fast.

They called the girls and agreed to meet them at Chili's for lunch at one o'clock. Because it took them so long to pick out their hats at Walmart— Dylan turned up his nose at hats with insignias of Diamondbacks, Coyotes, Suns, or any sports team—they were late. The girls were already seated, and Nick crunched his Diamondbacks cap low on his head as they approached the girls' booth in the back of the restaurant.

"You enlisted," Jennifer said.

Really, nothing got past that girl.

"Are you mad?" He slid into the booth next to her.

Jennifer reached over and took off his cap. "It's rude to wear a hat in a public restaurant. Dylan, you take yours off, too."

Sheepishly, Dylan complied.

"Oh, my god!" Melissa said. "Your ponytail is gone."

"Obviously. But it's in a baggie in the truck if you want it." Dylan seemed to have forgotten all about the Locks of Love.

Melissa shuddered. "That's a little creepy, Dylan."

Jennifer studied him so intently that Nick wanted to slide under the table. "You're still cute," she finally said.

"Are you mad?" he asked again.

"You didn't wait until August."

"No. Dylan and I stopped by the recruitment office, and we kind of got carried away with—"

"I don't want to wait either." Jennifer smiled her white, white smile.

Her tutoring really must have made him smarter, or else he just knew his girl. He grinned back. "Really?"

"We can obtain a license from the Clerk of the Superior Court at 601 West Jackson. It's sixty dollars, which I have in my purse, and there's no waiting period and no blood test. All we need is photo IDs."

"I've got my license," he said.

"Whoa, dude, are you guys saying what I think you're saying?"

"We are," they said.

"Let's order." Melissa studied her menu. "I'm starving."

"We're getting married," Jennifer told her.

"I know that. I think I'm going to get the baby back ribs."

"No, Melissa, we're getting married *now*." Jennifer took Nick's hand. "Right, Nick?"

"Right."

"We'll drive through McDonald's on the way," Dylan promised. "Dude and dudette," he said to Nick and Jennifer, "this is one important day."

"We also need to make another stop at Walmart," Nick said. He couldn't stop looking at Jennifer. "I need to get a bouquet of flowers for my bride." And a ring. He needed to buy Jennifer a wedding ring. It would have to be really cheap, but he would replace it as soon as he could.

After the stop at Walmart, on the way downtown, he called Annie. It suddenly seemed important to him that someone in his family knew he was getting married, and he was not going to call his parents. He was eighteen, a grown man, an enlisted Marine, and he was going to marry the love of his life. Really, it was quite simple.

Predictably, when he told Annie, she said, "Holy shit." And after he told her exactly where they were headed, she asked, "Can Carla and I come? We're at her house and can meet you there in ten minutes."

He said he would like them to come, and he was glad they did. They arrived late, and they had stupid boas around their necks, but they brought a camera and a big bag of brown rice.

"Sorry it's brown," Carla said to Nick. "But I'm pretty sure the symbolism is the same, not that I'm exactly sure what it's supposed to symbolize."

"Fertility and prosperity," Jennifer said, blushing. "What a nice gesture."

Annie gave him a big hug. "This is awesome, Nick. I really mean it. Now you and Jennifer scrunch together, and I'll take a picture. We'll take before and after pictures. You know, *before* you were married and *after* you were married."

"I get it, squirt," he said affectionately. He was so happy he felt like he could burst. No one, he believed, had ever been happier than him.

Later, he would barely remember the three-minute ceremony. But he would remember that all-encompassing feeling of utter happiness. And he would remember the four of them showering Jennifer and him with brown rice as they walked hand in hand down the steps of the Superior Court building.

He and Jennifer, shaking the rice that symbolized fertility and prosperity from their hair and clothes, laughing and crying at the same time.

He and Jennifer. Mr. and Mrs. Nicholas Carissa.

14

CHAPTER FOURTEEN

It was all too much. Alex wanted to take the baby and run away from home, *her* home. Where would she go—Aruba, Costa Rica, Mexico, Canada? Did babies need passports? It didn't matter, but it would probably be easier to take the baby somewhere in the United States. California and the East Coast would be too expensive, but perhaps she could find a small town in the Heartland—maybe Arkansas or Kansas—and rent a tiny bungalow and get a job waitressing at a diner along the interstate. Maybe women in small-town America would be more inclined to buy Avon products? She could try that again. Yes, that's what she would do. Sell Avon to lonely ladies in a desolate small town. And the added benefit of that was that she could take Sophie with her. She wouldn't have to worry about daycare. She could just plop Sophie in a baby sling and go door to door, selling gallons of moisturizers and perfumes.

She was thinking crazy thoughts, disjointed thoughts.

Her son had enlisted in the Marines.

Somewhere in Texas might be a good idea, some place warm. She wouldn't have to spend money on winter coats and boots for Sophie that she would quickly outgrow. Or for herself either. After all these years in Arizona, Alex no longer owned a winter coat. But didn't they get a lot of tornadoes in Texas? And wildfires? She vaguely remembered reading a newspaper article about a wildfire in Texas the summer before. Was it in the Austin area?

Sam was coming home today.

Hawaii! That was it. She could raise Sophie in a warm, balmy climate. She could rent a place on the beach, and she and Sophie could build sand castles and collect shells. She could teach Sophie how to swim in the Pacific Ocean. But wait a minute. They had hurricanes in Hawaii. And tsunamis. Hell, the Japanese had bombed Pearl Harbor in 1941. Granted, that had been years ago, but what were the odds of it happening again? Hawaii was a sitting duck.

Her son had gotten married.

Was she too old to join the Peace Corps? Did the Peace Corps let you bring babies? What about Teaching for America? She could renew her teaching certificate without too much difficulty. But what if they sent her to Appalachia or some inner-city school? Neither place would be ideal for raising a baby.

There were so many possibilities, and none of them were perfect.

Her son had come home yesterday afternoon and announced to her and Jack that he had enlisted in the Marines and gotten married. Drum roll, please: *Ta-da!*

(Could you go down to the recruitment center and tell them you'd changed your mind? Could you request an annulment from the Catholic church if you weren't Catholic?)

"Can we stay here for the next two weeks?" Nick had asked. He held tightly to his new bride's hand.

"I know how to cook," Jennifer had added.

As if that mattered.

She had been too speechless to reply. *Why?* She wanted to ask. Why in the hell did you go and do that?

"Isn't this great? We have a new member in our family!" Annie had a neon green boa around her neck, and as usual, Carla was in tow, along with Dylan and another girl Alex didn't know. (Obviously, she didn't know a lot about a lot of things.)

We already have a new member in our family, she thought. Sophie.

Jack found his voice first. "Is this legal?"

"It certainly is." Jennifer produced the marriage license.

The old Jack would have exploded; the new and improved Jack did not. "Congratulations," he said. He hugged them both awkwardly. "I'll see if we have some champagne in the refrigerator in the garage."

Coward, Alex thought. He used the first available escape route he could think of. And he knew there had not been any champagne in the garage since the first night that Sam arrived in Arizona. The bottles she and Sam had drunk that night almost a year ago had been the last of it.

Nick turned to her expectantly. It was her turn. The old Alex would have broken down in tears; the new Alex, the new mother, did not. She was exhausted. Getting up two or three times a night with an infant was exhausting. The entire year had been exhausting. And as they said, you can't fight city hall (Haha). "What's done is done," she said.

The disappointment from the group was palpable.

"Mom," Annie pled.

London. She could go to London. They spoke English there. The weather wasn't ideal, but there was so much history. She could push Sophie's pram past the London Bridge and Buckingham Palace. In the future, many years in the future, when Sophie was older than eighteen—say twenty-six or twenty-seven—maybe she would marry a prince?

She had a married child already standing before her. She had to say something, something that would not damage their relationship, something that could never hang like a rebuke between them. But what? Should she lie and tell them that she was overjoyed that her son very possibly would go to war, and on top of that, he had decided to get married at eighteen? It was already glaringly apparent to everyone in the room that she was not overjoyed. "I love you," she finally said. That, at least, was the truth.

She hugged them—she could follow protocol if she had to—and then went back upstairs to Sophie.

Sam would arrive any minute.

St. Thomas. She could take Sophie to St. Thomas, part of the American Virgin Islands. She'd read that they spoke English there, too. She could get a job at a souvenir shop that catered to cruise passengers disembarking from their massive ships. But how was the school system on the island? Would Sophie be able to get a good education? And the sun. She would have to slather Sophie with sunscreen every day. It would cost a small fortune to keep the baby from getting sunburned.

Sam would arrive any minute.

Alex needed a glass of wine. It would be her first since the baby was born. It was odd. During her pregnancy, especially at the beginning, she had craved wine, but with the baby here, she hadn't really thought about it. Until now. It was only three o'clock, but it was five o'clock somewhere (to quote Jimmy Buffet—maybe she should take Sophie to Key West?) The baby was sleeping peacefully, so Alex tiptoed out of the bedroom and down to the kitchen, which was mercifully empty.

That hadn't been the case this morning. After she gave Sophie her morning bottle, she went to the kitchen to make a pot of coffee. She planned on drinking the entire pot herself. She had been unable to sleep, imagining—trying not to imagine—what was going on in Nick's bedroom down the hall. They were all sitting at the kitchen table—Jack, Annie, Nick, and Jennifer—eating blueberry pancakes and bacon that Jennifer had made. She felt a pang of what could only be called jealousy. Her family had not eaten breakfast together in ages, and now Jennifer had waltzed into their life and prepared breakfast that everyone seemed to be enjoying. Happily. When was the last time she had made breakfast for her family? Alex had no idea.

"Have some pancakes, Mom," Nick said. "It turns out that my *wife* is a very good cook." Nick grinned. With his shorn head, he looked like a little boy.

Alex wanted to weep.

"Sit down, Mrs. Carissa. I'll fix you a plate." Jennifer hopped up to heap another plate with pancakes.

"They're really good," Annie said, her mouth full.

As a rule, Annie didn't like pancakes.

Everything had changed.

Jack pulled out a chair. "Come on, honey, join us." It seemed more like a command than a request. But then he said, "Please."

Alex didn't want to join them, but she didn't want to make a scene either. And then her stomach growled, loudly. Everyone laughed. She shrugged sheepishly and sat down. She would eat the pancakes, but she wasn't going to do the dishes. But as it turned out, that wasn't even an issue. Nick and Jennifer cleaned up without being asked.

Jennifer put a plate before her. "Here you go, Mrs. Carissa."

"You don't have to call them Mr. and Mrs. Carissa anymore," Annie said. "You're married to their son. I think it's some etiquette rule by someone ancient like Dear Abby or Emma Postman."

"Emily Post." Alex took a bite of pancake. It was delicious. "You can call me Alex." Not Mom. Not yet.

"You can call me whatever you feel comfortable with," Jack said.

"Okay—" Jennifer faltered, blushed. "Okay."

Alex listened to the banter around her, not contributing much to the conversation. But it wasn't bad. In fact, it was rather enjoyable. She could get used to this, she thought. But she couldn't let herself get used to it. In two short weeks, her son would be gone and so would Jennifer. She could already, as she ate her pancakes on this first day of their married life together, feel the loss of them.

"We won't be home for dinner tonight," Nick said as he started to clear the plates. "Jennifer's parents are taking us out to dinner to celebrate."

Cornelia and Charles Sang had taken the news surprisingly well. As it turned out, they, too, had married young and then gone to college and med school. To them, this marriage was a feasible, if not ideal, arrangement. Or maybe they were just more put together than Alex was. At this point in her life, Alex was not put together at all. She was not put together because everything had changed.

That afternoon in the quiet kitchen, Alex poured herself a hefty glass of chardonnay and took a good, long swig. Sam would be arriving any minute, and Alex needed to fortify herself. Sam was not going to take it well—to put it mildly—when Alex told her that she was keeping the baby. But Alex had given birth to the baby, and the baby was biologically hers.

Sam didn't deserve the baby.

Alex's list of grievances against her twin sister had grown long over the last year. Sam had coerced everyone to go along with her outlandish plan. Alex had slept with Chris at Sam's insistence, which had caused possibly irreparable damage to Alex's marriage. Sam had kept secrets from Alex about her own children. Sam had had an affair with Jack. Sam had been selfish and manipulative and demanding and secretive, all to achieve her own purposes.

Sam didn't deserve the baby.

Alex was going to break her sister's heart by depriving her of the one thing she truly wanted and couldn't have. Alex was going to break their promise, but she hadn't known how she would feel about this child, at the beginning. She had carried the baby for nine long months and then given birth to her. She had loved her from the moment she knew she was pregnant. Sophie was hers, and Alex needed another chance to get motherhood *right*.

And then Sam burst through the door in a flurry of excitement. "I'm back!" she called. She found Alex in the kitchen and embraced her in a ferocious hug. "Wine, it's a good thing! I'll take a glass. We can finally celebrate the baby's birth. I've missed you so much, Alex. I practically jumped off the plane before it even got to the gate. I'm so excited! Where's Sophie?"

"She's sleeping." Upon seeing her sister, Alex couldn't control the love that swept through her. It was so much easier to be mad at her sister when she wasn't standing right before her, her face mirroring her own.

"I don't care. I've waited ten long days—no, make that a lifetime—to hold my baby."

Alex needed time. This was going to be so hard. "She'll be cranky if we wake her up, and you want her to be in a good mood, don't you? Let's have a glass of wine first. You probably need one after your long flight from Chicago. How long is the flight? Four hours?" She was babbling, and she could feel sweat trickling down her breastbone.

"Three hours and forty-two minutes. I'm so excited!"

"Just give her ten more minutes. Trust me. She'll be in a much better mood if she finishes her nap." Trust her? Her sister should have never trusted her, not when it came to a baby. Alex's baby.

"I'll go up and take a quick peek at her, and then we'll have the wine." She turned towards the stairs.

Alex had to stop her. "Nick got married yesterday," she blurted.

It worked. Sam turned back around and picked up her glass of wine. "Oh, my god! You poor thing! I thought they were going to wait until July."

"They didn't wait." Alex told her the story, drawing it out as much as possible. She was buying time, buying time.

"How are you holding up?" Sam asked when she was finished. She rubbed Alex's arm affectionately.

"Not great. Everything has changed."

"Jennifer seems like a nice young woman, though—and smart."

Young woman. If Jennifer was a young woman, then Nick must be a young man, and Alex was persistently clinging to the notion that he was still a boy. She was going to have to let go—she knew that—but it was so fucking hard.

"I'm going to see Sophie," Sam said.

"You know what I could really use right now?" Alex was buying time, buying time. "A cigarette. I haven't had one in nine months."

"Then you don't want to ruin it by smoking now. I'm going upstairs."

"I'm dying for one." Alex really wasn't, but she needed *time*. "Please, Sam, it'll be like old times, the two of us with wine and cigarettes."

Impatience bloomed on Sam's face. "They took my lighter at the airport."

Alex rushed to her desk drawer and rummaged through the contents. She found it. "I have matches." She held them up. "Come on!" She led the reluctant Sam outside to the patio, and it wasn't easy. Sam begrudged every step.

"Leave the door open," Sam instructed. "I want to hear the baby monitor."

"This is her long nap. She might sleep for another hour." Please, Sophie, Alex prayed silently, *sleep*.

"Look, after this cigarette, I'm going to get my baby. I don't care if she's cranky. I want to hold my baby."

Alex knew that a Virginia Slims Superslim menthol cigarette took six and one-half minutes to smoke. There wasn't much time. She lit it and inhaled deeply. Immediately, she felt light-headed. This cigarette was not a good idea, but at least she had Sam farther away from the baby. She took another drag. Things were starting to spin in front of her eyes. Sam's face before her swam eerily.

"How many ounces of formula is she taking in each bottle?"

"Four," Alex said.

"How many times does she awake at night?"

"Two."

"I'll have to get the pediatrician's number before I leave."

You will not need it, Alex thought.

"I can't believe she's here," Sam said. "Finally, my dream has come true."

Alex could taste the bile rising in the back of her throat.

"I'm so happy," Sam said.

"I'm keeping the baby," Alex blurted. She couldn't keep her focus on Sam's shifting face.

"What did you say?" Sam's voice was a dry whisper.

"I'm keeping Sophie. She's biologically mine, and I want her, I need her, I *love* her.

"You can't do that. We made a promise, and we have never, ever broken a promise to each other. Sophie is *mine*." Sam's voice was no longer a whisper. It escalated with every word.

Alex shook her head, trying to clear her vision. "No, no, no. After everything you've put me through this last year, I deserve Sophie."

"After everything *I've* put you through? I didn't get Annie addicted to drugs, and I didn't force your son to elope, and I didn't turn your husband into a raging alcoholic. How can you blame *me* for all those things? Everything was happening right in front of you, and *you* chose to ignore it all. You can't blame me!" Sam's voice had now reached the level of hysteria.

Her words stung Alex like a slap. "Everything was fine before you moved across the street."

"Obviously, everything was *not* fine."

"You do not deserve the baby. You're *unfit* to raise her." Alex knew she had crossed the line even before she felt the slap on her cheek. Instinctively, she slapped back.

"You bitch!" Sam screamed. "Chris tried to warn me about you, but I kept defending you. I kept telling him that we had made a *promise*, and nothing would ever break a promise we made to each other. You cannot do this to me, your only sister, your *twin sister*." Sam moved closer.

Alex didn't budge. They were literally screaming in each other's faces. "You're the bitch, the *selfish bitch* who only thinks of herself, who will manipulate anyone to get her own way."

"We paid you to be our surrogate. You didn't have any trouble taking the money, did you? But wait. You don't have the money, do you? You were too *stupid* to realize that your husband was gambling it all away."

Alex slapped her again; Sam slapped her back.

"You are a Valium whore!" Alex screamed. "How are you going to take care of a baby when you're *high* all the time?"

They had never, in their almost forty-one years, had a physical fight. But they were having one now. They slapped and batted at each other's faces. They advanced and retreated the length of the patio, grappling, toward the pool. Neither one noticed.

Until they fell in, still grappling, still in a grotesque kind of embrace. They popped up, surprised, sputtering. "You ruined my life!" Alex shouted, water streaming down her face.

"You ruined mine!" Sam shook the hair out of her face. "You can't go back on a promise!"

"I wish we had never been born twins!" As soon as the heated, hateful words were out of her mouth, Alex wanted to snatch them back.

Sam stared at her in stunned silence.

"I . . . I didn't mean that."

"Being a twin has been the most important thing in my life. It's been the most important part of my *identity*." Sam moved through the water toward the steps.

It was almost impossible to tell whether Sam was crying because of the water streaming down her face, but Alex knew. Alex, too, was crying. For her, also, being a twin had been the most important part of her life and of her identity for a long time. But was it true now? She had loved Sam longer than any other person in her life. Then she married Jack, and loved him, and then she had her children, and loved them with every fiber of her being. In a strange way, she supposed, she had been *unfaithful* to her twin sister.

Sam climbed, dripping, out of the water.

"Wait," Alex said. She would apologize for the horrible thing she had said.

Sam kept walking toward the back gate.

"Wait," Alex said again.

"Our lawyer will contact you." Sam disappeared through the gate.

It was terrible to see his wife in this state. She didn't cry or scream or yell, none of the things she would normally do in such a dire circumstance. Instead, when she wasn't lying in bed and staring at the ceiling, she was going through minimal daily routines like she was on autopilot. She brushed her teeth without seeing herself in the mirror and smeared her face with hemorrhoid cream instead of Neutrogena. She heated a Lean Cuisine in the microwave and then forget about it until hours later when the lasagna or butternut squash ravioli was dry as a board. Chris found her bra in the freezer, and he found a half-empty cup of coffee in the medicine cabinet.

Things could not go on like this.

It had been less than twenty-four hours since they arrived back in Scottsdale, and the baby was still across the street. They had not seen her, had not held her, had not brought her home to the waiting nursery. He had been ambivalent about the prospect of the baby for months now, worrying about his age, and about money for private schools, braces, and college tuition. But all that had changed the instant—the brief instant—he caught a glimpse of the baby in Sam's arms at the hospital. As it turned out, he had been waiting for her all along.

He had to do something. When Sam had come home from Alex's with that horrible glazed mask of hurt covering her face and told him what had happened, he didn't say, "I told you so. You should have made Alex sign the contract." He would never do that to Sam, never. He had said, "I'll call the lawyer."

"I can't believe this," Sam had said.

Chris could. Unfortunately, he had suspected that this might happen all along. Alex had always been wrapped up in motherhood, and it was logical that, if she carried a baby for nine months, she would develop a motherly attachment. "We will get the baby," he had told her with a conviction he did not feel. Alex had a strong case; she was the baby's biological mother.

"I've lost my baby." Sam had started to cry.

Dear God, he did not want to go through this again. Once had been more than enough emotional pain for a lifetime. "We will get the baby."

"I've lost my twin sister."

There was absolutely nothing he could say to console her. Absolutely nothing.

He was still dealing with the death of Louise and the fighting over Mr. Peterson's will and all the *crap* that dying causes. The last thing he wanted to do was call yet another lawyer who charged $150 an hour. So, after a restless, sleepless night lying next to his quietly sobbing/soon-to-be comatose wife, Chris decided to take matters into his own hands. He would try to reason with Jack, which was an oxymoron to begin with. It was almost comical, the idea of reasoning with Jack the jock. Still, it was the only course of action that Chris could come up with. He would present Jack with the last check—*as agreed upon by all*—and persuade him to honor the original agreement. Unless, of course, Jack had slept with Alex around or during the time they were in Vegas. The baby looked so much like Annie. Chris tried not to think about it.

He wanted to speak with Jack alone, away from his house, but he wasn't keen on the idea of following the man, "tailing" him in his car like they did on ridiculous cop shows. Jack knew what kind of car he drove; after all, Jack was a car man.

When Chris wheeled his blue recyclable bin to his front curb, he saw that Jack was in the garage, once again working on their terminally fallible old van. But at least Jack had had the good sense to sell the ridiculous Lexus a few weeks before the baby's birth. No one else seemed to be around. The garage would have to do.

Quickly, Chris wrote out the last check, the final installment, and walked over to Jack's garage before he could change his mind. It was the first and only time he had written out a check to Jack and not felt resentful. How foolish he had been! That precious baby was *priceless*.

Chris had a strange sense of *déjà vu* as he approached. Jack's garage, with its oily smell, had been where Chris had given Jack the first installment, and it had been an awkward, painful experience. It was really the inciting incident, Chris thought, of Jack's and his burgeoning hostility.

"Knock, knock," he said. It certainly wasn't a brilliant beginning to this conversation, but he had to start somewhere.

Jack, bent over the engine, lifted his head. "Come in?" he said. "Or should I say, 'who's there'?"

Funny, very funny. Jack was quite the wit.

Jack straightened up and wiped his hands on a shop towel. "I'm glad you're here. We need to talk."

"We certainly do."

"Can I get you a beer?" Jack opened the refrigerator.

It seemed like a good idea to Chris. Anything to make this conversation go more smoothly would be welcome. "Sure."

Jack handed a beer to Chris. He didn't take one for himself. "We have quite a mess here, don't we?"

"I'm here to remedy the situation." Even to his own ears, he sounded pompous, and this was not the tone he was striving for. He wanted to sound reasonable, sincere. He wanted to logically coax Jack to acknowledge that the baby was his and Sam's.

"Someone needs to do something, that's for sure."

Chris took the check out of his shirt pocket. "This is the final install-ment—*as agreed upon by all.*"

Jack didn't move toward the check. "She's a pretty baby, Sophie, a very pretty baby."

"I wouldn't know. I've barely gotten to see her." The beer was not quenching his dry throat. In fact, it was making it worse. He looked for a place to set the can, but there was no available surface.

"She looks a lot like Annie. Looking at her sure does bring back a lot of memories."

What was he trying to say? Was he trying to say what Chris feared the most, that he was actually the baby's father? If that was the case, he and Sam didn't have a legal leg to stand on. "Did you . . . "How could he phrase this? "Sleep with Alex . . ." This was so awkward, asking a man if he slept with his wife! "Around . . . in Vegas?"

Jack looked taken aback, then recognition dawned. Chris could almost swear that he saw the light go on. "It's really none of your business, but yes, I did. The night . . . before."

Chris clutched the beer can so hard that it started to cave in on itself. "Then?"

"The baby is yours, Chris. I had a vasectomy a couple of years after Annie was born. We had decided that our family was complete: mother, father, son, daughter. There's no question that she's your little girl."

His little girl. Chris wanted to hug him—almost. "Sam is beside herself."

"Alex, too. Like I said before, we have a mess on our hands."

"I agree." It was the first time he had ever agreed with Jack about anything. And he agreed wholeheartedly.

"Oral agreements are binding," Jack said.

Chris didn't dare point out the fact that an oral agreement probably didn't matter at all in this case. However, his lawyer had been vague on that point.

"But I don't want any more of your money, Chris. I really don't."

"But it was part of our agreement, and I—"

Jack scraped his fingers through the hair at his temples. It had grayed considerably during the last months. "I've behaved like a complete asshole throughout this whole thing, and I apologize. I hated the whole idea from the beginning, and I only went along with it because I'd gotten myself in such a deep financial hole, such a fucking deep hole that I allowed you to sleep with my wife. And because of that, because of my self-loathing, I blew all the money—and then some. I've behaved unconscionably. I've been horrible, and I apologize."

Chris realized that his mouth had dropped open, and he snapped it shut. He had never thought that Jack would apologize to him for anything, not Jack the cock/jock. The baby, Sophie, was the one who had changed everything, and he suddenly, desperately wanted his little girl.

"Do you accept my apology?" Jack asked. "The twelve-step program and all that. Hopefully, the person you apologize to accepts the apology."

"I accept your apology." Chris meant it. He might have to change his opinion of Jack Carissa. But really, Jack was not the only one who had behaved less than admirably through all this. Look at him. He had gone along with his wife's outlandish plan, had slept with Jack's wife, and then gone behind everyone's back and hired a lawyer. "I also apologize." And Chris meant that, too.

"Accepted. Good. Now what are we going to do about our situation?"

"I would rather not get a lawyer involved," Chris said.

"Fine with me. I can't afford a lawyer anyway."

Which reminded Chris. He extended the check again. "Please take the money."

"Look, if I could, I'd pay you back all the money I've already taken, but I can't. Enough is enough. I'm working three jobs this summer, and we're making ends meet." He cleared his throat, embarrassed. "And it's not like I have to worry about college tuition. But I've accepted that," he added.

There was no doubt about it, Chris thought. The man had had a very rough year.

"Maybe Alex and Sam could come up with a joint custody agreement? What do you think about that?" Jack asked.

"Sam would never go for it." Chris knew this for a certainty, although the same thought had fleetingly occurred to him.

"Neither would Alex. I'm just tossing out ideas."

"Since we're tossing," Chris said, "perhaps I should hire a professional kidnapper to crawl in the bedroom window and take the baby."

"A cat burglar," Jack said.

"A baby burglar," Chris amended.

Unbelievably, they smiled at each other.

"We're going off the deep end here," Jack said. "We need to come up with *something*. Every day that Alex has that baby, it will get harder for her to let go. I know my wife."

"I agree. Time is of the essence." And Chris knew his wife. She had to have that baby—to save her sanity, to save her soul, to save everything.

They pondered the dilemma in silence for a few minutes, then Jack said, "Look, Chris, I love that little girl, too, and like Alex, I would like to keep her, but we can't. That baby is rightfully yours and Sam's. I'm going to do everything I can to help you get Sophie out of Alex's hands—and it might take a hydraulic lift—but I don't have a clue how to go about it."

"Neither do I." Chris sighed. "Neither do I."

Annie wondered if she was suffering from Post-Traumatic Stress Disorder. It was quite possible because PTSD was not limited to people who had suffered military atrocities. She had read this on the internet. Lately, in her dreams, she was having flashbacks to that night on the cruise ship. They were hazy, ill-defined images: a dropped glass, a boy's face leering over her, blood in her panties, a flash she could barely discern behind her heavily closed eyelids. She would wake up, heart pounding and bathed in sweat. She had buried all these memories almost a year ago, buried them deep in her subconscious, or so she thought. So why were they returning now?

It was a fact; she had PTSD.

But this was the question: What was she going to do about it?

She had her last session with Georgia a week before. And she wasn't particularly happy about it. She really liked Georgia, even when Georgia made her uncomfortable, made her explore her feelings, made her *spill her guts*. Pretty Georgia did not put up with bullshit, and Annie had to admit that her bullshit quotient had been pretty much demolished under Georgia's steady blue gaze.

"Does this mean that I'm cured?" she asked Georgia. She meant it as a joke, kind of. It would be a relief, really, if someone came out and said it: You are cured, Annie. You are well. You will never fuck up anything again.

"Cured of what?" Georgia asked evenly.

It just figured that Georgia would answer her question with another question. "Of everything that *ails* me," Annie said. That was a good one, she thought.

"And what would that be?" A smile played around the corners of Georgia's mouth.

"Oh come on," Annie said. "You know what I mean. Am I a complete person now? Am I *whole*?"

"You have always been a complete person, Annie."

Oh, brother. On second thought, maybe she wasn't going to miss Georgia at all. She could be maddeningly *elliptical*. (She had to grudgingly admit that the strenuous curriculum at SCDS had definitely improved her vocabulary the past year.) "Well, hooray for me," Annie muttered.

Georgia let the smile spread over her face. "You have made wonderful progress over the last few months, Annie. I'm very proud of you."

That was more like it. "I feel like there should be a graduation ceremony or something. At the very least, I should get a certificate of achievement or something like that. I don't suppose you have one hanging around?"

"No, I don't. But you don't need a 'certificate of achievement' to know that you feel better, do you?"

"I guess not." But it would have been nice to have a piece of paper with her name on it, announcing to the world that she, Annie Carissa, had *achieved* something. She was, in a way, the valedictorian of her graduating class of one supremely fucked up teenager.

But she wasn't fucked up anymore, right? She had to admit that she did feel better. And if Georgia said she was done, she was done, right? Unless her parents could no longer afford the therapy lessons. It was a distinct possibility.

"I'm going to miss you, Annie. You're a delightful young woman."

Great. Annie could feel herself starting to choke up. "I'm going to miss you, too, Georgia. You're a delightful older young woman."

Georgia laughed. "Oh, Annie."

"Maybe, if I'm in the neighborhood sometime, I could drop by and say hi?" Annie didn't live anywhere near this neighborhood, but she didn't want to let go of Georgia completely. She wanted a little sliver of possibility that she would see her again—maybe as a kind of outpatient?

"I'd like that."

Georgia walked her to the door and hugged her. Of course she was crying now. (She had been such a crybaby in therapy.) "Thanks, Georgia." And then she fled before she could break down completely, and Georgia would think she had *regressed* or something.

She had not told Georgia *everything*.

Now she had Post-Traumatic Stress Disorder.

Outside her bedroom window, she saw Carla's baby blue Mercedes—the car Carla's parents bought for her after Annie totaled the BMW—pull into the driveway. Hurriedly, she finished dressing in her McDonald's uniform. She and Carla had gotten lucky and landed summer jobs at McDonald's— that is, if you considered a job that could make you fat and made you smell like grease *lucky*—and today, they were working the same shift. Carla, of course, didn't need to work because her parents were totally loaded, but she said she wanted to get out of the house. Ron and Marge were around all the time now, and it was starting to drive her nuts. Plus, having a job made Carla's parents proud of her; it proved their daughter was not *anti-social*. She, on the other hand, needed to work. If she wanted gas money, she needed to work. If she wanted to buy a new pair of jeans, she needed to work. Work, work, work. Of course she bitched about it to her parents, but the truth of the matter was that she liked having her own money. It made her feel a lot more independent, a lot more *grown-up*, although she knew she was a *long* way away from that.

She galloped through the kitchen where Jennifer was at the stove fixing something for Nick's lunch, obviously, and Annie shouted out a greeting on the run. Jennifer was always in the kitchen. It was weird having her around but also nice. It was like having a sister suddenly plopped in your lap—no blood relations required. In fact, it was nice having the baby around, too, now that she'd gotten used to it— to *her*, Sophie—and had *almost* quit thinking about *Walter's baby*. In fact, it was nice to have the house feel full. You'd think that her Mom would be *rapturous*, but that didn't seem to be the case. Aunt Sam had gotten home the day before, but they still had the baby. It was more than weird. Something was going on, but she didn't have time to think about it now.

She had Post-Traumatic Stress Disorder.

Maybe she could talk to Carla? After everything that had happened to them in the past year, Carla would probably forgive her about the lies: the Norwegian boyfriend, the rose, the romance that had been the op-posite of what really happened with that horrendous Adam, her *first boy*.

(*Imagined scenario.* G: How did what happened with Adam make you feel, Annie?

A: You mean the rape? That ugly boy and his two ugly cousins drugged and raped me. They *raped me.* I want to kill them.

G: You have my permission. I have a registered gun. You have my *permission* to use it.

A: Gee, thanks, Georgia. You are the *best*!)

"Hurry up," Carla said when Annie got into the car. "I don't want to be late."

"You know what? I think I liked you better when you weren't so responsible." Annie was kidding, kind of.

"We have gotten a little bit boring, haven't we? The next thing you know, we'll be joining a church youth group." Carla had her cap at a jaunty angle again. Every single time, the pimply, bossy manager made her go into the bathroom and unpin it and put it on *properly.* Carla got a sincerely big kick out of this.

"We'll be joining the SADD group at SCDS." She and Carla used to make fun of the dorky kids who were in the Students against Drinking and Drugs group. And now look at the two of them. They were actually considering it, kind of.

"I've been thinking," Carla said. "Maybe we should join *something*? We need boyfriends."

Annie's smile froze. I'm not ready yet, she thought. I'm not ready yet.

Carla, her best friend, noticed. She said quickly, "I mean when school starts. Right now, we need to concentrate on being *career women.* We're ultra-chic career women."

"Working at McDonald's."

"Yep."

"That is so lame, Carla."

"Yep." Carla grinned.

When they got to McDonald's—true to form—the pimply, bossy manager, Roger, told Carla to go into the bathroom and put on her hat *properly,* and then he told them that they would be working the counter today. Annie was still rather terrified of working the counter. The computer was kind of high tech, and the customers could get really bitchy if they had to wait a *second* for their Big Macs and supersized fries. And if it got busy, she would get flustered.

Luckily, Carla took the first customers, two twelve-year-old girls already wearing make-up and skimpy halter tops. They each wanted a cheeseburger happy meal.

"What are you, *five?*" Carla said. "The happy meals are for *children.*"

They insisted on the happy meals; they wanted the toy that came with the meal in the cardboard box that looked like a house. "We're collecting the Barbies," one of them said. "They're going to be collectors' items one day, worth a boatload of money."

"Bullshit," Carla said. "The toys are pieces of crap, and besides, Barbie is a terrible role model for impressionable young girls like yourselves."

The girls gaped at her.

Roger, of course, was listening. He walked over. "What seems to be the problem here?"

"They want happy meals," Carla said.

"So?"

"Look at them. Look at the way they're dressed. They're probably having *sex*, for god's sake, and they want happy meals!"

Under normal circumstances, Annie would have thought this was hilarious.

But she had Post-Traumatic Stress Disorder. Another memory was swimming to the surface, a boy, unzipping his pants . . .

"Annie," Roger barked. "Ring up their order." To Carla, he hissed, "You better watch it."

After the girls left—with their happy meals and Barbies—Carla said, "Those little girls are sluts-in-progress."

"Maybe not." Annie kind of felt sorry for them. They were trying so hard to get noticed by a boy. Really, it was sad. (G: Do you think that you sometimes *act out* for attention? A: Been there, done that.)

It was an excruciatingly slow afternoon. The customers trickled in one at a time. Now Annie wished that they *would* get busy. She'd rather get flustered than have all this time to think—to try *not* to think—about things. Carla wasn't helping matters, although she had no way of knowing what was going on in Annie's mind, what she was trying to *suppress*, trying to *avoid*, trying to *not feel*.

"Raymundo thinks I'm sexually frustrated." Carla picked at her bright green nail polish.

Oh, great.

"Which might be true. I'm trying not to lie to him so much."

"Can we talk about something else?"

"Sure." Carla was a little hurt. She *loved* to talk about her therapy sessions with Raymundo. Annie was convinced that Raymundo was not a very good therapist if he hadn't figured out Carla by now. For sure, he was no Georgia.

The door opened, and a young man around their own age walked in. He was around 5'7" or so, with curly brown hair and hazel eyes. Annie didn't think she knew him, but there was something familiar about him all the same. "My turn," she said.

"Lucky. He's cute. You should so totally go for it." Carla straightened up and patted her hair.

She was so *not* going to go for it. She wasn't ready. (Would she ever be ready?)

"Hi, Annie," he said.

He knew her name? "Hi," she said. "What'll you have?" She searched her brain. Who could this be? It wasn't like she knew a hell of a lot of people.

"You don't remember me." He smiled. He had a nice smile.

"Sure I do." She looked to Carla for help. Carla shrugged

"I don't blame you," he said. "I grew seven inches this year, got my braces off, and got contacts. I don't look like I used to." He also had very nice eyes.

She smiled at him blindly, stupidly.

"I'm Preston. You know, the short nerd who used to bug you about smoking and stuff. And by the way, I'm sorry about that."

"Holy shit!" Carla said. "How could we not have noticed you?"

"You couldn't have. I transferred out last semester."

Annie blushed. Boy, had she and Carla been self-absorbed, or what? "Hi, Preston," she said. "You're looking . . . good." Her blush deepened.

"Thanks. You, too." He (thankfully!) blushed. "The last time I saw you, you had a Mohawk."

"Oh, the follies of youth," she said—and wanted to die. Would she ever learn to talk to boys?

"It looks nice now."

Her hair was shoulder-length now, and she and Carla had declared it her best feature. "Thanks. What can I get you?" (Did that sound sexual?)

"A strawberry shake." He reached for his wallet, not quite looking at her. "Are you seeing anybody?"

Did he not remember how unpopular she was? "I—"

"She's not seeing anyone," Carla interrupted.

"Would you like . . . to go out sometime?" He blushed again.

So did she. Was he really asking her out on a date?

"She'd *love* to go out some time." Sometimes—a lot of times—Carla just could not help herself.

"No offense, Carla, but I'm not talking to you." Preston didn't say it in a nasty way. He had a nice voice. It didn't crack anymore.

"No offense taken."

"Well?" he asked.

Did she dare risk it? She was scared shitless, because obviously, her previous meager experience with boys had been either horrible or *tragic*. But there was something about him. He seemed nice. "Maybe," she said. "I think I would like that."

"I'll give you a call." Carla had magically furnished the milkshake.

"Okay."

After he left, Carla said again, "Holy shit! Who would have thought that Preston would turn out to be so hot?"

"I know." And even more amazing than how he looked was that he had asked her, Annie Carissa, out for a date. Was she ready? Did she dare risk it? "Would you cover for me?"

"I've always got your back," Carla said.

Annie went to the bathroom and made a phone call. When she returned, she said to Carla, "Could you drop me off at Georgia's on the way home? "I just made an appointment."

She wanted to be ready. She wanted to be *totally* ready. She wanted to risk going out on a date with a nice boy. So now, she was going to tell Georgia *everything*.

Nick hoped he hadn't made a mistake. Now that he and Jennifer were married (two days!), he was having second thoughts about joining the Marines. He had to keep his promise to Dylan, of course—he was not the type of man who went back on his promises—but still. There was Jennifer, his lovely wife, and it was going to be hard to leave her. Every day that went by, he knew, would make it harder for him to leave his lovely, adorable, terrific wife. How had he gotten so lucky? She could have married someone smarter or richer, but she had chosen him! He couldn't believe his good fortune.

When he brought up the subject with Jennifer, she simply said, "We will make this work. We love each other, and we will make it work."

How had he gotten so lucky?

He dropped Jennifer off at her parents' house on his way to Fry's. He was going to work up until the day he left for boot camp, even though that meant being away from Jennifer for some of the crucial hours they had together. He hadn't wanted to, but when they discussed it (and they were going to discuss *everything* in their marriage!), Jennifer had pointed out, rationally, that they could use the money. Of course she was right. He now had a *wife* to support!

He was in the break room drinking a fast Coke when Loretta walked in. They hadn't worked the same shift in weeks, and he was glad to see her. However, knowing Loretta, she might be a little hurt that he hadn't kept her in the loop about everything that had been going on in his life. So, he just blurted it out: "Hey, Loretta, I joined the Marines, and I married Jennifer!"

"Whoa, baby cakes, you what and what?" Loretta had her dyed blonde hair pulled up into a lopsided bun, and she wore dangling butterfly earrings.

He repeated, "I joined the Marines, and I married Jennifer."

"Well, you could just knock me over with a feather, honey. For a darling boy who was afraid to ask a girl out, you've certainly turned into a hunky young man who moves *fast*, huh? Lordy, lordy, a soldier—that explains the hair, although the buzz does not ruin your good looks, sugar—and a married man! You and that sweet little oriental—I mean Japanese—girl."

"Korean." Loretta was never going to get it right.

"Yes. Well how do you like that? You went straight from the *big ta-da* to the *grand hoopla*, didn't you? I'll be damned—I mean, *darned*." She grinned at him.

He grinned back. "I'm sorry I didn't invite you to the wedding, but it was kind of spur-of-the-moment."

"City hall?" she asked.

He nodded.

"Well, that's okay. I just bawl my eyes out at weddings anyway, sugar. I can go through a box of tissues before they even get to the 'I dos.' I even bawled at my own weddings, but as you know, there was probably good reason for that. Hindsight is—" She tied on her apron, thinking.

"20-20," he supplied.

"I'll take your word for it, honeybunch," Loretta said. "I've never had my eyes tested, but come to think of it, it's getting a little blurry when I have to read the code numbers on the produce."

"I'm so happy," Nick said. Boy, Loretta could get off track so easily.

Loretta's eyes welled up. "I'm happy *for* you. You give an old lady like me hope that there is true love. Of course, I've always believed in true love. I will be a silly romantic until the day I die."

"You're not silly, Loretta. I think you're great." And she wasn't old either, he should have said. She had helped him so much over the last year. He needed to buy her some kind of present before he left. What would be appropriate? Jennifer would know. He hugged her; he didn't want her to see that his own eyes were getting a little moist.

"I think you're pretty damn—darn—great, too, baby cakes. Now I want to have you two lovebirds over for dinner."

"We'd love to," Nick said. He took Loretta's arm as they walked out of the break room, vowing that he would always stay in touch.

He was just getting off work when he got the phone call from Annie. "Can you pick me up? I'm at Georgia's." Her voice was thick.

Something must be up. Annie was supposed to have had her last session with Georgia a week ago. "Sure," he said quickly. "I'll be there in five."

She had been crying. She climbed into the van with red-rimmed eyes. "Thanks," she said.

"No problem." He had picked her up many times from her therapy sessions before she got her driver's license, and Annie usually had red-rimmed eyes. He always thought it was better not to pry, but this time, for some strange reason, he felt compelled to ask, "You okay?"

She sniffled. "Georgia says I will be."

"That's good," he said lamely. He wondered what they had talked about. No, on second thought, he didn't want to know. It wasn't any of his business. Therapy sessions were supposed to be private, and he respected that.

"Confession is good for the soul and all that crap, right?" Annie stared straight ahead.

"That's what they say." And then he thought about his own confession, about finally telling everyone that he had been a thief. It had been painful and embarrassing, but he had felt better after he told and after he had done the right thing. "It took a while, but I felt better after I told everyone that I stole all that stuff. I was such an idiot."

"I was such an idiot," Annie said sadly.

He wasn't exactly sure what she was talking about, but she sounded so forlorn—so hopeless—that he would do anything to make her feel better. "No, Annie, you are not an idiot. I've made some poor choices this past year, and you've made some poor choices, but you are not an idiot." (She had made some seriously *rotten* choices in the past year, but he was not going to add insult to injury.)

"I'm emotionally exhausted," Annie said.

"I'll take you to Taco Bell." Maybe it would make her feel better.

She managed a small smile. "That's your solution for my emotional exhaustion? Taco Bell?"

"Taco Bell can cure anything," he said, trying to sound jovial.

"No Taco Bell. Not this time." They were almost home. "Can you drive around a little longer? I don't want to go home yet."

He was anxious to get home. Jennifer would be waiting. By picking up Annie, he had already lost ten precious minutes that he could be spending with Jennifer. However, he would soon be leaving her, too, right? (That was what Jennifer would remind him.) "Sure. Where to?"

"How about Cactus Park? I need to tell you something."

They drove to Cactus Park in silence, and Nick felt a growing uneasiness. Annie hadn't said she wanted to tell him something. She had said she *needed* to tell him something. There was a big difference.

Annie headed directly to the swings, and he followed. The swings had always been Annie's favorite playground toy. Not the slide. Not the monkey bars. The swings. Their mom used to say that, if Annie had her way, she would swing for days.

"This is going to be hard," Annie said, scuffling her flip flops in the sand.

He sat in the swing next to hers. "You don't have to do this." His unease was growing into dread. He knew that he didn't want to hear what she needed to say.

"Yes, I do." Annie took a deep, ragged breath. "You were the one who found me. In a way, you were my *rescuer*, as Georgia would say, and you deserve to know the whole story. Plus, if you know the truth, you might kind of understand where I've been coming from the past year, although I don't think Georgia would want me to say that. I'm not sure. After this last session, I'm confused. I'm *emotionally exhausted.*"

When had he ever rescued her? He was beginning to taste the dread.

"That night on the cruise, when you found me passed out on that chaise lounge?" Annie spoke slowly. "You were right, I had been drinking—one drink, I think—but it wasn't what you thought."

Oh, no! he thought now.

"Adam and his cousins must have drugged my drink."

She had been fully clothed when he found her. He was sure of it.

"When you found me, I was still pretty much out of it, I think. And when you took us back to our room, I was already trying to convince myself that nothing had happened."

The dread tasted metallic, and heat was working its way up his neck, to his cheeks, to his forehead. He wanted her to *stop*, but was unable to open his mouth, unable to tell her that he didn't want to hear anymore.

"But then the three Polaroid pictures fell out of my purse, and I knew. All three of them raped me."

It felt as if his head had exploded. "Those *motherfuckers!*" he screamed. "I will kill them. I will hunt them down and kill them with my bare hands!" The tears streamed down his face. How could those motherfuckers have done that to an innocent, fifteen-year-old girl? He was never going to let those motherfuckers get away with it. Never.

Annie was crying again, too. She grabbed his arm. "Nick, I know this is horrible, and I'm sorry to dump this on you."

He had never felt real anger before, he realized, nothing had ever come close to the red hot, burning, searing emotion that was coursing through his veins now. "You have nothing to be sorry for, Annie. Those *motherfuckers!*"

"It was partly my fault. I was naïve—"

"It was not your fault! How can you even think that? You were fifteen!"

"Shh, Nick. People are staring."

A mother pushing a stroller toward them quickly turned away. "Let them stare." His heart thumped in his chest. Was he going to have a heart attack? "It was not your fault!"

"You're right. Georgia said that today, too. I finally told her today. But that was the thing, Nick. All these months, I thought it was *my fault*."

"It was not your fault!" He sounded like a broken record. He felt broke.

"After that night, I felt like damaged goods, you know? So I guess I kind of thought *what the hell*. I've never even told Carla about that night. I made up this stupid, romantic story about this Norwegian guy, thinking I would tell her eventually, but then time went on, and it just got too embarrassing to tell her the truth."

How could she have kept this inside for so long? It was no wonder she had started drinking and taking drugs. He probably would have, too. Well, probably not, but still. It was understandable—in a way. But how could guys do that to a young girl? What kind of sick, twisted person would do that? He would never understand that kind of behavior. Never.

He took a deep breath, trying to still his racing heart. It didn't work. He really did want to kill those guys, but of course, he didn't want to go to jail for the rest of his life. He needed to try to be reasonable here. "I'll track them down on Facebook. We should report them to the police."

"I didn't know his last name. Besides, he told me he went to college at Santa Barbara, and that turned out not to be true."

"They need to pay for what they did to you." He hadn't liked them from the moment he set eyes on them, he remembered. And then he remembered that he had followed her one night—a secret mission—and then he had gotten distracted when he discovered his dad in the casino and had to take the drunken Iraq vet to his room. If he had followed her, could he have saved her? "Oh, no," he moaned, burying his hot, wet face in his hands.

Annie put her hand on his arm, stroking. "I'm so sorry, Nick. I knew I shouldn't have dumped this on you."

She was apologizing to him? Her sympathy made him cry even harder. "I was going to follow you one night—maybe it was that night—and I got distracted. I might have been able to prevent that terrible thing from happening."

"Nicky, it's not your fault either. You're right. They were *motherfuckers*."

He would give anything—even his life—to make this not have happened to his sister. "I'm sorry, Annie." He couldn't think of anything else to say, and that sounded so woefully inadequate.

"I'm going to finally put this behind me," Annie said. "That's what Georgia said, and I believe what Georgia says to me. She was right about Walter's baby. It's taken some time, but I'm almost there."

"Walter Caldwell was the father?" Nick felt sucker-punched for the second time. He hadn't really let himself imagine who the father had been. He didn't want to let his mind wander to some skuzzy, nameless, faceless guy she had met at some party. But of course his sister wasn't like that, and he should have known that all along.

"You didn't know?"

He shook his head.

Annie seemed embarrassed. "Well, uh, I might as well tell you the basic facts, since I'm spilling my guts here. I always had a huge crush on Walter, and the one bonfire party Carla and I went to, I hooked up with him. Nina had just dumped him. I loved him. He was drunk. I don't think he even remembered. I'm kind of done with that story."

It was a good thing. Nick was *emotionally exhausted*. He felt utterly drained. And one thing was certain: He would never become a therapist. He was having a hard enough time absorbing all of this as her brother.

"Can I ask you a favor?"

Nick choked out, "Sure. Anything."

"Don't say anything to Mom and Dad just yet, okay? I'm going to tell them—eventually—but I'm not up to the challenge yet." Annie seemed calmer now, a weight lifted. She started to swing.

"Okay," he said. His poor parents. It was going to break their hearts when they heard this horrible story, when they found out about the motherfuckers who raped their daughter. And poor Annie. She was going to have to tell the story again, relive the humiliation *again*.)

"You can tell Jennifer, though. I really like Jennifer. I'm glad you married her." Annie pumped her legs, gaining speed, gaining height.

"Me, too." And even though it was far too little, far too late, he added, "Is there anything you want me to do for you, Annie?"

"Just be my brother," she answered.

"I'll always be that." He started to swing with her.

"I'm going to miss you when you're gone."

"I'm going to miss you, too." He hadn't realized how much until just that moment.

"I just thought of something else you can do for me."

"Anything."

"Come back safe and sound." Annie was really soaring now. "Or I will be royally pissed off."

To get her out of the house, to make this plan work, Jack was going to have to stop being an enabler. Even though he was working three jobs (driver's ed instructor, summer soccer camp coach, and part-time mechanic at Shell), he still managed to make sure that he brought up trays of food, prepared by Jennifer, to Alex.

Alex refused to come out of the room and leave the baby now.

He was enabling her to do this. Since her blow-out with Sam four days ago, he was enabling his wife to become a hermit with the baby, upstairs in what used to be their shared bedroom.

"Why don't you take the baby for a walk?" he asked her.

"The baby is safe here. She's happy." Alex rocked her. She rocked and rocked and rocked the baby, barely taking the time to shower.

He knew what she was thinking. (Was she totally losing it?) "Sam is not lurking around some corner, waiting to snatch the baby," he said, trying to reason with her.

"I wouldn't put it past her."

Jack wanted to snatch the baby and march over to Chris and Sam's house and say, "Here's Sophie, your baby girl. Sorry about the inconvenience."

But in the long run, he knew this wouldn't accomplish anything. In that scenario, Alex would demand that they hire a lawyer, which they couldn't afford. In that scenario, his wife would never speak to her twin sister again. In that scenario, his wife would never speak to him, nor trust him, ever again. So much would be destroyed. So much would be lost.

It had to be Alex's decision to give the baby to Sam.

He tried another tactic to at least get her out of the damn bedroom. "Your son and his new wife are downstairs. Your son is leaving soon; you need to spend time with him. For god's sake, Alex, you also need to spend time with Annie."

Her response to that? A blank stare.

His wife was losing it, and he was enabling her.

He met with Chris to confer on the situation. They still had not come up with a plan to reconcile their wives and put Sophie in the right mother's arms. It was strange, but after all these years, he was actually starting to like Chris. They had absolutely nothing in common. Except for their wives and the baby. Which was huge.

"I went to the store today to buy Alex sanitary pads," he told Chris. "I have reached a new low." They were walking at the far end of the neighborhood. Both of them had the strange, ridiculous notion that they should meet in secret, that Alex and Sam shouldn't know that they were talking. Each wife would feel betrayed.

"Your first time? I'm a regular in the feminine hygiene aisle at Walgreens." Chris gave a rueful laugh. "You're looking at the definition of a classic enabler when you look at me. When Sam says *jump*, I ask her how high."

"What in the hell is wrong with us?"

"That's a good question."

"I don't know why I can't just take control of the situation. I don't know why I can't tell Alex that she must give the baby to Sam. Period. A year ago, I couldn't have imagined this situation." He paused. "But a year ago, I would have taken a drink or two to gather my courage."

"It's a very complicated situation," Chris said.

"Shit, yeah."

They walked in a companionable silence for a couple of blocks, then Chris pulled out two cigars from his shirt pocket, two cigars with pink bands announcing: "It's a girl!

He handed one to Jack. "I couldn't resist."

Jack probably smoked one cigar every five years, but this occasion seemed to call for it. "Thanks." They lit up and continued walking. It was dusk and still hot, but as everyone in Arizona said, it was a dry heat.

"To answer your question—what in the hell is wrong with us—I would have to say I'm terrified. I'm terrified to see Sam go through another loss." He blew a perfectly round smoke ring. "She almost didn't make it after Grace died."

Jack realized that he, too, was terrified. He was terrified of losing Alex. "There's that."

"And I love her, maybe too much."

"And there's that, too."

They walked and smoked a few more blocks before Jack spoke again. "The way I see it, we have to get them together to talk."

"In a rational manner," Chris added.

Jack snorted. "Yeah, right."

Chris laughed. "One can always hope."

He was really starting to like Chris. Sometimes, he almost had a sense of humor. "We could drop them off some place, like Cochran's, and leave them there to talk."

"Or throw things."

"Or duke it out."

"They already did that."

"Yeah." Jack couldn't believe that Alex and Sam had gotten into a physical fight, but Alex had the scratches and bruises to prove it. Well, she *said* she did. He still had not seen his wife naked. Her asking him to make love to her a few days ago was only a ruse to distract him. And it had worked.

"They can't know that the other one is coming," Chris said.

"Exactly. We can each tell them that we're taking them out to dinner—and what a coincidence—who should be in the restaurant but the other one. And then you and I run like hell." It sounded like such a corny idea, but he didn't have a better one. "Are you in?"

"I'm in," Chris said. "But you know, they could just turn around and walk home and not talk at all."

"I know."

"But we have to try something. I can't take one more night of a comatose wife. Let's do it tonight. Eight o'clock at Cochran's."

"Tonight?" How in the hell was he going to get Alex to Cochran's? He couldn't even get her out of the bedroom.

"Tonight," Chris said firmly. "This has got to come to an end." He realized how ominous that sounded. "I mean, this situation has to be remedied."

"The baby has to be given to Sam." Jack knew it was the right thing to do, but he could already feel an ache of loneliness for Sophie.

"And they need to make amends."

"Let's head back now. I'm going to need all the time I can get to drag Alex from the room." If he had to carry her, he would.

When he walked into the house, he went directly upstairs. He didn't even knock on the door of his own bedroom like he usually did. He just barged right in. "We're going out to dinner!" he announced.

"No, thank you," she said, overly polite. She was rocking, rocking Sophie.

Of course he had expected this. "I mean it, Alex. I'm not going to take *no* for an answer. You need to get out of this house."

Alex didn't answer him. Instead, she cooed to the baby, "Mommy's not ever going to leave you, honey."

This was bad, really bad. His wife, in fact, was *losing it*. "Thirty minutes," he pleaded. "We'll just grab a quick bite to eat."

"I'm not hungry," she said, nodding toward the tray with a half-eaten sandwich. Jennifer, sweet, overly conscientious Jennifer, must have brought it up. Evidently, he was not the only one in this family who was enabling Alex, and come to think of it, neither Nick nor Annie had even mentioned the fact that the baby was still here. No one had pointed out to Alex that this situation was blatantly wrong. No one had said to her: *What in hell are you doing?*

"Please," he said. "We need to spend some time together."

"Sit down," she said. "You can join us."

Not knowing what else to do, he sat down on the edge of the bed. He glanced at the clock on the nightstand: 7:45. He was going to have to think of something, fast. What could he say to get her to move?

And then inspiration struck. "Okay, Alex, I'm not supposed to spoil the surprise, but I guess I have no choice."

She actually looked at him. "Surprise?"

"Yeah, Amanda organized a surprise party for you." Jack hoped he wasn't stretching his luck too far by saying that it was Amanda's idea. "I mean, I think it was the entire Bunco group that came up with the idea. They're waiting for you now at Cochran's." He was starting to sweat.

"Why would they give me a surprise party?" She looked suspicious.

"Because you just had a baby. It's what people—women—do when someone has a baby. They throw you a party—a shower, a baby shower." He was grasping at straws here, totally out of his element.

"They already gave me a baby shower."

Had they?

"Don't you remember the shoe party?"

Oh, shit. He gave a feeble laugh. "Right. The *footwear* instead of *cookware* party. Haha. Well, I guess they thought that now that the baby is born, you deserved a proper baby shower. I'll bet they're laden with little pink dresses and booties and all that stuff." The sweat was starting to pour off him. The room felt like a boiler room.

"Are they really throwing me a shower?"

"They sure are!" he said with hearty, fake enthusiasm. "We better get going! You don't want to keep your friends waiting, do you?"

"You aren't just saying this to get me out of the house, are you?"

"Why would I do that?" Instead of lying outright, it was a good rule to answer a question with a question.

She looked almost convinced, but then she asked, "Is Sam going to be there?"

"At *your* baby shower? What do you think?" A question answering a question, a good tactic.

"They've been my friends for a long time, way before Sam moved into the neighborhood."

"That's right. Let's get going."

"It might be nice," she said thoughtfully.

"Yes! It's going to be great!"

She got up. She miraculously got out of the damn rocking chair! "Sophie could use some pretty little dresses. I haven't had a chance to buy much for her yet."

He didn't want to ruin her momentum by stating the obvious: You haven't been out of the house. "Right," he said.

"What should I dress her in for the shower?" She placed Sophie in the bassinet and started sorting through the basket of laundry next to it.

Shit. Wait. Alex couldn't bring the baby. He had a flashing, terrible image of Alex and Sam having a tug of war, the baby being the rope. "They're not expecting you to bring Sophie," he said. "They're having it in a bar, Alex. I think it's a girls' margarita night type of thing." This flash of inspiration, this bogus story, had as many holes in it as a colander.

"Of course they'll want to see the baby. She's the star of the show, the main attraction. Aren't you, sweetheart?"

But Sophie, God bless her little soul, was fast asleep. "She's going to sleep until her next bottle," he pointed out. "She's not going to wake up until around midnight."

Alex looked torn. "Well, I could make an exception this once—"

"I'll tell you what," he interjected. "I'll drive you there—Annie can watch her the five minutes I'm gone—and then in an hour or two—whenever you call—I'll bring her by for a short visit. How's that?" He was practically panting. He glanced again at the clock: 7:55.

"Well," Alex said doubtfully.

"Come on, Alex, your friends are doing something nice for you, and you don't want to keep them waiting."

It took another fifteen minutes for Alex to try to find something to wear that didn't make her look fat, to fuss with her hair, to apply some make-up. As they pulled up to Cochran's, Jack was relieved when he spotted Chris's Saab. He wondered, briefly, if Chris had as difficult time as he had, but that didn't matter now. They had both somehow managed to get their wives within close proximity of each other.

Now for the hard part. To keep them there.

"Amanda told me that they would be on the back patio. I'll walk in with you."

"Why on the back patio? It smells like garbage back there."

"I don't know why." He let out a huff of exasperation. He couldn't help himself. His patience with her was frayed.

"You don't have to walk me in," she said testily.

He took a firm grasp of her elbow, just in case she decided to bolt. "I want to see the look of surprise on your face." Honestly, that was probably the last thing he wanted to see, knowing that the surprise would be followed immediately by anger.

"Don't worry, Jack, I can fake a look of surprise. I do it every year when I open your Christmas present."

"What?"

"You hide it in the same place every year. I always know in advance what you're going to give me." She smiled at him. "You didn't know?"

"No." She was crafty, his wife. Evidently, she had unknown, hidden talents. However, after the "baby shower," she might never want to receive another Christmas or birthday or anniversary or Mother's Day present from him again.

The back patio was crowded. With the misters spraying their pressurized stream of water, it was a pleasant night to eat outdoors. He saw Chris and Sam sitting in the far corner first. He stifled a gasp. Sam looked terrible: skeletal, hollow-eyed, hunched, zombie-like. Chris had not been exaggerating. "Over here," he said.

Alex turned toward the table, and when she saw them, it was not a fake look of surprise on her face. "What have you done?" she asked him with the expected anger.

"You're going to talk to your sister." He still had a firm grasp on her elbow.

"I have nothing to say to her." Alex couldn't get her elbow out of his grasp.

"You have everything to say to her," he said as he propelled her unwillingly toward the table. "Everything."

Sam looked up when he pulled out a chair and pushed Alex into it. "It's you," she said.

"It's me," Alex answered.

They stared at each other, long and hard.

"We're going to leave the two of you to talk," Chris said, rising from his seat.

"Don't even think about making a scene." Usually, Jack would have directed this toward Sam, but tonight, he meant it for his wife. "It would be all over the neighborhood by tomorrow." There were a few families from the neighborhood here, couples he knew only by sight. He hoped this ploy—what will the neighbors think?—still had some merit for Alex.

Alex and Sam still stared at each other.

"I'll tell the waitress to bring over a bottle of chardonnay on our way out," Chris said, and walked quickly away.

Jack was right behind him. He stole a quick glance over his shoulder. The women weren't moving, and he and Chris were practically running by the time they got to the parking lot.

"You got Sam here. Congratulations," he said to Chris.

"Congratulations to you, too. How'd you get Alex out of the house?"

"Fake story about a baby shower. You?"

"Fake department dinner."

They managed tired smiles. They were in the same boat, on the same page, and it was nice to have someone to share it with. "Nice touch with the wine."

"Lubrication," Chris said.

Jack was really starting to like him.

They each had a glass of wine in front of them, and the waitress had put the bottle in an ice bucket. They hadn't said a word to each other yet. Where to start? Sam had been waiting for this moment, imagined it, had gone over and over in her mind what she would say. But now she didn't know where to start.

Sam took out a cigarette and pushed the pack and lighter across the table to Alex. "They think they're so smart, don't they?"

Alex took a cigarette and lit it. "I really made Jack squirm. A baby shower? Really. You think he could come up with something better than that."

"Good acting job." If she didn't know what was going on, she would have believed Alex's shocked look was real.

"I wasn't acting. When I saw you, I—"

They had never liked to criticize each other's looks, and Sam knew that she looked terrible. A makeup artist couldn't camouflage her despair. "I look like shit," she said. She took a big sip of wine and a big drag off her skinny little cigarette. "I look like shit because I feel like shit."

"I'm fat," Alex said.

As if that balanced things out? "You just had a baby." *My baby.* But Sam wasn't going to continue harping on this essential fact. So far, it had gotten her nowhere. In the email that Alex sent her, all Alex had said was this: I MISS YOU. Cochran's on Thursday?

It was such a simple email, but Sam knew it represented a spark of hope. Alex possibly wanted to apologize about what she had said during their awful fight in the pool, but whatever the reason, she was offering an olive branch. Sam—the writer—deliberated for two hours before sending: I'LL BE THERE FOR YOU.

She hoped it spoke volumes to her sister.

So now they sat. It was time for the big heart-to-heart discussion. It was time to clearly define who was going to be Sophie's mother, and Sam didn't know where to start. Her heart felt like it had been put through a grinder during the past few days, but in a strange way, she wasn't surprised at Alex's adamant wish to keep Sophie. Hadn't she expected this for some time? Hadn't the signs been there all along? She couldn't really blame her sister because, if the tables were turned, the roles reversed, and she had been the one to give birth to Sophie, she would want to keep the baby, too.

And she had to admit that Alex had valid points. She had behaved like a selfish bitch during a great deal of the last year, a selfish bitch motivated by—not the hope she had originally thought— but by *fear*. This was the closest Sam would ever come to having a biological baby. It was her last chance. She was terrified that it wouldn't happen, that the bottom would drop out, the trap door would open, and she would fall into the abyss.

And it had opened. And she had fallen.

"Sam, I just want to say that—" Alex leaned forward earnestly.

Sam wasn't ready yet. She didn't want everything to be over. She leaned forward, too. "Remember how hard we campaigned for cheerleading in seventh grade? It wasn't anything about whether you could turn a cartwheel or do the splits. It was a total popularity thing." During the past few days, she had been thinking a lot about their past. Their shared past.

Alex managed a small smile. "We thought it would be the end of the world if we didn't get it."

"Or even worse: One of us got it, and one of us didn't."

"I remember," Alex said.

"We had a plan. Every day, we would assign ourselves a group to talk to, the popular clique or the band kids. You would go one way, and I would go another. We could cover more ground that way. And remember how we practiced the different way that we could work into the conversation—oh, so casually—that the Murphy twins would love to be cheerleaders, that the Murphy twins had more school spirit than anyone else trying out."

"Subtlety was not our strong suit." Alex laughed.

"We were as far from subtle as you could get. But it worked. We both made it."

"You couldn't even turn a straight cartwheel. In fact, you were probably the worst cheerleader in the history of Fairview Junior High." Alex was really laughing now.

"That's beside the point. The point is that we made a good team."

"We did."

"Do we still make a good team, Alex?" After all her reminiscences about the past, that was the crucial question.

"We grew up," Alex said quietly.

"Supposedly." Sam lit a cigarette off the ember of the first. This was certainly a situation that called for chain-smoking. "When we were growing up, we always had each other's back. When you broke Mother's porcelain baby Jesus in the Nativity set, I told her that the cat had jumped on the table and knocked it off."

"I only wanted to hold him. He was so cute and tiny, with that tiny flush on his cheeks and those blue, blue eyes."

"And I told you there was no way that Jesus would have had blue eyes because He was from the Middle East."

"You said there was no way in *hell* that Jesus would have had blue eyes. It was the first time I ever heard you swear. We were nine. That's why I dropped the baby Jesus." Alex reached for the wine bottle and filled their glasses.

"I'm still right about that," Sam said.

"When you were dating Teddy Donner in high school and stayed out way past our curfew every Saturday night, I always told Mother that you were already in bed, and then later, I'd go unlock the back door so you could sneak in. At the time, I thought you were being very promiscuous. It was thrilling."

"I know I let you think that for a while, but I eventually told you that we were only playing very competitive games of Scrabble. Teddy was a good friend, and he was gay."

"I wonder what ever happened to little Teddy Donner?"

"Someone in the Fairview beauty shop told Mother that he died of AIDS about fifteen years ago. She thought I would want to know."

"That's so sad."

"I cried when I heard the news."

What were they doing here? They were dancing a *long* way around the real issue.

However, Alex didn't seem particularly eager to get to the subject at hand either. "Mother and Dad didn't make it to Nick's graduation," she said.

Or Sophie's birth, Sam thought. "Where in the hell are they?"

"Apparently, somewhere that doesn't have cell phone service," Alex said dryly. "Even if Mother did answer her phone, would we really want her advice?"

"Only if it was what one of us wanted to hear." Sam had no idea what their mother would advise in this situation. Would she be on her side, or Alex's? Would she take any side at all? When they were growing up, when they had their rare arguments, their mother would generally listen to both sides of the story, nod sagely, and say, "I'll let you two girls work it out. I'm sure you can come to a mutual agreement."

Alex took another large sip of wine. "Have you ever considered the possibility that we simply wore our mother out?"

"And that's why they roam the country in their RV, to avoid us?" They certainly had not been bad or disobedient kids, but they had been a handful—demanding, even willful. Well, if Sam had to face the facts, she had to admit that they had both been stubborn. Very stubborn. Obviously, things had not changed in their almost forty-one years. "Maybe so," she conceded. "So now, they only have to contend with *Ginger*. Piece of cake."

Alex choked on a laugh. "If they were going to go with a *Gilligan's Island* theme, why didn't they name the RV Mary Ann? I always liked Mary Ann better."

"It was Ginger for me. She was a *movie star.*"

"We'll agree to disagree."

"On that topic, at least."

They stared at each other. They were definitely going to need some more wine.

There was a commotion at the back door, and Amanda burst forth, all honey-streaked hair, fishy mouth, and big boobs barely contained in a tube top. "Shit," Sam said. Of all the people to enter their sphere now, Amanda would have to be the last name on the list.

Alex looked toward the door. "Crap," she said. "Read the menu, look busy, act like we don't notice her," she instructed.

Sam picked up the menu, but it would never work, not with Amanda.

They were definitely going to *need more wine.* Sam motioned to the waitress.

Amanda spied them with her gossip radar, of course, and sailed over. "Gals!" she exclaimed in her high, breathy voice. "The whole neighborhood has been wondering what's going on with you two! The other gals and I are dying to see the baby!"

"I'll bet," Sam said icily.

"Hello, Amanda." Alex's tone was equally cool.

"I'm waiting for Curtis. You know how all successful husbands are: work, work, work. He just got another promotion, and I have to tell you," she leaned closer, conspiratorially, "we're thinking of moving up, you know, to a bigger house in a nicer neighborhood. Not that our neighborhood is shabby, of course."

"Not shabby. Of course," Alex mimicked.

"Congratulations," Sam said. "You'd have a whole new ballgame to play in." What a joy it would be to get Amanda out of the neighborhood.

"Ballgame? Don't be silly! I'm not going to a ballgame!" Amanda trilled.

Sam rolled her eyes and gave Alex the look that said: Just shoot me now.

Alex stifled a smile. "Nice seeing you, Amanda."

Amanda looked around. "I have a few minutes before Curtis gets here. I'll just pull up a seat, and you can tell me all about the baby."

"No!" she and Alex cried in unison.

"What?" Amanda took an involuntary step back at their outburst.

"We're having a private conversation," Sam said. If the nosy bitch sat down, she was going to have to strangle her.

"Well!" Amanda said huffily. "I was only trying to be neighborly."

And wring out every bit of gossip that you can, Sam thought.

"Another time," Alex said.

Luckily, at that moment, Curtis appeared. "Amanda!" he called. "We're eating inside. Come!" He snapped his fingers at her. "Come now!"

Without another word, Amanda obeyed. She turned on her heel and followed him into the restaurant.

"Well, that was something," Sam said. "It's like he was calling a dog."

"Maybe there is justice in the world. Imagine the scale." Alex held her hands in front of her. "On the one hand, you drive an Escalade." She flipped her right hand over. "And on the other, you get treated like a dog." She flipped her left palm up. She wagged them up and down. "Seem fair to you?"

"Hell, yeah."

The waitress brought the bottle of wine, and they fell into silence. Sam lit another cigarette and slid the pack across to Alex. How much longer were they going to avoid talking about Sophie? She was enjoying being with Alex, and it was the first time in a year that they hadn't talked about a baby, but she was starting to feel the strain like an iron bar in the middle of her shoulder blades. How much longer before they got down to the nitty-gritty?

Not long.

"I want to apologize for what I said in the pool. I didn't mean it. I've loved being your twin. I spoke out of anger—and idiocy. Please forgive me."

The tears rose up swiftly. Sam had not been hurt by Alex's remark; she had been *wounded*. She couldn't speak. All she could do was nod.

"I will never say anything so terrible again." Alex was crying, too, tears trailing down both cheeks.

This was it, Sam thought. They were going to be so *civil* about reneging on a promise, about reneging on the only remaining chance she had at motherhood. Alex had carried her baby, and now Alex was going to keep her baby. As simple and as complicated as that. The end.

There wasn't going to be any King Solomon scene where two women claim a baby and the king says bring me a sword and cut the child in half, giving half to each woman. The true mother says let the other woman have the *living* baby. And then King Solomon says that she is the baby's *true mother* because she wanted to keep the baby alive. There wasn't going to be any of that.

"I've been doing a lot of thinking, too," Alex said slowly.

Sam took a sip of wine and swallowed hard. They were going to be civil, rational, calm. No hysterics. It was too late. She would have to respect Alex's decision. *Even if it killed her.*

"I've been thinking about college and the abortion. Remember how you wanted to run away and raise the baby?"

Sam nodded.

"You would have done it, too, if that's what I wanted. But then when I decided to have—I still have a hard time saying the word—*abortion*, you were right there by my side. I couldn't have made it through the ordeal if you hadn't been there for me." Alex's voice caught.

Sam still couldn't speak.

"Part of the reason I agreed to be your surrogate was to try and make up for that mistake, to *atone* for the loss of that baby. Does that make any sense to you?"

Sam nodded. She knew all about trying to atone for loss. In fact, in certain ways, wasn't Sophie an atonement for Grace? And if so, wasn't that a good thing, a wonderful thing?

"And after everything we've said and done to each other during this last year," Alex continued, "you didn't bring up the subject once. Not once."

Another sip of wine helped to dislodge the lump in her throat a little. "We made a promise. We were never going to mention that baby again."

"We made a promise. And you kept it."

Sam realized she was holding her breath. She slowly exhaled. "What are you saying, Alex?"

"I still want to keep the baby."

There. It was done. The abyss widened, deepened. Without realizing it, she let out a strangled cry.

"No, Sam, no." Alex was at her side in a second, kneeling down, putting her arms around Sam's shoulders. "Let me finish. I love that baby, but I know that you do, too."

Sam was sobbing. What was Alex trying to say to her? She didn't understand.

"I tried to pretend that it was all right to keep her, but I couldn't totally convince myself that it was the right thing to do. I told myself all kinds of stories, Sam, all in a desperate attempt to convince myself that it was *right* that I keep her. I rocked that baby for hours and hours, trying to rationalize my position."

"I think I'm going to faint." Sam's head spun. She needed more wine. No, she probably didn't need any more wine. Could this really be happening?

"You've never fainted in your life," Alex said, patting her back.

"There's a first time for everything." She put her head between her knees and tried to breathe deeply. When she looked up, Alex was smiling at her.

"Sophie belongs to you," her twin sister said. "We made a promise, and I'm keeping it."

15

TWO YEARS LATER

Alex paced up and down the front hall, to the kitchen, and then back to the front door. She opened the door and looked out yet again. Nothing. Where in the hell was Sam? Their plane had landed an hour ago. Granted, baggage claim was undoubtedly a nightmare with all the baby paraphernalia—car seat, stroller, portable crib—and they had to get a rental car. But still. Where in the hell were Sam, Chris, and Sophie?

She was a little disappointed when they couldn't make it to Annie's graduation the night before. She understood that Sophie had an ear infection from a late spring cold, and the doctor wouldn't let her fly until today. Alex swallowed that tiny pill of disappointment rather easily. She was finally learning to not sweat the small stuff. A good part of that education came from having a son in Afghanistan for ten months and in an overseas military hospital for another ten. When your son is in a war zone, you count your blessings for every day that goes by without bad news. You send weekly care packages that contain homemade cookies, socks, razors, and something to make him laugh, like a whoopee cushion or silly string. You wait for internet contact. And you hope, and you pray.

A baby's ear infection, a late plane. Nothing.

"Dad wants to know how many hotdogs to put on the grill," Nick said behind her, startling her.

"They're not even here yet. Tell him to wait." She reached out and touched his arm. She was always touching him these days, every chance she got. He didn't act like it annoyed him. But even if it did annoy him, she would do it anyway.

"Everyone's pretty hungry," Nick said. He looked so much older now. Two years of experience, experiences no one could have foreseen, had contoured his jaw and cheekbones into that of a man's, a handsome man.

She sighed. It was wonderful to have a full house. She loved having a full house. However, the only downside was this: Someone was always hungry. "Tell him to cook them all. They'll get eaten eventually."

"Roger." Nick gave her a quick peck on the cheek.

She grinned at him. She did this every chance she got, too.

Nick had come home safely. Not *home* home first. He had spent the last four months in Palo Alto with Jennifer, naturally. (He was in the USA! He was safe from gunfire. It was fine.) But Jennifer's semester was finished now, and two days ago, they had moved back to Arizona. She had transferred to Barrett Honors College, and Nick was enrolling at Scottsdale Community College. They had an *arrangement*, they said. Fine. Good. She knew all about *arrangements*.

"I.e.," she said to them, "you've realized how much cheaper it is to live in Arizona than the Bay Area."

"Palo Alto is very expensive," Jennifer said.

"We want to do this on our own. We don't want to ask anybody for money, and I can get in the manager's training program at Fry's."

Although she and Jack's financial situation had improved somewhat over the last two years, it wasn't as if they had a lot of extra cash to help. She hated that. She really hated that they couldn't give their kids more financial support, and it still rankled that Jack had gambled so much away. Oh, well, water under the bridge.

"I'm proud of you," she said to her son and Jennifer, who was becoming a daughter to her. "You're welcome to live here as long as you need to."

So Nick was moving back in, and in August, Annie would be moving out. Gain one, lose one, gain one, lose one. Alex had a feeling that this was a cycle repeated in many families during this era of economic uncertainty.

Alex heard a car turn into the driveway and flung open the front door. It was only Carla, exiting from her baby blue Mercedes convertible, with a pink-wrapped package and an assortment of balloons.

"Sorry I'm late, Mrs. C. Have you ever tried to transport balloons in a convertible?"

"I can't say that I have." As much time as Carla had spent in this house over the years, she might as well move in, too, Alex thought. And it wasn't an unpleasant thought. At the very least, you could say that Carla was entertaining.

"It was *murder*," Carla said. "I had to stop three times to retie them. First, I tied them to the steering wheel, which was a huge mistake. They were flopping around my head, and my hands kept getting caught in the strings . . ."

This had the makings of a long Carla story, so Alex interrupted. "You're not late, honey. The birthday girl hasn't arrived yet. Why don't you go tie those pesky balloons to something on the patio?"

"Will do, Mrs. C."

Alex resumed her pacing. Annie and Carla were going to room together at U of A, and she had mixed feelings about it. She loved Carla, and she loved that she and Annie were such good, close friends. However, she did think that it would be beneficial to Annie to meet some new people. Granted, the two of them had brought Preston into their tiny group during the last two years. He was a nice kid, responsible, polite. He and Annie had gone on a few dates but decided—with the enduring wisdom of the teenager—that they were "better off" as friends. Fine. Good.

Her pacing circuit landed her, once again, in the kitchen. Something smelled peculiar. No, something smelled *rotten*, and it was coming from the pan on the stove. "Annie!" she called.

Annie bounded down the stairs, Carla right behind her, and stopped at the stench. "Holy shit," she said.

"What is that *smell*?" Carla pinched her nose with her fingers.

Alex turned off the gas burner. "I believe your boiled eggs are done." She carried the pan to the sink. The water had completely boiled away, and the egg shells and the bottom of the pan were charred.

"I was going to make deviled eggs," Annie said. "Are they still any good?"

"I don't think anything that smells like that could be considered *still good*," Carla said.

"I burned boiled eggs," Annie said. Then she started to snicker.

"You burned boiled eggs!" Carla hooted.

Alex started to laugh, too. There were so many things about her daughter that she hoped would never change. "I think I'll just throw these out."

Annie, through her giggles, said, "This incident does not leave this room, agreed? I'd never hear the end of this if Nick found out."

"Or Jennifer," Carla added. "She could be a contestant on *Top Chef.*"

"Agreed," Alex said, smiling. She reached under the kitchen sink and pulled out a bottle. "And this is why they make Febreze."

For some reason, this set the girls off again. Alex supposed that they had a huge case of graduation giddiness. Good. Fine. They were entitled to their happiness.

Since she wasn't on guard, wasn't at her post, she didn't hear Sam's car pull in, but she certainly heard Sam's voice: "Where in the hell are you, Alex?"

"The baby's here!" Annie cried.

"Let me at that *munchkin*," Carla said.

I will cry when I see her, Alex thought. But which *her*—Sam or Sophie? Since Sam and Chris had decided to move to Wheaton, IL, shortly after Sophie was born, she had seen them twice. Last year on Sophie's first birthday, she and Jack had driven to Illinois, staying at KOA Campgrounds along the way, which was luxurious compared to what they used to do, with the four of them in a small tent. And this past December for Christmas, all of them had met with Emily and Paul at another KOA/RV Park in Texas. The trip had not been good. Emily and Paul were noticeably slower, older, and hard of hearing. For months, they had not answered their phone because they couldn't hear their phone. She and Sam had taken them to get hearing aids.

And Sam was Sam. The weather was cold and windy, there was no room service (obviously, but she still seemed surprised about it), and the electricity went out the second night they were there. Enough was enough, Sam said. It was freezing, and she didn't want the baby catching pneumonia, bronchitis, strep throat, measles, chickenpox, mumps, scarlet fever, etc. Her list was as long as it was ridiculous. The next morning, she and Chris left with the baby. Suffice it to say, Sam was not a *happy camper.*

This was Sam's first visit to Arizona in almost two years. She did not disappoint. "It's so frigging hot here!"

"Yes, but it's a dry heat."

"Dry, wet, it's frigging hot."

"I want to hold Sophie," Annie said, holding out her arms. "Look how big you are, Sophie. How old are you today? Are you two?"

Sam handed the baby to her. "Come on, Sophie, you can do this. We've been practicing this for three weeks." She held up two fingers, a peace sign. "You're two, right? Show your cousin Annie how old you are."

Sophie started to wail, and Annie practically tossed her back to Sam. "I'll hold her later," she said.

"She doesn't like to perform on cue," Sam said apologetically.

"Most children don't," Alex said.

"And she's tired."

Carla piped up. "I always performed on cue. At least that's what my mom says. It's become a family legend that by the age of two, I would strip off my clothes in front of anybody and everybody."

"That figures," Annie said.

"Burned boiled eggs," Carla retorted.

Sam looked from one to the other, confused. "Am I missing something here?"

"I'll fill you in later," Alex said. She was dying to hold the baby, who looked nothing like Annie now. Sophie nestled her face in Sam's neck, trying to hide. Alex felt a pang. Sophie didn't know them. She didn't know her aunt, uncle, or cousins. Alex was going to have to change that during this three-day visit.

Chris lumbered through the door, loaded down with Sophie's necessities. "With Sophie, we don't travel light," he said. He looked good. His face looked leaner, and his paunch looked smaller.

And Alex thought: Well, that's what chasing after a toddler will do for you.

"If you change her, I'll get a bottle ready," Sam said to him.

Sophie was still taking a bottle? Wasn't she a little old for that? Alex wasn't going to judge. It was all good. Fine.

"Speaking of bottles," Alex smiled. "I've got one open."

"Wine, it's a good thing."

In the kitchen, she and Sam finally hugged, then stepped back. There was no need to hide their assessment of each other. Alex thought Sam looked good. She had cut her hair short, very short. (No time to fuss with it now, she said.) And it looked as if she had gained a couple of pounds. (Of course Alex would never dream of pointing this out.) It was clear that moving back to Illinois agreed with her. It was clear that Sophie agreed with her. Her blue eyes sparkled.

"You look terrific," Sam said appraisingly.

"Yoga. And ballroom dancing. And long walks in the neighborhood. Since Jack quit drinking, we have a lot of time on our hands. You'd be amazed at how much more time we have, actually." She poured them each a glass of wine and handed one to Sam. "Cheers," she said.

"Cheers." Sam clinked her glass to Alex's. "Have you heard from the school yet?"

"Any day now." She had applied for a position as a kindergarten teacher at the neighborhood elementary school. She had been substituting regularly at the school for the past two years, and the principal had told her in confidence that she would get the job. Teaching a room full of five-year-olds could probably be considered her dream job. And she was never going to try to *sell* anything again. She stank at it.

"You'll get it," Sam said confidently, "and you'll be terrific."

Alex smiled. "I hope so."

They drank in companionable silence while they got the food ready for the party. It wasn't like they had a lot of catching up to do. They talked on the phone at least twice a week, after Sam put Sophie to bed. It was just like the old days, each had a drink before her and a lit cigarette in hand, and they would talk and talk. It was just like the old days—except for the fact that Sam had a toddler. They talked to each other more now than they did in the year that Sam lived across the street, the year that will live in *infamy*, as Sam liked to put it.

It was strange, Alex thought, how that year seemed so long ago. There were weeks she couldn't recall at all. (She referred to them now as her shock weeks or the weeks of pounding, painful revelations.) She remembered being pregnant, of course, and she remembered Sophie's birth. She remembered not wanting to give the baby to Sam. But strangely, she didn't feel those events anymore, and really, she was grateful for the distance—in her mind and heart—of that year.

She was older and wiser now. Well, she was definitely older, but she would have to admit that the "wiser" was questionable. She would do it all again.

Chris carried Sophie into the kitchen. "The birthday girl is ready for her bottle and her party." He carried his daughter naturally, as if he had been doing it all his life.

She was a cute little girl (but not as cute as Alex's babies), with soft, blonde hair, blue eyes, and delicate bones. "Can I hold her?" she asked.

"Sure." Chris handed her over.

The little girl stared at Alex, her eyes round, then she glanced over at her mother, noticing the similarity. She was too startled to cry.

"She's a little confused," Sam said.

"You certainly can't blame her for that," Chris said.

"Hi, Sophie. Do you remember me? I'm your Aunt Alex," Alex said softly to the little girl.

There was no doubt about it. She would do it all again.

It was Sophie Alexandra Connor's second birthday party. They were all gathering on the back patio at the long table Jack had rented for the occasion. The misters did little to alleviate the heat. It was June. It was Arizona. Of course it was as hot as hell.

Jack manned the grill, turning over the hot dogs and bratwursts with a set of long tongs. It was, of course, hot work, and he was sweating profusely. Even after eighteen months of sobriety, he still longed for a beer. He would probably always long for a beer.

He had fallen off the wagon once during his long road (one day at a time) to recovery. And it had been a dramatic fall. Shortly after Nick left for Camp Pendleton, Annie had come to Alex and him and said she had something to tell them.

"You better sit down for this one," she said.

He was in a hurry, late for something that, at the time, had seemed important to him. But he no longer remembered where he had been going on that terrible afternoon. "Can't it wait, honey?" he said.

"No," she said firmly.

And then she told them what had happened on the cruise.

And then he did something he had never done before. He went on a bender. He locked himself in the den and drank scotch for three solid days as he searched the internet for the damn prick who had raped his daughter. He didn't have any luck, since the piece of shit had obviously given Annie a fake name. At the end of those three, long, bleary, wretched days, he called the cruise ship to get the roster for the passengers on that fucking trip. He thought he found him. A Reginald Hurst, aged twenty, might be the scumbag. He was going to call the fucker, and . . . do what? He couldn't kill him over the phone, but he sure as hell would *terrorize* him with his wrath.

That's when Annie knocked on the door. Alex had not come near the den during his bender, and to this day, he did not know what she did with her grief. "Please, don't, Daddy," she said.

She looked so young and defenseless. His rage boiled over. "I have a name," he said. Or slurred. He definitely slurred.

"Please don't, Daddy," she said again, softly.

He took her in his arms and wept. Finally, when he couldn't cry anymore, he dumped out the rest of the scotch, showered, choked down some dry toast and black coffee, and went to an AA meeting.

Jack wiped the sweat from his brow just as Annie appeared at his side by the grill. "Mom said you look like you could use this." She handed him a frosty mug of lemonade.

"Thanks, honey." He took a grateful gulp.

"It's kind of stupid to be grilling when it's one thousand degrees outside, huh?" She looked very pretty with her brown curly hair resting lightly on her shoulders. She didn't wear much make-up these days. The Mohawk/eyeliner days were safely behind them, or so he fervently hoped.

He shrugged and grinned at her. "It's a party," he said. "People do stupid things for a party."

Annie rolled her eyes. "Tell me about it."

That revelation, too, was out in the open: her mad crush on Walter Caldwell, the bonfire party, the drinking. Annie's quest for total honesty—after the fact—had been as difficult to deal with as his struggle with the bottle.

And his struggle to save his marriage. After Alex had finally given the baby to Sam, and two months later, when Sam, Chris, and the baby moved to Chicago, things had been tough. Alex didn't regret her decision to give the baby, rightfully, to her sister, but when Sam told her that they were going to move to Chicago, that Chris was taking a higher paying job, Alex had lost it for a while yet again.

"Sam and I can now be friends again," she had said. "After this screwed up year, we can finally talk to each other like we used to. We can be sisters. And she's taking the baby and moving away? Why is she doing this?"

Secretly, he thought it was a good thing that Sam would not be living across the street, but he consoled his wife as best as he could. She had a few private sessions with their marriage counselor, and they went to joint sessions for a year before they both felt on solid marital ground again. It had taken a lot longer than he thought it would; it was like peeling away the layers of an onion. And the more they got into therapy . . . Well, the onion had a lot of layers that needed to be peeled.

That was the thing about pain and loss: You don't heal overnight.

"Do you need some help, Dad?" Nick called from the table. He was, of course, sitting next to Jennifer. He had not left her side in the two days they'd been home, and even now, he was holding her hand as if he would never let go.

"That's okay," Jack said. "I'm almost done here, but thanks for asking."

His son and his wife were home safe and sound. That would have been enough to make him happy after the fretful months of Nick's deployment. One night after watching the news and hearing about another bomb exploding in another Humvee, killing four more American troops, Jack had gotten into his Jeep. He had no particular destination, but when he drove by St. Mary's Catholic Church, an evening mass was just letting out, and something compelled him to stop.

He sat in the wooden pew, staring at the stained-glass depiction of Mother and Child for some time, trying to find the words to pray for his wife, his son, his daughter, and for all the hurt he had inflicted upon the ones he loved most. (So true, that saying. You hurt the ones you love the most.) The words did not come.

He realized he didn't know how to pray. He wanted to swear in frustration, but of course, he couldn't. He was in a church. He was getting ready to leave when he felt a tap on his shoulder.

"May I be of some assistance?" The priest looked to be in his mid-seventies. He was bald, except for a fringe of white hair encircling the back of his head like a fuzzy half halo.

"No, I'm fine," Jack stuttered, even though it was clear he was not.

"The confessional is open for another five minutes," he said kindly.

Jack felt trapped under that kind, blue, penetrating gaze. It seemed a little too late to tell the priest that he wasn't Catholic, that he had just stopped by to have a chat with God and failed miserably. And it would be worse than cowardly to bolt for the door.

"Thanks," he said, and headed toward the confession box—or was it called a booth or a stall? To Jack, the thought came unbidden: It looked like an inverted coffin. He shuddered, hesitated. Was he supposed to knock?

"Go on in," the priest said.

Jack was beginning to think that under that priest's kindly, fatherly façade was a hard rock will. He took a deep breath and entered the cramped space.

He had seen enough movies to know to get on his knees, and when the priest slid open the panel, say, "Forgive me, Father, for I have sinned. It has been—he mumbled something unintelligible—since my last confession."

"Please speak up, son," the shadowed priest said.

"Sorry," Jack said.

The shadowed priest waited expectantly.

Jack cleared his throat. Where to begin? "I have done some really shitty things in the last year or so." Damn. He had sworn to a priest. "Sorry."

And because of the darkness and the enveloping feeling of intimacy that came over Jack as he knelt in the inverted coffin, he started talking, spilling out his shame, his wrath, his mistakes. When he was done (way past the allotted five minutes), tears rolled down his face, and he was exhausted, wiped out, emptied. Could it be possible that his sins were gone? The shadowed priest told him to do something with Hail Mary's and the rosary, and Jack slipped out of the church.

The funny thing, though, was that he felt much better after that confession. Maybe his sins were truly gone, or if not gone, forgiven? He had been praying—trying to pray—every night since then. He still wasn't sure that he was doing it right, and he couldn't quite picture the face of the Being he was praying to, but he was trying. He was going *all in.*

He scooped the last of the hot dogs and bratwursts onto a platter and carried it to the table. They had enough food to feed an army, but he refrained from saying so. He didn't want to make any references to the military. Nick was still in a fragile state after what he had gone through, and he didn't want to upset him. Jack gave thanks in his nightly prayer that Nick had Jennifer to talk to.

"Is everyone ready to eat?"

"I could eat a cow," Carla said. She looked at the platter. "Or whatever hot dogs and bratwursts are made of."

"We've *been* ready, for, like, *hours*," Annie said.

"You are still the queen of exaggeration, squirt." Nick teased.

She stuck out her tongue. "This is for Nick, not you, Jennifer. I like you."

"Thank you," Jennifer said politely.

"You're still rude," Nick said.

"You're still lame," she retorted.

They grinned at each other, and Jack thought: I am a happy man.

Sam and Chris walked out the back door carrying bowls of potato salad, corn on the cob, coleslaw. Alex followed them, carrying the baby. She settled the little girl into a high chair that they had borrowed from Amanda Williams. Amanda had given birth to a little boy about a year ago, an event that seemed to surprise her as much as everyone else in the women's Bunco group. To Alex's great glee, Amanda had not regained her Barbie doll figure, nor had she and Curtis been able to afford to move out of their "shabby" neighborhood.

Jack searched Alex's face. She had assured him that she would be *fine* when she saw Sophie. He wanted to believe her—tried very hard to believe his wife—but you could never tell what was going to happen when Alex and Sam got together. Their feelings were so strong for each other that they created an explosive situation. When they were happy with each other, they were very, very happy. But when they were angry with each other, they were mad as hell.

His beautiful wife sent him a dazzling smile, and winked.

Oh, yes, Jack Carissa was a happy man.

Chris was in love, head over heels in love, *besotted*. His little girl had changed his life in ways that he could never have imagined. Why would he even think about being on his computer if he could spend time with his darling daughter instead? When he looked back at how dubious he had felt about

Sam's plan to have her sister be a surrogate, he shook his head pityingly at that man. When he remembered how fretful he had been about his age, that he would be too old to have a child, he wanted to laugh at that poor, misguided sap. He had never been happier in his life.

Of course he had, on numerous occasions, been mistaken for Sophie's grandfather. He didn't mind at all. He would just smile at the woman (always a woman), and say, "No, this little girl is my daughter. I'm a late bloomer." One of the women had had the audacity to sniff disapprovingly and announce, "Well, it seems as if men can get away with being late-in-life fathers." Even at that remark, he had smiled, nodded, and said, "Lucky, aren't we?"

It was on the occasions that Sophie was mistaken for his granddaughter when Sam was with them that things got tense. If the unfortunate woman said something along the lines of, "What a pretty little grandchild you have," Sam would immediately have her boxing gloves on. "She's our *daughter*, you old biddy. Why don't you mind your own business?"

When the woman would huff off, he would say, "Sam, it's an honest mistake."

"Do they actually think I'm old enough to be a grandmother?"

"It's me. You obviously don't look old enough to be a grandmother," he placated.

"You're not that old either. And can't they see that she looks just like you?"

It was true, and he couldn't believe how thrilled it made him. With every day that passed, Sophie was starting to look more like the baby picture of himself that he had found in Louise's locket. In the past when he had allowed himself to imagine their theoretical daughter, he had always imagined her looking like Sam.

Sam had, too. But she wasn't complaining. "I guess Sophie's your mini-me, not mine," she had said. "She's still pretty, though."

"Gee, thanks, Sam."

"You know what I mean."

Yes, he did. His wife was vain. What else was new?

However, he still loved his wife as much as he always had. Sophie simply brought a new dimension to that love. And even though motherhood had not come as easily to Sam as she had always envisioned, she deserved an A for effort.

But it was still a fact: Motherhood had not come easily to Sam. The peaceful baby they brought home from Alex's *woke up*. She became colicky, and Sam would walk the floor with her night after night until they were both crying with frustration and exhaustion. After they moved to Wheaton, Sophie was prone to colds and ear infections.

"What am I doing wrong?" Sam would wail. "I've read every child-rearing book I can get my hands on. I bundle her up when we go out, and still we're at the doctor's office every damn week. What am I doing wrong?" It had been the end of an extremely long day, and Sam was still in her spit-up stained bathrobe, her hair straggly and greasy.

"You're not doing anything wrong, Sam." He took the baby from her. And Sophie quieted immediately. She was a lovely little traitor, his Sophie.

"See? My baby hates me!"

"Don't be ridiculous, Sam. You're overwrought. You're tired. Go to bed. I'll take it from here."

Sam wrung her hands. "I don't have any maternal instincts."

Chris calmly changed the baby's diaper. He knew that this tirade would pass, as they all passed. *All* the tirades.

"We should have stayed in Arizona. Alex would know what to do."

Once Alex had put the baby in her arms, Sam had been as anxious to leave Arizona as he had been. He didn't point this out.

"Why is my baby always sick? What am I doing wrong?"

He remembered something. "Louise once said that I was a sickly baby, that I had a lot of ear infections. Maybe it's hereditary?"

"Louise said? *Louise* said? Look how *that* turned out! She was a lousy mother!"

"That's enough, Sam." Three months after his mother's death, the pain of her emotional barrenness was still fresh. He was never going to understand Louise, never. And now that he had a child of his own, one he grew to love more with each passing day, Louise's behavior was even more perplexing, more hurtful. Yet he was still fighting with the Peterson clan to recognize the marriage. Yet he still brought fresh flowers to his mother's grave every week.

"I'm sorry," Sam said, finally subdued.

"Go to bed," he ordered.

"I'm sorry I'm in such a state." She crossed over to stand beside him at the changing table. They stared at the now peaceful baby whose eyes were almost closed. "I'll be better tomorrow, I promise. I'll get the hang of this. Eventually. I think. I hope. I can do this. I can do this *right*. Eventually. I think. I hope."

"I know you can," he said.

She kissed him lightly on the cheek. Then she kissed the baby lightly on her forehead. "Blissful slumber. What's a gal gotta do to get an Ambien around here?"

He smiled at her. "It's a good thing you don't need one."

"Right," she said forlornly.

Chris knew that she still longed for her stash of "helpers" weeks after she had flushed the stash down the toilet. On the night they finally walked with the baby from Alex's house across the street to theirs, the night the baby was finally theirs, she had called him into the master bathroom.

"The end of an era." Sam had bottles lined up on the counter, bottles of Valium, Ambien, Xanax, Prozac, and Percodan.

He was surprised—no, shocked—at the array of drugs. She must have done some doctor shopping in Illinois, too, when he was busy putting Louise's affairs in order. "Jesus, Sam," he whistled.

"Pretty pathetic, huh?" Looking at the line of bottles, she nodded. "Now go get the stash that you've been hiding from me that you think I don't know about."

He had squirreled away a sizable assortment, too. He brought them. He brought them from his locked desk drawer, from the extra watering can in the garage, from underneath the rocks in the potted Saguaro on the back patio, from the shoe box on the highest shelf in the guest bedroom. He brought them all to her.

And he watched as she ceremoniously uncapped each bottle and dumped its contents into the toilet and flushed. Each bottle received a farewell: Bon voyage. Good riddance. Adios. Die, you suckers. It's been nice knowing you—not. Too little, too late. Free, free, I'm free at last. Thank the Lord, I'm free at last.

He had never appreciated more her penchant for the dramatic.

Things improved. As Sophie got older, she and her mother developed a routine, although there were still good days and bad days. There had been days when he got home from teaching, and Alex thrust the baby at him before he had even taken off his coat or set down his briefcase. The Gymboree experiment had been a disaster. Sophie had screamed, terrified of the giant parachute, for the duration of their one and only class. And then there were days when they were over the moon with their lovely, brilliant daughter's milestones: rolling over, sitting up, crawling, taking her first steps. He was sure this was normal when you had a baby in the house, the roller coaster of each day, and slowly, they got used to it.

However, as he observed his wife and daughter together—and he loved to do this, especially when they didn't know he was watching—one thing was becoming crystal clear. The two females in his household were both fiercely stubborn, and at times, between the two of them, it was a battle of wills.

Like now, at Sophie's second birthday party. Sophie was not in a particularly good mood. It was way past her nap time, and she viewed the people surrounding her warily. Her little face seemed to be saying: What are you strange people *doing*? She eyed the cut-up hot dog on the paper plate in front of her with utter disdain, and every time Sam tried to feed her a bite, she shook her head fiercely. "No!" she said. "No, no, no, no!"

No was currently two-year-old Sophie's favorite word.

Sam did not like to take *no* for an answer.

"Come on, sweetheart," Sam coaxed. "Eat a bite for Mommy."

"No!" Sophie's blond curls whipped about her face as she shook her head.

"Yes!"

"No!"

"Just one bite." Sam's face was flushed. Everyone at the table was watching this exchange. "Just one bite, Sophie."

"No!"

"Maybe she'd rather have a bratwurst?" Annie suggested.

"She loves hot dogs," Sam said through gritted teeth. "Sophie Alexandra Connor, you will eat a bite of hot dog. *Now.*"

"No!"

"Pick up a bite of hot dog and put it in your mouth, Sophie." She glared at her recalcitrant daughter.

Sophie stared back. Without taking her eyes off Sam, she picked up a piece of meat. And threw it.

It hit Sam's cheek. "Oh!" she said, surprised.

Jack was the first one to laugh, then everyone joined in, including Chris (who had rather enjoyed the show). He knew that his daughter was behaving like a tired, spoiled, little girl, and he knew that Sam was mortified. She wanted everyone there, especially Alex, to think that she was a good mother. And she was a good mother, but really, what was the point here? It was a damn hot dog.

"Sophie Connor, you are going to—"

"That's enough, Sam," he said quietly.

"Is everyone ready for cake?" Alex asked brightly. She started to clear the plates. In a low voice, she said to Sam, "We need to learn how to choose our battles, and it's not easy. I'm still learning."

"Good advice," Sam admitted. "It was only a damn hot dog."

Precisely. He felt a rush of pride for his wife and his daughter.

"We'll sing to the birthday girl, and then she can take a nap," Alex said.

"No!" Sophie said.

As they all laughed again, even Sam managed a smile. It was going to be the ride of a lifetime to watch as the battle of wills dramedy played out between Sam and Sophie, his two girls, his two loves.

Chris couldn't wait.

Camp Dwyer was situated in Afghanistan's Helmand River Valley, but the Marines referred to the camp as "Hell Man" because of its unforgiving weather. The temperature would often reach 120 and above, and at certain times of the year, there were constant, unrelenting sand storms. Thankfully, many of the tents—at Hell Man, there were no permanent structures—had air conditioning, and there was an internet connection and a post office.

"Home sweet home," Dylan said when they arrived, which happened to be in the middle of one of those stinging, unrelenting sand storms.

"I guess we've made it," Nick said. They were going to live here for a year? Of course they would periodically be sent out on missions, but this was going to be home? And what would happen after that? More deployments? In their rash excitement to enlist in the Marines, they had not stopped to consider that they had signed on for an eight-year commitment. Nick tried to tamp down a sense of unease that had started as soon as they boarded the plane to come to this distant country. After all, he had the most important thing to be thankful for: He and Dylan had been deployed together.

They had emerged from basic training tougher and stronger, which they had to be because their chosen MSO was to be riflemen in the infantry. (Nick was having second thoughts about that, too.) However, they had also emerged from basic training with a far more realistic notion of what serving in the military truly meant. It certainly wasn't as romantic as they thought it would be. Not even close.

On their third day of defending their country in Afghanistan, over the powdered eggs offered for breakfast in the mess tent, even Dylan's bravado was starting to lag. "Everything here tastes like sand. These eggs taste like sand."

"We grew up in a desert," Nick reminded him. "We should be able to take it."

"Yeah, right. A desert filled with eighteen-hole golf courses, swimming pools, and palm trees. So not the same thing, dude."

So not even close. Nick didn't know which was worse—the boredom or his homesickness. Or perhaps the worst thing was the uncertainty. They could be sent on a mission on a moment's notice. They could be attacked at any time of day or night. Nick felt both a heightened sense of awareness and a numbing dread.

"I miss Jennifer," he said. It was an ache that never went away. He had been writing her three letters a day.

"I can top that, dude. I miss Melissa."

"I miss my family, too," Nick added.

"I even miss my mom's stupid horses."

They needed to stop dwelling on the homesickness. It wasn't going to do them any good. Only three days into their war experience, and they needed to *buck up*. They had hundreds of days to go. "We are soldiers," Nick said.

Dylan knew he was changing the subject, and he knew why. "We are fighting machines."

"We are Marines," they said together.

"I'll feel better when I get to shoot my rifle," Dylan said. "If I can shoot at something, I know I'll feel better."

Shooting his rifle was the last thing that Nick wanted to do. God forbid, he didn't want to *kill* anyone. He was starting to believe—too late, way too late—that he might be a pacifist. Good going, dude, he thought to himself. You wanted to go to war. No, you *demanded* to go to war. And now you're here. And now you're scared shitless. You can talk the talk, *dude*, but you can't walk the walk.

Really, the worst thing about being here—he might as well admit it to himself, at least—was the death. There had been more than 400 casualties at Camp Dwyer. Troops were sent to the battlefields. But not everyone came back. The living would bring back the bodies of the dead and bury them near the base. At the entrance to the base, there was a tree. Hanging from the tree were metal nametags etched with the names of the ones who didn't come back, the ones who would never go home.

Nick shuddered with dread and fear every time he looked at that tree, the makeshift memorial. But at the same time, he had a hard time tearing his eyes away from it. It was touching and ghoulish.

Maybe this whole war was touching and ghoulish? Maybe it was just ghoulish?

He believed in America, and he believed that her freedom should be preserved and honored. He believed in the American flag and the national anthem. (He had always placed his hand over his heart when reciting the Pledge of Allegiance or singing "The Star-Spangled Banner.") He believed that America's veterans should be honored. He believed that terrorism should be stopped and that all people should have a chance to live in a democracy.

He just no longer believed that he should be fighting in a war in Afghanistan.

He longed for Jennifer. They hadn't even gone on a honeymoon. Jennifer, of course, never complained, but it bothered Nick immensely. During the short time he had with her between boot camp and deployment, he had said this to her after they had made love. She was nestled in his arms (where he wished she could stay forever).

"We'll go on a honeymoon when you get back," she said, her lips whispering on his chest.

"Where would you like to go?" he asked her.

She thought a moment. "Niagara Falls," she said.

"Didn't people used to try to go down the Falls in a barrel, or something like that?" It's the only thing he thought he knew about Niagara Falls. He didn't even know where it was.

"Yes. I don't know if anyone's ever survived the fall, though."

They fell silent. The unspoken thought hovered above them.

Finally, he said, "Why Niagara Falls?"

"I don't know. It's kind of old-fashioned and corny at the same time. Like me."

He kissed her then. He drowned himself in her one last time, trying to ignore the unspoken thought, but it still hovered.

Was he going to survive the war?

"Private Taylor!" It was Staff Sergeant Gonzales.

Nick and Dylan jumped to their feet. "Yes, sir!" Dylan barked.

"Come with me. I need to take supplies to Bravo Company." Gonzales turned and walked briskly away.

"Finally, I'm going to see something," Dylan whispered excitedly to Nick. "Sorry he didn't order you to go, too."

"That's okay. I'm sure there'll be plenty of other supply runs." Again, that feeling of unease crept up his spine. He was being a big baby, he told himself. Dylan would only be gone for a couple of hours, and he could certainly manage being alone for that amount of time. He'd write another letter to Jennifer.

"Maybe I'll get to shoot somebody!" Dylan hurried after their sergeant, cradling his M16A2 service rifle.

Those were the last words Dylan spoke to him.

For Dylan, there would be no more supply runs. For Dylan, there would be no more war.

On a rutted back road in a desert in Afghanistan, Sergeant Gonzales's and Dylan's Humvee ran over an IED, a buried explosive. They were killed instantly, their bodies ripped apart by the blast.

The only comfort that Nick had during the days, weeks, and months that followed was the knowledge that Dylan had not felt any pain. He had probably not even had time to recognize what was happening to him. The explosion had happened in a split second, the blink of an eye. Dylan was alive, and then he was gone. Dylan, Nick's best friend since kindergarten, was dead, another casualty, another fallen soldier.

There was no time for tears when you were a soldier. Nick etched Dylan's name —-Dylan Thomas Taylor—on a metal nametag and hung it with the others on the tree by the entrance to the base. And then he went to work. He hardened himself to the atrocity around him, he slept with his eyes open, and he did what he was told to do. He put one foot in front of the other, and he didn't think. He didn't feel. He merely functioned until he could come home.

He began to thaw in the weeks he had with Jennifer in Palo Alto. He slept a lot, and he watched TV, although he was very selective about what he watched. No more war movies. No more military shows of any kind. And certainly, no "reality" shows, with all of their staged, shallow "problems," with all their bitching and complaining. They enraged him. They didn't know what a real problem was. You go to a home ransacked by insurgents in a tiny village in Afghanistan, and you see a dead mother and father and a squalling baby lying in a pool of their blood for who knew how long. Now, *that* was a *real problem*.

And that was when he had snapped.

He lost it totally, completely, absolutely.

They had to pry the screaming baby from his arms (or so they told him later). He had threatened to shoot five men in his own company (or so they told him later). He had threatened to shoot himself (or so they told him later). He must have been in bad shape because they transferred him to a military psych ward in Germany (or so he thought; he wasn't exactly sure where he was during those weeks.) Eventually, the experts decided that he wasn't *fit to serve*. He wasn't mortified by this. He was glad.

His discharge was not honorable, but it wasn't exactly dishonorable.

He had killed three men—that he knew of.

And he had always thought that Annie was the craziest one in the family. Not even close.

During the weeks in Palo Alto with Jennifer, they decided that what he needed to feel whole again was to go home. It had been an easy decision for Jennifer and him to make. They told everyone that Palo Alto was too expensive, but the real reason they moved back to Arizona was because of him. He needed to be near his family. He needed to be near Dylan's grave.

He had visited the cemetery early this morning. Jennifer had wanted to go with him, and he appreciated her support, but it was something he needed to do alone. That's what he said to her, "I need to see him alone."

She looked at him, concern spilling out of her dark, dark eyes. "Are you sure?"

"Yes," he choked out. But suddenly, he wasn't sure at all. Seeing Dylan's grave, seeing the tombstone with Dylan's name etched across the top might be more than he could take. He had etched Dylan's name—Dylan Thomas

Taylor—on a nametag, sure, and hung it on the tree in Camp Dwyer. However, this etching on a marble tombstone, this remembrance of his friend, was going to have the date of Dylan's birth, and the date of Dylan's *death*. Whatever remained of Dylan was buried in a hole in a ground in a cemetery in Phoenix, Arizona, far, far away from where, on a fateful, nondescript day, he had gotten in a Humvee on a routine supply run and crossed over a buried IED planted by insurgents.

Nick was sick with fear that seeing this tombstone would finally make it real.

And Nick did not want it to be real.

Even now, months later, he woke in the middle of the night, bathed in sweat, disoriented from the dream of exploding bombs and mangled bodies and blood, blood, blood, and for a blessed fraction of a second, he thought it had only been a nightmare. Even now, months later, he would hear a voice call his name and turn around, expecting to see Dylan, expecting Dylan to grin and say, "What's up, dude?"

Would this ever stop?

Probably not.

Survivor's guilt, that was one name for it. Why hadn't Staff Sergeant Gonzalez ordered him on that run instead of Dylan? Why had some of his buddies in the platoon lost arms or legs or sight and he had not? Why was he one of the lucky ones? They had all been over there doing their jobs, and some survived and some did not. Why?

Wrong place at the wrong time.

Yeah. Fuck yeah.

As he approached Dylan's grave, his chest tightened. He hadn't known what to bring. Jennifer had suggested flowers, but that seemed too ordinary to Nick. (Besides, Dylan was not a flowers type of guy.) He stopped by Walmart—the ultimate symbol of America?—and bought an American flag. Not a tiny paper flag, but a real honest-to-God American flag. Like the kind people put out on Veteran's Day and Memorial Day and the Fourth of July. It felt unwieldy in his hands as he approached the spot that Dylan's parents had told him where they had laid their younger son. ("A fucking waste," Dylan's father had said on the phone. "My baby," Dylan's mother had wept.)

It was a small stone nestled among a row of equally small stones. A bucket of wilted spring flowers was its only adornment. A tiny card stuck in a plastic prong was still in the seared soil. Nick dropped to his knees and leaned forward to read the card: Love you always, Melissa.

It was too much.

He had planned on saying, "How've you been, Dylan?"

And Dylan, from somewhere beyond, would say, "What's up, dude?"

And they would have a conversation, just like they used to do.

Impossible, implausible, of course. Stupid.

Dylan was dead.

Nick cried for a long time. It was a lonely place, this cemetery. Not another living soul came or went while Nick cried on his knees in front of Dylan's grave. He cried for the loneliness of death, and he cried for the guilt of those who survived. He cried for the injustice of preserving justice, and he cried for the need to do so.

Finally, spent, he leaned back on his heels and wiped his face with the back of his hand. "I'm so sorry, Dylan. I'm sorry I couldn't save you."

It was beyond weird, but it was like a voice came to him through his heart, Dylan's voice. "Not your fault, dude, not your fault."

"Dylan?" It felt like he was close, very close, and just then, Nick knew that Dylan, the best friend he would ever have, was not in the ground before him. Not even close.

"Semper fi, man."

"Semper fi."

And Nick stuck the flag in the ground and unfurled it. The stars and stripes managed a small flutter in the wan breeze, and Nick knew that Dylan would stand at attention and salute, so he did, too.

On the way home, still filled with emotion about Dylan—feelings which would never leave him—he almost forgot to stop and get the hot dog buns at Fry's. It was his only responsibility for the birthday party. Both of his parents had been tiptoeing around him with concern since he got home, not knowing if they should ask questions or offer sympathy—or what. He could understand. They had lost Dylan, too, had cried at his funeral, but there it was again: They were incredibly thankful that their son had come home safely. It's just the way things were.

He hadn't been to see Loretta yet because . . . Well, he just wasn't ready. Loretta was a talker, and she was certainly not shy about asking questions. He hoped (and felt guilty about it) that she wasn't working today, or if she was, he could slip in and out of the grocery store without seeing her.

No such luck.

"There's my boy!" Loretta shouted from checkout lane four. "Heard you were coming back! Come over here and give old Loretta a big, fat hug, sugar cakes."

Loretta could still make him blush. The store wasn't busy; there was no escape. Sheepishly he walked to her lane, holding the packages of hot dog buns. "Hey, Loretta, good to see you."

She walked around the lane to the customer's side and gave him a big hug, crushing the buns in the process. She stepped back, holding him at arms' length. "Let me get a good look at you, sugar."

He felt his cheeks redden even more under her scrutiny.

"Tough, huh?" she said thoughtfully.

He nodded and felt more tears rising. How could that be? He had just cried an ocean. He needed to *buck up*.

But Loretta surprised him. "I ain't going to ask you no questions, baby doll. You come and visit me when you're good and ready, and we can catch up then. And bring your little oriental wife, honey. She's a cutie-pie."

"Korean," he said, and smiled.

"Sure," she said, patting his arm tenderly.

"What's new with you, Loretta?" he asked, even though he knew he shouldn't.

"Oh, baby doll, the shit did hit the fan, indeed it did. When husband number three got out of the joint, he wasn't no better than before, no better at all. I had to dump his sorry ass—I mean, buttocks—and *move on*, you know? I met a real nice guy, who will be husband number four as soon as we scrape together enough money for a new trailer. My Molly has had two more babies, and she's still with that sorry, good-for-nothing asshole—stinker—and the trailer I have now is just not big enough for the all of us." Loretta worked the hairpins into her dyed blonde bun with fingernails the color of gazpacho.

"Number four?" he said, even though he knew he shouldn't.

"Oh, yes, sweetheart, you know I always did believe in love. I'm a true romantic, I guess you could say."

Nick grinned. "Me, too."

Loretta patted his cheek. "I know you are, sugar buns, I know you are. Old Loretta has taught you good."

He got out of the store with the crushed buns fifteen minutes later, but he didn't mind the time after all. Loretta had lifted his mood, despite himself. There was, he thought, something *contagious* about that woman.

"I'm so glad you're home," Jennifer said to him when he walked in the front door. "Are you all right?" She looked anxious.

"I will be," he said to her, kissing her on the top of her head. "I think I will be."

"Nick, there's something I need to tell you."

"Can it wait, honey?"

She seemed disappointed. "I suppose so."

Nick felt bone-tired throughout Sophie's birthday party, but he tried to put on a good face. He kidded Annie a little, and he offered to help, but really, he just wanted to stay next to Jennifer. Everyone seemed to be enjoying themselves, especially when Sophie—a cute kid—threw the hot dog, and it was hard to remember how tense things had been two years ago.

To him, it seemed like a lifetime ago.

Finally, they finished the cake, which Sophie mashed all over her face and into her hair, and Nick was hoping that he and Jennifer could finally go upstairs and take a nap. Mom and Aunt Sam were clearing the table.

"Come on, Jennifer," he said. "Let's go upstairs. I'm beat."

"I'm tired, too," she said. She looked at him with her dark eyes and gave him her dazzling white, white smile. "For a good reason."

"What reason?" (He was never going to keep up with her, never.)

"I'm pregnant," she whispered into his ear. "I just found out this morning after you left, and I've been so excited to tell you. I didn't want to phone. I wanted to tell you in person. We can tell the others later."

They were going to have a baby? "Really?"

She nodded, her eyes gleaming.

He had never felt anything like it before, this feeling coursing through-out his entire body—incredulity, adrenaline, elation? It was a natural instinct for Nick to get up and shout to his family: "We're going to have a baby!"

As he did so, the voice in his heart applauded. "Way to go, dude."

She, Annie Carissa, was a high school graduate, an alumna of SCDS—not that she planned on *ever* going back to a dorky high school reunion. Yeah, rah, sis boom bah! She could hardly believe it. In a few short weeks, she and Carla would be rooming together in a dorm at U of A, and she couldn't wait. Carla's parents had wanted her to go to school somewhere in the East, some place like Wellesley or Vassar—a women's college—but Carla, true to form, had thrown a fit of gigantic proportions, even for her. She locked herself in her room for an entire week, refusing to eat, refusing to speak, and refusing to go to school. In desperation, they finally called her therapist, and Raymond, bless his heart, had sided with Carla. Her parents admitted defeat.

Little did they know that Carla had been sleeping with Raymundo for over a year at that point. Her "therapy" sessions consisted of unbridled sex on every surface of his office. Her *feelings*, since then, had remained largely unexamined.

That was fine with Carla. "Thank God," she had said after the first time they had sex. "It was getting harder and harder to make up interesting psychoses."

Annie was appalled by the whole thing, but as usual, she didn't want Carla to think she was prudish or naïve or something like that. "Couldn't he lose his license for sleeping with a patient?" she had asked timidly. Georgia, she knew, would never sleep with a patient. Georgia, she knew, would also be appalled. Even though she no longer saw Georgia—she went a few more times after she told Georgia *everything* and had to be *cured* again—she still heard Georgia's voice in her head. Really, it was annoying.

"Who's going to tell?" Carla said. "We're having fun. Besides, he thinks I'm nineteen, and the sex, therefore, is consensual. What's the harm? No one is going to get hurt."

Yeah, right. Until Raymundo's wife found out that her husband was fooling around with another woman/girl, although she never found out it was with Carla. Until Raymundo abruptly folded up his practice and left town.

Carla was the one who got hurt. "I loved him," she wailed. They were in her redecorated room (no more pink ruffles and porcelain dolls) with a bottle of Jack Daniels. Carla thought the severity of the trauma deserved bourbon.

"You did not," Annie stated firmly. The one glass she had sipped emboldened her to speak her mind. She hadn't wanted a drink, her first in months and months and months, but she thought that, as Carla's best friend, she should show some solidarity. And boy, did it feel good burning down her throat—even though the taste wasn't so hot. (G: You do not need to be a follower, Annie. You can make your own decisions. A: If someone jumped off a bridge, I wouldn't follow. And it was only one drink. Then two. Then three. Whoops, I did it again. Sorry, Georgia. Hiccup.)

"Who needs men?" Carla was weaving around the room at that point. "I think I'll become a lesbian."

"Don't look at me," Annie said. She loved Carla, of course, but even she wouldn't go that far. She couldn't even imagine *kissing* Carla. (A to G: Aren't you proud of me, Georgia?)

"Not you, silly. You're my best friend. And you're already taken. Besides, it's only a thought. Wow, this Jack is fucking great. I am flying, high as a kite." Then Carla went into her bathroom and threw up.

Annie threw up shortly after that.

The next morning, hungover, Carla said, "We're out of practice."

Annie, head pounding and mouth dry as dirt, was wondering: Was a hangover always this wretched? Why had she ever thought this was fun? "This sucks."

Carla downed an entire bottle of Gatorade. "Big time."

However, it wasn't as if they had *relearned* the lessons of their *youth*. It wouldn't be the last time they got drunk during their senior year, but they certainly didn't make a habit of it. That much they had learned.

No, she and Carla weren't saints, but they weren't exactly fallen angels either.

They figured they could live with that.

And they tried. They really did try to fit in, to be what everyone else considered to be *normal* teenagers. They got jobs at McDonald's for heaven's sake! What could be more normal than that? For an entire month during the summer between sophomore and junior years they had showed up for work when they were supposed to and did what they were told to do—kind of. Carla wasn't so hot at taking orders from pimply Roger and flatly refused to wipe down tables. (I'm not a maid, you dork," she said to him.) Annie, on the other hand, didn't mind wiping down tables. It was the customers that threw her for a loop. Hungry people were downright nasty. If she accidentally gave a customer a large order of fries instead of a *supersized* order, you would have thought she had committed a *felony*.

One customer had said to her, "Are you lazy or are you just stupid?"

Annie had eyed his large body up and down and said, "Are you large or are you just obese?"

At the cash register next to her, Carla had said, laughing, "Good one, Annie."

Annie had felt pretty proud of herself. "Thanks." Then she had given the obese man his supersized fries.

He had complained to pimply Roger anyway.

So really, they should not have been surprised when pimply Roger called them into his office at the end of that month. "I have compiled your trainee probationary performance review." His voice was solemn, but he had a stupid smirk on his face.

"What in the hell is a performance review?" Carla said.

We are in deep shit, Annie thought. She hadn't known that they had been on probation. She thought they had been hired, period. Chalk up another one for clueless Annie. (G: You are not clueless, Annie. You are a very bright young lady. A: What in the hell is a trainee probationary performance review?)

They were fired, basically, for being rude to customers, although Roger had compiled an impressive list of petty infractions. They didn't obey orders, they didn't wear the proper attire (Carla's hat), they were slow to serve customers, yada, yada, yada. All in all, he pronounced triumphantly at the end of his spiel, Annie and Carla did not possess the right *attitude* to work at the sacred, holy church of McDonald's.

"Can we get any lower?" Carla asked after she threw her hat in Roger's face and they left the restaurant.

"Nope. McDonald's hates us. I don't think we can get any lower than that. We're disgraced." She was never going to eat another Big Mac again, which was no big deal. She preferred Taco Bell. Then she had another thought. "I don't think we should put this on our college applications."

"Not even a mention." They walked to Carla's car. "But you know what?" she said thoughtfully. "We are going to have to start joining clubs or volunteering or something. College admissions people eat up that kind of shit."

"We're not really joiners," Annie pointed out. Neither one of them belonged to a single club or sports team.

"We're just going to have to become one of the masses," Carla said matter-of-factly.

"Holy shit," Annie sighed.

So they *joined*. Unwillingly.

Science Club was out of the question. "Too many nerds, even by SCDS standards," Annie pointed out.

Ditto for the Math Club.

Students against Drunk Driving wasn't an option either. "I'm not totally against students driving drunk," Carla said.

They ended up joining the badminton team, which didn't suck too much, as far as sports went. (They rarely broke a sweat.) And they ended up joining the Drama Club, which naturally, turned out to be Carla's true calling. She got the lead in every single production junior and senior years and was going to major in theatre at U of A. Annie, on the other hand, wasn't so hot at being on stage. She froze every time she tried out for a small part. "That's all right, Annie," the drama teacher said. "We can always use *bodies* backstage to design the props and paint scenery." Well, Annie could paint a decent tree, and she had a body, didn't she?

The only problem was that she still didn't know what to do with it. When it came to boys.

Take Preston, for example.

They went out on a few dates, to the movies and to a Diamondbacks game (which bored Annie out of her mind), all perfectly normal stuff. And Preston was a perfectly normal boy. He was nice. He opened the car door for her, and he walked her to her front door after dates and gave her chaste kisses good night. He smelled good, too, kind of like Granny Smith apples. But she just didn't feel attracted to him, not like she had with Walter. Her heart didn't pound, and her armpits didn't sweat, and she didn't even try to imagine him naked.

The only time he had taken her parking had been a *disaster*. It was after their fourth date (the wretched baseball game), and Annie supposed it was a perfectly normal assumption on his part that he should get some *action*, something more than an awkward goodnight kiss at her front door. She figured she would go along with it. After all, it was the first time she had been in this situation with a boy who wasn't drunk and/or stoned (and who wasn't a *rapist*)! (G: There are nice boys out there, Annie, nice boys who don't take advantage of girls. A: I'll have to take your word on that one, Georgia.)

The making out part went okay, although Annie still didn't feel any spark. Rather, she was wishing that Preston had not had onions on his hamburger at the ballpark. Had he not been thinking ahead? When he asked her if she would take off her shirt, Annie thought *what the hell?* and complied. He kissed her breasts for a while (slobbered on them, actually), and Annie still didn't feel any spark. Instead, she was thinking that she would rather be home watching *The Bachelorette*.

When he reached for the top button on her jeans, Annie decided she had had enough. She didn't know much about sex—even now, after *everything*—but she did know this: It shouldn't be *boring*.

"I think I need to go home now, Preston," she said, reaching for her bra and shirt on the floor of the car.

"What's the matter? Am I doing something wrong?" His breathing, naturally, was heavy.

Was he doing something wrong? Why didn't she feel anything? "I don't think so," she said. She was trying to be kind. After all, he was a nice boy. She wasn't going to tell him that she'd rather be home watching television with her mom.

"I brought condoms, if you're worried about that."

She had not been thinking about condoms at all. (Holy shit, hadn't she learned *anything*?) "No, it's not that," she said. It seemed, somehow, too intimate to put on her bra in front of him, so she stuffed it in her purse and pulled her t-shirt over her head.

"Are you a virgin?" he asked. "Because if you are, you don't need to worry. I'm a virgin, too."

And then she did something that was totally *not nice*. She started to laugh. Hysterically. And she couldn't stop.

Poor, poor Preston. He didn't know what to do. "Annie," he kept saying, "Annie, why are you laughing?" When her laughter turned into sobs, his refrain became, "Annie, Annie, I'm so, so sorry. I would never make you do anything you didn't want to do."

Poor, poor Preston. He did not deserve this. He was a nice boy, and she was such a crybaby. (G: There is nothing wrong with tears, Annie. A: Would you *shut the fuck up*, Georgia?)

She finally collected herself. "It's not your fault, Preston. It's really not your fault." He handed her a tissue, which almost made her start

629

bawling again. He was that kind of nice boy; he carried tissues in his glove compartment. "It's a long story, and it doesn't have a very happy ending."

He didn't press her. He took her home and left her at her front door with a quick peck on her cheek. He did call her again, but it was an unspoken, mutual understanding that they would just be friends. Eventually, she did tell him about Walter, but not the cruise ship fiasco. She felt like she owed him that. He hung out with her and Carla a lot after that—he seemed to get their sense of humor—even though he was dating someone else. He was going to major in physics at Princeton in the fall. So why couldn't she fall in love with a nice boy who was also extremely smart?

Go figure.

Eventually, too, there came the day when she had to tell Carla about "Adam" and his cousins. Carla listened, wide-eyed, tears rolling down her cheeks. "Why didn't you tell me, Annie?"

Telling Carla had been as bad as telling her parents. She could only shrug and give the explanation, whispered, "Damaged goods, you know?"

"You are not damaged goods, damn it, Annie. Fucking A. They are *criminals*. They should be put in jail." And then, like the rest of her family, Carla got mad. Her rage was astounding—scary, really. She demanded to know every detail. When Annie told her the name her dad had found on the internet—Reginald Hurst—Carla went pale. "I know that prick! He was a lacrosse buddy of Drew's at prep school. It just figures that the two pricks would know each other. We are so going to *nail* him now."

It took Carla less than twenty minutes to nail Reginald. Only he had already been nailed. He was serving 10 to 25 years for statutory rape in a prison in Connecticut. Carla was elated. "The fucker got what he deserved, Annie. Doesn't it make you feel better?"

It did, and it didn't. Reginald Hurst wasn't doing time behind bars for what he had done to *her*, and he had hurt another young girl. Maybe she should she have told Carla sooner? But he was in jail. That was something.

Annie could live with that.

And so could her parents. She had felt so awful when she told them the whole stupid, crappy story. Her dad fell of the wagon (such a stupid expression! What wagon?), and her mom fell to pieces. Then—and she was very proud of her parents for this—they rallied. Aunt Sam, Uncle Chris, and Sophie moved away, and Nick was serving his country in Afghanistan. In their family of three, they never said Nick was gone, or that he had left home. They said he was *serving* his country. Important distinctions when you are terrified for your son's life. When you're terrified for your brother's life.

She hadn't known she would miss her brother so much. She even missed his stupid jokes, missed him calling her *squirt.* She felt bad for every time she had called him *lame,* or a *dork.* When she went to Fry's to pick up a gallon of milk or a loaf of bread, she unconsciously looked for him. It was really terrible—Annie knew this—but when they heard that Nick had been transferred out of Afghanistan because of some kind of mental disorder (i.e., a nervous breakdown, why didn't they just say it?), they were relieved; they were almost happy. At least he would be safe. He could get professional help. He could come home.

When they heard about Dylan, well.

Your brain didn't really register that kind of thing. The skinny kid with the pony tail who was your brother's best friend was gone. Just like that. He was never going to walk in your front door again.

Life was so unfair.

No, it was *death* that was so unfair.

Dylan was dead. But he had died for a noble cause, right?

Walter was dead. But he had committed suicide, and that was wrong. (G: You are not responsible for Walter's death, Annie. A: Should I have that tattooed on my butt, Georgia? G: Annie? A: I know, I know, I know.)

Mom took the news about Dylan hard, but she didn't fall to pieces. She baked: chocolate chip cookies, banana bread, *baklava,* apple pies. She baked way more than the three of them could even begin to eat. So Mom had the bright idea to take the mountain of baked goods to the V.A. Hospital. Annie went with her once, but it was painful to see the hurt and maimed soldiers. It was painful to think that one of them—in a split second—could be her brother. Still, it made her mom feel better, and she kept going. Every week, she would gather the latest batch of sweet-smelling treats, plaster a smile on her face, and take them to the men in the hospital. Annie had to give her a lot of credit for that. It took guts.

Of course her mom needed a glass of wine when she got home (or two or three—who could blame her?). Annie often joined her in front of the television on those nights, although Annie would drink diet Coke, obviously. It was on one of those three-glass nights that her Mom told her about getting an abortion in college.

Thanks, Mom. Way too much info.

"It was part of the reason that I agreed to be a surrogate for Aunt Sam. I still feel guilty about it. I was young and afraid. Aunt Sam helped me through it."

So even your parents could make some really crappy choices.

"That baby would be twenty years old now."

Her mom didn't seem to expect any kind of reply; it was more like she was talking to herself.

"Oh, Annie, the choices we make."

Walter's baby would be fourteen months old. Abortion or miscarriage—either way, the baby was gone. Would she be like her mom, always mentally aware of how old that baby would be?

Yes, she would.

Everyone made choices—some good, some not so hot, and some downright fucked up. Everyone.

She, Annie Carissa, a newly minted high school graduate, would probably mess up again in the future. Those were the odds for everyone. After all, she was never, never, *never* going to be a saint. But she wasn't actually a fallen angel either.

She could live with that.

Her daughter had not behaved well today. That was an understatement. Her daughter had behaved atrociously today of all days, her second birthday, when Sam had wanted her to behave perfectly.

Hah! The laugh was on her, she supposed.

After Sophie threw the hot dog and hit Sam in the face (perhaps she should be glad that her daughter was a good aim?), Alex brought out the pink-frosted cake with two lit candles perched in the middle.

"No!" Sophie yelled and pummeled her two little fists into the cake and pulled out two gooey fists of cake and frosting. She threw them. One fistful landed on Jack's shirt, and the other landed in Annie's lap. Before Sam could stop her, she did it again. And again. Sophie was quick. No one at the table was left untouched.

"That little girl has quite an arm," Jack said, dabbing ineffectually at his shirt with a shredded paper napkin.

"Gross," Annie said.

Chris smiled proudly.

Sam wanted to wring his neck. Why didn't he do something?

"Do all two-year-olds act like this?" Carla asked. She looked at Sophie like she was some kind of alien.

"Only when they're tired," Alex said kindly.

"We're going to have one of those." Nick looked dazed. Pink frosting dotted his forehead.

"Maybe we should move the cake to the middle of the table?" Jennifer suggested. She rested her hands on her flat, newly pregnant belly.

In the past, Sam would have felt jealousy pierce her like a knife at the announcement that this young couple—seemingly, without even consciously trying—was expecting a baby.

Now she wished them good luck. They were going to need it.

She picked up Sophie from the high chair and plopped her precocious daughter in her lap. "Say you're sorry, Sophie. Throwing cake at people is *not* a nice thing to do. Say you're sorry." Sophie knew the word *sorry*, although she rarely used it.

"No!" Sophie said. Of course.

Sam wanted to cry in frustration as her daughter wiggled in her lap. But she would not. That would signal defeat to the family gathered at the table, especially to Alex. Especially to Sophie. Why was her daughter so stubborn? She could repeat her demand that Sophie apologize, but she knew what the outcome would be. Sophie wriggled from her lap and started to run crazily around the backyard. Instinctively, Sam glanced at the pool gate to make sure it was securely closed.

She apologized for her daughter. "She doesn't usually act like this." But she did when she was tired and cranky. "She's just getting over an ear infection, and she's exhausted from the trip."

"She looks pretty wired to me," Annie said, as they all watched Sophie dart back and forth across the yard.

"She can run, too," Jack said. "Really, Chris, you should get her into some kind of toddler tee-ball program."

"She's in a toddler tap dancing class," Chris said proudly.

Why in the hell wasn't he doing something? Sam seethed. Sophie was making a mockery of their parenting skills—hers in particular—and he sat there with a stupid grin on his face. Sophie usually listened to him, but he was just sitting there, watching her act out.

She's only two, barely two, Sam reminded herself. It was no big deal if her daughter behaved like a little shit in front of her aunt, uncle, and cousins. No big deal. But to Sam, it was a big deal.

Sophie stopped for a moment to rip her little yellow sundress over her head, and Sam knew that the diaper would come off next. This was a newly acquired, irritating habit of her daughter's—stripping.

"A girl after my own heart," Carla piped up. "She seems to really like an audience."

Nick and Jennifer gave each other an uneasy glance.

Sam flushed. They were probably thinking that their kid would never act like this, and Sam couldn't blame them. Two years ago, she would have thought the same thing. Out of kindness, she didn't say to them: Hey, you never know what you're going to get. It's a crap shoot.

The sodden diaper hit the grass, and Sophie was running naked.

Alex sat, watching.

Sam saw the smile play around the corners of her mouth. "It's not funny, Alex," she said.

"Yes, it is."

Maybe it was, a little—if it wasn't your kid.

"Should I go get the sunscreen, honey?" Chris grinned broadly.

"Oh, shut up!" Sam snapped. Enough was enough. She stood up. "Sophie, it's nap time," she called, trying to keep her frustration out of her voice, trying only for a firm tone. All the child rearing experts seemed to think this was best. Sam was beginning to think that none of them even had children.

"No!" Sophie shouted. Of course.

Sam strode across the lawn and picked up her sticky, sweaty, now screaming child. "We'll take a bath first," she said. Sophie loved her baths but *hated* getting out of them.

This calmed Sophie, a little. "Fishy?" she said. Her favorite bath toy was a phallic-looking blue rubber fish. To Sam, it looked like a dildo, but Sophie loved Fishy. (Maybe Sam should be worried about this? But there were so many things to be worried about!)

Oh, great, Sam thought, as her heart dropped. She had forgotten to pack Fishy. How could she have done that? It was going to be inconceivable to Sophie that her stupid mother had forgotten to pack her beloved, ugly toy. "Yes," she lied. Maybe Alex had a dildo lying around? Should she ask her? It was amazing how low she would go to appease her child.

Chris—who was again in Sam's good graces—had remembered to pack Fishy. She wanted to run down the stairs and throw her arms around him when she found Fishy nested in the suitcase next to Sophie's baby shampoo. But of course she would never leave her child unattended in a bathtub, not even for one-tenth of a second.

The bath did the trick. Sophie's eyes were already closing when Sam lifted her from the tub, rubbed the sweet-smelling Johnson's baby lotion on her small body, and dressed her in her Barney pajamas. Chris, naturally, had assembled the portable crib, and Sophie was sound asleep when Sam laid her down.

She stared down at her sleeping, peaceful child, and the familiar, helpless, all-consuming wave of love washed over her. She loved her child with all her heart at these moments. It was just when Sophie was awake that things became difficult.

She didn't mean *difficult*, exactly, maybe *trying* was a better word. She had been so naïve. In her desperation to have a baby, she had not really thought much past the infant stage. She had not really considered the reality that babies grow into toddlers, then grade schoolers, then teenagers, then adults. Every phase was going to demand something else from her, something more for her to give, new needs to be met. (Dear Grace. She would always be Sam's baby.)

She had been so stubbornly naïve. She should have listened more to Alex.

God help her when Sophie became a teenager. What if she started asking questions—and Sam knew that she would—about her birth? What if she found out that Alex had given birth to her and that Sam had played no genetic role in her conception? And what if she found out that her mother and father had never officially adopted her? She and Alex had finally convinced their dubious husbands that it wasn't necessary, not at all. They *promised* each other that it wasn't necessary to get the legal establishment involved, and it wasn't necessary to pay all that money to lawyers. They *promised* each other that things were as they should be: Sam and Chris were Sophie's rightful parents.

The Murphy twins did not break promises made to each other.

Still, what if a pierced, tattooed, sixteen-year-old Sophie said to her, "Aha! I always knew you weren't really my mother. I always knew you were a fraud!"

When she voiced these concerns to Chris, he would always say, "You are Sophie's mother. I am Sophie's father. Period."

She hoped that he was right; she prayed that he was right. And she did the only thing she knew how to do. Every day, she tried her hardest to be a good mother to Sophie, to be the best mother she could be.

Some days were more successful than others. That, as Alex had said to her over the phone one late night, was the definition of motherhood.

She tiptoed downstairs and found Alex sitting under the misters on the back patio, the table clean, all globs of cake and icing gone. Alex (bless her heart) had a glass of wine waiting for her. Sam sat down next to her and took a grateful gulp.

"She's sleeping?" Alex toyed with a pack of cigarettes.

"Down for the count." She leaned back in the chair. Suddenly, she was deeply tired. "I'm sorry that Sophie made such a mess. I'm sorry that she created such a scene."

"Don't be," Alex said. "She's adorable."

"Are you blind? She was a holy terror today." Sam eyed the pack of cigarettes. She desperately wanted one, but she was trying very hard, for Sophie's sake, to quit.

Alex laughed. "She's very entertaining."

"She's stubborn."

"She's two."

"I give up." Sam reached for the cigarettes. "I'm trying to quit, but one won't hurt anything."

"Same here." Alex lifted the sleeve of her t-shirt to show Sam the patch. She ripped it off. "Just one."

They lit up simultaneously and sighed, contented. For the time being.

"You're going to be a grandmother, a granny," Sam said.

"I'm not going to be a granny. I'll be a *nana*. It doesn't sound so old."

"You'll be whatever the kid calls you."

Alex laughed again. "So true."

Sam could tell that Alex was happy, but she asked anyway. "How do you feel?"

"Ecstatic. But probably not as ecstatic as Jack feels. He's already in the garage building a rocking horse for the grandbaby."

"Does he know how to do that?" Sam had never seen Jack work with wood.

"He says he'll learn. Besides, Jesus was a carpenter, and you know—-"

Sam did know about Jack's new conversion. She knew about everything that was going on in Alex's life, and Alex knew everything that was going on in hers (except that she planned to divide the money she had finally gotten from Mr. Peterson's estate among Nick, Annie, and Sophie). Really, they talked all the time, more so than when she lived across the street. She had barely glanced at the house when they pulled into Alex's driveway. She had been a different person then, a person fueled by grief for one child and desire for another. Thanks to Alex, her twin sister, she would never have to be that person again. She was the mother of Sophie.

They looked at each other and smiled.

"What are you thinking?" Sam asked her sister, although she already knew.

"I think we need more wine," Alex said.

Exactly.

TO MY READERS:

Thank you for reading *Across the Street*. I have completed seven additional novels, each a distinct and interesting story with great characters. If you liked *Across the Street*, I believe you would like my other novels as well, and of course, I would love for you to read them.

Please visit the Library page on my website at LaurieLisa.com for more details on each of the other completed novels and their upcoming release on Amazon:

- *The Wine Club*
- *The Light Tower*
- *Hollister McClane*
- *"star-cross'd lovers"*
- *David's Women*
- *Family Mythology*
- *Queen of Hearts*

You can also join my Reader's List at LaurieLisa.com to receive updates on the pre-orders and release dates for my novels. Feel free to make personal requests to me directly or ask questions about my books.

I look forward to hearing from you!

Laurie.

Printed in Great Britain
by Amazon

40848657R10364